KILEY KNOTT

The Heart of Lafayette

For me, but I am willing to share.

Contents

Preface

While this is a dramatized work of fiction, the moments and people you come across in this story have existed, and most of the letters shared are honest words from a man who lived and loved over two-hundred years ago. He was far from perfect, but I think he meant well in all he did; and his wife — a woman, who, like many in history — deserves so much more praise for all she went through. There is a power in love and loyalty, and the Marquise de Lafayette is the perfect example. It was a privilege to get to know her, to spend almost two years by her side, in her head and heart, and I hope whether through this story or in private research, you may get to know her too.

If you would like to find further reading, I may recommend my main sources. "Lafayette Comes to America" by Louis Gottschalk — a fantastic biography in which my friend Rachel snatched the book straight from under the President of the Lafayette Society's nose for me. Sorry, sir — no regrets.

"The Marquis: Lafayette Reconsidered" by Laura Auricchio — wonderfully organized, an easy read for any age.

The Memoirs, Correspondence, and Manuscripts of General Lafayette — preserved by the Project Gutenberg — was a great help for easy access to Gilbert's words. *The Founders Archive*, likewise, was perfect for letters between Lafayette and Washington, Hamilton, Adams, Jefferson, and Franklin. This man writes so much, it is difficult to be bored with his lexicon.

If you admire the cover and back cover of this novel, they are works of art done by Jean-Honore Fragonard; the Progress of Love series. While they are in the public domain, you can find them in the Frick Collection c.2024. Please support our museums!

Acknowledgement

I would first be like any good child and thank my mother — who was, in a way, my first beta reader and listened to my story after long work days, even though she fell asleep after a while — and my father, who is just a good man and a better dad. I'll like to thank my auntie Giselle, for fanning my ego and confidence through the whole journey and encouraging me to follow everything through. To my beloved friends in *The Ladies of the Greene*, who, although did not all beta read for me, did listen to my passionate rambling and bragged for me to other people. And to everyone who donated — Josh, Geoff, Vinny, JJ, Zav — to help bring this story to the market, you wrought my loving tears.

I would like to thank the *American Friends of Lafayette* for simply existing — there was no better motivator to finish this story than the exciting news of historical anniversaries. You all promote a great man and uplift an arguably greater woman. A gratuitous thank you to my students who always checked up on me as I wrote this story at work, I couldn't have done it without you guys quietly not causing problems in class, and specifically to Angie, who was my greatest hype girl in the final stages and wanted to be mentioned. To those who pursue and preserve historic letters and make them available to the public, my life would be very mundane without you all; the memoirs and correspondence plays an important role in highlighting the humanity of people in our past (and makes me cry and laugh and pace the floor as I get to share in a private moment between husband and wife.)

And finally, I would like to thank me. You did it. How proud twelve-year-old us would be to know we still tell stories, and grateful to the teachers who enlivened us to never stop. Keep going, there are so many more to tell.

<h1 style="text-align:center">Prologue</h1>

"Jean, this is outrageous, you cannot possibly still be thinking of such a thing!"

The Duchesse d'Ayen knew better of such patriarchal schemes. In fact, she always knew better of practically everything. She was built with a firmness of mind and feet that never tired as she stalked her husband's retreat from room to room. The candlelight flickered off the bronze silk of her gown as if she were a fireball from the heavens.

She had kicked the duc out of Paris once and she could do so again.

"For goodness sake, Henriette, an arranged marriage is nothing out of the ordinary," Jean replied, sitting down at his desk. He rapped his middle knuckle against the well-polished wood, as it was the only finger without a heavy ring adorning it. "We were an arranged marriage and I think we did quite well for ourselves. But alas, if only I had known that d'Aguesseau *heiress* had such a tongue on her." He clicked his teeth, glancing up at his wife for a fraction of a second before he returned to the piles of letters in front of him.

Henriette crossed her arms. "I was eighteen years old when I married you," she said, a deep line creasing between her brows. "She is a *child*."

"Louis and Louise are engaged and she is but a year older."

"You know that is not the same. I disapproved of that as well, but I've known Louis since he was a babe, and as he is your cousin, they will have as long an engagement as I wish. I do not know this boy you propose for my dear Adrienne. She's only turned eleven, Jean."

"They wouldn't meet until next year, regardless. The boy is in *de Plessis*."

Henriette slapped her forehead with the back of her hand. "Oh, in school, how lovely! Both of them: children!"

"This boy-child makes over a hundred-twenty-thousand livres a year," Jean retorted in a forced whisper, as if another noble family would hear and try to throw their own daughter at the prospective match. "You've given me five *beautiful* daughters, *ma chérie*, and I love them – I do. But now I am charged with finding suitable husbands for them to better this family. There is no better opportunity than this. I've already spoken to his uncle and he agrees it is a fine arrangement."

The duchesse lifted her skirts and marched around Jean's desk before she knelt at his feet, her folded hands on his knee. "I beg of you, beloved, don't send my little girl away like this. I can compromise, but let us discuss the matter. If they are both children then let us wait, let them wait. If you men worry that one or the other will be taken by a better suitor, then… Well, an engagement is a contract, no? If Adrienne were to just be engaged for a few years to this boy, then their commitment is secure." Henriette shook her head. "But not *marriage*, please. Not at this age. Would you send your daughter to lie in a wedding bed tomorrow, Jean, would you?"

The duc sat still, his eyes flicking from hers to the paperwork, then to her soft hands on his lap. He took them in his and bent over in the chair, kissing the supple skin with care. "No, *chérie*, I would not," he said into her knuckles. Still, his brows furrowed and the heirless frustration settled into his lines. "I will write to the Comte de la Rivière and the Comte de Lusignem and request that the contract be amended. Perchance, if it pleases you, to also meet the boy to confirm that a prolonged engagement is acceptable?"

"A prolonged and *discreet* engagement, Jean," Henriette added sweetly, batting her lashes. She played her cards well and her husband knew it.

If there was one thing she would pass on to her daughters it was how to win arguments with any man.

"Very well."

"And I *would* very much like to meet this young man. Perhaps invite him and his uncle to the house for dinner and a soirée. Allow the two to meet in our usual comfort at home."

"It would wait until he has finished his time in du Plessis, but yes, I suppose that could be arranged. His tenure with the King's Musketeers should be up by next spring." He twisted in his seat to pick up his quill, his left hand still holding onto Henriette's as she popped up next to him to look at the letters.

"Then I finally must know," she said, eyes flitting over the paperwork, "who is this child you're convinced must be a part of our family?"

Jean tapped his pen on the corner of the inkwell and sighed. "He is the Marquis de la Fayette."

Part One

Pity the caged girl who loves an impatient, caged boy.

Chapter One

Paris, November 1771

Being twelve, Adrienne decided, was far better than being eleven. She must have grown another inch since the beginning of the month because the bottom hem of her gown was revealing the silver buckles that kept the shoes firmly on her feet. A tall lady intimidated boys, her mother had said, and so she took it to heart to try and grow as tall as possible.

It wasn't going very well.

Picking up the side of the mauve wool petticoat, she marched herself over to her boudoir to find her hat. Her maid had pinned and teased most of her hair up and lightly powdered the brown tresses until it took on the shade of milk in tea. She wanted it higher, the way her mother wore it, and being twelve now essentially meant she was allowed to do anything. But she was planning on going riding before her lessons, and her maid managed to deter a style that was usually saved for court. Despite the expensive riding habit and perfectly pearlescent earrings to match the buttons down her jacket, Adrienne considered herself decently plain. She inherited her father's brown eyes, but they were not dark enough to be mysterious; and her mother's oval face, but lacked the cheekbones that gave the duchesse that beautiful regal touch.

That was fine, she thought. If she were too pretty, then she would be considered vain.

It rained in the early hours of the morning. The droplets that stuck to the glass windows slipped down the panes, collecting each other until they grew too heavy to remain in Adrienne's company any longer. Most things did that though – left her. Her sister's kitten, a small, fluffy grey thing always dressed in lace and little bells, would wander through Adrienne's room from next door before deciding the space wasn't good enough to play in, nor her lap comfortable enough to lay.

That was fine too, being independent was important for a strong lady.

She took her hat and pinned it through her hair, giving the wool one last smoothing before she escaped the bedchamber and hurried down the marble halls of the grand mansion known as the *Hôtel de Noailles*. The center rooms glittered with gold embossing and too many mosaic arches to count as added by her mother for the delight of her guests – she ran her salon with detailed care. However when the parlor was not in use, it was merely a room for Adrienne to continue to run through, slowing down ever so slightly to walk through the entryway with *some* sense of decorum – she was a lady after all.

Monsieur Dameron, the Duc d'Ayen's secretary, entered the home from its imposing center door with his usual pile of paperwork in hand. He always wore some shade of brown; seeing him amidst the marble was like spotting a brown cow among the snow. Adrienne slammed her back against the adjacent wall. Her heart raced like a frantic violin. Every Thursday she would go riding in the morning, and every Thursday Monsieur Dameron would arrive at the same time. It was a game of sorts: trying to avoid him. Not that there were any consequences, but the twenty-eight year old gentleman had started playing along at times, slipping behind the house staff.

He didn't seem to be in the mood today, with his footsteps quick and steady until he turned the corner and almost crashed right into her.

"Christ Almighty, Mademoiselle," he wheezed, clutching his chest. "You've almost shocked my spirit right out of my body."

"I could not think of how, Monsieur, you have always expected the unexpected," Adrienne replied. "Pray, could you have forgotten that? Hopefully it isn't your mind aging, I still believe you've a bit of youth left."

Monsieur Dameron shook his head with a smile, his hands carefully straightening the documents kept under arm. "Yes, yes, I am gripping to my youth for as long as I am able, Lady Adrienne. I, *erm...*" He patted the paper. "I am in quite the rush for your father. I apologize for forgetting our game. Next week, I promise."

"Verily," Adrienne said. She clasped her hands together behind her back while she watched him disappear down the hall by the stairs where her father kept his office. "Disappointing," she mumbled, picking her skirts back up. *Oh well.*

An uncomfortable chill nipped at her nose as she flew down the stone stairwell, the streets of Paris already in a bustle. The *Rue Sainte-Honoré* was perfectly situated near the Plâce Louis XV and the Tuileries that sat beyond the house's own gardens. She usually could manage one lap before her governess dragged her back inside. Mademoiselle Maron was a small woman; so small that when she was first introduced to Adrienne and her older sister, Louise, by their mother, Adrienne feared that all unmarried older women would be stuck at such a ridiculous height.

"Adrienne! Adrienne!" The panicked voice was easily recognizable and right on time just as the stablehand brought the young girl her horse. Adrienne's mother carefully side-stepped down the stairs, fisting her copper silk petticoats. *"Adrienne,* you cannot go off without an escort."

"But Maman, everyone knows who I am," Adrienne groaned, foot already on the mounting block. The stablehand awkwardly remained in place; she pointed for his hands to assist her in climbing to the saddle, but the servant gawked at the duchesse.

"Precisely! What if you are kidnapped? What if they wait for you on your route?"

"Then I'll take a different direction this time."

"That is worse, for then my men cannot properly follow you," Henriette said with a shake of her head.

"Maman, if I'm followed, then are they not my escorts?"

Henriette tsked sharply, her bare forearms taking on goosebumps without mittens. "My spies do not publicly count as escorts. You will take your cousin as he is here for the week."

"Louis? But he takes *eons* to just put his boots on if they aren't properly polished."

"No, no, he won't, dearest," Henriette assured her, glancing back at the house. She sighed and patted her daughter's cheek. "That was lovely use of your Greek."

"Thank you."

"Your other studies are going well, I hope?"

"Maman, you are stalling for him."

Henriette gasped at the correct accusation. Louis de Noailles was of the martial side of the family and took too great of care in getting ready for a morning ride. The fifteen-year-old vicomte of his illustrious father was a kind boy though, if not a little bold and coquettish. His recent engagement to Louise was taken decently; Louise did not dislike their cousin and found him handsome enough, and Louis thought Louise an easygoing and pleasing companion.

To Adrienne's word, Louis did take a while longer to present himself at the gates. A valet retrieved a cloak for the duchesse who had Adrienne's reins gripped in her hand to prevent her from riding off. Adrienne had taken to staring at the architecture of the row of apartments across the street, looking quite cross until Louis had mounted his own chestnut gelding.

"Good morning, Adri," Louis said, pushing his fur-lined hat further down his forehead. He had bagged the rest of his peruke's hair, the hair powder still apparent on his shoulders.

"I go by Adrienne in full now," she replied, holding her chin high.

Louis looked at the duchesse and cocked his head. "Of course, as all girls become ladies when they are twelve," he smirked.

"Louis, please do be careful," Henriette said, still rubbing at Adrienne's skirts. "Watch for holes in the road, and if anyone approaches you two, strike them."

"You know I have Adri's best interests at heart, Auntie. We will do a tour around the gardens just in time for her to be back for breakfast."

Adrienne rolled her eyes, her heels itching to get underway. She let her head fall back, staring up at the clouds that were retreating from the sky. The birds swayed by, hay and trash in their beaks to build their winter villas. With her mother's parting squeeze, the gate opened and she was free to start her trot on the open stone.

Louis was a hard rider, so keeping him at a pace below a canter brought something of a mischievous grin to Adrienne's face. He would stop and go and stop and go, finally settling on forcing the two of them to simply walk because "their horses' gait was too different to match up a trot." Adrienne smoothed out the mane of her champagne-colored horse. She had named him *Chouchou* when she was younger, and had since thought perhaps she should have chosen something grander for the gelding. Louis' horse today was *Conqueror of the Earth* — which sounded a little too sumptuous for the steed who enjoyed munching on grass whenever they stopped.

The Tuileries was a promenade favorite of the city's center quarter. From the fountains and statues, to the remaining orange and yellow leaves that clung to the trees, it was a tiny little countryside among the bustle of the greatest city in Europe. New winter fashions were beginning to arrive and if anyone wished to make themselves seen outside of a salon, it was here along the stone walkways. But it was spring when the gardens truly flourished – when the daffodils and daisies struck color across the land and the park smelled of the lavender and jasmine that bloomed. Adrienne preferred spring far better. In autumn, everything was dying and the cold brought more loneliness than she cared for. Sure it hosted the anniversary of her birth, but the year declined from there.

"You're in your thoughts today," Louis said after several nods to passersby. "Planning some trouble?"

"Even if I were, I would not tell," Adrienne retorted, sticking out her tongue. "But do tell me, has Papa set a wedding day for you and Louise? He was arguing with Maman last week strongly enough that I believe Grandpère intervened."

"Uncle Lou was involved? Oh dear…" Louis shook his head, the feathers in his hat bouncing lightly. "No, I haven't been told anything. If I were to guess, probably in a year or so, but if Auntie has any say, we will be waiting until your sister is an old maid."

Adrienne reached over to swipe at Louis' arm. "She'd *never* be an old maid!" she said, making a particularly unladylike sound in her throat that she covered as another couple walked by. Louis suppressed a laugh long enough to ride out of earshot. "You're going to have me embarrass you if you make me shout again."

"It is awfully funny though," Louis sighed. "Louise is a fine girl, I don't mean to disrespect her… or *you*, for that matter. Lord help me if I do. I feel like I would wake up one morning with my bed covered in chickens."

Adrienne idled on the thought, merely pursing her lips. "Are you excited to be getting married?"

They rounded the corner of the gardens, some rogue raindrops pattered down from the tree branches and blotted their shoulders with a sudden icy tickle.

"I do not mind the notion of a wife," Louis shrugged, brushing the droplets off his woolen shoulder. "Such as I do not mind titles or succession lines – I'll educate you, dearest Adri, that men truly look towards three things and these things thus: glory with the sword, enlightenment of the mind, and pleasure for the body," he counted. "Only few are capable of attaining all three, thus you have the categories of men through soldiers, philosophers, and, well, degenerates."

"Are you just to be a degenerate then, Louis?" Adrienne pressed, giggling while she moved Chouchou ahead in a trot to avoid the vicomte's wounded scoffing. "A minister, maybe?"

"I will be a soldier as my father is," Louis said, catching up with her as they crossed through the row of trees back towards the Hôtel de Noailles. "He has great favor in court, as does most of our family, you know."

Adrienne thought of Versailles often in the stories that her mother and father shared. While their response to attending court was in the sphere of negativity, her cousins were always returning with gossip that supplied the Noailles sisters with tantalizing ideas. The year prior, France received a new dauphine, and with rumors from Louis – his mother, the comtesse, was on the receiving end of a very distraught Austrian princess who had *no* idea about proper French etiquette. Her Aunt Anne was serious in her business as the future queen's primary lady-in-waiting, a position she held for two generations.

Adrienne had tried to place herself in the young dauphine's shoes, to have to learn a new country's customs and ways – from dancing to curtsying and eating to speaking – and how different it must be for the high expectations of the Versailles court. It was unpleasant, and that was the only word she had been able to apply to it.

Mademoiselle Maron was tapping her foot impatiently on the top step as the nuns were leaving their convent next door. Her blonde hair was perfectly pulled back under the lace cap that hid any mess of a bun she would have to have done to be out and about so early in the day, Adrienne concluded. Maron lifted Adrienne by the elbow after she dismounted, bade adieu to her cousin, and was promptly pulled inside. Then rushed back to her rooms to change and prepare for prayer and breakfast, where, no doubt, her mother would be hosting a guest or several.

With her riding habit replaced with a simple cream gown and hat swapped for a lace cap, Adrienne joined her mother in the drawing room by the fireplace, where she met with her four sisters. Louise sat next to their mother who still bounced Rosalie in her lap despite her no longer being a toddler; yet she was still the baby of the family, and was doted on accordingly. Little Pauline waited for Adrienne to kiss their mother on her cheek before claiming the other side of the duchesse. Being last to arrive typically meant all seating by their beloved mother was taken, and Adrienne settled down between Louise and Antoinette. Antoinette must have had a tantrum getting out of bed as her brunette curls were hardly contained in her cap and the eight-year-old refused to have anyone fix it.

"What happened to you?" she whispered, tugging at the dark green sleeve. Antoinette pulled it back, crossing her arms as she slumped on the sofa. The edge of her skirt revealed mustard yellow stockings and Adrienne clicked her tongue. "Aw, they didn't let you pick your stockings today, hm?"

"They don't match," Antoinette grumbled. "I told them they *don't* match."

Adrienne nodded knowingly. "I'm sorry no one realizes your superior knowledge of fashion, Anne. How about I help you change them before we join Maman again this evening? Then you can show her how nice you look."

"That would be acceptable," Antoinette said. She remained in her hunched position until their guest arrived. A woman, older than their mother, slowly stepped through the doorway. Any guest who was new to the house always took their time admiring the raised ceilings and artwork that was placed meticulously in an order pleasing to the eye. Yet this guest was not new, in fact, the face of the middle-aged woman was very familiar to all the young girls who greeted her with soft smiles and ready ears.

"Thank you for coming today, Madeleine," Henriette said with a gentle inclination of her head.

Madeleine de Puisieux curtsied. "There is truly nowhere else I would rather be, Madame, it is always the deepest pleasure when you invite me into your home. Good morning to you all, ladies," she said, rousing giggles all around with the excitement she carried in her tone. "I've brought some of my newer publications with me today, but I believe you all have been reading the seventeen-fifty piece? Perhaps we shall discuss that first." She sat across from them on a circular stool that her skirts consumed.

Puisieux was a favored guest of the Duchesse d'Ayen, and her books were commonplace along the daughters' bookshelves. Every night between knitting and playing the piano, Henriette would read to them a passage from Madame de Puisieux's *Woman is Not Inferior to Man* and had Louise and Adrienne reread it several times after. There were several publications that were aimed for young Antoinette and Pauline to understand, and Rosalie was always allowed to read the titles for everyone, thus Madame de Puisieux handed her the book.

These morning gatherings were full of laughter and high-toned proclamations, as both the writer and the duchesse encouraged the young girls to express themselves as boldly and as loudly as they pleased. Tea was served with small cakes for the ninety minutes, the time always slipping by as they perused the newer pamphlets on advice. Adrienne leaned onto Louise as the eldest read through the introduction. Her sister smelled like the lavender satchels she would always be sewing.

"Maman?" Adrienne said, and Louise lifted her shoulder at the gross tickle of her sister's breath on her neck.

"Yes, Adrienne?"

"Wouldn't it make more sense for men to be here with us *now* to talk of equality of our sexes? Why don't we invite Papa or…"

Louise gave a single, short laugh. "I do not think you would find Louis in a salon like this," she said, resting the papers on her lap. "And Papa already knows you are his equal, Maman, isn't that right?"

Madame de Puisieux covered a smile with her teacup as Henriette raised her chin. "Your father is well aware who makes the rules in this family," she said to her daughters. "We split our duties equally between each other. Unfortunately his schedule makes it difficult for him to have the pleasure of joining us for these chats, but I am sure he would agree, Adrienne, that you and your sisters are extremely intelligent and would conquer any challenge set upon you like the Maid of Orléans herself."

"I think having men involved in the conversation is a great notion, Adrienne," Puisieux said. "These are arguments that, after all, men have to acquiesce to for any real change to happen in this society. Perhaps one day, we wouldn't have to wait so long."

"Not every man is like Papa," Adrienne said, picking at the embroidery on Louise's sleeve buttons. "Won't we all be at the mercy of our *future* husbands?"

The duchesse set her jaw and the room was quiet save for the crackling of the fire and the tiny tinks of tea cups. She plucked some fluff from Rosalie's hair and turned to embrace Pauline further before her eyes glanced towards Adrienne. They were the color of glass, and the look was just as fragile. "Madeleine," she said, turning towards their guest. "It was so nice having you join us today. How does next week sound, same hour?"

Chapter Two

❧

Paris, April 1772

A *guest*, they were told. No more information other than *"a guest"* was what was given by their mother before she left them in the parlor. Most guests were hardly announced to them at all. Usually an older gentleman or lady from court or those from the duc's science practice resulted in the daughters eating their dinner with Maron so that the adults could talk and drink the night away. If it were family, then the girls would be welcomed to join the company in the dining room.

Louise, when their mother was not around, sat in the center sofa of the room. She was always said to have a face like a summer peach when she was stuck in thought, the deep blues of her eyes reflected the sky itself while she stared out the lofty windows from her spot. Her gaze shifted only fractionally to Adrienne, who leaned against a table next to the open window, her own attention split between the gardens of their house and her sister.

"I'll ask Papa," Louise sighed after they shared a long, silent look. She put her book on the pillows, dusting the cover ever so slightly with the edge of her sheer lace apron that served no real purpose. Adrienne nodded and let her curiosity fall back to the servants who bustled through the gardens with their trimmers and waterpails.

The daisies were already blooming ahead of their budding rose neighbors, joining the forsythias in covering the garden's path with yellows and pinks. The lilacs surrounding the cherry trees gave the air a sweet note that Adrienne breathed in happily. With the sky so clear, it was bound to be a fine day, and even the mysterious guest wouldn't put a damper on it. She draped herself across the console table to not be seen eyeing the day-to-day love story blossoming between the gardener and the servant sent out to collect flowers for the inside vases.

"What if it's the King?" Antoinette asked. She laid on the rug between chairs with her cat, fluffing up the frilly collar.

"Is it?" Pauline squeaked from her embroidery circle. Adrienne's finished piece was perched next to her to follow along. "Should we be getting painted?"

Adrienne pressed her forehead to the table's marble top. "I do not think Maman would leave that detail out," she replied. "But she probably isn't too happy about this guest if she was so blunt about it."

Antoinette brought the kitten to her lap. "Maybe it's someone here to take us away."

"Anne," Adrienne scolded. "Maman would never!"

Pauline held up her embroidery – some flowers that encircled where she would practice her letters. "Maman would sooner *die*," she added and Adrienne stood up to her full height, looking at her two young sisters.

"That is just as awful to say, Polly! You two are the strangest girls on this planet," she said, throwing away her hope for them, and finally crossed the room to check on quiet Rosalie, who sat on a chair with her wooden dolls.

She silently bounced one dressed as a shepherdess alongside another that wore men's clothing that was perhaps fashionable when their father was young.

"Are they courting?" she asked her. Rosalie furrowed her little brows and looked at the dolls with a stare the duc gave to some of his letters.

"I don't know yet," Rosalie decided. "They just met."

"I see, I see," Adrienne said. "You'll have to tell me all the gossip when you find out, alright?" She brushed the dark blonde hair from the girl's forehead. "Are you feeling well?"

Rosalie nodded.

"Tired?"

She nodded again.

"Thunderstorms kept you up last night?"

"Yeah."

Adrienne knelt down next to the chair and balanced her chin in her arms. "I didn't hear you cry out or go into someone else's room. You must have braved that whole thing by yourself, huh? That's a very big girl thing to do, you know. You should tell Maman when she comes back, she'll be so proud!"

Rosalie's round cheeks flushed as she looked away, hugging the dolls to her chest. She nodded once more, seeming content to continue playing with her toys. Adrienne leaned back, digging her nails into the rug below. The breeze that twiddled about the room rocked the crystals dangling from the chandelier, filling the silence with soft melodies. A clicking of the short heels from Louise's slippers echoed down the hallway, and the door to the parlor opened a crack, the sunlight catching on the blue satin of her skirt. She looked at Adrienne with raised brows, and gestured for her to come quietly. Adrienne rose as nonchalantly as she could, swiftly walking until Louise shut the door behind them.

"It's a boy," she whispered.

"A *boy?*" Adrienne said, and Louise covered her mouth with a hand.

"He and his uncle, Papa says," Louise hushed. "You and I are to attend the dinner, then they are staying for Maman's soirée afterwards."

Adrienne waited for her sister to take the hand from her mouth. "What's so special about this boy? There have been plenty of Papa's friends bringing their sons and nephews."

Louise kept her lips puckered into a mischievous smile. "I don't know," she said, "but why would Maman be so secretive about it?"

Her brows fell heavily forward. If they were told in the first place, their mother would normally be plain with ranks and all the formalities so that the daughters didn't embarrass the guests at first greeting. Adrienne cocked her head. "She did want to say some extra prayers last night," she thought aloud. "Maybe he's a Protestant… or *English*. Papa has had English scientists over for dinner before."

"Regardless," Louise said, waving a hand. "We are to wear our best this evening. Maron will be watching the girls until the soirée, then they can join us. That'll appease Anne at least."

"Stick her and Pauline in front of a chessboard and they'll be occupied for an hour," Adrienne replied. Pauline was perfectly content in winning against her older sister in multiple rounds; Anne refused to lose, and thus rematch after rematch took place until the game was taken away. Adrienne frowned and looked down the hall. "I wish we knew something about this boy so I could prepare some conversation. Maybe he'll be sitting far from us and we won't have to worry about it. I hope you're next to me, Louise, so that we may talk more."

Louise shrugged, her hands coming up to play with the choker around her neck. "I suppose we will find out when everyone gets here. I'm going to be wearing periwinkle – don't wear the same or I'll make you change."

"I'll pick something else," Adrienne sighed, already needing to think of a new outfit.

☆

The silk was a soft blush pink – hardly touched by the dye. Adrienne didn't mind the adornments with it, they were quite cute: little bows were held together with pearls at the sleeves where layered lace dangled down her arms; her stomacher was embroidered with pink and white roses that matched the small white buds on her shoes. She fiddled with the pearl earrings while her maid laid the back pleats of the gown delicately behind her. With her hair as powdered as it was, she felt as if she were going to court for the first time, with a bit of rouge to add some color back to her washed out complexion. She hadn't worn something so elaborate since both her grandparents, the Duc and Duchesse de Noailles, hosted the Epiphany dinner.

However, instead of the monochromatic blooms and velvet drapings of winter, the house was now a flourish of color, as if a rainbow was sent through the halls, reflecting in every crystal and mirror that cast its rays upon the floor and wall.

She met her parents in the drawing room, the two in the throes of a faint argument that ceased as Adrienne approached them and gave the most curt of curtsies. Her father smiled warmly and left his wife to her agitation to kiss Adrienne's cheek. He was perfumed, Adrienne could smell it through his wig's new powder, and freshly shaven. Dressed to impress, she noted.

Just who were these guests?

"You look beautiful, Adrienne," he said, and turned to Henriette, a sturdy hand on Adrienne's shoulder. "Does she not, *mon amore?*"

The duchesse's glare eventually softened and she nodded with a sigh. Taking a glass of wine from a servant, she promptly consumed half of it.

"Well," he continued, "as your sister probably told you the summary: we will be hosting the Comte de Lusignem and his nephew tonight among other company with whom you are familiar."

A comte? Not at all the title Adrienne was expecting with all the decorum.

The duc must have seen the confusion cross his daughter's face and added, "Said nephew is the Marquis de la Fayette. He is about your age."

"Jean," Henriette said, eyeing him over her glass.

"So as you know from meeting other courtiers," the duc said and Adrienne nodded along, "refer to them by their titles – good, good. They should be here presently. Your mother and I were discussing final dining arrangements."

"That's very last minute of you, Papa," Louise said, entering the chamber on Louis' arm. The two made themselves out to be a walking garden – with the sister in her soft blue, like a cascading marble fountain, and the vicomte in a green ensemble with an embroidered waistcoat of yellow and green flowers and figs. He held a cane in his other hand, as if they returned from a stroll, but from the perfection of Louise's hair, it was evident they did not. Adrienne looked towards her mother, who appeared to have polished off that wine and was taking a second one.

"You all look darling," she said, finally composing herself enough to be at the duc's side once more. "I feel like we should have a portrait done right now with how mature you all look, my babies…" She breathed through what was an encroaching sob and shook her head, the small crack in her composure mended instantly. "Like any meal, I have final say in who is sitting where, and have taken into consideration our guests and their station for such a gathering. Regardless, girls, I expect your best behavior."

At promptly three in the afternoon, Adrienne, Louise, and the rest of the family greeted their first round of guests, and wine and music played as some brave or cocky soul took up the piano to entertain. Mostly men and their wives or mistresses, speaking in groups as if in several separate conferences, continued to arrive at the Hôtel de Noailles. Adrienne nursed her glass, counting the numbers while realizing the average age of the salon was only growing older and older. While her mother socially and successfully combated any of the old widowers from approaching her daughter, Adrienne was already growing increasingly bored. She stood next to the duchesse and watched her sister and her fiancé mosy about together, mingling with gentlemen of whom Louis was acquainted with from his father's time at court. Louis was due to be formally introduced in Versailles in the next year, and he was certainly assuring he had allies there right away.

How simple Louise made being a fiancée look, Adrienne thought, as she bobbed and weaved with relative ease. She answered many questions about her Aunt as if she spoke to her on a daily basis, knowing exactly what the *Madame d'Etiquette* was thinking of the Royal Family. Adrienne could tell that Louise was peppering in some lies amongst her story; little ones, nothing that would hurt their Aunt's reputation by any means, but certainly there to bring smiles to the company.

Adrienne picked a chip at the bottom of her wine glass with her nail and moved on to finding her father with her eyes. She heard him talk about his chemist work before she spotted him and his dark suit amid the spring colors. The brief moment of paternal affection had disappeared entirely and returned to his business demeanor, his hands restrained in their animation of whatever new science was being discovered.

She wondered if somehow she got away from her mother, that anyone would notice she was gone.

Alas, she didn't have to ponder that thought for much longer, as the door opened once more and her mother's hand shot out to grip her arm. Four men walked in, well, to be precise, three men and a *boy*. The gentleman in a red brocade, who must have been the Comte de Lusignem, was immediately greeted by her father, the bow of the guest followed with an overly excited handshake. Behind him stood another man, younger, who reminded Adrienne of Monsieur Dameron with his secretarial stature. Whoever he was, the duc accepted his welcome as well. A gesture to the left and the attention flitted over to the youngest, and at this, Adrienne saw her father make eye contact with her and her mother and waved the two of them over. The duchesse's feet almost dragged, but there was a vehement curiosity on her face that Adrienne had never seen before.

"May I introduce my wife, the Duchesse d'Ayen, and my second daughter, Lady Marie Adrienne Françoise," Jean said, taking his wife's hand. "Ladies, this is the Comte de Lusignem."

Adrienne dipped her head; the older men returned a bow.

The comte looked just a little older than her father with a straight brow and a dimpled chin. "It is a pleasure to make your acquaintance Duchesse, and yours as well, Mademoiselle. This miserable looking man behind me is Monsieur Lambert, my secretary, who isn't staying long, I assure you Madame..."

Adrienne was too caught up in stealing glances towards the boy next to them to hear what else the comte had to say. From where her skirts ended, the silk matched almost perfectly with the pastel pink of his suit, down to the large pink bows on his jewel-encrusted shoes. Where she wore silver and pearls, he wore gold – the glimmering thread woven intricately into his waistcoat and frock. His buttons were embroidered with the smallest of suns. The lace cravat at his neck was delicate and tied in an unfamiliar way from what she had seen in Paris, almost backward.

The boy himself wasn't too handsome – he had a prominent nose and small, pursed lips; his large eyes were not quite brown, but not quite green: a hazel hue to them, with brows filled in with burnt clove that made him look in awe of everything. His hair was heavily powdered and pomaded, with several curls pinned neatly on the sides. He was taller than Louis for certain, Adrienne found, as she had to look high just to see the forming blush across the boy's cheeks as those hazel eyes glanced down to her.

The Comte de Lusignem's foot nudged the boy impatiently and suddenly the lanky teenager sprung to life like a wind-up toy.

He stepped back on his right foot and dipped into a very practiced bow. "I am Marie-Joseph-Paul-Yves-Roch-Gilbert du Motier, Marquis de la Fayette. Thank you for the invitation to your lovely home," he said with an awkward flair that Adrienne found both embarrassing *and* a little, dare she admit, charming.

"What a name," Henriette said. Adrienne watched the blush on the Marquis' face grow even redder.

"Ah, y-yes, my parents baptized me like a Spaniard, I am afraid," he replied. There was something about the way he spoke; the calm, foreign song-like nature was immediately a tick towards someone from the southern parts of the country. Adrienne only heard a few guests speak in such a way, but it sounded like the Marquis was trying his best to mask the un-Parisian accent.

His attention returned to her briefly. She watched his eyes dance the same dance hers did while she looked him over, but only for a moment; he kept his chin pointed towards her parents as the older men spoke on. Behind him was a clergyman who kept his head low, but nodded politely when he spotted Adrienne looking. His older appearance was abated by the genial way he continued to acknowledge the Marquis.

Perhaps he was to the Marquis as Mademoiselle Maron was to her.

In a mock call-to-arms, the Duc d'Ayen announced to the salon that dinner was to be served, and with a slow pace, the guests began to filter into the dining room. Adrienne never knew if guests were whispered where they were to sit, or if it was included in the invitation – though as a future lady of someone's home, it felt like something she should learn. There certainly were no place cards nor escorts. The Duc de Noailles also made an appearance here. Her father's father was a plump old man, with kind dark eyes that made his smile all the more welcoming. He usually lived in the family apartment in Versailles, but visited Paris as often as his schedule allowed. Adrienne knew there was an awkward air between her grandfather and father – they both wanted a male heir to pass the line down through. The content composure of which he carried himself was expertly practiced, greeting the visitors to the Hôtel with great care, knowing each face without needing an introduction.

"Ah, my petite Adrienne," he cooed, kissing her cheeks as he passed her. "Not so petite anymore. You are becoming a beautiful woman."

Adrienne beamed. "Thank you, Papi. You're looking very well. How is Grandmère? Has she received my letters?"

"Yes, she has, and she is absolutely horrified she cannot be here to thank you in person. But she has been recovering well knowing she has such a loving granddaughter." The Duc de Noailles' eyes crinkled while he spoke. He seemed to idle in front of her for another moment before the movement of the *other* young person in pink caught his attention and an interested "*ah*" escaped his lips. With a kiss to Adrienne's knuckles, the old man excused himself and sauntered over to the newly arrived comte and marquis.

Adrienne felt her mother back at her side before her name was whispered quickly, a chair pointed out for her not too far from where the duchesse was to sit. Adrienne took up her skirt and walked over, eyeing the parties that sat around the long table.

"Allow me." Louis appeared to her right, taking the chair out for her. "Auntie has been scheming, hasn't she?"

"What do you mean?" Adrienne sat carefully as he pushed her in. He sat Louise down on his other side – who looked at her with a soft smile – and dropped himself between them, throwing his coat pleats behind him.

"Take a look at who's not sitting next to us," he said. They watched as the young Marquis was seated across from them. Physically close, yet not socially accessible in polite society – conversation partners always came from the immediate left or right. "It's almost cruel." Louis gave the Marquis half a smile, to which the boy returned in kind.

The Duchesse d'Ayen proved herself more of a schemer as she approached the Marquis' left to sit. The poor boy jumped from his seat, apologizing for not assisting her sooner. If Adrienne's mother was going to judge anyone, she would always sit them on her right hand. She wished she could tell what her mother was doing giving the guest a fright. It was clear he had no idea what *he* was doing.

"A marquis amongst the ducs, duchesses, and peers," Louis mumbled, polishing off another drink. "He's like a pony in a stable of mustangs and mares."

"A very tall pony," Louise said. She leaned back in her chair to look at Adrienne. "You were next to him, is he taller than Papa?"

"The same, I think," Adrienne replied, trying her best to not be heard across the table. She didn't want to embarrass him, nor herself, for being so forthright in the company of others. "He seems shy, but kind at least." She liked his voice; it made up for the rest of the awkwardness that the teen exuded.

"Shy and kind," Louise repeated. She giggled lightly, the one glass of wine enough to bring color to her ears. "That won't last long in Paris. I hope Maman doesn't eat him."

The speaking companion to her left arrived as the first course was being served. The Comte de Lusignem set a glass of champagne down next to his dinner wine with enough care that the liquid inside hardly moved. He held himself like a young courtier, yet in his hands was where Adrienne started to see his age. Displaying the prominence of his knuckles and deep lines where a youthful man's hands were usually smooth; if she were to choose again, she'd place him in his upper forties. Her father was hardly thirty-three.

"Mademoiselle de Noailles," he greeted. She kept her fiddling fingers in her lap, hidden under the table while she politely dipped her chin. A bowl of soup was placed in front of them. "Your family name is very well-known, Mademoiselle. I must say, there seems to be a Noailles in every corner of the court."

Adrienne sipped at the broth while she contemplated her words. She didn't speak to older men often, or at all if her mother had any say in it. "My grandpère and Papa work hard to keep our family in His Majesty's highest honors, Monsieur Comte. I am merely grateful to be part of such a name."

The comte nodded. "And your mother is quite the lady ahead of her time. You and your sisters are educated like sons, I hear?"

It was an odd way of putting it, but the man made no motion to alter his wording. Adrienne sucked in a breath and looked at her mother across the table. She dominated her conversations with such ease; whatever she said was taken with respect and admiration. How Adrienne longed to be like her – the perfect mother, the perfect woman.

"We are all taught in Latin and Greek, history and arithmetic," she said, watching for his reaction. "Of course, we are learning everything proper to be a lady."

"Of course," he replied. "And your hobbies? Do you keep any?"

"I enjoy needlework with my mother, but I also ride and read contemporary literature."

The comte hummed, his eyes flicking up to the other side of the social barrier. "My second wife took up riding as well. It is a…*fine* hobby for a lady, I believe. Unusual, but makes pleasant companionship for the unsuspecting gentleman."

Adrienne wasn't expecting the response; *was that a compliment or a slight?* She set her spoon down as they finished the first course. "You used past tense, Monsieur? Has your wife passed?"

"Unfortunately so," he replied. "As did her sister, of whom I was married beforehand. Alas, I am still close to the Rivières and their offspring." He looked over at the Marquis – who was hesitating on where to place his used spoon, taking seconds too long to just set it back down in his empty bowl. "My current comtesse is seeing to the estate's further construction today, but I will not bore a young lady with such a topic."

The second course was a variety of sizable fish, seasoned with lemon and salt that Adrienne swallowed down with her wine. A roast with the vegetable courses followed. What she was truly waiting for was the desserts. The platters of cakes and puddings set the table in a sweet delight that brought the child in Adrienne right out to the surface. Her hand, upon reaching for one particular pastry, was intercepted like a hawk diving for its meal – the Marquis all but over the table to take the delectable piece. The two startled each other. Adrienne drew her hand away and the boy promptly abandoned the dessert, falling back to his seat as blood rushed to his face while the other guests looked on. Whatever powder he wore on his cheek did not assist in camouflaging the shame.

Adrienne nibbled on her lip and gestured to the lost chocolate macaron. *Perhaps he hasn't had any where he was from*, she thought, and as the hosting family it would be rude for her to take it. The Marquis shook his head a fraction of an inch and simply looked down into his lap. Adrienne heard the hard click of a tongue from the comte to her left and felt the unfamiliar air of public humiliation rising.

After the final courses, the ladies excused themselves from the table per custom and floated in droves back into the halls and continued on through to the drawing room. Coffee was already prepared for the women upon entering. The rainbow shuffle of skirts was overtaken by the gossip, some kept quiet, others less discreet with their sudden shouts of laughter. Adrienne felt out of place, standing in the room as her mother flit about from group to group, combining some and filtering through others. She moved her hand under the slit of her petticoat to the pocket underneath, assuring herself that the little chocolate pastry was still there.

Louise didn't take long to find her. Her arm looped through Adrienne's as she stared at the door. "You're going to look mad if you don't blink, Adri," she said, patting the top of her sister's hand. "You know they never keep Louis in the men's talk for long, he gets bored out of his mind whenever Papa brings up his sciences. It certainly was interesting getting to eat with the courtiers today; a rarity that I found was rather fun. Monsieur Lefebvre sat to my right and could not help but be a gossip."

"It was… a little mundane," Adrienne admitted. "Everyone talks of the same old things, and Maman doesn't let me wander."

"Mm, once you are older and engaged, I'm sure she'd feel more comfortable with you making your rounds. Or maybe not," Louise shrugged. "Maybe you are destined to be Maman's companion for the rest of her life."

Adrienne pinched Louise's arm. "I thought we already decided that role was going to be Anne. She's never been interested in boys to begin with."

Louise seized her elbow and dragged her to the table nearest the door as Louis sauntered in with his square jaw high in the air, another glass of wine in hand. Reaching over and snatching his arm too, she pulled him into their little group. A few of the older women drew out their fans as they glanced at the trio of adolescents looking like they were to become the cause of trouble.

"What was tonight's topic of discussion?" Louise questioned her fiancé with vigor, but Adrienne's attention focused behind their cousin, to the tall, lanky marquis in pink who quietly had followed behind him into the room.

He stood with his hands behind his back, his breast forward slightly as if he were a goose of sorts. She watched him watch the floor, his gaze occasionally slipping to the drawing room's light blue drapings and paintings of the Noailles family. A finger went out to touch a crystal candelabra that stood on a glass table behind one sofa. The crystal bead promptly fell with a *clack* and the Marquis reeled his hand away. Adrienne softly snorted, covering her mouth.

"Louis," she said, hiding her embarrassment on her sister's shoulder. "Please go collect the poor Marquis before he burns our house down. I feel absolutely awful that we should leave him out of conversation when he is our age."

It didn't take much prodding to send one teenage boy to rein in the other. The Marquis' eyes seemed to light up at whatever Louis had said to him and they returned to the girls before the clock struck a new minute.

"I do wonder, Marquis," Louis said as he settled his elbow on the console table. "Have you always been so tall?"

The Marquis brought his hands up to his waist to spin a ring on his forefinger. "Well, I was a baby *once*," he said with a small smile. It was an odd statement, Adrienne thought, because of *course* he was a baby, everyone was at some point. The Marquis glanced hopefully between the three of them as they slowly raised their brows.

Oh, Adrienne realized, as it hit her straight on. It was a *joke*.

The smile flew to her face as soon as the Marquis appeared to grow a blush again. "I personally came straight from my father's head, fully grown like Athena herself," she said with a nod and a shrug of one shoulder.

"*Bah!*" Louise cackled. "The only thing true about that statement is that you're as fully grown as you're ever going to get. Small forever."

"You are only taller because your head is so big," Adrienne shot back and Louis laughed aloud until Louise smacked his chest.

"Oh my," the Marquis said. He pressed his lips together to quell a grin. "I'm afraid I do not know what it is like to have a sibling, but I imagine it could not be better than this. I apologize, I haven't been around... *ladies* in some time."

Louis waved his hand dismissively. "These two are only ladies when their mother is around," he said, earning another prompt smack to the gut. "I mean, yes, excuse me. I haven't introduced you. Monsieur Marquis, these are my cousins' daughters. The elegant beauty in blue is Mademoiselle Louise de Noailles, future vicomtesse. The short one with a mouth is –"

"Mademoiselle Adrienne," the Marquis answered. "I had the pleasure of her acquaintance when I arrived." He lowered his voice and took up Adrienne's hand, giving it a polite kiss. "If I were Paris, I would have given my golden apple to Athena."

"The Marquis comes from a military background, like myself," Louis said, but Adrienne was only focused on the heat drawing to her knuckles as the boy let her hand go gently. Her cousin prattled on. "How old are you, Monsieur?"

"F-fourteen," he said, "but I turn fifteen in a few months."

"I turn sixteen myself in a couple days. Are you new to Paris? I haven't seen you very often at the local clubs."

"I've been living with my great grandpère in Luxembourg Palace while I attended school for the past few years and then with some uncles afterwards. I must admit, I didn't cross the river often at the fault of my own stupidity."

Louise clicked her tongue. "Oh, Marquis, that can't be true. Perhaps your uncles simply are protective of you as our mother is of us. Children do that to some guardians, I'm told."

The Marquis tilted his head with a frown. "I don't think they are as protective of my person than they are of other things, but... *ah*, it doesn't matter; I am across the river now and for some time it seems."

"Oh?" Adrienne asked. "Where are you staying? Perchance we may call on you to join us for a promenade this week?"

He looked at her like she turned into a hydra and sprouted several heads. The fidgeting hands returned as he glanced around the room full of women, like he was suddenly lost in the wrong house.

"I was, *erm*, I was told by my uncle that I was to stay... *here?* For the time being?" he mumbled. Again, the three of them raised their brows. Louise and Adrienne looked towards Louis, as if he would have the answer, but the young vicomte simply brought his wine glass to his lips and finished off the rest of it. The Marquis cleared his throat, took a breath and added, "Uncle Philippe, that is, the Comte de Lusignem, was speaking with the Duc d'Ayen about my rent? I'm not sure for how long; I've been shipped off from place to place before with no consistency."

"You're staying in the Hôtel?" Adrienne asked as Louise inquired about which room.

"I am at your mercy, Mesdemoiselles," he replied with a bow of his head.

He really was at the mercy of the Noailles. As the guests filtered out, the family remained behind. The Duc d'Ayen shook the Comte de Lusignem's hand as the Marquis remained affixed, pinched on the shoulder by his uncle as he received a long talk before the nobleman departed as well, and the Marquis stood in his pastel suit in the empty marble hall.

Antoinette had settled next to Adrienne when the little daughters were allowed into the soirée. She pushed a pillow into Adrienne's lap to make it more appealing to sit by.

"He looks sad," she said over Pauline's slow piano-tapping with Louise guiding next to her.

Adrienne felt the macaron still sitting in the handkerchief in her pocket. She shimmied it out and unfolded it; it was miraculously still in one piece. Handing the pastry over to Anne, she said, "You should go give him this. It may cheer him up a little."

Antoinette carefully took the sweet in her hands like it was made of porcelain and slid off the sofa. Her tiny heels were muffled on the rug before they clicked over the glossy wood floor. Adrienne idly watched. Her intrigue in the boy had only increased with his clumsiness and bumbling composure. Too many times they were hosts to young heirs who stuck their noses in the air and scoffed at the attempts the Noailles sisters made to speak to them – so many times, in fact, that Adrienne was convinced most boys did not know how to speak at all.

When the eight-year-old reached the Marquis and held up the welcoming gift, he had snapped out of the daze he was in, and looked down at the girl. He gently lowered himself to one knee, his eyes level with Antoinette as he accepted the handkerchief. Adrienne didn't hear what Antoinette had said, but she covered her face with a hand when the Marquis turned his head towards the sofa.

Why was she suddenly shy? Adrienne was not a shy girl by any means. Yet, here was all the heat rushing to her cheeks as the Marquis stood and took little Anne by the hand to escort her back to the family.

"Maman," Antoinette said to the duchesse as she sat with her needlework. "Are we keeping him, truly?"

The Marquis couldn't help but laugh a little under his breath as Antoinette did not let him go.

Henriette looked up slowly from her work, her gaze shifting from her daughters to her husband – a deep churning, mischievous fire burning in her eyes. "Marquis, do please have a seat, we never got to finish our conversation over dinner." She waited until the boy picked one of the stools to sit on, keeping his feet firmly on the ground. "You were telling me about your family, hm? I know of your mother's family, the de la Rivière's – very well-established here in Paris. I was sorry to hear of her death last year; and your grandfather's as well so soon after, that is just terrible."

Adrienne's hand went over her heart. She didn't hear about such things! Here this boy was, only two years older than her and had already lost his mother?

"Thank you for your condolences, Madame," the Marquis replied, his voice returning to that soft and slow timber it had earlier in the evening. "I loved them dearly."

"La Fayette is a southern name, isn't it?"

"Yes, Madame – Chavaniac, in Auvergne, near the mountains of Le Puy. The house goes back to the fourteenth century, but my family began far earlier during the crusades." He smiled. "I am told my many great-uncle's served with Jeanne d'Arc. We are a line of soldiers, of course."

Henriette twisted her needles. "And your father?"

The Marquis' smile twitched. "I am afraid I never knew him. He was killed during the Seven Years War when I was only two."

"Michel du Motier," Jean said from his book. "Battle of Minden, was it? An embarrassing loss for our country and King."

If the Marquis was going to say something, as his shoulders tensed, nothing came out. He just looked at the duc with apprehension, then back down to his lap.

Adrienne glared at her mother. Henriette subtly shushed her with her pinkie. "Truly then, your father was as honorable as his line has been, serving his country with much needed courage," she said, carefully folding her knitting in her lap to look at the young man.

"Thank you," said the Marquis with a swell of pride.

Henriette glanced back at Adrienne with a knowing tilt of her mouth. She continued, nevertheless, "Now as for your time in our home, Monsieur Marquis, I expect the same honorable behavior as you are around my daughters. You are *not* to be alone with them unless a chaperone is near, and you will not interrupt their studies and lessons while in the house. While we sojourn in Paris, you will have to journey to Versailles at your own expense to continue with your Musketeering should the King wish it. Your apartments here are in the northeast wing; your baggage has already been taken care of. We take prayer every morning at nine-thirty, allow guests into the salon at ten, and often conclude our public days by eight or nine. Do you have any questions, Marquis?"

"I… don't *think* so, Madame," he replied.

"Very good, then. You must be tired from all the sudden change. Louis," she said without looking at the boy helping himself to the last glass of wine. "Would you be a dear and show the Marquis to his rooms?"

The Marquis rose from his seat. Adrienne noted the macaron still folded neatly in his hands. Antoinette, who had been picking at the golden threads in his coat, sat back with a small complaint. "Thank you all for having me," he said quietly. "I had a lovely dinner, Madame, my compliments. Monsieur d'Ayen. Mesdemoiselles."

Adrienne smiled with a nod as she watched him follow after Louis.

Adrienne found the next day that she had completely forgotten they were housing a guest; and said guest was a boy; a boy with a very long name and a very tragic life story. While she had gone to sleep thinking about what it must have been like not have her mother and father constantly in her life, to be dragged from house to house with different uncles and aunts, to have Papi suddenly pass away – she had even *cried* a little while wiping the makeup from her cheeks – by the time morning came and the soft pillows of her bed consumed her, her mind went to her stomach. It growled incessantly. Did she not have a multiple course meal last night? Did she not eat everything in front of her?

No, her mind replied, *you didn't have the dessert.*

Without the bookend of ending a meal with something sweet, her belly was quite displeased.

Adrienne threw her arms atop her blankets with a grunt. The curtains over her windows were still dark, the sun not strong enough to push through. She would have time to sneak down to the pantry for a snack before her mother rose for morning prayer.

Rolling off of her bed, she pushed down her chemise, as the gown somehow managed to bunch up at her hips every night. Slipping on her robe and a well-used pair of slippers, she tiptoed out of her room, careful of the creak of the door's hinge. The house was in its dawn hour prepwork, where the servants silently moved to dust the artwork and mop the foyer. Adrienne took the servant's stairs, a small rounding stairwell that was hidden between two large plants. It led close enough to the kitchen for her to pop her head in, eyeing the girl who stoked the fire.

The maid glanced up at her with a sighing grin and rose from her knees. With a towel, she picked up the kettle that hung over the flames and took it over to the prepping table. Adrienne waited in the hallway for the woman to hand her a steaming mug.

Ah, her stomach was ready for it. Content, she shuffled along to the morning room, ready to sit on the chaise lounge and watch the birds fly into the nest that balanced on a branch easily seen from the window.

Walking into the room, a tall shadow already stood where the window was. Adrienne leaped back with a sharp gasp before it quickly turned around to reveal the memorable wide eyes of the Marquis. He stood in his banyan — a damasked teal robe — and a matching morning cap to keep the hair out of his face. Some of the powder had worn off over night, bringing the stark white shade to a light blond. Adrienne's hair itself had maintained its overall shape with the amount of pomatum in it. She quickly collected herself, making sure the mug's contents did not get on her clothing nor the expensive imported rug beneath her feet.

"I'm sorry," the Marquis whispered. "I didn't mean to frighten you."

Adrienne coughed lightly, bringing the mug to her lips to blow off the steam. "I wasn't expecting anyone else to be awake," she said. She looked down at the untied center of her robe and quickly turned around to adjust for decency. "Forgive me, I am not usually so immodest."

"I will turn around then and not look, Mademoiselle," he said, and she heard the fabric of his robe crinkle. She peeked over her shoulder, and true enough, he was facing the window again where the baby birds bobbed about their nest. "The gardener always removed the nests from the shrubs at Luxembourg Palace. I have missed seeing them so close."

"I like how small and round they are," Adrienne mused, looking at the blue and yellow feathered mother returning with a worm. "And how their maman sits on them like they are little pillows."

"Only for warmth!" the Marquis said, grinning. "I can't imagine it to be very comfortable."

"Mothers make that sacrifice, don't they? To keep her babies safe."

"That is true. They do…"

Adrienne mentally slapped herself.

The Marquis carefully tilted his head, keeping his eyes on the window. "You may make yourself comfortable, Mademoiselle. This is your home; I can leave."

"No, no," Adrienne sighed, "it's alright. I'll be quick." She sipped faster by the doorway.

"What are you drinking?"

"Hot chocolate."

"Dessert for breakfast?"

"Why not? I didn't have it last night, did I?" she said. The unsettling silence that followed made her insides churn. "I meant that in jest, Monsieur, I am not angry."

He brought his fingers up to his waist to crack a knuckle, the whites of his eyes reflecting the rising sun as he spoke over his shoulder, but like a gentleman, continued to avert his gaze. "Thank you for the pastry," he said. "I had hoped I wouldn't make an enemy so soon into the evening from taking her sweets. It was my one goal upon arrival and I had failed it."

His jokes were terrible, Adrienne thought, but they continued to make her snort. It wasn't as if they were funny themselves or delivered in a mocking way – they were blunt, and simply self-deprecating.

"Hot chocolate makes for the best morning drink, Monsieur. I have tested all options and concluded that is so."

"All options?" He cocked his head.

"Well, ones proper for a lady to drink, of course."

"Ah, of course, only those. Perhaps I will request some tomorrow, then? If the lady scientist thinks it best for my health?"

Adrienne smirked. "I do."

He had joined the family for prayer – something not even Adrienne's father did – which pleased the duchesse and most definitely pleased the girls. Rosalie, asleep the night before, was very interested in this newcomer, but held back her tongue, only wanting to look at him through the whole of the mass. Antoinette was easily more tactile, her curiosity with poking the poor noble led Pauline to grab her hand before their mother had the chance to scold them. The Marquis never complained.

When he went away for his lessons, Louise and Adrienne went away for theirs. The days of the week seemed to go about normally, more or less, save for Adrienne gaining a new morning hot chocolate follower, much to her sister's tea-favoring roll of the eyes. If he joined them in the drawing room at night, he'd sit quietly and read while the girls knitted. On occasion, he'd sit on the ground by little Rosalie with her dolls and prop his chin in his hands.

"What are their names?" he asked, and Rosalie pursed her lips shyly.

"Madame Bergerie," she held up the shepherdess doll, "and… the Chevalier de Rose," she said of the gentleman.

"A chevalier!" the Marquis said, his voice piqued with genuine excitement. "He is knighted, then?"

Rosalie nodded. "They aren't married, though," she explained and the Marquis bobbed his head.

"Of course not. Madame Bergerie has all the cards, little miss." He carefully asked for the boy doll to which Rosalie hesitantly supplied. "The Chevalier de Rose is at your service, Madame," he said in a deeper voice, putting the doll into a graceful bow. "No trouble shall come to you as long as I can help it, if you'll allow me."

Rosalie bounced the shepherdess in front of him. "The country is a dangerous place!" she said.

"Ah, but no beast nor man will raise a fist – or claw – to you, Madame, I promise…"

Adrienne bit back a smile as she traded glances with Louise and her mother. Her mother was hesitant to allow him regularly into their family's drawing room, but within the week, she had relinquished to him an hour before they retired as long as everyone was still in their evening wear. Adrienne never mentioned the run in with the Marquis, both in their dressing gowns, to her mother for certain she would be banished to her chambers for the rest of the month.

☆

When the family found themselves together for a promenade through the Tuileries, Louis was among them. He walked sometimes with Louise, and other times with the duchesse, leading her arm as they spoke of family and his duties. Louise, then, slowed her pace to fall back with Adrienne, who spent much of the promenade tugging a reluctant Antoinette along.

"I need help," Louise said. Her hat covered most of the panic in her eyes.

Adrienne hummed. "I do not know if there is a doctor who knows your problems, dear sister."

"First of all, that was rude," Louise replied, "but more importantly, I was talking about Louis. I want to get him a gift before he turns sixteen on Friday. I've been giving him the same kind of satchels throughout the years, but now that we are engaged, I need to do *something* better than satchels."

"You think *I* know what sixteen-year-old boys want?" Adrienne said, then shook her head. "You really do need help."

"Adri, please!"

Antoinette yanked at Adrienne's hand until she was freed, the adolescent falling back until she stopped and pulled at the Marquis de la Fayette's hand instead, almost taking him down sideways. He *"la'd"* lightly, correcting his misstep, and looked up at the sisters ahead.

"She has not escaped," he said, with a small salute.

Adrienne sighed and pushed the hat away from her face – the straw covered in silk and daisies. Louise politely smiled and said, "I believe she merely caught her quarry, Monsieur. Sorry about her, she's a picky one; but no one likes Adrienne's hand. You may be stuck with her for the remainder of this jaunt." In her pause, she looked between Adrienne and the young man, the clockwork gears clicking before her smile split. "Actually, Monsieur Marquis, perhaps you may be of some assistance?"

"I will try," he replied. The four of them now walked in tandem.

Louise spoke in a whisper, and so he leaned in as if she were sharing the intelligence of the nation. "What do boys your age like? It is the important anniversary of the vicomte's birth this week and I want to surprise him with something special."

"A lavender satchel wouldn't suffice," Adrienne added, looking at her hand as if Antoinette abandoning her for the Marquis was its fault.

"Oh yes, he was mentioning his plans for the day," the Marquis said. "Something about his brother, the prince de Poix… and *drinking*, I believe."

"Well, he certainly isn't getting wine from me," Louise said, rolling her eyes. "It wouldn't last the day. I wish for something that will last. And thus, we ask you, Monsieur Marquis, as you are also from a similar type of family."

The Marquis looked off as he thought, the most minute expression changes in his brow or in how much he pursed his lips were evidence of the debate going on in his head. He would not be a good liar, Adrienne thought plainly, though if the Marquis was one to *try* was something she had yet to discover.

"I think every gentleman awaiting his time to be a soldier could use a new sword," he finally said with a firm nod. "Something nice and balanced; not for court fencing, but like a colichemarde for duels, or a saber, even."

"If Louis starts to find himself in duels, Louise may faint," Adrienne said, "but a saber sounds decent! Is that something that can be customized?"

"Yes, absolutely," he replied, the smile returning ten-fold. "There are many hilts to choose from, if you think he would prefer a decorative guard or something simple, then you can play with the design. You can also add engraving to the blade, but I will warn you, Mademoiselle, you will sacrifice its strength for the poetry. If you frame it as an officer's sword, which is more ceremonial, you see, then that strength won't matter as much. So it truly depends on if you'd wish the Monsieur Vicomte to use it or not."

Adrienne looked at Louise. "You know he would want to use it."

"It could be dangerous though," she said, bringing her fan up to tap her chin.

"He'd still use it," Adrienne and the Marquis said together, the former out of knowledge of *the* boy, the latter out of wisdom *of* boys. Adrienne worked her lip as she smiled. The Marquis simply twirled his walking cane in his other hand.

"I want a sword," Anne said, popping into their traveling triangle. "Can I have a sword?"

"You cannot have a sword," Louise said, "you are a girl."

Adrienne nodded and waited for Louise to walk ahead a step or two before she bent down and added, "Yes, Anne, you must wait until you are a *woman*. Then you may have your sword."

"Excellent. Oh Monsieur Marquis, will you teach me how to fight with a sword?" Antoinette pulled at his hand. "You will, won't you?" She looked at him with such large, brown, doe eyes that he simply drew out a long sigh and smiled.

"If your mother says I may, then I will, Mademoiselle."

They followed the line down the lush walkways. The sun warmed the speckled spots on the path where it could squeeze through the tree branches. Music was floating far in the distance, carried from an open window, a cello playing a piece from Bach. Every few yards, the Duchesse d'Ayen would be greeted by another, and the entourage slowed to a stop as customary conversation was made – the how-are-yous, the discussion of husbands, the latest of the King's movements with court… And all the while Louise stood with Louis again, looping her arm through his to rest on his elbow. But Adrienne for once was not standing alone behind them, as the Marquis kept Antoinette busy by her side. He twirled her like a ballerina, let her hold his cane, and showed her how to hold it like a foil should she ever need to give an unwanted suitor a good smacking.

Adrienne hugged herself, letting her gaze linger on the boy. With less makeup on, he still wouldn't be considered as handsome as someone like Louis, but something was there, she thought, that made him quite agreeable to look at.

"You're very good with children," she said when the walk picked up again. "If I wasn't told you had no young siblings, you could have fooled me."

The Marquis' shyness gradually returned to the blush in his cheeks. "I am, perhaps, a little too talented at *embarrassing* myself," he said, "but children seem to mind a little less. I could be fun, even, instead of a nuisance."

"I don't find you a nuisance, Marquis," she said. "My word, has someone told you that?"

He laughed. "I wish they did. Nay, I hear it from circles and can see it in their faces. *Ah*, excuse me, this isn't the type of thing I would normally say to a young lady."

"No," Adrienne shook her head, "please, I don't mind. I like when people are frank as well. Believe me, Marquis, I'm not a liar – I know Antoinette here can attest that you are far more fun than a nuisance… Unless you are trying to be one, then by all means, Monsieur, I am sure you have the *capability* to excel at that as well."

"I think my grandmère would agree with you, so with that evidence, I shall take your compliments," he said through a smirk. "She lives back home in Chavaniac – my father's maman. She's a good woman." The smile remained affixed while he looked out at the passing families and couples.

"I like my grandmère too," Adrienne said. "She hasn't been feeling well since the Epiphany, but I've been writing her letters every week so she knows her granddaughter loves her. Papi says she is recovering, so I'm hoping she visits soon. They usually live in our apartments in Versailles. Do you write to your grandmère often, Marquis?"

"As often as I can," he said. "Although letters can only alleviate some homesickness, not all of it."

"I cannot imagine…"

"Oh, please don't," he exclaimed, letting Antoinette go as she ran up behind Louise and Louis, nudging herself between the couple. "You shouldn't have to try and imagine homesickness, Mademoiselle de Noailles. I hope you are never at such a distance from your loved ones." His mouth tilted into a small smirk. "Unless you find that you feel sick *at* home, then I pray for an epic adventure and the fair countryside for you."

Adrienne covered a snort with a snap of her fan.

Chapter Three

❧

Paris, December 1772

Summer had come and gone rather mundanely. The Duc d'Ayen had enrolled the Marquis in the *Academie de Versailles*, and thus the young man who entertained his daughters so fervently through spring was away in their court apartments with fellow students his age who both outranked him in title and in class. Whether it was from how he rode his horses, to the way he lacked any and all elegance when learning to dance, it went without saying that the Marquis had a rough first season with them – and the Duc d'Ayen read through it all from the letters he received from the boy and his tutors.

Adrienne still went riding every Thursday, and Louise eventually was told by her mother that she and Louis would be formally married come spring. The teenage girl had slipped into her sister's bedroom soon after to leap and squeal atop her bed.

As the summer months in Paris paved the way into autumn, and slowly into winter, the Noailles sisters did their utmost to keep each other company while their father's temper brewed about things he would not speak of besides minor complaints that the boy was too foolish for his own good. Adrienne couldn't say what was the norm for boys who attended school for the families of the Sword; the Marquis had mentioned most of his classmates who attended *du Plessis* with him were from families of the

Robe, which placed him in a social sphere much higher than usual. He was spoiled there, according to her father, gaining too much hubris for where he should normally belong. For once, however, it was the duchesse who often came to the Marquis' defense after the evening's salon, especially when the young gentleman was returning from Versailles with some members of the family as the first snow fell late December evening.

Their carriage was shared, full of boyish hearsay and teasing, with swords on their hips that clashed as they pushed each other around in the confined space. Yet when the door opened in front of the Hôtel de Noailles, only two stepped out with care under the watchful eye of the duc: Louis smiling boldly to his old cousin, and the Marquis quietly giving the man a long and humble bow. The sisters watched from the northern drawing room window, faces pressed against the glass while their sorely missed company was escorted inside the warmed house.

Shoes left behind, several stockinged feet raced down the staircase, Antoinette almost taking the tumble as they reached the ground floor.

"Welcome back, welcome back!" Pauline shouted as the young men had their cloaks and hats taken from them, leaving a dusting of powdery snow on the ground. "Look at how many teeth I lost! I'm like a *worm* now," she said, opening her mouth.

"Pauline, come now, that's not ladylike," the duc scolded.

"Ah *là*, you are the prettiest little worm I have ever seen," the Marquis replied, bending over to investigate. "Have you been putting them in your shoes for La Petite Souris?"

"Yes, she's made ten whole livres in this past month alone," Adrienne said, crossing her arms. "Spent it all on a new desk and pen set."

The Marquis quizzically raised his brow. "Oh really?"

"I'm going to be an author," Pauline said with a nod. "Like Madame de Puisieux!"

Before he had the chance to reply, the firm hand of Jean de Noailles gripped him by the shoulder, and his posture straightened immediately, the color to his cheeks faded as his warm expression cooled at the touch.

"My office, boy, before the night settles, if you will," the duc said, stealing the Marquis away from his daughters like a pail of water from the withering crops. "You as well, Louis."

"Papa," Adrienne started, but Louise took her arm and hushed her. Louis followed behind, giving the girls a genial smile before he turned down the hall and under the stairs where the office lay.

There came no yelling, for their father's voice would most definitely carry in the long corridor. Adrienne wished there was something – *some* noise, some sign of life. Minutes flew by and she couldn't imagine her father would outright murder the Marquis for not being the greatest dancer. He danced fine with Rosalie when she had asked him in the spring; it isn't his fault that a bunch of noble boys were trained well with their *living* parents around to guide them.

"Adrienne, calm down before you grow faint, will you?" Louise said, fanning her face. "You being moody in the direction of Papa's office isn't going to do anything for them. Come on, Maman is waiting upstairs. They'll come up when they are done – there's nowhere else for them to go."

"You don't know that," Adrienne replied. She fought against Louise's pulling. "Papa could throw him into the gardens for the rest of the night, or the streets; he's too skinny to have any natural warmth, Louise, he won't last in the cold!"

"Goodness, then we will throw a blanket out for your Romeo."

Adrienne felt her face burn. "He is not my Romeo! How could you say that, Louise?"

"Sure, sure," she replied, finally having the lead to drag her sister up the steps.

"Wh-why would you call him my Romeo?" Adrienne asked again. They hadn't done anything to warrant *anyone* thinking they were anything more than just friends… have they? She looked back down the staircase. No, there was nothing that would insinuate that – her reputation was secure, it must have been. The Marquis was away for several months and they hardly traded correspondence.

Sure, she sent him a letter here and there to check in – another new place to be settled in was intimidating to be certain. Telling him where the best chocolatier was in town or where the secret spots around their Versailles abode were was not written in any flirtation. The Marquis had only replied to two of her letters and they were short and frank, not suggesting she had mentioned anything out of line.

"Louise!" Adrienne spat, stopping them before they saw to their mother. "Why did you say that?"

"What?" Louise said, her light brows pulled taut. "Adri, I was teasing. I didn't mean anything of it. I just thought since Louis and I are together, it was queer when you and he end up in a pair. Nothing improper was meant by it."

Something improper drifted through her mind as she sat on one end of the sofa while the Marquis sat beside her in silence. It was late, and the hour was showing on the boys' faces while Antoinette tooted away at her flute. Louis and the Marquis had quietly followed the duc into the drawing room, chins tucked low and tail between their legs. Adrienne watched Louis approach Maman to greet her, then took Louise's hand to kiss before he settled next to them on the adjacent sofa. The Marquis bowed mindlessly before he had taken his seat. His gaze never quite made it up to watch Antoinette play. His nail picked at the buckle of his dark blue breeches instead, watching a piece of lint from the duc's frock settle on the ground.

Adrienne looked to her mother. It must have been evident that he was scolded, *right?* She wondered why no one else could see it – the redness that trailed from the tip of his nose to the sides of his eyes; it was unlike his usual blush that stained his cheeks like spilled tea. Adrienne had never seen the Marquis so upset. Her perturbed stare turned to her father now – the duc sitting in his chair, leg crossed over one knee. There was a pressure of being a son in an illustrious family, Adrienne knew that, but the Marquis was their guest, not a brother nor a nephew or a cousin. The thought that her dearest Papa would criticize their guest made her heart squeeze until it hurt. She crumpled the edges of her dress, trying her hardest to listen to her sister play. The tune did nothing to stop her from stealing glances every time she heard him sigh or see his shoulders slump in her periphery.

This was ridiculous, she fumed. She was allowed to speak to him, for goodness sake, he had been a friend for months on end and if her mother didn't smite him on the spot, she wouldn't do so now.

She leaned over, gently inclining her chin towards him. "Marquis," she whispered. He continued to stare in his thoughts, not even sparing a blink. Adrienne huffed. She scooted over a few inches and leaned again, careful not to attract the attention no one gave her anyway. "Monsieur la Fayette," she tried.

His shoulders shot back up, adding more powder from his wig to the wool. The hand that was picking at his buckle retreated to his lap. "Mademoiselle?" he said, his filled in brows pulled up into his familiar look of surprise.

"Are you alright?" Adrienne asked. "I hope my father wasn't harsh on you."

"Oh, I'm fine," he said. "He just heard that I am too talented for my own good. They were not prepared for someone like me at l'Académie; many a scolding."

He said it with a smile, but the shame in his eyes brought Adrienne to frown deeper.

"Is there anything I can do to convince you that you are not as foolish as you think you are?" she said. "I was taught to be very persuasive. I'm sure I can win if you start to disagree, so you are welcome to try. But I insist you simply take my word for it."

The tiniest smirk pulled at his lips. Adrienne latched onto it.

"You see, Marquis, while you were away in Versailles, I must be frank in telling you – if it were not already obvious – you were sorely missed."

Louise's glance from beyond the Marquis gleaned with a smug look that Shakespeare himself would covet. Adrienne blushed and straightened her posture, simply turning her head to look at the young man.

"Anyway, if you are not completely tired from your trip back to Paris…"

she said, and she caught her mother's passing look as well, her whispers ceasing. Adrienne continued to listen to Anne play – the girl frustratingly glaring at her music sheet. The duchesse's contentment with how close Adrienne could get to the Marquis seemed to fluctuate with the weather. Snow, apparently, was not a good enough reason to sit too close.

"Marquis," the duchesse took over, "we are attending the opera tomorrow evening. You will join us, yes?"

"I am your servant, Madame," the Marquis said. Adrienne heard his exhaustion.

It bothered her more than she expected.

The Marquis' wing was opposite Adrienne's, but she was discreet when she snuck up from the kitchen with the platter in hand, trying to keep the silver from clinking against each other. She kept to the walls, feeling like an assassin while shimmying between pillars and art towards the bedchamber doors. With everyone retired for the night, it was just her and the maid that tended the fireplaces that were out and about.

Adrienne paused by the Marquis' door when she heard the back and forth creak of pacing feet. She didn't expect him to be asleep yet, perhaps reading or writing as he tended to do when alone. Many times she had walked into a room when he was at a table, buried deep into a letter, the outside world a blur around him. If she peeked over his shoulder, the small handwriting revealed itself, his script sharp and slanted – unexpected from a boy who presented himself rather demure around her family.

Thus the aggressive pacing caught her off guard.

Pressing her ear against his door, she decided he couldn't have been very close to the entrance. If she could manage to open it quietly, then she could slide the platter inside and run away as fast as her legs would allow. He wouldn't be the wiser.

Ever so delicately, she lowered herself to the ground.

A few candles were lit, their dim glow reflected off the hall floor as she cracked the door an inch… two inches…

She should have shut it as soon as she saw a glimpse of his bare leg –

the Marquis was stalking to and fro in his shirt and banyan, mumbling to himself. The wood panels were still damp from what must have been a tub, the candlelight flickered around tiny puddles, a starry night at his feet. He wore no peruke, and the powder from his hair was cleaned off, revealing the rather short locks that curled about his ears and nape of his neck. He was a redhead, not a blond as Adrienne thought before. It suited him, the copper hair with his pale complexion.

Her heart had drummed so loudly, with a start, the silver platter clinked on the herringbone pattern beneath her. However lightly, it was deafening. As the Marquis stopped, so did Adrienne's breathing, and the two of them gawked toward each other in the shadows without a word between them. Only the heavy ticking of a clock down the hall provided some anchor to the world.

Adrienne should have ran when the Marquis approached the bedchamber door – it would have been a little embarrassing, but anything would have fared better than looking up from her pitiful hiding spot as the young man carefully pulled the heavy post open.

Oh, she bit her tongue, *the curls on his forehead really did suit him.*

The Marquis had opened his mouth before he looked further down at the silver platter, filled with a pot of hot chocolate and a plate of pastries. His brows, which were no longer filled in with the dark clove, were light and rounded, and softly pulled together.

"Are you alright?" he asked, eyeing Adrienne who had not moved from her sprawl.

"I'm well," she quipped. "I brought you hot chocolate. Thought maybe they had neglected you in Versailles, so there is enough here for several months at least."

He pressed his lips together in a tight line. Lifting himself on his toes, he glanced down the empty hallway before he sharply pulled his banyan closed.

Adrienne cleared her throat, staring down at the desserts. He had nice calves.

"You didn't have to do this for me," he said, sitting down on the ground with her like they were at tea together and not in the frame of his chamber in the middle of the night. He took the cup and saucer that Adrienne handed him.

"No one else has hot chocolate with me," she shrugged, "and I wanted to apologize again if Papa said anything against your honor. He was worried about making sure you have the best education that is afforded to you. Papa already receives chiding for allowing Maman to have my sisters and I educated beyond the basic etiquette for a lady. Believe me, Monsieur, that you have done no wrong here."

The Marquis sipped the chocolate thoughtfully, letting the mug warm his hands. "I admire your warmth, Mademoiselle," he said. Then he tilted his head. "It was not just my lessons that earned me a reprimand, however. I must admit, I am quite cross with another student." He pointed his finger down towards the hall. "He rode in the carriage with the Vicomte and I here."

"Cross with him? What has he done?"

"*Bah*," he replied, his mouth disappearing back into the mug. "The Comte de Ségur owes me a duel. I've confronted him to take up the sword plenty of times and he refuses each."

"A duel?" Adrienne said, her voice raising in alarm. "Marquis, you can't do that!"

He shrugged, and divulged in a macaron. "Apparently not," he said, bluntly.

Adrienne had never seen the Marquis' temper flair so much. "You must truly detest the Comte for whatever he has done," she said.

"Yes, but he is one of my only friends, so he will have to deal with me until he accepts my challenge. Although it is apparent that your father, as well as your grandfather, have been communicating with Ségur's father, the Marquis, and well..." He shook his head. "Excuse me, I keep ranting about things that do not interest you."

"No, no, I am interested," Adrienne replied, engrossed with the boy's shift in attitude.

"No, it's not appropriate."

"We are on the floor in our nightgowns, Monsieur," she reasoned. "We'd already be imprisoned by my mother for indecency."

The Marquis set his empty cup down and paused with his hand on the kettle for another serving. His blinking outnumbered the seconds, and he poured the hot chocolate while he pursed his lips, mumbling, "I think that frightens me more than the idea of losing a duel."

His stubbornness was delivered in such a casual way, it could have been read as cold, but Adrienne was catching on. They both were older now – thirteen meant a girl was much more wise. What *fifteen* brought to young men, she didn't know yet, as Louis was her only example, and he would certainly be an outlier in any experiment.

"I visited home while I was gone," he said, bringing Adrienne back to attention. "Maybe that's why I seem to have forgotten all the intricacies of a courtier's life; the country hills of Chavaniac do that to a man. I have missed it."

"Seeing your grandmère must have been nice," she replied, thinking of the way he would speak of her in the early spring.

"Y-yes," he whispered, his voice trailing off to nothing. The tiniest of sniffles could have been from the cold halls or lingering from his long carriage ride into the city, but Adrienne was no stranger to a stifled sob, and her heart began racing again.

"Monsieur?" she said. She set her cup down and leaned over the platter, a hand to his arm. He shook his head, breathing deep before he smiled.

"She passed away not long after I returned to school," he said. "Peacefully in her bed, I was told. There's no better way for an old woman to go, I suppose."

"I'm so sorry," Adrienne said, hand drifting to his elbow. "I am so sorry, Marquis."

"My aunt and cousin were with her, so it is alright. It's comforting to know that she was not alone."

"And you are not alone, Monsieur," Adrienne exclaimed. "We are all here for you."

He was silent for another moment or two, his gaze drifting up from the platter of chocolates to her. Like looking at a newly unveiled painting, he nodded slow and gentle, the pained smile settling into something a little more consoled.

There was one curl atop his head that must have dried like that – bouncing straight up amongst the rest of his hair. Adrienne wanted to touch it, to fluff up the rest of it.

"Little Pauline wants to be a writer, hm?" he said finally, picking at the leftover croissants. "I never caught what sort of things she wishes to write."

Adrienne clicked her tongue. "She gets inspired by something different every day. Madame de Puisieux is a very forward thinker and we read a lot on the equality of men and women, but then Pauline is also interested in myths and legends, so I believe she will be a novelist of many stories."

"And Anne?"

"Still wants to be a musketeer thanks to you. Maman can't seem to shake that idea from her just yet. We're trying to convince Rosalie that Anne has high hopes for a young girl."

The Marquis smirked into his mug.

"Louise is ready to be married this upcoming spring," Adrienne said, picking at the seam in her robe. "She's been trying to have a say in the menu, but isn't having much luck. But I believe she's already decided on her gown and that's been sufficient enough it seems."

They had barrelled through most of what she packed onto the platter – all of it was meant for the Marquis, but she picked at it too. She hadn't intended on sticking around.

"And of you?" he asked. "How was the rest of your year?"

"I've been… existing, I suppose," Adrienne said. "Nothing special. That's alright though."

He settled his hands in his lap, the mug cooling from the time. "Well, thank you, for all this. It was welcoming with your company included. And I am certainly *happy* for your continued existence, Mademoiselle," he said warmly. "I think that is special enough."

Adrienne beamed. "It was nothing, Monsieur Marquis, I enjoy *your* company as much as I do the chocolate's." She gathered herself, knowing the hour was growing late and heaven forbid her mother took a late night walk through the house.

"Gilbert," the Marquis whispered, watching her rise. Adrienne froze in place, holding her robe closed.

"Pardon?"

"You may call me Gilbert, if you wish," he said. "It is what my family called me."

"Is… is that appropriate?"

"We did just picnic on the floor," he replied, pulling a watch from his banyan's pocket, "at two in the morning."

She grinned, and passed a glance towards the curve of the hallway before she looked back with a nod. "Very well," she said. "In private, of course."

"Of course," Gilbert said, bowing his head from his seat on the floor. "Good night, Mademoiselle."

"G-good night."

Adrienne slipped down the wing's hall, her face burning from a smile that didn't fade while her cheeks ached. Like a ghost through the passageways, passed her parents' rooms and into the wing that held all of her sisters, she spun herself into her own chambers, the fire dimming in its hearth. Beats of her heart hammered against her chest, threatening to burst. As she pushed her back against the sturdy door, a mass of giggles escaped her lips before she had the chance to cover them.

"Gilbert," she breathed – alone, to herself.

Parting is such sweet sorrow.

Chapter Four

Outside Paris, February 1773

He was always told that he grew at inopportune times – surpassing even his tutor's height when he was but eleven. The Marquis de la Fayette was, more often than not, the tallest man in the room even at the fruitful age of fifteen. There were occasions he didn't mind the height, there was a sense of authority about it, and many ladies found him interesting to look at. But he knew he stood awkwardly, and never figured what to do with his hands nor how to hold an expression that didn't betray his inner thoughts, making the attention he garnered absolutely atrocious. Any attempt to come off as nonchalant made him look too serious – truthfully, in l'Académie, in the operas, or dinners with the courtiers and their sons, he had little to say for their conversations. Whether it was about lands they owned or the gambling games they played, it was boring, and Gilbert found himself staring off into the corner of every room, or at the missing spots of powder on every man's wig.

His own wig was itching the back of his neck like it was a pine tree's branch. His cravat had pulled slightly down when he threw on his waistcoat in a rush to meet his uncle, and there was no decent time to fix it from when he was tossed into his carriage, banging his forehead in the process, to being pushed along from the Hôtel de Noailles to the apartments in Luxembourg Palace, then abruptly to the home of Monsieur d'Aguesseau – the Duchesse d'Ayen's father.

The Comte de Lusignem's grip on his neck was pinching a nerve. Maybe if he skewed his head slightly, he could get one of the man's rings to itch that spot.

"If it's only family, Uncle, was formal attire so necessary? I have drilling today with my regiment," Gilbert asked, skipping a step or two as the doors were opened for them. The feathers on his hat were fighting back against the fierce wind that had been causing quite the mischief in the city over the week, stealing hats and throwing up skirts.

"It is not just *'family,'*" the comte replied. "And after your stupid fiasco with Ségur's boy over that silly girl, you owe it to me to be a proper gentleman." They barrelled through the hall, their heels clicking loudly on the wood.

"I had fancied her and he tried to seduce her behind my back," Gilbert argued. "I had it in my right to challenge him!"

The Comte de Lusignem whirled around so suddenly, the buttons at the back of his frock pleats clicked like muffled cannonfire. "Listen here, boy. From now until this contract is sealed, there is no chasing primadonnas or actresses nor any daughters of the court. Save it for when you are married and have an heir – do you understand? Imagine, all this time living with the duchesse and her daughters and you've been trying to gallivant off like a buffoon!"

"All the boys in Versailles have been," Gilbert said. "You cannot say it's not normal."

"I'm not saying it isn't, Marquis," the comte said through gritted teeth. "But for one, all those boys rank higher than you in court, and two, I do not give a *damn* how their guardians are dealing with their incompetence. I have you for that. You will not ruin this for us. This is for *your* benefit. A wealthy orphan whose name means nothing in Paris. The Noailles' are diamonds in court. They can get you somewhere."

The door to the office opened and the familiar stern face of the

Duc d'Ayen greeted them. Inside the room felt like a secret meeting place, complete with the Duchesse d'Ayen, the Duchesse de Noailles, the Madame and Monsieur d'Aguesseau, as well as the Comtesse de Lusignem, Comte de la Rivière, and Monsieur Jean Gerard – Gilbert's lawyer. Not long after the young Marquis arrived and stood in the corner of the room did Abbé Murat enter – the cousin of his auntie who remained south in the Château de Chavaniac.

"Good morning everyone," Monsieur Gerard said, setting his hand on the paperwork along the large table. "At long last we are finally getting somewhere, yes?"

There was a quiet chorus of murmurs and nods. Gilbert leaned against the bookshelves, tapping his hat against his leg, silent as he always was in these more frequent meetings since the year had started.

"We have confirmed that the lady's dowry of four-hundred-thousand livres was attainable and reliable from the duchesse's sum, given to her by right from Monsieur d'Aguesseau. Any opposed to the proposal? No? Excellent, please sign here…"

The contract was long and detailed, clearly something that had been worked on for quite some time if Gilbert were to make any guesses. Although he was central in the document's pages, never did any adult ask him a question nor his consent on the matter. While he considered himself growing mature, fifteen was still young to think about something like *marriage*. He thought of his father, wishing he could ask him how he felt when he was engaged to Maman… he probably *knew* about it at least.

If there was one thing that he hated, it was that: he had not known. But he digressed, he was standing amongst them now, and yet his future wife was left in the dark.

It became the subject of debate now that the document was signed by all parties and the declaration that his Majesty, the King, would approve by the end of summer was read.

"Duchesse, by now, don't you think it wise to let Mademoiselle de Noailles know of her future?" Murat said as they toasted to the deal. "She is bound to find out, it is the talk of the town. With your eldest's marriage,

I am shocked that the matter has not already perforated your home's walls."

"When I see it done, it will be by my own word," the duchesse replied. "I will approve when the King formally gives his consent."

"I have not even seen my future in-law," the Comte de la Rivière said, finishing the champagne.

"Abbé Fayon described her as a fair embodiment of both her mother and father," Murat exclaimed, a small smile towards the d'Ayen's.

"Good, good, perhaps she will keep my zealous nephew in line, then," the Comte de la Rivière laughed. Only a few glances were spared toward the boy in the corner.

"A pretty face and a pretty dowry to match, I can't think of anything more agreeable," Lusignem nodded. "To your family, Monsieur d'Ayen, Monsieur d'Aguesseau." He held up his glass before he set it empty on the table.

Gilbert was only spoken to when Murat told him of his new living arrangements. While he attended school and lessons, living in the Noailles apartments of Versailles, he was to return to Paris every other week to visit on Sunday and Monday. It felt like he was a dog, being shunted around from shelter to shelter with a leash that tightened around his neck.

His neck that *still* itched, damn the formality.

He remembered many of his academy mates and thought maybe the dauphin's brother, the Comte d'Artois, would be interested in having his horse stamp on it.

Versailles, June 1773

The Duc d'Ayen was more conscientious to Gilbert's standing at Versailles now that the two were officially to be in-laws. It wasn't long into the year when the Marquis held his lieutenant's commission to the Noailles Dragoons. The uniform wasn't Gilbert's favorite – the change from the regal red of the Musketeers to a summer green coat with white facings washed the young man's complexion out completely. And if he were not already immensely tall, the helmet of the regiment made him all the more so.

"You look like you'd be a good grenadier," Louis said, riding up next to him on their route back to the riding grounds. "If you put on some weight, that is."

Gilbert cocked his head, the fur of the helmet swaying like a horse tail to one side. "My father was a grenadier," he said. "It's the only physical idea I have of him besides one portrait and, well, my unfortunate face."

Louis raised his brows and laughed. "You're not so bad looking, Marquis," he replied, leaning over in his mount to pat Gilbert on the leg. "I'm sure once a lady gets her hands on you, she'll work her magic."

"Is that what happened with you and your new vicomtesse?" Gilbert asked, straightening his back as their captain trotted by for inspection. His shoulders automatically slumped slightly as soon as the horse had passed.

"I was handsome since birth," Louis said, "but Louise always has ideas for what I should wear when we are together, and what color powder I should buy. Women are interesting like that. Trust me, when you find yourself married, ask your wife how she would prefer to see you. Then when you go out, you can dress the opposite and find a girl to dally with, eh?"

"Louis, not a few weeks from your vows and you've already a mistress?" Gilbert asked. Sure, the vicomte was seventeen, but the idea of seeing him stray so soon from Louise was surprising.

"No," he replied, then smirked. "But a little flirtation never hurt anybody. Being presented at court has that coming. There are a lot of painted ladies ready to thrust their bosoms at you and your wallet, my dear Marquis."

The campus of the academy was a skip and a jump from the palace; a slightly curved building with stables lined the inner walls like doorways to a hundred rooms. Thankfully, the day was dry, as, if wet, the stone walkways could be slick enough to slide a *cannon* through with relative ease, let alone the horses and their riders. It was a breeding ground of young men with ambitious goals and lofty family names to uphold.

Without being too pompous, it was full of first-borns or even wealthier second sons whose families preferred the lessons of chivalry over that of the clergy – which was where many second sons ended up. Gilbert was an only child, and thus any teasing of siblings or competitive nature surrounding it went right over his head.

Though he *was* becoming well acquainted with what it was like to have young sisters. He half-expected Antoinette de Noailles to appear among the gaggle of boys, sword in hand ready to jab at them all like he had shown her; or Rosalie to be at his feet – still wanting to play with her dolls, but now telling him what actions he as the Chevalier de Rose should do next; Pauline sent him copies of her stories to read on the rides to and from Versailles – which were honestly decent work that kept him well entertained while Louis hastefully wrote his new wife in their carriage. The Noailles sisters were eccentric bundles of joy, and Gilbert did enjoy their company when he was with them. Yet the confinements of the house and having to powder and prissy up to every social interaction was driving the young Marquis a little mad.

He hadn't expected to see Adrienne on the floor outside of his apartments while he was blowing off steam over winter. After screaming under the surface of a scolding bath and perhaps hitting too many pillows, he begged she hadn't witnessed such a tantrum.

Adrienne had a delicate kindness – with good taste in late night snacks. She always seemed to match his energy, at least, to the best of her ability; her attempts in making equally bad jokes meant more to Gilbert than he let on.

When he was told he was already engaged a year prior, he was more confused than angry – he was so young? Pity the wife who would have to deal with his juvenile nature. When he was told it was Mademoiselle Adrienne who would be that wife, *now*, Gilbert's thoughts twisted. They were both too young, and he expressed that blatantly to the Duchesse d'Ayen. She agreed with him, yet here they were still forming a contract.

Gilbert liked Adrienne, but then again, he liked any pretty lady that gave him attention. Although, not every young girl that spoke to him expressed as much tenderness as Adrienne did – and she still didn't know he was her fiancé. It made him feel a little defensive when she was brought up in conversations, as if he was her own personal knight to fight for her honor.

And that's how he kept it for the past several weeks. He would be there for her by the carriages and to walk her to the theatre, an escort for whatever she needed. Sometimes, he thought, it didn't really seem like acting – the smiles she gave him and the tiny self-deprecating jokes she returned brought a warm color to his cheeks.

"Thinking about something fun?" Louis asked, helping to pull the saddle off of the Marquis' horse.

"Only about how fast I would take down Philippe if he wasn't a *coward*," Gilbert smartly replied, turning to look at the Comte de Ségur in the stall next to them.

The young man was almost twenty and already enlisted in the army, and if it were any other brazen student who said such a thing, he would have every right to backhand them then and there. But Ségur merely coughed and sputtered, a mock offense as Gilbert gave him a prolonged, yet friendly scowl.

"Only you would be so bold as to think I would dare take any woman away from you, Monsieur," Ségur said. "After all, with your receding hairline, those women are saints to approach you. I am too close to God to intercede in his work, for that is what it will take to have a pretty lady enjoy that." He gestured to Gilbert's face as a whole, his lips pursed in a humorous smirk.

Louis howled and clapped Gilbert on the shoulder. "Best to just take it, Marquis," he said. "His father would whip you with his *one* arm if you touched a hair on Philippe's horse-shaped head."

Ségur took up his riding crop and sent it like a catapult to Louis' ass. "You shut your mouth, Noailles, I have two arms to smack both of you." He shook his head. "Honestly, it's a wonder why I keep friends my little brother's age. Go finish your drill before the colonel hounds me for keeping you. I don't need Pierre's shrill voice in my ear, I leave that for you two."

Louis smoothed out his uniform. "Yes, we also will enjoy Pierre's far more handsome face. A normal shaped head, wouldn't you agree, Marquis?"

"Y-yes," Gilbert replied, firmly nodding to whatever tomfoolery came out of his future brother-in-law's mouth. Ségur idly rolled his eyes as he did too often and waved them on.

"I expect you to be at my apartments later," Louis added to Ségur, pulling Gilbert along to where the dragoons lined up outside with their swords. "You and I have a card game to finish!"

"Another party?" Gilbert whispered, fixing the helmet under his arm. "You had one three days ago."

"Well I received a new shipment of cognac that I wish to try with my beloved friends. I can't drink *alone*, can I, Marquis? You're coming too, of course."

"I mean, yes, of course," Gilbert said. They were neighbors after all. "But won't the vicomtesse be expecting you?"

"Is it that time of week, already?" Louis asked, standing amongst the line. Gilbert nodded. "Hm. I guess we will be showing up late and slightly inebriated, *non?*" He elbowed the Marquis in the side, a wide grin splitting his features. "I'll save one glass for you – Heaven knows you're a lightweight."

Gilbert opened his mouth to retort, but shut it as their captain strolled by, merely setting his jaw and staring ahead as drill orders were given.

Drilling with the Noailles' Dragoons was similar, in a way, to with the King's Musketeers. But he missed the freedom he had belonging to the Musketeers – the prestige he felt in protecting the King and his family, the tougher fencing, the fact that the Duc d'Ayen's eyes weren't constantly boring into his soul…

Gilbert set his sword lightly on his shoulder and marched in time with the other men. His head whirled with one thought too many, a character flaw his mother once told him he had that he must have inherited from his father.

Adrienne's eyes were brighter than her father's, a candlelight in the dark. He liked when they crinkled with her smile.

Paris, August 1773

"It's as if they don't have bones," Adrienne whispered to him as they watched the acrobats perform in the Plâce Louis XV. It was an impromptu street show that delighted many of the aristocracy – some players from a small French colony in India. The two of them had been walking the gardens with family company when the performance kicked off, gathering a large crowd in a few minutes. She gripped his arm and made a gagging noise as one performer bent backwards in half. "Oh my God."

Gilbert grinned. "You don't have to watch," he said, as she turned her head again.

"No, no, I want to, it's fascinating," she replied, hesitantly eyeing the players as they threw themselves into the air and tumbled with exact precision. "The height they achieve is marvelous – like a bird taking flight."

"It is rather impressive."

"And that one there holding up two people," she said, pointing at one middle-aged man, whose arms seemed larger than his head. "Oh to be picked up like that!"

He heard her laugh over the immense applause of the crowd and watched as her smile relaxed as the show went on. Gilbert looked back at the strongman, eyes narrowing. He could probably pick Adrienne up like that if he tried, he thought, how hard could it be?

Not that he would try out in public with her. If his uncle didn't strike him on the spot, the Duchesse d'Ayen would no doubt smite him from above.

"Are you well, Marquis?"

Blinking towards Adrienne, he nodded more aggressively than he intended, for the young mademoiselle raised her inquisitive brow. "I am distracted as of late, I suppose."

"Would talking about it help?" she asked. "We can abscond to the

Tuileries, I'm sure that no one will notice if we went walking."

"Without an escort? Your maman would kill me," Gilbert said.

"Oh please, she knows you well by now. How couldn't she, you are essentially part of the family."

The Marquis de la Fayette certainly knew that was truer than Adrienne was aware of. Tapping his walking stick to the ground, he glanced over to their company: his uncle and his family, some of Adrienne's relatives, and Louis — who was staring at him with the stupidest smirk on his face.

"Perhaps we can get away with the strip just behind us?" Gilbert offered, moving his body to shield the fact that the youngest among them was escaping with him into the crowd. The sun was on its slow descent in these summer months, and casted long shadows across the square; no one would notice if two of those shadows retreated away. He was conceivably feeling a little guilty for possibly causing some controversy with being with Adrienne *slightly* alone. Should rumors spread too much, the typical resolve was to marry each other.

Ah, the *scandal*: two people engaged to have to marry. Gilbert rolled his eyes.

What he wasn't anticipating was to actually say something to Adrienne when they reached the garden's outer wall. He couldn't tell her the truth, that is, if he mentioned their engagement then he was a dead man walking. But he couldn't lie to her – she had a countenance that made it absolutely impossible.

"Gilbert?" she said, and he felt the spotlight burn his ears. "You're fidgeting again; what's wrong? You did not stab the Comte de Ségur, did you? Gosh, I've never thought about having to hide a body, but –"

"Goodness, no, no, nothing of that," Gilbert replied, waving his hand. "It's…" he paused, backtracked, and asked, "you would help me hide a body?"

Adrienne blinked. "If I must."

They walked side-by-side, their hats tilted to block what remained of the sun from their eyes. Every few trees hosted an empty nest, the year's new hatchlings having grown and taken off already to their wide skies.

"Hopefully we will not have to dirty your hands with such a thing anytime soon," he said with a small smile.

She was silent, only looking up at him expectantly, the bottom beading of her bodice on the receiving end of her own fidgeting. Carefully reaching down, he took her hand from its nervous prattle and raised it up as if he were bidding her adieu. They had stopped walking now.

"What are *you* so nervous about?" he asked. "I swear I haven't stabbed anyone."

Adrienne laughed, the apples of her cheeks growing rosy as if dusted by petals. "It's nothing," she said. "I'm just curious about what has you so distracted as of late. To be truthful, you've been acting a little off for a few weeks. Not a *bad* off, but unusual. I want to make sure you are well, so… are you well? You aren't ill?"

"No, I'm not ill, I am – maybe – a little tired from the academy. That's all. All the back and forth travel between housing is a bit wearisome," he admitted, trying his best to teeter around the truth of his anxiety by answering one question of the many she proposed. "I miss simply riding through woods without being reprimanded for my posture."

The coo that she made was quickly covered by her free hand, the quiet laugh following to mask it made his heart squeeze. He started to worry if his hand was becoming clammy; he should have let it go by now: her hand. But it rested relaxed in his, their fingers taking each other's warmth.

"Your posture isn't so bad, Gilbert," she said with a shake of her head. "Maybe you'll come riding with me this Thursday? If you'll stay longer, that is. I understand that you have your duties and the like to get to; far more important things than me –"

"You are important," he interrupted, the shared self-deprecation beginning to bother him. Hearing Adrienne speak down about herself was unacceptable. "I will happily entertain you this Thursday."

Her face glowed as her eyes crinkled. "You need not entertain me," she said. "I enjoy your company even if we ride in silence. It's nice to not be alone."

Gilbert nodded. He knew that sentiment better than most. Enclosing her fingers in his, he finally brought her knuckles up to his lips before he released it and offered his arm for their promenade. Part of him wished someone saw and called them out; let Adrienne know already, he thought, *it wasn't fair.*

Chapter Five

Versailles, November 1773

The Noailles apartments in the tight-knit city of Versailles were outside the palace walls. The family *had* apartments inside, but the Duc d'Ayen detested being there longer than he had to, and with a family the size of his, a humble house in the city fared much better. Adrienne considered it their country getaway home, which was a bit of an oxymoron with all the courtiers strolling about, with only a row or two of buildings separating them from the working people.

While Adrienne's room in these apartments was smaller, the window looked out to a large tree that hung over the street, as if reaching out to their neighbors. It was a favored spot of squirrels, and she would find herself merely watching a pair chase each other up and down the trunk before escaping to the other side.

They were to be here for the winter quarter – the Duc de Noailles and the Duc d'Ayen served the King's bodyguard directly over these weeks; a task that befitted their station.

Her parents, as well as her sister and Louis, were invited to the dauphine's eighteenth birthday dinner – which was unfortunate to Adrienne, for she shared a birthday with the future queen. Very rarely would King Louis XV be in Versailles for longer than a month, preferring his other homes around France. She had spent most of her birthday rolling around her bed – a boring Tuesday with only her younger sisters for the occasional stimulation. When she wasn't laying across her bed, she draped herself over the drawing room sofa, listening to Pauline as she recited the drafts to her current piece, a complete memoir of her life. Comparing it to what other seven-year-olds would be writing, Adrienne mused, it offered a unique perspective of a young, adolescent girl's thoughts on gender and social status. She couldn't help but give a little clap when Pauline finally looked up from her writing.

Antoinette, at a haughty ten and still intrigued by the sword, used her knitting needle to parry the small cane belonging to Rosalie's dolls. Rosalie had begun learning how to make more outfits for her chevalier and shepherdess, so instead of simply asking for new dolls, she and Antoinette started to knit armor for them to "wear into battle together."

The sofa was becoming strenuously uncomfortable while Adrienne rotated around it, letting her head hang upside down while she looked around the polished wood room. What felt like an hour had passed, yet it was more likely just a few minutes before the door carefully opened, and a very formal powdered wig leaned into view.

"Am I interrupting anything?" Gilbert asked, glancing from sister to sister.

While he trained at the academy, he had been using these apartments. His rooms, due to the size of the house, were a little closer than those of the Hôtel, but it was apparent that Adrienne's mother had a say on where he would be.

"We are making Madame Bergerie into a knight so the chevalier doesn't have to go to war alone," Antoinette said, raising a small knitted cuirass.

"Oh? Wouldn't the Chevalier de Rose wish to keep Madame out of harm's way if he could help it?" Gilbert said, stepping into the room. He was dressed in the Noailles family's dragoon uniform, sans helmet, a small flat box in hand.

Rosalie shook her head, as if the answer was obvious, "he could not stop her if he tried!"

Adrienne heaved herself back up on the sofa, not missing the curious look from the Marquis. "I don't think we've seen you in our uniform before," she said, propping her elbow on her knee.

Gilbert stood up straight, clearly under intense inspection by the lady of the room. "How does Mademoiselle de Noailles find this mere soldier?"

She tilted her head. "You look splendid. Although, the green doesn't suit you. It's too summery and I think you are more of a spring. I do enjoy the boots though, I think they make you look sturdy, that is, very soldier-like. Give us a spin."

He complied, carefully teetering in an ungraceful circle, his coat's pleats pulled together to reveal quite a pleasant rear view as well with his breeches, Adrienne would think if she weren't a lady.

"Can I braid your peruke, Marquis?" Pauline asked, setting her pen down. Rosalie and Anne both looked up from their work with wide smiles.

"Can we? Please, Marquis, can we?"

Gilbert pulled out his watch and sighed. "I suppose we shall have time for a simple queue, if that is comparable enough," he said, moving around the chairs to sit on the ground in front of them. He looked up at Adrienne with a dimpled smile while the young girls went off in undoing his powdered wig's previous style. "Keeping busy?"

Adrienne gestured to her discarded distractions at the edge of the sofa. "As busy as one can be when they're inside all day," she said, pulling at the frilled edges of her lace cap. "Why aren't you at the palace?"

"I wasn't invited," he said plainly. "Viz, since I'm not officially introduced at court yet. Sometime next year, I'm told. The king prefers spring for receiving new people, or something bizarre like that. Took up my morning with drills instead."

"And what was today's drilling like?"

"Shot some targets on horseback – that is, while I was on horseback, not the targets – the targets were… hay."

"How many hay targets did you slay?" Adrienne asked, leaning forward when the Marquis' head was pulled back, his hand moving to hold onto the top of his wig.

"I am sure I hit at least one."

"At least one."

He nodded. "At *least*."

"Impressive," Adrienne also nodded.

Antoinette glanced up from the plaiting. "Can I shoot a –"

"*No*," Adrienne said, with Gilbert echoing right along.

In a few minutes, the three of them successfully tied off a neat queue, adding back the black ribbon to the base. The Marquis gave their knuckles a quick kiss before he stood up again, holding the box he carried in now with two hands. His face was reddening even before he looked towards Adrienne.

"Box," he said.

Adrienne nodded once more. "Box."

"Hallway?" he asked, tilting his head towards the door.

Adrienne pulled her dress' petticoats up off of her feet and stood, smacking Antoinette's hand away from the sheath at Gilbert's side. She followed him into the hall. The only other company were maids that scrubbed the floor in the foyer, the wood dirtied by the road's mud and early snow mush.

"This is for you," he said, holding out the box, then pulled it back slightly when Adrienne reached for it. "*But!* You must wait to open it until your mother speaks with you, understand?"

"Maman? What is it?" Adrienne said, curiosity piqued. "A birthday gift?"

"Of sorts," he replied. "It won't make sense until your mother tells you, so… Promise me you won't open it until she is home."

Her brow raised. "But you know what she is going to tell me?"

Gilbert's shoulders tensed. "Yes."

"And *you* cannot just tell me?"

"No."

"Why not?"

"Adrienne," he whispered through gritted teeth, nerves slipping into his composure.

She clasped her hands together under her chin and sighed. "Yes, I promise. No opening the box until Maman has spoken to me."

He handed it to her, and she took it carefully. It was much heavier than she expected. From the shape of the box, she had some inklings of what could possibly be inside. She kept it to her chest and looked back up at the Marquis who smoothed his hands over his coat.

"Now what?" she asked.

Gilbert blinked. "Now what what?"

"Are you taken for the rest of the day?"

He clicked his tongue. "Ah, yes, technically. I am to speak with my uncle over supper."

"Oh."

"I'm sorry," he said.

Adrienne shook her head with a smile. "It's alright. Family is important."

"It is, but…" Gilbert bit the inside of his cheek. "It is."

"We will see you for breakfast tomorrow?" she asked.

His face appeared to be stuck in a nervous twitch, not as cutely innocent as he once had now that his baby fat was slowly leaving. "Perhaps, yes, I believe so." He brought his shoulder up in a half shrug. "I cannot say for certain, but –" with a deep breath, "I will try."

"Hot chocolate?" She cocked her head.

There was a bustling at the entryway down the hall – the voice of the Comte de Lusignem.

It was quick, Gilbert's bending over at the waist to kiss her exposed cheek, all the blood rushing to his face. Not a *faire la bise*, it wasn't cheek-to-cheek, but a *real* kiss. He straightened upright, frankly unable to look her in the eye. He looked over her instead while his uncle appeared behind him from Adrienne's view.

"Marquis!" the comte called. His voice rang through the corridor. "How long did you intend on keeping me waiting?"

Gilbert half-turned on his heel, his hands clapping behind his back. "Apologies, Uncle, I lost track of time."

"Clearly." The comte bowed his head politely towards Adrienne and then gestured to the door where the impatient clomping of horse hooves echoed in the house. "Come now or we'll be running late."

"Of course, Uncle," Gilbert said. He took a step back and dipped himself into a parting bow to Adrienne, keeping his eyes on the floor. The queue the sisters made remained in place down his back as he spun to meet his uncle down the hallway.

Adrienne curtsied to no one, as neither looked back at her. Lusignem only gripped Gilbert by the shoulder, the young man still growing taller by the day, and pushed him along out of view. Adrienne leaned to catch a longer glimpse of the Marquis. She kept the box firmly clutched in a tight hug, the spot on her cheek aflame as the rest of her body started to spark and shudder; her feet needed to hop in place as she split a grin. When the door closed with a reverberating *bang*, a sharp giggle escaped from the young lady who forwent all sense of decorum over the adolescent sin of a simple kiss to the cheek.

Would she have to admit this in confession, she wondered, covering the spot where the warmth lingered.

The Marquis, in fact, did not join them for breakfast the following morning when the other members of the family returned from the palace. Most of the day went on in continued boredom. Even Mademoiselle Maron's shrill reaction to Antoinette's unladylike responses to her questions about the Church didn't provide much entertainment or argument for once. Adrienne was distracted, awaiting her mother to call for her.

Continuing the next day, she propped her chin on her hand, watching out the windows to the squirrels below that picked at fallen acorns, tapping at the closed gifted box with her finger. During prayer, she stared at the painting of the Virgin Mary along the wall, glancing reverently towards her mother as the duchesse glanced away. It was going to drive her mad, but she didn't pry, she didn't outwardly complain. God heard enough of her lamenting and pleading.

At least she thought so.

By the time night came, Adrienne washed her face and sat on the edge of her bed. Her hair set in paper curls that had already been heated by her maid. The wood in the fire was damp from a soaking rain the night before, and so it popped and crackled as she read from the gazette she swiped from her father's hands. Nothing extraordinary in the news; perhaps some sailor exploring the South Sea was the most riveting story on the page.

Steps from outside her door were almost silent, the only betrayal was a creak from a pane of wood right along the corner. Adrienne glanced up, then immediately back down to the papers – she shouldn't seem so impatient about such things – as the duchesse carefully opened the door.

It was the way Henriette looked at Adrienne that made her feel as if what her mother wanted to say wasn't all good news. She put the gazette down by her pillow.

"Maman, what's wrong?"

The duchesse walked in, her red velvet robe dragging behind her. In her hands looped a rosary, the same one she was clutching throughout mass. Henriette took a seat at the bottom of Adrienne's bed; her daughter immediately crawled to meet her, worry building up like a flood in her lungs.

"There's something important I must speak to you about, *ma petite chou,*" she said, brushing her hand under Adrienne's cheek. Adrienne clenched her jaw and gave a small nod. "I've spent the better part of the day wondering how I was going to tell you."

"Tell me what, Maman? Did something happen?" The sudden panic that her mother was going to tell her something along the lines of *'the Marquis is dead'* brought spontaneous tears to her eyes.

Did she know about the kiss? She wouldn't have killed him herself truly, would she?

"No, nothing happened," the duchesse replied, then sighed, bringing her sleeve up to wipe Adrienne's watering eyes. "Well, something has happened, but it isn't something you should cry about. Your papa and I have been talking about this for a very long time. And like your sister, I wanted to wait until you were old enough to understand some things."

She gathered up Adrienne into her arms as if the young girl were still a babe.

"You know I would never agree to anything I didn't fully believe you can handle, my strong girl." Her chin rested on her daughter's shoulder. And she was silent for another minute; even the crackling fire ceased its noise under her dominion. "What are your thoughts on the Marquis?"

"Oh my goodness, is he well?" Adrienne shuffled in the restricting hold, looking at her mother as if she admitted the boy was anything but. "Maman, please tell me you didn't send him away – he did nothing wrong!"

"Adrienne," Henriette said with a breathy laugh. "The Marquis is well and still part of this household. Should I understand you care for his well-being then?"

"He's been a good friend, Maman," Adrienne said. "He listens to me."

"Hm, doesn't Louis listen to you too on your rides, *chérie?*"

"Louis *hears* me, maybe. It's hard not to. But Gil – I mean, the Marquis, he…"

The duchesse tsked lightly, a knowing smile on her face. "I thought the same of your father."

"You did?"

"Mmhm," Henriette mused. "Although I may have pushed some of his buttons as a borderline old maid."

"Maman!" Adrienne cried, "You could never be an old maid. You're the most beautiful woman in France."

"Just in France?"

"Well, I've never been anywhere else, I can't prove the world. I can maybe predict more beautiful than any woman in England as well – they are quite lackluster."

The duchesse laughed and pulled back some of the wrapped curls that bounced on Adrienne's forehead. "There's that Adrienne candor. I think the Marquis is also very honest; a rare trait in boys, don't you think?"

"He is honest to a fault, certainly. Why are you asking me about him?"

She held back the inquisitions about the duchesse potentially knowing that they had hallway picnics, or snuck away from chaperoning groups, or God-forbid, if she knew he kissed her cheek. Watching her mother struggle with saying something was like watching the sun forget how to shine or the tides not knowing how to rise and fall.

"Nothing you can't handle," her mother said again, squeezing her into a hug. Adrienne shifted to kneel in front of her as she took her hands. "Your father and I have been talking about your prospects in marriage, and this year, we have confirmed the match."

Adrienne's chest started to tighten as she held her breath. *Marriage.* After Louise, she would have been next in line. But Louise's engagement to Louis was a fairly long one. For once her mouth was dry of a response, the gears in her brain slowly clicking.

"We were thinking of spring for the ceremony, but we need to have some of his paperwork shipped up to our parish – it does take a disgusting amount of time from the south."

Spring was hardly five months away, that couldn't have been right, Adrienne thought. Who has such a short engagement in a family like hers? "Marriage, Maman?" she asked. "So soon?"

"Well, we have been letting you and the Marquis get to know each other for some time first. I did not want you to meet a boy under the presumption that you were bound to him. You have every right to form your own thoughts and feelings."

Adrienne's fingers went cold as the blood from them rushed to her cheeks. "The Marquis," she repeated. "I am… to *marry* the Marquis?"

"Yes, dear."

"*De la Fayette?*"

"I hope you were not thinking we were speaking of some other Marquis who has been living with us for almost two years."

Her heart pounded with such ferocity, Adrienne had to peel her hands from her mother's to cover her gaping and a quickly rising gasp. The tail-end of arguments she heard between Papa and Maman suddenly made sense when they were hushed at the sight of her and the Marquis;

the gradual allowing him to join them for events, to take up Adrienne's arm when Louis had Louise's, the hallway, the box.

The box.

"The box!" Adrienne tumbled off of her bed sideways, scrambling over to her boudoir where the thin, square container rested untouched, as she promised. Henriette followed her with her eyes, caught off guard from Adrienne's volume.

"What is this?" the duchesse asked, getting to her feet.

"It was a gift," Adrienne said, "from the Marquis. I figured it was something for my birthday, but now I'm not so sure." She slid the ribbon off the wood and held her thumb to the crease to open it. The thought that, maybe, it could be *inappropriate* for her mother to be here to see what Gilbert gave her crossed her mind, but it wasn't in his warning, and she trusted that he would still be a gentleman.

Pulling the lid up, she balanced the weight on an open palm, the light from the fireplace cast the gift in a glittering barrage. A gold-backed pink topaz necklace, speckled with diamonds, sat in the satin lining and circled the rest of the parure with matching earrings and a cross-shaped brooch. The shade of the topaz was the same soft pink both she and Gilbert wore when they had first met.

"An engagement gift," the duchesse said, coming around to look over Adrienne's shoulder. "How wonderful...ly expensive, oh my."

"Y-yes, it must have been," Adrienne whispered, unable to stop thinking about Gilbert's face and how nervous he was to give this to her. The Marquis was a giver by nature, gifting horses to Louis when asked, distributing his wealth as if it were a bottomless pit, a sparkly jewelry set to his betrothed would not be out of his wheelhouse.

He knew.

Of course he knew, she thought, *men are always in the know first.* But how did he feel about it? Was he as satisfied with her as she was with him?

Did he get giddy like she had become? It was a weird feeling, like a million needle pricks, when he was around, when he looked at her like she was, for *once*, the only person that mattered; and he didn't seem to mind being with her alone.

But he did know then, too?

"Adrienne, dear?" Her mother's hands squeezed her arms. "I know how you are usually so well articulated. Why the few words? If you tell me you do not want to marry this boy, just say so and I will wreak havoc for you. But I have grown fond of the Marquis. I think he will make you happy."

"I am happy, Maman," Adrienne said. She turned to face her mother and smiled. "I am happy to marry him, I'm surprised, that's all. Tell Papa, would you? I think I'm overwhelmed enough that I need to sleep."

Henriette hummed. "Certainly," she replied, and pressed her cheek against Adrienne's. "Let's talk about it more in the morning? There are some new lessons Maron and I must teach you right away."

"Goodnight," Adrienne whispered. She watched as her mother went, taking up a candle to escort herself down the hallway.

Remaining steadfast until the door was closed, Adrienne gasped until her lungs went concave, sinking to the polished floor. She held out the parure like a platter and carefully set it down on the floor in front of her. A custom set like this must have taken months to orchestrate. It was heartwarming that Gilbert remembered what color they were wearing when they first met – a small detail that not every man would recall. Adrienne knew this by fact because Louise was in yellow when she first sat down with Louis post-proposal, but when asked, Louis didn't even remember what day it was, let alone the color of her dress.

A follow-up groan followed as Adrienne covered her eyes and rolled back on the floor. Topaz was her birthstone, of course Gilbert would choose for her the expensive jewel. She was going to go mad with how perfect he was. All she's ever given him has been a hot drink and sweets.

Adrienne smacked the ground with an open palm, the echo swallowed by the pop of the firewood. *She would have to do better*, she decided. Never would twelve-year-old Adrienne let a boy unravel her like this, fourteen was to be no different!

As she removed her banyan and set the jewels safely back on her boudoir, she shuffled back to her bed. The lights from the windows wheeled by with a carriage as it stopped in front of the Noailles apartments, the lanterns and torches waving. Adrienne paused at the glass while the carriage door opened and out stepped the tall, lean, young man in his winter cloak. Another person sat in the carriage, and the two spoke to one another for a moment longer before the Marquis closed the door and stepped back to watch it depart. She couldn't make out much detail of his face from her window, but covered her own as he turned to walk up the steps and paused – looking up towards her room.

Gilbert removed his hat and, with his left foot forward, dipped into a bow just as awkward and deep as when they first met.

Adrienne smiled behind her hands. If a small motion like that was enough to bring color to her cheeks, she was doomed.

Chapter Six

Paris, April 11th, 1774

If there ever were a date when Adrienne would witness her entire family flying about the Hôtel, it was the second Monday in April. Adrienne was sure her father had expressed the date for the wedding was to be on the Sunday, yet just several days prior, there was a fit between the joining families about the whereabouts of the Marquis' baptism record – the parish he belonged to, *Saint Sulpice*, was over three hundred miles away and he had never formally switched to belong to the *Saint Roch* church they frequented up in Paris. Gilbert's Abbé Murat was throwing himself at the boy's uncles for weeks, trying to assure them and the Noailles' that it was on its way. The Marquis' lawyer had been drawing up a list of the numerous la Fayette land ownings that were scattered throughout France: a list that was not even completed on the day.

There was almost *too* much to learn in the last few months. It was a monumental task, not only understanding the responsibilities of a Marquise, but accepting to forgo a part of her personality; everything she was to be now would reflect on Gilbert, and embarrassing him was the last thing she ever wanted to do. And he was terribly kind to her on his days they spent together, reassuring her that if anyone were to embarrass him, it would be himself. In her lessons, it was *she* who was to be serving *him* — yet at every door, he opened it, and every time she went to mount her horse, he would have his hands at the ready to hoist her up.

He did it all with a smile on his face and it hurt her twice as much that she could not match his generosity.

Louise had told her to enjoy it for the time being, that once a man was married and passed through the honeymoon phase, that the real work and arguing began, just like Maman and Papa did.

But when Gilbert returned from Versailles – from his formal presentation at court to the King – he was swept into the same chaos Adrienne was in, the two unable to speak for the days prior. He looked tired, as the two caught each other's eye across the corridor.

She peeked at the menu for the dinner. It was long and one of the only things she could vaguely approve of while her hair was being fixed.

"It's arrived, right?" she asked her maid as she pinned a curl as high as it could reach. "You saw it?"

"I took it from the courier myself, Mademoiselle. It is ready whenever you are."

"And no one else saw you, right?"

"We are as sneaky as you command," the woman said with a wink. She took another hair pin and dressed the high roll with fresh powder.

"Have it sent, then, with his shirt."

Adrienne ducked under the first petticoat of what was an ivory and gold gown, the lace threaded with the precious metal. It was a miracle, she thought, that she did not suddenly become shorter from the weight. Her stays supported layer after layer of linens and silks. The matching gold shoes were encrusted with jeweled buckles.

"The topaz, Mademoiselle?" her maid asked, gesturing to the set on Adrienne's bed.

"Please," Adrienne said. The pink jewels brought a wave of nostalgia with them as she waited for the maid to clasp the necklace around her neck. "Do you think he'll like his gift?"

"It's from you – of course he will. Now stop looking in the mirror, it's bad luck."

The routine of a wedding morning was different when one was in the wedding party. She remembered waiting for Louise to come out from her bedchamber; wishing her all the happiness in the world before she and Louis met in the chapel for their vows. Only the men were technically witnesses to the affair, while most of the ladies, herself included, grew impatient to begin the festivities as soon as the couple kissed and returned to the salon.

Now it was her sisters and her mother who waited for her, all dressed in some of their finest silks. The Duchesse d'Ayen kept her chin held high, as if receiving the queen. Adrienne almost choked up when she curtsied to her mother. Louise was characteristically bawling, her handkerchief dotting at her cheeks before the tears ruined her rouge application.

"Are we sure *I* can't marry the Marquis?" Anne asked. The duchesse plopped her fan against the top of the middle child's head.

"You are going to be wonderful," Henriette said, kissing the air on either side of Adrienne's painted face. "Your Papa is downstairs to escort you. Do you feel ready?"

Truthfully, Adrienne wasn't sure if she felt anything except the almost painful pounding inside of her ribcage, but she nodded at her mother, and took her time to descend the main staircase.

Seeing the duc at the bottom brought about a nervous smile. Her papa was dressed in a dark blue and silver suit, the embroidery something grander than she usually saw him wear. He took her hand and, in turn, she tightly squeezed it.

"If there were any woman to overshadow her husband, Adrienne, it would be you. Worry not," he said. "It will be a few words, you two sign a piece of paper, and then it's over." The Duc d'Ayen lowered himself briefly while they walked and added, "You can eat to your heart's content afterwards. I know I did."

Adrienne's anxiety-induced smile teetered as she saw the other gentlemen of their two families at the corner of the chapel hall; the Comte de Lusignem and the Marquis de Bouille were Gilbert's great-uncles; the others, the Comte de Noailles and the Comte de Tessé, her own. They gave her a look long before entering, and she heard the ringing of church bells follow. From the chapel, Louis' head poked out, his knowing smirk tilting.

"We're ready, Cousin," he said to the duc. "Auntie is going to sign as well, yes?"

"She will, no doubt," Jean replied, listening to the clicking of heels behind them as the duchesse pinched his elbow before entering the chapel. "Let's get this over with. I think we're all hungry, hm?"

Performing the ceremony was Abbé Murat's honor, his voice was something Adrienne had become accustomed to in the past several weeks. His order for the guests to rise only tightened Adrienne's hold on her father's arm. She wasn't used to so many eyes on her. She knew her family would never judge her so harshly, nor her grandparents who watched her closely. But she could not say for the la Rivère's and Lusignem on her fiancé's side.

Her fiancé.

Gilbert was distinguished, in his own way, at the end of the aisle – his rose red suit was corded with golden embroidery that shimmered in the glow of the stained glass windows. At his hip balanced a new sword in its sheath, Adrienne knowing that the details inside were as pristine as she could afford. He looked at her softly, with a tender smile that matched her nervousness. His eyes only flicked to the duc's as her hand was traded off to his own – the men exchanging words she did not hear as her heartbeat was deafening. Her hand must have been freezing. Gilbert rubbed her knuckles with his thumb a few times before they both turned to face the Abbé.

Stand, kneel, bow the head… It was a mass routine she was familiar with, just that the prayers were for *them* and that the Abbé had to promptly smack Gilbert's hand off of hers when it wasn't time to touch on *several* occasions. Adrienne glanced at him, trying her hardest not to laugh.

Perhaps it was when they were standing, turned to admire each other, when their humor jilted, and the saturation of Gilbert's coat moved up into his cheeks. A ring was placed into his palm, and all at once Adrienne realized they had already made it to the vows when Gilbert proclaimed:

"I will."

Abbé Murat seemed to know the verse by heart in its repetition, "Will thou have this Man to thy wedded Husband, to live together after God's Ordinance, in the holy Estate of Matrimony?"

Adrienne's voice eventually found itself. "I w-will," she whispered.

"Will thou *obey* him, *serve* him, love, honor and *keep* him in sickness and in health, and forsaking all other, keep thee only unto him, so long as you both shall live?"

She nodded, finding his eyes only on hers. "I will," she said.

Murat motioned with his eyes for Gilbert to lift Adrienne's left hand, ring carefully balanced between the Marquis' fingers. "As practiced, boy," he murmured.

Gilbert's brow furrowed. Adrienne's ring finger lifted slightly. "With this Ring, I marry you," he said, "and I promise to be caring and kind, to keep you from harm, and provide you comfort for all of your days. In the name of the Father, the Son, and the Holy Ghost... Amen." And the ring, a simple golden band, slipped easily onto Adrienne's finger; and the two carefully knelt once more, hands gripping each other as one more benediction was spoken.

"What therefore *God* has joined together, let no man put asunder."

Her knees were wobbling as he helped her rise. Before the hands of their relatives closed in a clap, Gilbert had closed the distance between their lips with a kiss so gentle and earnest, it felt longer than the second it was, as if the sun had set and rose again, throwing the colors of the stained glass windows across the room. Some of the rouge on Adrienne's lips had transferred to Gilbert's, and gone unnoticed as he pressed his together, only to spread the color more. Adrienne finally let the laugh that was building up go, listening to the celebratory applause that caught up to her ears.

Signing the marriage act was somehow more of a hassle than it was suggested it would be. As several people signed it, it took minutes of Adrienne holding Gilbert's fidgeting hand to finally have the opportunity to leave her name next to the small, and nervously written *"du Motier de*

Lafayette."

Louise and Louis, the clearly veteran, young married couple were waiting in the hallway, ready to embrace their new family member.

"You are so b-beautiful," Louise cried, draping her arms over Adrienne's shoulders. "And oh, my beloved new brother, welcome!" She pulled him down and planted a kiss on Gilbert's cheek.

"Brother," Louis extended a hand and Gilbert took it firmly.

"Brother," he smiled. His left arm remained propped for Adrienne to grasp.

The two had traded what parts of themselves were inoperable, balancing each other's weight. Gilbert maintained a sudden rehearsed smile as they went through the entire family with greetings and cheers. Adrienne's hand was bowed to from the gentlemen more times than she could count.

"Hi," he said to her, when they finally had gone through everyone on the way to the salon, where the decor had shifted to splendid wedding bouquets and long tables already full of the hors d'oeuvres.

"Hi," she breathed.

"You look very lovely today."

Adrienne beamed. "Thank you. You look very handsome yourself. Is the sword to your liking? I was worried you wouldn't want to wear it."

Gilbert guffawed. "I wish I had it when I was in the King's antechamber last month. With all the courtiers gawking at me, you would think I were some hog they were ready to hunt. This would have given me the courage to stand there without faltering."

"Was it so awful, truly?"

"I'm a noble of the *old extraction,*" he exclaimed, "so the King at least pitied a glance at me, but that was enough to last a lifetime. I dread returning. No one speaks to you, they just speak *of* you." He paused, his hand moving to cover her own as he grazed the ring on her finger. "I am sorry now you must endure that with me."

"I will fight them should they slander you," Adrienne replied firmly, then pursed her lips. "I mean, only if you would want me to."

A small puff of air escaped his nose. "Versailles would not see it coming," he said. "I will protect you as you protect me, then, Marquise. Respectably, of course."

"Of course," Adrienne agreed. They were nobility after all.

The Duc and Duchesse de Noailles were apt to return to the couple, glasses of champagne in hand to share.

"What a perfect arrangement," the duc said, his hand resting on the curve of his belly. "Does the bride have room for a dance with her Papi this evening?"

Adrienne lifted her hand from Gilbert's arm to look at the dance card dangling from her wrist. "I believe you are the first to ask, Papi, so you may *have* the first."

The duc laughed and clapped Gilbert on the arm. "I have beaten your husband to it." He looked at his wife and grinned, "I have a nose for such things, what do I tell you."

Gilbert stood a bit thunderstruck. He opened his mouth and, when the duc finished writing his name in Adrienne's tiny booklet, took the hanging pen. "Then I will claim the second, third, fifth, ninth, and fourteenth," he said, scribbling his own name down.

"You hate dancing," Adrienne said with a learned shake of her head.

"But I would love to dance with you," he said. "There, I left some open for others. I am a very generous husband."

At that, the Duchesse de Noailles laughed. "Evidently, so," she said, tapping her fan to the side of her brow, giving Adrienne a quick wink.

Gilbert, by courtesy, offered the duchesse his hand to lead her in the first dance as others flocked to Adrienne to fill up the rest of her card. Wine balanced high between everyone's fingers as they picked at the food and flocked to the floor. The orchestra sounded off for the first minuet.

Comparing men and their dancing was like comparing horses to their canter. They all performed equally the same motions, just with different flairs or faults, or in Gilbert's case, with such concentrated precision that his face was stuck in a pinch for the whole second act. With Adrienne matching his silly bobs with her own, he slowly relaxed, making the duet feel like it should have been performed in such a way. Before dinner was served, she had danced with Louis, the Comte de la Rivière, and the Comte de Noailles – Louis' father.

Yet from the circumstances of being a newly married couple, sitting at a large table doomed them to entertain different people on their lefts and rights. He met her eyes from down the row as they were served their soup course; he was at the mercy of Louise to one side and Adrienne's exuberant Aunt Tessé to the other.

Conversation with Gilbert's relatives went as well as she could manage. Any prying into the topic of heirs brought the mighty Duchesse d'Ayen's hand into the fray, pulling the comtes to speak with her instead. Adrienne took up her wine to cover the growing embarrassment of talking about such private matters with men thrice her age. Several courses later, she simply wanted to have Gilbert return to her side to parry any other talk, but she nevertheless smiled and made pleasantries for the next hour… or two… Until the strings of the violins and cellos were humming with the next wave of dance and Adrienne sprung to her feet.

It was her father who took her hand, having parted the sea of company to walk her into the eighth dance of the evening. His face was clear from the lines he often carried with him. Adrienne thought that he looked much younger when he wasn't frowning or tensed up, the lack of stress suited him. The Duc d'Ayen was graceful and pleasant, taking the steps on the toes of his shoes, but after two sets, Adrienne realized he hadn't spoken a word.

"Papa," she said as they came around another pair of dancers.

"Yes, darling?" he asked.

"Are you well?"

He lifted his brow. "Yes," he replied. "Why ever would I not be?"

Adrienne nibbled her lip. "I don't know. You usually always have something to say, don't you? Was the ceremony to your expectations?"

"You were wonderful, as we told you you would be."

"So you and Maman rehearsed those lines?" Adrienne teased, tapping her fingers on the top of her father's hand.

Jean's sober countenance slipped slightly. "Your mother and I always discuss all matters of you and your sisters together. She's a wise woman. Your husband would do well to follow in my footsteps and come to you for the same."

Adrienne beamed at the prospect. "I will try my best to be like Maman."

"You need not try, Adrienne," he said. "It is the Marquis who must rise to the occasion."

"You're too hard on him, Papa."

"If he is to be my son, then it's my duty as father to be so. I am the same to the vicomte."

"You adore Louis," Adrienne tittered. "As your cousin and son-in-law, he has a home advantage. Please give the Marquis an opportunity to prove he isn't as bumbling as you see him. I think he is rather sweet and forward."

"I know you do," the duc said, finishing their dance. "I only wish for him to succeed."

Not having sons must be hard for men, Adrienne thought, when they must find another to extend their paternal affections. She did have brothers briefly, but they died as infants, much to her parents' woe.

She gave her father a deep curtsy as he returned a bow. The bold color of Gilbert's coat cautiously approached him, exchanging a soft "monsieur." If there ever was a slow transaction of giving away a woman, it was between Adrienne's father and her newly acquired husband, as her papa took more time handing her over now than he did before at the altar.

"Marquise," Gilbert said, taking her for their third go around once the duc departed.

"I don't think I'll ever be used to that title," she replied as the orchestra switched their flow to another tripled tune. "Just as I think you won't get used to a minuet." Smiling as she watched him plainly count his steps under his breath, she turned about. "How was the dance with my sister?"

Gilbert puffed out his cheeks. "I believe she's with child," he whispered, grasping her arm before Adrienne almost tripped over herself at the news.

"Why would you say that?" she asked, turning red. "Did she tell you?"

"No," he replied, "well, not exactly. It was Louis who cannot keep a secret to save him. But the vicomtesse was also counting her steps, and if I remember correctly, your sister is one of the best dancers I know of."

"She can't be far along, she hasn't told me!" Adrienne said, then gasped. "Do you think Maman knows?"

Gilbert looked over all the heads at the party, searching for where the duchesse had gone. "She is dancing with Uncle Charles, so, *eh*," he shrugged, "I think if she does then she is not up in arms about it. Then again, she knows Louis' character; I don't think she would be surprised."

"Is he trying to catch up to his brother, you think?"

"The Prince de Poix has *one* three-year-old son, there isn't much to catch up on. Our vicomte is several years younger than his brother as well, I think it's reasonable to say that Louise and Louis simply, ahh," he paused to fix his footing, "… did what came naturally."

Adrienne hummed, her petticoats crunching softly as she hopped in time with the other ladies. "I suppose they *have* been married for a year. It has passed so quickly."

Gilbert didn't have to raise his arm very high for Adrienne to circle under it. The blush that tinged his ears matched hers as several eyes shifted in their direction. "May I ask you something, Adrienne?"

She raised her chin. "You may."

The delay in his question lasted until the end of the dance when Gilbert's fingers hovered over where his sword would be if he weren't participating. "Were you angry with me?" he asked, and at Adrienne's incredulous look, added, "for not telling you about our engagement?"

Oh, Adrienne frowned. "I don't think I was angry, no. I think I was very pleased with the prospect, in fact. But I was thinking…"

"That is a lot of thinking," Gilbert replied, narrowing avoiding a quick swipe of a hand.

"You once said you preferred if people were blunt with you – if they were honest."

He nodded. "I do."

"I prefer that too," she said, throwing up a waiting hand to her next dance partner. "In the future, let us be just that to each other. No more secrets."

Gilbert cocked his head, his eyes hovering over her face before his smirk softened, and he ducked down to steal a kiss to her temple before her Maman turned her gaze. "I submit to your superior judgment. No more secrets."

Adrienne was thoroughly exhausted by the end of the night, and daresay, a little tipsy from all the wine and the flourishes around the ballroom. Gilbert was not faring well either as he tried to keep up with Louis' drinking in between the vicomte's dancing schedule. There was some solace against a wall, whose minimal space between paintings and curtains left the alcoves private and bare. Wedding celebrations went on for days if the attendants were bold enough, and many were – the Duc d'Ayen and Duc de Noailles played a hand in calling for carriages or setting up guest rooms for those who were so inebriated they could not do so for themselves. It must have been four, maybe five in the morning. Adrienne couldn't locate the clock that usually was right out in the open. *Who would move the clock?*

Gilbert, sans coat, his wig slightly askew, stumbled over to the alcove where Adrienne leaned against the cooled wall. His ears were bright and pink; and Louis, a foot or two behind him, finished off what must have been Gilbert's drink.

He kept a napkin in hand, carefully opening it when he mirrored Adrienne on the other side of the nook. "I owed you a wedding gift," he said, taking out a small chocolate macaron.

Adrienne's shorter curls were starting to fall into her eyes while she laughed. "You didn't owe me anything, I'm wearing the gift you already gave me," she replied, tapping on the heavy jewels adorning her neck and ears.

He waved his hand with a short *"bah"* and said, "that was months ago, this is right now."

"Gilbert."

"It's a pastry, not a block of gold," he argued, waving it in front of her face with a gradually forming pout. Rolling her eyes, she opened her mouth and let him place the macaron between her teeth. He followed through and stole the rest with his own quick bite, snapping the macaron in half while Louis cackled like a little boy behind them. "Tastes better than gold, I say," Gilbert declared.

Louis shoved his nose between them. "Especially on the wedding night," he said, only to be sharply pulled back by the ties of his breeches.

"That's enough, Louis," Adrienne's mother exclaimed, sending him away with a slap to his rear. She looked unfazed by the long hours of the night, not even a crease in her powder. Gilbert moved his hand over his mouth, trying to swallow the shared dessert with enough panic one would think he were caught in a scandal. She smiled politely at him. "Hello, Gilbert."

"Hello, Maman," he replied, and Adrienne's face warmed.

The duchesse folded her hands in front of her. "You will be returning to your own apartments tonight," she said, "and Adrienne, to yours as well. I won't be having any scurrying like little mice back and forth with you two, is that clear?"

Adrienne huffed, "But Ma–"

"Yes, Madame," Gilbert said with a curt nod.

"You and Louis will be returning to Versailles when the festivities are over for your training?"

"That's right."

Henriette hummed. "We will sincerely miss you. Do take care of each other if I do not get the chance to wish you well before you go. Congratulations, my boy, I am happy for you to be a part of the family."

Gilbert looked to be trying hard to sober up as he glanced at Adrienne before he and her mother exchanged *la bise*.

They were to go without consummating the marriage, then, Adrienne realized. Not that she would know what to do if they did, that is, but she wouldn't have minded a little dalliance. He had all that curly hair hidden under the powder and pomade she wanted to touch.

When all was said and done, and Adrienne found herself deposited back into her chambers with nothing new save for the golden band around her finger, she ran to the window and pressed her nose against the glass, hoping maybe she would glimpse Gilbert as he passed by the windows of the other side of the house. But the sun was streaking through the treeline now, perfectly aligned to cast shadows of the branches to block her view.

"He will still be here in a few hours," Louise said, letting herself in through the door in the wall. Adrienne lifted her cheek from the windowpane, the makeup still clinging to it.

"Do you think I'm being too desperate?"

Louise laughed and sat at the edge of bed, picking idly at the ties to her banyan. "Come here, let us get you out of that, dearest sister of mine." She held her hands out until Adrienne reluctantly sauntered over and let her pull the pins from the bodice and free the ribbon from her stays. "I think you're smitten with the boy who has been courting you *very* well since he arrived here. You know, I'm a little jealous of the fact he has been with us as a friend and companion without realizing it. Louis isn't awful, I do love him, but knowing him as part of the family is different. He's ostentatious, while the Marquis is quite the opposite."

"He's not *really* the opposite," Adrienne said. "He has many opinions and voices them, they just aren't all… polite. He's very frank." Her grin slackened, and she nudged Louise's arm aside to grab her wrists. "Are you with child?" she asked, eyes wide. "Gilbert said you were acting off – I mean, he said Louis was being a chatterbox about, you know, the *hhhh* and the *haaa* between you two, but you never told me you were having a baby!"

Louise sat up to clap a hand over Adrienne's mouth. "Don't go letting the whole house hear it, Adri!" she whispered harshly. "Why are boys so awful at keeping their mouths shut? You whisper one thing about missing a cycle and boom, all of the Dragoons know the next morning."

"So it's true," Adrienne said, muffled beneath a palm. "Oh, Louise, congratulations, I'm so happy for you." She kicked her shoes off as she wiggled in place and climbed up on the bed, arms flailing to enclose her sister into a tight hug. "It is going to be the prettiest baby in France, I know it."

"Pray he has my countenance," Louise giggled, falling onto her back. "If our son is anything like Louis, then I'll have two young men to restrain."

"You think it's a boy?"

"One always hopes so," she said, her hand resting on the small bump of her belly. Without her stays or the tight garments of a gown to hide under, the once flat skin was beginning to look full now, as if she had eaten twice her fill at supper. "Boys carry the legacy of their father's names. You know Papa…"

Adrienne let her head fall on her sister's chest, the elder's hand coming up to stroke her hair. "I always hoped we would be enough to make Papa proud."

Louise sighed. "It doesn't mean he doesn't love us, stupid," she said. "It's tradition; and why he always treated Louis like a son even though they're cousins, and now the Marquis. Which, *Madame*, you outrank me now. I should be jealous of you."

Adrienne snickered, snuggling into Louise's bedgown. "The Vicomtesse de Noailles jealous of little me? What, with such a large family as ours, and your new maman at the right hand of the dauphine, you are going to be far more important than I am at court. Everyone will know you; will want to befriend you."

"At least not make enemies out of me," Louise said, tugging a blanket over them. "I bite."

"Are you leaving when Gilbert and Louis leave?" Adrienne asked, feeling the fatigue of the day circling back around.

"Not so soon. I believe I may retire later in the year at the Château de Maintenon, but as soon as Maman finds out, I'm sure she will want me near her. Regardless of how old we get, Maman will always want to have us in her company."

"That one is in *Eure-et-Loir*, right? The half day ride from the palace?" Louise hummed.

"I wonder how long a ride I would have to take to Gilbert's château."

"Goodness, several days at best," Louise said, crinkling her nose.

"Perhaps I am not so jealous after all. More than a day in any carriage is havoc for your back."

Adrienne closed her eyes. "But Chavaniac is important to him, so it is important to me. I can handle it, I'm sure." And if he wanted a son, she could give it to him if that was so essential.

"I'm sure you can handle every problem the dear Marquis brings to you, Adri, even as mundane as a faraway castle in the mountains."

Chapter Seven

Chaillot, September 1774

Dominoes began to fall as soon as Gilbert swore a lifetime oath to his new wife and then was shipped back off to Versailles.

The largest, upon being in the company of the King and his party for supper at the Grand Trianon, Louis XV startled the entire audience with his violent outburst of illness. Never had Gilbert seen a man break out in blisters and hives so suddenly, a poison that pocketed the skin's surface like war horse hooves in dirt. Gilbert pulled back with the crowd as if the plague had overtaken the palace, handkerchief to his face, while he watched the guard and the King's servants rush to his aid.

Louis XV died no more than two weeks later.

It was a bit of a panic inside of Versailles where Gilbert would catch glimpses of *Louis-Auguste* being shuffled around like he were made of porcelain, the new young king only three years older than Gilbert himself. Several times when Gilbert loitered in the library, sifting through books on smallpox and other ravaging diseases, he spotted the Comte d'Artois, stealing kisses with women who were most definitely not his new wife – whom he had described as a clumsy idiot several weeks earlier.

"Everyone is looking at my dear brother, not *I*," d'Artois would say when he caught Gilbert eyeballing him from across the bookshelves. "And you know how well he takes to *that*."

Married for four years with no heir, nor any child for that matter, did not paint Louis-Auguste in a good light among his compatriots, although most public blame slid towards the dauphine. Gilbert had gone on one or two hunting trips with the now-king and not one conversation was about his wife, whom Gilbert noted had taken a sabbatical to decorate the gift of the Petit Trianon on the palace grounds with her confidante, the Princess de Lamballe.

There was almost too much happening throughout summer for Gilbert to truly pay attention to, so instead, when not drilling, his nose was in books. It didn't take long for him to decide that if any intelligent person were to live a life free of the fear of dying of the pox, then they *had* to be inoculated.

"My boy, I am not against variolation by any means, but I am worried. You are young, you've just been married. I've suffered the pox before and I can tell you it is no laughing matter," the Duchesse d'Ayen was saying as she and Adrienne followed behind him. He strolled merrily down a distant Parisian street where the grand houses shifted into smaller cottages of a half-dozen rooms. Gilbert flipped through the items hanging from his equipage and removed the key there as they approached one cottage's door.

"The mortality rate is nothing to be worried about, Maman," he said, unlocking the cottage he had rented for the procedure. "Voltaire's studies prove that it's actually quite safe."

Adrienne's arm slipped through his as they walked inside the distant abode. She and her mother had insisted on being with him as he underwent the procedure; the doctor was a few hours behind with the supplies, and his dear lawyer was having a fit with the *tiny* chance Gilbert could die from the inoculation. Still, Gilbert was very confident he would be alright.

"I'll write to him tonight, then," Henriette said, crossing her arms while her studying gaze swept the little foyer.

There were simple brass decorations on the furniture, the walls taken up by sparse but large paintings of the European countryside, a small staircase that led up to the second floor, and a floral needlepoint rug that ran the length of the short hall. To the left was a study, furnished with two cases of books, a desk, and two sofas that bordered the unused fireplace. To the right, a powder room that appeared to be freshly cleaned. A kitchen laid hidden by the stairs, with a parlor on the other side, enveloped by glass windows that stretched around the room to the private, tiny garden amongst the rest of the city. Upstairs were two bedrooms of equal size, with sloped ceilings and loosely woven blankets draped over the beds.

"It's so quaint," Adrienne said, gliding her hand over the ceiling as they inspected the chamber that Gilbert would be confined to for as long as his recovery took. "Makes me feel tall."

Gilbert smiled, narrowly avoiding hitting his head on the highest part of the room. "Me too," he replied, sliding his coat off. He draped it over a chair that stood lonely against one wall and rested his hands on his hips. "I feel good about this."

Adrienne untied her hat's ribbon and held it between nimble fingers. "I do hope that means you have every intention of developing no symptoms at all and can come home with us right away."

"I suppose that is a possibility," he said. "I would be the one to somehow not be inoculated correctly."

"Marquis," the duchesse scolded from the doorway. "Don't put that kind of talk into our heads; we have the best of doctors for you. A few weeks at best and you will be on your feet, tripping around our halls again."

"Maman!" Adrienne covered her smile. She glanced at Gilbert with a rising blush as he pressed his lips together. School had not changed his character.

On the days he would spend in the Hôtel de Noailles, despite his apartments on the other side of the house, when the family retired early, he may or may not have had nights of quiet escapades to Adrienne's room. She was an honest girl, and he wouldn't abuse her kindness by allowing him into her bedchamber, so they truly did *nothing* except sit and speak on her sofas. Perhaps the occasional brushing of fingers or her weight against him while they looked out her windows to the stars above. With every creak to the floors outside of her rooms, they would leap several feet away from each other. Gilbert — at various times — had been thrusted inside a chest, thrown into the inner walkways between rooms, and even deposited out the window just as the duc or the duchesse opened her door. If anyone were to know of their late night antics, it was the *gardener* who rose early to tend to the budding flowers. Twice Gilbert made eye contact with the worker as he bustled through the stone pathway in his nightshirt and robe, fixing his nightcap as if he did not fall several feet into the bushes.

The surgeon at Chaillot was young, probably in his mid-twenties, and carried with him a locked wooden box. He spoke in whispers to the duchesse in the hallway while Gilbert removed his waistcoat and shoes. Adrienne tugged on his stockings one way as he fell back the other, she rolling backwards on the floor in a fit of giggles. The two of them red in the face while he carefully removed his silk breeches as well.

It wasn't as if it were scandalous, he thought, making sure his shirt remained for modesty. They were married, after all.

He was settling into bed when the gravity of the situation began to nibble at his mind. There were a few other young men he knew that had or were going through inoculation and *they* survived; symptoms were foretold to be unpleasant for some, and for others very little happened. Gilbert did not fall ill often, but when he did, he would be the first to admit he didn't take being bedridden well. He got restless; and when he got restless, he got moody.

"You're already pouting and he hasn't yet come in," Adrienne cooed, smoothing out the blanket as she sat on the edge of the bed. "There's no shame if you've changed your mind."

"No, I want it done," he replied with a firm nod. "I just want it… done."

"I did peruse the books downstairs. They seem interesting. And we can play games, or you can listen to me droll on and on about whatever comes to mind for the next few days."

Gilbert let his head fall back onto the pillow as he looked at her. "I suppose I could think of worse things," he said. The light from the window lit up the back of her cap like a soft halo. It couldn't all be bad if he had such an angel watching over him.

When the surgeon came in, Gilbert's sleeve was unbuttoned and rolled up above his elbow. He spoke of the procedure steps frankly and without any hesitation, seeming very confident in what he was doing, which was great because Gilbert and his women companions were eyeing the bloodletting fleam in the surgeon's hand with growing anxiety. It was a short prick as Gilbert's arm was cut and the pox was applied. The smell was absolutely abhorrent. Having to turn away and stare at Adrienne's hand in his to distract himself, he wiggled his fingers up into her palm; she wiggled hers back. Overall, the process was quick and rather uneventful. With how fast the sores appeared on the late King's body, he was somewhat expecting the same in a matter of minutes.

"There's an incubation period, Monsieur," the surgeon explained, "of about a week. If symptoms arrive, they will start around then or perhaps a bit later. You should rest for today to let the inoculation manifest naturally."

"Wonderful," Gilbert replied, staring at the ceiling.

"Once the scabs appear, it is best not to touch the patient. But I will be back regularly to check in on you, so I will happily provide updates for your family."

"Thank you, Doctor," the duchesse said as he collected his things. She eyed the two younglings knowingly while she escorted him down the stairs.

Gilbert brought Adrienne's hand to his lips as soon as they were out of sight. Her skin smelled like orange blossoms; so much more pleasant than the odor from his other arm that he kept his nose pressed to her knuckles until her laughter bubbled up beside him.

"You can have my fichu, you know," she said, carefully pulling the tucked fabric out from her bodice. Her revealed bosom was pushed up from her stays; Gilbert crossed his legs discreetly under the blankets. The flower oil permeated the fabric as he pressed his nose into it, breathing it in.

"Perhaps my kind wife may provide her to-be *ailing* husband with a softer pillow for his head?" he asked, blinking up at her from the neckerchief.

"Not five minutes in and you're already so bold," Adrienne said with a shake of her head. She scooted around on the bed until she was laying flat enough for Gilbert to rest his cheek on the supple skin of her chest.

"Fortune favors the bold," he smiled, perfectly content listening to her heartbeat. It fluttered under him, warm and gentle. Her hand rested along his shoulder and onto his hair, smoothing through the pomade that kept his curls tamed and off of his forehead. This was something he couldn't get with just any lady from court, he thought, this *domestic bliss* as one of his more happily married friends had put it. Those who enjoyed the bosom of other women argued against that notion, but Gilbert was certain now that no other girl would be lulling him to sleep so easily. It wasn't even night yet.

His arm tingled for most of the evening. As the duchesse returned upstairs with plans for supper and smacked the two of them apart, he found himself against a pillow once more.

It took a few days of dawdling about for anything to happen. The first few were full of activities Gilbert could do on his feet: running up and down the stairs while Adrienne counted the seconds it took; he showed her a proper fencing form in the small garden outside, using sticks fallen from branches; she taught him a single song on the harpsichord that sat in the parlor, sitting shoulder to shoulder. He liked the way she sang. Not high in the throat like he heard in the operas or at the palace, but deeper, softer, like how his grandmother used to sing lullabies.

During one of these quarantine outings, Gilbert suddenly felt the pinch of a headache strike up his spine. He wished he could say it settled at the back of his head, but it did quite the opposite, bouncing back and forth like a pendulum. The room circled, tilted on a mysterious axis, while Gilbert fumbled with the sheets of music. Nausea crept up his throat.

"Gilbert, hold on," he heard Adrienne say before her hands were on his waist. "Can you make it upstairs?"

Clapping his palm over his mouth, he gave a single nod. She called for her mother who was reading in the study around the corner. Getting up the stairs was harder this time, lacking the sport that was made out of it as his back started to tense and cramp. Back to his bed he went, groaning as he fell on the stuffed mattress, his limbs suddenly too heavy to unbutton his waistcoat.

"Regretting any choices, dear boy?" the duchesse asked, pressing a cold, damp cloth to his forehead while Adrienne removed his cravat.

"It's all necessary," he said, squeezing his eyes closed. "Just is awful, that's all."

"But it just started," Adrienne said.

Henriette laid his shoes on the floor. "Worry not, *ma petite chou*, men of all ages complain about pain as if it is the end of the world. Gilbert, *cher*, I will call for the doctor and let him know it's begun."

He merely whimpered through the second wave of nausea that followed another coursing throb. At some point a chamberpot was thrusted into his arms and he held it like a small woman would hold her lap dog. He emptied his stomach into it the moment he sat up.

"That's upsetting," he said, disappearing into his pillows. "I liked that dinner."

"I'll make it again for you when you can handle it," Adrienne said. She brushed her finger down his nose, giving the tip a quaint bop.

"I can handle anything," he argued. It wasn't his fault that his insides were not helping sell his point as he curled up into a ball, which aided his belly, but pained his back.

He heard Adrienne hum before she rubbed at his shoulder blades. "God will lead you through this."

"If God can lead me faster, my dear Adrienne, I would appreciate it tenfold."

The fever that often left most people debilitated for three to four days could only hold Gilbert for two, as even while he was wobbling around his room to get some energy out, he insisted on picking up the gazettes from the downstairs foyer. When caught by the duchesse, like a housecat, he would bumble back up the steps before she followed with light scolding. Adrienne sat by the window and read for him the news of France and her enemies, of the palace, of the British colonists across the ocean rioting against taxes. She would bring him soup and tea, the smallest cups of hot chocolate accompanied by a gentle kiss to his probably now very sweaty hair, and small gifts to entertain him for his seventeenth birthday which rolled by as a drizzly Tuesday.

When the doctor returned the fourth time, Gilbert had started showing the small dotting sores up his arm and neck, and so any tiny, pleasant touches he would have with Adrienne abated, as she could no longer do most of the caretaking; the duchesse would feed him if he were too tired, and wipe his face like he were a young boy playing in the mud again. No longer was he allowed to get away with leaving his bed, and the true boredom of quarantine began.

"You have to bring the needles under before you pull them through," Adrienne had said, raising her knitting up from where she sat on the other end of the room. She had been showing him how to make mittens before they settled on a simpler scarf after Gilbert lost his temper and threw the project across the room while trying to knit a hole.

"Like this, right?" he asked, holding up his work.

"Yes, there you go! Would you like to add a different color?"

"I'd have to rewind this yarn, wouldn't I?" Gilbert grimaced when Adrienne returned a pitiful smirk. "I'll stick with this."

Tap.

Gilbert looked at Adrienne as she jumped in her seat, both glancing toward the window as another pebble was lightly thrown at the glass. Adrienne stood up and pulled her daygown straight before she boldly tore the window open, clearly ready to fight whoever was disturbing them.

"Oh, good afternoon, Mademoiselle!" Gilbert heard from the street below, the voice eerily familiar. "I didn't mean to interrupt. I am looking for a friend of mine, you see. I believe he is trapped in one of these houses. Looks like he was dropped as a child; a tall, awkward boy of a man."

Gilbert sat up straighter in his bed. "Is that Ségur?" he asked. "Looks like a horse?"

Adrienne leaned against the side of the windowpane and replied to the voice, "well, sir, if you are the man that had your friend up in arms years ago, forsooth he is still waiting for the opportune moment to strike. Best you be careful in a narrow street like this."

There was a pause, and Adrienne quietly giggled at whatever display was going on below. Gilbert leaned forward as if he could see the street through the wall.

"Goodness, be careful!" Adrienne peeped, stepping back as the face of the Comte de Ségur appeared over the window.

"Marquis!" he said with a wide smile. "Dear friend, you look absolutely atrocious. And with the pox too, how *awful* the two intermingle."

Gilbert smirked. "It's a miracle that ivy is able to hold your weight, Philippe. Clearly my *wife* is in such good favor with the divine that you are saved from a terrible fall in her presence. Best to thank her."

The Comte de Ségur rapidly turned his head to look at Adrienne, eyes blown. "So this is the famed Marquise. I should have recognized you, you have the Noailles' pouty lips. Thank you for sparing my life; I am Louis-Philippe, a treasured friend of the Marquis. I'm sure he has spoken many a thing about me, but trust, Madame, that only the best things are true."

"You are at the mercy of Gilbert," she said, crossing her arms. "As soon as he tires of you, I will snip the ivy away from your hands."

Ségur gasped with a smile. "Marquis!" he replied. "Now if I *were* to steal a woman from you, it would surely be this one. What a family of pretty faces. Tell me, Madame de la Fayette, do you have any unmarried relatives...?"

"Cut the ivy, Adrienne," Gilbert sighed. "Save yourself."

"Nay, hold on, allow me to deliver your letters from the lads. I come as friend *and* courier." He carefully adjusted his hold on the house to pull a small stack of papers from his coat pocket. "Many well wishes, some ask for a loan, I believe d'Artois has included his most recent affair for you to read for he knows how much you fancy the details – pardon my vulgarity Madame – and then there is one from *me* for you to stare lovingly at, my dear Marquis. Perhaps you may use it to balance all that yarn on as you explore your feminine side with your beautiful young wife here." Ségur smiled with all the gusto a good friend could summon as Gilbert sat under his bedsheets, unable to go over and push him from the ledge himself.

Adrienne, ever the witty one if Gilbert had come to know no woman better, tapped Ségur on the shoulder and whispered quietly enough that Gilbert couldn't catch the whole of it. But his friend had paled and his smile had gone lopsided as he glanced towards the open door in view of the other bedroom where the Duchesse d'Ayen sat with her bible.

"I, uh, well, I better get going then," Ségur said with a quiet laugh, his hold slipping slightly on the ivy. "Doing some last minute naval exercises or something like that…"

"You are not in the navy," Gilbert replied.

"I'm not, no," Ségur nodded, his head gradually disappearing. "Marquise, it was the utmost honor to meet you."

"My compliments, Monsieur," Adrienne said, taking the letters. She let her head loll to the side as she watched him abscond down the road. Gilbert fell back to the pillows, the short interaction draining enough. "He does have a particular shape of his head," she said after a moment, and Gilbert coughed through his laughter.

"He does," he mused, closing his eyes. He heard the dripping of water before her hand gently fiddled behind his head. The tingles peppered down his back.

"You need a bath," she whispered, pulling him up slightly. "Here, Maman said we have to keep you thoroughly quenched or you could shrivel up."

Gilbert tried his best not to spill the drink. "I'm attempting not to sweat to save you two the trouble of having to make one up." The idea of fully being naked in front of the women heated his cheeks as if he didn't think about the prospect on their wedding night. Opening an eye to watch as

Adrienne set the cup on the table, her face was composed, completely serene in her countenance; a long, wavy strand of her brown hair was loose from her cap and tumbled down her back like chocolate falls over her lilac linen dress. He could reach out and touch it, coil it around his finger if he wanted to. It was probably soft.

His attention shifted slightly to the duchesse in the room across, her eyes set upon the two of them from her chair, the bible she was reading rested on her lap. He let his hand fall against the bedding.

Compared to other patients, the doctor was saying, Gilbert was taking the pox with relative grace – the only grace he would ever have. While the marks were plentiful up his arms and scattered widely across his chest, not many made their way up to his face. The likelihood of scarring was less so, and for that, all three of them were relieved. No one would admit to seeing it, but even the Duchesse d'Ayen had one or two scars on the curve of her cheekbones from her time with the infection.

Meanwhile, Gilbert was trying his best not to itch the scabs, nor rub them vigorously together under the blankets to relieve some of the annoyance. The duchesse was always walking by as if she were a guard on patrol, ready to smack his hand from making the condition worse. He didn't suffer any more fever, just occasional bouts of fatigue, which led him to almost fall asleep in the tub that the Madame eventually did require him to get into.

He kept his hands in his lap, awkwardly staring at the edge of the bath while his mother-in-law scrubbed his shoulders with a cloth, biting back a wince at every scab she scraped over. She spoke to him, but he was only half listening, glancing over to Adrienne who remade his bed with all the care of a housekeeper, bending over to fluff his new pillow, tucking the loose strands of hair behind her ears. She sighed and set her hands on her hips, looking over her work. He didn't miss her quick glimpse back at him.

"Adrienne," the duchesse said, snapping the two of them to attention as she dropped the cloth into the tub for Gilbert to handle more sensitive areas by himself.

"Yes, Maman?"

"I am going to go down to find some of the oils the doctor left for the Marquis when he is done. Would you tend to his hair, darling? It shouldn't take too long."

Gilbert didn't see what expression Henriette gave that made Adrienne fidget with her hands like she did when she was nervous, but she nodded and disappeared behind him. When the duchesse exited the room, he brought his knees up instinctively to his chest as he heard Adrienne pick up a warming bucket of water.

"Careful now," she said with a glimmer of amusement as she poured the water over his head. It splashed in, out, and around the tub, promptly soaking the floor beneath them. His hair was greasy without fresh powder and pomade, sticking flat to his head with the soak. Pushing his bangs from his face, he tried to rub the sleep and water from his eyes.

"Thank you," he said, wondering if this was what a cat felt like when Adrienne's hands put the soap to his scalp and combed her fingers through it until his hair started to curl again.

"It is my pleasure," she replied. Her hand ran up the back of his head and behind his ears. "I can get more hot water if you're chilly. I'm counting some goosebumps over here."

Gilbert nabbed the cloth the duchesse left behind and added the extra layer to his lap. "It's… sure, yes, more water would be nice," he said, brow twitching wildly as her hands left his hair while he damned the rest of his body for being so weak in a *bath* of all places. He jumped in place when Adrienne appeared back with another warmed bucket, almost slipping on the mess they had made.

"I'll be more careful this time, watch out," she giggled, aiming the water to fill in the space between his back and the wall of the tub before she knelt down above his head once more. "Is it too hot?"

"It's perfect," Gilbert squeaked, pressing his forehead to his knees.

"I need your head back if I'm to work this soap in," she said and the two soft pats to his back only made him curse himself more. He slowly leaned back again. "I was reading the book you picked out yesterday, by the way."

"Rousseau?" Gilbert asked. "I didn't know you were into treatise. How did you find it?"

Goodness her fingers scratching his scalp felt so nice.

"I've only read a few chapters so far. I think he's right on the argument about slavery – what an awful thing we've subjected innocent people to when they have every right to their freedom," she exclaimed, "and I am a bit biased, but I agree about his stance on women."

"The book is banned here, so don't tell your Maman."

"I remember Monsieur Voltaire mocking some aspects of Monsieur Rousseau's work, but I do not think I agree with all of his critiques."

"True, there are parts of the Social Contract that I have a hard time imagining," Gilbert said, content on discussing politics. "When Monsieur Rousseau mentions democracy, he does so without any inclination of a monarch and I… cannot imagine France *without* one."

Adrienne hummed. "That would be difficult to do, I think."

"But that is also why it is so interesting to read about, to speak of the different possibilities of the future."

"You said it was banned in Paris?"

Gilbert clicked his tongue. "Some things could be taken in a treasonous manner, I suppose. Enlightenment challenges tradition."

There was humor dripping into her tone. "Where did you get the book?"

Oh, he thought. He tilted his head back to look up at Adrienne, who had pursed her lips as if she already knew the answer.

"Louis may have slipped it to me during drilling last month, but I don't know where he could have possibly acquired it," he said, but then the immediate guilt set in under Adrienne's rising brow. "Except maybe he could have bought it from a fellow who attended our… club. Like how you and your sisters sit with your Maman with guests, the boys and I discuss things similarly. Usually it is a bit more raucous, but we are gentlemen, and the conversation never sways from these topics!"

"You seem intent on persuading me you're not getting into any trouble,"

Adrienne replied, cupping some of the water to pour over his hair, wiping the excess from his forehead. He blinked and she laughed lightly. "I would love to hear anything you learn and discover. It isn't every day I get to skim through banned treatises. But maybe be mindful of Louis' incorrigible kidneys. We are convinced his blood may be wine, but yours certainly is not."

"No, it is very much normal," he mused. He slinked deeper into the tub, the back of his neck at the rim. The soap may have been out of his hair, but Adrienne's hand remained, fingers carefully itching and massaging through the strands. "I will speak to you of everything as often as I can then, for I find I am quite keen on the subject."

"Then I am as well," Adrienne smiled.

"And you must tell me everything you are fascinated about. I'd like to hear anything from your heart. For if it is in *your* heart, then it is in mine as well."

She hummed and looked about the room. "*You* take up so much of the space in here," she said, holding her hand over her chest.

"You will make me terribly conceited, Madame," Gilbert whispered, the annoying festering of his scabs had gone unnoticed since he watched her. The rogue strand of hair had slipped out from its prison behind her ear, dropping ever so lightly on his cheek. He took it gently before she could move it back. It was as soft as he thought it would be; and was warmed by the fire and highlighted with gold.

Maybe the hot water was getting to him. Perhaps the pox had some unknown side effects that made his mind think things that would get them both in trouble. He couldn't blame Adrienne and her sweet smile, nor the way her eyes were tenderly watching him, or the dutiful manner in which she felt so devoted to him since they made each other's acquaintance. He could only blame himself – a rare thing, really, but then again, maybe he was already a little self-centered – for what question came from his mouth.

"May I kiss you?" he asked, the strand of hair still captive in his fingers.

Adrienne's look of innocent surprise had allotted itself into one of

Gilbert's favorite expressions he had been blessed to witness. He waited for her reply, content in watching the affair upside-down. Very gladly he gave this power to her, for Adrienne, if any woman could, would wield it wisely.

He was also naked, indisposed, and at her mercy.

"M-my heart says you *may*," Adrienne whispered, and Gilbert let his hand drift further up and hardly grazed her jaw before they locked lips for the second time.

Such a divine thing could heal him, he thought, as Adrienne lifted her face slightly only to kiss him again. He would crane his neck more if it meant prolonging the touch.

"You are so ridiculous," she breathed, bumping his nose.

"Why is that, *mon coeur?*"

"Because *we're* ridiculous."

He would argue against it, but the conveniently timed clicking of heels up the stairwell brought the two of them sliding away from each other, Adrienne wiping the water from her chin while Gilbert threw more suds on himself. The duchesse arrived with a towel draped over one arm, the medicinal vial in the other, and a trained smile as she explained it took longer than she thought to find the ointment.

Chapter Eight

Versailles, December 1774

They were becoming rather skilled in traversing the halls of Versailles while avoiding Adrienne's father, who was back in court for his annual stipulation as guard. There was talk of the King promoting the Duc de Noailles, Adrienne's grandfather, to a *Maréchal de France*, which was a great honor, but also brought a wave of new eyes and expectations to the family. The Duchesse d'Ayen had no desire to be inside the palace for the multiple winter balls, but as soon as Adrienne accompanied Gilbert, she forced herself to join them, keeping a steady eye on both of her eldest daughters while she conversed with very few of her friends.

Versailles, Adrienne decided, smelled like it was soaked in perfumes. Perhaps it was to hide the smell of a water-closet every time a hidden door opened to the servant hallways where courtiers went to relieve themselves before rejoining the party. Snuff boxes were passed around like wine under the polite guise of lace handkerchiefs. She hadn't accepted any at the duress of her sister, who shoved people aside to push the young entourage – the Vicomte and Vicomtesse de Noailles alongside the Marquis and Marquise de la Fayette – through.

Meeting with Louise's in-laws was a regular occurrence the longer they were at Versailles. And with every passing, the young Queen Marie-

Antoinette was closer and closer to her named *Madame d'Etiquette* –
despite replacing her as senior lady-in-waiting.

The queen's youth was radiant, Adrienne thought, watching the
Austrian smile and dally with Louis as Louise spoke with her mother-in-
law before the old couple departed. She was thin with a fair complexion,
and the powder that made her hair stark white led Adrienne to conclude
she must have been blonde; she had a dimple in her chin that seemed to
be a favored resting place of her fan; and some of the bluest eyes Adrienne
had ever seen.

"Ah, Marquis!" she said, slipping out of Louis' hold to saunter over. She
was a few inches taller than Adrienne, aided by her intricate hairstyle.
Gilbert's back straightened, and Adrienne let her arm slip from his as
he greeted the queen with a bow to her hand. "I must thank you for
your efforts last month in introducing me to the people I care little about.
Frankly, no one else would have bothered to do the job, but I admired
your resolution."

It sounded like an insult, yet her smile was completely sincere.

"I expect a dance this time, since you denied me before."

Gilbert's smile wobbled. "Y-yes, of course, your Majesty."

Adrienne slipped her arm back through his. She kept her mouth shut;
of all the people, she certainly couldn't fight the queen, but whenever
Gilbert cast his eyes at the ground with the shyness only the court brought
out, Adrienne debated that maybe she *could* fight the queen.

"Marquise." Marie-Antoinette nodded her head.

"Your Majesty," Adrienne replied with a curtsy.

"My apologies for stealing your husband, but a debt is a debt," she said,
holding out her hand for Gilbert to take while the orchestra fired up
across the room.

Adrienne smiled. "Be gentle with him, please, I only have the one." She
watched as he was pulled away from the group, already seeing his mind
churning with the numbered step of the current quadrille playing. If the
anxiety was rising in her, she could only imagine his own.

Louise slipped in where Gilbert's arm once was, pressing her cheek against Adrienne's while they watched the pairs begin. "Can I get you anything? Wine, a snack? Her Majesty is quite generous when it comes to providing for her company. Here," she said, taking one of Louis' glasses of sherry, "he doesn't need this one."

"How are you fairing? That baby must be due any week now," Adrienne said, sipping at the sweet drink. Louise's gown sloped around her rounded belly in the elegant way that only she possessed.

"I'm well enough to be here. Although it's exhausting at times that I have two kickers in the same bed as me on some nights," she replied, eyeing Louis who merely downed his drink with a cocky grin.

"What can I say? I'm an athletic man and so is my strong heir," Louis said. "Forgive me, Adrienne, for not offering to dance this one, I promised my lady I would limit my gallivanting to five and I have already serviced three."

Adrienne rolled her eyes, finding the awkward hopping of Gilbert's navy frock between the skirts. She could see him from here with his brows pulled tightly, easily comparable from his height to the three other couples he danced with.

"You worry too much about him," Louise said, nudging her arm. "Men make it out of every situation somehow; he'll be fine in the end."

She would like to believe her sister, but Gilbert was not just any man. The dance felt longer while watching it from the side. Prayers whispered that her husband would not fall or knock into the queen were answered with more of his usual gracelessness that stuck out amongst the elegant swaying of the dancing couples.

The growing laughter bubbling up from the dancefloor struck a deep chord at the parting bow of the quadrille. There might as well have been a ring of fire encircling Gilbert while Marie-Antoinette and the courtiers around her laughed harder. He had stood still, his chin all but tucked to his cravat, his hands folding together at his front. Adrienne stepped forward, catching some of the embarrassment that radiated from him as he bowed and exited the chittering fray. His steps were long and fast, almost passing the lot of them that waited, Adrienne's hands barely catching his sleeve.

"I do not believe court is suited for me," he said, the flames of the candelabras reflected in the gloss of his eyes. His hand curled under her arm, squeezing it softly.

"Do you want to leave?" Adrienne asked, but Gilbert was already lost in a conversation with Louis, who had come to relieve the man's embarrassment with another round of sherry. Louise was beside her husband and gave her a grand shrug, as if boys will always take each other's shame and throw it to the dogs to make room for other bad decisions.

Her gut twisted. It wasn't *jealousy*, she didn't get jealous. She was very used to things and people not paying her much attention. Why would things change now?

Yet despite her silent fuming, Gilbert's hand was still holding onto her forearm, his thumb ever-so-softly tracing circles onto her skin while he spoke to Louis about their club. Adrienne couldn't be mad with him. It was a little embarrassing to think that the probability she could bring herself to whine about *not* getting his attention was so minuscule.

A twirl of pink brought Adrienne's eyes to flick over to the queen as she danced with another man. Perhaps she could be angry with Marie-Antoinette for bringing the court to insult Gilbert; the queen should have known better than to force him out onto the floor, surely. That she should *continue* to dance and smile like embarrassing someone was nothing more than the happenstance of one of her parties…

"Adrienne," Gilbert whispered and she snapped her attention back to he who deserved it. "I would like to go home now, if you are ready."

The sky outside was littered with stars fighting with the torches' attempts to drown them out. A carriage ride from the palace was short, and with them was her mother, taking the first opportunity to get out from the social obligations. Gilbert had kept his face toward the window as they bustled through the streets, his hand overturned on Adrienne's lap for her to grasp it between hers. The duchesse didn't add any commentary on their closeness together, not since Louise's belly really began to show. When they reached the apartments, the couple split from their hand holding, and Adrienne sat in her room alone while she fiddled with the strings of her robe.

She lifted up her hairbrush and held it aloft, in how Gilbert showed her with their stick-swords over the autumn season. Not that she could take out courtiers with her brush, but she could pretend to smack every single one of them that laughed. If her Aunt Anne was able to strike fear into the hearts of many with her regard to etiquette by simply *showing* up to events, then Adrienne would be able to bring out the same.

But then again, maybe not.

She was too small to be intimidating, her sisters assured her of that. Although, she thought, she did have her wit, and with her wit, she had words to put to paper. Her father would tell her *not* to go about committing things to letters that could be used against the family; she could hear him giving her a stern scolding if she ended up writing to the queen that she was a cruel woman for finding Gilbert's untalented dancing amusing.

The caveat was that Gilbert's atrocious dancing skills *were* funny, but it wasn't something to make him feel bad about. Adrienne thought that him trying was sweet.

"Your arm will cramp if you don't parry or advance, *mon coeur*," Gilbert said from the doorway. Adrienne almost fumbled her hairbrush, catching it with both hands as she pulled it back to her chest.

"I wanted to advance," she said. "I was just second guessing myself."

He rested his head on the frame, his hair poking out from under his cap. "That's dangerous. If you wait too long, your enemy will advance instead."

"What if you don't know if they are an enemy or not?"

Gilbert's face was set in a frown. His forehead creased in the center. "Would you be fighting them if you did not know?" he asked.

Adrienne shrugged, twisting the brush that still had some of her loosened hair between its bristles. "Aren't you philosophic tonight?"

"Is that *indignation* in your tone?"

"No," she replied, pouting. "I am not angry, I'm..." She sat on her bed. The tree outside her window had a thin but growing blanket of snow across its branches. "I do not know."

Hearing him quietly shuffle across the floor, she let him take the brush from her hand, and he went to work combing through her hair. He always had a soft hold; he would brush Rosalie's when she didn't let anyone else back in the early years of living with them. With Adrienne, he was even more careful.

"About my blundering today," he said. "I'm sorry I must have put you in this mood."

Adrienne turned to face him. "It was not your fault!"

Gilbert raised his brow, and brushed the front part of her hair over her eyes. "What I do is always my fault. It wasn't the first time I've made a fool of myself in front of Her Majesty. What she was referring to with introductions… I thought she had not known some Mesdames so I did her the honor, but it turned out she knew them well, and did not have a favorable opinion of them. I am afraid that it was an embarrassment for us *all* that she feigned estrangement."

"That's so cruel," Adrienne replied, pulling her hair from her face only for Gilbert to gently place a kiss to the tip of her nose.

"She is mocked and slandered every day, *mon coeur*, I think it is very human of her." He paused, their nuzzling ceasing as he pulled back to hold Adrienne's cheeks in his hands. "Do not go fighting Her Majesty, she is just like us."

"Gilbert, you were going to cry there. You can admit she hurt your feelings."

"Fine, yes, I was ready to weep like a babe, but you need not remind me. We're grown ups, essentially, we don't cry in public. We wait until we are in our lover's arms and then we may mewl into their bosoms."

Adrienne shoved the brush aside, her fingers tapping across his knuckles. "Would you like to mewl now, then?"

He laughed despite the tears that started to flow immediately. "You make it sound so childish for a man to ask his wife to hold him… and maybe play with his hair… tell him he's at least a *decent* swordsman even though he cannot dance."

"Oh, he's a fantastic swordsman, the best," Adrienne replied, discarding his embroidered cap while he nudged himself under her chin. He pulled his legs up on the bed, laying as if he were a large house cat. "And he's sweet and courageous. Maybe needs to gain some weight," she added, scratching his neck.

He gasped. "I thought that disappearing when I turned aside would be great for avoiding cannonfire. If I put on weight, then the English would have something to shoot at. Ah, there's an answer to your query… if they are English, then more likely than not, they are an enemy and you may slash away at your pleasure."

Adrienne knotted her fingers in his small curls. "I will keep that in mind should any decide to show up for Papa's science experiments. I believe he has an English friend or two that frequents those conferences in Paris."

Gilbert's muffled words didn't form a complete sentence as his weight shifted slightly in her embrace. Like a soft tickle of butterfly wings, whatever tears he had dried on her skin.

She would have to talk to the queen in her own time, she thought, when she could manage to get her by herself. It shouldn't be too difficult – now that Adrienne was a Marquise of the old extraction, and her sister was already in close proximity to Marie-Antoinette's friends in court, Adrienne simply had to show up to the queen's chambers during her levée, and if she were the highest ranking lady in the room, she'd be right by her side.

A sigh towards the ceiling.

She couldn't plot like this; she shouldn't, rather. But her brain kept going back to it. Twelve-year-old-Adrienne popped up in her mind like a feisty, little minx ready to openly mock anyone who got in her way. No wonder Maman always seemed so calm and graceful – it appeared the older one girl got, the more confined her situation became.

Comparatively, Adrienne's *situation* wasn't anything horrid. Here she had her affectionate, young friend as her husband, asleep in her arms, and that was already more of a blessing than many women had. The queen's marriage couldn't have been this happy even if she and the king got along diplomatically, she thought. If Gilbert was right, and it seemed he *was* on many opinions, it wouldn't be the queen's fault for finding laughter at the expense of others, when so many impolite remarks were made at the expense of her.

She still would speak to her, Adrienne decided. Maybe not within the day or the week, maybe not for the year, but she would share her words. Eventually.

Gilbert gave the softest of snores and Adrienne swallowed down a wave of giggles, kissing the top of his head. This was something Louis nor anyone in his club could enjoy; this side of Gilbert was all hers.

Paris, March 1775

Gilbert was preparing to go to Metz with the regiment he was soon to captain, but he was currently in a long-strided walk with the Duc d'Ayen hot on his heels. Adrienne only caught a glimpse of them as they angrily passed by upon her exiting the drawing room, a book in hand.

"How *dare* you!" her father shouted, painfully reverberating across the walls. "Shameful, ungrateful!"

"You did not ask for my permission, Monsieur," Gilbert replied, continuing on his escape route. Adrienne had hopped on the tail end, worry slipping onto her face. Arguments between the two of them were the opposite of few and in-between these days.

"I need not your permission, boy. You are in *my* family, in *my* house. You've insulted me; you've insulted the Maréchal de Noailles! This was for your benefit, how dare you throw it all away for your fantasies!"

"Papa?" Adrienne said, catching up to him. She pulled at his arm, the one he used to point and shake angrily at the Marquis. Her father was red in the face and gray at the roots of his hair. It appeared as if he pulled half of his cravat off amidst his fit. Gilbert pounded down the stairs, stopping halfway.

"I am not your puppet, Monsieur," he said between his teeth, but he opened his arms and gave a short bow. "Forgive me for corrupting your good name, it was not my intention. Please inform His Highness if he wishes to duel, I will settle the affair."

"A fool," the duc spat.

Adrienne's head was spinning. *A duel? Permission? What was Gilbert doing?*

She squeezed her father's arm. "I will speak with him!" she said as she followed her husband down the stairs, leaving her father to fume while the duchesse emerged from her chamber. She threw the book she carried across the floor, the cover squeaking on the wood. Gilbert stalked straight to the back gardens, throwing the doors open before the sun struck him, the tails of his frock caught in a gust of wind. Adrienne, gripping the train of her skirt, hopped down several of the stone steps before racing to grab him. "Gilbert, what has happened now? You worry me when you are angry."

"It is of no consequence. What's done is done."

"'Of no consequence?' You mentioned a duel, Gilbert, how could you say that it is nothing?"

He stopped in the gravel between hedges, kicking a stone or two as he turned about. The gears rapidly turned behind his eyes. "The duc and your Papi thought to make me a member of the Comte de Provence's staff with those newfound Maréchal honors."

Of the many names Adrienne had memorized, this one was unexpected. "The king's brother? The Monsieur?"

"I spoke with him at the masquerade the other week and insulted his character. He came to me at court recently to try and *rectify* the situation – as we were in masks and thought I did not know who he was at the time."

Adrienne crossed her arms. "Alright… did you truly not recognize him at the ball?"

Gilbert scoffed. "Of course I knew who he was. And I told him again that he who wore that mask then was now wearing that ugly green coat."

"Gilbert!"

"Verily enough, I didn't call it an *ugly* coat when I made the comment."

"No wonder Papa is furious!"

"I don't want that silly position, Adrienne," he argued. "It would make me a *retainer*, some clerical servant who would never see war and good God, *mon coeur*, there is something brewing out there, I can feel it and I want it so badly like I have never wanted anything before in my life." He wriggled her hands free from her elbows and squeezed them, bringing them up to his face where it was warm. "Please don't be upset with me, I know Papa means well, but you know how he suffocates me so."

"You've put me in such a difficult position, Gilbert," Adrienne said. If she could not calm her father's anger, then her mother would have to. But there was a more pressing matter. "And you mocked the King's brother – my Lord, what if he *does* want to duel you? You cannot accept that! You must apologize!"

"I do not think he would want to speak with me at any point in the future, truthfully," Gilbert said, resting his cheek upon her hand, giving her palm a soft kiss.

"Then speak to the Comte d'Artois. You are his friend, and he is Monsieur's brother as well. He could – I don't know – leeway a peace between you so that both sides are satisfied. Provence may recover some honor and you are free to make your own decisions for your better happiness." She rubbed her thumb over the soft of his lips. "And I do want you to be happy."

The frustration pulling at Gilbert's brow lessened. He fiddled with her hand a little longer while the birds in the trees sang away. Winter's chill was stagnant this year; the tips of her fingers were pink and cold. He turned her hand about and kissed the tips of them with care before holding them between his hands. "You have always been very wise," he murmured. "It makes me anxious for your approval."

"So you will speak with d'Artois," Adrienne said, raising a brow.

Gilbert puffed out his cheeks, bobbing on his toes as if he were on the verge of a temper tantrum. "Yes, yes, I will see him later this season."

"And what about Papa?"

His lip twitched, he looked towards the house, eyeing the windows to see if her father was in any, watching them. "Would your father duel me?"

"Gilbert!"

"Fine, I will figure *something* out with him. Once he wants to look at me again. Maybe I'll bring Louis with me as my second…" He turned to look back down at Adrienne, both of their noses growing red in the chill. "You poor thing. Having to deal with me. It is not too late to sneak some hot chocolate into our rooms before dinner, *mon coeur*."

"Having to deal with you is the job I consented to." Adrienne sniffled and smiled, her fingers fiddling into the folds of his waistcoat between the shiny buttons. "And I could think of one *other* thing I can sneak into my rooms before dinner," she said, enjoying the view as Gilbert's face lit up, looking back-and-forth and back-and-forth from the windows to her.

"Madame Marquise, you find me at your mercy."

Paris, May 1775

He was already gone for the summer when Adrienne woke up alone in her bed and, after prodding around on her mattress, stared at the ceiling in utter horror. The month prior she thought it was a fluke, that she didn't eat as much or the stress of him leaving again played with her heart so greatly that she skipped all of April. It was something that happened to all women sometimes.

Even Louise with her new baby girl had said so, that missing one was nothing to worry about every now and then.

But two in a row?

Adrienne dipped her hand under her bedsheets, cupping the bottom of her belly.

"Hello?" she whispered. Nothing answered her, obviously, not the slightest sign of movement. It would be too small, smaller than a pearl. "You are going to send my Maman into a bout of madness once I tell her." With the lack of soiled bed linens, *well*, she thought aloud, "if she doesn't know already."

Chapter Nine

Paris, October 1775

Adrienne was informed she was taking this particular pregnancy rather elegantly throughout the months. With the few exceptions where she'd rush to the chamberpot at various times early on in summer, or grow the desire for copious amounts of lemonade, which only meant she needed to relieve herself almost every hour, Adrienne managed to keep up with her daily meandering. As soon as she told her mother, however, back in the spring, her weekly riding ceased. Instead she was left to walk with no less than two chaperones on either side of her whenever she wished to stroll through the gardens. Unless it was her sisters, she did not care for the company.

She'd read every letter that came in from Metz, even if it wasn't written by Gilbert. Nose over her father's shoulder, she asked for news from the regiment and their training. The Marquis was given his promotion for his birthday the month prior, and according to letters from Louis, was taking on the role exceedingly well, which appeased the duc enough that his anger and disappointment for Gilbert sabotaging his early career moves were quelled for the time being.

Pauline would sit with her while she knitted, her face close to Adrienne's belly and read from her writings various topics stemming from her lessons with their governess. "It will be a very intelligent baby," Pauline had said before switching to a poem about the change of seasons.

Rosalie enjoyed resting her hands on the bump, asking her or Louise on her visits a thousand questions about how it moved, or how long until it would pop out, or what were the signs to tell if it was a boy or a girl. Anne would answer that Louise thought hers would be a boy and was wrong, so it was best just to leave it a surprise – which everyone agreed on except for Rosalie, who sulked with her ear pressed up to Adrienne's belly.

Adrienne found she avoided mirrors if she could. It wasn't that she thought the sight was atrocious, but it was a picture of the guilt that rose in her conscience. Her mind was at a constant battle with itself. She had pulled Gilbert into her room, this was of her doing – as fun as it was – and God was no doubt boring His eyes down upon her.

But you are married, the smaller part of her brain replied, flailing its imaginary arms. *And it was consensual!*

Yes, but the *Sin*, she mulled.

It isn't a sin!

Avoiding the mirrors was simply the most reasonable answer to avoid thinking about it. There was always some other distraction to occupy her. Louise was a great help mediating the stories their maman would tell about her various pregnancies. She loaned Adrienne the pair of stays she wore in later trimesters, helped her with putting stockings on and stayed long into the night to comb her hair. Whereas Louise had a country home nearby to escape to, Adrienne's was too far away to travel without Gilbert, and so Louise brought some of the country to her, slathering Adrienne's face with mud. Too much giggling was bad for the baby, the duchesse would say whenever she heard them from the halls. Walking for too long was bad for the baby; eating too much, drinking too little, all *bad* for the baby.

Adrienne was ready to scream.

Unlike Louise, Adrienne did not go to parties so far along, but the family was still preparing for the two hour ride to their Versailles apartments.

The doctor said that was where Adrienne would likely give birth so her parents were doubling down on efforts to make her chambers there as comfortable as possible. She would be trapped there for weeks on end after all, to watch winter from her bed.

Which was why she was *trying* to enjoy her autumn.

Gilbert's relatives stopped by several times a month to the duchesse's salon to catch a glimpse of their future great-nephew or niece. Adrienne heard their talk about a potential heir for the vast fortune that the Marquis was privy to, bringing to mind the image of her slightly disappointed father when Louise gave birth to a daughter and not the expected son. Louis didn't seem to mind too much, declaring they had plenty of time to produce a son, but Adrienne saw Louise's bittersweet look she gave the infant.

It wasn't a healthy baby. Louise was, in honesty, too afraid to name her. Georgette was a name that was passed around, included in the babe's Baptism, but she was in and out of fevers, remaining under care in *Eure-et-Loir* for Louise to push out of mind as to not be so gloomy when she was with Adrienne.

She prayed her own baby would be healthy. The utmost fear that Gilbert would return for Adrienne to simply have a miscarriage or a stillborn gripped at her heart. Every doctor reassured her that everything was going perfectly, but like everything else, God could punish her at any moment He pleased.

Pacing. *Pacing*, she thought, helped in no manner, but it definitely kept her upright. If she was going to mull in one depressive episode after another, at least she would do it on her feet.

She paced until she heard the clopping of horses make their way into the Hôtel de Noailles' grounds. The gaggle of young men dismounted and chatted amongst themselves as servants rushed out to take their horses to the stables while the rest of the entourage continued on their way. Adrienne's knees wobbled while she watched them from the window, spotting the ginger hair in the middle of blonde and brunette. She hadn't met a handful of the men he was speaking with; and he spoke to them for a long while, his hands flailing about as they did when he got too excited.

Goodness, she swore he grew taller whenever he went away, standing almost a whole head above Louis as they shoved each other, disappearing from Adrienne's view. Their chatter echoed through the foyer.

She smoothed her dress over and wiped the sweat from her palms on the nearby sofa. Through the months he was away, she didn't think about if he would find her repulsive to look at – it wasn't his character – but now that she thought of it, it was all that possessed her mind. If she looked at a mirror just to check… But *no,* she was avoiding mirrors… She could ask her sisters, but they would lie sweetly, she knew it.

Pacing – she would pace again.

"Mon coeur," she heard as the door flew open, and her pacing was halted by his hands on her jaw. They were warm hands, and despite the smell of sweat and horse that accompanied the bestowal of kisses, Adrienne couldn't think of anything more comforting.

"Your face," Adrienne whispered, gently tracing over a small bruise at the corner of his brow. It matched the color of his eyes.

Gilbert shook his head. "Whacked myself with my own stirrups on the way home," he said. "Can't go too long without doing something ridiculous."

She tsked softly. "You poor thing."

His hands flowed from her cheeks to her shoulders, stepping back once to look at the whole of her. "And you," he breathed, "like an angel from heaven." His fingers hovered over the rise of her stays, to where the pleats of the dress covered the soft swell of her belly. Adrienne swallowed, letting him caress where she was told the baby's head would be. "It's more firm than I thought it would be," Gilbert chuckled, then gasped.

Adrienne smiled and took his hand. "You feel that?" she said, putting his palm to where the last kick was. Another came right on cue. "I think it hears you."

"Does this hurt?" he asked.

"Sometimes," she said, and took a breath. "But it's manageable. Better now that you're back."

"I'm sorry I was gone for so long."

"You should tell the baby what you were doing," Adrienne said. "Maman says if we talk to it often, then it will know who its parents are when it's born."

Gilbert carefully knelt down, his nose bonking into her skirts. "*Hello*," he said, silly enough that Adrienne snorted. "This is your Papa speaking." He went into extraordinary detail about what Metz looked like in northeast France, the different drills that the boys ran, some more disciplined than others; how he met and befriended many Germans in the area, where they dined by the Moselle river. Parties were held almost every night, but Gilbert insisted he only attended one or two a week at the behest of his friends – he did not lie that he flirted here and there with no success; but most evenings were among his club and local enlightenment speakers. "Truly, *mon petit*, you should hear of the talk of liberty across the Atlantic. Something new is stirring; something profound. What do you think? Can your Papa be a part of that?"

"Careful," Adrienne said, "or I think liberty may be its first word."

He smirked. "Liberty, liberty, liberty," he cupped his hands around his mouth to say to her belly. Adrienne knotted her fingers through his hair and gave him a little tug as he continued to tickle her. "What, *mon coeur?* It is better to save our babe from having to say Marie-Joseph-Paul-Yves-Roch-Gilbert du Motier."

"Typically it would just be 'Pa,' you know."

"Our baby is too intelligent for just *Pa*." Gilbert kissed the spot he spoke to and stood up, gracing Adrienne's lips with another. "You must tell me how you have been, now. Do not spare me of the details."

So she told him of her growing confinement, of Louise's sick infant, and the worry she had for theirs. She gave a summary of Pauline's writings, of what the other sisters were up to, of how her parents were both suffocating and not around enough at the same time. She told him how much she missed him, a topic that brought him great pleasure and simultaneous guilt. In admission of the subject Gilbert was growing to cherish more and more, she told him of the conversation heard from her grandfather and her father as they whispered about the American colonies and France's involvement in beginning to ship them supplies.

"Really?" Gilbert almost shouted it before Adrienne clapped his mouth shut. "So it's true? I'll tell you, it was a great deal of conversation in Metz."

"It's rumored through the Maréchals," she said. "Shush! I wasn't supposed to hear anything. And neither did you! This can't go into that club of yours. Let someone else get in trouble for admitting affairs of state."

"With the amount of time I spend with the king, it shouldn't be too long before he mentions something. All of his ministers are so old and crotchety, he likes to confide in better company. So there, no slip up on my behalf, your spying is safe with me."

She shoved him onto her chaise. "I'm not spying, I am *listening*. Men forget that women have ears and a brain."

"That's because we men are incredibly dense. We need our women to remind us," he teased, wrapping his arms around her. His ear rested gently against her belly as he quieted. The wind outside was building up with incoming rain, stray leaves slapping against the glass like wet towels. "I'm sorry to hear about our little niece," he said. "How has Louise been handling it?"

"I don't think she has been."

"Ah." Gilbert's silence returned for another minute. "If I know anything about the fairer sex it is that they are *very* strong. My grandmère once told me when my maman left for Paris after my father died, she did so because she had such a large heart, it was difficult for her to carry all the love and anguish she had for him through the mountains. But I later understood that it was because she had people in Paris who she could confide in, who could help her. And I know it wasn't easy for her to leave me behind in Chavaniac as a toddler, but she did it because she had to – that was a very hard thing for a mother to do. My maman was one of the strongest women I've ever known."

"I would have loved to meet her," Adrienne replied, pushing the powder through his hair.

"I'm sure she would have loved to meet you as well, *mon coeur*. And Louise is lucky to have you and your sisters, and your maman as well to support her. Louis, too, even," he said with a tilt to his head. "When he's around."

☆

Little Georgette did not make it through the month.

In the carriage ride to Versailles, Adrienne snuggled close to Gilbert. With her head on his shoulder, he drew his cloak around her, and they both sat in silence with Louis and Louise across from them, having considerably worn themselves out. Louise was asleep against her husband, her eyes rimmed with red. Louis let his cheek fall atop her cap, half-dazed while he watched the trees go by. Their carriage followed the d'Ayen's, and behind them trailed family friends, everyone's luggage piled atop. They rolled through the better parts of the city, the roads less frequented by highwaymen from the sheer amount of guard presence. Still, wandering paupers made the trek out to the wells on the parameters of Paris to avoid the more contaminated ones inside. Women whose aprons were fraying and dirty, well-used from work, glanced up at the carriages as they passed.

Adrienne kept the toe of her shoe over Louise's. It wasn't much in terms of comfort, but the four of them have always been so close over the past few years – the grief was a black cloud.

Louis' attention flitted back towards them. He didn't look like he had cried, but the darkened circles under his eyes betrayed his calm demeanor. For the first time in Adrienne's memory, the haughty Vicomte de Noailles looked exhausted. He gave her a small smile, his glance moving up to meet Gilbert's sympathetic face.

"A long winter this will be," Louis said while the coach rattled along the road. The leather of his glove crinkled softly as he adjusted his hold of Louise's hand.

"There will be plenty of things we can do to make the time go by easier," Gilbert replied. "Our grand cage is full of toys and good company. I am quite lucky to have you all. Shame you must have me."

Adrienne pinched his knee, mindful of her sleeping sister.

The bulk of the two hour trip brought them along the King's Road, a hundred-year old route that the previous Louis XIV had transformed from a country backroad to a busy path from Paris to Versailles. It was framed with trees on both sides that stretched across the sky, casting splotches of shadow and light through leaves and bare branches. Every now and then, the wheels of the carriage would slide over the piles of wet leaves that hadn't been blown away, or the breeze would cut through the row to rock the coach as if they were on a ship instead. Inside, Adrienne thought the seats were too straight, too rigid; if the creators simply thought to design the benches with a slight recline and softer cushions, long journeys would become less of a strain on the back. It was likely that the driver had better seating arrangements for the trip.

"Are we still on to do the Court Club?" Louis asked, and Gilbert responded with a muffled snort.

"By all means, I cannot think of a better way to attend frivolities at court."

"The Court Club?" Adrienne asked, a brow raising for concern that the gentlemen of the family were already losing their minds.

"That is our name for those discussions on literature and the news I was telling you about. Although lately we were thinking about rebranding ourselves. The Society of the Wooden Sword was brought up in jest, but..." Gilbert exchanged a long look with his brother-in-law. "I think it is growing on me."

"Sounds more republican," Louis nodded. "I also think switching names may make our past transgressions with His Majesty's ministers, *ahh*, in the past."

Adrienne pinched the bridge of her nose. "What past transgressions?"

"Nothing a lady should worry about," Louis said.

"We were simply critiquing the Parlements," Gilbert said. "And we didn't get in trouble — We *nearly* did. Ségur saved us all."

Adrienne was going to bite his shoulder. "What did you *do*?"

"We put on a little play, that's all," Louis replied. "A little burlesque show. The king's brother was even in on it. Dear Gilbert here played the procurer-general. And it was fantastic and *hilarious* and would have been a regular event if the ministers didn't find out. Thought we were being disrespectful."

"I thought we made them look better, honestly," Gilbert added.

"Monsieur Maurepas, that is, the king's chief minister, went to snitch on us, but our blessed Ségur beat him to it."

"The Comte told King Louis you all were making fun of the Parlements?" Adrienne asked. Such a thing was not usually taken lightly. Why were the boys she loved like this?

"His *Majesty* thought it hilarious," Louis smiled. "When Maurepas told him he wanted us banished from court, he laughed. I have to say, dear Marquis, my appreciation of the king has grown this past year."

"My appreciation of Ségur has grown likewise," Gilbert whispered as Louise stirred lightly. "But *mon coeur*, worry not for us, the most dangerous thing we do is smack each other with foils."

Versailles, December 15th, 1775

Adrienne was dealing with something far more dangerous than Gilbert gave her credit for. He walked the length of the drawing room, his banyan tied tightly around his waistcoat and breeches. The speed at which he paced threatened to kick his shoes right off of his feet while cries and shouting echoed down the hallway.

"Calm yourself, have a drink," Louis said, holding up the glass he had helped himself to while the rest of the men sat around and waited.

"Get that away from me else I may be sick," Gilbert replied. He had already drank his fill for the whole month the day prior – attending another party without his wife. Where games and gambling took place betting on horse racing and cards, there were many contested drinking affairs. In hopes to impress his brother-in-law, Gilbert had consumed several rounds too many, promptly tripping over a table and several other courtiers. He didn't remember how he was brought back home, or who had put him in his carriage, but amidst his mumbling for everyone to inform the Vicomte how much he drank, he later learned Louis was not even in attendance. The throbbing was still present in his mind when Adrienne went into labor in the early hours of the day. It was now late evening.

The Maréchal de Noailles and the Duc d'Ayen stood in the corner of the room by the window, watching the snowfall while they smoked their pipes. The young Noailles daughters were with their governess while the duchesses and Louise remained with Adrienne and the doctors.

He was elated to be a father. That was something he couldn't suppress since he had received the news during training. For the whole day he held the letter in hand, babbling about the prospect of fatherhood. There was an air of mystery around it, only having mother-figures in his life, the role of a father had always been partially obscured by the guidance of his uncles, his grandfather, and the men of his wife's family. Some ideas from his great-grandfather came to mind on how he would be a decent patriarch. For one, he would leave the rule-making to his matriarch, as any intelligent man would do. Adrienne's career was to be a mother now, and he was acutely aware that the role of father was a minor part in a man's life, but he still wanted to be what his own father could not.

"Thinking about names?" Louis asked. He leaned back against the sofa, one arm thrown lazily over the back while he sipped his wine.

"Not really," Gilbert said, coming back around for the thirty-eighth time.

"Are you thinking about anything?"

"Yes. No. I don't know."

Louis cocked his head, then nodded. "That's fair," he said. He toed a half-written letter on the cushion far from him. "Were you going to add anything to our letter to Broglie, or shall I just sign it off?"

"I don't care," Gilbert replied, then spun around, "I mean, tell him I send my best regards, of course. That I am impertinently interested, but at the *current* instant, I am indisposed." He hesitantly eyed his in-laws and their hushed speaking. Any talk about his friends' interests in the happenings of abroad would not do well in the duc's ears. If Gilbert was curious about something not proposed by his family, the Duc d'Ayen would do anything in his power to prevent him from attaining it.

"Very well." Louis paused as another shout came down the hallway, followed by a chorus of incoherent responses. "Well, it sounds like something is finally happening."

"Pray it's an heir," the duc said, lowering his pipe.

Louis tilted his head over the sofa. "What, dear Cousin, you don't think my brother's son is enough for the Noailles lineage? Fret not, I will provide for you and Uncle next time, I swear it. Do not put pressure on Gilbert's loins, here."

"Adrienne may have also inherited her mother's inclination to birth daughters," the Maréchal replied, sounding hopeful, yet already resigned to fate. Gilbert's brow furrowed as he remained silent, watching the door intently for someone to come with the news. News on *anything*.

The halls had gone quiet – the first time in hours. Gilbert nibbled on his nails, willing to pay any amount of money from his ever-growing fortune to hear that Adrienne was alive and that the baby was well. He imagined the secretary rushing in with a wide smile saying those two things exactly – *Adrienne is alive and the baby is well.*

Eventual clicking of a man's heels down the hallway was fast enough to be a stride, not a run nor a solemn approach. The four men in the room twisted their attention to Monsieur Dameron as he pushed the drawing room door open. He didn't look distraught, Gilbert noted, as he swallowed his heart that was rising up into his throat. Dameron's hands clasped tightly together in front of him as he looked towards the duc first for several seconds before turning to Gilbert himself.

"You have a daughter, Monsieur," he said with a short bow of his head.

Gilbert hardly heard the clicking of tongues as the Maréchal made a sanctimonious display to his son and nephew. "Another girl to the Noailles entourage," someone said; it could have been the duc, it could have been the Maréchal.

"Monsieur," Gilbert said to the secretary. Dameron looked up at him expectantly. "How is the Madame?" he asked, stepping forward, having to hold his fingers to keep himself from fidgeting.

"You may go and see her, Monsieur Marquis," Dameron replied, keeping the door open. "The duchesse will meet you down there."

If he counted the steps he took as he hurried down the hall, he'd damn decorum as his pace turned into a nervous jog. Hardly having time to compose himself as his mother-in-law was waiting in the doorway, he slid to a stop at her feet. She breathed a slow sigh, her hand resting on the straight line of the front of her bodice, but she was smiling with her eyes, holding out another hand for Gilbert to take. He kissed it while he caught his breath.

"Is she…?"

"She's awake and waiting for you," the duchesse said. "The babe was taking her time to arrive, but there were no complications." Tilting her head into the room, she whispered, "Go on, then. See your wife and child."

The room was lit up only from the fireplace, keeping the winter outside at bay. Besides the crackling of the wood, it was silent, quiet enough that the gentle blubbering bundle laying on his Adrienne's chest was the only thing Gilbert could hear. Louise stood up from the bedside, stepping away as Gilbert searched for his wife's face.

She looked enchanting. Her brunette hair was down around her shoulders, loosely tied into a braid that disappeared behind her back. Her cheeks were flush and seemed to glow from the firelight, a perfect spot for Gilbert to kiss as he knelt by her.

"I'm sorry," she said, blinking slowly. He wanted to kiss her again.

"What would you ever need to apologize for?" he asked, smoothing Adrienne's stray hair back.

"I was hoping to give you a son."

God, his heart was breaking. Gilbert cupped her head, making sure no tears came from those eyes. The baby cooed, and he was drawn to look at the small, chubby-cheeked daughter who watched him with a wide hazel look. There was a single patch of ginger hair that refused to remain flat as he stroked it with his pinkie.

"She's perfect," he said.

"She looks like you."

He smirked and shook his head. "Thankfully, she looks like *you, mon coeur.* Look at her nose, her pout! It would be me apologizing if she inherited any of this," he replied, gesturing to his face. Adrienne tiredly smiled, unconvinced. "She is so much you, that it would only be the right thing to name her after you," he said, standing up only to sit atop the mattress, politely wiggling himself to embrace both of his girls.

"After me? Oh goodness, Gilbert. We can't call her Adrienne, it would confuse her."

"It's actually good we haven't had a boy – the poor thing would inherit my names as well, and I couldn't bear to do that to a child. But Adrienne is a perfect first name. I can only think of naming her after all the beautiful women I know, but to save her the pain of several names, I will settle on Adrienne Henriette."

They heard the duchesse let out a small cry from the doorway.

"Then we will also add Catherine for your grandmère," Adrienne said. They softly bickered over other name options, turning towards the babe's namesake, to which the duchesse provided Charlotte, for Gilbert's aunt.

"Mademoiselle Adrienne *Henriette* Catherine Charlotte du Motier," Gilbert said, tapping his nose on Adrienne's head before he kissed her crown. They watched little Henriette blink in and out of a doze, her small, chubby hands reaching for the heavens.

"Ah, Maman," Adrienne called, "I think she's hungry." The duchesse walked over like a mother on a mission, carefully taking little Henriette. A woman Gilbert didn't recognize but must have been a wet nurse waited in the hall.

With their firstborn borrowed to be fed, there was a vacancy in Adrienne's arms that Gilbert slid down to fill. He kicked his shoes off and shoved his stockinged feet under the covers, snuggling into the gentle curve between her breasts. Her hands went to his hair, to his back, and lightly scratched away — an expert on the craft. He purred into her skin.

"Stop this, I'm gross," she was saying, but Gilbert only mushed his face further into her hold. "Louise is still here, Gilbert, please!"

"Louise knows where the door is," he replied, mumbling into her shift.

He heard Louise tittering, a few steps before her heels left the rug and hit the wood of the hallway's floor.

"Papa must be upset," Adrienne said after a moment.

Gilbert looked up with a frown, the stirring of anger in his chest. "I don't care what Papa feels. I love our daughter. She is of our blood and my heart, not his. *Du Motier de la Fayette*. That is the name I willingly give to her; what she rightfully inherits from me. It doesn't matter what d'Ayen or the Maréchal de Noailles think. She will be a strong and intelligent woman one day and I will have the pleasure of shooing all the young men from her hand."

Adrienne's dark eyes sparkled. "Would we pick her husband for her, then?"

"I think all three of us are far too young to think on that matter," he replied. "To imagine she would know the man who would fall at her feet before they are engaged would be preferable."

"Yes, I believe you are right." Adrienne yawned, and Gilbert heard the slow beating of her heart. "We'll raise her to have good tastes."

"That will have to come from me," Gilbert also yawned. "Lord knows how you said yes to *this* in the chapel."

She was the first to fall asleep, hand still tangled in his curls. Gilbert wearily watched the fire from the bed. He was a father. A strange feeling. A good, strange feeling. He made something with Adrienne that was their own.

Chapter Ten

✦

Paris, June 1776

To settle into motherhood wasn't so bad a fate. Her weeks at little Henriette's side were full of ups and downs. While the ginger waves continued to grow on her head, Henriette babbled and reached for every new thing her mother showed her while they walked through the halls of the Hôtel de Noailles. Adrienne's mother had said she was a very talkative baby, which must have come from Gilbert because, as an infant, Adrienne was quite the mute.

Gilbert was frequently away all throughout early spring; sometimes with his regiment, others with his club, or sometimes off somewhere where Adrienne couldn't even place him. When he was home, however, they would welcome guests of their own – men young and old who Gilbert spoke of about *liberty* and the American colonies that Britain continued to molest. Adrienne happily listened, for seeing Gilbert speak of his passions with the intensity she would see her father speak of new science warmed her heart.

Through the Maréchal de Noailles, she let more information slip to her husband and his companions of the foreign minister, the Comte de Vergennes', support for the war and the king's agreement to supply the Americans with arms and ammunition. It was, perhaps, riling the young man up a little too much, but Adrienne rejoiced in seeing him so excited.

Little Henriette took great pleasure in shrieking with Gilbert's boundless energy. Days when her papa would be away from Paris were the days when her papi would enjoy her innocent prattling. The Duc d'Ayen would hold her when he was out of his office, pointing to all the flowers in the garden and naming them for little Henriette to try and grab at. Sometimes, after Adrienne's mother and father would borrow the baby for a short stroll, she would receive Henriette back with little buds in the baby's strawberry hair.

There were moments, still, when Henriette was a stubborn eater, and refused to let any spoon into her mouth unless her papa was there. Adrienne was so convinced that Henriette was the perfect mixture of her doting parents, that she couldn't bear to be away from the babe nor her husband, and *definitely* not the both of them, for any long period of time.

Adrienne forfeited more public outings for the time being. Every day was spent in the company of her infant. It wasn't a slight towards her sister, who had kept her late baby miles away from her with wetnurses and a governess, but Adrienne disliked the lonely feeling that sat in the pit of her stomach when her lovely two gingers were out of her sight. Gilbert didn't seem to mind that she was taking a break from parties and balls, for when he went to present himself to court and to the operas or ballets, he had a reasonable excuse to depart early that no respectable courtier would bark at.

Earlier in the day of a warm, clear June morning, Adrienne laid across her floor in her wrapping gown, jingling Henriette's silver-belled rattle in front of her eyes. She had twisted the red hair tufts to stick out of her lace cap like Gilbert's hair would if left to dry uncombed, smiling as it bounced while Henriette reached for the musical toy. It was only this week that the baby had been able to sit up straight. She sat in the sun blocks of the window, basking and glowing, babbling about *philosophy* probably, Adrienne pretended, while attempting to eat the rattle.

There was a clicking of commotion coming from the foyer. It echoed through the open doors – a gaggle of young men and the tapping of toe-caps on some of their riding boots.

Riding… Adrienne missed it. She'd take Henriette on a jaunt one day when she was old enough.

The sounds went leftward beneath her room, likely to the parlor, save for one that tapped up the stairs and took long strides towards her bedchamber. Adrienne bopped Henriette's nose while she waited for Gilbert to appear in her doorway. And that he did, with his face red and his brow twitching, another day of a passionately angry man.

"What's happened now?" Adrienne asked, sitting up. Gilbert moodily sauntered over to her and the babe, kissing Adrienne's forehead before he lifted Henriette high into the air. She wiggled and squealed, flying like a bird.

"What's *happened* is that I'm – and the rest of us, Ségur, Louis – we-we-we…" Gilbert puffed out his cheeks, one arm flailing about while he held Henriette with the other, pacing around the room. "We've been placed in the reserves. The reserves! You know what that is? It's unemployment! It's lackadaisical! I've been given rank only for it to go directly into the chamberpot!"

"*Bah!*" Henriette shouted, holding his nose.

Gilbert nodded. "Bah is right, my little lamb," he said, swapping the babe in his arms while shoving his coat off on Adrienne's bed. Adrienne rose from the floor, shaking her head.

"Who has done this? Why? The Noailles Dragoons are one of the most highly regarded men. The king wouldn't possibly do such a thing."

"No, it was not King Louis," Gilbert said, grabbing his housecoat from where he left it the night before. Henriette disappeared beneath it before she popped back out of the large sleeve. "Well, of sorts. His Secretary of State for War is the real antagonist here. Thinking he can shrink the army when we will need it most!"

His proclamation of frustration as well as Adrienne followed him down the hallway. Adrienne kept an eye on their baby that bounced happily in Gilbert's fluid walking. She was, traditionally, in indecent attire for non-familial company, but if she and Gilbert were both to walk into the salon in their banyans, who would stop them?

Louis and the Comte de Ségur she recognized on sight. They sat together on one sofa that by now must have been indented from their weight with how often they visited. Across from them stood a gentleman, maybe in his late-twenties or early-thirties, with shoulder length dark hair and a small, perfectly groomed moustache. To Adrienne's utter delight, the man was hardly taller than herself.

"Aw, you brought the baby!" Ségur said as Gilbert returned to them.

"Oh, yes, I did," Gilbert replied, somewhat snapping back into reality as he looked at Henriette before turning to Adrienne. "She's just very easy to carry around. I'm sorry, I did not mean to take her from you, *mon coeur.*"

Ségur raised his arms. "Oh, but could I hold her, Madame? I've always wanted to bounce a baby on my knee, and with the amount of nerves we've all been penting up, my knee will be bouncing regardless."

Henriette had ample amounts of enjoyment by it, giggling away while her father and his friends continued to express a great deal of annoyance at the decision of the Comte de Saint-Germain.

"I would not be the first Pole to cross the Atlantic, nor anyone here the first Frenchman," said the slight man, seemingly continuing off where the discussion was.

"Of course not, Monsieur Pulaski, but there is a difference between regular volunteers and those of us who are not only nobles, but inside the King's social circle," Louis said. He crossed his foot over his knee while he spun the spur at his ankle. "Let alone, we would need permission before we…" Adrienne didn't miss his glance in her direction. "Got involved."

"Is this about the Americans?" Adrienne asked. Three of the gentlemen looked at her; Gilbert merely nodded. "There are soldiers already leaving France for the New World." Another nod. "And… you four wish to join them?"

"It is a righteous cause we all believe in," Gilbert replied. "But as Louis said, it is almost impossible at this point to do much of anything."

Monsieur Pulaski took a watch from his pocket and clicked it open. "I only have a few more moments with you all before I'm collected," he said. "Should any military opportunity arise while I am still behind bars, by all means, write me. I won't take much convincing to depart from Europe to live or die for such a thing as freedom."

"Behind bars?" Adrienne mouthed to Ségur.

"Debtor's prison," he mouthed back.

"Rumors are that there are some Americans en route here," Louis said. The sofa under him was becoming more of a bed with how far he reclined. "Not that they'd say anything when Britain's eyes are on Versailles, but oh, how I cannot wait to see one. Distant country folk, probably wearing undyed linen, uncocked hats, and oh! Maybe some old English fashion. It's very exciting, actually, don't let my lack of enthusiasm dissuade you from thinking I am not going to run up to the first American I see."

"Rein it in, Noailles," Ségur exclaimed. "Your family would have a stroke if they witnessed that. Think of your mother."

"She and Pa have my brother. As a *spare*, I'm allowed to be embarrassing once in a while. You wouldn't know what that feels like though, Ségur. Being a spare, that is – I know you embarrass yourself all the time."

"Noailles, I swear this baby is more intelligent than you are. She's judging you with these big Fayette hazel eyes, look."

Gilbert walked back over to pick up Henriette from Ségur's knee and folded her against his chest. The conversation with Adrienne in the room, to her ears, became regulated. Less talk of overseas journeys, although the stories from the American war continued to be their spark of excitement between the complaints against the Parlements. Adrienne watched Gilbert attentively: the way he leaned his head against the top of Henriette's while he spoke, or rocked her with ease under the warmth of his banyan. Imagining him among his regiment actively involved in a war, a captain leading charges, dodging bullets and bayonets, or remembering the way the previous Marquis de la Fayette perished in battle when Gilbert was hardly a toddler wrought hot tears in her eyes. She blinked them away, not wanting to be the wife that wept over the *idea* of anything bad happening. Gilbert was there in front of her, and he said it himself: there was nothing for them to do to leave while France maintained a neutral stance.

It would have been easier to keep that belief if an American didn't arrive in Versailles the following month. Monsieur Silas Deane was a merchant according to Adrienne's papi, but even he sent the rest of the family sideways glances at the reasonable doubt. For now, all of France seemed to go along with the ruse, that this *English colonist* was just around the courtiers to sell his wares to a wealthy market.

Louis was right in saying that he would rush the man. The trio in which Adrienne had been seeing connected at the hip would often leave Paris to attend the soirées and dinners hosted with Deane as a guest. While she was growing increasingly interested in hearing about what they were speaking about, the Duchesse d'Ayen shuffled her in the classic direction of every woman who avoided court: into prayer and her small and intimate salon days. Her sister, Anne, had suddenly become a teenager, and much to Anne's dismay, followed the social obligations she now had to attend as a young woman. The duc and duchesse would have a tough time finding a match for her, Adrienne thought as Anne kept her arm looped through hers, biting almost every boy who looked in their direction.

Their Maman didn't seem to mind too much, and there didn't appear to be any secret engagements lined up for Anne or any of the younger Noailles sisters for the time being.

The Noailles family gatherings only grew larger with more visits from the *de Tessé's*, the Duc d'Ayen's sister and her husband, who were ever the quirky and sociable couple who doted upon their nieces because they had no children of their own. Madame de Tessé loved gardening as much as Adrienne's mother did, and often the girls would find themselves covered in soil as they planted more fruit for the season. Baby Henriette squished the dirt between her palms like it was dough and she the baker, sneezing as it fluttered over her nose.

With so many family members smothering the days with talk and tea, it would be reasonable to not notice the absence of a young, rambunctious husband. Adrienne wasn't as reasonable as she hoped to be though. She looked towards the door whenever it opened, willing the appearance of Gilbert to walk through. Whatever was filling his days, be it with his friends or around the court, if he were with other women – which was completely normal for young men of his station, but the thought brought a dark cloud over Adrienne's head – or starting some secret organization behind the backs of the Maréchal and duc, at least Adrienne had the comfort of knowing that he would be in their bed each night. She could hold him while he mumbled himself to sleep.

Paris, October 1776

It was a bad habit: Adrienne eavesdropping on her father. It wasn't her fault. Louis and Gilbert had hustled through the hallway with a flame to their step, only to nudge and push and slap each other upon nearing the Duc d'Ayen's office. Adrienne happened to be returning from a ride around the Tuileries with her aunt and uncle; and she happened to miss the stairwell that led upstairs, walking over to the window by the duc's office. She fiddled with her gloves, eyeing the squirrels that bopped around outside.

Louis spoke clearly. "To be plain with you, Monsieur, I am here to request permission to join General Washington in the Americas…"

Adrienne held her breath. She couldn't hear Gilbert. He must have been nervous, as after a moment, a tiny *"too!"* cracked from the room, and that was when she heard the slamming of the desk.

"Absolutely not," the duc said.

"But, Monsieur," Louis said. "Monsieur Deane is giving Frenchmen ranks if they sign up. We have military experience. Since these American colonies stripped their connection to England, there's no –"

"You've asked me this before, Louis, and I told you it was not wise."

"But you have influence with Monsieur Maurepas. If you put a word in for me – I mean, for *us* –"

"So what? You can go over and die? You think your father would be pleased with me if I gave my blessing for such a thing? It is not the place for young nobles in a time like this. This declaration of independence means nothing while France is neutral. His Majesty and the ministers would not blatantly allow it."

"The king already told us he can't put anything in writing, but he did not say no. You would just have to speak with them, Monsieur," Gilbert said, finally loud enough for Adrienne to hear.

"I will do *no* such thing for *you!*"

Adrienne stepped back. She had never heard her father say something so bitter in their arguments. Shouting, yes, of course – names and curses between them – but never something defiled with so much degradation. Cupping her hands over her mouth, she leaned against the opposite wall. If they were to open the doors and see her standing there, having heard the shameful reprimand, what would she even say? The office was silent, deafeningly so. Lifting herself onto her toes, she tapped over to the stairwell, linking her arms through the marble banisters while she waited to hear the boys return.

"I told you not to," Gilbert had said.

"We're minors, we can't *not* ask."

"I told you he would refuse. I'm going to see Broglie; see what he can do for us."

"Gilbert," Louis whispered, and their footsteps paused. "I don't know if it's a good idea."

"I'm not giving up on this. If you're backing out, then back out. Ségur already did. But Louis, you know it will not leave your mind. It cannot leave mine either."

"Broglie already told you he wouldn't be the cause of the death of your line," Louis said, biting back a shout. "He won't do more!"

"He will," Gilbert replied. "I won't give him a choice."

Adrienne remained silent, her forehead pressed to a post. Louis walked by her, chin down and his eyes to the floor before he retreated down the hallway. She'd never seen him so defeated. If Louise could handle his disappointment, perhaps she could handle Gilbert's.

"How much did you hear?"

She looked back to where Gilbert waited, his frown deepened. Adrienne stood up on the steps and cocked her head. "I don't think it matters how much I heard more than *what* exactly I was hearing? What are you *doing?*"

"What am *I* doing?" he asked, waving his arms like she had asked him the stupidest question. "What is *anyone* in this country doing? I am trying to be useful! To make a name for myself! Whose goal is it to be a court-hanger? To waste away drinking and eating and dancing and gossiping and fucking every day when there are people out there making history." He shook his head and slapped his hands to his side. "No one likes me anyway, my absence would make little difference."

"Gilbert," she said, catching his arm as he turned to ascend the stairs. "You know that is not true. Papa – he… he's trying to keep you alive."

"I don't wish to speak of Papa for the remainder of, well, *forever*, right now. And I am very capable of keeping myself alive, thank you! It is a learning opportunity."

"Do you truly want to go to the Americas that badly?" Adrienne asked, keeping her voice tamed. She squeezed his arm with all her might as she hugged him.

Gilbert looked away. "Please don't try to discourage me, *mon coeur*, I couldn't take it from *you*."

"I'm just trying to understand. If you are happy then I am happy, remember? Does this war mean that much to you? Would it make you happy to be there?"

His eyes remained on the wall until Adrienne moved to place herself in front of him on a step above. She waited until he looked at her.

"You care for these strangers' liberty so much that it brings you to tears," she said, wiping his face.

"I can't think of anything else," he admitted, falling into her touch. "It's calling to me."

He spoke with a lightness of breath that one would reserve only when speaking to their angels, a quieter than whispered prayer. Adrienne went soft at his pleads. Regardless of how she felt, and damn it all, she cursed herself for placing her needs at the mercy of Gilbert's sense of divine purpose; she wanted to see him smile with true happiness that she couldn't seem to give him.

"Promise me," she said, "that you will tell me before you go."

"Mon coeur…?"

"Promise to kiss me long enough to last a war. Don't leave without taking my heart with you." Smoothing his hair back, she nudged his nose with hers. "You have my blessing to fight, but please, please promise me that."

His hands at her waist could have engulfed the whole of her. "Leaving you and Henriette would be the greatest challenge," he said. "But I have yet to go anywhere. I will give you a thousand kisses before I depart, I promise."

Louis' stomping of heels returned to the foyer. "Gilbert, we *demand* general officer ranks or nothing at – oh *Adri*, hello," he said, clicking his teeth into an awkward smile. "I am interrupting. Gone for two minutes and suddenly I am intruding into la Fayette time. Don't know why you're picking the hall for this; I feel like you would *hit* me if I was assaulting Louise's face like that in broad daylight. Get a room."

"Thank you, Louis," Adrienne replied. She huffed a laugh. Gilbert rested his forehead on her cheek while they waited for Louis to abscond once more. His hands moved to the buttons of her riding habit.

"I'm realizing you just came back, but would you like to come out again with me for a ride? I could use the air. Perhaps Henriette would enjoy a respite from the house as well before it gets too cold out for her." Gilbert tucked Adrienne's silk cravat back into her waistcoat.

She nodded. "I'll get her then," she said with a smile. "You better prep the horses."

Henriette bounced happily in Gilbert's saddle as he led the horse on a slow walk through the golden gardens, one hand on the reins, the other wrapped safely around his daughter. Adrienne kept to his right, taking in the pleasant silence between them. There was an increase of people in Paris this season, she noticed, watching groups of men in heavy conversation meander by, their walking canes gripped in their hands. They didn't use them, their attention too caught up in their speech to let it fall. Wives, if they had the ladies on them, were several steps behind in their gossiping. No one else brought an infant along; which was normal for the nobility. But Adrienne never claimed to be normal, nor had Gilbert, but all of Paris already knew that. Henriette was taking in her first autumn with wide eyes, pointing at the red and orange leaves and apples that dangled from trees.

Gilbert reached up and snatched an apple from a branch.

"Puh-puh!" Henriette said, grabbing for it.

"Pomme," Gilbert said, holding it for her to squeeze between her hands. It was too heavy for her to lift to her mouth, and far too big for that matter, so it hobbled in her lap before the horse's gait wiggled it out. It rolled off the saddle, Gilbert catching it with the curve of his boot. "Oh, goodness, it's stuck there now."

"I've got it," Adrienne said. She leaned over and took it, her own saddle creaking from the imbalance. "Your long legs are ridiculous," she added, rubbing the apple against her petticoat before she bit into it. "In a good way."

Gilbert took a soft piece of the apple that Adrienne handed his way and let Henriette nibble at it. His brows were furrowed as they were when he was deep in thought – if Adrienne didn't know him completely, she would think he was angry.

"What is it?" she asked.

He didn't answer for another several seconds. She wondered if he didn't hear her over their horses' clomping.

"You," he said. "You are… I mean, I don't know how I have lucked out with such a perfect wife. Few of my friends enjoy their lady's company, and I feel spoiled in this friendship we share."

"It is I who am fortunate enough to have such a tender-hearted man as a husband," she replied, "and who makes a loving, doting father for a daughter. Papa must have thought himself a genius when he matched us."

Gilbert tsked. "He matched us financially. It is the first reason why any parent makes arranged marriages. My lands bring in thousands every year, but I couldn't tell you the specifics. When we spend, I know that we have the funds unless Monsieur Gerard or my Abbé Fayon tell me to stop."

Ah, financials. "I might have spent a little on silks over the summer," Adrienne admitted. "I've never had so much at my disposal. Not that I wish to bankrupt you."

He smirked. "I've already vowed that what is mine is yours. I don't think some new dresses will bleed my account dry."

"And what is mine is yours as well," Adrienne said before she thought. "I have not much of interest to you though unless you wish to borrow my jewels or clothing. The house, I suppose."

"*You* are what interests me," he said, waggling his brows. Henriette danced in his hold.

Adrienne covered her mouth as other people promenaded by. "Well then," she said, clearing her throat, "I am all yours."

The clouds in the distance were growing shadowed as the sun dipped below the highest tree branches. With the days growing shorter, their time outside of polished cages was shrinking minute by minute.

"May I ask you something?" Adrienne said after they rounded the garden.

"Anything, *mon coeur*."

"Who is this Monsieur Broglie? You mentioned speaking to him."

Gilbert gripped the reins tightly, his eyes searching the path in front of them. "He was a soldier and diplomat under Louis XV. An old gentleman, now. Hosted a dinner last year while I was in Metz," he said. "The Marquis de Ruffec is his courtesy title, but we've just been calling him Broglie. I like him. He knew my father."

The death of his line made more sense now, Adrienne mulled.

"I will not die," Gilbert exclaimed, reading her face. "I promise you that."

She looked up at the sky, to the birds flying over. "If you say so," she said. They didn't lie to each other. If Gilbert said he would not die, then she would believe him.

She wouldn't consider the other option.

Versailles, December 1776

Even when they were stuck for ages at the queen's balls until the wee hours of the morning, Adrienne at least enjoyed having Gilbert at her side when he wasn't parading off with older men that she didn't recognize. She knew they had something to do with the Americas. A newer gentleman to Adrienne by the name of *de Kalb* was hosted in the Hôtel de Noailles several times throughout the autumn season, and traded pleasant conversations with him and the constant riveting news. Piles of letters were exchanged daily between her husband and his friends when he was not in their company. Monsieur Deane, no longer holding the façade of a merchant, appeared swamped at every event he was presented at.

Gilbert was in a fine mood. They stood together along the wall of the ballroom, sharing a glass of wine. He kept an eye on the new American arrivals, Messieurs Franklin and Lee, whom the French ministers buzzed around like wasps to sway other prospecting French nobles away for the time being. It was like watching a perfectly carved ice sculpture of neutrality melt from within. Adrienne was not completely versed on all things politics, but she had attended enough salon talks to know that France couldn't possibly upkeep the mask with Britain. Everyone knew *any* self-respecting Frenchman would take the first opportunity to assist in ruining a Briton's day, or in helping to free a colony from their grasp. After all, France was all but kicked out of North America in the last war, and every heroic story needed a triumphant revenge plot to take out the villains.

Adrienne leaned against Gilbert, pinching the beads on his blue frock absently. *He would make a grand hero, wouldn't he?* Tall and handsome enough. If not for his age and lithe figure, he would sound like how the noblemen described the rebels' leader, General Washington. Washington was spoken about as if he were a mythical figure, by Gilbert, by the delegates: a tall, majestic man from the Virginia colony. The one who had started the war with France in his youth now led one against Great Britain; it was, without a doubt, a Greek legend come to life.

It was amusing to see the Americans in their browns and gray-colored suits amongst the bold color of Court. Franklin even danced with a duchesse early on in the night before he retired. It was unusual for anyone to leave before the queen; frowned upon – not that it stopped Adrienne and Gilbert from slipping out from time to time – but Franklin was an older foreigner and so the slight was excused.

"Are you not in the mood for a drink tonight?" Gilbert asked. He held their glass that still remained half full. "Does your stomach hurt? You've been rubbing it for the past ten minutes."

"Oh," she said, looking down at her bodice. "No, it doesn't hurt. It's just been flipping every time I take a sip. You can have the rest."

"Like that's a good idea," he replied, setting it on a passing tray. "Are you sure you are well? Is there something I can do?"

A flutter of mischief came up with another wave of nausea that she swallowed down. It wasn't this bad the first time; nor did the sickness come at night so often. She shook her head and glanced up at Gilbert before she placed his hand at the top of her petticoat. He froze in place as his fingers smoothed over the velvet. "You could tell your progeny to stop rejecting the food and drink I'm trying to consume, else we'll both starve."

Watching him work the words through his brain was her favorite part of his reaction. His brows journeyed upward, eyes wide and twitching while he bounced up on the tips of his toes, not caring for the couple behind him as they stepped away at the display.

"You're joking, *mon coeur*, you cannot be," he said, his smile only growing. He kissed her forehead, her nose, her lips – he would go lower if they did not stand in the company of others. "Oh, this is better than learning from a letter."

"It could be a boy," she said, but he shushed her.

"Don't pressure it nor yourself," he whispered. He squeezed her hands. "It's job is to grow and yours is to be safe and healthy. I'll call the doctor for us *and-and-and* I'll get the kitchen staff to make you your favorites. Oh! Perhaps hot chocolate will help. They say dark chocolate is healthy for –"

"Gilbert, it's alright," she laughed. "It's not the first time. Let's just tell Henriette she gets to be a big sister by next summer. It is a great honor for any young girl."

"Next summer," Gilbert said, coming to a halt. His smile waned, but he sighed longingly. "How exciting."

Part Two

Pity the caged girl who loves the boy with wings.

Chapter Eleven

Paris, March 1777

After the festivities of Mardi Gras, Louis' brother, the Prince de Poix, made the suggestion that he take Gilbert on his next trip to England to see the Duc d'Ayen's brother who served there. It would somewhat satisfy the young man's needs to travel – and he would certainly find London interesting to explore – but Adrienne knew it would be under the confines of ambassadors and diplomats. Still, she clung to him as often as she could while he remained in France.

He was there for Henriette's first steps all on her own; her once pudgy legs were starting to shape up, and no doubt she would be tall like her papa and agile like her mother. She was becoming as sassy as them too, mimicking their tones when she didn't want to take a nap, or waving her arms around when toys were taken away when it was time to eat. Henriette's one flaw was her weight, which was below what the doctor desired. And so times to eat became more frequent, which upset the toddler a great deal unless Gilbert was there to press it. It would be hard, she told him, to keep it up without his help. But he regularly replied that she was a perfect mother and had no doubts of her care of their babies. He kissed Henriette a dozen times until her round cheeks were pink and turned to embrace Adrienne for a long while before he left with de Poix.

"I love you," he had said. "I love you so very much."

She could still feel his fingers on the strand of hair she left hanging from behind her ear.

London wasn't too far away, especially when they shifted their living arrangements back to Paris. It would just be a few weeks.

So by the time the end of March rolled around, it shouldn't have been a shock to see her father busily running to and fro in the house, his secretary and other men from court racing after him. He could have been preparing for something grand for the spring like she had seen him for his work colleagues. Her family was involved in almost every sphere of influence in the country and her father was, of course, a very busy man. Adrienne watched from the top of the stairs as two kingsmen from Versailles entered the foyer in their scarlet and blue uniforms, and with that, her father's powerfully angered voice screamed up the walls.

"You stop that ship! I don't care under whose jurisdiction he was allowed there, you tell His Majesty to forbid it to launch at once!"

"Monsieur, Bordeaux is so far, the likelihood of its arrival in time –"

The duc slammed his hand against the wall, the frames of paintings shuttering under his fury. "If he wishes to escape France without the title of a *traitor*, he will wait for the King's permission. Tell that boy that should he aim to preserve any ounce of honor, he will meet me in Marseilles. We will tour Italy if he desires to get out of France so badly. Might educate him."

"Jean, he wouldn't possibly have just left," Adrienne heard her mother interrupt as the soldiers swarmed out with letters in hand. "This isn't like him."

"Oh, it is exactly like him," the duc replied. "Brazen fool thinks of finding glory like his ancestors. He'll get himself shot like them too. Why can't he listen to reason? Why must we repeat the same mistakes month after month?"

Adrienne's knees began to tremble. She turned around, hand gripping the side of the railing until her knuckles turned white.

"All boys desire glory, you've said it yourself, Jean."

"Yes, but he could have waited to achieve it *in* France! *For* France! These are colonists – farmers with hunting rifles, not an army! Do you know how often these Continentals win a battle, Henriette?" the duc said. "There hasn't been news of a large-scale victory for them since they freed a port city called Boston in seventy-five, which counts for nothing as the British captured their largest port city in New York last autumn. If we are lucky, then their Congress will send Gilbert right back to us. No pauper's government would want to pay for foreign officers."

Adrienne's nose burned like someone had struck a candle and poured the wax over her face. Rivers of fire ran down her cheeks. She willed herself forward, falling on her feet in some semblance of walking, running, crumbling towards her room. The floor had never been so hard, yet not solid enough to balance on. She couldn't feel her legs before she surrendered to gravity, a childlike whine stuck in her throat.

Gritting her teeth, Adrienne heaved and silently panted into her rug.

Oh God, she thought, *oh God, oh God, oh God – why was this happening? This wasn't like Gilbert – he wouldn't have just left like that – he promised to tell her, he...*

But *did* he? A small part of her mind asked.

Adrienne searched back in time for his word, the promise to take her heart with him, yet she could not find it. He made no promise but to kiss her, and he fulfilled that much. She could not call him a liar, but she was empty and she was alone. Void of thought and feeling, her tears wet the floor in silence.

She always ended up alone, the feeling like an old friend returning with its cold embrace. Gilbert did not take her heart, he had shattered it instead.

Her nails embedded homes within the soft muscles of her palms as the room slowly darkened around her. She did not fall asleep, but relented to rolling to her side, watching the flames of the fireplace sink to glowing embers.

A sharp pain whipped her back as if she were a man on the rack.

Adrienne winced, curling up around her growing belly. Gilbert would usually massage her gently when the cramping started; he would kiss her and hold her until it passed, he seemed so attentive, so ready to be a father again, following Adrienne as often as he could. Nothing made sense to her anymore. Why wouldn't he tell her? She conceded to his desire to fight. Was it too much to ask to know when he was leaving?

Am I not important enough?

An ember cracked, falling as ash to the bottom of the fire.

"Madame, are you well?" she heard her maid ask from the inner chamber door. "Is it the baby? Shall I call the duchesse? The doctor?"

Adrienne closed her eyes. There were too many questions.

"I'm alright," she lied. "Just a dizzy spell. I laid down beforehand."

She wouldn't know what to say to her mother if she came in. No doubt she would be babied and cooed through the retelling of Gilbert's desertion with a small crew of thirteen Frenchmen and other European nobles; that he bought the ship with his *own* money; that he absconded somehow without a word or anyone knowing. She wouldn't believe it. Gilbert was a meticulous planner even when the plans included some improvisation. It was why she thought he would be a good soldier, he wasn't *stupid*.

The soft warmth of a toddler's hands pressed up against her cheek. Little Henriette was there, moving faster than a racehorse.

"Maman," she said, followed by a babbling of words that Adrienne deciphered early in her speech to mean sleep.

"No sleep for Maman yet, little lamb," Adrienne whispered, surprised at how weak her voice was, taking Henriette into her arms. She smelled like roses.

"Baby?" The small hands wriggled to hold her belly.

"Baby is sleeping, that's right."

"I kiss," she said, and like her Papa, planted a carefully aimed kiss to where Adrienne's stays ended before she crawled back to the hug. Her eyes continued to be the largest of any child that Adrienne had ever seen, with long ginger lashes and smooth, pale skin. Where Gilbert proposed he saw Adrienne in Henriette, Adrienne could only see him.

"You are so sweet," Adrienne said. Some pieces of her heart she now held in her arms, embracing the warmth. "You're going to be such a good big sister, you know that? Like Auntie Loulou."

When the duchesse finally came to Adrienne's room, Adrienne was sitting on her sofa with Henriette and a book. She didn't tell her mother she already knew, she didn't say she wept, she instead just stared hard at the words of the novel while her mother spoke.

Gilbert was gone. Taken his ship to a bay in Spain. There was a chance, she said, that Papa would get him back. If the King declared that leaving was forbidden, then Gilbert was bound to bring himself in or face arrest.

Adrienne nodded compliantly and twisted a piece of Henriette's hair around her finger. Gilbert wasn't going to come back, she knew. He had already made up his mind.

Gilbert show-boated his tenacity in *April* when the Duc d'Ayen received a letter agreeing that he would meet him in Marseilles, and the duc along with a handful of the family prepared the voyage down to the southern country to meet with him. Adrienne turned down the trip. Her energy was taxed every day by noon, sitting in the morning room with her young sisters to entertain her.

It didn't take too long for the madness to return to Paris.

Gilbert never went to Marseilles, had no intentions of lollygagging around Italy. Letters were sent to Versailles, she learned, from Gilbert requesting permission to travel and then following up with that he had not received word and therefore his departure must have been sanctioned – for silence was a tacit consent. Adrienne would have laughed if she wasn't sick to her stomach. He was so clever.

Louis and Louise showed up one morning while the Duc d'Ayen temper was matched by the Maréchal's. The room was the only safe space, it appeared, where the shouting was muffled only by the chitter of birds outside the window where spring was blooming as it did every year. Louise was bearing a small belly of her own once again.

Putting his hat on the table, Louis took a hesitant seat. "I'm sorry, Adri," he said.

"You were right, Louis," she replied, watching the nest by the glass.

Louise sat by her, fiddled with her hair, silent in her comfort.

"I can't imagine this is a good thing, for once," Louis replied after a moment.

"About what men want."

It was clear Louis didn't remember the wisdom he had shared a handful of years ago, but Adrienne unfortunately remembered most things. Louise's chin rested on her shoulder, and a folded paper tapped at her hand. It was a roughly handled thing, the seal broken in haste that half had chipped off. Adrienne glanced at it, then to Louise.

"I took it from Papa's desk," she admitted. "It was a spur of the moment decision. He doesn't know."

The scribbling along the front was Gilbert's handwriting, addressed to the duc from London. If she were to just lift the fold, set her eyes on the words given to her father and not her, the first line read: *"You will be astonished, my dear father, at the news I am on the point of giving you..."*

She closed the letter. It mattered little: the news she had already known now.

Louis leaned closer. "He did what we could not," he said. "And trust me, this travel will be good for him. When I go to America and set eyes upon him, I will write you to confirm it."

"You still intend on pursuing this? Seeing how Papa responded?" Louise asked, shoving her slipper against his leg.

"D'Ayen will allow me," Louis said. "I will be one-and-twenty this year anyway. At the first notice of war with England, I shall take the trip, as will many Frenchmen, you'll see."

"Gilbert doesn't even know English," Louise said, taking back the letter Adrienne let fall into her lap. "I can't imagine the American colonists know French."

Adrienne watched a second bird return to the nest with a worm in its beak, wiggling past the other who sat on her chicks and unbroken eggs. They fluffed out their feathers together to keep the hatchlings warm.

"How long would it take for his letters from America to reach us?" she asked.

"Gosh, I think two months? Depends if he can find a ship coming back to France to give the correspondence to. I hear it takes longer to get to America than it does to return. Monsieur Franklin was sharing his charts at Madame's salon the other week." Louis crossed his legs, then uncrossed them, formulating words in his discomfort. "If we are to write him, best we do so sooner than later. I'll see what men are heading to the continent that could carry them for us."

"Come to Versailles with us," Louise said, twisting her fingers through Adrienne's. "Just for a week or two. You cannot stay cooped up in here for so long, I don't care what Maman says. A good distraction of friends and family there will do you some good. Let these to-be cousins get to know each other better." She cupped her bodice. "I want all of our children to be best of friends like we are."

"I don't know if I'd consider the vicomte to be a best friend," Adrienne mused, allowing herself a small smile at Louis' outrageous guffaw. "But dear, to be sure."

"Thank you," he said, throwing himself back against the sofa. "But anyway, yes, please join us this spring. I'd feel like a proper ass if I allowed you to sulk alone."

Versailles, May 1777

The duchesse had put up a fight when Louise and Louis turned to her for permission to steal Adrienne away for a few days, but nothing would deter the vicomte and vicomtesse from getting their way in the family. The Duc d'Ayen acquiesced to their wishes despite the glares from his wife, his manner still fuming, but now on the worried end about Gilbert's gallivant. Having his heartbroken daughter distracted was, without a doubt, an ease on his mind. Little Henriette would stay with her grandparents. Versailles was not the place for children. Its gilded fences and mazes of gardens and fountains were only for the accustomed and experienced – a chessboard floor emphasized the game that was maneuvering through Court.

Ladies were adorned in the Franklin fashion with their hair coiffed like the beaver hat he wore over the winter months, wearing spectacles as if they truly needed them to see. Intriguing talk was only about the Americas. And so, when promenading through the vast expanse of shrubbery and flowers, Adrienne could not escape the mention of her husband's name.

The Marquis de la Fayette's blatant disobedience to the crown and his father-in-law was hot on everyone's tongue.

"I've heard he had the courier assassinated –"

Adrienne shook her head, the breeze taking her sigh with it.

" – taking an entire *fleet* to the colonies –"

Where some people heard these types of things, she would never know.

"He left his whole family in the dark –"

She picked at the threads holding her fan together, her grip growing tighter.

"His poor wife."

Her fingers went stiff, the fan hit the ground with a light clack. She watched the gossipers with dark eyes, her mouth pressed into a thin line, as straight as a rapier that she was willing to stab them with. The breeze that whipped through the gardens was cold, but Adrienne could only feel the sweat building up on the back of her neck. Her palms were itching to hit something, someone, to the point where the only reasonable response was to grip the silk flowers lining her gown, squishing them like snowballs until the courtiers moved on by. She felt like she was going to be sick; the mere idea that people were thinking she was someone to pity, to make up stories about. That Gilbert cared so little for her and their family that leaving them was so easy.

Adrienne had already sent out at least four letters. Louis had promised they would find their way to America through different couriers, but all the letters expressed her feelings: her love, her anger, her devastation. What did a bunch of strangers know? They took any word they heard in passing and fantasized it to suit their entertainment.

She didn't think any further on the matter, not wanting to be persuaded by the rumors, she hugged her belly that pressed angrily against her stays.

"Madame," a voice behind her called. The Comte de Ségur approached, his hat pinched between his pinkie and his walking stick. His face seemed to have aged a year since the last time she saw him. "Forgive me, Madame, I didn't mean to frighten you."

"No," she said, shaking her head. "You didn't frighten me, I've just been in thought." Clearing her throat, she let her hands drop back to her sides. "How have you been, Monsieur? You did not arrive with your father when he dined with my Papa last week."

Ségur managed a small smile. "Forgive me again, I am afraid I was enjoying my short honeymoon with Elisabeth. It's been a peculiar time as of late."

"Is my auntie well?" Adrienne asked. "You managed indeed to squeeze your way into the Noailles family after all these years."

"She is well and joyously managing her new household, I can hope. She's been reading through my family history this past week. Happy is she to entertain herself," he replied. He crouched down to pick up Adrienne's fan. "I wished to speak to you during the wedding, but I… I was afraid that I submitted to my cowardice when a word from me may have eased some of your burden. About the Marquis, Madame, I am sorry."

"You have nothing to be sorry about," Adrienne said. She curled her hand around her fan, leading it to the pocket under her skirts. "No one could have stopped him from going."

"No," Ségur agreed. "But… he *did* return to Paris after his trip to London, Madame."

Adrienne's head shot back up.

"He was invigorated to start his journey, yes, and in truth, he still wanted permission to go from the duc. Of course the king as well, but he desired your father's approval so much that he dallied around the city, in Chaillot, that is, hoping to get it. He was talked out of waiting for so long there, which is why he left for Bordeaux."

"Why… why didn't he come to say goodbye?" *To me,* she wanted to add selfishly.

Ségur tilted his head towards the sun. "He was scared that if he looked at you, he would lose the bravery he spent so long building up. He'd be at your beck and call, Madame, trust me, you were his sole source of hesitation. And the babes, of course, he – ah, stupid me," he said, shifting through his pockets. "This was for you. The Marquis wrote it on his journey back from England. Know that he wrote another one for you, but ah, forgive me Madame, I have misplaced it in the bustle." He handed her a neatly folded letter, the addressee written in Gilbert's small hand.

She was scared to take it.

Don't be foolish, she thought, willing her doubt to take it from her new uncle and husband's dearest friend. The paper felt hot, like grabbing a steaming cup of hot chocolate right from the pot. She carded through the folds, it was at least four pages.

"He apologized for the brevity of it; but insisted he would write to you again during his voyage, and when he arrives, and every step going forward," Ségur said.

The seal had not been broken, nor any sign that it had been read and resealed. True to Ségur's character, this letter came straight from Gilbert, bearing with it no other eyes.

"Thank you," she replied, stepping back into the bushes with it.

Her nail snapped the wax seal bearing Gilbert's crest.

Gilbert would be a fine biographer, she thought, reading through his manuscript of his time in London, of the people he spoke to, of how not pleasing to the eye an English woman was. He poured his every thought onto the paper, his emotion drawing on every sentence. Reading his words was like seeing his face. When the ink grew dark and heavy, she saw his brows pull in tight in annoyance; when light and arched, his smile and cocky self-deprecation. He sent his thoughts to the family and at the bottom of the last page, something newer, angled as if he wrote it inside a carriage.

For my promise to one, I have broken another, mon cher coeur. It pains me like no other to not bid you a proper farewell. In my mind I kiss your lips, your eyes, every tender finger. Let my sorry self remain in your warm embrace, I beg. Papa will tell you all the news of my venture. I sail on the Victoire. That is what I will bring back with me, mon coeur: a victory for America and for myself, and for you to have a brash husband who has hopefully made you proud. Give our Henriette ten thousand kisses from me. Adieu adieu.

Affixed at the bottom: *Lafayette.*

"He loves you, Madame. Unequivocally. Fervently. Though I need not say it, he turns into a poet whenever he speaks of you. What these people have been saying here about him, about you, these leeches know not the *lionheart* of the de la Fayettes."

How Ségur always knew exactly what to say was beyond her. Never had she known a man to be so kind. She fiddled with the letter, pressing the words to her chest. She would not cry in front of others when he first left, she would not do so now. Gilbert never liked to be the center of attention, he hated the whispers of himself and the crude stares; he would hate court now more than ever, and the fury compounded into Adrienne; there was one person she could think of who would be able to cease this nonsense.

☆

The speed at which she threw her feet in front of her masked the anxious tears brimming in the corner of her eyes. Courage comes, she learned, when one didn't have time to grow afraid. Hurried steps of Louise trailed several paces behind. Never had the court seen two heavily pregnant Noailles sisters strutting like the kingsguard, and so early in the morning to boot. They swept through the Hall of Mirrors – aglow with the rising sun's light, full of those who rose with it, or who had yet to sleep from the night before – and into the queen's apartments, the line of attendants already quite long. The rooms were brightly lit, covered in the queen's favorite flowers and colors for spring. Adrienne's attention flitted from one courtier to another as she walked past them towards the front. Louise's hand grabbed at her fingers.

"Whoa there," she whispered. "Don't go barging in with your tongue aflame. The toilette is usually quiet unless you are spoken to."

"I know how courtesy and etiquette works, Louise," Adrienne replied, her heart in her throat. "I am a lady."

"Right," said Louise, eyeing where the duchesses were in front of the marquises. "Well, since Madame de Noailles is no longer the first lady-in-waiting, I'm stuck back here. If you're called in, please, for the love of *God*, don't make an enemy of the queen. You are unpredictable and it makes me nervous."

"Dear sister, it makes *you* nervous? Imagine that."

"Come right back to me when it's done. I promised Maman I would be a decent chaperone."

"I never promised I'd make an obedient little child, but we will see what happens."

It was a little daunting, sliding into the line with the other women of her rank. So many were far older than she was. Their makeup settled into the lines on their faces as they glanced at her and then to each other, daring whispers behind their fans and gloves.

From the bedchamber, the light was glittering gold, much warmer than the antechamber they waited in with its pastel green walls and pale circular rug that swallowed the floor. It vaguely looked like the top of a parasol, as if one was small enough to walk above it like raindrops.

Scarcely, the line would shift and all ladies took a step forward. Adrienne went over her plans in her head; like performing a play in front of her sisters when they were young, committing lines to memory. She would demand the queen to put a stop to the slandering of Gilbert's name, she didn't care how – the queen's circle was quite large, and her influence was deviously astounding. Adrienne couldn't get Gilbert's face out of her mind when the court laughed at him; when the queen embarrassed him those years ago. It left a displeasing taste in her mouth whenever Adrienne attended court afterwards. Gilbert was always there to keep her calm.

She closed her eyes. His hands were at her waist, his breath on her ear as he showed her how to hold a sword as one would on the dueling grounds. Of course in that little garden of the Chaillot cottage, there were no other people to practice on, and all duels ended in their own laughter as he swung her over the grass.

The queen stood silent in her abode, arms out as a duchesse fastened the ties of the panniers around her waist. She looked bored, finding the clock on the mantle of her fireplace far more appealing to look at. One lady fixed her hair while another handled the morning gown with care, as if it were crystal. It gave the *appearance* of crystal, the pale blue fabric was almost white. Adrienne felt like the darkest shadow of the room, if not from the almost russet shade she wore, then from her nerve abandoning her when she needed it most. The piercing gaze of Marie-Antoinette met hers from across the chamber, and Adrienne's jaw clenched.

Whispers. *Oh* how Adrienne was growing to loathe them.

The marquises in front of her seemed to part like a bullet rushing over water as the queen's lady-in-waiting eyed Adrienne curiously from head-to-toe.

"Come then, Madame. She requested you," the Princesse de Chimay said, gesturing to where the queen and the Princesse de Lamballe sat. Adrienne bypassed the line, her shoulders squared.

"You may replace her buckles," de Lamballe said bluntly, handing her ones encircled with pearls before she returned to adding more pearl clips into the queen's hair. "She recently changed her mind about diamonds today."

Adrienne smoothed her thumb over the glossy gemstone and cleared her throat. Needing to look diagonally down at the queen's shoes, it would be quite the crouch. She cupped her belly, her legs quaking to support herself as she moved to bend down. *Humility was a virtue*, she repeated, hobbling to her knees.

"Oh, good heavens Thérèse, stop this. The Marquise de la Fayette is pregnant, are you blind? *You* may do it if you will not allow me to simply get it done myself," Marie-Antoinette said, waving the princess from her hair. Adrienne hovered painfully where she was, the buckles still in hand. "Do please stand, Madame, I do not mean for you to strain yourself or your infant. Trust me, I find all this so silly." She took the pearls and plopped them in her friend's hand.

Adrienne straightened herself, forcing her breath to come out of her nose as silent as she could manage. She was handed the hair pins.

It was unexpected; her advance stagnated.

Situating herself behind the queen by her mirror, the lines she rehearsed in her head suddenly didn't seem to fit into the perfectly planned situation she had imagined. Not that she expected an empty room all to herself with Her Majesty, nor that she would suddenly speak out boldly in front of the highest noble women of court about her wayward husband. To whisper would make her a hypocrite and Adrienne had not the audacity to start speaking into the queen's ear like a common gossip.

"Wherever you think they should be added, Madame," Marie-Antoinette said. Her blue eyes crinkled, watching Adrienne through the reflection. She stuck the pearls in aesthetically random places around the powdered blonde pompadour before she met the queen's gaze again.

It was strange, the way Adrienne was being looked at. No doubt the queen had heard of everything, especially of the insult to the king by Gilbert and his revolutionary entourage. Like the way others gawked at her, she expected the same pity or disdain. But the queen was sober, looking from one tiny detail to the other, with the quiet, gentle poise of any fine woman of her station. Adrienne felt naked.

"Marquise, I don't believe you have ever joined me at my levée before," exclaimed the queen, not breaking eye-contact.

"I am not in Versailles often, Your Majesty," Adrienne quickly replied.

A hum. Just a simple one. "You should come by again. I like to get to know everyone I can at court. If you join us more often, we could chat longer. I've hosted many of the Noailles family; especially dear Madame d'Etiquette."

Adrienne raised her brow. It was very well-known that the queen, in fact, was not so friendly and dear with her Aunt Anne.

Marie-Antoinette smirked, continuing, "I hope to be bringing my friends to my estate this evening for some much needed music and fun. Perhaps you will join me for the promenade over? I very much enjoy the walk on nice days like these."

She made no allusions to Adrienne's predicament, but she knew, Adrienne knew she did. And so Adrienne agreed with a simple nod and a tight smile to join her on the fifteen minute stroll towards the Petit Trianon.

Waiting another few hours didn't make much of a difference when every second felt the same since Gilbert left. Abandoning Louise to the palace salon, she waited by the outside fountain for the queen to come. It was like a parade of parasols and feathers marching its way down the paths towards her, Marie-Antoinette in her lavender evening wear leading the fray. When she caught sight of Adrienne, her rouged lips broke into a smile. Seeing it appear so sincere was unfamiliar, alien, even.

"Marquise," she said, holding her arm out like a gentleman would to a lady. Adrienne looped hers through, politely pulled along into the parade. "I am so happy you decided to come. I must say, the ministers have been incredibly dull up until this week; it is like someone lit a fire underneath their rears, stirred them up a bit. My Louis has been escaping to more and more hunting mornings to avoid them, but he gets nervous when they catch him at supper." She puckered her lips into an o-shape. "Forgive me, don't tell anyone I've told you that."

Adrienne's mouth teetered. How hard could it be to ask if the queen was already willing to overshare?

"Actually, Madame," Adrienne said, "I wished to speak to you about something as well."

"Not politics, I hope."

"No, not exactly."

"I imagine not." Marie-Antoinette's smile softened, her hand cupping over Adrienne's. "Go on, then. You've been looking like you may pop off like a firework since you were in line this morning."

She swallowed. "It is about the Marquis de la Fayette."

Marie-Antoinette nodded. They walked under a canopy of trees in a straight line, passerbyers bowing as they went. "Your husband is a grand topic as of late," she exclaimed.

"Yes," Adrienne replied. "And I wish for you to put a stop to it."

The queen raised a brow as she looked down at Adrienne. "Me? Madame, I think you overestimate my power. One cannot stop gossip. Dare I say, not even God can put a stop to it."

"Everyone wishes to be like you, Your Majesty. If you put down the ridicule to my husband's name, then they would surely follow. All these accusations against him are false and if he were here then there would be plenty of rebukes."

"But he is not here."

Adrienne's jaw clicked. As they walked, she never failed to keep up the pace set by the queen. It was bringing a rising ache to her feet, and weight to her belly, but she didn't falter, merely bringing her outside hand to hold the bottom of the swell. Marie-Antoinette's studying stare moved down to where Adrienne's maternity stays laid up over her like a perfectly round globe.

"This is your second child, is that right?" she asked, far lighter.

"Yes."

"May I?" Marie-Antoinette halted the party, her hands gesturing to the skirt. She waited for Adrienne to nod before she gently felt along the fabric. "Do you enjoy it?"

"Enjoy it?"

"I've heard some women love the feeling of carrying a child with them; others detest it and what it does to them. I try to imagine how I would feel."

"It is a rotating feeling," Adrienne replied. "I enjoy it more when they are in my arms after it all. When I can hold them with my husband next to me."

Marie-Antoinette in all her glory that Adrienne had ever seen her, suddenly appeared somber. Neither would breach the topic; the queen still had not laid successfully with the king after seven years of marriage.

"Surely though," the queen said after a minute as they continued on towards her estate, "some rumors must be true. You two always looked like the perfect couple – his departure must have wounded you severely.

He forwent being with you for this child's birth."

A pang set off in Adrienne's chest. Her throat tightened. "The Duc d'Ayen was going to bring him to Italy anyway," she said. "I would miss him regardless." It was the half-truth; he may have been back for the day if the trip had turned into a short one. Men missed out on plenty of important dates, she was lucky that Gilbert was around for Henriette's birth.

"I know what rumors do to a young woman. I am sorry you're subject to them," Marie-Antoinette whispered while she rubbed a wrinkle out of Adrienne's forehead.

"So you'll help me," Adrienne pushed – vaguely a question, moreso a demand.

Marie-Antoinette spared a single glance to the group behind them, hardly turning her head as she did so. "I would like to," she nodded.

The Petit Trianon was a humble mansion amongst an illusion of the country, with a pond and several paths through wildflower gardens that disappeared over a rolling hill. Too many parties were held around the estate throughout the year for anyone to count on their hands. The façade of the château casted a pink hue in the setting sun. Marie-Antoinette's inner circle enjoyed the grounds and the games and performances inside regularly.

Slowly, as the courtiers flounced into the cottage, Adrienne became acutely aware of the discrepancy. She'd be more established as a Noailles, although with her aunt's reputation between Marie-Antoinette's circle, *perhaps*, she thought, *it wouldn't be the best foot forward.* She clinged to her country-husband's name like a blade, following the princesses and duchesses and the macaroni up the stairs.

Adrienne didn't gamble, but she did watch absently while the women tossed their dice and turned over cards on the tables. The queen didn't waver from her side despite circling around to chat with every lady they passed. It was like a dance, if Adrienne had to give it a name, a minuet with the queen through the parlor, finding wine on the way.

When would she become like her mother, she wondered still. A woman who hardly needed to say a word for others to listen to her. Adrienne was going to scream at every passing glance that followed the whispers. Maybe she was imagining it; it would not be the first time her imagination created anxieties. Perhaps the thick smell of perfume was making her woozy.

"Let's have some music," Marie-Antoinette said, waving over the servants who carried in violins and cellos.

"Aren't you going to say something, Madame?" Adrienne asked, the heat rushing to her face.

"Marquise," she replied with a small smile as Adrienne's heart dropped, "it is not *I* who can change their minds, as it is not *I* who they are looking at or speaking of."

Fight her, her brain said.

"The one who has to say something is yourself. No one can stop gossip, but you *can* point it in a new direction. Here you have the wives and lovers of the most *influential* men in France who speak and speak and speak. We do love a performance, we listen to a show." Marie-Antoinette lifted her glass to her lips, watching Adrienne with an unwavering gaze. "Give us your opening monologue to this *play de la Fayette*."

Her fingers went cold. She was led into the lion's den, a lamb set in front of the feasting eyes of the wolves. If she were smart like her sister, she would take herself and leave; or excuse herself politely like her mother and accept the gossip alone going further – words were just words, why should she care? Save herself some honor, live the life of the woman whose husband abandoned her, accept the pity, deal with the future if Gilbert made it home sometime then.

But what if he didn't make it home? Not only would she be a young widow whose silly husband left her, but she would be a widow whose said husband was a rash fool who died for a cause that had no large impact for France.

A kick to her belly snapped her back to the present. She rested her hand where the babe moved, the infant who still would bear its father's name. It was a grand name, a proud name, and Adrienne was too stubborn to let it be slandered any longer. If she embarrassed herself, it would be on her, not on Gilbert. She walked to the center of the parlor, looking up at every face that now regarded her with curious tilts of their head despite their continued conversations and stringing of bows.

A show. They wanted a show.

Adrienne grabbed a chair from a table and politely dragged it out to the floor.

She could give a show.

Stepping up onto the cushion that covered the neatly curving wood, her heels sank into the seat, but with the tiniest of hobbles, she stood up straight and cleared her throat. It wasn't every day for a courtier to see a short, pregnant woman stand on the queen's parlor chairs. That shut them up. It was too late to talk herself out of anything now.

"G-good evening," she said, her nerves settling. The queen took a seat on a sofa to the side, quietly listening. "I am conscious of the fact that I need not introduce myself to any of you, for my name and the name of my husband has been invoked on many tongues since his departure in April."

A pause for effect, she thought, forcing eye contact.

"You have heard he boarded a ship bound for America. This is true. You've heard he had left without His Majesty's permission, though he waited for *weeks* to depart our shores for such a blessing. We have met Messieurs Deane, Franklin, Lee, these American delegates who many of you have hosted in your salons," she said, nodding her nose at those whose hair reflected the beaver style. "Their cause has stirred something different in the hearts of many of the French people, of the Austrians, Poles, Spaniards. It is something akin to enlightenment, I imagine: this liberty."

She could picture Gilbert's passionate tears when he spoke of it, like nothing she had ever seen before.

"The Marquis de la Fayette has one thing that the other men in here do not have," Adrienne continued, and she felt the audacity rising in her. "It is not wealth or high regard, nor piety or the inclination to make decisions without his wife… But he has the courage to go out to a foreign land and *do something*. Putting his life on the line for a cause – a just, noble cause he believes in – instead of throwing dice on a table in exchange for land or pretty silks! The Marquis is half the age of many of our military leaders in France and yet he has more gall than *all* of them combined."

Strikings of fans as they opened thundered through the room as the women looked to each other with wide eyes. Adrienne's hand fluttered to where she kept Gilbert's last letter in the gap of her bodice.

"Shame on cowards," Adrienne cried. "Blaming a young man with so much to lose for making history. Well, I will tell each and every one of you – I know whose names I will see in the history books, and whose will be lost to time and disgrace." She was drunk on adrenaline, the nerve bringing a laugh to her lips. "What Frenchman is too much of a coward to face an English foe?"

"Here, here!" Marie-Antoinette clapped, her eyes lit up with utter delight.

"Why are we not pushing for a change? Our husbands, who once served in France's most prestigious army are wrongly stripped of their honor as they sit around like meager housewives, deserve the glory of victory. Versailles is not a court of mice in the face of Britons, are we?"

A chorus of no's and the shaking of heads brought the image of the Duchesse d'Ayen's salons, when the air of philosophy was potent, or in her father's meetings when she heard slamming of fists upon tables from spirited men, to Adrienne's mind.

She held her glass high above her head. "I believe the Marquis may bring France back from behind Britain's rotten curtain. But will he do so with his countrymen, I wonder?" She took a sip. "Sometimes it takes a woman's hand to stir the pot," Adrienne ended, her voice leaving her as her belly was taking a beating from the inside. By no one's fault but her own, she remained on the chair, unable to get down unaided. It took another minute before the few gentlemen inside the room came to assist her to the floor. She did not receive an ovation by any means, but the courtiers no longer looked at her with pity, instead bringing a louder chittering to their game tables, and that was good enough for her.

Setting her wine on a tray, she quickly absconded to the halls to catch her breath, gasping like a fish against the cooled stone walls. It appeared she had woken the baby up, and it was stretching and rolling, probably wanting to listen about its father as well. At least it had the patience to wait until the end of Adrienne's passion-ranting before flipping over. She blew out a stifled sob, maybe two, holding the curve under her stays, watching the ceiling to keep any tears from falling.

How strange, it was, that the ceilings of such a luxurious home were bare.

"That was invigorating," Marie-Antoinette said, poking her head out of the parlor. "You will be pleased to hear that I haven't heard the Marquis' name used in any negative connotation in the slightest."

"Good," Adrienne replied, quickly wiping her lashes with her pinkie. "I hope you've a very talented painter in there to immortalize that performance on account of me never doing that again."

The queen grinned. "It is immortalized in my mind, I tell you. Will you stay for the music? I expect the games to get rather silly into the night."

"If it is alright with you, Madame, I am feeling tired and would like to retire."

"Of course," she said. "Let me get you a carriage for you and the baby." She snapped her fingers to summon a servant before they rushed off and her hands returned to a neat fold in front of her. "I assume you will be returning to Paris before the birth, so may I wish you a safe and successful trial, Marquise. Maybe one day I may be so lucky to look as lovely as you."

Adrienne flushed. "Thank you, Madame," she curtsied, "for your generosity."

"Please do not be a stranger to me any further in the future. I enjoyed your caprice very much," Marie-Antoinette said, covering a giggle with the back of her hand. Adrienne curtsied again, her mind a blank slate. As the queen returned to her circle, a carriage rolled to the side of the château.

Chapter Twelve

Paris, August 1777

I am writing to you from a great distance, mon coeur, and with the dreadful uncertainty of time in which I am to receive any news from you. How have you taken my second departure? Do you love me less for it? Do you forgive me?... All these reflections did not prevent me from experiencing the most bitter grief. Your sorrow, that of my friends, Henriette, all rushed upon my thoughts, and my heart was torn by a thousand painful feelings. I could not at that instant find any excuse for my own conduct.

An abundance of letters from Gilbert arrived from a captain who sailed from the colony of South Carolina, and with it, the man's assurance that the young Marquis who entrusted him with the correspondence was well and in safe hands of the welcoming Americans. The Duchesse d'Ayen delivered the parcel to Adrienne's rooms, where she lay under her covers well into the afternoon, tracing his writing with her nails. Little Henriette was half-asleep by her side, picking at her mother's loosened hair.

The first letter was several pages long, pouring out his guilt and sorrow for wounding her. He reassured her countless times of his safety, that an officer was hardly in the line of danger, in-between his begging for her to never stop loving him else he would be a miserable man. She smiled at his gloomy retelling of his seasickness, and how life aboard a ship was so mundane. All these things could have been avoided if he simply remained at home in her arms, but alas.

Let us speak of more important things: of yourself, of dear Henriette, and of her brother or sister. Henriette is so delightful that she has made me fond of girls. Whatever the sex of our new baby, I shall receive it with utmost joy. Lose not a moment in hastening my happiness by informing me of its birth. I know if it is because I am twice a father that my parental feelings are stronger than they ever were...

What good news, she thought, wiggling her position where their second daughter slept upon her chest. Anastasie Louise Pauline du Motier was easily like her father with her small, rounded lips and rosy complexion. Her eyes had darkened to a light brown over the weeks of summer, with the tiniest hints of brown hair fuzzing at her scalp. She was already a proper lady, her pinkie never wanted to close with the rest of her fist whenever she fed with the wetnurse or held onto Adrienne's finger. Henriette found the new baby very interesting to squeeze when she arrived on the first of July.

A second letter was folded along with the first.

I am still floating on this dreary plain – the most wearisome of all human habitations. To console myself a little, I think of you and of my friends. I think of the great pleasure of seeing you again. How delightful will be the moment of my arrival! I shall hasten to surprise and embrace you. I shall perhaps find you with your children. To think only of that happy moment is an inexpressible pleasure to me.

To be a "good American" is what he asked of her. Adrienne thought of the prospect: an American wife. It felt fantastical, like he was asking her to be in a fairytale. His passion for the country's happiness brought warmth to her cheeks when she imagined the warmth of his as he wrote of it. He mentioned his practicing of the language, which must have been difficult. English never sounded like it made much sense – too blunt and ugly – but Adrienne would have to pick up an English book somewhere to surprise him. Gilbert sent his compliments to Louis and Louise, to Adrienne's little sisters, to his Abbé, and to so many other friends and family. Too nervous to write to the Maréchal de Noailles, he admitted, but offered gifts of trees from the New World in return.

Adieu, night obliges me to discontinue my letter, as I forbade the use of light after dark on my vessel. See how careful I am being! Once more, adieu, if my fingers were guided by my heart, it is not necessary to see clearly to tell you that I love you, and that I shall love you all my life.

For a moment, she slapped the paper to her side, staring up at her bed's drapings. How dare Gilbert be so romantic, she mulled, it was not fair to her failing composure, to be a weeping girl, lovestricken for her husband like they were in an early courtship.

Anastasie rubbed her tiny nose against Adrienne's collarbone.

The last letter was more of a note, the first written on paper that was laid differently: *American* paper, it seemed. By the grace of God, there was a French vessel about to depart when he arrived, the captain being the man already met. Gilbert was already in love with the American people, and his journey took him next to Philadelphia – a city Adrienne only knew from listening to the talks of Monsieur Franklin.

Is it not true that you will always love me?

His last written words called for another slap to the bedding. She sighed and kissed the top of Anastasie's fuzzy head.

"Do you know your Papa is a perfect nincompoop? A brave and very lovable man, but a nincompoop. That's between the family, though, don't tell anyone," she said, folding the letters neatly. They were over a dozen pages in length but she longed for more. Nothing would compare to having Gilbert here to speak these lovely words into her ear. She sighed again, and once more for the sake of it, until Anastasie was popping her lips. "Do you think Henriette would eat something if you showed her how much of an expert you are?" she asked the infant as she ran her hand through her eldest's growing hair while she snored.

Henriette was not as well as Adrienne would wish. The doctor continued to pry at her to feed her baby more, but it was a hassle to keep the food down. Henriette kept coughing it back up, even hours later.

Just the thought of it made her sick so she tried to *not* think of it, but it was an impossible task.

At least Louise's pregnancy was going well. And the girls enjoyed the drama of Anne embarrassing a young man who was fencing another in the nearby courtyard of the city. Their papa must have been wondering how he managed to produce such resolute daughters, partly blaming their maman's character and the visitations from too progressive of women in the salon. Last dinner, the duc tossed a napkin over his face and refused to look at Anne until she apologized to him; a sight most amusing to Pauline and Rosalie.

It was not but a week later when Adrienne was taking tea with her mother and father that more letters arrived for her by the hands of both French and American captains. To what joy she felt, that if the continuation of his words were like this, the separation would be a little easier to bear.

"The house is going to start to smell like fish if sailors keep coming," said the duc, sipping his cup while thumbing through the letters. "Would you look at that: he writes to his ladies, but not I." He took the correspondence meant for himself, and handed the rest to the duchesse and Adrienne.

"Perhaps if you wrote him one first," the duchesse said, "he would feel as though you still love him and wouldn't fear a scolding."

"I do love him. He is just a troublesome pain."

Adrienne was too busy picking the wax off her letter to pay the conversation any mind. Gilbert opened the several paragraph-length essay with a repetition of facts from the last letter of his *lucky star* keeping he and his letters safe from the English. Adrienne prayed on that star immediately, for it must have been an angel, reading on the happenstance of God's will that his ship arrived without crossing the English fleet.

How he loved these Americans, she read, flipping to the next page, as he went into adoring detail of their form and character. They received him well, his presence was lauded over a five-hour dinner.

From the agreeable life I lead in this country, from the sympathy from its people that make me feel as if I had known them for twenty years, the similarity in their manner of thinking and of my own, my love of glory and liberty, you might imagine I am very happy. Yet you are not with me, mon coeur; my friends are not with me; and there is no happiness for me when I am far from you and them. Often I ask if you still love me, but I put that question even more to myself and my heart ever answers: yes. I trust that heart not to deceive me. I am inexpressibly anxious to hear from you; I hope to find some letters in Philadelphia.

"Papa, did Louis say that our letters would go to Philadelphia?" Adrienne asked, holding the papers in her lap. She was stressed to think that they would go wayward and lost to the sea.

"If their jaunt was to join the American army, their Congress would be the first place they must present themselves," the duc replied. He licked his finger and flipped his own letter over before adjusting his spectacles.

The duchesse perched at the edge of her seat. "Jean, we should send him money. It isn't safe without something tangible – not every colonist merchant would take a check from a Frenchman."

He hummed. A statement he rightly agreed with. "I will write and have some funds from our account sent with a trusted vessel. I would simply need a day to organize it and find a suitable courier who planned on taking a trip to the Americas. Men are becoming more robust now, it seems, about this war."

Adrienne pressed her lips together. She couldn't take the credit for that. Still, it was pleasant to know that Gilbert wouldn't be without his countrymen for much longer. She glanced down at the parting passage of his writing.

Embrace most affectionately my Henriette: may I add, embrace our children? The father of those poor children is a wanderer, but he is nevertheless a good man – a good father attached to his family, and a good husband also, for he loves his wife most tenderly.

By this time, Gilbert must have received his commission by Congress. Perhaps, Adrienne mused, he has already met his venerated General Washington. She threw her thoughts to the sky and prayed that the Americans had not invited him to dance. She longed for him, daily, until it hurt. Her tea had gone cold before she picked it up again.

Paris, October 1777

Most things hurt.

The world was cruel and pitiless.

She laid alone on the wooden floor of her bedchamber, the place where no one else would see how she crumbled to pieces. Her grip on a rosary cracked a bead, the floor stained with her tears, her spit, as she dry heaved again and again. What nails she may have had at the beginning of the month had worn to the skin, red, sore, raw, scraping against the wood like an animal.

God had blessed Louise with a baby boy, and how beautiful and small he was. It was a joy throughout the house, so much so that the Maréchal called for fireworks the following day. Tiny Adrien de Noailles was a loud crier when he came into the world, his screams echoed through the halls with the popping of champagne bottles. And for once, as Adrienne looked on at the shining son of her sister, she felt the twinge of jealousy sink its teeth into her neck.

She had sat in the chapel for hours during the celebrations staring at the statue of the Virgin Mary. How a girl as younger than Adrienne took on whatever the Lord asked of her; how venerated and divine, the Mother of God at fourteen.

Where God had sent a blessing for the Noailles name, He also took a price, and after a week of a simple cold, He had whisked little Henriette away in silence, without a sigh from her perfect lips. There was nothing the doctors could do – it happened so fast, Henriette was too tired, too weak to put up a fight.

What had she done to deserve such misery? Whenever Adrienne thought she found a speck of happiness to mend her heart, it crumbled in her hands. Her whimpering sounded like a wounded dog. That was what she must have been in another life – a homeless, crying dog.

She could not be like the Virgin Mary, watching her child die in front of her. Adrienne was just a person and no divinity could save her from the pain; Henriette was not Christ, she did not die for the world, she would not rise on the third day – she was a little girl, and the stone that covered her tiny tomb would not be swept aside again. Adrienne locked herself away instead; like she did before, she mourned alone.

Letters. More letters lay in front of her, scattered with her desk's belongings along the floor. Some candlelight in the darkness. Adrienne reached for one, her sole companion, bringing Gilbert to her face.

You must know that I set out in a brilliant manner in a carriage, and I must tell you that we are now all on horseback – having broken the carriage in my usual praiseworthy custom – and I hope to write to you that we have arrived on foot...

I am always meeting, mon coeur, with opportunities of sending letters... I have received bad news here; Ticonderoga, the strongest American post, has been taken by the enemy; this is very unfortunate, and we must endeavor to repair the evil. I am every day more miserable from having quitted you, mon coeur. Adieu, my life; I am in such haste that I know not what I write, but I do know that I love you more tenderly than ever; that the pains of this separation were necessary to convince me how very dear you are to me, and that I would give at this moment half my existence for the pleasure of embracing you again, and telling you with my own lips how well I love you...

She hiccuped, finding the last of the letter on the other side of the paper, but simply turning it around was more arduous than pushing open a vault door.

If you knew how much I sigh to see you, how much I suffer at being separated from you, and all that my heart has been called on to endure, you would think me somewhat worthy of your love! I have left no space for Henriette; may I say for my children? Give them a hundred thousand embraces; I shall most heartily share them with you.

How could she write him? What words could relay the horror and grief? To give him a share of this pain would no doubt cause him agony in a war where his attention should be for his own health. Adrienne could not do that to him, he did not deserve it.

But the false assumption that he had his two daughters waiting for him only to find one departed upon his return would do more harm, and he did not deserve that either. Adrienne wept. Eight months had turned into an eternity. The lucky star that reigned over Gilbert in its brilliance and adoration had forgotten to include her in some of its light.

Chapter Thirteen

She still allowed herself, when composed enough, to venture out for a ride. That was one thing that would never change; a brief moment of freedom and air. The snow that was falling on Paris melted when it touched the stone walkways, leaving only floury dust over the grass and atop of hats and shoulders of cloaks. Her dear Chouchou was getting old, but was always reliable, clomping heavily on the slow walk. His whiskers and coat were thick for the winter, and his purple freckles were more obvious around his nose. Adrienne thought he was aging gracefully.

There *was* a destination in mind. If she followed the river westward for longer than usual, she would come across a small neighborhood that bordered Chaillot. Quieter than a country village, but maintaining all the charm, was Passy. It seemed fitting, then, that Monsieur Franklin lived in an apartment here by the water. He remained here more often than not with his teenage grandson unless he was called to Versailles. If a Parisian admirer was lucky, they would catch him on an evening stroll with or without said grandson.

Adrienne wasn't staking any money on if Monsieur Franklin was home, and she didn't make any appointment to see him. Her family's spies had mentioned him being very busy as of late, many visitors coming and going; including a British representative the month prior.

She just wanted to look.

Chouchou's clomping was so resounding, she had forgotten that Louis rode several paces behind her in prolonged silence. Adrienne held the reins and glanced back at the young man. They both wore black velvet, as they have been donning the color together for a few days. He was breaking decorum, being out in public with her in a state of grieving, but Louis' respect for decorum fell away long ago. He had grabbed his cloak and followed her to the stables when she expressed her desire to go on a very long walk. Much of the family was in Versailles, as they did most winters, and the Hôtel de Noailles remained largely sparse save for the duchesse, the vicomte, Adrienne, and baby Anastasie. Many days, her Maman filled the salon to distract from the bleak winter weather, and Adrienne filled her thoughts with the dozens of letters Gilbert sent.

Louis' eyes were cast against the passing rows of apartments. He looked different without his peruke on, his brown hair curled around his cheekbones, powdered lightly. It was the first time he'd been out of the house without looking completely his best; and no one would dare bat an eye at it – losing an heir was taboo conversation. Louis' dark circles and set square jaw would dare anyone to mention "proper etiquette" to him.

Papa said that a child was always in danger until they turned four or five. Then a parent was allowed to properly show affection to them. It saved the heart from too much sorrow.

Adrienne didn't think she was capable of such a thing.

"Are you well?" Louis asked, catching her stare.

"Just seeing how much you've grown," she said.

Louis' inner brows rose. He shook his head with a puff of warm air from his nose. "It's *you* who has grown, dear Cousin, not I," he said. Then added with a shrug, "maybe an inch. Two at most."

Adrienne scoffed. "Here I thought you'd be philosophical." She turned forward in her saddle. They kept to the road by the river as a carriage squeezed by, its driver tapping his hat to them.

"I'm only philosophical after three drinks at least," Louis said. He rode up to her right to block the next carriage from driving too close to them. "Still, I wait to be a soldier again. I grow more jealous of the Marquis after every letter. To take a musket ball to the leg and walk it off like it is nothing!" He shook his head, disbelieving. "I never thought that boy who broke a chandelier on his first night here would grow so profound."

"He did *not* 'walk it off,' Louis, he was in a hospital for weeks," Adrienne snapped, remembering her horror when Gilbert's letters from September and October arrived. In fact, letters from him to *all* of the people in France seemed to pour in en masse before the year was up. The Marquis was back in everyone's conversations, albeit he had become something of a heroic phenomenon over the winter.

"I'd spend a few weeks in a hospital to have a notoriety like that."

"Louis!"

The Hôtel de Valentinois looked larger than that of the Noailles home, but the front entryway was merely a raised, covered hallway, connecting the two houses. The river in view was not far beyond an inner courtyard that hosted two grand fountains and a luxurious garden. The estate itself was vastly longer, covering all the ground upon the hill that it sat on until the banks of the Seine. The smaller of the two dwellings was where Monsieur Franklin resided. Like a flag, his famous lightning rod stuck out in the otherwise clear sky.

It would be rude if they crossed the stone arch unannounced, which was why Louis went first. There were very few people roaming the grounds in the cold, some gentlemen in heavy cloaks and hats perused in circles around the frozen fountains. The sight of the south of Paris from the courtyard was worth the ride alone, even if they did not see the man himself. Through the windows, the rooms were still. There was the prattle of a kitchen preparing an evening meal, the smell of cranberries in the air. It stirred Adrienne's stomach.

They loitered. She felt like she was a young girl again waiting around where she wasn't supposed to be, but Louis didn't seem to mind. He let his horse roam without steering him; Chouchou nibbled on a small piece of dead grass sticking out from the stone.

Clicks of a cane to the inside of the yard lifted both of their heads to the familiar gentleman they had seen so often surrounded by large crowds, looking pleasantly alone and content in his beaver hat and brown wool coat. He gave the guise of a wise and mirthy grandfather.

"Ah," Franklin said, setting his cane center. "*Bonjour* to each of you. I am afraid I did not know I had guests for today." His French was passable for an English-speaker, erred by his accent and limited vocabulary. From what Adrienne heard from his contemporaries, he did understand others fairly well, and so she didn't feel ashamed in speaking plainly.

"We beg your pardon, Monsieur. We did not send an advanced word," she said.

He squinted at her as she let her reins rest on her horse's neck. His spectacles were large, and made his eyes appear ever the more so. "What do I owe the pleasure of this visit?"

Louis glanced toward her. He was an escort, he said with his shrug.

Adrienne rubbed her thumb to her forefinger, the leather gloves gliding lightly. "I do not know, Monsieur," she admitted. "I believe I just wished to see you."

That caught Franklin off guard – in a genteel, kind way. His brows raised only slightly, and the firm line of his mouth curved up on the sides. "You are the Marquise de la Fayette."

"I am."

"I recall meeting your husband this time last year. He spoke fondly of you. It is a shame I have not formally introduced myself to you since then. I hope you can forgive an old man with a fleeting memory."

"Your mind is still sharp, Monsieur," Adrienne said. "It has been a busy year and you have been engrossed in your noble work. I took no offense. Consider our folly in not warning you as even recompense."

Franklin chuckled, leaning forward onto his cane. "Madame, you have made a good day into a great one with your kindness," he said, his eyes crinkling. With a nod towards Louis, he looked up at Adrienne and smiled. "I expect good news from France to reach your husband by the end of this spring."

"You jest, Monsieur!" Louis started, a goofy grin splitting across his face. "You have accomplished your mission, then?"

"One of many, but perhaps the most important one at this time," Franklin replied.

Adrienne admired how, in his excitement, his tone never swayed into mania. He was resolute; ready to continue working for his country. She lacked, however, the knowledge of what her cousin and the doctor spoke of. There were plenty of rumors in Versailles, of course, of the King's support for America; of how far he was capable of persuading the other ministers to agree to send more aid, or if he could: join the United States in the fight.

Adrienne tilted her head. Franklin and his American delegates had already secured much of France's financial and material aid with their persistence. There weren't many options left.

"An *alliance*?" she dared to breathe, as if English spies were around the corner.

"Word is already sent to our foes in London. I imagine they will not receive it well."

Pride swelled in Adrienne's chest as Louis clapped, his intensity only quelled by his gloved hands.

"Then I will see my dear brother by year's end!" Louis said, wiggling in his saddle. He brought his horse around to shake Franklin's hand. "Thank you, Monsieur, for pushing this old nation out of her stupor. I await to call your country a second home."

She should write to Gilbert, she thought. Although the news was very likely already on its way across the ocean. How many of her letters ever made it over, she wondered – it was impossible to know. Gilbert was always complaining of not hearing enough from her.

Adrienne looked at Louis. It would be reassuring to have both of them together if they must continue to fight. Louise would certainly protest, but nothing could be done to stop them; it was a fact Adrienne was already resigned to.

"I would invite you inside for some coffee, but I'm afraid I will receive a scolding from my grandson if I do not rest. Forgive me, again, Madame Lafayette," Franklin said, issuing a small bow.

"Think nothing of it," Adrienne replied. She bit her cheek and said, "thank you" in as enunciated English as she could manage. Franklin's gentle smile grew, and he took her hand to kiss.

"You are *very* welcome, my dear."

Louis could not shut up on their walk back to the Hôtel de Noailles. Even without the decorum, seeing a man dressed for mourning while happily babbling like a schoolboy was unusual to be sure.

The fireplaces were burning through wood supply in the hours that the Duchesse d'Ayen hosted her intimate gatherings. The smell of roasted nuts and pomegranates clung to the air, drawing any passersby to approach the grand doors to the chamber. Adrienne made out a few voices. There couldn't have been more than a dozen guests in a period like this; although the vicomte and vicomtesse were the primary mourners for the loss of their son, everyone partook for some time; the guests her maman invited surely must have been important then. Adrienne's goal was to simply crack the door open to let her mother know that she had returned home, and then was ready to return to her abode and dote upon Anastasie – who had been very complicit in allowing Pauline and Rosalie steal her away from her crib.

Her maman looked beautiful in all her gowns – in mourning dress, her skirts rolled like fog on a late evening, dancing over the floor to keep all the company entertained and full of wine. Adrienne could watch her for hours. She eyed a few writers she knew, those who had come to the Hôtel before when she was younger; some of the wives of the duc's scientist compatriots; and others whose faces were obscured by the attention diverted to them, save for the familiar smile of the Comte de Ségur. They all seemed so content, blithe with each other's company. Adrienne waited for her mother's glance, a graze of her eyes.

Several turned her way instead, as if she had knocked the door from its hinges – which she in no way did, she hardly touched the thing. But there they looked, and with nothing else to do but curtsy amongst the attention, Adrienne dipped her head.

"Marquise!" an older, well-used voice pricked her ear. Its owner stood up from one sofa, the gentleman still comfortable in the fashion of his prime. Adrienne wasn't expecting to see Monsieur Voltaire. The man had entered self-imposed exile years ago outside of Paris. His smile lines were deep, and he had grown lithe in the years since she remembered seeing him last – as a young girl in the previous decade. Voltaire approached her, a hand to his heart. "Ah! How joyful I am to live long enough to see, face-to-face, the wife of the Hero of Two Worlds. The youth have graced me with a future I am content to dream about in my eternal sleep. May I live long enough to salute to him as liberator the Old," he said, and to Adrienne's horror, he fell to his knees in front of her.

"Monsieur," she whispered. She looked up in a panic – here was Europe's most influential and profound philosopher, gripping to the edges of her gown, kissing the velvet as if she were his Holiness, the Pope, and he the most devoted Catholic. Her cheeks warmed beyond repair, red as the wine they drank.

What had she come into the salon for?

Oh, that's right – her mother.

The Duchesse d'Ayen faltered for a fraction of a second before she encouraged the remaining gentlemen of the room to assist Voltaire to his feet. He had no shyness about the action, kissing Adrienne's knuckles. Had someone like Voltaire ever fallen to the feet of Marie-Antoinette, she wondered, and she truly did wonder, for next time she saw the queen, she thought to ask how on Earth she was supposed to handle it. All she could do was stand there and let the guests escort the eighty-three-year-old writer back to his seat. Her mother smoothed her hand down Adrienne's arm.

"Why don't you join us for a few minutes?" she said. "Have some food, *chère*, you're getting thin. We were discussing Monsieur Voltaire's next play that is set to perform in the following month." The duchesse lowered her voice and added, "and there are even more letters for you to read from the Marquis by my seat. He talks about defeating *Hessians* in a place called New Jersey. Come, come, you've been holed up in your room for too long and I've missed your sprightly opinions on these things."

Paris, May 1778

It was earlier in the month prior when a dozen French ships left the shores of Europe under the Comte d'Estaing. The Noailles had held onto Louis by the scruff of his neck to keep him from running off with the navy of all the military branches. He had permission to leave with the army once that was organized and secure. Ségur assured it, as he was to join him. Ségur attended to Louis' impatience ardently, with his newborn daughter in attendance every few times to be used as a distraction whenever the young man grew antsy. It took some pressure off of the Maréchal de Noailles and the Duc d'Ayen, the latter of which had called for Adrienne to visit his office in the early hours of the evening.

The last time she stalled outside of the room was when she was listening to her father insult her husband. She didn't look at him for days afterwards until he ultimately begged her to open up. No wife wished to see their husbands shamed by their father, especially when Gilbert had done nothing different than Louis had.

At the time, that is. Adrienne looked out the window – Gilbert did fly the coop. The frustration from that whole affair last year was undoubtedly excused.

Sometime over the winter, the duc must have had the hinge of the door oiled, the creak it used to emit disappeared. A man startled upon seeing Adrienne waiting outside of it – his periwig made his face appear rounder, the rest of him already quite stout. Mid-forties, for certain, Adrienne decided, and maintained an expression of annoyed constipation. Of course, Adrienne didn't think such a thing – she was a lady.

"Excuse me, Miss," he said in English between pinched lips. His scurrying down the hallway, if Adrienne were not from polite society, would have brought about a laugh. But she swallowed down the temptation, merely peeking into the office where her father stood, leaning against his desk.

Where his windows often were closed, they were open, letting the light make itself at home. He wore yellow today; Adrienne never recalled seeing him in such a bright color. Truly, something must have been wrong.

"I didn't know you hosted Americans," she said, nodding her head towards the hall. "He made it out alive, I see."

"You sound like your mother," he replied. He hummed, turning to his belongings. "It would have been rude if I didn't host them every now and then. Monsieur Adams just arrived a few weeks ago to assist his Americans in securing the alliance."

"But that was done in February?"

"Yes, it was," the duc said, smirking. "The man is in limbo. And speaks French like an infant. It's been years since I had to resort to speaking the petty tongue; a diplomat cannot even learn the language of diplomacy."

"I'm sure you did not mean to summon me to speak of Monsieur Adams' lack of purpose here," Adrienne said. She smiled as her father sat back onto his chair and sighed, looking up at her with relaxed, calm eyes.

"No, I did not," he said. "I was speaking to the Comte de la Rivière in the days past and discovered something. I thought it was important to speak with you about it."

"What is it, Papa?"

He fiddled with his rings. Adrienne watched him glance between his hands and a letter that sat by an open inkwell. If she looked carefully, she could see the tiny ink stains on his fingers that matched the dots lining the paper. It wasn't every day that the Duc d'Ayen was nervous to say something to one of his daughters, but Adrienne had been growing increasingly patient in waiting for men.

"I owe you an apology," the duc exclaimed, "and I owe Gilbert an apology as well."

Adrienne slowly sat down. "Papa…"

"There has been a division between us for a long while. I've been bitter in my grudges, and am shameful for my response to his desires that led him to go astray and leave you."

"Papa, nothing could have been done to stop him from going. It isn't your fault," she said. She reached over and took his hands. They were aging, the lines grew deeper.

"Even so," Jean replied, "he has written me several times since departing, and I have not been a good father-in-law for returning the favor. I have… drafted a reply." He pulled one hand away to slide the parchment closer. "If it wouldn't be too much trouble, I would like you to read it. Check for errors."

Her father did not make any grammar mistakes, she knew, but she took the letter from him. Whether or not this newfound respect for Gilbert began when his name grew in popularity, or if it stemmed from the news of his successes and bouts of honor from America, Adrienne did not care. Her father wrote most graciously, casting his benevolent paternal affection into words that, although without poetry, struck Adrienne quite deep. There was no reprimanding nor spite, just simplicity of comfort in its finest form.

"I believe you will bring Gilbert to tears," she said, rereading.

Her father tsked, resting his chin on his knuckle. "Perhaps I should be more blunt then."

"No!" Adrienne smiled. "I love this. He will love it. Let him cry, Papa, he deserves this."

Jean de Noailles would have never admitted to her that he may have cried as well, but she could see the gloss over his eyes as he rubbed at the stubble on his chin.

Chapter Fourteen

It was warm before the sun had touched the tent city's canvas coverings. Those soldiers who had the misfortune of sitting in the cabin filth over the winter were ordered to clean them out and replace the roofing over the spring – burning the soiled and mold-covered hay around the border of camp – and now they enjoyed the dark shade the cabins brought from the incoming summer heat.

Sounds of drilling came with the early morning. Miles across the encampment, the voice of the industrious Baron von Steuben overcame the farmland roosters. Angry German was echoed by only slightly softer, angry English as the man's aide-de-camp translated the vulgar language.

Gilbert was awoken almost daily from it all. He'd welcome the warmth of Valley Forge over the cold of upper New York – his winter was spent wasting time away from General Washington as a plot to have the General replaced was conspiring under their noses. It was unhealthy for Gilbert to be away from His Excellency for so long. He had let the returning embrace last far longer than was socially polite simply because he knew that Washington would let him. Gilbert took great comfort in his relationship with the General.

He had plenty of correspondence to reply to, so the short rest was not so terrible. As a Major-General, he was afforded two aides-de-camp:

Major Edmund Brice of Maryland and Lieutenant Colonel Gimat. Both men accompanied Gilbert on the ship from France, the former having been studying art at the time, and the latter: a volunteer officer whom Gilbert regarded fervently. Alongside his breakfast, they would leave a stack of generic letters for him on his tent desk for him to peruse at his leisure. Of course he would answer any from Washington first. Planning for the summer campaign had hogged up all his time since he arrived to Valley Forge at the end of April, and now the summer was upon them and the Continental army was ready to claim some victories.

Most days in Valley Forge followed a schedule, with an occasional sunny day allowing Gilbert to join Washington's staff in what the General *called* exercise, but were, in reality, games with the excuse that tackling one another was for their health. Hamilton's hair was still attached to his shirt from when his sleeve buttons were caught in the man's curls. There was an attempt to untangle it, but Laurens conceded that Hamilton had enough hair for Gilbert to rip the few red strands out.

He dressed himself, picking the pollen off of his uniform until it was smooth and pristine. While reading Washington's letters, he had to be careful if he were drinking; he smiled too much and was prone to spilling the wine over his waistcoat. He had made eye contact with Brice and Gimat too many times after doing so — subject to their stifled laughter — to attempt it again.

Today, his aides were nowhere to be found. Not that they slept in his tent, they had their own officer tent next door, but when Gilbert poked his head out and wandered over, they were gone. Nor were they inside of the Marquis' headquarters of the Brookside Inn's lower rooms. If it weren't a city of a camp, perhaps he would have been more concerned. If Knox or Greene needed to borrow them, Gilbert wouldn't mind – being informed would have been nice.

A few artillery soldiers from General Knox's regiments saluted him as they ran by. The gear that they used to clean cannons was balanced over their shoulders. Their faces were heavily freckled and pink and toothy, happily calling out to him.

Gilbert cocked his head.

It wasn't unusual to see Knox's boys giddy and excited to clean cannons – just like their general, they were serious *and* jolly – but the *"long live King Louis"* was a new exclamation to hear from a ragtag bunch of Americans. Perchance he was still dreaming.

Several beats of horses echoed down the road as Gimat and Brice arrived, flaming with joy. Hamilton rode behind them, waving papers in hand, his voice high.

"Lafayette! You must join us posthaste," he said in French, and his French was wonderfully accented to Gilbert's ears. He pointed towards the horse that Brice held the reins to next to his own.

"I have not finished my meal," Gilbert replied, holding up his bread. Still, he threw himself on the saddle, eyeing his friend's glowing cheeks.

"Trust me, your stomach will feel full with the news."

"Will you not tell me, Hami? Good news I hope, if the redness of your face is from excitement and not the exertion of coming all the way down here to find me." They turned around to trot their way back up the two mile stretch.

"It is of excellent news, but I exercise great restraint in holding my tongue. Dear Tilghman opened it this morning for translation and it had caught all of us off guard. Congress' letters too have confirmed it. I have never seen His E so elated; he's called for you."

"Colonel," Gimat said. "I thought you were holding your tongue."

Hamilton bit his cheek. "Laf knows it is my *one* fault," he said, glancing at Gilbert.

Gimat shook his head, and shifted a hand through his inner pockets to fish out a small packet of letters. He leaned over and handed it to Gilbert, saying, "personal correspondence for you as well, sir. Just arrived this morning."

"Thank you." Gilbert tucked them away for safekeeping.

He hated that his quarters were so far from Washington's. If he could fly up the river like a fish to reach Potts House, he would. *Distance makes the heart grow fonder* – he knew that one well. With every hill, Gilbert knew exactly when they were getting closer to Headquarters, and as the regimental waistcoats shifted to red and the cocked hats to the helmets of the Life Guard, they were upon Washington's office in an instant.

Gilbert should have expected something insane as he met eyes with every other general currently making their way inside. Brice took his horse as he dismounted, catching up with General Greene as the man huffed through his asthma, having walked the whole way out of spite. The Rhode Islander gave him a pleasant smile, clapping him on the shoulder while using it as a polite excuse to hold onto him for support. Gilbert enjoyed Greene immensely; the man was blunt and committed to the cause, and treated Gilbert like the major-general he was. They also shared the same sense of humor, which helped bypass the time when they went out on orders together.

"Congratulations, Harry says I should tell you," Greene said as the men piled into Washington's office. "And before you ask me about *what*, he didn't say. I do not know why nor how that man finds out things before the rest of us."

They looked over at General Knox who stood in the corner donning a wide smirk. The others were left speculating with rumors and whatever information their own aides were able to snag from Washington's. Gilbert glanced warily at Hamilton as he loitered by the room taken up by the rest of Washington's military family; all seven faces of the young aides piled along the length of the door, grinning, secretive, gnawing their lips as they waited for their leader to rise from his desk and speak.

"Gentlemen," Washington said, and the entire room hushed. Gilbert could see the inkling of a smile from his stoic features. He had stared long enough in his time with the man to recognize it, all the better when he was the cause of such a smile. "I have received confirmation word from Congress that has been long overdue."

He met Gilbert's eyes and the stern crease of his brow melted away like wax to a flame.

"France has signed the Treaty of Alliance with our delegation in Versailles and ships have already departed for our shores. It seems many have been enthused with what this army is capable of, and how beneficial even *one* Frenchman may be for our country. Monsieur Marquis," Washington said, and the wide eyes of the generals followed suit towards Gilbert, "your efforts to persuade your king to join us have not been overlooked. We are indebted to you, my friend."

Gilbert was not going to cry. He wasn't, he lied to himself. Even while Greene, Lord Stirling, and Knox flew over to kiss his cheek or shake his arm, he wasn't going to blubber like an idiot in front of Washington, as his eyes went glossy keeping his gaze on his General.

"There is nothing that needs to be repaid, *mon général*," Gilbert said. "It is my duty and privilege to do all I can for this country." The air he sucked in burned his nose.

France was joining the war. The United States was going to be free and his home would have a helping hand in it.

Gilbert barely heard the talk of what came next, when French ships were bound to arrive, how many in number would be sent… All these things were sent over his head. He was floating in bliss. When did he end up back in the hallway kissing and hugging his friends? He didn't know. Suddenly he was kissing Washington's cheeks, and they were warm and wet with tears. Did his letters have a sway in France's decision? *They might have*, but they might have *not*. He felt humbled at all the attention; he was not the only Frenchman in the army, far from it, there were more volunteers than Gilbert could properly list. So many Europeans here deserved praise for their efforts.

Word got around Valley Forge like the wind as the generals relayed the information to their officers and they to their privates and the militias: France had allied itself with America and help was on the way. To many it was reasonable to think that the war was going to be over by next year once the French military arrived to meet the British head on with similar weaponry and might. Gilbert wondered which men would be chosen to command the French army; he could think of many eligible people who would fit the role perfectly, but King Louis and his ministers were still likely debating the topic.

Traveling back to his quarters to bury himself in writing more letters, replying to the ones with thoughts he forgot to simply tell to the General, toasting with his aides, he went up again to the Potts lawn as celebrations had taken over. He dressed himself in the Bourbon colors, leading the French troops in the camp through the growing assembly. Freshly cleaned cannons were now firing off sparks as fireworks were lit.

Despite horrible supplies over the winter, the boys passed around ale, clapping and cheering and singing the good graces of another monarch. It was inconceivable to hear it all, Gilbert thought, fighting back a laugh. He was thrusted a whole mug of something strong from Colonel Laurens, the man who proceeded to throw himself into the aides with Meade and Hamilton. Gilbert would be lying if he said he didn't miss the times he acted as an aide earlier in the war – the boys in the Family were truly that: *family*.

Family! He smacked his head and dug through his coat's pockets for the neatly tied correspondence from France. Very few ever made it to him; whether lost or intercepted, he hoped whoever had his love's words enjoyed them as much as he would have liked to. He daydreamed often of returning home to envelop all of his dear girls in his arms. Anastasie's birth came from a letter from the Maréchal de Noailles, an immense joy to hear after months of silence. Gilbert interrogated every Frenchman who arrived at camp about who they knew and what quality of intelligence they could supply about his family. It was a tedious task – many men claiming visitations to Versailles knew nothing of any aristocrat.

Carding through the letters, some were notable replies from the ministers he wrote to while confined to a bed post-Brandywine, others from his aunts or friends from his old regiment, but there was one, he stopped at, that was quite worn – a well-traveled letter from home. Gilbert could recognize the Noailles seal even if it was faded and flat. He had walked several paces away from the laughter and noise, stepping up into the Potts House now void of secretaries. It still smelled like ink and pounce from the morning.

It was written not long after he first arrived at Valley Forge, which still was several months ago. The distance agitated his patience for how long it took for letters to travel. The dots in every *i* appeared more like slashes, which was typical of the Duchesse d'Ayen and so Gilbert prepared for his mother-in-law's typical family report with ease. Leaning against the wall, he took his time imagining everyone's faces in his head as he last remembered them. Anne's societal introduction? *She must have hated that*, he thought, suppressing a chuckle. There was even some news from Chavaniac that Gilbert divulged in – the duchesse was truly spoiling him.

His Adrienne was not mentioned until the last page, which was a terrible fault itself – she should have been one of the first. She turned eighteen while he was away, his beautiful lady. How he longed to embrace her, to kiss her and Henriette, who must have been a sprightly toddler by now…

Ah.

The letter crinkled as he adjusted his hold. Perhaps he read it wrong. Gilbert cleared his throat, read the sentence once more, and then cleared it again. His smile faded; his chest squeezed his lungs.

"My God," he breathed, and a hand fought for purchase along the wall, a desk – anything. A whine escaped his lips, *"oh God."*

It had been almost a year, and in every letter he sent his beloved wife he had mentioned Henriette's name, wished Adrienne to give her his love and she… she…

She wasn't even alive.

Gilbert was mortified.

In his ignorance, his letters meant to bring Adrienne peace of mind and reminders of his affection must have only brought her pain at the reminders of their lost child. To grieve without him there – he imagined Adrienne alone in a dark, cold room and his heart mourned. He was a terrible man, a worse husband.

Gilbert hardly heard the excited calls of his name as two pairs of boots shuffled around the corner accompanied by their laughter. He was on the floor – he didn't remember falling to the floor, but he looked up at Hamilton and Laurens, his face stinging with tears.

Their smiles fell away instantly.

"Laf?" Laurens said.

Hamilton fell to his knees by Gilbert's side. *How he loved them both dearly.* "Gilbert, what's happened?"

Gilbert opened his mouth, speaking no words, but whimpered French nonsense. The hand that gripped the letter's pages could not release them even as he tried to show them. His poor Adrienne, his poor little girl…

Laurens' palm was on his leg, a thumb digging trenches into his thigh. Hamilton pulled him into a hug – hands calloused by years of writing and working brushed at his cheeks. It would not be the first time for anyone to see the young trio cuddled into a pile.

Gilbert sniveled, making a mess of Hamilton's cravat. Why wouldn't his shoulders stop shaking? His uncle Lusignem would smack him for acting like a woman in hysterics, needing to be consoled. Yet the silent rubbing to his back was soft and the hand in his hair was just as gentle. Did Adrienne have someone there to comfort her like this? He cried harder.

"I need to go h-home," he panted. He knew he couldn't – not yet – not with the summer campaign about to begin. Battles would be a distraction from the anguish. The lads held on tighter, a good deed as Gilbert thought his spirit would simply up and float away if not tethered down so firmly.

He didn't settle at his desk inside of his own headquarters until several days later. He stared at a blank piece of paper. Very few opportunities presented themselves to let him sit and expound the long tale of his late spring emotions. Writing her name came naturally, he didn't have to look at the quill to do so.

Chance has furnished me, mon coeur, with a very uncertain opportunity of writing to you, but I shall take advantage of it, for I cannot resist the wish of saying a few words… My expressions of heartfelt grief must even add to your distress. What a dreadful thing is absence! I never experienced before all the horrors of separation. My own deep sorrow is aggravated by the feeling that I am not able to share and sympathize in your anguish. The length of time that elapsed before I heard of this event had also increased my misery. Consider, mon coeur, how dreadful it must be to weep for what I have lost, and tremble for what remains. The distance between Europe and America appears to me more enormous than ever. The loss of our poor child is almost constantly in my thoughts: this sad news followed immediately that of the treaty; and whilst my heart was torn by grief, I was obliged to receive and take part in expressions of public joy.

Several pages, as always; he could always write novels to her. Writing of the treaty, of Barren Hill, of his anxiety and sorrow for being unable to return. He could not help but grow gloomy as he went on with the usual pleasantries in the closing lines.

Embrace, a million times, our little Anastasie — alas! She alone remains to us! I feel that she has engrossed the affection that was once divided between my two children: take great care of her. Adieu; I know not when this may reach you... I even doubt it is ever reaching you.

"Sir," Gimat said, opening the door. "General Washington has called upon you to join him for dinner. Shall I reply yes?"

Not many weeks had passed since he was granted command of two thousand men to survey General Howe's troops as they occupied Philadelphia. A great distraction and a show of Washington's trust for him, Gilbert excitedly had accepted it. The mission didn't completely go to plan – Gilbert may have camped a little too long in one place despite being advised not to, and the British descended on the hill very quickly with hopes of capturing him. But Gilbert always had his lucky star when it came to his time in America, and his order to retreat was perhaps the most expertly enacted order of the year to date. Washington could not be angry with him at risking capture when the retreat was so perfect. He even drew a laugh from the General when informing him that the Americans managed to take out some British soldiers along the way. He also selfishly relished in his friends' embraces upon his second return.

Gilbert let the wax drip over the folds of the packet, and sealed his words.

If only his star was a bit brighter.

"Yes, of course," he said. "I shall be right over."

Tiverton, Rhode Island, September 1778

If summer were kind to him, it was a fluke, for Gilbert was on the verge of committing heinous acts after heinous acts. His seemingly limitless patience had cracked. The Admiral d'Estaing and the French fleet had fled to Boston after storms and ill-luck damaged the ships too much to sustain a fight or provide coverage for General Sullivan's troops on land. Both Sullivan and the British peace commissioners slandered the French forces – a slight that Gilbert took seriously, challenging one commissioner to a duel and then angrily writing d'Estaing that he would shoot the damned Briton in the head. The man declined, as typical cowardly Englishmen did. Gilbert wrote to Washington with delicate, but growing agitated words to allow him to do something.

Perhaps there was a second chance to invade Canada, he thought.

In his letters to General Washington, he expressed these thoughts as well as the intelligence his spies had gathered, his wishes to return to headquarters, to be *useful*. Not to frighten the inhabitants of the family who housed him in their home by the harbor, Gilbert swallowed his growing urge to scream and break something. He had already damaged a pillow after beating it against the bedpost, pretending the wooden beam was General Sullivan.

Pacing the second story floor, Gilbert passed a mirror.

He hardly recognized the reflection.

He was not suicidal, although the feeling tended to linger that his current predicament was all too similar to simply laying in a grave. An unexpected letter from the Duc d'Ayen full of kindness and affection raised his spirits ten-fold, and he had spent the utmost of an hour writing a reply back, trying not to spoil his ink with rolling tears with how much the good opinion of his father meant to him. In his youth, he had longed to fight in a French uniform, and if he were asked to, he would have left America to fight for their freedom abroad. His father-in-law assured him that there would be no land campaign in Europe or elsewhere, nothing nearly as important as the one fought where Gilbert already was. It eased his conscience dearly. Love for his General tethered him to these shores;

and Gilbert would do what was asked of him by his commander *or* his king.

King Louis, Gilbert imagined, was still waiting on an apology to his expedient departure from France. There were many possibilities of how the monarch would react to a return – from his friendly nature, Gilbert hoped the king wouldn't imprison him in the Bastille, but he doubted it would be a simple slap to the wrist. A fugitive: that was what he was. And if he returned to France, he would have to eliminate that moniker.

An open, lengthy letter lay on Gilbert's bed from General Washington. Gilbert nibbled on his knuckle as he looked at it from across the room.

If you had entertained thoughts, my dear Marquis, it read in the General's firm hand, *of paying a visit to your Court – to your Lady – and to your friends this winter, but waiver on account of an expedition into Canada, friendship induces me to tell you that I do not conceive the prospect of such an operation so favorable at this time as to cause you to change your views.*

No invasion, no large scale prospecting battles, the army was compelled to lay in wait. Washington, to his generous credit, invited Gilbert and his dear Adrienne to his cottage in Virginia for when the war was won. A more pleasing image for Gilbert to imagine, than that of a sad, lonely wife. He closed his eyes, and for the first time in a while, he prayed.

He could smell the ocean from the open window. The air held onto more salt here than it did at home, the waters greener from the seaweed. When he sat to write to Adrienne, the breeze had pulled his hair back toward the window, out to the sea, to France, to her.

Adieu; when shall I be permitted to see thee, to part from thee no more; to make thy happiness as thou makest mine, and kneel before thee to implore thy pardon? Adieu, adieu; we shall not be very long divided.

Chapter Fifteen

Paris, February 12th, 1779

There were no birds on the branch this year outside of the morning room's window, so the evening was quiet and still. Little Anastasie, instead, had covered the glass with her fingerprints. She had moved along to reach up for every book and dangling crystal, her Auntie Pauline following behind to show her the novels' covers or to push the candelabras away. Once Anastasie took a book and gave it half a glance, it no longer interested her and so found its new home on the floor. Pauline looked at Adrienne with pursed lips, cleaning up the mess as it traveled around the room.

Adrienne sat on the sofa with her sewing. She planned on embroidering a fichu for Anastasie when she was old enough to wear one – little silver stars on the deep blue silk. She was getting a little carried away with it, intending on making the thirteen, but continued without thinking, and now she didn't know how many she stitched.

Anastasie's brown hair had grown into a soft, wavy crop. No matter how often she rolled around or tore off her cap, the hair always fell perfectly back into place. It was easy to manage and looked adorable with a bow. Pauline was always picking out new colors. Today's bow color was a ruby red and made her look like a little Valentine's Day angel with her white dress. Perhaps for mass on the saint's feast day, she would put Anastasie in pink, she thought, still chuckling at her daughter's curiosity. Another book met the floor.

Watching her grow was a joy that melancholy slinked not too far behind. Anastasie was still two months shy from the age Henriette was when she passed away; the fear was ever-present. But unlike dear Henriette, the doctors reassured Adrienne and her family that Anastasie was a perfectly healthy baby. She ate everything Adrienne fed to her, slept the correct amount, and met every monthly goal. Her one fault, if she had one, was that she was *too* curious – which was a Noailles characteristic that everyone in the family was used to handling. Regardless, Adrienne didn't take Anastasie outside as often as she did with Henriette. Just in case; she wrapped her like a gift on every cold night.

"Anastasie!" Adrienne called. Her little one's brunette head popped up over a table. "Would you like a muffin?" She held up a small piece.

Anastasie waddled over, hands already outstretched to receive it.

"Would you like some butter on it?"

"Yes!" she replied, nodding her head. Adrienne added a little bit to the top and let Anastasie climb onto her lap before she handed it to her. The treat was her favorite, a surefire way to summon the toddler if she ventured off out of sight. She had tackled stairs in the past month and too many times it was Monsieur Dameron or the Duc d'Ayen who caught her before she scurried out the door with Adrienne or Mlle Maron not too far behind.

"What do you think," Adrienne said, tickling Anastasie with kisses to her cheeks. "A bedtime story or a song tonight?"

Anastasie dragged her mouth all over her muffin. "Mm wah," she replied, dancing her hand like she was a maestro.

"Song? Very well, we can do that." More often than not, that would be the case; it was amazing that Adrienne did not lose her voice after fifteen minutes of putting Anastasie to sleep every night.

Pauline had collected the last of the fallen books in the room, some including little pamphlets she wrote herself – unique copies that only the Noailles owned. Last July, she had written a short children's story for

Anastasie that was enjoyable for the entire family; applause was joined by the jingle of the baby's rattle. Pauline was going to turn thirteen when the summer came, and was far more calm about being introduced to society. Their mother was done allowing her daughters to be married so young, none had to worry about being wed at fourteen like Adrienne was.

"Do you hear that?" Pauline asked, tilting her head towards the door. "Maman's not hosting her salon tonight, is she?"

"Not that I know of," Adrienne replied, allowing Anastasie one more little muffin. "But you know I am the last of anyone to find out."

"That's because you sit here for most of the day," Pauline said, sticking out her tongue.

"I do not!"

"Then are you going to come with me to investigate?"

Adrienne coddled Anastasie. "No," she said, falling back into the pillows. The sofa was too comfortable on busy baby evenings like these. "It's probably Papa having another piece from his laboratory brought in. You know how fragile some of them can be and that building could never be heated properly."

"I don't know," Pauline said, disappearing behind her to approach the door. The noise from the hallways echoed with delightful screams from Anne and the shuffling of feet. "Are those soldiers? Anne, what is going on?"

Adrienne couldn't hear what came next; Pauline had closed the door behind her. Anne was always excitable when there were more men for her to spar with, the bustle wasn't unusual. Adrienne would happily dote on her daughter.

Anastasie laughed like no tomorrow when Adrienne spun them around the room; she loved to be thrown, although Adrienne could only do it once or twice before her arms ached. Anastasie also loved mirrors. Not in a vanity way, she was far too young to be obsessed with looks, but seeing her maman twice was like a fantastic puzzle, her confusion bringing rouge to her cheeks as she giggled, reaching for Adrienne's reflection. And

Adrienne loved it too, seeing her baby so perfect. Adrienne's reflection had changed slightly since she last cared to look at it. Nineteen brought her cheekbones out but after two children, her features felt more round — defined, yet soft.

Not much taller, of course. That was typical. Maybe next year.

"Maman," Anastasie said.

"Yes, darling?"

"Miaou miaou," she said, pointing at Antoinette's gray cat that wandered beneath the curtains and sat down with a ceremonious *poof.* He had grown fatter with age, but still wore plenty of lace and bells around his neck.

"Let us go pet the miaou miaou," Adrienne replied, walking her over to the window drapes. Anastasie wiggled her fingers over the soft fur, sitting down by the tail to hold it gently. If Anne's cat was any other, Adrienne would be wary of the claws, but he was the laziest, nonchalant feline in Paris, no doubt, and Anastasie loved treating him like a pillow. "Soft, yes?" She patted the cat's head, guiding the little hand with hers.

"Ah."

"My *God,*" a voice whispered from behind so softly it could have been a ghost; the hair on Adrienne's arms stuck out like it was. A shiver ran so quickly up her spine, she had to stand to avoid falling over. And it *must* have been an apparition for the visage of her husband stood in the doorway.

She swallowed. Never had she hallucinated him before so vividly. What he wore was different than how she pictured him: a dark blue uniform, a pink sash wrapped neatly around his waist; he wore his wig densely powdered, but that was not what she normally imagined – she liked the red of his hair, she'd always picture him with it freshly clean.

When the form carefully walked towards her and rounded the sofa, she could only place her hand out, a silent *halt* at her lips. And he did, frozen just out of reach. From there she could see the newborn freckles on his nose, the fresh lines that deepened as his brows rose, his eyes glassier than a crystal lake.

"*Mon coeur,* I..." he breathed, and shook his head. She could see the guise of frustration pass his face as no other words followed.

Adrienne's vision wobbled. He sounded just like she remembered.

She had forgiven him in her letters; a thousand times over she would have swept aside everything and engulfed him in her arms. In her delaying a response, he too had faltered, the couple hovering in a crack of reality. With her legs too stubborn to move, or perhaps, they knew if she dared take a step forward, she would fall, Adrienne ventured to simply blink. Warm tears curved her cheeks, the underwater film that seemed to cover Gilbert fell away as he dropped to his knees in front of her.

"To you do I come, before you I stand, sinful and sorrowful," he said, a wistful prayer, but once again, he whose words often came from poetic verse and blessed by the muses, one move from Adrienne – the parting of her lips or the rise of her hand – rendered him speechless.

Never before had Adrienne felt so powerful in front of a man. Stealing words like stealing air, no doubt a thief as cruel as her would be thrown into the Bastille. They stood in silence for eons.

"Beloved," he whispered. "I beg you to spare me a word. Admonish me, damn me, but love me the same, I implore."

There were the smallest hints of whiskers on his chin that were not there when he had left her. Two years had ticked by; when he departed France as a boy and somehow aged into a man, as Adrienne left behind her girlhood so long ago. She allowed herself to reach out and touch his face, following the contour of his jaw, her fingers drawing over the peach fuzz. Gilbert's eyes closed. His skin was warm. He didn't seem to need to know where she was as she took a small step forward into his reach before his large hands grasped her waist, bringing her fully to him. Her petticoats were like a safety blanket, wrung in his fists while he burrowed himself into her skirts. The last time he did such a thing, Adrienne was in the early weeks of her second pregnancy.

"Maman?"

Gilbert's grip on Adrienne tightened. His eyes were already red when he lifted his face from her, so full of fear she imagined if he bore such an expression in the throes of war.

Adrienne comfortably let her hands rest on the slope of Gilbert's shoulders – he was so damn tall, even kneeling they could kiss with ease. She dragged her thumb over his lashes.

"Yes, Anastasie?" she said, watching Gilbert's every move.

"You sad?"

Despite wiping her own tears from Gilbert's face, she shook her head. "No, darling," she said, "Maman is very, very happy." She looked at the ceiling and wondered, if it were clear, would she see that star above them. Adrienne felt the familiar grasp at the back of her skirts from Anastasie's small fist as the toddler climbed to her feet, eyeing the tall stranger that clung to her maman like a child. Gilbert eyed her too. A tiny pull to his smile let his sobs shift into the gentlest weeping as he looked over their daughter.

Anastasie, wary and hidden behind a pleat of Adrienne's skirt, seemed interested at least in the gold buttons that adorned much of Gilbert's uniform. She had reached up and pinched one on the cuff of his sleeve that had dipped to hold Adrienne's thighs. He lowered it completely, as entranced as the babe was, as she investigated every button. But soon she grew tired of it, finding the fabric of her mother's skirt far more enticing to nibble on.

"It's her bedtime actually," Adrienne said, bending over to scoop Anastasie up, draping her over a shoulder with ease. Gilbert sat back on his heels, silently watching his girls. "If you'd like to join us, Gilbert," she whispered, "you may, but I will warn you that tonight is a lullaby night."

He rose to his feet, a steadying hand on the sofa. "I would love that more than anything."

The sash around his waist was the same dark pink he wore on their meeting day, Adrienne noted. Sheer coincidence, surly, she thought, as they walked down the hall together. His arm hovered under hers, there, but shyly, like he was afraid to touch her while she held their child who did not realize the man who followed them to the bedroom was her father. Adrienne tried to go about their normal nightly routine sans maid – who nary approached the door when she saw the Marquis with them.

"Maman," Anastasie said, eyeing the man as Adrienne combed through her hair. Adrienne set down the brush, watching Gilbert loiter from the mirror.

"Come introduce yourself to your daughter, or you'll both simply stare at each other all the days of our lives." She turned Anastasie in her lap. Gilbert pushed his sword back as he knelt on one knee and took little Anastasie's hand with his fingers.

"Hello," he said. "I'm sorry it has been so long, my sweetling. I am your papa." He kissed her hand with delicate ease, narrowly avoiding her pinkie which still liked to stick up into the air. She bobbed her head to the side, taking him in for a long moment before she nodded, content that the tall man was good enough to stay for bedtime. Gilbert rubbed his neck and sighed, "Oh Lord, she looks just like me."

"She's as talkative as you too," Adrienne replied, letting her slide down to wobble to her crib. It was a beautifully carved thing, adorned with wooden flowers and swirls of the sea. Anastasie, whether she knew it or not, was acting as a tangible crutch for her parents to lean on as they continued to pass glance after glance. "Now, my dearest, what song would you like tonight?"

"*Belle-qui?*" Anastasie requested after a long minute of debating the very few favorites she had. *Belle qui tiens ma vie* was meant to have four singers, but Adrienne was a talented mother and Anastasie was a pleading daughter who it was almost impossible to deny anything to.

"Oh, alright," Adrienne said, settling herself on the floor by the cradle. She pulled up the blanket to her brunette baby's chin. "*Dearest Beauty, my whole existence is captive in your eyes; Joys, at my soul's insistence, upon your smile's arise...*" she sang, tracing soft circles over her face. There were several verses that Anastasie fought hard to stay awake for, mumbling after her mother's softly low singing, but her lids were growing heavy. "*My soul, in fear, had wanted of Passion to be free; but Love came in undaunted, and mastered all of me...*"

Watching her fall into her dreams was the best part of every night.

When Adrienne could tuck her in nice and safe and kiss her perfectly round cheek, she then could rest easy. Could a parent ever get used to seeing their babe sleep? Could the adoration ever fade?

Her hand hovered atop the blankets as the slight clicking of a sword's belt came free, being placed lightly on the table. She wondered if her legs would support her even if she tried to rise.

"Then, lovely girl, come near me; come close, my little one," he hummed behind her. She turned her head, eyeing Gilbert as he removed his court wig, the flames of the fireplace lighting up the back of his head. And oh Lord, his hair had grown. *"Do not rebel or fear me, for my heart you've fully won."*

Adrienne carefully rose, as if a string was tied to the top of her head. Gilbert looked dashing in blue, he always had, and the gold detailing brought warmth to his face. She left behind her slippers, sacrificing the inch of height they gave her in exchange for the chance to run into his arms.

America must have done something to improve his balance for he hardly needed to take a step back to embrace her, to pick her up off the floor with ease. Adrienne tucked her fingers through his hair, it curled down his neck to his shoulders, and dug her nose into the soft linen of his cravat. He smelled like the sea, with the slightest perfumed hint of Versailles.

"How long do I have you?" she dared to ask. Forever, she hoped, but knew it was too wishful of thinking; she would never be so lucky.

"I am under house-arrest, so you surely have me all day, every day, *mon coeur*," he replied into her hair.

House-arrest, Adrienne could strangle him. That would have to be unpacked later. She felt him remove a pin from her hair with his teeth, the tiny piece of metal clinking lightly to the floor.

"Not in the baby's room," Adrienne said, biting his shoulder. Anastasie wasn't a heavy sleeper. Gilbert cupped his arms under her legs, sashaying to the inner chamber doors to shove one open with his hip. She suppressed a giggle, tilting her head to kiss his ear. They maneuvered and dodged through doorways and arches until they stumbled into the apartments of the Marquis on the other side of the Hôtel. Gilbert's legs finally gave way, the two of them rolling to the floor with Adrienne landing neatly on his hips.

"That was very impressive of me, I didn't know I could do that," he said. "And what an impressive sight before me now."

Adrienne tore his cravat from his throat, eliciting a sharp gasp from his end as he allowed her to continue to tear open the top buttons of his waistcoat. Two years. Two *damned* years she had sat with only his letters. Her hands pulled the pink sash from his waist, wrapping it over her shoulders like a shawl as she freed the rest of his chest from the waistcoat. From the ground, Gilbert watched her, biting back a mewl while she ran her fingers underneath his shirt. She sat on his lap, she could feel the impatience.

"Kiss me, General la Fayette," she commanded, "you owe me thousands more."

Gilbert sat up in an instant, leaving behind the coat and weskit like a butterfly leaving its cocoon. He held her face with hands that felt a little rougher than a typical aristocrat; his shoulders were broader, his arms took up far more sleeve than she remembered. She could melt into him, breathing him in as they kissed and kissed and kissed until their lips were red and swollen. The pins keeping her bodice closed were plucked away, one by one. Gilbert shoved the gown right off her shoulders, following it down her back where his hands found the cording of her stays. His fumbling with it somehow made her smile more – clearly he had no practice in these past months, Adrienne could still say she had all of his fidelic attention. She led his hands through loosening the garment until he could slide it over her head.

Gilbert, like any man, Adrienne supposed, enjoyed a fair bosom. After two babies, Adrienne was almost embarrassed by hers, but Gilbert was more than content to smother himself in the softness of her breast, holding her like a comforting blanket. He kissed her sternum, nuzzling and humming into kissing each breast as he followed the lines of her body back up to her lips.

"Why are you crying, *mon coeur*? Did I hurt you?" he whispered, kissing the tears away from her eyes. "I am here, *amour*, I am here. You are not alone."

Adrienne bit her lip as a rising sob caught itself in her throat. It was all so much. Like a terribly beautiful dream, if she woke up and he was not in her arms, if he was not kissing her and loving her, she would go mad.

She smoothed back his hair, the winding strands behind his ears, and traced the bridge of his nose with the tip of her pinkie.

He squeezed her fingers and brought them to his lips. "Tell me what you want, Adrienne, and I will have it done. Are you angry with me? Strike me if you hate me for putting you through such agony, I will accept your blows. But if you are not angry, if you love me still, allow me to love you in full –"

"You can't," she replied, shaking her head. He looked like she indeed had struck him, denying him of her. But she merely smiled and cried a small laugh. "I am on my courses."

His hands padded around under her petticoats until they found her pantaloons. The doe-eyed look sank into displeasure, as if Ségur instead had kicked in the door and stopped them from making love on the floor.

"Well, that hasn't stopped me before," Gilbert said. "I'll have you know, war has been far bloodier than –"

"Gilbert, gross!"

He wriggled them both until he was able to safely roll her over, his knees on either side of her half-dressed body. Disposed of his shirt, gone were the boots from his feet. Adrienne could happily pinch and pull the fine fuzz down his chest while he hovered over her.

"You're the one who has that over your shoulders," he said, flicking the sash away. "Mind my own bloody marks there, it has been used as a tourniquet in the early days of its life."

Adrienne's attention flitted to his leg. "Does it still bother you?" she asked. Gilbert ducked his kisses under her jaw.

"No, *mon coeur*, only the mark remains; the bother had gone by last spring." He nipped at her collarbone, his thumbs circling the soft of her inner thighs until she squirmed. "May I be so bold as to persuade you? I've been a neglectful husband and wish to repair the injustice I've afforded my wife."

There really was no need for persuading – Adrienne would ravish him in an instant, but she enjoyed listening to him prattle on for why he deserved to send her into bliss and how he would not let her sleep until she heard how much he adored her. *A little death was a good reward for such things*, he said. So patient he was, surrounded by American generals and their wives over winter encampments, so regretful for not loving her more while he laid sick in bed for weeks before he returned; so many fairly presented arguments that Adrienne had worked off his breeches in the meantime, kicking them down to their feet with the rest of her petticoats.

"Very well, General," she said, locking her ankles over his back as she brought his face back to hers. "If you remember how to do it, you may execute your attack."

☆

She hadn't woken up naked in quite some time. Despite the weather, she was sufficiently warm, nose pressed into a feather-filled pillow. Wiggling her toes, she stretched them across the bed, searching for a warm leg to press them on.

Her heart stopped when she couldn't find it.

Shooting up from the pillows, Adrienne panicked to find the bed empty.

Was he even here? Did she hallucinate that intensely? Her belly ached, like she was going to be sick. The chamberpot was several steps away.

The door opened quietly, the tall form tip-toeing in with a platter in hand. Gilbert was still in his banyan and cap, shuffling along like a little spy to close the door behind him. He turned around and saw her clutching the blankets, on the verge of crying, and cooed.

"Oh, *là*, you were supposed to be sleeping. Pretend you're sleeping so I can surprise you," he said, walking over with the smell of hot chocolate steaming from the pot.

Adrienne slumped back to the mattress, her heart up in her throat. She closed her eyes simply to rid them of the tears. Of course he didn't leave like that again, she mulled, there was no need to worry. Still, she felt for his hand as he climbed back into the bed, his bare leg sliding up against hers.

"Good morning, *mon coeur*," he chirped. "I have made you your favorite. At least, I hope it's still your favorite. I don't recall the vicomtesse saying that she has converted you to the tea-cause."

"Chocolate is still the superior," she replied, content as he kissed her hair. "Thank you."

"Is there anything else I can get for you? A rice bag? I can massage your feet or comb your hair…"

"Holding me would feel nice," she said. He immediately scooted down to wrap his arms around her. His skin smelled like soap. "How long have you been up?"

"Not too long. Went down to the kitchen, went through some of my things that were brought in this morning. I have some letters I wish to deliver to Monsieur Adams today if you would like to join me. But if you're not feeling well, then you should rest."

"Hand deliver? Gilbert, you are under house-arrest." Let alone, one of the last times she had seen John Adams was when he dined with the Noailles and she had to politely inform him of every single person at the table, down to her great-uncle's English-speaking mistress.

"What are they going to do – send me *home*? I haven't seen a sentry. And why not, anyhow? There's so much to be done."

"You are impossible."

"But you still love me, I hope?"

"Oh, why not," Adrienne said, holding his hands to her abdomen.

"I've invited Monsieur Franklin to the Hôtel," he said, "and scribbled a letter to Vergennes. Maybe in my confinement, we may have some friends and dine on some American delicacies? It's likely been a long while since they have had a home-like meal, and you may like some of the dishes as well, I've grown quite fond of them. I have stolen a few recipes from Lady Washington…"

He had switched into English, a sudden change. Adrienne didn't believe he even noticed he did so. The names of his General and the honorable man's wife came up often in his monologue, he spoke of them like they were his parents, and she imagined they must have been like that for Gilbert. In all of his letters, he had sung their praises. Adrienne shifted in his hold to face him, watching his joy as he spoke the jargon she didn't fully understand, but knew it was important to him.

War, it seemed, made brothers and fathers for all men who bared it together.

If any other woman's husband continued talking as much as Gilbert did about politics and war, he wouldn't make a good bedmate for her; very few young ladies Adrienne knew cared for the nitty-gritty details of how their husbands were hunkered down with other men in tight spaces night after night in pouring rain, or that the most admirable thing a soldier could do was to have his arm blown off by a cannon while saving another man… Adrienne's brow twitched at the insinuation that Gilbert was so close to cannon fire knowing his family's repertoire, but hearing it from him was better than reading it in a letter. She could feel his heartbeat like this, drumming strong and steady.

They must have laid in bed for another hour or two, talking and enjoying the hot chocolate on a fairly windy morning. He presented her with all the compliments of his friends, and proceeded to name them all, providing small biographies of each man so that Adrienne could picture them without need for a portrait.

The door had opened again, just a little, slowly. From the bed, neither Adrienne nor Gilbert could see any servant or family member poke their head in. It couldn't have been the wind for the windows were closed.

Tiny footsteps patted their way towards the bed.

"Maman, found you!" Anastasie giggled, her hands raised high as she leaned against the frame. "Found Maman!"

"My goodness, you have!" Adrienne said, slightly appalled that Anastasie had crossed the house without anyone watching her. She stared hardily at Gilbert, who grabbed his robe from the edge of the bed. Their child continued to wave for the chance to be picked up. "Who woke you up, sweetling?"

"All by myself," she said.

"That's a *you* trait, *mon coeur*," Gilbert whispered into her shoulder. "We've made a dangerous combination. Good morning, Mademoiselle." He nodded politely at Anastasie, slow to toe the line of becoming acquainted with his daughter.

Anastasie faced Adrienne, but spared a glance as she hid her nose in the crook of her mother's neck. "Hi," she said.

Gilbert watched her from the few inches they laid from each other; Adrienne could feel his lashes on her arm as the two continued to glance. It would take a long time for Anastasie to open up to the man if both continued to simply gawk at each other. She sighed, her arm reaching over to the bedside table where a bible lay.

"Here," she said, lobbing it over to Gilbert. "You can read Anastasie her morning prayers. Pick a Psalm."

"Any?"

"Any." Adrienne turned Anastasie over on her chest to take her small hands in hers, folding them for prayer. Gilbert flipped through the holy book like a man who hadn't opened one in some time. "It's near the back," she said, and Gilbert skipped ahead.

"I knew that."

Adrienne did join Gilbert on his wayward gallivant to Passy, where all Americans seemed to reside in the capital. He tightly secured her fur capelet around her neck, properly ensuring she was warm and bundled before he called for their horses. She didn't understand a lick of what he and Monsieur Adams spoke of save for some terms and names, standing idly like a quiet and good wife, but she derived a great deal of joy watching Gilbert speak so freely and boldly. As if he were the sun, she tried to bask in as much of his light as possible in case he was gone tomorrow.

Chapter Sixteen

❦

They rode often with the queen in her various gardens throughout Versailles. The pace was kept slow except for when she declared an impromptu race from the gentlemen in the party, and Gilbert stirred his white mount to keep up with the ducs and comtes. He still rode with distinction, albeit a more relaxed Americana style than the goose-like prance everyone had come to know.

Marie-Antoinette kept to Adrienne's horse as they cheered the men on, casting bets with the other women in the party, some with Louise, keeping to the grass.

"The Vicomte de Noailles has always been an aggressive rider," Louise said, juggling a small pouch of coins in her hands. "I would not be surprised if he passes the leader on their venture back. Dear Marge, that's your husband up front, isn't it?"

"I cannot say I can tell, Madame." The duchesse flipped open her fan to hide a smirk.

Adrienne turned to the queen, who watched with squinted eyes at the boys hollering to each other.

"How are you, Madame, and how is the princess?" she asked, lowering the front of her hat. The queen shifted her horse, meeting her gaze with the same pleasant look.

"She is fine, as am I," Marie-Antoinette replied. "I think I enjoy the role of being a mother. It's a fair distraction from hearing all the ministers' talk of money… and proof that I am not as inept as they thought I was." She pursed her lips and subconsciously scratched at her horse's neck. "A son would have been nice, though."

"That is what we all think until we get to know our girls better," Adrienne said. She watched as Gilbert reached out to shove his brother-in-law, who in turn kicked him back. "I believe men *think* they cherish their sons more, but I've seen them melt into puddles for their daughters. I am sure His Majesty is the same."

"He's grown more fond in the past few weeks. Ever since your husband returned, to be certain. I see the Marquis provides an enthusiastic view of this war of ours, and it brings the king plenty of reassurance that he is doing the right thing. For you must know, Madame, the king cares very much for the opinions of others."

"Perhaps it is well that the Marquis de la Fayette enjoys his hunting trips with His Majesty more now that they speak on equal footing. France will soon get to know all the wonders of America and their liberty if he has the king's ear."

"Yes, well, hopefully we may all reap some reward after claiming victory over Britain so that France will soon remember relief. Some islands in the West Indies would do well for our treasury, and I imagine the people of Québec would like their monarch returned to them. The fur from those colonies sell quite nicely here now that Monsieur Franklin has made it so fashionable. Never thought an old American man would set a standard over myself."

Adrienne held her tongue, but nodded all the same.

The queen laughed once, glancing down at Adrienne's posture. Her eyes lingered for a long moment. "You have raised your waistline, Madame," she said casually, and turned to applaud the vicomte for his excellent win – the men huffing louder than their horses. Adrienne rested her hand in front of her, pulling down the jacket before she locked eyes with a very red-faced Gilbert.

"It is no loss," he said to her, reaching for her hand from his saddle. "I will lay waste to Louis when we depart for training. I did not wish to embarrass him now."

"Of course not, General," Adrienne replied. She smiled as he did. He brought her knuckles to his lips.

"You have me by the throat when you refer to me like that, Madame," he said.

He had purchased command from the King's dragoons through Marie-Antoinette three days before he was released from the unenforced house-arrest. Typically, as if he had never left France, Gilbert was bound to train over the summer months. Fear wavered in Adrienne's mind; she didn't want to call it *distrust*, but the little part of her brain reminded her that it had no other name. If she could truly hold him by the throat, she would. But he was bound for the coast in the following days, and she was bound for home.

"I have to talk to you before you go," she said, spurring her horse to keep up with the queen as they continued on their garden ride. If she had to worry about him for the entirety of summer, it wouldn't be too much to ask if he worried about her just a little bit. Not enough to be wholly concerned – but slightly worried.

It shouldn't have been a surprise to either of them, and certainly not Gilbert. They had been tearing clothes from each other almost every night that he was with her. Nevertheless, when the queen's promenade came to an end, and they found themselves walking down the Hall of Mirrors to the king's side of the palace, Adrienne tightly looped her arm through Gilbert's. He had occupied the otherwise whispering hall with talk of General Washington and how often he wrote him without receiving any line back. But Gilbert was an avid correspondent and Adrienne prayed for the American general who must have possessed such patience and love for the young man, that she loved him too like a second father despite never meeting.

They were bowed to as they walked by. Not in the way one would to their Majesties, but as if the Marquis was a veteran soldier who had seen countless years of war; a small, but extended tilt of the head, and generous smirks from the women. Adrienne tightened her grip. Gilbert had no mistresses that she knew of; he would tell her if he did, or at least ask permission if he felt so inclined to seek one. Men were needy, she already knew that much.

"*Mon coeur*, I have filled our conversation for the past fifteen minutes. People will think I am monologuing like an old man," Gilbert said, swinging them into an alcove. "Interrupt me, would you? You know your silence tortures me. Have I done something wrong? Are you angry that I am leaving? It is just for a few weeks, and I will write to you constantly from my seaside bed. The Irish Sea excursion likely won't get approved – you should have seen Vergennes' face when I proposed it, like a horse when its lips are pulled back in a sneer – so you will not lose me to any naval advance, which is actually fine, I think, for you know how I am on water for too long, but it is important that I am close to accost England at any short notice. And if I were to abscond from your tender embrace to fly to America, then I would arrive at a winter encampment void of work and excitement... Please, Adrienne, *interrupt* me at any time, truly."

"No, no, please carry on. If it delays your leaving, I will allow you to perform Shakespeare as well."

"Madame," Gilbert titted. "If you keep me waiting in such agony, I will have no choice but to punish you. I'll love you a little less if this teasing persists."

"Oh no, Monsieur, that won't do," Adrienne sighed. He was so dramatic. But she could be as well. "I'm afraid what we need is the opposite of that: *twice* your love will suffice, although I may be so bold as to ask for *three* times it since you must split it up between me and your children."

Ah, such bliss, watching his brows knead in soft humor, taking her in for all the trouble she was worth. Adrienne would wait; she could wait some time, following Gilbert's thought process as it ticked away on his face. She cocked her head and gestured to her bodice.

"*Amour*," she said.

"No, no, hold on, I've been counting your courses, you cannot trick me like this," Gilbert said, folding his arms. The pink was rising in his cheeks as his lips began to curl into a grin. "You're jesting."

"You have not been counting, you've been too preoccupied with work," Adrienne replied. "Just last week you thought it was still Lent."

His spurs jingled as he bounced a little in place. Very quickly he dropped into a crouch, cupping his hands around the loose jacket. "Good afternoon there, this is your Papa. Now, I wish you no pressure, but if you happened to be a son, that would be most grand. If you are a girl, I will dote on you a little too much, I think. Girls are too easy to spoil, and your Maman needs more spoiling, so if you are a boy, I believe that would relieve some pressure from my shoulders."

Adrienne covered her mouth with the back of her hand, sinking into the alcove as a few courtiers sauntered by.

"I am to be a father again!" Gilbert said to them from his position beneath her.

The polite chorus of *congratulations, Marquis* and *bless you, General* only boosted his ego. Adrienne should have waited until they were in their own apartments.

"Heavens, next time I will tell you over dinner."

"Oh, yes, next time. I do love the idea of a next time," Gilbert said, climbing up her skirts to kiss her one less too many times.

Paris, September 1779

Receiving over the summer: a painting of General Washington that Gilbert had commissioned. It offered quite the talking piece for visitors to the Hôtel de Noailles while France was increasing its speed to organize an army to depart for American shores. It seemed to follow the bustle of patriotism, joining everyone in Monsieur Franklin's home for the anniversary of the Declaration of Independence, and moving from the salon to the dining room so that everyone over dinner could see and enjoy it. Adrienne saw Washington more than her husband in the last three months, her loneliness ebbed only by her sisters and the gallantly painted man to whom she spoke about Gilbert like a senile old woman.

Gilbert desperately wanted to be named commander of the French army en route to America; his letters scored essays on why he would be the best suited for the role, ignoring the fact that there were plenty of men who outranked him in France. Despite the doubt that Adrienne had for the ministers to grant him that honor, she still wrote back to him of her unwavering faith. He would make a wonderful commander.

Louise provided her support in wishing Gilbert the best of luck telling Louis what to do – a comment which received his utmost praise in that he was already beginning to break the vicomte in to the idea. On occasion, within the margins of Gilbert's letters, there were crass doodles from Louis showing his light displeasure at the prospect.

Monsieur Franklin's grandson had shown her a sword that the American congress had commissioned for Gilbert, a beautiful silver thank-you with encrusted Latin and French, including the la Fayette motto: *Cur non?* Many letters from Havre arrived after it was sent to him about his adoration for it, how it was permanently attached to his side now in lieu of his old. Adrienne couldn't help but be amused at the present, like he was now married to the United States and this was their wedding gift. She wrote to him to be careful of the bigamy, she would have to fight hard to reach the glory that America had in his heart.

Every day passed with at least one line coming from the family's trio of gentlemen that the Noailles sisters still gathered in their mother's room to read them to each other, omitting any marital details that may have weaseled their way into Louis' letters to Louise.

They had not tried for a baby this year. Louise was too concerned about the on and off cold she was fighting and Louis was altogether fine with dallying elsewhere to let her rest. Adrienne's Aunt Elisabeth and her now uncle-Ségur had produced the *future* Comte de Ségur, a rather chubby baby who they named Octave-Henri. Elisabeth brought him with her to the Hôtel to show off to the Duchesse d'Ayen and the girls, with her little daughter, Laure, in the arms of her governess. Anastasie chewed on a handkerchief by Adrienne's feet, content watching while she teethed. She would look up whenever Gilbert's name was mentioned in conversation, murmuring into the fabric before she tugged on Adrienne's skirt for attention.

She wished she could give Anastasie more of her time, but fatigue struck her hard almost nightly, and she found herself half-asleep on Louise or Pauline's shoulder during their chats. Pauline had taken to being an auntie with the intensity of a man at war, playing with Anastasie when Adrienne could not, including tiny sword fights with Anne during dinners with legumes acting as the dueling weapon.

"I enjoy the children," Pauline had said, echoing Anne's sentiments, "it is the majority of men that make me gag at the idea of them."

Men were obnoxious and didn't like when women were smarter than them, she argued, which was difficult to provide a counterpoint to when Louis arrived back from his training a month earlier than everyone else, flipping and tossing the coattails to his new Soissonnais uniform. He had been given a rank of colonel in the regiment, making him second-in-command of the famous armed force, and all that awaited was the official appointment of the French general.

There was no way that Louis would act the way he did at home in front of his superiors, Adrienne thought, he was too venerated in the papers he had on hand for the elders to realize how much of an oaf he really was. Lovingly: *an oaf.*

The evening he arrived and the ladies were enjoying their tea and sewing, Louis bent to where Adrienne laid back on the sofa and supplied her with a soft kiss to her cheek.

"That's from the Marquis," he said, before moving on to Louise to supply his kisses. "He should be back well before your birthday, Adri, so no need to look so mopey. I am sure he will bring you a garden of flowers or *la Manche* or the ship he's been staring at for weeks hoping his little raid with Captain Jones would be granted, but ah," he shrugged, "he only gets that luck when he is on foreign shores." Louis twisted in a circle to regard all of his cousins. "I'm surprised Ségur has not joined you all. He's been getting in touch with his feminine nature, I was expecting him to produce me a new waistcoat or whatnot with embroidery and embellishment…"

"The only thing he would embroider you would be a phallus," Anne said, and Louise choked on her drink.

"That is not appropriate, Anne, watch your mouth! God forbid Maman was in here to hear that from you of all people." Louise gave Adrienne discerning wide eyes, expecting her to step in like a parent to add to the scolding, but Adrienne was hiding a grin behind her circle. Ségur would indeed do such a thing.

Louis puffed out his cheeks. "If only France knew how awful we Noailles are," he said with an exaggerated shake of his head. "Do we deserve to be called nobility when we embroider genitalia onto weskits?"

"Louis, stop it," Louise hushed. She reached out to slap at his passing behind. Rosalie, Pauline, and Anne divulged into a fit of giggles.

"We could color it like a cute, little mushroom," Pauline added under her breath, so that her little sisters gasped for air behind their covered faces.

"Rosalie, if you add another comment, I swear," Louise said.

"I didn't even say anything!" Rosalie slapped her sewing to her lap, mouth agape. "You cannot yell at me when I didn't say anything."

"I am not yelling. I'm just telling you not to add to your deranged sisters' conversation."

"I wasn't going to!"

"Adrienne, are you really going to leave me to be the adult here?"

Adrienne nibbled on her bottom lip and shoved her needle through the fabric. If she made eye-contact with Louise, she would break the well-practiced composure she worked so hard on. Louis poured himself a drink from the tray along the wall, glancing at her from over the glass' rim with a wink. It was different to see him in an army uniform that did not belong to the family. The thought of him and Gilbert leaving with thousands of Frenchmen in tow, where it should have brought some sense of national pride, only started digging a deeper pit into her stomach. Adrienne offered him her smile instead, and Louis took it graciously, his laugh shaking the wine in his cup.

☆

When Gilbert returned from the coast, Adrienne buried her worry into his chest. He smelled like salt, his cheeks burned from the wind that grew colder by the day. But his bosom was warm and his arms cupped around her, holding her head to his heart. She counted every beat.

"I've missed you," he said, nuzzling his nose into her hair that was curled and pinned to the top of her head. "How have you been faring?"

"He's been gentle, but takes all my energy," she complained, holding her belly as his hands moved down to find hers. "Some days I find it hard to get out of bed."

"*He?*"

"It has to be a son, your daughters didn't exhaust me so much," Adrienne mumbled into his coat, locking her fingers around his. She could hear his smile. "Will you come to bed with me early tonight?"

Gilbert hummed. "I have a short meeting about loans soon this afternoon, but I will rush headlong back to the bedchambers, I promise. To run with such speed, they shall be picking my shoes and shirt from the hallway floor." He took a step back, but Adrienne merely shuffled forward with him, the two shuffling through the parlor in a young lovers' embrace. Upon walking by, the Duchesse d'Ayen simply sighed loudly.

"You two are worse than Monsieur Ségur," her Maman said, taking her books into the library.

Gilbert guffawed, picking his head up from Adrienne's hair. "I'm sure there are stories tied to that. Has he been torturing the poor duchesse's sister that much?"

"He sings your praises, don't go teasing him," Adrienne said, as they continued shuffling down the hall, passing the grand painting of General Washington. She looked up at it, to the face that occupied much of her husband's thoughts and of her private soliloquies. "Has he returned your letters?" she asked as Gilbert stared at the portrait.

"Not as much as I would like," he said. "Though I blame the miscarriages. There is no way he would not drop me one line. I wrote one last letter to him before I returned here about d'Estaing's West Indian exploits among other matters. I made copies if you would like to read them. If you are to be a good American wife, it is best that their interests you continue to make your own."

Adrienne nodded, she had already expressed those prominent American values her husband preached in her own salons with guests to the Hôtel. Many times, with the emboldened hearts of the French citizens, she found it much easier to lead conversations about Gilbert's beliefs on slavery in the Americas, the intermingling of people of all nations, and their willpower to continue fighting despite the odds. She wouldn't brag to Gilbert, nor anyone else, of her little fame in Paris and Court, but she was handling their attention far better now that he was back.

Her nail was drawing a little line in the wool of his frock. "Will he come here, you think – General Washington, I mean?" she asked.

Gilbert huffed through his nose. "I have told him thousands of times that we would welcome him most graciously. He knows of my love, and I have informed him of yours as well, *mon coeur*, I shall take great insult if he declines."

"Ah, but you would forgive him right away," Adrienne said, wrapping her arms around his neck. He drew down to kiss her, bumping her nose with his.

"Don't call me out so easily; you are like Hamilton," Gilbert said. Adrienne made a motion to bite his nose that he dodged.

"Then your Hamilton sees you for how you are," she laughed. "He should visit as well. I'd love to host your friends. I want to ask them for all the stories about you that you do not share."

"I tell you everything!"

"No, you don't," she said, "not the things you don't notice you do. And Gilbert, you should know you do a *lot* that you don't notice."

Gilbert scrunched his lips and shook his head.

"Like that expression you're giving me."

"What expression? This is my face."

He tucked his arms under her rear, squatting only to lift her up with a dramatic grunt. Carrying two people was his threshold, and he wobbled them further down the hallway where he could plop her on the second step of the staircase. "I will not risk killing us all challenging God by bringing you two up. Now, go pamper yourself, *amour*, I can bring you dinner and kisses and desserts of course when these old men leave."

"I'll take my time then, because I know *you know* I know that you'll get carried away in talking with them."

Gilbert put his hands on his hips. "Then I shall look forward to surprising you when you are in the bath if I am lucky enough." He walked his fingers down the curve in her stays. "This one won't be long, I swear. The gentlemen find me very persuasive so I doubt that any argument will be had."

"Papa," Anastasie appeared at the top of the stairs, gripping onto the railing like she was taught when she wanted to come down. Adrienne turned on her heel and hurried to stop her rogue daughter from trying to reach them first.

"We're going to have to get her another leading string to stop her from wandering off," Adrienne said, picking Anastasie up.

"Or little bells so we hear her coming," Gilbert said, skipping every other step to kiss the girl on the forehead. "Forgive your papa, sweetling, he will be back in a few hours."

"You read to me?" Anastasie asked, catching one of his sleeve buttons.

"Yes, of course, I will. Whatever you wish, I will do it."

Adrienne adjusted her hip. "Be prepared for the same story we've been reading all month."

Gilbert smiled. "Ah, but it is new to me, so I will read it a thousand more times for my girls. *Adieu, adieu*, I shall return to you both."

He wasn't leaving the manor, he was hardly leaving the hallway as the salon was just down the stretch of portraits and sculptures, but as soon as he was out of sight, her heart cramped. Yet, she simply sighed and nibbled softly on Anastasie's round cheeks to elicit her giggling and squirming. Not having Gilbert again for an hour or so wouldn't be too strenuous as long as Anastasie was near.

"Have you been practicing your letters?" Adrienne asked, bringing her down the hall to their apartments.

"Done *M*," she replied. "For Maman! And Mo… Mot…" She babbled slightly trying to pronounce *Motier*, but all the same, she was sure to get the name across.

Adrienne smiled, bouncing her on her hip for a few strides. "That's fantastic! I'm so proud of you, my smart girl. Wait until Papa hears how smart you are! What do you think, should we surprise him when he gets back?"

Anastasie nibbled on her fingers as she smiled and nodded. Her mischief was a dangerous mix of her parents to be wary of.

Paris, December 24th, 1779

"Will Maman be well?" Anastasie asked, holding her hands to her ears. Her eyes glossed over with tears as Adrienne's cries flooded the Hôtel de Noailles.

Gilbert took a drink from Louis this time, wiping his mouth with his thumb. He didn't recall Henriette's birth being so hard, and he missed Anastasie's but was told it was *fast* at least. This had dragged on for hours in bursts – the clock on the wall ticking past midnight: Christmas Eve. Anastasie could not sleep, having run into his room bawling in fear. He wrapped her in his banyan and moved to pace the room where, once again, all the men of the family gathered with their cigars and liquor, chatting amongst each other like Adrienne could not be in danger of dying several rooms away.

"Maman is the strongest woman I know, sweetling, but we must be brave for her, understand?" Gilbert said. He could be brave; he was a general, *dammit*, he had seen men die with limbs missing, others covered in their own shit and vomit… but none of it now compared to his Adrienne. He wouldn't know what he would do if the worst happened. The idea as it crossed his mind the first time *should* have resulted in the prospect of having to remarry, but it didn't, he couldn't contemplate marrying any other woman. Adrienne had been his girl since they were children, he…

He just wouldn't.

The second glass of whatever it was that Louis poured him burned harder. His thoughts were louder than the usual conversations of the Maréchal and duc, although now they looked on him with more fondness than they did before. His own uncles arrived a few minutes into the holiday, dressed nicely despite the late hour. Gilbert balanced Anastasie in his arm as Lusignem grasped his other hand in a tight shake before the familiar pinch to his shoulder followed. Maybe it was meant to be more reassuring, but nothing about the additional pain was assuring at all.

"She's going to pull through," Louis whispered as Gilbert passed him again. His pacing was lulling Anastasie to sleep. At least *someone* could try and rest.

The room paused as they heard footsteps hurrying down the hallway, only for it to be Pauline grabbing more water. She had made the run five times already, if she were a young man with a sword, one could think she was drilling.

"I doubt labor will last another twenty-four hours, so it's lucky this one doesn't have a Christmas day birth. So much mass, not enough celebration." Louis stuck his leg out to try and stop him from running a path through the rug, but Gilbert stepped over it. "Gilbert, there's nothing you can do, sit down before you hurt yourself."

He set the empty glass down a little too hard, he heard the rim chip. The wound in his calf, despite being healed for two years, panged like phantom pain, an unsteady pulse that pushed him to limp back over to the sofa and stare at Louis, whose joking manner had subsided and left behind a sober frown.

"Sit," Louis commanded. "I'm going to war with you in America, Brother, let me be at war with you here." He pulled his robe aside for Gilbert to carefully fall into with his daughter enveloped against his chest. Her hand was curled around his cravat and those soft brunette brows twitched slightly at the movement, but settled. Louis pulled Gilbert's banyan further over her sleeping form. "I'll take her back to the room when you go," he said.

"Thank you," Gilbert whispered. He stared ahead at the fireplace, seeing the campfires that soldiers huddled around for warmth through the biting winters in Albany, burning through wood faster than if they simply lit the forest aflame. Too cold, too lonely, all the things soldiers hate in war when they would rather die on the battlefield with their brethren; Gilbert felt it all coming back to him like a frozen wind slapping him in the face. He didn't see Louis put his glass on the table and throw his arm around behind him, but his shoulder hit his brother-in-law's as Louis tightly gripped his arm. Gilbert relaxed into the hold.

"Well damn," Louis said, his chin atop Gilbert's head. "Just when I thought we'd have some peace, Ségur is here."

"You're so kind, Noailles," Ségur replied, walking around to shake Gilbert's hand. "Hello my favorite friend and nephew. Sorry I'm late; my steward took his time retrieving the carriage."

"Welcome to my agony," Gilbert said as further cries echoed down the hall. "Please make yourself comfortable. There is a very strong drink somewhere on that table…" He gestured vaguely to where the older men settled into a silent conversation.

"*Bah*, I don't need anything." Ségur sat on the couch on Gilbert's other side, his eyes settling on Anastasie before they crinkled. "Goodness, you and the Madame produce some beautiful offspring."

"It's because she is beautiful," Gilbert replied plainly, his eyes growing red.

There was a moment of silence before Ségur's hand settled in a gentle clap over Gilbert's knee. The three of them huddled in a sheltered snowstorm, surrounded by gilded gold and velvet rather than whittled trees and old canvas tents. Ségur was already in the army for years – his attained command in the Regiment d'Orléans was passed down his family line.

His two French Colonels.

"You know, Marquis," Ségur said, "this American experiment we are readying for… I hope we may be of merit to you and its outcomes."

"You are already of great merit to me," Gilbert replied. He broke off his trance with the fire and pressed his hand over his old friend's. "We will find glory in creating the foundation of a new republic. What other Frenchman could say such a thing?"

"As long as I hear the singing of praises to my name as heroes when we return," Louis said. "It isn't fair you've earned that so easily."

"'*Easily*,'" Gilbert repeated with a shake of his head. "I'll shoot you in the leg when you land in America and we will see where you go from there."

"If we can achieve the goals of enlightenment for the Americans, what do you think of bringing it back here to France? Imagine," Louis said, though his thoughts drifted off into contemplative silence. It was a good distraction, Gilbert could think about his American brothers for hours, their work and struggles and accomplishments that he could help introduce to the court and to the French people.

Over the distant chatter of women down the hall, Ségur pulled a pamphlet from his coat pocket. "Shall I read to you both the most recent of Monsieur Diderot's thoughts?"

Gilbert listened, flinching only when the shouts grew more constant and loud as the clock ticked into one-thirty... two in the morning. He longed for sleep, but his mind would not let him. Images of Adrienne intermingled in his imagination of living in the American countryside, settling somewhere in Virginia close to his general, or attending the small theatre productions there with her, planting a garden, becoming humble farmers. Adrienne would look perfect standing in a field of golden wheat and unexplored green hills rolling behind her. She can let her hair down there, let the sun warm her face. They could run and fall in the grass in their shifts; he could show her how the fireflies dance above the forest floors like fae, make love under America's celestial bodies...

The Duc d'Ayen broke off the daydreaming as he walked through the room. Not even he was as composed as he usually was. The young trio lifted their heads as the sounds of steady clicking heels down the hall arose. Louis grabbed Anastasie from her father, her hands easily gripping to her uncle's cravat instead, as Gilbert stood up from the sofa. His hands were clammy, his heart was in his throat. The duc stopped when the door opened to his secretary, and Monsieur Dameron, growing prematurely gray at his roots, stopped in the opening, presenting the company with a polite bow.

"Congratulations, Monsieur Marquis, on the birth of your son."

A boy. He had a son to carry on his name.

Gilbert did not know what to do with himself as the men around him bustled with excitement and approval, several hands clasped his shoulders, his neck, his arms. Perhaps this was how the late Marquis de la Fayette felt when Gilbert was born: his skin buzzing, existing like a dandelion that could be blown away at the slightest touch. He slipped away from it all, stepping into the hall to follow the panes of wood to the bedchamber. There was no running, not this time – he walked as if he were aboard a ship, careful on the deck not to be thrown sideways and off into the depths of the ocean. The duchesse waited for him, as she always did, with a bundle already in her arms.

Why was it not in his Adrienne's?

He treated the duchesse with a kiss before he was handed the wrapped baby. The head was perfectly round, a dimple on his lips that made him look like a tiny, carved cherub. Far more appealing than Gilbert was as an infant. He cradled the babe higher, his cheeks already warm at how perfect this child was. Being led into the room, he was greeted by the entourage of the Noailles sisters as their mother escorted them out – their tired faces smiling as they curtsied to him and passed along their embraces. Truly the kindest sisters Gilbert could ask for. Louise kissed his cheek.

Madame d'Ayen smoothed out the bed while a servant collected the wet and bloodied towels. A doctor quietly collected the rest of his things, giving Gilbert a courteous bow before leaving the chamber. The father stood holding his son, merely watching the people pass with the buckets and the afterbirth and trays of diluted wine. He watched his mother-in-law tuck back the hair of his wife, who lay silently in the center of the bed, paler than he had ever seen her before.

He approached without his shoes, leaving them where he had stood. Too afraid to touch her, but too desperate not to, he fell at the bedside to his knees, never taking his eyes from her. The baby mumbled under his breath, a little hiccup, a second of blinking to look up at his papa before he fell back asleep.

Adrienne stirred slightly, her face turning to them as an exerted smile formed. Gilbert's breath left his lips.

"Mon coeur."

"We did it," she whispered.

"You are perfection," Gilbert replied, letting their son rest on the mattress between them in the curve of his arm. He took her hand in his other. "I love you so much."

Her smile split, a shadowed brown eye gracing Gilbert at last. "I love you too." She took a deep breath. "What would you like to name him?"

Gilbert adjusted himself now, sliding into the bed as a well-practiced man slipping under his wife's sheets. He could feel the wet warmth through his stockings, but he couldn't care enough to mind, content holding Adrienne and their son. Brushing away the sweat along her forehead, he gave the infant a long lookover.

"I had a thought," he said, "on the chance we did have a boy."

"For your father…"

Gilbert cocked his head. "Michel would be a fine name."

"No," Adrienne breathed, the lightest laugh in her tone. "Your American father."

Ah. Gilbert blushed. She knew him too well.

"Little Georges," she said, brushing a pinkie down the baby's nose. Gilbert was so still in listening to her breathe, a part of him longed to call for the doctor to return to assure him that Adrienne was going to recover well.

"If you'd like," Gilbert said, combing his fingers through her hair, "Abbé Murat can baptize Georges tomorrow, that is, Christmas day. I think that would be auspicious – a very holy day for our boy." Very carefully, he allowed Georges to be taken by the duchesse and laid in a prepared cradle by their bedside. "I'd like to lay with you tonight if you don't mind. And all morning thereafter. The family can begin celebrations but I will wait for you to be fully rested and restored to your full glory."

"Mm, my *glory*," she said, "lying in my filth. Let them get you a chaise so you won't smell horrid with me." She tried to raise her hand to get the duchesse to summon one, but Gilbert held it back and waved his mother-in-law away politely.

"I think you smell delicious," he replied, firmly laying back to stake his claim as master of the bed and his wife and child mere renters. "Better than a soldier, I'd say." He kissed the top of her head, feeling the slight fall of her cheek on his chest as she started to nod off once more.

"Thank you for being here," Adrienne said into his heart.

Gilbert wiggled himself down further until he could kiss her nose and lips. "I am always at your service, Madame."

"Here in France. I'm happy I could have you, even if for a short time."

Oh how she could twist the knife he gave her; the terrible line between leaving her again and returning to the fight he longed for. He closed his eyes, wrapping his arms under hers, breathing her in. Four years had passed since he was able to do this, and how four years have flown by.

"I will not be gone long, *mon coeur*," he said, "and I do not leave you yet. I will be here through all the cold days, like a blanket to keep you warm, your knight to keep you safe…"

"You keep talking," Adrienne mumbled, clearly trying to sleep.

"It is part of my charm," Gilbert replied. "I'll keep going until you hear me comfort you in your dreams."

The fireplace cracked as a servant silently added another log, their shadow disappearing into the stretches of darkness in the room. He thought of the chance to wash Adrienne this time in the morning, to card his fingers through her hair and massage her back, steal some soapy kisses, maybe hold her breast.

Gilbert pursed his lips, his hand shifting back and up a few inches to cup one.

Ah, there we go, he thought.

Georges gurgled his assent from his cradle – a young man of good taste, Gilbert mused, definitely his son to be certain.

Chapter Seventeen

Rochefort, March 1780

Adrienne had seen to escorting Gilbert to the harbor this time, white-knuckling his arm as they watched the docked ships come into view from the small window of their carriage. His shoulders were stiff since they departed Versailles, his farewell to the king in his American Major-General uniform, with the sword Congress gave him by his side, warranted the silence it wrought. Gilbert was not selected to lead the French army to America – that honor fell to the Comte de Rochambeau, a decorated veteran who deserved it as any other. Still, Gilbert felt a little slighted, and Adrienne knew when he saw how dearly his American brothers and General loved him, his spirits would be raised.

He was sailing weeks before the French forces were scheduled to depart, bearing with him the responsibility of informing the Continental army of their ally's imminent arrival with a number not even Adrienne was privy to.

She smelled the scent that so often stuck to her husband's wool clothes: the salt and wood and musk that carried on the breeze. If she could only keep the smell inside a locket, she would keep it safe within her pocket to bring with her everywhere. Instead, she had wrapped a small curl of *her* hair inside of one, and placed it carefully within Gilbert's pocket. He kept his hand tightly clasped around hers as the carriage bustled over the cobblestone streets with his luggage in tow, his thumb rubbing against the soft of her skin.

The *Hermione* looked like a sturdy vessel, which it better have been, else Adrienne would challenge the heavens to a duel herself. There were a few men of which she became acquainted with, those of the Americans who traveled with their General to France, and a few columns of sanctioned Frenchmen. All had the blessing of Louis XVI to depart this time, their faces reflected the pride and excitement to get underway; save for Gilbert's whose excitement was still shrouded with wounded honor.

"Your American troops will adore having you back," Adrienne said as the carriage stopped. She held the growing Anastasie to her side, the almost three-year-old was curious to explore the harbor. "I can hear the reception now," she added, cheering softly into his ear before she gave it a little nibble.

Gilbert took his hat from the opposite seat, bending his neck to escape the tickle and extracted immediate revenge on her ear. "If it were not war, I would take you with me," he murmured.

"And me!" Anastasie said, crawling across Adrienne's lap into Gilbert's. She flung her arms up and over his epauletted shoulders, planting a kiss to his freshly shaven jaw. "Take me with you, Papa. You will, won't you?"

"Ah, my sweetling," Gilbert's brows pulled tightly. "You're the only one I trust to be the greatest big sister to Georges. Your Maman and I rely too greatly on you."

"No! Take me, Papa," Anastasie shouted. Her grip grew tighter, catching on Gilbert's queue. But her father was a patient man for the ladies, and Adrienne needed not rip her off of him; he pulled her into a gentle hug, his hand on her back.

The carriage door opened to the friendly face of Abbé Fayon – the man who first accompanied Gilbert to Adrienne and now was to be the one to assure her safety home as Gilbert left her. Gilbert stepped out first, with his daughter still holding onto his uniform and hair, and assisted Adrienne with descending the carriage step.

No man had regarded her with more respect than the gentlemen making up the *Hermione's* passengers and crew; to that she lent to the venerated figure of her husband at her arm, as they removed their hats and bowed their heads. All the cargo had been loaded, minus the remaining men who basked a little while longer in the sun on the solid footing of earth. General la Fayette would also be one of those men, never faring well on sea voyages, but he loitered by her side in keeping his promise to her.

"I already miss you," he exclaimed, bringing her fingers to his lips. "I will write you and the family as soon as I port in Boston, and every opportunity I can afterwards."

"Send His Excellency my most tender affections. He must know I think of him as a father as you do," Adrienne said. She smoothed the folded sash around his waist, its color matching the gown she wore under her cloak.

"If I were a painter, I would capture his expression when I tell him of his namesake."

"But you are a poet, so I will wait for that portrait in your words."

"Don't go," Anastasie mumbled into his neck.

"Hug me tighter, dear Anastasie," he replied, "so that I may feel it for every day of my journey." She must have, for he made an exaggerated groan to praise her strength. The quartermaster shouted from the ship as the rest of the men began to board, but Gilbert still held onto Anastasie with all of his might. From over her shoulder, he looked at Adrienne with glossy eyes. "Take care of each other," he ordered.

"As long as you are safe, so are we," Adrienne replied, pulling his face to hers. His skin had smoothed during his time at home, back to the care that the court-life gave to many noblemen. Another few years; she acquiesced to the pain and longing it would cause, content to dreaming of his return. "I've snuck some macarons into your luggage for the trip."

"You are the greatest wife," Gilbert laughed, nibbling on her lip until Anastasie was tactically swapped into her arms.

"I know," she said, and she didn't cry, she wouldn't cry. She stared up at the sky to keep the tears in her eyes. If she could hold onto him a little longer while his men brought his trunks and supplies on board, it wouldn't be unreasonable in etiquette standards. No man here would dare call them out on excessive displays of affection, she would take the sword from Gilbert's belt and start swinging if they did.

There went her American hero, the awkward, lanky French boy who broke and fumbled everything he touched, off to lead armies of men who loved him. He looked better in the blue than the white, he was glowing. He followed up the gangplank, his knuckles protruding as he gripped the wooden rail of the ship. The details of his face were so small from where Adrienne stood with Anastasie and Abbé Fayon, but she could see his smile.

"Madame," Fayon said from behind. "Shall I prepare a room for you to stay the night?"

She watched the ship until Gilbert disappeared from her view, whispering prayer after prayer for a safe voyage. "That would be best, Monsieur," she said. "I think he would like us to see him off."

Fayon comfortably folded his hands behind his back. "He's come a long way, hasn't he?"

Adrienne smiled sadly. So much of the way was without her. "Yes, he has," she replied, helping Anastasie wave goodbye to her papa.

☆

The following two months, the Comte de Rochambeau and his army of several thousand soldiers boarded ships in the harbor of Brest. Among them was the Noailles' vicomte, dressed in a finely pressed uniform, his sword by his side. His departure from the Hôtel was no less teary than Gilbert's, but he was invigorated to leave, the metal adorning him bouncing with every step. He carried with him a bag full of letters from several members of the family, by the American delegation, by the French ministers… By the time Louis launched with the French army, it was very likely Gilbert had already landed in the American state of Massachusetts, the cities and land described in as much detail as Monsieur Adams could relay of it in his sorry excuse for French. Nevertheless, he tried, and Adrienne appreciated every word of it.

Her hosting of American figures continued, and although her grasp of the English tongue continued to be strained, her vocabulary grew word by word, until she was at least able to delight her guests with a simple English sentence here and there. Their praise for her efforts were perhaps excessive, Adrienne knew she didn't speak it well, but there they were: a salon full of those who spoke the other's language poorly, but attempted anyway. With skill she did have, she managed to persuade them to drink hot chocolate as a treat instead of their coffee, sitting content with her power of persuasion as the Americans delighted at the pleasure.

Still too early for letters. She leaned back into the job of a mother, making sure Anastasie was schooling well and that Georges remained healthy. He was the spitting image of his father, comparable to the little portraits that Gilbert had shared with her of him in his youth, more youthful than the teenager that she first met. Georges had the complexion of a to-be ginger if his cheeks were any hint of it, always rosy, especially red when he laughed. And he laughed a lot. The Duchesse d'Ayen enjoyed holding him, complimenting on how well-behaved he was. Anastasie liked hugging him from behind whenever the little family settled on the floor for a book or a song.

While it was maddeningly cute, it also prevented Georges from rolling away from them. The House of la Fayette had a knack for being restless.

Versailles, July 1780

"Perhaps it would be best if we had someone bring the poor Baron here with those drinks, the man is past the point of no return," Marie-Antoinette said from her seat in the theatre box. She and Adrienne watched the older gentleman struggle, drunk himself, while bringing the ladies the exotic wine he recently purchased from a Chinese tradesman in the city.

The theatre they sat in, although as luxurious as the ones in Paris, was only recently completed, hidden amongst the queen's makeshift countryside estate. Its blue walls were welcoming and gold sculpted statues looked legitimate despite being made of paper. A light perfume settled into the air, the cushions of the chairs were too new to have soaked in decades of oils and wine, and the orchestra was winding up like an approaching storm.

"It would wound his honor if another were to offer help," Adrienne replied, picking at the fruit platter placed between them. She hadn't spent much time in Her Majesty's company alone in the past few months – not that attending an opera was meant to be alone, but the queen certainly took notice and Adrienne had not left her side since the levée that morning. "But if, perchance, the Marquis de Cernait simply took them in a friendly manner, I believe the Baron would find it a relief."

Marie-Antoinette hummed her consent, reaching her fan back to tap the pruning gentleman behind her. "Henri, be a dear and fetch those glasses for the Marquise and myself, we're shriveling like these grapes," she said, picking one green one from the vine. They were fresh and full, naturally, perfectly shiny and plump.

Adrienne looked down at the simple yellow linen jacket she wore with its tiny eggshell blue stripes; the pearl earrings were a thousand times lighter than the crystals and gemstones of court. No one imagined it was the undressed, informal style that Marie-Antoinette preferred amongst her intimate company; the imagined dress of the working class and peasantry permeated the Trianon grounds. The queen herself looked quite pastoral in her blues and whites. Such was the theme, when the performance began and a quaint shepherdess walked on the stage, her voice high and twiddling.

Adrienne was careful in her spending of her husband's money – that said, he had a fair amount of it. His lawyer had informed them earlier in the year of the serfs that still worked on the land he owned in Brittany and Tourraine as he went to retrieve more of his sums to fund his American war efforts. However, after hearing how much the Americans struggled to keep shoes on their soldiers' feet, she felt terrible splurging on mere silk to dress herself in. And France alone was spending an exuberant amount of money on aiding them.

She looked at the profile of the queen, to the constructed display around them.

Surely, Marie-Antoinette had cut corners with this theatre as well. She was not blind to the financial burden that continued to climb.

Or was she?

There were a few things Adrienne noted that pinched and prodded on her mind. Not all faults were with her fellow country folk, as she eyed the Americans with ample judgment too. Often, they avoided the edict King Louis X passed hundreds of years prior, declaring that any slave that stepped on French soil was *free*. And so, she bore witness to them renting out enslaved servants in their time in Paris, leaving the people they owned on board ships. She was not blind to Marie-Antoinette's treatment of the Chevalier de Saint-Georges, the mulatto composer; her word absolved his chances of rising in the Paris music scene. Adrienne knew by God's word – and by sheer common sense – that even the subtle acts were as abhorrent as the grand displays of racial prejudice. She would bite her tongue until it bled to keep from saying something to the queen about it, a horror in its own right, she admitted. If she thought about the stories Gilbert shared with her of the Black soldiers of Rhode Island, or the valet of General Washington, and their valiant and chivalric character, she thought, perhaps when he returned, they may do something to help them after the war was won.

Only God could see the turmoil stirring inside of Adrienne's otherwise perfectly still form. She clapped when the queen clapped, and fanned her face as the summer night's heat squeezed her from all sides.

It couldn't have been likely that she was the only noblewoman who had noticed all these things; they lived in the era of growing enlightenment – something could be done. She twisted a strawberry between her teeth, a little idea bubbling in her mind. There were some people to write to, she thought, but it would take some time. Emancipation would be a fine thing to put their money towards, and definitely something Gilbert would approve of.

Lambs were led onto the stage with the arrival of what Versailles thought a day in a working woman's life was like, full of color and ribbons and dance.

There was a woman on the roadside that flashed into Adrienne's memory from her journey back from Rochefort. It was a few days' ride going through much of the western country. The woman was incredibly filthy, her petticoat must have been brown or black for there was no other color to it but the dirt and grime; the bedgown she wore under a pieced together apron was worn away enough to see her shift underneath. A prickly rope led a goat behind her while she balanced a bucket on her hip.

As the carriage ambled by the woman, there came a low note from her: a song, like no one else was around her, carrying over the fields. It was haunting to hear. Adrienne sat further back in the carriage, holding her sleeping daughter as if they were all caught up in a dream. *That* was the French countryside shepherdess Adrienne saw – not this pastel lady on stage before her.

"You haven't tried this yet, Madame," Marie-Antoinette said, holding the arrived glass of clear Chinese wine. "It's definitely a strong one," she laughed. Thrusted into Adrienne's hands, the liquid had no smell, like a drink to oblivion.

Chapter Eighteen

⸎

Passy, March 1781

Sometimes, when Adrienne was invited to afternoon tea with Monsieur Franklin, he let her read his correspondence with his American friends, and at all times except where Intelligence was concerned, his letters with her husband. It was becoming easier to find the English words that she memorized when the writing was neat and clear, but also evident that many of his lady friends from the colonies were not as well educated on grammar as she was. Another thing she thanked her mother for among the long list of privileges granted to her. However, it was sweet to see the life of a woman so different from herself, but also incredibly close – this Catharine was, too, a young wife of an American general, the name Greene stirring Adrienne's memory of a patriotic man Gilbert loved dearly.

Whispering some English words to herself over the steaming cup, Franklin's grandson, Temple, made himself busy around the aging man. Monsieur Franklin's gout was always paining him after the week's end, Sunday allowing ample rest. He took up an armchair by the open window. The breeze was a little chilly, but refreshing, and *healthy* according to him. Adrienne sat on the edge of a sofa, keeping the papers organized by sliding a corner under the folds of her petticoat. Franklin seemed happy to help correct her pronunciation, the two amicably babbling like schoolchildren.

A knock at the door stirred Temple from the corner desk's chair. He hopped passed them, mumbling about the ill timing of arrivals, to disappear into the hallway.

"He's early," Franklin chuckled, glancing at the grand clock along the wall. Adrienne quietly collected the documents, looking from the man to the hall.

"Shall I leave you, Monsieur? I don't wish to interrupt a meeting –"

"No, no, my dear, I enjoy your company far more than my work. I suspect you also would like to stay to meet this particular young man." Franklin adjusted his posture, an attempt to sit up a little straighter as three pairs of shoes made their way into the room.

Temple Franklin pulled his waistcoat down as he cleared his throat. "Lieutenant Colonel Laurens and Major Jackson to see you, sir."

Adrienne peered over the edge of the sofa at the two men in American uniforms. They were both fair of hair, the one who bore the silver epaulettes, standing behind the other, styled his in the European way, fluffing around his ears and bagged in the back; his face was clear and soft like a baby's – he could not have been any older than Adrienne herself. The man in gold was definitely a few years older than Gilbert, and kept his hair natural in a simple queue that laid just past his shoulders. He was handsome, but did not look like he enjoyed breathing European air, let alone air at all.

"Doctor Franklin," he said with a curt bow of his head. "I've come with the disquisition of General Washington to give to the King, expressing the army's impertinent and immediate need for twenty-five-thousand..." His voice tapered off as a glance towards Adrienne turned into an outright stare. The younger man looked her way as well and pressed his lips together, hiding a quaint smile behind a subtle cough.

Adrienne lowered her gaze. She really shouldn't have stayed.

Franklin spared no expense for the man's propriety, leaning forward on his cane as it rested between his knees. "Colonel, you need not pause your mission statement I am sure you have practiced on your journey here on account of my guest."

"With all due respect, Your Excellency, it is of important matters of the *army*."

"I assure you, if there is any lady here in France who is with you in the cause of America, it is the Marquise," Franklin said, and turned to Adrienne. "Isn't that right, Madame de la Fayette?"

Adrienne swallowed, looking between the doctor and the soldiers. "That's right," she said in English, then quickly switched to French in a panic, "but I may leave if I must, I do not wish to intrude."

"Ah, *Madame!*" the younger of the men, Major Jackson, exclaimed. His eyes lit up and an elbow was sent into the Colonel's back as Laurens simply gawked at her. She was familiar with the time it took for some men to catch their thoughts up to their tongues, and she took no pleasure from the redness that occupied the blond man's cheeks.

Colonel Laurens' jaw clenched before his features softened. He pivoted on his heel and gave her a longer bow. "Forgive me, Madame Lafayette, I did not recognize you," he said, his French perfect. "I am afraid your miniature does not do you justice."

Gilbert showed her around. It was her turn to go red.

"Perhaps I shall have one done and send it with you to give to my husband?" she said.

Laurens flitted his hand back to Jackson, the two fumbling through the satchel at the younger's side before they produced a large packet of letters. He removed a thick one from the pile, flipping it over before he handed it to Temple to give to her. It was graced with Gilbert's handwriting. She noted the soldiers had silenced as she opened it.

The person who will deliver this to you, mon coeur, is a man I am greatly attached to, and whom I wish you to become intimate with. He is the son of President Laurens, who has been lately established in the Tower of London; he is lieutenant-colonel in our service, and aide-de-camp to General Washington; he has been sent by Congress on a private mission to the court of France. I knew him well during our two first campaigns, and his probity, frankness, and patriotism, have attached me extremely to him. General Washington is very fond of him; and of all the Americans whom you have hitherto seen, he is the one I most particularly wish you to receive with kindness. If I were in France, he should live entirely at my house, and I would introduce him to all my friends; and give him every opportunity in my power of making acquaintance, and of passing his time agreeably at Versailles; and in my absence, I entreat you to replace me. Introduce him to Madame d'Ayen, the Maréchal de Mouchy, the Maréchal de Noailles, and treat him in every respect as a friend of the family: he will tell you all that has occurred during our campaign, the situation in which we are at present placed, and give you all details relating to myself.

"He brags about you," she said aloud as she read. "You are Monsieur Laurens' son? I had written about him to Monsieur Vergennes this past October when I found out about his capture. I am sorry, Colonel, for such a horrible circumstance."

Laurens' brow raised. "Thank you, Madame. I did not know you knew him."

"I don't, not really. But he is important to your country, and so he is important to me. Some letters are the least I can do to help. And so it seems the Marquis wishes me to help you in any way I can as well." Her eyes quickly skimmed down the page of Gilbert's news about the French at Newport, Rhode Island, of Gilbert's favored Colonel Hamilton, of the American traitor, and all the trust that this Colonel Laurens here would relay to her all the information she pleased. Adrienne glanced back up to him – the man certainly did not look like he wished to be adopted by her family, but if it was Gilbert's wish to smother him in her company, who was she to refuse him?

Embrace our children a thousand and a thousand times for me. Their father, although a wanderer, is no less tender, no less constantly occupied with them, and no less happy at receiving news about them. My heart dwells with peculiar delight on the moment when those dear children will be presented to me by you, and when we may embrace and caress them together. Do you think that Anastasie will remember me?

"The Marquis is a good friend," Laurens said, "and speaks very highly of you as well."

"Well, goodness," Major Jackson said, "perhaps Doctor Franklin and the rest of us should be the ones to give you two privacy." He wheezed as a quick elbow jabbed him in the gut.

"Forgive my secretary, he's fresh from his mother's bosom."

"Aren't all secretaries," Franklin said, receiving a slow stare from his grandson.

"Have we slandered all the decorum in front of the Marquise now?" Temple exclaimed with a shake of his head.

Franklin huffed a laugh. "She has spent ample time in the company of Mister Adams, there is nothing she has heard worse than a Bostonian's temper. But ah, yes, Colonel Laurens, you will not find a better guide through the halls of Versailles than the Marquise. If you have not done your research, allow me to inform you that her family is famous in every corner of France and even within England."

Adrienne handed Temple the stack of his grandfather's letters.

"I am grateful for any introductions that can be made," Laurens said, looking back at Franklin, "as I hope to speak to King Louis as soon as possible."

"No one speaks directly to his Catholic Majesty," Franklin deterred. "It is ill advised for anyone to approach him without being summoned. I recommend you allow the Marquise to introduce you to the Comte de Vergennes. I can write up a letter of introduction as well, but I assume the Marquis de la Fayette has also already done so. He is your easiest way to reach the king's ear."

Adrienne stood from the sofa, signaling to Franklin that he may remain seated. "If I may be frank as well, Vergennes will already find it pleasing that you speak French, Colonel," she said with a smile.

Major Jackson cocked his head. "Perhaps it is not all pleasing if he can understand *everything* Colonel Laurens says."

Laurens turned around. "Should I have left you outside, sir?"

"No," Jackson replied, his eyes glimmering with tears of laughter. "Oh, *aha*, Doctor Franklin, sir, the Colonel had asked me to write you requesting a list of accounts for the shipments General Lafayette had ordered. Since we are here in person, it is my honor to inform you of this now." He winked at Adrienne and under his breath added to Laurens, "See, I'm a *fine* secretary."

"I'll start compiling the lists for you, Grandfather," Temple said, snatching the paper from Jackson. Franklin merely nodded. Laurens found a fine spot on the wall to bore a hole into.

Adrienne clicked her teeth together, somehow obliged to alleviate the growing awkward air. "Do you gentlemen have accommodations in Paris?"

"I believe Mister Paine is securing us a room for the time being, but Doctor Franklin will be unfortunate enough to see me many times in the following weeks," Laurens said.

"In your time at Court, allow me to welcome you to the Noailles' apartments, and of course here in Paris. What is ours is yours. My husband financed a small hôtel nearby, that although it is being rented out, will happily accommodate you, the Major, and any other staff you've brought with you."

"No staff, Madame," Laurens said with a polite wave. "I do not need anyone I cannot pay."

That's right – Gilbert mentioned Laurens as the one who abhorred the notion of slavery the most in Washington's military family. An odd conundrum, knowing his father brought a small entourage of enslaved servants with him to the Netherlands before he was captured, yet hopeful, in a way, that the Colonel — being from such a well-known family in the United States — wished for emancipation.

"But thank you for your offer. I do not wish to intrude upon your family."

"Gilbert will be angry if you do not," she argued.

Laurens opened his mouth, shut it, then replanted his feet on Franklin's fine wood floor. "Well then," he said, "I would hate to bring about the Marquis' fury for disobeying his wife."

☆

Colonel John Laurens was a little like the Noailles' Louis with his zeal and immense republican opinions, but without the familial immaturity that was allowed to the vicomte. Upon meeting with the Duchesse d'Ayen and Adrienne's grandfather, he spoke factually about the campaign, fighting in his home state, his capture, and time in Philadelphia that led him to being chosen as emissary. He wasn't as poetic as Gilbert was when describing action, but his discussion still brought about the horror that the Americans were facing and why it was so important that France send more money and supplies. He did not stay in the Hôtel for long as the evening grew into night, but agreed to allow Adrienne to meet him for his journey to Versailles, where she would visit with her father beforehand.

She felt a little weird being the bridge that helped Gilbert's dear friend navigate through Court. Too many eyes had already been on her, yet now with *another* American uniformed man whose arm her hand carefully rested on, *all* the eyes shifted. Laurens walked with her like he had been kicked in the back by a horse. She swore she could almost feel the uncomfortable static on his sleeve.

"May I ask you something, Colonel?" she said as they slowed their step in the halls of the palace. Laurens didn't move his head while he looked around at the decor and paintings – the overindulgence of France's nobility in plain sight. "I have been trying to culminate a plan to be a part of the emancipation movement, and was hoping to talk with my husband about it when he returned. If you could offer me your *opinion* on my idea, I'd feel greatly at ease. I admire your plan to have enlisted slaves freed for their service, and I think it would do well if, perhaps, the Marquis and I purchased a plantation somewhere and freed those who worked on it? Is that something you think would work well?"

Laurens crossed his arms, finally snapping to attention. "I admire the idea, although I am not certain many American farmers would agree to sell you land if you intend to grant the people freedom outright, even if you offer a lot of money, unfortunately."

Adrienne puffed her cheeks. "That is what my father said. A French colony, then. Slavery is still legal in my country's South American holdings."

"I think Gilbert will be in agreement with you. He's a smart man, hates the irony that America is privy to," Laurens said with a nod. "Perchance we will live long enough to see some change come to fruition."

"You're not too old, sir, I think it's very possible."

"*'Not too old,'* Madame, you wound me. I am but six-and-twenty."

"Gilbert has told me he, yourself, and Colonel Hamilton have gotten each other in and out of trouble on many occasions," she shared. As they continued their walk, she kept her hands to herself. "And that you two comfort him when he is melancholy."

Laurens rested his palm on the hilt of his sword. "He's a dear friend. I… and Hamilton, of course, love him very much."

Adrienne smiled. "It's comforting to know that. Thank you, for *all* you do. I admit that while he said goodbye this time, it still hurts not knowing his day-to-day business; meeting some of his closest friends makes me feel like I am with him there." She pointed out a few of the maréchals and ducs that spoke to each other in the alcoves, and the entourage that would normally follow the king on his hunting rides. "Do you have a wife, Monsieur?"

Laurens' cool demeanor shifted cold. "Of sorts."

Adrienne took upon her fan; *of sorts* wasn't the greatest reply to such a question. An unhappy marriage could be at one end, a dead wife at the other. She looked away towards the windows.

"She was in England last I heard of her. She and her daughter."

And *that* was the end of that topic, Adrienne decided, her mind emphasizing the othering of his child. Unhappy marriage indeed. She wondered what had happened, although would dare not ask.

"You know," she said instead, "Gilbert and I would often cause some mischief here in court, mostly between each other at the balls. He's shown up many a time in the Elizabethan ruff and codpiece to the queen's soirée with my cousin and his friends. Though I cannot imagine he would do such a thing in front of General Washington, I'm curious about his conduct in the army. What *exactly* was it you three got into?"

There was a smirk, she noticed, on Laurens' otherwise serious face.

"Truthfully, most times we simply sit under the stars and talk politics. Nothing to bore you with, Madame. And you know our commitment to General Washington; we would do anything to protect his honor from disrespectful slander. Let's just say that other generals find us a formidable force, a couple of rooks in a game of chess castling with the king."

"I didn't think you a metaphor-type of man."

"I spend too much time with wordsmiths, I'm afraid. It may be a redheaded quality, Hamilton and Lafayette could write letters that crossed the oceans."

She laughed. "That is true. I feel so guilty when I cannot write as much as he does."

Laurens eyed the ministers that swarmed like ducks from one door and waddled to another. "You could always do what I do whenever my Hamilton writes me long essays," he said, seeming to gravitate towards the men with only Adrienne to hold him back with some decorum.

"And what would that be, Monsieur?"

"Don't write back."

He delivered the response so smoothly, she almost missed his amusement with it. *Outrageous,* she thought, to not write Gilbert back at every opportunity she had when too many were already misplaced – ignoring the fact that she had, too, given her husband the silent treatment at times. Adrienne hopped several steps to keep up with Laurens' stride towards the ministers. She could already see the Comte de Vergennes' face shift through a theatre production of expressions as he looked the American soldier up and down before he glanced over to her. Laurens had another letter from Gilbert already in his hand – likely an introduction and whatever else Gilbert wished to say to Vergennes, which was definitely something of some length and importance.

"I can only imagine what your congress has sent you to ask of France," Vergennes said, politely stopping himself from escaping with the other ministers. The sixty-two year old man looked tired of his job of Foreign Minister, although he was the most qualified for the part, having been extremely well-traveled throughout Europe.

"Lieutenant Colonel John Laurens of the Continental army, aide-de-camp to His Excellency, General Washington," Laurens said, holding out his letter of introduction, which, at this point, was now just Gilbert's personal letter. Adrienne would have shrugged if she weren't a lady. Gilbert did not warn her of his friend's tenacity *continuing* on his diplomatic mission.

"I see," Vergennes replied, cracking the wax seal. His gaze fell upon Adrienne again and his head tilted slightly. "Marquise, a pleasure to see you."

"And you, Monsieur."

Vergennes looked long at the letter, holding it at arms length from his eyes. His left brow twitched skimming the words. There was no way he would read it in its entirety out of his office; Gilbert's hand scrawled several papers front and back.

"Ah, well," Vergennes said, folding the lot. "I will have to take the rest of this to my desk, but I'll have my secretary schedule a meeting to discuss the matters at hand."

"With respect, Monsieur, I am here now," Laurens replied.

"Here in the drawing room where other courtiers should not be privy to talks of money," he said, the smile not reaching his eyes. "With respect, Colonel Laurens, I have already spoken to Monsieur Franklin about France's numerous gifts to the United States."

"And now you will speak to me."

"Colonel Laurens, you arrived so *recently* from the American army that you forget you are no longer delivering the order of your Commander-in-Chief, but you are addressing the *minister* of a monarch."

Adrienne snapped her fan. Laurens was like Gilbert when he was angry, but intensified. Unlucky for him, at least Gilbert was on friendlier terms with the comte, and she was positive that Vergennes was holding his temper on the account that Laurens was also friends with Gilbert. She cleared her throat, lightly tugging on Laurens' sleeve.

"Monsieur," she whispered, "the Comte de Vergennes is the king's most trusted minister. It is best if you yield. An appointment is a respectable enough conquest for this day. He will get your words to the king, I promise." That, and Vergennes was so close in throwing out the current Finance Minister, who just made the country's income and spending *public* to the people. If Laurens wished to speak of money, he had to follow Vergennes' schedule.

Laurens' jaw clicked. Whatever thoughts he had, he didn't make verbal, which in this case was completely fine by Adrienne's account. He needed not make his friendship with Gilbert frowned upon by the Court. Laurens bowed his head, letting Adrienne keep him from pursuing Vergennes any further.

A little diplomatic victory, Adrienne thought to herself. Maybe she was good at something.

Versailles, May 1781

She reveled in her small accomplishments until Colonel Laurens completely disregarded all warning signs and had walked right up to King Louis during the royal reception. The horror on her face mirrored everyone else's. Even the king, in his shy demeanor, was caught off guard by the soldier who approached him like an equal.

Twenty-one million livres. That was the number Laurens continued to say. That was three lifetimes of the la Fayette annual income; Adrienne couldn't fathom such a number.

Neither could Vergennes, it seemed, on the days where she stood near the Americans as Franklin, Laurens, and Vergennes bickered. She would listen when she could, but her grandfather was quick to escort her away from the men's talks of politics.

Men's talk.

Adrienne humbled herself before she could roll her eyes.

She would politely pry the men's talk out of Colonel Laurens when he dined with the Noailles in their apartments, which was as recent as the Maréchal pleased, enjoying the tales of his grandson-in-law's exploits as well as the campaign in the American south. Laurens was convinced that was where the war was to be won now. The north had met a stalemate, only waiting for the British to leave York City for the patriots to win it all. Before Laurens left for France, he described Gilbert being sent down south with the American General Greene and the Prussian Von Steuben. Laurens also read his Hamilton's account of the betrayal of General Arnold in full, the Noailles finding the idea of traitors and cowards abhorrent.

Maybe Gilbert will be the lucky man to capture Arnold, the Maréchal mused.

Wherever he was, Adrienne thought, she hoped he was being smart. She wanted him to feel successful and useful, but not at the expense of his life. She'd take a cowardly husband over a dead one.

Regardless, she felt Gilbert with her when she was in the company of her children. When Anastasie arrived with her governess, and Georges was brought to her in the arms of the Duchesse d'Ayen, Adrienne rejoiced in their embrace. Anastasie was growing fond of learning English, and enjoyed sitting on her mother's lap while Monsieur Laurens spoke it at her request. In return, she'd sing a few lines from a French children's song, always met with rounds of genteel applause. Georges was growing like a miniature of his father, quiet, but with wide attentive eyes while he chewed on his rattle. All the American visitors were pleased at seeing their General's namesake, wishing him the best of luck as the infant in turn simply stared at them.

When Adrienne was away from other adults, and was able to bask in the sun shining through the windows of her grandparents' home with her children, she wrote. In her letters to Gilbert, Georges would often try and snag her pen, interested in the feather that constantly floated by his eyes. Anastasie enjoyed drawing, working on a portrait of the family until her fingers were covered in charcoal.

"Can we send this to Papa, Maman?" Anastasie asked, holding up the little circular blobs that held hands. Adrienne wouldn't let her forget Gilbert, always talking about her father and showing the children his portrait and pointing out the similarities they shared.

"Of course, sweetling," Adrienne replied. Oh, how it was ugly, but the drawing made her smile all the same. "How about we ask Monsieur Laurens if he may bring Papa some letters back for us? Should we send some to Uncle Louis? I'm sure he would like to hear from you. We can ask Auntie Lou to include it in her packets."

"Is Auntie Lou coming back soon?" Louise had gone to the Noailles' country home with their Aunt Tessé for the winter.

"She should be on her way home as we speak. Are you going to make her something? I think she'll like it."

Anastasie nodded, slowly taking another large paper to turn into one of her masterpieces. Georges nibbled on the feather, surprised when Adrienne tickled it down his nose.

So many events had passed day by day, that the spring and summer had gone on like clockwork. Adrienne doted on her children, Adrienne dined with Americans, Adrienne attended mass, Adrienne spoke with Gilbert's lawyers, Adrienne hosted more officers and dignitaries with her mother in the salon… A diary, if she bothered to keep one this year, would list the same transactions in a variety of orders. Her riding on Thursdays was limited to just an hour when she was in Paris. Very few letters arrived from Gilbert. All news came from word of mouth; letters at this stage of the war were too prone to being intercepted and any information given away could be crucial. So she settled with listening to their stories and asking the right questions when they paused. Spoken English was becoming easier; the tutors she hired for her children did her some kindness on the side as she practiced the written language.

She hoped she was doing him justice – it brought great pleasure to hear her visitors liked her. A good wife, a doting mother, all that she was brought up for and she loved it all.

Truly, she did.

Only sometimes did she wish to scream into a pillow, but Adrienne had a terrible habit of patience. While being with Gilbert made time go by easier, she relented to being a bother to Louise upon her arrival. Going shopping together wouldn't be too much of a burden to their finances, she thought, if it kept her mind off the mundane routines.

Colonel Laurens would have to be satisfied with his pull of six million livres and a loan of several million more from Vergennes and the king. And just like that, she was watching the man who was closest to her husband prepare to depart France after a few months. If only Gilbert did that, she thought. But Gilbert was awful on the open ocean, it would be cruel to send him back and forth to be sick and mopey the entire time.

"You will give him these right away," Adrienne had said to Laurens upon his last dinner at the Hôtel.

"Yes, Madame," Laurens said, taking the packet of letters.

"And this to the Vicomte de Noailles," she said, with another packet.

"Of course."

"And you will present my compliments to General Washington."

"Madame, because you are the only person in France who says his name correctly, I will be sure he receives your regards the moment my feet land back on my native soil." Laurens shoulder-checked his secretary as Major Jackson brushed by with their things. "Anything else I can do for you or your family?"

Adrienne held her elbows. Unless Colonel Laurens was God, capable of keeping back danger, there wasn't much he *could* do. Instead, she simply leaned up and planted a quick kiss on Laurens' cheek. The man lit up bright red. "Would you give that to the Marquis for me? That's the only thing I have left to give him."

"I – I, um – yes, I can… I will see what I can do." He took up Adrienne's hand, bowing politely to her knuckles.

There went her last solid line to Gilbert, off into a carriage to depart from these shores, she mulled, watching from the door as the last of the luggage was hooked up and the driver signaled to ride on. She nibbled on her lip; maybe she should have written more, longer letters, including her ideas she had so that Gilbert could keep them in mind for when he returned to her. Already she was passing the line of what a usual wife was supposed to do, but she couldn't help it. When Gilbert was away, all her efforts went into trying to be as bold as he was. She desperately wanted him back if only to let him guide her.

He did have a nice arm to hold onto after all.

Chapter Nineteen

Very rarely did Adrienne see Paris so aglow in revelry. Celebrations had continued for months after the queen bore a son – *the dauphin* – in late October. From beautiful festivities in Versailles, the Noailles followed the cheer back to their city home, attending events with the queen before the king even arrived. There were carts and carriages and people hogging the streets like a sheep's pen; one could see the king's carriage stuck in it all *blocks* away as Louis XVI tried to join his wife in the multiple masses she went to. The grand Hôtel de Ville had never been as full of nobles in Adrienne's lifetime, decorated with an army of candles and gifts for the baby prince, tables draped in white silk were set aside for gaming and conversation, and servants flooded through the doors with platters of champagne and hors d'oeuvres. It was Paris' own palace, and the extravagance was well placed.

Adrienne kept her arm looped around her mother's and Louise's, whose arms were, in turn, looped through Anne, Pauline, Rosalie, the older gentlemen and so forth. The Noailles were always a sight to behold in their extravagance and size. She saw distant cousins in attendance, and her favorite aunt, the Comtesse de Tessé, joined with many stories to tell the young girls while they watched the performances from the side. Ségur was only there in the last few months before he was deployed to the United States to relieve their Louis from his work. Letters had finally come of Louis' excitement for being chosen with Colonel Laurens to be the peace negotiator after a long battle at a place called Yorktown. Gilbert had led men into storming redoubts, proving that the French and American Alliance was at its strongest.

October was full of good news for the country. Adrienne felt the weight soar off her shoulders. She listened to her mother politely scold Anne for avoiding another potential match – Anne was turning nineteen this year and even Pauline had acquiesced to allowing some gentlemen to call on her. Her favorite was the captain of the Comte d'Artois' regiment, a young man who would be the future Marquis de Montagu; he was polite and enjoyed listening to Pauline's literature, and that was good enough of any man. Yet Anne would rather gnaw her own arm off than let their parents propose possible suitors.

The Duc d'Ayen was growing only slightly impatient, his incessant staring at the duchesse to do something about their daughters was never amiss. Too many times, their Maman would have to smack Anne during mass as she prayed to be a virgin forever.

Joining a monastery was never frowned upon by the duchesse and her daughters, but they were too high up in the aristocracy to have any one of them become a nun. They had enough understanding of the religious path by simply looking over at their monastic neighbors.

Rosalie was enjoying her first grand event, the baby of the family was already fifteen and they all saw their Papa growing misty eyed – either out of joy of getting them out of the house, or that his last child was no longer the little girl who played with dolls anymore. She was partaking in ample amounts of games with other courtiers at a card table, doing quite well for herself if the pouch of coins next to her was any sign.

Adrienne fiddled with her wedding ring, spinning it in circles around her finger. The floor broke out into lavish dancing while others toasted and clapped for their Majesties as they took their seats at the head of the grand table. Marie-Antoinette beamed, happy as she ever saw her. The king looked shyly glad, and Adrienne would imagine so — the man truly took his time in sharing the royal bed with his wife again.

Cool air from the revolving back doors to the garden allowed the perfume to circulate, and the sweat of the late afternoon subsided. Very soon, the color of the sky was beginning to match the shade of Adrienne's gown, a fact that Marie-Antoinette noticed right away.

"Why, you look like a starry night, my dear Marquise," she said, approaching Adrienne with two glasses of champagne in hand. She handed the spare to her before turning to acknowledge Louise, with a "Comtesse" and a nod. Louise curtsied.

"Congratulations, Your Majesty," Adrienne replied.

"Look at us, we match now with our eldest daughters and baby boys." Marie-Antoinette's smile was blinding. "Perhaps if the rules weren't so strict, they could be lovely playmates."

"I think they would like that. Anastasie speaks about nothing else now but wanting more friends." Adrienne glanced at Louise and added, "Once the vicomte is back, I imagine that wish may be fulfilled."

Louise's face flushed. "One can only pray, dear sister," she said.

"I believe the Vicomte de Noailles will be looking forward to that," Marie-Antoinette said, "if I know his character well. Thank you both for coming, I had to be sure I saw to you first since I know you have a knack for sneaking off."

It was Adrienne's turn to blush. "Madame, I would never! This is yours and France's celebration. I will be here until you leave, I promise."

Marie-Antoinette put two fingers to her eyes and turned them to her. "I am counting on it," she said with a smirk before she walked off to other guests.

Louise shook her head, the feathers in her hair bouncing lightly. "I cannot believe the queen criticized your bad habit like that."

"She meant it in jest."

"Did she?"

Adrienne smiled confidently and looked at her sister. "She did," she said.

The sun cast a red line across the horizon as the courtiers shuffled outside or to the windows as the king and queen walked together to the steps. Adrienne smelled the smoke from the hall, spotting the men with torches a few yards away. The smoke was accompanied by a quick hiss and a spark, several fireworks shooting off into the sky in reds and blues and greens. Only the music rivaled the explosions, drumming with every beat in her chest. A symphony of celebration, one that must have echoed with that of America's. The war wasn't over, but everyone saw that it would be soon. Adrienne prayed every mass that it would, that the next ships arriving in France would carry her heart back to her.

She allowed herself to dance a few sessions – her uncle-in-law Lusignem held her hand with care, even the Comte de Vergennes led her slowly through another, but she enjoyed dancing with her father the most that night. He spoke of nothing, simply twirling her around, meeting hands and hopping to the tune with ease. It was a silent conversation. He wore simple court attire that day, without the intensity of too much embellishment. Lately, the Enlightenment had been living within their house, the duc hosting many scientists and thinkers for dinners and his wife's salons. Adrienne would have thought there was a republic outside with some of the talk she overheard. Her father was still loyal to the king, that was never called into question. Somewhere, she felt in her soul that her family was only going to grow in prominence in France's future.

Through the south windows, one could see the Cathedral of Notre Dame, and if they listened carefully enough, heard its bells ringing through the night. An hour or two to midnight was when the royal couple decided they had enough. Their leaving signaled to the rest of the company that it was acceptable to depart and return home. Like any other event, the d'Ayen's and the rest of the Noailles were exceptionally fast in calling for their carriages.

Her mother was halfway upon the step to one coach when a footman approached the family, dressed in the royal attire of Versailles.

"I beg your pardon, Monsieur," he said to the duc. "Her Majesty has requested that the Marquise de la Fayette join her in her carriage. She would like to escort the Madame home tonight."

Adrienne stumbled. No one rode in the royal carriage outside of the royal family. She looked at her mother, then to her father. They looked at her in prolonged silence before nodding towards the footman. Tucking a curl of hair behind her ear, Adrienne curtsied to her family, and strode up to the front of the carriage line where the large and ostentatious, gold-gilded, beautifully painted coaches waited. They were the size of small rooms, set upon grandiose wheels only superior to the Noailles'. On the top, above trumpeting angels, sat a crown, the highest point in the entire entourage. Marie-Antoinette poked her head out from the doorway.

"Come on then, the whole of Paris waits on you," she said, gesturing to the procession line behind them; only the king's coach preceding.

Adrienne was assisted up to the body, all of the gold and the beading on her gown glittered in the lantern light of the city. The insides were covered in satin cloth and silk embroidery overtook the ceiling; seat cushions were the softest Adrienne had felt in a long time, that reclined back enough that if she sat there, her feet would not touch the ground. Pieces of gold and beetle wings were sewn delicately in the designs. The entire thing was a rolling piece of artwork.

Marie-Antoinette smirked, sitting happily on the edge of her cushion. She took Adrienne's hands and squeezed them. "You look terribly confused," she said.

"Madame is very observant," Adrienne replied. "I've never seen anyone but the princesses join you in here before."

"That is true, I'm very particular about who I invite. This is quite unprecedented." Marie-Antoinette tapped the wall. "To the Hôtel de Noailles, Monsieur Empharie!" she called, and after another beat, the carriage started underway. Because the royal coaches only moved as fast as one speedily walked, they would have a fair twenty-five minutes before the Hôtel came into view.

Adrienne remained quiet, watching the queen as she dipped into a slip in the door, pulling out a small box.

"Chocolates?" she offered, opening the decorative lid.

"I shouldn't," Adrienne said as she took one.

"Neither should I," Marie-Antoinette replied, taking one as well. "I don't like eating in front of big crowds, so these secret delights are my vice."

The chocolate had a sprinkling of sugar over the top that melted in her mouth.

"So," the queen said. "Tell me about how you spent our birthday. I was still recovering in bed and missed the potential festivities."

"I'm not sure if I'm the right person to ask, Madame," Adrienne admitted. "I didn't do much celebrating, although on my name day there was some gift giving. In truth, I was too caught up thinking about Georges' day. Christmas is already such a busy time, I have very little thought to myself between mass and my children."

Marie-Antoinette smiled, relaxing to the side. "You're a very devout, young woman, Madame Marquise. I think some of us could learn a thing or two from you."

"Oh, no, Madame, I just do what my mother taught my sisters and I to do."

Take the compliment, her very small pride screamed.

"But thank you for noticing."

"I had a lot to think about on the birthing bed," the queen said. "After begging for a son, he finally came. Now I can only pray that he's healthy and strong." She twirled a strand of her hair. "He has my complexion, you know," she smiled, "a small head of golden locks. I wonder if it will turn brown when he gets older. It does that on many boys, I hear."

"Georges' is growing in copper. Anastasie is brown like myself."

"Ha, my girl is brunette like her father. How quaint we are with our little families."

To be compared to the monarch by the monarch herself… Adrienne looked out the window. She must have been in some bizarre dream. A few market-women stopped along the street to watch the row of splendor roll by, their arms full of goods. Why they were out so late, Adrienne couldn't place; maybe the common folk had their celebrations as well this day. She pictured little taverns full of the working class, clinking drinks and dancing without decorum. The reflection of Marie-Antoinette joined her in the window, watching in pleasant silence.

Who was more of a show, she wondered. Did the normal people of France look upon the nobility in some sense of idolatry? Did they scorn these carriages as they drove by? Adrienne didn't fantasize about living a life with less than she had, she didn't dream of being a white-cotton-clothed shepherdess like Her Majesty often did. It wasn't practical. Like the tales of the women of America, if she were to shepherd sheep and goats, she wouldn't be doing it with flowers in her hair – she would be covered in mud and worn out petticoats.

Adrienne's dreamlike smile fell from her face.

Well, at least the Parisian women didn't appear starving.

It was more or less a straight path from the Hôtel de Ville to the Hôtel de Noailles, passing rows of townhouses and city estates. An earlier passing shower left the stone reflectant of the lanterns and lights, like stars upon the ground. The City of Light was a fair moniker, she doubted places like England could walk the paths of London unaided.

"Madame," Adrienne said, almost whispering, "what do you think France will do once the American war is done?"

Marie-Antoinette sat back, the many layers of her gown crinkled and poofed out by the doors. Her hair had speckles of gold in it that sparkled when she wasn't in shadow. "I imagine we will celebrate a well earned victory," she said and entered a long pause. Her eyes crinkled. "And I hope: return to normalcy. I would rather retire with my children than be witness to another historical event. But that's every mothers' dream, isn't it?"

Adrienne nodded.

"What about you? I think the Marquis has grown too accustomed to the cheers he receives when he walks through doors to simply enter retirement when the war ends," Marie-Antoinette said.

"He has spoken about General Washington's wishes to retire to his country home," Adrienne replied. "I imagine, maybe one day, he would like to as well. We haven't traveled to his home in Chavaniac yet, but he speaks fondly of it. He loves France, though, and wants to do all he can for its betterment. I'd be willing to wait for retirement if it means he can feel like he accomplished all he is able."

The long stretch of the Tuileries that became the Hôtel de Noailles' back garden started to come into view. It was an unusual ride, sitting with the queen alone. She could hear the stories people would spin of why the queen would invite her in, let alone give her passage home.

Marie-Antoinette seemed to read her thoughts. "Go on and ask," she said.

Adrienne fiddled with her fingers. "What should I tell my sisters when they ask why you've called upon me?"

She grinned. "Well, you do know I love a show," she said as the carriage turned along the road to the front of the home. "And sometimes the *play de la Fayette* is my favorite to bear witness to." The coach rolled to a stop, the humming of a bustle outside on the courtyard.

Adrienne couldn't tear her eyes from the queen, the woman sitting pleasantly with her coy smile. With the footmen dismounting from the back and the guards surrounding the other side, the door was open for her to the familiar smooth stone of home.

"Have a good night, Marquise," the queen exclaimed, leaning into the gap between the seats as Adrienne rose to exit.

A hand was offered to her to descend the step; being so short, the steps down were more nuanced than she cared to admit, so before she attempted it, she took the hand – slightly roughed at the pads of the fingers, but smooth in between, a slowly broken-in hand, newer to work. A well known hand, Adrienne thought, her gaze rushing up from her feet to meet the hazel eyes of Gilbert. He was crowned in laurels, his red hair long enough to tie back into a neat queue behind him; and *oh*, his smile, wide and gleaming. Adrienne's knees buckled. It couldn't have been real.

He caught her, naturally – he always did. The crowd around them were near yet absent, Adrienne could only hear the pounding of her heart and his voice whispering sweet nothings in her ear as his arms kept her warm and safe a few feet above the ground.

"She is returned to you in excellent condition, General!" Marie-Antoinette said behind her.

"I thank you wholeheartedly, Your Majesty," Gilbert replied, snuggling his nose into her hair. His voice sounded deeper, reverberating in his chest. He didn't try to put her down; Adrienne's legs were not going to work if he did. She grounded herself in him. Months of no letters, no expectation to see him, not knowing if he was alive for the last month…

Oh no, she was getting his uniform wet.

Happy shrieks and further crowding pushed them into the Hôtel as her sisters, aunts, and mother ran to kiss his cheeks. She never felt his arms strain to hold her. Every time he returned from war he felt more firm, steadier. The procession kicked off and disappeared on their way from the detour, dozens of carriages to disperse through the city or back to Versailles. But Adrienne was still stuck on his neck, breathing him in.

"I came back and only the children were home," he whispered to her amongst the rabble. "I asked them: where is your Maman? And *mon coeur*, I cried when they spoke. We have such intelligent children, you did so well."

Adrienne broke a sob in his cravat. "You're here," she said.

"I am here," he said.

"Is the war over? Are you done?"

"It isn't yet," he replied, "but I am in France to make sure it does. America will be free, *mon coeur*, most fighting is naval now. Washington thought it was best I help from home."

"I owe that man so much." Adrienne finally lifted her head from his neck. He looked perfectly perfect in that victory wreath. Gilbert smiled up at her, his nose bumping hers.

"It was so strange," he said. "Sometimes I felt like the goddess Athena was with me in battle; I recall I needed to give her an apple. But I wondered if my goddess would prefer it in pastry form?" He blinked innocently while Adrienne pulled herself together.

She laughed, the tears leaving lines where her face powder and rouge succumbed to the river. "Apple pastries sound delicious," she said.

Pauline wiggled on their side. "You two are so sweet," she said, making it very apparent they never made it out of the foyer. "Can I have some too?"

"Oh, yes! I want some!" Anne said.

"Girls!" the duchesse scolded, and Adrienne turned to look at her mother and Louise as they rounded up the rest of the family, shoving them up the stairs. "Leave them be, you will see them in the morning for breakfast and mass…. Hush, Antoinette, don't speak back to me like that, you're too old now to complain like a child."

Gilbert returned his smile into her hair, nuzzling behind her ear. "We need to get our own place," he said, carefully lowering her until her heels hit the wooden floor. Adrienne's hands lowered from his hair to his shoulder blades, rubbing down his muscle and back up again as he bent over to continue to embrace her. "Perhaps that will be my mission this year: find us a home. You can have your own salon and decorate with me."

"And how would you like to decorate?"

He stifled a chuckle. "Well I did preemptively buy some furniture in Boston. So it is very simplistic at its core, just the way you like it."

"We'll look like an American getaway in Paris," Adrienne mused. "I think I will like that."

Gilbert hummed. "May I stay the night with you, Madame?" he asked, his hands encompassing her waist.

Adrienne leaned her head into his, his breath tickled. "You may," she replied. He scooped her up again, from her legs and over his shoulder. She yelped, her hands coming down on the slight curve of his ass as he hoisted them up the stairs towards her apartments. "Gilbert, you –" A smack to his behind only seemed to encourage him to go faster, a racehorse spotting the finish line.

He was gentler when laying her out on the bed, softer when he hovered over her to bestow her lips with plenty of kisses. There was no easier effort than his disposing of his coat, a gift for the floor alongside his boots, his waistcoat, the ribbon in his hair. Adrienne took the laurels from the top of his head to place it amongst the curls of hers.

"No courses this month," he said, almost narrating to himself as he started digging through the layers of her skirts. Under he went until Adrienne felt the tickle of his lashes upon her inner thigh. "I know because I kept count. Am I a good lover?" She saw her left stocking fly off out of view. "Although, *mon coeur*, I would understand if you were tired and wished to sleep. I just ask that you let me rest down here."

"Gilbert," Adrienne laughed. Somehow he managed to untie the panniers at her hips. The baskets were yanked to the floor, leaving her gown rather shapeless. He reappeared, pulling his hair from his mouth.

"What?"

She wiggled her fingers out to him, beckoning for him to climb back up to her. He rested on his elbow by her side. The highest points of his cheeks were tanned from the sun, a little bronzer at the tip of his nose; she wondered how many freckles he earned that she could count when they laid together like this. Why did men have such long eyelashes? He seemed to catch on to her studying him, his cheek squished into his hand as he returned the loving gaze. A coarse finger ran down the contours of her face.

"It'll be ten years in April since we first met," she said. "It is hard to believe the time has passed when you've been gone for half of that."

Gilbert hummed quietly. "You are still the very same princess I told myself I would keep safe and serve with all that I have. Prettier, even. I could stare for an eternity into your eyes and still find new secrets hidden in their shadows. How I envy God when He gets to be with you for every moment and I am restricted to our waking hours."

Adrienne burned. "You must have taken some literature lessons in those camps."

"My wife makes poetic verse come naturally, what can I say?"

Pulling the pins from her bodice, she was sure to place them carefully along the rim of the gown; no need to be laying in bed and suddenly pricked from a hastefully removed needle. Her stays were embroidered underneath, a design that Gilbert had a fine time looking at as he helped push the sleeves from her arms.

"Lacing in the front," he observed, "how fashion keeps changing. And your hair, I like it like this." Most of her curls were piled on the sides instead of high above her head. "We will have to have you sit for a portrait or two. I'd say let's do the children as well, but I do not think either of them can sit so long for the painter not to scold me for having energetic offspring…"

Adrienne tucked her hands under her cheek, once again a happy witness to Gilbert's rambling. He was in France indefinitely, hers to have almost every night. Any impatience was, of course, immediately forgiven when he spoke to her like they did as adolescents. She could still see the fourteen-year-old Gilbert within him, but bolder, experienced, and maybe his hairline went back a little bit… but he always had a high brow and it didn't make him any less handsome.

"I have some things I want to talk to you about when you're not in meetings," she said when he finally talked himself dry. All her ideas she kept in a small journal, waiting for the right time to bring them up to him.

The traveling of the day hit him hard all at once, and the two of them laid half-clothed on top of her bed.

"Of course," he replied, blinking slowly like a cat would. "I love you."

"I love you."

Paris, June 1782

Gossip. Adrienne hated it. She hated it when it was falsified, dramatic stories woven to please the ear of the listener, but she hated it all the more when it was true, when the past stories of Gilbert's youthful crush with Madame Aglaé came back to haunt her.

It shouldn't have been a surprise – he had written to her as well when his letters from America came in. He returned a grand hero from the war and she was an easy woman to contact. Gilbert would look nice on any woman's arm – he was promoted to Maréchal-de-camp, knighted by the king, skipping over dozens of noblemen in the hierarchy.

But the Noailles did not like this affair, they did not like Aglaé, and what the Noailles did not like, the court did not like, and very soon Madame Aglaé's reputation in the eyes of her peers was chipping away like paint; even the Madame's mother wished it would end. In fact, the worst part in Adrienne's eyes, was that the only one who seemed to want it to continue was Gilbert himself. The days he returned from her abode, he was always in a sour mood, and the longer he persisted in this dalliance, the more the court began to glance his way from their circles.

It wasn't that he *had* a mistress that bothered Adrienne, she expected that inevitability to happen to her someday – she was four months pregnant, she couldn't have been beautiful to him *all* the time – but it was that Madame Aglaé never acknowledged her. She wished Ségur was around to leeway some peace. It was with him, after all, that Gilbert once challenged a duel over this woman. Ségur would tell Adrienne that Gilbert was a bit stupid sometimes, she could hear him say exactly that. But Ségur was gone, and Louis instead was back, returning to Paris a few weeks after Gilbert, to receive a stern slap from Louise for not mentioning he had returned the same *day* as the Marquis, on the same *ship*. And instead of offering solace to the ladies of the family, Louis merely cheered Gilbert on with his passion, although a different woman *would* have been preferable.

Familiar scoldings from her father echoed down the hallways as Adrienne sat with her mother in the parlor. She jabbed the needle at her embroidery circle. The duchesse's glances were burning into the side of her face, but she kept her attention down. She would not be the weeping wife.

She didn't do much but sit around and keep her hands busy. Even walking through the gardens with Anastasie and Georges proved immensely difficult with pain striking up her spine, and headaches splitting enough that she would sometimes sit down in the soil until it passed. Personally, she was grateful she was even able to get herself out of bed in the morning after retching all through sunrise.

Gilbert hadn't spoken to her in detail about the affair, and why should he? A man was allowed to do as he pleased, to seek comfort where he found it. Adrienne had tried to be attentive in the past few months, forcing herself to stay awake to greet him when he came home from Passy or Versailles or another appointment in Paris. She still attended to both of her children's education: Anastasie was so pleased she was able to write a whole sentence in French and in English and dance a few steps of the minuet with her tutor, and Georges was naming all the colors of the flowers in the garden and pointed out all of the horses in the Hôtel's paintings. And when Gilbert came home, he was still as loving and doting a father as he had been before. If Adrienne kept her teeth clenched, she could pretend as if nothing had changed, and all of France would see that she was a good wife and mother.

All of France, save for *Louise*, of whose lap she occasionally wallowed into. Her sister's hand continued to draw down her back in soft strokes. Being the wife of a man like Louis made her all the wiser, having dealt with the vicomte's flings and couple hour interests, understanding his promiscuous behavior since the beginning.

"He still loves you," she said, combing through Adrienne's hair. "I've never known anyone who loved a woman more than he does you besides Papa and Maman. It's not like he has to spend *every* night in your bed."

"He gets nightmares since he's come back," Adrienne drolled. "Doesn't like sleeping alone if he can help it."

"He needs to pick a different mistress, one that you like."

"How could I like someone who touches him the way I do?"

"In one way, think of it like a friend who you can confide in about him. Make sure she isn't just using him for his station; she should be intelligent and admired by her compatriots."

"Wouldn't Gilbert find it uncomfortable if he walked in on his wife taking tea with his mistress?" Adrienne asked, feeling like a child plotting vengeance again.

Louise looked down at her, smoothing back her hair with a pinkie. "All the better for it, I say. But again, this Aglaé woman needs to go."

"He is too stubborn to simply agree to Papa's terms."

"Then make him agree to yours."

"I don't want to embarrass him."

"Adrienne, he's embarrassing *himself*."

Adrienne squeezed her eyes shut. "I will *not* admonish him," she said. But he would have had to have known how much she suffered with this affair, she thought, he must have known. He must have.

☆

She timed herself well. When Gilbert returned to the Hôtel from his time with Monsieur Franklin and kept to himself in his apartments, where he was very likely writing or pacing as he so often did, she carefully approached his door and sank to her knees. She set a platter before her, with a small plate of macarons and croissants, and a fresh pot of hot chocolate. It was a little too warm outside to enjoy it completely, but that was beside the point. Adrienne made herself comfortable with her growing belly and the light robe that covered it.

And she waited.

The decor in the hallway had altered slightly over the past decade. A few different paintings, and the sculptures and plants were gifted from all over the country to Gilbert and the Noailles family. How incredibly proud one must have felt to be the recipient of so many marvels and adoration.

She knew Gilbert was busy with securing more money for the United States until the war officially came to an end. He wanted to represent it abroad despite not being a citizen; he wanted to be useful, and always be useful. He always *needed* to be loved, and Adrienne was very well aware of that.

A gust of wind accompanied the opening of the door, where Gilbert skidded to a stop upon seeing Adrienne at his feet.

"Ah," he said. "I was just on my way to you… what is this?"

Adrienne poured herself a cup of the cocoa. Her appetite wasn't what it used to be these months, but she pulled apart a croissant as well. "Will you sit with me?" she asked.

"I'd always like to sit with you." He lowered himself in the doorway, sitting cross-legged. The robe he donned wrapped tightly around him. Adrienne pressed her lips together as she poured him his cup. "Are you well?"

"How were Monsieur Franklin and Adams today?"

Gilbert looked at her and she looked at the desserts before them. "They are in good health; busy as ever," he said. He followed the journey of her cup up to her lips. "What's the occasion for a hallway picnic, *mon coeur?* It is not an anniversary, I am sure of it."

"I know it has been a strenuous few weeks for you," she stated. She pushed the plate of macarons toward him. "You should have some, you haven't been like yourself."

Gilbert's brow suddenly couldn't stop twitching. His agitated composure shifted to soft for only a mere moment, then his shoulders shot up. "This is about Madame Aglaé isn't it?" he asked, and Adrienne said not a word. "You and Papa, the Maréchal, *my* uncles even; you all cannot leave me be about it." His voice raised higher, ready for a debate, an argument.

Adrienne quietly sipped at her drink.

"Am I not allowed to enjoy the things that every other man like me enjoys? It is not like I am the Duc de Chartres – there is no harem I own nor orgy I attend. One woman whom I have known for several years and the entire family erupts! What do you want from me? Shall I visit brothels? Would that fare better for the family name?"

Adrienne thought the chocolate needed a little bit more sugar. She'd have to mention it to the kitchen staff.

"Adrienne!" he said, his face red.

She spared him a glance. Anger didn't suit him well, but his temper had always fluctuated. Adrienne managed to keep her expression stoic, yet her chest was squeezing her ribcage, her lungs pressed between stones like a witch on trial.

"Anastasie asked me why her Papa was yelling at Grandpère yesterday and why Papa missed dinner the night before," Adrienne said, and some anger leaked into her tone. "I had to lie to her."

He sat back, pushed himself even, until his torso was back in his room as his arms crossed his chest. He looked at the walls inside the bedchamber, licking his lips as if they'd gone dry. There must have been some answers on the inner paneling because he stared at it for a long time.

"No other man would take this from his wife, you forget yourself," he said to the empty air and shook his head. "And all this rabble is just making Madame Aglaé a victim to wicked fictions about her and me. We've done nothing more than what the vicomte does, than what Ségur or any man does in this country. You are in a constant state of exhaustion. I *cannot* force myself upon you whenever I feel the inclination. I *would* not – am I so terrible to seek female company elsewhere? Do you love me less for it?"

Adrienne finished her small portion of the hot chocolate and reached for the rest of her croissant. She had said her piece.

Gilbert rolled to his knees. "Answer me. *Do you love me less?*"

She said nothing. Did nothing. She let him get to his feet before he huffed a pent up scoff through his nose, rubbing quick and small circles into his temples, and retreated into his room, the door slamming shut in her face. The sound struck her head like a chime of a church bell, and she took her time collecting every small piece of crumb from the floor before she wobbled to her feet with the tray.

Her heart was buried deep within her, as if it dropped to the bottom of her body. The empty cups caught a stray tear that missed her cheek entirely as the tray quaked in her hands.

There was a bench several paces down the hall for her to rest on if she experienced another dizzy spell. She could make it; better than falling to the floor. But she had done what her sister advised, she let Gilbert know how she suffered. Mlle Maron would have told her she was an unwavering mountain if she were still with her governess.

Adrienne missed the support that came from youth; she may have lived in her parents' home, but she still had yet to learn to run her own.

She felt her belly shift, the baby move, and what thrice-refined memory served her as what *would* have been a surprising but pleasant feeling, couldn't replace the *horrible* burn it was. The bench in the hall wasn't close enough. The silver rattled in her hold but her knees rattled harsher.

"I'll take this," Gilbert said, coming up from behind her. His left arm hooked under hers while his right hand took the tray.

How did he know everything? She forced a breath through her lips, holding onto his arm like it was a beam. He took a few steps with her, stopping every now and then as she kept breathing, holding her belly. His brows were furrowed in all the mirrors they passed while he watched her, walking her to her bedchamber. The tray went to a table, and his right hand returned to lift her up.

Adrienne couldn't feel anything but shame as he doted on her once again, his stern brow still creased his forehead. Some tears came naturally now, hopefully under the guise of the pain she was in and not of her rising depression. If Gilbert didn't speak his thoughts aloud, it was agonizing, and he said nothing while he prepared her bed and helped remove her robe; nothing while he gently massaged her feet and opened a window to let the warm night breeze in. Only when he stood by the bed in his cap did his hands anxiously return to fiddle with the strings of his nightshirt.

"May I still lie with you tonight even if you do not love me?" he asked, gesturing to the space he had taken up every single night before.

It hurt harder because she loved him too much.

She nodded. He carefully climbed under the covers. Her fingers burned to touch him, but she was also incredibly displeased, and her mother had never taught her what to do when she couldn't get angry with a man she tried to hate a *little,* but couldn't. It wasn't blasphemy to hope that maybe she would simply ascend like the Holy Virgin, escape the whole situation; but then she would find she missed the temperamental ginger that laid next to her. And as he rested his head, she could feel his eyes shift from the ceiling to her face.

"None of this is a discredit to you, *mon coeur,*" he whispered. "Please understand."

The bed grew cold; Adrienne curled over on her side, facing the wall that displayed a lovely painting of a castle on a hill draped with a morning mist. If she closed her eyes, she could pretend she was there, hearing the breeze rustle a long lane of trees, counting how many birds she could see bringing meals to their nests. Being in Paris was starting to make her sick, there were too many people, too many stories.

She felt a lock of her hair twist and the shiver from it rake down her spine. There was no stronger feeling than her desire to forgive him immediately if it meant she could just curl up in his hold, let his arms engulf her, to fall asleep listening to the steady drumming in his chest.

Left Bank, Paris, September 1782

"Monsieur Mouton, I asked for the wood I imported and sent to you to be made into a *cabinet*, not a desk," Gilbert was saying, following the gentleman who was walking them through the recently purchased home. "It wasn't like I asked you to round up sheep, Monsieur, I cannot understand where the miscommunication was. Tell me at least Monsieur Folitor delivered the mahogany bookcases for the library."

The townhouse was on the Rue de Bourbon, a modest block of land by the river. Gilbert had sold some land to fund the price and the renovations he was putting into it. Glancing at the receipts his attorney was gathering, the Parisian home was *three-hundred-thousand* livres. Still, it was far different from the Hôtel de Noailles, smaller in size and decorated less like Versailles and more, as Adrienne would put it, *Americana*. Gilbert prattled endlessly in showing his family the home, walking Adrienne and the two children with him alongside his Protestant architect. His office that joined the library was intimate, but hosted grand windows that overlooked a balcony and mirrors that lined the opposite walls; white, marble top tables and luscious drapings lightened the room. If one could imagine a house inspection given with the greatest care, it would be from Gilbert. His hand hardly left his chin as he stared at blank walls inside and out of the house, carrying Georges in an arm to point out his thoughts to the toddler.

Anastasie was elegantly strolling down the hall of windows, looking out at the construction of the stables that would house the horses and carriages they owned. Adrienne watched her shift into hopping from window-light to window-light from the oval salon that Gilbert had been elated to show her, adorned with French doors and mirrors that reflected the shifting shades of autumn from the garden outside. She admitted Gilbert did a fine job in finding a simple home away from the hub in a stylish quarter of the city. If she squinted across the river, she could still make out the Tuileries and the rise of the Hôtel behind it.

"Maman, watch me, watch me," Anastasie called, balancing on one foot as she tried to leap the yard distance to the next rectangular panel of light. Adrienne held her belly, breathing quietly through constant pain.

"I'm watching, sweetling," she answered.

The five-year-old girl was confident in her chances, but didn't see her father approaching behind her, crouched with his son on his back and his arms open to grab her. Anastasie flew for a moment, caught gasping and laughing as her legs wiggled and kicked through the air to the next spotlight. Adrienne was staring down Georges, whose arms were too small to fully grasp Gilbert's neck, but instead held onto his hair.

"Careful, Gilbert," she said, pulling Georges before he slid right off.

"He's a strong boy, he wasn't going to fall," Gilbert replied, straightening only to hold Anastasie up instead, nibbling kisses to her cheek. "So, my girls, what do you think? Do you like it?"

"We get to live here?" Anastasie said, clapping her palms to Gilbert's face. "What happened to Papi's house?"

"Papi and Mémé are still there, we will visit them often. If they are ever on a promenade, and we shout loud enough, they might be able to hear us," Gilbert exclaimed, gesturing to the river. He lowered his voice and glanced over to Adrienne, "Although our neighbors may think we're a little crazy."

Adrienne swallowed down rising nausea and smiled. "It wouldn't be the first time."

"Do you like it?"

"I think it's lovely."

The weather outside coolly rustled the trees, with the sun providing some warm spots, but Adrienne was breaking out into a sweat. She wasn't feverish – at least, she wasn't that morning – feeling well enough to agree to take the growing strenuous carriage ride over the bridge. It wasn't as if she was overworking either. In truth, the most she was doing was keeping herself together for the children whenever mentions of Madame Aglaé rose.

Adrienne was less agitated at the woman – after hearing that Aglaé was trying to get out of the affair for the sake of her position and reputation, she could not hold anything against her. Gilbert was stubborn, but he held his tongue and didn't bring much talk of her in front of the family. His frustration was for his letters, and Adrienne made a hard point not to look at them.

Anastasie wanted to see the paintings that Gilbert had delivered and hadn't hung up yet, and he obliged, walking them over to pull the white cloth keeping the dust off of them. She, as talkative as he was, pointed and joined in his explanation of each as he moved on to the next covered portrait. She was very pleased to inform her Papa what people she recognized up until the architect returned with papers in hand of the final plans for the outside details of the house – just aesthetic points; after all, the home was hardly thirty years old.

Adrienne lowered Georges to the floor, his still chubby legs finding his footing with a wiggle and a little grunt of independence. He wasn't as much of a runner as Anastasie had been at his age, but he enjoyed slipping into a crawl and back up again while he explored the room. It was a salon that Gilbert would use as often as she. Adrienne imagined how many of his American friends, Protestant and Jewish friends, Black friends they would host here, a mixed gathering that Gilbert viewed as what France could be in a few years: diverse and welcoming of all peoples and faiths.

Sincerely, Adrienne agreed to that future dream of France, imagining how many new minds and stories could be added to the nation. In turn, when they had time alone, Gilbert listened intently to her ideas that she mentioned to Colonel Laurens, his hand on her lap, indulged with the idea of starting a plantation somewhere on the path of emancipation. He'd look into his contacts, he had told her, to show the Americans who held onto their slaves with such might, that freeing them could be done without chaos. It was a little victory that Adrienne relished in, having his attention and praise.

Small pleasant memories amidst Gilbert's fleeting time between work, family, and his departing lover.

A *twang* split up her back so sharply, so brutally, she doubled over before she realized it. Like a demon had ferociously slammed his fist into her gut, there was no breath to find. She tried to gasp and cried out instead.

What's happening, what's happening, eyes widened while she cupped her belly. In an instant, the entire room shrank around her. It was too early – she wasn't even eight months pregnant yet – it's too early, too early.

"No, no, no, no," Adrienne pleaded, feeling the shooting pain course up from her abdomen to her head. Black dots splayed around her vision like ink blotting parchment. She must have called for Gilbert, or Georges must have wailed, for in her next blink the man was in front of her. His hands felt cold on her face, and they pulled at her skirts to the growing warm puddle between her legs. "Please, please," she moaned.

Why did it hurt so much?

Gilbert was speaking, shouting maybe, but Adrienne couldn't hear anything over the blood rushing through her ears.

She wasn't at home with her mother, nor any sister near to comfort her. Just herself, Gilbert, their children, and a man she only met a handful of times before. Was she going to vomit? She didn't want to be sick in front of them all. When did she close her eyes? She forced them open to see Gilbert still in front of her, his forehead to hers as he gathered her up in his arms. It hurt like she was a child experiencing pain for the first time again, and then a thousand times that.

"I can't do this," she whined.

"Hold on, *mon coeur,* hold on, we're getting a doctor," he said. She wished she could watch him instead of curling up in his hold. The green in his eyes would be so much more of a comfort, if she could just look at him, if…

She was screaming when she woke up again. If the feeling that she didn't know where she was didn't add to her anxiety, it was the three sets of hands pushing and pulling and tearing at her legs. There were indistinct shouts of *Madame* and *breaching* where Adrienne clawed at the blankets beneath her, clawed at herself.

Wasn't the pain supposed to go away? Why wasn't it over yet?

"Please don't hurt yourself," she heard Gilbert whisper in her ear, his hands taking one of hers between his palms. He kissed her fingers. She found his face. He looked so scared. It immediately fell to the top of the list of expressions she didn't like on him – she'd take anger over this. "Breathe, *amour*, breathe," he said. Her breathing came out in desperate pants, between sobs bitten back until her lip bled.

Would she die from this, a passing thought came. Too many women she knew of died in childbirth, including Gilbert's dear cousin, Marie, who died with her baby at the same age Adrienne was now. It was a thought that seemed to have crossed Gilbert's mind as well, his grip on her hands tightened with every cry that rose from her throat. He had never been in the room with her during the births, when Adrienne looked utterly disgusting and would rather disintegrate than let anyone see her, but now all she wanted in the room was him. *Damn* to the lovers he may have, he was with her now and that was good, that was enough.

The light through the window was soft and gentle and warmed the room, reflecting off all the tiny pieces of dust that floated in the beams. It felt delicate, perfect if someone were a cat to bask in it. For Adrienne, everything was sore.

Burning yet empty, hot yet barren, a wasteland either way, she laid aching on her back, looking up only at the simple light green ceiling. Some trimming met the top where golden faux beams held up the corners. Her throat grew hoarse, her stomach already started to eat itself, and her skull endured a hundred pounds of weight upon it.

She tilted her head towards where the bed moved, slowly blinking up at Gilbert. There was a small lapdesk propped on his knee, his hand scribbling away. His brow was creased, an unhappy stress that brought pain back to Adrienne's chest.

"Did I lose the baby?" she asked, horrified at the sound of her own decaying voice. Gilbert righted himself, the desk placed by their feet.

He cleared his throat, discreetly wiping a tear from his eye. "Good morning," he said, lowering himself to her. His nails combed through her hair, still somewhat dressed from the evening prior. "I was actually scribbling a line to Monsieur Franklin to tell him of our daughter's birth."

Adrienne whimpered. A girl.

"She is very small, but in perfect health. We've Christened her just in case, but oh, *mon coeur*, she fits perfectly in my hands," he said, his smile excusing the tears. Adrienne was silent as he said her name: *Marie Antoinette Virginie*. "I've asked Monsieur Franklin if that was perhaps too much to ask offering her to America, but I think he will excuse my ardor."

"Virginie," Adrienne said. It was beautiful. His eyes sparkled while he watched her, but the smile on his face wilted.

"You must drink and eat something; would you like your feet rubbed? Ice? A warm rice bag?" Gilbert listed. "I was told to call for the doctor when you woke up, but I think Maman will beat him here once I open the door… if she's not already waiting with her ear pressed against it."

The duchesse was, indeed, waiting for her cue. She had pushed herself in, carrying her skirts like they were baggage, a bible held between some fingers, a toilette pinched between some others.

"Ah, my little girl, look at you," she cried, falling upon the bed, somehow displacing Gilbert entirely. Adrienne didn't need a mirror to know how awful she must have appeared if her mother was teary eyed. She imagined gaunt cheekbones and dark circles, a skeleton who also was very swollen; a perfectly baked meringue.

Goodness, she was hungry.

"No more," the duchesse said, cleaning her collarbone. Adrienne raised a brow; Gilbert's jaw pinched. "Do you hear me? She can't take any more."

"Maman," whispered Adrienne. She shook her head. *Don't say that*, she wanted to plead, *not to Gilbert*.

"I know," Gilbert replied. Adrienne couldn't help the awful sniveling objection that came out of her mouth. Sure, Georges birth was troublesome, and Virginie's may have ended her life, but to deny that they ever laid together again was…

He had all the reason now to seek lovers elsewhere.

If she were not void of energy, she'd glare harder at her mother as the towel pushed her cheeks around. But her mother was only looking at Gilbert, and Gilbert was looking at his hands.

"A few things," the duchesse said, pulling up the blanket. "The infant is under constant care as she must be kept warm, that means if you would like her to lay with you, we must keep the fires burning hot and the windows closed tightly. The drapes must be closed as well to ensure that no drafts come in."

Gilbert nodded. "Yes, Madame."

The door opened with the doctor sliding in front, Gilbert's secretary behind him.

"Adrienne, you must exercise with great care. Nothing too strenuous for your health, but laying for too long is ill-advised." The duchesse snapped her finger at the doctor to stop his input on the matter. "I speak from experience with my several children, you'll recover faster with some stretches, diluted wine, and lots of prayer. I will visit every day until you are up on your feet again. And we will get you some fish to eat, my poor girl."

Behind her mother's doting attention, Adrienne eyed the secretary whispering to Gilbert, and the two exchanged correspondence packets. The large, curling spelling of the Madame Aglaé was poignantly obvious and everyone knew it; Gilbert shoved the letter between his others, his nostrils flaring. He covered the red in his cheeks with his handkerchief, dabbing at nonexistent sweat.

"The Marquis has a meeting to attend to," his secretary said, giving a bow. "Please excuse us."

Gilbert clicked his teeth. "Take care of Madame," he told the doctor. His brows were too tightly pulled together for Adrienne's liking.

As he kissed her hand, she asked, "whom are you meeting with?"

"Vergennes," he replied, a little too quickly, but maybe Adrienne was simply being skeptical. She nodded, a faint smile pulled her cheek up if only for a moment before it fell back into its pained frown.

Virginie was tiny. No bigger than her forearm, her pink skin was almost translucent in some areas, and covered in a ginger fuzz. It would be a miracle if she survived for long, Adrienne thought, tiredly staring at the baby as it laid on her chest. Virginie was bundled in thick blankets, only loosened in the front to give her the opportunity to steal some of Adrienne's body heat. Virginie was too young to look like either of her parents, moreso like a blank slate baby.

Adrienne should have been happier; despite her sisters visiting to dote on her and meet the child, with Louise coming in to share that she and Louis started to try again for their own baby, and Aunt Tessé joining to exercise with her, she felt empty.

She would let the wetnurse and the doctors take Virginie back to her heated pot, and she would allow Anastasie and Georges join her during her baths as her mother and maid cleaned her weekly, but she wouldn't feel a damned thing until Gilbert returned late every night and climbed into her bed. And she then could feel bitterness or relief, whatever it was that made her heart pound hard enough to remember she still had one.

Chapter Twenty

Chavaniac, June 1783

He actually made the decision in *March* that Paris was starting to chew his patience to the bone. If it wasn't political, as many things ought to be in an age when one was trying to build up a nation to surpass all others, it was Aglaé. The woman who flowered his return with praise and kindness suddenly continued to push him away with her letters, her family's letters, things that he could ultimately choose not to receive from the postman, although his curiosity always got the best of him. Gilbert knew he was not in the wrong for doing what was normal for his station. He had spent years in war, living in plain tents and marching through mud and disease — why would he not take his opportunity to live the life he was born into? He didn't do it often; he loved liberty but certainly was no libertine.

Aglaé had pulled her final card and that was something Gilbert was too proud to admit won her their separation. She was off to a convent, to find a life closer to God. It was a cruel move. But Gilbert was an honest man and withdrew from her, sauntering aimlessly home until he could locate his beloved — *another* woman who held faith in such high esteem, but one he could not pull his affections from even if she were to hate him with all of her heart.

Adrienne had been bedridden for so long over winter, recovering while their youngest lived on and ever so slowly grew. She missed much that happened around Versailles and Paris; Gilbert was apt at relaying the stories of Monsieur Mesmer, and the marvels of the new hot air balloon that launched, showing her the illustrations from the newspapers; even the Duc d'Ayen was enthusiastic in his talks about it.

Spring in Paris fared better for the family than for himself, when the windows could be opened and the children could shout their messages across the river, mostly to be replied to by a passing elderly fisherman who became such a *common* occurrence that Gilbert tended to buy his catch every Monday so Anastasie and Georges could give a proper hello. Astute Pauline was married to her proper match in May, a time when Adrienne felt well enough to come out and celebrate with her sisters.

But that was about it with the niceties. For work, any expedition he proposed and meticulously planned was rejected, with word that the British were likely breaths away from surrendering the war. Several packets of letters sent to Washington entailed all of his thoughts. Sometimes he wrote them blindly, expecting his adoptive father would know exactly what he meant by them. He would write to Hamilton as well, and the man hardly replied, but when he did, his heart would ache – his American brother was a father, the war was still laboring away, their dear friend Laurens was dead…

Gilbert simply wanted to roll himself into the largest rug he could get his hands on.

Their little Parisian townhouse had slowly been growing in decor and friendly company and while that was a pleasure, it was her and the three little ones that wrought excitement to come home. Adrienne always stole his breath away when he walked in on her with the children. She sat on a chaise in the parlor, her robe acting as the blanket for their two oldest, one hand holding a novel, the other curled around the baby, who suckled on her thumb and listened. Gilbert leaned against the door, fiddling with a newly arrived reply from his aunt, listening to Adrienne tell the tales of far away lands and a princess. He curled his fingers as Anastasie gasped at every twist and went wide-eyed upon the little spun-in romance; even the paraphrasing Adrienne *definitely* must have made up on the spot when the story turned a little too adult for their children's ears.

"Oh, that is so romantic!" Anastasie cheered, rolling back into her mother's lap. Georges was almost pushed from the chair, his pout as grand as his smile when he locked eyes with Gilbert.

"Papa's back!" he declared, crawling off the chaise to run towards him. Gilbert crouched down to grab beneath his arms, throwing him upward as he stood again. Georges' hair had grown very fast and very straight, any queue was proving difficult to maintain, so they alternated between cutting it and letting it sit on his shoulders like the gentry of last century. He had been inoculated for the pox earlier in the month, the small marks on his neck already in their healing stage. It made Gilbert far more comfortable knowing his son was well-recovered.

"Hello, Papa," Anastasie said, wiggling her fingers at him from Adrienne's lap.

"You've stolen my spot," Gilbert replied, walking into the room. "That's not very nice, sweetling."

She laughed and only clung onto Adrienne's skirts tighter. "It's not your spot," she said, presenting her cheek for Gilbert to bend down to kiss. He grunted, Georges clinging to his lapel, and managed to cast a kiss for all three of his girls in a row.

"*Mon coeur*," he said, tilting his head. "Let's get out of Paris for a while."

"What?"

"Just our little family for a few weeks. It will be healthy for you and for the children. And for me as well until work's correspondence finds its way to my hand, but at least some days will be peaceful together."

She looked around the room like he had presented them with ship tickets to Africa instead of something far more sane and practical. To be fair, it would be something he would do, but he was trying to be smart.

"I haven't made any inquiries into my family's estates – where would we go?" she asked.

And so, they presently sat in the carriage headed south to Auvergne.

Gilbert was familiar with the handful of days it took to bustle along country roads into the mountainous region of France, but it had been years since he had visited his birthplace. There were people there who worked on his land and paid rent towards their property whom he hadn't even met in person before. All that paperwork had been handled by his aunt, Madame de Chavaniac.

Some of the woods they passed sparked faraway memories that brought out a laugh. He pointed to the forest, holding Georges in his lap as he retold the story of the *Beast of Gevaudan* – the hyena that ate the heads of lone shepherds and farmers, man, woman, and child alike until King Louis XV ordered for it to be slain. When he was younger, he too went out to try and find the beast, as there were talks that it never truly was killed.

"Gilbert, stop it, you're going to give them nightmares," Adrienne said, cupping her hand around Anastasie's ear, shoving the other one to her bodice.

"Bah, I don't think our children are afraid of anything," he replied, fluffing up Georges' placid locks. "As long as we are always together, no one will hurt a hair on any la Fayette head. Besides, I haven't heard of anyone being snatched by the hyena since I was Anastasie's age. Chavaniac is perfectly safe, I promise."

"How big was the beast they delivered to the king?" Anastasie asked, trying to escape her mother's hold as the carriage rocked left and right. "Bigger than you, Papa?"

Gilbert smirked. Adrienne stared him down and shook her head. He sighed and lifted his hand. "I cannot say for sure," he exclaimed. "If it were to stand on its hind legs, I still think I have the upper hand. But your Papa is a tall man and very strong, which is not common for other Frenchmen, so they must have been more frightened than I would have been."

That must have been decent enough to avoid a scolding. It did earn him a roll of the eyes and a suppressed smile — a victory.

"Papa, are we there yet?" Georges whined. He pressed his face against the glass window, fogging the pane and left a mark from his lips.

"Count how many mountains you see, I'd like to know," Adrienne said, her gaze still firmly on Gilbert.

Virginie was the luckiest among them, sleeping through most of the journey, keeping Adrienne and Gilbert awake all night when they stopped to rest at inns along the way. She would continue to do so until the final reprieve of the trip.

The entirety of the Château de Chavaniac was not quite a hundred years old yet; part of it had burned down at the start of the century and had to be rebuilt, but it was never less of a sight to behold. Black stone towers flanked the manor that stretched nine windows across — the medieval design could be an explanation to why Gilbert was so enamored with knights and glory growing up here. Standing on top of a mountain, it could be seen from the hamlet that surrounded it from over the trees. Townsfolk gathered along the street to watch the carriage roll by; the word of their lord's arrival must have spread. Gilbert's knees couldn't stop bouncing as he looked back at them and smiled at their cheerfulness. *Here* was where he was appreciated in France, where people loved him, he recalled that well.

He had opened the carriage door before the driver had stopped in the courtyard, taking in the smell of the fruit trees that blossomed. One could forget how few trees existed in the city until you were surrounded by them in the country. It was warmer where the sun shined, graced with comforting wind rolling up and down the hills. He was happy to replace his silks for linen, formality for the sweet guise of an eight-week retirement.

When had he ever been patient, hopping out of the carriage with a little stumble that only his wife saw as she pursed her lips and fanned her face. Sometimes his clumsiness returned to quell his hubris, and because his pride was impossibly strong, it meant that God had to have made him *very* awkward to balance it.

"That was a close one," Adrienne said, taking the hand he held out for her after Anastasie and Georges exited. She held onto Virginie with practiced care, being so petite a woman, the steps of every coach were unfairly placed to accommodate her. Gilbert frowned. He would have to order a custom made step-stool for her… maybe make a whole new coach, after all, Adrienne had been recovering so slowly, it wasn't right for her to have to take long steps.

"Chavaniac has seen me do far worse," he admitted. "As long as Auntie didn't see… she is right behind me, isn't she?"

Adrienne smirked, glancing back to him from the rest of the courtyard. "There's no guarantee she saw," she said before she waved the children into an orderly line to meet their hostess.

Gilbert spun on his heel. Aunt Charlotte was a head shorter than him, with silver hair that was perpetually perfectly coiffed, kept in place with a simple lace cap, and blue eyes that matched the Ligurian Sea. He had more portraits with his aunt than he did with his own late mother, and she treated him like a son all the same. Gilbert took the madame's hands and kissed her cheeks.

"Your letters, although satisfactory, do not replace your visits, Gilbert," she said, her voice as smooth and warm as he remembered. "It has been years. How was I supposed to guess you had grown another five inches since you were last here?"

"My deepest regrets, Auntie," Gilbert replied. "War keeps a man very busy whether he is on the field or not."

"War is no excuse not to visit your homeland, but I will forgive the discrepancy if you make these visits more often now. I may keep your house, dear, but I am not the housekeeper. Oh, but do introduce me to this lovely fold you have – there are never enough Motiers for France."

Gilbert's ego was bursting introducing his daughters and son, who, besides the babe, gave respectable and well-practiced curtsies and bows. "This is the Madame de la Fayette, my wife, Adrienne," he said.

"Of course, a kind writing partner," Aunt Charlotte said, taking Adrienne's hand. She leaned in close to her, whispering in her ear as they exchanged *la bise*, and Gilbert watched Adrienne's cheeks grow warm as her mouth struggled not to smile at whatever secrets his aunt was sharing.

Gilbert puffed out his cheeks. "And children," he continued, "this is Louise Charlotte de Guerin du Motier de la Fayette, the Madame de Chavaniac. She is *my* papa's older sister."

"Like me!" Anastasie said, grabbing Georges by his shoulders.

"That's right, Mademoiselle," Aunt Charlotte replied. "That means you must keep a careful eye on the little Monsieur. The château grounds are large and we cannot lose you to its many hills." She took Adrienne's arm and linked it through her own while they walked towards the manor. Gilbert followed behind, slouching to the side to hold his precocious children's hands. "Madame, I suggest you have their governess keep them to the main garden for their perusing pleasure. Although it has been some time since children roamed the halls, it is embedded in my memory watching your husband and my daughter tumble one time too many into the trees below. Horrifying for a mother, even worse for an aunt."

Gilbert huffed. It was an error of trajectory in their rolling races, they didn't mean to continue down a hill at the speeds that they gained. The astonishing joy of feigned flight outweighed the bruises and split lip it cost.

The entrance to the château was surrounded with a tidal wave of vines and topiary sentries. Oculus windows peeked through the ivy on the ground floor, offering the cool-stoned tunnels the servants' hall as well as the kitchen – with a hearth the size of the many mural-painted walls – a soft light to guide them along. A curving stairwell displayed two indoor balconies above it: used often by a young Gilbert to spy on visiting guests as they walked up to the formal reception room. He was already overlooking modifications and repairs needed for the interior; not that his aunt wasn't taking the finest care of the home, but it *was* his fortune that paid for the thing.

Madame de Chavaniac was meticulous in showing Adrienne every detail of every room, informing her of the names of every servant she would need to speak to, of the typical domestic management and records – Gilbert was melting in his shoes waiting for the opportunity to take his wife back. He eyed Anastasie as she climbed up on a sofa to view the painting of Gilbert's great-great-grandfather, Virginie crawling behind her. Georges must have fallen asleep standing up, still holding onto Gilbert's hand, for he wobbled in place like a puppet.

Chavaniac was a maze of corridors, it would take ages for a full formal tour to conclude, but they had weeks to get Adrienne and the children acclimated to their country home. Gilbert handed a loose-stringed Georges to his governess, intent on catching his aunt before she ruined the *surprise* he didn't warn anyone about through no fault but his own.

"I can show Madame our home from here, Auntie, thank you," he said, slapping Adrienne's hand to his arm. "Also, Georges likes a snack whenever he wakes up from his impromptu naps," he added, pointing to the boy with a tilt of his head.

"I'll have the kitchen prepare a meal for you all since you arrived so late in the afternoon," Aunt Charlotte stated, folding her hands in front of her.

"You say that like it is my fault," Gilbert replied. "I'll have you know my presence only broke one wheel, but it was our luggage cart, not the coach. A few hours delay is not the worst of my feats. Now allow me to steal my wife."

He pulled her away, whisking her down the hall like they were teenagers again, escaping from their chaperone. In his directions included in his past letters, he had instructed a certain room be stripped of its furnishings and detail, and that the architect be ready for any alteration to come within the week of their arrival.

Gilbert stopped at the double doors, spinning Adrienne in circles until she laughed like music and gripped his coat to keep from falling.

"Goodness, Gilbert, you've pulled all the air from my lungs," she gasped. "You are so impatient; Madame was pleased to be giving the tour."

"I am also selfish and wished you only for myself," he replied, tickling her elbows.

"What is it," Adrienne asked, glancing towards the door. "You're bouncing."

He bent over, pushing his nose against hers until they were forehead to forehead. "Well, I can only wonder why. Perhaps I should open the doors then? I think it might stop my bouncing, but I hear it is a very contagious thing in my little family." She looked up at him readily. He put his hand on the door and pushed.

It was one of the brightest rooms in the château. The doors opened like the gates of heaven to tall ajar windows, the white light bounced around the bare walls and floor. Hidden exits lined one wall leading to its conjoined room, also empty and ready to be decorated as its owner saw fit.

Adrienne stepped into the chamber, a prima ballerina taking her stage. She looked at the flooring, up to the ceiling and the chandeliers that remained much to Gilbert's twitching-brow disdain.

"What's all this?" she asked, her skirts coming to a stop as she completed another rotation.

"It is to be your salon," he replied, "and your boudoir, of course. I expect to visit often if you'd invite me."

Her eyes squished at his tease, her hands rising to the familiar nervous wringing her fingers. "My salon," she said, her silence adding a little question mark. Gilbert leaned against the doorframe, soaking in her glow.

"You are the lady of the house; this is your castle, Madame. I know I sort of, maybe, overwhelmed the Hôtel with my choices in furniture and art and color and the like… but this is all yours to do with as you please."

Adrienne stepped lightly to the walls, her hand grazed over the blank canvas. "All mine?"

"I relinquish all claim to this room; you are its sovereign."

He could tell she was lightly bouncing on her toes. The tiniest of heel taps echoed off the floor while she examined every inch of her new abode. He wanted to give more to her – crown her if he could.

"Thank you, Gilbert, it's perfect, thank you," she said, all the fatigue she had been living with for months abruptly vanished in front of his eyes, but he pulled himself away from the entrance when he saw the glimmer run down her cheek.

"Why the tears?" he asked. Crying was not good, he didn't like that at all. She didn't let him touch her face, her hands swiping at him like he were a bee while she wiped her lashes. "Adrienne."

"You're always so sweet and I have nothing to give you."

"I want for nothing, *mon coeur*. You are my gift every morning and every night – no man has a better wife and partner than I."

"That doesn't count."

"It does, though," Gilbert said. "We promised no lies, so I am obligated to inform you that you are indeed the best wife in France. May God smite me if I do not speak the truth." He held his hand up and waited for lightning he knew would not come. "And *voila*, the Lord agrees."

He beamed when Adrienne slowly lowered her guard, letting him smother her with affection.

"I will try to run the house the best I can."

"I know you will," he said, bending back to lift her from the ground. Rocking to and fro while her legs dangled, he would hold her until she laughed again. They were too young to be wallowing. Trepidation did nothing helpful in an ever-changing world. Gilbert knew if mankind were burning around them, Adrienne was fully capable of keeping their home and family infallible. And she wore his favorite perfume. "Mm," he added, pressing his nose to her neck. "You're making it impossible for me to want to let you go."

"You don't have to then," she replied. "Although, your aunt may be concerned if your back gives out before dinner."

"Did we tell her the children eat with us?"

"… No, I don't think we did. You were very eager to bring me here."

"Can you blame me? I like surprising you."

She snorted and Gilbert shook with their combined cackling.

"One of these days, I'll surprise you," she said, "and it will be the greatest surprise you have ever known."

Gilbert carefully let her down, slow to pull back as her hands were in his hair. "I will look forward to it," he replied. He still had several places he wanted to show her, the mysteries and hidden corners of Chavaniac were ripe to explore again after all these years.

The meals never lacked a little Italian flair in Southern France. The children had their first taste of dried pasta and a wide assortment of vegetables to chew on diligently, sorting their favorites on their plate. Everyone enjoyed laying on the stone of the ground floor afterward to escape the heat of the floors above. It wasn't at all proper, but Madame de Chavaniac could never be surprised by the things Gilbert allowed his family to do; so if the lord and lady *wanted* to lay on the floor with their kids, then they certainly *ought* to.

They ended the evening with a small performance on the harpsichord; Adrienne covered the harmony on either side of Anastasie's simple, but well-maintained, cheerful melody. Their daughter had been practicing on the piano, so the baroque sound was newer to her ears; all the same, Gilbert didn't notice a single error in their playing.

The bedchambers were less apartments than they were just rooms, squished and placed particularly around what the castle foundations allowed. Some rooms were circular, others could have been mistaken for inner chambers with how small they were. Gilbert's bedchamber was modest, the one he was born in, that is. The fireplace would easily heat the space within minutes when lit, and the open window cooled it just as quickly. A starburst design took up the wood floor. He traced it with his steps, the lucky thing…

A warm, colorful sunset lit the clouds in a lavender hue. It got dark in the country. There were no lanterns lining the roads, only a few along the church walls and those held by the occasional watchman. It didn't mean that the horizon line was indiscernible, however. Thousands of stars dotted the sky, outlining every mountain peak and jagged line of the treetops.

Gilbert tucked his hair into his cap when night fell, and journeyed his way down the hall to where the children slept. Without a sound, he peered into the room, waiting for Adrienne to rise from their bedside. He took her fingers, sliding her out into the corridor.

"Come with me," he said.

"Alright," she immediately replied.

He led her up spiraling stone stairs used only by the servants, recounting the way by memory. They passed the great hall and the hidden sauna, up an old wooden staircase where Gilbert pushed against the low ceiling with his shoulder until the secret door opened, receiving them with a cool gust of summer night air. It had been a dry week and the roof was not old enough to collapse with the addition of two lithe people, so Gilbert climbed to the top and pulled Adrienne out to join him.

"Gilbert," she cautioned, holding onto his shirt as their robes blew out around them. He held her close, shimming along the red tiles until their footing was flat.

In the daylight, one would be able to see the deep slope that the château was built on, one side of the manor completely exposed to rolling hills and gardens behind it, the other deceptively simple where the grounds sat three floors below them. Most of the breeze swooped up from the river, zigzagging through the village, and caught their banyans and hair in a warm tumble of windy waves.

"We can't see this in Paris, can we?" he asked, pointing up at the sky. Adrienne hugged his waist, following his finger to the silver speckled stardust of the galaxy that beheld them. If he had a telescope, he would let Adrienne wander the thousands upon thousands of stars that made up the night's stream from one horizon to the other. "Some of the stars are different in America. It's amazing to try and spot where the constellations hide themselves."

Adrienne was silent, looking up at the watercolor masterpiece. The flecks glimmered and dimmed as other stars shot across the sky like cannonfire. Her hold on him tightened before her fingernails massaged at the small of his back.

"Which one is yours?" she asked, and her head rested against his chest.

Gilbert squinted at the endless possibilities. To choose one like the north star would be far too cliché, but others were impossible to locate every night. "I'm not sure," he admitted. "Certainly one that has been with me since birth. But it is like trying to find the chamberpot at a party when you're several drinks in."

Id est: you do not, and are sick all over the floor in the corner, he thought, but Adrienne already knew every gruesome detail about his misfortunes.

"It must be the sun, then," said Adrienne after a very contemplative moment. Gilbert smiled and shook his head, making the top of hers a fine place to rest his cheek.

"The sun was too cruel to me during the southern campaign."

"Cruelty is not the antithesis of luck."

"It caused so many men to desert and burned my nose until I shed."

"But it gave you so many freckles for me to count."

It wasn't fair that she could tease him and not expect him to want to love her harder. They had been a cordial pair since the birth of Virginie – their *last*, a phrase that haunted him and had been a severe hit to Adrienne's pride. Finding her alone in the chapel or sitting in the garden with her thoughts while Gilbert had to attend ceremonies and meetings and drills did strike him like a fist, raw to his heart. The few moments when he was able to call to her in the day when her frown was at its deepest, she performed the happy woman ardently. Gilbert conceded to the point that while he was naïve at times, he was not blind. Their private lives were not to be a performance, not to each other.

Until work was to find him down in his land, he would be the most doting husband any woman could ask for.

Which meant no talk of lovers, no grumpy mention about politics unless she brought it up, bringing her breakfast in the morning and taking long promenades with her on the grounds and around the village so that she could be introduced to every one of the townsfolk. No doubt the people of Chavaniac would love her, it was difficult not to.

"You've gone quiet," Adrienne said. "Please say something."

"I was thinking about how the thought of anyone angry with me would be fine, save for you. I don't ever want you to hate me, *mon coeur*. You are too important to me."

"Who has been angry with you?"

"Oh, I've had some disagreements with Adams and some ministers —

oh, oh no, *no*, we are not getting into this discussion." He shook his head. "I tell you that your melancholy wounds me, and you only heard that others have crossed me?"

"Well my feelings are of no consequence," she replied, pushing against him to catch his face in full view. "I do not want you in ill repute with your peers! What on earth has gotten you and they to disagree?"

His tongue went to reply, he could go on in a passionate speech about how ridiculous it was that his plans for a French government were sidelined so quickly, and he knew he just allowed himself to speak of it if she brought it up, but seconds were too soon, and although she cast the line, he would not take the bate.

"What is this 'feelings are of no consequence' nonsense?" he stammered, his head shaking like the whole château was rumbling beneath them. "I will have you know that they are of *incredible* consequence. I am happy only when you are happy, and not pretend-happy, I want you to be sincerely happy – joyous, even! I want you to look at our family that you've dutifully raised to be as perfect as they are, and know that I could not love anyone as much as I do you and them; and you have every right to be content with that." He bit his cheek to stop.

"I do not wish to argue with you, Gilbert."

"There is nothing to argue about when we are on the roof. I have trapped you up here and as lord of this castle, I am declaring that, while it may be unhealthy for us to have any more children, it is still my marital duty and obligation to ensure and provide for your happiness." And with all the breath he had in his lungs, lifted his head to the sky, and consequently to the village below them, and shouted, "I am going to make love to my wife tonight!"

"Gilbert!" Adrienne's hands clapped over his mouth, falling into him as the breeze took his proclamation and her balance with it.

"I can still be a good lover to you," he mumbled. "I want to know if your happiness is genuine, and that I can be the cause of *that* instead of your sorrow." If her hands continued to prevent his words of affection, he was going to start licking them. He tucked his own hands under her robe, feeling the warmth of her back through the light linen nightgown. Adrienne's hands drifted closer to herself, and so he followed them with his lips until the only thing blocking him from kissing her were two layers of very delicate fingers.

Stars reflected in the dark pools of her eyes where not even a telescope would be powerful enough to explore all of them. "You are *not* the cause of my sorrow," she whispered, and although Gilbert knew she would not lie to him, he shook his head.

"I do not believe that," he replied.

"You've already given me so much, Gilbert, I hate it when I can't reciprocate."

"I've already told you, I don't need anything but you. I enjoy giving gifts to people I love, it makes me happy."

Adrienne sniffled and one hand fell away to wipe at her eyes. "And I just enjoy being with you," she said, "but I know you're so important to the people who need you, I can't…" Her other hand pivoted to cup his cheek, and they filled the space with an anxious kiss, followed by another for safe-keeping.

"You can," he said, agreeing with whatever hesitations she could have. "*Mon coeur*, you can." She could push him off the roof if she desired, although it would be better if she simply let herself take control of their late night dalliance. "I am yours to do with as you please."

"I'm sorry."

"Beloved, I will need to kiss you for every useless apology I hear."

Her nose squinched. "… Sorry."

Gilbert rolled his eyes and kissed down her cheek to her jaw to her neck until she tried to weasel her way out of his embrace. "Sorry, sorry, sorry," he said, clicking his tongue. "It is a word I never need to hear from your lips. Maybe from Anastasie's if she paints on the wall again, but not yours."

"You don't think she would paint over the murals here, would you?" Adrienne asked, suddenly very aware that their daughter may think that the art on the walls from decades past would mean she could add her own. "Oh, Gilbert, we should warn her right away in the morning."

"I was thinking of showing them the swimming pool after breakfast. Have them bring their studies down with us, and we can float and test them on their numbers."

The night air was prickling Adrienne's arms; their time on the château's peak should eventually come to an end.

"That does sound nice. I think they'd enjoy the water."

"And I may enjoy you in a wet chemise, perhaps," he thought aloud, biting his lip when Adrienne pinched his side.

"You're really thinking with your head tonight," she said, "and not the one attached to your neck."

"You are so lovely and amiable, it is hard to resist thinking about it." He avoided another pinch, stepping around her towards the door. She twirled once to keep facing him, her braid waving like a flag. "If it would please you, Madame, I will follow you to your chambers if you find the present environment too gauche." On one hand, their passion would certainly keep them warm, but a hard roof would leave more bruises and scrapes than a feather-filled mattress.

The softness in which his Adrienne regarded him – it robbed him of any thought. She clasped at his arm, her slippers struggling to remain on her feet as the tiles angled.

"Don't let me fall," she commanded, and Gilbert laughed, guiding her down the slope to the ladder. "And you may, if you'd like, accompany me *every* night to my room."

Gilbert lowered her gently back into the château, trying his best not to trip himself and crush his fingers in the door or stumble down the short-pronged steps. "Y-yes, Madame," he replied. Her fingers caught the strings of his robe as she tugged him along.

Chavaniac, August 1783

True to his word, Gilbert did show her around the village at the start of their summer. The people who worked the town were polite and sweet, happy to introduce Adrienne to their local wares and their families. She would return to the château with plenty of gifts from the workers; so many, in fact, that it was understandable where Gilbert's background of giving may have stemmed from. The southern French accent was delightful to listen to, Adrienne went out to the surrounding farms every other day to hear more of it – asking the men and women if they were in need of anything from supplies to money, and taking note of their responses in her journal. It was nice to feel useful after months of being housebound, she mused, and that Gilbert trusted her unconditionally with the affairs of his estate.

She hadn't seen him button his waistcoat at home since they arrived; he looked like a true country man in an uncocked cream hat, his sleeves rolled up to his elbows as he led the horse she rode on down the curving path of the château's large park. Neither of them had powdered their hair in a fortnight, having dunked themselves into the pools almost every evening. The children loved picking the wildflowers and chasing each other to exhaustion. It made for quiet, late afternoon walks together – just the two of them.

Heavy clouds rolled along in the distance, rumbling softly over the mountains, but the sky above them was still cerulean and amber, with feathered clouds that wouldn't know of the storm. A rustle in the trees, the grass was swaying, and Adrienne could smell rain from miles away. Gilbert still led them along, ambling over the path with the reins looped around his wrist.

She let herself close her eyes and listen to the muted clomping of the horse; thought of home – Louise had given birth to a son, Alexis, who thankfully was in perfect health. The new Marquise de Montagu, her dear sister Pauline, wrote often of her visit to her husband's medieval château a few hours outside of Paris: a perfect place to write unbothered. Her mother checked in constantly in weekly letters spanning pages long; Adrienne read them over dessert before Gilbert read his General Washington correspondence that came few and far between. One dated from May arrived that consumed Gilbert's attention as he updated himself on America's war, and of his friends; and the Washingtons' cordial compliments to Adrienne herself, which she accepted right away. To be remembered by the equivalent of the United States' royalty was an honor she held as highly as her husband did.

Gilbert had also been somewhat swarmed with letters from their Congress and spent the end of July responding and relaying information to Vergennes and to the American Peace Commissioners in Paris. The Franco-American Alliance, it seemed, was to be primarily carried on Gilbert's back. And if that was the case, Adrienne was going to do more for the estate so that he didn't have to.

The salon was coming along; she had decorated it modestly, but it still bore the familiarity of home in the way the floors were laid, the elegant drapery, and the lightly painted walls. She didn't need any intense sculpture or large paintings to cover the room – there was space to breathe and focus on the guests. And her first guests were people from their little hamlet, who were delighted to visit and discuss pleasantries alongside their home-life stories. Adrienne was determined to know as many people of Chavaniac as she could.

"Should we bring anything from here back with us for our Monday dinners?" Gilbert wondered out loud, breaking through Adrienne's thoughts. She opened her eyes to see him glancing back at her with a lopsided smile. "I didn't wake you, did I?"

"I wasn't sleeping," she said. "I think we should bring up some potatoes for a large cheese fondue."

"That was an easy answer."

"Ever since I visited Monsieur Gambol's fromagerie, I have just been *craving* it. The smell of it has been stuck in my nose. Let's bring other vegetables with us so we may all decide what tastes best with cheese and what we leave aside."

He scratched the horse under her snout and nodded his agreement; it was impossible to deny fondue. They pulled aside to the tiny pond hidden behind golden bushes and drooping tree limbs, where a steady gurgle of the river's water poured over a shoot made from a thick tree branch. A tower from the château was visible from where Adrienne sat atop the saddle, but once Gilbert helped her down, they truly disappeared into this tranquil oasis.

Birds twiddled from their high branches, using the shoot as a quaint running bath. Several racing dragonflies drew quick lines across the surface of the pond, dodging the splash of the little falls.

Gilbert's stockings were thrown high into the air, consumed by the long grass a few feet away. Adrienne settled into the little poof of linen her skirts provided as she sat down to watch him strip himself bare. The smallest glimpse of his rump from under his shirt as the breeze rustled it had her smile aching. She leaned forward to her elbows at the pond's edge while he dunked his head under the three-foot depths. He popped out to meet her in a quick wet kiss, the rest of his body floating to take up the length of the pool.

"Are you going to join me?" he asked. She smoothed back his hair. It was past his shoulder blades now, curling around his ears and precariously along his neck where the strands escaped his braid.

"Only if it's warm today," she replied. He reached up and pulled the pin keeping her braid wrapped around itself, the thick hair falling right to her lap. Fashion dictated that the front tresses were kept short, and without pomade and powder, framed her face with unusual bangs that Gilbert had taken a liking to twist and shape with his wet hands.

He rolled onto his back, his shirt sticking to his chest as he floated. "You'd be warm with me here," he said. "You cannot deny me this. We return to Paris before the month ends and there are no nice ponds in Paris. Just work and work disguised as leisure... and friends, but then there are friends who are actually just work disguised as friends."

"You enjoy work more than you think you do." She could easily push him under the water with a bop to his nose. "If helping democracy is involved then you love to have a hand in it. Don't forget I've read some of your letters; you are very persuasive."

"You too have been busy by your desk, *mon coeur*, but I have not been privy to enjoy your writing," Gilbert teased and that bop became a little more enticing.

"I am a busy woman."

"*Oh, là?*"

She picked at the fichu covering her chest, pulling it from her gown while she watched Gilbert fight not to glance at her bosom; his lips pressed tightly together. "Your aunt and I have been ardent in handling domestic affairs, but I've managed to squeeze in my own American ones." Trading correspondence with Lady Washington was one of many things she enjoyed behind the gentlemen's backs. How difficult it must be for the mistress of Mount Vernon to continue on alone without her husband – how blessed Adrienne felt to have hers here in front of her. Hopefully with the end of the war, Lady Washington may too enjoy marital bliss once more. She cocked her head and thought aloud, "I should write General Washington as well."

Gilbert sputtered out the water that snuck its way into his mouth. "You saying that while torturing me with how slowly you are undressing yourself is both cruel and exciting. I think he would love to hear from you. Any of my friends, really, would benefit from your words. You may write my heartless Hamilton; he writes me so little, and he likely needs to practice his French with a lady. He is more likely to respond to a woman, you see, he's a little bit rakish."

Adrienne shrugged her gown off, the breeze tickling at her collarbone while she sat in her stays and petticoats. A young, flirtatious, brazen red-headed man, she thought. *Hm, where has she heard that one before.*

"I better write to Lady Hamilton, then," she exclaimed. "She would need it more if that is the case. I do not think America takes as kindly to mistresses as the court of Versailles does."

Gilbert rolled back over, using his elbows to push himself up out of the water. "You are teasing me."

"That I would be your Hamilton's mistress or that you do not think you'd still be flirting with other women if we lived in America?" Adrienne met his face halfway, nudging his head back with her forehead. She fell forward in the grass until her arms could lay lackadaisical in the tepid pond. Not quite bathwater, but refreshing nevertheless. "I appreciate you at least bringing up Madame de Simiane to me."

She didn't mean to break the romantic gestures they were sharing, the words out of her mouth tasted bittersweet. No wife would want to acknowledge more affairs of their husband. But unlike Aglaé, Simiane by reputation alone was a very honorable woman in Versailles. She also was very pretty. Adrienne pinched the wet dirt under the water between her fingers.

"It changes nothing of my adoration for you," Gilbert said and Adrienne merely nodded. His hand found hers, digging between to entwine them. Even with his ass floating, he managed to tug her a little more forward into the pond. She squeaked as her shift's sleeves soaked through, water finding its way down the front of her bodice.

"You siren," she gasped and he flashed a mischievous toothy grin, yanking her into the pond, her petticoats be damned. His knees kept to the bottom, holding her like they would the children to rock them to sleep. She was the sailor that lost her way into the siren's clutches, to be dragged as deep as the creature pleased, to drown, to change, to be food or a prize. Her siren was hard to resist, she couldn't be blamed.

"I won't tell Hamilton you insinuated leaving me for him, it would go to his head," Gilbert mumbled into her neck as they bobbed around.

"I'll take his wife on a holiday, I think she would deserve it," Adrienne said. "I'll take all your friend's wives and we may sojourn to Italy or the like."

"You would leave these poor men without the comfort of their ladies? How you use your dagger to strike my heart so shamelessly."

"Your minds will be preoccupied with your talks of the future as they always have been. Tell me, Gilbert, if the opportunity came for you to return to the breast of your American father and family, you would not hesitate in the slightest to go. It has been almost two years since you've sojourned yourself."

Gilbert ducked his mouth under the surface, blowing bubbles as he looked at her. "Are you kicking me out of the country, *amour?*"

"Never would I have you out of my sight," she replied. "But you are rejuvenated from whatever fountains flow through the United States; the trip may do you some good. A little escape from politics."

"Would you come with me? See the lands we have fought for, bask in the Virginia sun together?"

Adrienne lifted her face to the sky, the warmth that bathed her cheeks dyed them rose over the weeks they've spent in the country. Washington's hands must also be warm, she thought, imagining he would bow most graciously to her if she arrived with Gilbert. And the tour that Lady Washington would give of their little villa would be marvelous to listen to if Adrienne worked harder on her English. But there was a tether around her wrists – she couldn't leave the children. They were too young to travel over an ocean, and she could not bear being so far from them.

"One day," she answered, running her hand over his jaw. "We can bring the whole family to meet their adoptive grandfather. Georges will have to meet his godfather and namesake, and Virginie: the land that she is named for."

"Poor Anastasie, without cause."

"She can see where her father had run off to when she was born," Adrienne said, pinching Gilbert's chest. He only sank further, bringing her weighed down petticoats to the bottom of the pond, her chin hardly above the water. "Gilbert! This isn't very mature of you, come now."

"No," he replied. "Every time you bring me guilt, I shall dunk you further."

"I was only stating a fact."

"But I felt a pang in my heart."

Adrienne rolled her eyes. "You poor thing," she said, brushing the wetness away from his lips before she claimed them as her own. She knew a thing or two about pangs.

Once they returned to Paris, he would be thrown back into his work, his idle time split between many characters until the sun fell below the horizon and she would wait for him to return to bed in the late hours if he wasn't called away for a few days at a time. Still, while it lasted, it was nice to have him every day over the summer. She was young again with him, as if they were still those teenagers who met that fateful spring afternoon. Combing through his hair with her nails, there weren't any that were graying just yet; which was a relief. The man was only about to turn twenty-six.

Chapter Twenty-One

Paris, April 1784

"I do not understand why he is treating me like this!" Gilbert marched back out of his office and into the parlor where Adrienne sat with Georges and a book on her lap. He had been returning with a different letter every few minutes, the line of his scowl only deepening. "It is not like the American delegation had anything to *pay* for when we French soldiers joined the Society – I've paid for it all – *I've* gone into debt for Cincinnati. Why is Adams acting as if *he* has? Have I missed something? Did I spite him somehow?" He shuffled through his paperwork. "Ever since the negotiations have started between the delegates and Britain, he has been nothing but rude to my offers and support. Do you know what he wrote me when he learned of my trip to America? Adrienne, you would not believe..."

Adrienne put her thumb into the novel's pages, readily waiting for him to return with another letter from Monsieur Adams, who had been ill in the Netherlands for the past month.

"*'As to your going to America, surely I have no objection against it. Being asked whether you were going to America, I answered that you talked of it, but I questioned whether you would go, as the War was over, and I knew of no particular* motive *you might* have *to go*,'" Gilbert read, throwing his free arm about. "I am sorry, did he miss the fact that I have every motive to visit my adoptive father and see my brothers whom I have fought and shed blood with? I love them and they, me. That is reason enough."

"Have you already written him back?"

"Yes, but he has not replied. I'm waiting to hear about my departure date from l'Orient and was going to ask if any of the delegation have letters or parcels I could carry to their loved ones." Gilbert frowned, folding and unfolding the letter. "I want him to not hold any amnesty against me, but whenever we argue in person, I find I cannot speak English correctly and it makes me feel like such a fool."

"Whatever strains Monsieur Adams may be going through, it may be because of his illness or that he is a homesick man who is jealous that you are returning to his land and he is not," Adrienne replied. "Think of the more important things. Have you written to Washington?"

"Only four times on the same day a few weeks ago. I fear he may tire of my scribbling. I can picture his face as he receives the stack one of these days; he'd sigh through his nose and give a slight shake of his head. If he's happy to get them, he may give the smallest of smiles, otherwise it will be a *thump* right to his desk. I told him I would see him come June, but that is not going to happen at this rate. End of the summer at best."

Adrienne was also waiting on a response to her letter to the retiring general as well that she wrote one inspired night in late December. How desperate she was to rejoice for him, to hope that she may meet him in France one day and to show him the country with Gilbert at her side. As American as she was French, any celebrations she heard from across the Atlantic sparked fireworks in her soul. Virginie was already learning how to speak Washington's name the proper way – not to sound like any other horrid Frenchman who had tried.

"You're going away?" Georges asked. He had only heard in bursts about Gilbert's foreign trip.

"It will be but a few months," Gilbert replied, finally settling on the sofa. He stole the child from Adrienne's lap. "You will be so busy with your lessons and with your sisters, you won't even notice I'm gone."

Anastasie, curled up with her own book in the far chair that overlooked the river, poked her head up. "I am going to notice, Papa. You're going to be gone when I turn eight. What am I supposed to do if you don't take my anniversary walk with me?"

Gilbert pursed his lips. "Sweetling, you can still promenade with your Maman. I'll bring you something from America; tell me what you would like before I go." He let his head fall back on the cushion, glancing at Adrienne with glassy eyes. "Do you think Virginie has any objections as well that I should get over with?"

"She will be none the wiser as long as you're back by Christmas," Adrienne said.

"Just a few months, *mon coeur*, I promise."

Anastasie's dark eyes rose from the chair. "May you carry a letter from me, Papa?"

Gilbert laughed. "A letter? To whom?"

"I want to write Washington."

Adrienne's cheeks warmed. She turned to Gilbert, who looked at their eldest with a tender smile.

"Absolutely. I'll make sure it is the first one he reads when I see him."

☆

Throughout May and into June, Gilbert and his fellow soldiers amended some points to the French faction of the Society of Cincinnati that had made the American delegation so irritable. Even then, Monsieur Adams ignored all of Gilbert's olive branches; an obtusely rude gesture, but Adrienne held her tongue. It would be easy for her to pen a letter to Madame Adams. In fact, while Gilbert was sailing to America, Madame Adams was sailing to Europe. A perfect opportunity to invite the amiable woman to the la Fayette home.

Anastasie perched herself on the edge of a chair as she held her pen with determination. She wrote in English, heavy-handed, but still lovely and legible.

I hope that papa whill come back Son here, I am verry sorry for the loss of him, but I am verry glade for you self. I wich you a werry good health and I am whith great respect, dear sir, your most obedient servent... anastasie la fayette

She watched wide-eyed at her father as Gilbert skimmed the note with an approving nod, tapping his chin as if he were a professor of the English language. "Very well said, Mademoiselle," he stated. "I believe he will be taken aback with such a lovely correspondent."

"I want to fold it!" she replied, taking the paper to gently line up the page. "Can I seal it too?"

"Let your Papa add a little something and then you can stamp it."

After a quick scribble, he melted some wax and held it firm for Anastasie to press the house seal to the paper. Adrienne lifted Virginie up to receive a long goodbye nuzzle and kiss; her small hands held Gilbert's ears as he whispered countless affections into her round cheeks.

"Would you like to add anything for your father to bring with him, Georges?" Adrienne asked the boy. He stood with crossed arms in the corner of the room, his shoulders hunched as he held back some whimpers. "*Georges.*"

"I don't want P-papa to g-go," she heard him mutter.

Adrienne, with Virginie in hand, stared long at Gilbert. He was not a man that needed much prompting to console his son, to whom he sneaked over and scooped up from the corner. Georges wailed, kicking his feet out until Gilbert smothered him into his coat.

"No child of mine is going to be crying out of sadness if I can help it," he said, finding Georges' wet cheek to blow a raspberry into. He fought through the attempts to repress some giggles until Georges' forced frown surrendered to a smile. "I will miss you all so very much. But I will return with many stories and regards from our American friends, it will make up for the time lost." He picked Anastasie up along his walk back to Adrienne, groaning like an old man at balancing his two children in either arm. "Forgive me, your Maman deserves the next raspberry."

Adrienne beat him to it, eliciting laughter from all around until the kids groaned and covered their eyes at their parents farewell kisses.

"None of my friends' parents kiss as much as you do," Anastasie complained. "You're squishing us."

"No one loves your Maman as much as I do," Gilbert said, squeezing his small family more. He kissed Adrienne once again for good measure. "Keep up your studies, you two. I want to hear some beautiful singing when I get back. Someone must give me a whole presentation on everything you have learned or I shall be very cross."

His coach was already packed with everything he could possibly need for an American autumn. Some friends and family took his offer to be the courier for their letters, and he added them to his own stack. Louis stopped by to personally reprimand him in case his correspondence was to not make it to their intended, ending his scold with a tight embrace. Adrienne watched from the door, arms full of their children until the governess came to her side to take Anastasie to her dancing lessons and Georges for his numbers. Gilbert admired her through the carriage window, bowing his head as the coach lurched forward, leaving only the odor of horse and dirt behind.

She could handle a few months. Her knees wobbled slightly, but with Virginie wiggling in her hold, she was determined to remain upright, eyeing the road until Gilbert was out of sight.

The Hôtel de la Fayette grew more *l'Américaine* in decoration and no doubt would continue to do so if Gilbert thought to purchase and mail home items from his trip. From the friendly compliments they had received from guests, Adrienne lived as close to America as she could in France. Even the gardens bloomed flowers and trees from seeds and saplings sent from Boston, Philadelphia, and Albany. Bursts of violets and ferns enjoyed the sunny Paris days. Adrienne nudged the windows open, the breeze kicking up a few goosebumps on her arms.

She couldn't say why she thought what she did, as she stared past the young trees in the yard. For some reason whenever Gilbert left her, there were some rogue decisions that struck a match in her head, and her tongue was sharp and cutting. The idea had already been stirring in her head, planted by a roused Louise years ago.

Virginie pulled at the necklace adorning Adrienne's neck, glancing up at her with light-eyes that she eventually decided on a few weeks after her birth. Her hair had grown curly and ginger-touched brown. She was a Noailles child, no doubt, Adrienne's features all over except when she played far away, and the proportions of her face were every ounce her father's.

Adrienne ran a pinkie down Virginie's nose. She was a quiet baby, ever attentive and calm when in Adrienne's arms. So intelligent she was, that one could never have guessed she was born prematurely.

Stress was what the doctor had said was the cause of that whole affair. Adrienne had said nothing; affairs, no doubt, were the reason for any wife's anguish.

She clicked her teeth, turning from the window to walk the length of the parlor to where the home's valet was often found amongst the servant's quarters.

"Madame?" he said, rising from his small corner office.

"I'd like you to invite someone to the Hôtel as soon as her schedule permits," Adrienne said, waiting for the valet to collect a calling card from its quaint chest.

"Right away, Madame. Who is the recipient?"

"Madame de Simiane, if you please."

Paris, July 1784

She wrung her hands out as she paced the parlor. It was a miracle the silver gown didn't reveal her sweat underneath. Evening was settling in the sky, dyeing the clouds lilac and the gulls a dark inky black while they flew from the sea down the Seine.

Words. Rehearsing some words. She didn't know what words – just that her brain kept repeating "words," but it kept her heart from racing too frantically as every carriage noise tightened a noose around her throat.

It was her home, Adrienne thought, she was the lady of the house – the queen, arguably, as long as Marie-Antoinette never actually visited the Hôtel de la Fayette. If a guest scorned her in her own abode, it was Adrienne's choice to do with them as she pleased. There should have been nothing to worry about. She left the children in their bedrooms with plenty of books and sewing to work on with their governess, all the servants were at their most ready for anything Adrienne could need from drink to a riding crop.

"Madame, the comtesse's carriage has arrived out front. Will you receive her here?"

Adrienne nodded and carefully sat on the edge of a chair as the valet left. Then she stood up, then sat back down. No, she decided, she should stand. No need to look shorter than she already was.

The Comtesse de Simiane was quite a fine young woman who worked in the queen's social circle, a lady-in-waiting for the king's sister. Adrienne dared to admit that she was as beautiful as the court said – intelligent eyes, clear as quartz, with lips perfectly strawberry-shaped. She stood half a foot taller than Adrienne, a ribbon draped over the back curls of her lightly powdered hair. Simiane still retained youthful smooth skin and a long, unmarred neck that bore no jewels or decoration. She stepped quietly into the salon, her gaze to the floor as she met Adrienne with a deep, polite curtsy.

"Marquise," she said. "Thank you for the invitation to your home. I admit, it came at a surprise. Please forgive my delay in responding, my duties prevented me from leaving Versailles for some time."

Adrienne felt the heat from the candles several feet away. Her jaw clenched as she resisted giving her knuckles a tight crack. She opened her palm and gestured to the sofa across from her. "Please, have a seat, Madame," she said, finally lowering herself to the chair. Nothing creaked, her satin gown did not even crease.

Simiane smoothed her skirts as she sat. She was two years younger than Adrienne, and up close, the lack of deep lines in her makeup – as minimal as it was – revealed just that. The hesitation to meet Adrienne's eyes told her that Simiane knew exactly what she was doing there. They had never spoken before, not really. Gilbert had met the girl in Versailles, telling Adrienne he found her quite amiable and a good talking partner… among other things.

"How may I be of service to you, Madame de la Fayette?" Simiane asked. Her hands folded on her lap, palms up to the ceiling.

A breath sucked through her teeth. "Tell me about yourself, Madame, if you will. I am afraid I do not get to Versailles often enough to make new friends."

"Oh," Simiane said. She pressed her lips together, and looked up at the decor of the room before she smiled softly. "A short synopsis of me… My father is the Marquis d'Antigny, I have plenty of brothers. One served as the Comte de Rochambeau's aide-de-camp during the American War of Independence, though currently he is employed under the Comte de Provence." She paused, finding interest in the books that lay on the table to her side. "I love to read. Though sometimes my efforts are in vain, I am attempting to grow my library. Some English books are difficult to find translations for."

"What do you read?"

"Anything I can get my hands on," she replied. "Much of what I currently own is fiction in nature, but I enjoy a talk of politics between ladies and enlightened men as much as the next persevering woman. I've always admired the salons the Duchesse d'Ayen hosted and am sorry to have not earned an invitation."

Adrienne glanced at the books on the table: Diderot and Locke, as well as the old pamphlets she and her sisters read with Madame de Puisieux when they were but mere adolescents. The pages were worn, the binding marked with years of opening and bending.

Simiane shrugged. "No one believes I have read all of Shakespeare. Frankly I'm not sure if it is embarrassing to admit or an impressive feat."

A huff of laughter escaped Adrienne's nose so fast, she didn't have the chance to suppress it. Simiane perked up, finally meeting her eye, and her shoulders lowered.

Self-deprecating, how odd a trait to all have in common. Madame Aglaé had no ounce of humility in her body before the Noailles family began to shame her for it. Simiane, by contrast, was already in the family's good graces. Did Adrienne want to like her? No, not really. It would be normal for her to dislike any other woman in Gilbert's life; but then again, her utmost affection for the man was already unusual. She had the money and her family, all of it provided, any other woman would enjoy her independence while their husbands were off dallying.

Speaking of husbands, Simiane hadn't mentioned hers.

"How is the Comte de Simiane?" Adrienne asked, waving over a servant to lay out a small platter of cheese and fruit.

"He is well, last I have heard. I only see him in passing, and he has been training for the season."

"You do not write each other?"

"No, Madame, I cannot say we've had much of a relationship since we said our vows. We are on a friendly plane of existence, but," she swallowed, "he prefers a different kind of company that I cannot supply him with."

She was smiling, but it was empty. Adrienne felt her hands grow cold; she took a piece of brie, breaking it apart.

"I'm sorry to hear that. Forgive my ignorance."

"That's alright, Madame, it's been several years since I came to accept it. Makes me appreciate the bonds I have since formed with genuine people."

Adrienne's tepid expression faltered, a tiny twitch to her brow.

"You've invited me because you wish to speak of my connection with the Marquis," Simiane said. Her face softened.

"This is too awkward, isn't it," Adrienne said, staring blankly at the food dish. "I thought you would be threatened to speak with me, but you are as composed as any dignified queen would be."

Simiane let the quiet carry as she took a berry from the platter. "I was. I am. But your kindness and modesty precedes you, Marquise. I do not think a wife who did not love her husband would invite a woman with amicable relations with him into her home. When I received your call, I thought – no – I *knew* that it was because there is a strong bond between you two. I do not wish to form a chasm, but let us mend this awkwardness between *us*."

"I cannot see how it can not be but a little unusual."

"Unusual is quite fine, don't you think?"

Adrienne smirked for a moment. "Tell me how you first came to know the Marquis."

The comtesse went into polite detail about Gilbert's coming to see her portrait being completed; how he was charming and glowing since his return from America. They spoke of their interests, how he let her say all that she wanted to say before he added his remarks instead of interrupting like so many men did. Their duties, the philosophical gossip of the week, current news coming from Britain and the like, all fit into their conversation and eventually to their correspondence. She was Aglaé's fallback, in the polite sense. Gilbert never made her feel like she was lesser than his first mistress, they had never fought like the first, disagreements were discussed instead.

"We do have opposing opinions on many things, but I think that is why I enjoy his friendship. He doesn't try to change mine, although he does give some long, thought out arguments," Simiane exclaimed.

"Yes, he does that," Adrienne replied. The embellishments on her gown were loosening under her constant fidgeting. She didn't want to ask about how extensive their affair was, she wanted to know, but she didn't, but did they kiss like she and Gilbert did? Did he hold Simiane as firmly, twirl her hair around his fingers and lift her into the air?

Her nose was beginning to sting like she had breathed in water.

"Does he, ah… Is the Marquis…" Adrienne squeezed her fist.

"He is," Simiane provided, "a tender man. A good man."

Adrienne felt the burn of a tear tumble down her cheek before the salt contaminated her tongue. The comtesse rose from the sofa, rounding the table to kneel on the floor beneath her. It was something one of the Noailles sisters would have done, to clasp her hands between theirs in an effort to quell the inevitability that was grief.

"He is lucky to have you, Madame. You cannot fathom how often I see him look forward to returning home." She removed a handkerchief from her pocket and lifted it to Adrienne. It smelled like roses. "I do not wish to replace your prominence in his heart."

"And I do not wish to remove the happiness you bring him either," Adrienne replied, dabbing at her eyes.

Damn it, damn it, damn it.

Sorry, God, don't listen to my head, Adrienne pleaded.

Bells chimed from the resident church, deep and distant, filling the space of silence. Simiane's hands were pleasantly warm. Adrienne practically played with them in her lap. It could have been worse – the comtesse could have been an ugly, terrible woman. If Adrienne could like Gilbert a little less for taking a mistress, at least his choice was kind and intelligent, she couldn't dislike him for having bad taste.

"Would you tell me about yourself, Madame?" Simiane asked, having made herself comfortable on the rug.

"Does he not speak of me?"

"He tells me how wonderful a mother you are; how clever you have always been since you two met so young. I thought sixteen was young for me to marry, but to have been together at fourteen…"

"I met him when I was twelve," Adrienne replied. "He was a terribly awkward boy."

"He still is… a little awkward," Simiane said, color coming to her cheeks. "In an endearing way. He tries."

Adrienne sobbed another laugh. "Yes, he does try."

"Do you also like to read?"

"Our library is just in the other room. I read with our children daily."

She leaned against the sofa, attentive to Adrienne's description of the authors they had in their collection. Simiane had no children of her own, nay, she believed she never would have any. As difficult as it was to consummate her own marriage, no progeny would ever likely come to being.

Wine came out from the halls, something chilled to pair well with the food, when the candlesticks sank low in their sconces. Simiane seemed delighted to listen to anything Adrienne had to say; and when she made the comtesse laugh, she decided then and there that she was going to bring the woman so close to a confidant that it could border on a scandal of its own. It would never not be awkward: a wife befriending a mistress. Yet in comparison to Aglaé, where Adrienne was left to mope alone in the house, Simiane would be invited back to Adrienne's salons as often as she pleased; even if it was during the times Gilbert went alone to Versailles, she could invite this new friend over to Paris.

Adrienne bit into a strawberry, sitting on the floor with a second glass in hand. "So," she said, letting her head rest on the cushion seat, "I personally believe Gilbert's waist is perfectly proportional, but he has argued that he put on weight."

"The Marquis most certainly has not. He could use a few pounds still. Although I have seen when men get older that it happens naturally. He may have something akin to a belly when he reaches thirty."

"Thirty, my gosh," Adrienne mulled. "That feels so far but so close. Our Anastasie would be ten by that time. The thought makes me nauseous."

Simiane sipped the last of her wine. "You said she likes to paint, yes? May I send her some? Elisabeth is a friend of mine and would know where to find the best pigments."

"You may. And may I call upon you again in the upcoming weeks? I can use another hand when I take the children out for a promenade. Sometimes my sisters are not available in Paris, and my mother has been recovering from a cold and I do not wish to cause any further strain."

"With your children?" Simiane exclaimed. She set her glass down, searching the little space in the middle of their skirts. "I would be honored, Madame. And please, call me Adélaïde."

Versailles, December 1784

When she wasn't replying to the farmers of Chavaniac to help with the year's harvest collapse, or writing to Madame Chavaniac about the construction and organization for the women of the village to attend a weaving school, or going through the *loads* of paperwork that the family lawyer had sent her on account of their finances, Adrienne still enjoyed the company of the Noailles. Opportune times throughout the year allowed the young la Fayette children to meet and greet their cousins, including the tiny, future Vicomte de Noailles.

Louise, Pauline, and Adrienne had a grand time poking and prodding and teasing Anne for finally getting married to the far older Comte de Thézan, a maester for a cavalry camp among a long list of titles. He was a southern gentleman as well, with a strong arm to keep Anne from flying off. Rosalie was the last, although never wanton for lack of suitors according to their father – who took the interviewing process very seriously for the family's final opportunity to spread their influence even further.

Papi was having a splendid time in the company of his great-grandchildren, holding Virginie's hand as he pointed out all the artwork he acquired since their last visit. Ségur was actively reading while standing in an also-active conversation. He was to leave immediately for Saint Petersburg, delaying his coach until he had one final opportunity to cuff Gilbert when the man returned. It was to be a "strike to last years" according to Ségur, who kept his sleeve prematurely rolled back. His youngest son, Philippe-Paul, ran through the rooms and adjoining hallways with Georges right on his tail. Laure and Anastasie discussed fan positions in the corner. Octave stood silently by his father's side, a hand gripping the cane Ségur leaned on.

Adrienne kept her arm looped with her sisters', keeping watch of the children while Anne discussed her plans to go south for the late winter and early spring before the Comte de Thézan had to return for training. All wives should have some beautiful getaway, Anne argued, when their husbands went off to play with their swords all summer.

"I couldn't leave the children," Adrienne replied, cupping Georges' hair as he ran by.

Louise smoothed her gown over her still rounded belly. Baby Vincent had surprised them at the end of autumn. A carbon copy of his father. "The wetnurses, and your governess, are responsible enough of the babes to get away for a week or two," she said. "Imagine nights without hearing the crying."

"You couldn't catch me sleeping peacefully without them under my roof," Adrienne said. She shook her head. "They would have to come with me. Virginie and Georges need a few more years, then Gilbert and I are going to bring them to see America."

Pauline's face scrunched into a grin. "Have you written to Gilbert about your biweekly tea with Madame Simiane? That is the drama I am waiting to hear."

"It hasn't specifically made its way into my letters," Adrienne replied, poking one finger to another. "I've only received two letters from him in the past four months. I think Monsieur Washington's home had successfully held him hostage; it was to bookend his trip."

"Maybe she wrote him about you."

She didn't think Adélaïde had. It would be more appropriate if Adrienne was the one to admit she invited his mistress into their home.

"I still think you should let him find you in conference with her sometime. I believe it would be poetic justice," Louise exclaimed, plopping a strawberry macaron into her mouth.

Adrienne puffed her cheeks. "You're just projecting what you'd like to do with Louis. Gilbert and I are honest with each other."

"So he knows how uncomfortable you are?" Louise asked under her breath. Adrienne's hair stood up under her sleeves.

Anne looked at Louise. "Louis would produce the most ridiculous expression if you were taking tea with every woman he had affairs with. Perhaps if we hired a painter to recreate it?"

They all turned to glance at the other end of the room where the vicomte was in deep conversation with their father. The Duc d'Ayen's face was in its practiced frown, poised for listening to one of the many radical ideas that Louis came up with: many government plans, peppered with vague treason. Clearly, there was always something exciting happening in the Noailles household.

Silent as ever, the Duchesse d'Ayen appeared between Louise and Adrienne's shoulders, and whispered to Adrienne, "his coach has pulled up outside. Go now if you want to beat the announcement."

Stepping backward out of the conversation, she excused herself to the hall. He was late. He may have stopped in Paris if no one had reported to him at the dock that the family was in their Versailles residence. He might have stopped elsewhere.

Adrienne squeezed her fist. It was unlikely. He was always at his best when he returned from a long voyage.

The hall grew cold without all the family to warm it, lit with a few candles down the way. A thud of the front door opening, whispers from the manservants, an echo of footsteps – Adrienne kept moving towards the foyer, her velvet gown doing nothing to keep her anxious body from shivering until Gilbert stepped into her sight.

She disappeared under his cloak, wrapping him completely in her arms.

"Lady Washington fed you well," she mumbled into his chest. He had some squish to work with. "I should write a thank you letter."

His laugh warmed them both. The cloak's ribbon cried as he tore the bow apart, revealing her once more as it dropped to the ground. It was becoming too easy for him to bend down and pick her up, letting her drape over him as he leaned until his back cracked and they could only laugh more. His smile lines had slightly deepened.

"Mount Vernon crafted the best meals. I've been given some recipes that I hope you will share with our cook."

"I would love to."

"And everyone is so well, *mon coeur*. Many have started their own families, become so important to their country. Retirement suits General Washington very much, but ah, I cannot see him remaining there long with how the bustle of Philadelphia was churning. There is so much to share with you," Gilbert said. He kissed her neck. "But, here I am in the Maréchal's home. Where are my children? And all our brothers and sisters?"

"In the music room now," Adrienne replied. "You've missed dinner."

"I was held up before I even disembarked the ship, I'm sorry." He swayed back and forth; her feet dangled like a doll's. "Are our babies upset with me?"

"No, they've been playing. Like I said," Adrienne slid back to the floor and took his cheeks between her hands, "before Christmas and everything would be fine."

"Did you hear I am a doctor of law now?" he asked, happily looping her arm around his as they made their way back to the soirée.

"Must we call you Doctor la Fayette?"

"Mm, no, I don't think I get that additional title. Harvard wasn't very clear about it. I think Hamilton would have told me if I did. I was a little more excited about my honorary state citizenship." He was growing slightly scruffy, as if he shaved a few days prior and forgot to freshen up before arriving. Fair ginger hairs revealed themselves in the passing candlelight. "I believe you would enjoy the piety of Massachusetts, but the climate of Virginia. If we are to retire to the American countryside and become farmers, perhaps somewhere in the middle."

Adrienne nodded. "And how were the Washingtons? In good health?"

"Very," he replied. "The General and I embraced at the stoop of his home and cried for half an hour before we broke apart." His smile waned. They stopped outside the salon doors. "I am afraid that I have seen my General for the last time though," he whispered. "He is an aging man, of course… Not an immortal nor a god."

Adrienne squeezed his arm. "You will return to Mount Vernon to see him again, I promise," she said. "You must enjoy his letters and be his best correspondent in the meanwhile, that's all. He is the one man I know could never tire of your letters; rivals only myself in this world."

"We're about to greet the family and you are going to make me cry," he mumbled, swiping a handkerchief from his coat pocket to dab at his eyes dramatically. "But yes. You will come with me next time and it will be all the better."

He was prepared to catch a flying Anastasie as they entered the room, her happiness reverberating around the family at his return. Georges latched onto his leg like a shackle; the combined effort of the eldest children brought their general-of-a-father down to the floor, aided by their cousins for an opportunity to lay atop an adult, and eventually of Louis and the Comte de Ségur despite the judgmental brows of the mature company.

"Mercy! Mercy!" Gilbert cried underneath them all. His hand fished a packet of letters from his waistcoat. "I have brought offerings!"

Louis snatched his right away, but Adrienne was ten-times more enticed by the neatly folded envelope from Washington that Gilbert handed to Anastasie. She bounced in place, the ringlets of her hair flying free from her cap as she carefully broke the seal and allowed her papa to sit up beside her as she read it.

"Mount Vernon, the twenty-fifth of November, one thousand-seven-hundred and eighty-four," she said in English.

"Very good," Gilbert replied. The foreign language attracted the family's ear to the words of General Washington to the young girl.

"Permit me to thank my dear little correspondent for the favor of her letter of the 18th of June last, and to impress her with the idea of the pleasure I shall derive in the continuation of them. Her Papa is restored to her with all the good health, paternal affection and honors her tender heart could wish..." Anastasie grinned as she leaned into Gilbert's shoulder, letting him correct her on pronunciation. He eyed Adrienne as she settled on their other side.

"Continue, sweetling," he pushed.

"He will carry a kiss to her from me, (which might be more agreeable from a pretty boy), and give her assurances of the affectionate regard with which I have the pleasure of being her well wisher."

Gilbert pressed a hard kiss to Anastasie's cheek, which followed up with a loud, immature raspberry that lit her entire face pink until she escaped into a warm embrace and all Gilbert could do was hold her to his chest, his own cheeks rosy. "We will have to keep this letter very safe, isn't that right, Maman?" he said, looking at Adrienne.

"Yes, we will," she said. "We can frame it if you'd like to show it off to guests. A correspondent of Monsieur Washington? Oh, sweetling, what an honor." She tickled Anastasie's back.

"For you as well, *mon coeur,*" Gilbert whispered, handing her a slightly thicker letter with Washington's familiar hand addressing her. "You must tell me what he said about my character."

"If he has not already revealed it to you," she replied, tucking the letter into her bodice for later, "then it is to be a private confession."

Noailles gatherings stretched naturally into the early hours of the morning when the skies were brightening behind passing winter clouds. Ségur departed with his family in tow after many kisses, bound to Russia. Gilbert rubbed his shoulder as the family waved their goodbyes to his carriage; in his other arm, he carried a half-conscious Georges. It went without saying that the la Fayette children were the only ones remaining by the time the party ended, albeit sleepily, if awake at all. Virginie was contently snuggled in Adrienne's arms after trying her first sip of chocolate. They opted, like they all used to, to remain for the morning, resting in their old apartments – that was, Gilbert found his way into hers as she was putting Virginie back to her cradle.

Adrienne was too nostalgic, too often, keeping watch on the reflection of Gilbert while he changed. He was facing his own mirror and, after shedding most of his clothes, had focused on his hairline with a disapproving frown that caused a single annoyed line to crease between his brows. Adrienne sat on the bed, still watching him until his attention flitted towards her little form behind him.

"You don't think I shall be bald before thirty, do you?" he asked, pulling the ribbon from his queue.

Adrienne shook her head. "You've lasted this long. I haven't noticed much change. You've always had a very noble-looking face. It is probably why I fancied you so much."

He turned around, his frown shifted into a smirk. "Oh goodness, you liked me?" he asked. The bed thumped as he threw himself onto it, rolling until he bumped into her on the other side. He immediately ducked down and nipped at her thigh.

She pinched his belly. "You're such an oaf sometimes," she said.

"Yes," he replied. "I was told if I didn't sleep the final night of the sea voyage, I would be a complete lunatic by the next evening, but I was too excited to see you, I could not rest. Although I believe I have avoided losing most of my faculties."

"One more hour, however, I'm not sure," Adrienne said, scratching her nails through his hair.

Chapter Twenty-One

"There's so much I want to tell you."

"And I have things to share too, but beloved, you're already half-asleep."

"No, I'm not," Gilbert said, opening his eyes.

Adrienne rolled hers. "Like father, like son. You're worse than Georges."

"No, I'm not," he yawned.

She kept quiet, gazing at him relaxing as he slowly did fall asleep. Like clockwork, after two minutes, his lips parted slightly, his head lolled to the side… Given he was lying slanted with his head at the foot of the bed, above the covers, Adrienne easily snatched the pillows and readjusted the blankets. There was no headboard to sit up at, so she laid on her stomach and opened Washington's letter. It was addressed the same date as Anastasie's.

Madam, If my expression was equal to my sensibility, I should in more elegant language than I am master of, declare to you my sense of the obligation I am under for the letter you did the honor to write me, by the Marquis de la Fayette, and thanks for this flattering instance of your regard. The pleasure I received by once more embracing my friend could only have been increased by your presence, and that opportunity I should therefore have had of paying in my own house, the homage of my respectful attachment to his better half... The Marquis returns to you with all the warmth and ardor of a newly inspired lover. We restore him to you in good health, crowned with wreaths of love and respect from every part of the Union. That his meeting with you, his family and friends, may be propitious and as happy as your wishes can make it — that you may long live together revered and beloved — that you may transmit to a numerous progeny the virtue which you both possess — is consonant with the vow and fervent wish of your devoted and most respectful Humble Servant.

The man was a poet, like Gilbert was. A modest one, that appealed to all of Adrienne's affections. Even he and Lady Washington pleaded for a completed family visit. Virginie was still so tiny, she would have to be at least ten before Adrienne considered putting her on a ship for an entire month's journey. If the mid-nineties wasn't too much for the Washingtons, that would be the perfect time to travel.

Adrienne rested her chin on a curved arm; Gilbert hugged her around her waist. They would be in their mid to late thirties by that time, she thought. Even at twenty-five now, she thought of how twenty-four was far better than this: she kept finding new lines on her forehead, new scars on her thighs and belly. Thank goodness for an early marriage or it would have been her that would be considered an old maid.

Gilbert didn't seem to mind. His hands still could easily hold her, and she didn't care that he was slowly aging too. She left the letter on the chest next to the bed and descended deeper under the covers to observe her quarry. The smile lines she noticed before had relaxed, as did the lines of his forehead. Gilbert would still be very handsome if he had to shave his head; his face could suit it. But she loved his hair, it had grown considerably through autumn. She kissed the tip of his nose, tucking herself perfectly into his arms.

"We should cast your face," she whispered.

Gilbert grunted, something nondescript. "Family portrait," he added, nuzzling into her hair. "To send to… 'shington…"

They would immediately sit for a portrait upon their return to Paris and Gilbert presented Georges with a small, replica continental uniform. Anastasie stood above a sitting Adrienne, looking dear at her father. Virginie sat in her mother's lap holding a bible. Adrienne, content in looking forward towards the painter, still kept an open hand towards Gilbert on the arm of the chair. It was their first family sitting and the children had done so well. The sittings lasted a month, every Saturday afternoon for an hour at a time. To be shipped to Virginia, at least the la Fayette family likeness would have the first opportunity to see their adopted nation.

Part Three

Pity the woman who loves the man who flies too high.

Chapter Twenty-Two

Paris, January 1787

I f the past two years could be written in Adrienne's diary, they would be full of completely domestic and household itineraries. How very content she was to enjoy the uninterrupted bliss of her role as mother and wife, and as a trusted financial advisor to all household incomes and expenditures. It was time-consuming work: keeping track of numbers and land-holdings, who they owed and who owed them. When Gilbert was busy touring the German states, she kept a stern eye on their *emancipation* experiment at a modest plantation on the coast of Cayenne, guaranteeing each worker was paid and provided for, and that there were no additional purchases of slaves or cruel punishments for the undeserving. She maintained contact with the estate's nearby seminary to ensure that each of the workers had an education and a religious teaching. Gilbert trusted her explicitly, and at many times, the two would be bent over their desks, back to back for hours of the day.

Adélaïde had visited nine times in the last year alone, typically happy to read with the children or take tea with Adrienne. *"Auntie Di"* had come from Anastasie's mouth one afternoon several months back, causing Gilbert to choke on his drink at the dinner table. With his mistress visiting their Paris home so often, it appeared to Adrienne that he saw her outside the home less and less. Adélaïde's own husband wasn't pleased with the arrangement at all, claiming Gilbert was stealing all of her company. Though the Comte de Simiane loathed Gilbert for it, no duels came from the affair, and Adélaïde was never hurt, so the la Fayette's merely ignored the man. He could complain and fret, but the Madame was a happy guest of their little home.

Frost danced up every window of the Hôtel. The ivy they had imported from America was supporting an inch of snow along the outside stone, never wavering under the weight. It was a powdered blanket over their gardens, a soft and delicate sight to accompany their dinners. An American dinner, the family entertained their usual repertoire. Monsieur Franklin had been replaced with Monsieur Jefferson – a far younger man, of similar complexion to Gilbert, with skill in the French tongue as well as his remarks. The Noailles had already spoiled the man with French culture. He differed greatly from the company across the table of the Adams' who visited from Britain as often as they could. Adrienne enjoyed Madame Adams, an intellectual and sincere woman who reminded her of her own mother with her wit and forwardness. Gilbert enjoyed the banter between the American gentlemen, happy to mingle in his comments or two or five whenever talks became political.

When the hors d'oeuvres finished, Gilbert rang a small bell and the servants poured in to take and replace the plates and departed the room: quick, discreet, and allowed guests to speak comfortably without the aristocratic pressure of a dozen strangers watching their every move.

"I am hesitating to feel either insulted or honored about the difficulty it was to nominate me for the Second Estate," Gilbert said, holding up the recent gazette. "First I am on the list, and then I disappear from it because I am too young and 'know nothing of government administration,' but now here I am again."

Jefferson spun the wine in its cup. "The Assembly of Notables is a fine opportunity to speak on our two countries' future relationship," he said.

"If they even get to that stage," added Adams, shaking his head. "Heaven knows why his Catholic Majesty bothered with it. I've never seen any worthwhile decisions come from so large a gathering. It was hard enough for Congress to agree on anything and they are a fraction of the size."

"Well, it is at least encouraging to know that the king desires some action to correct the flaws France has accumulated. We have a substantial amount of debt that has been hurting the people of this country. Perhaps I shall use the opportunity to introduce to the Estates the socio-liberal ways of the United States – where all people matter." Gilbert's brow twitched as he set his fork down. "Most people," he corrected, passing a glance towards his guest before he looked at Adrienne. It was no secret that Monsieur Jefferson had a considerable sized plantation; Jefferson himself confessed his beliefs were contrary to his actions, but used the *economy* as a reason why he could not follow the manifestations he wrote of.

Jefferson took a slice of pear and slid it under the table.

"I imagine the common people of France are still unhappy with the expenditures of their Majesties," Madame Adams said. She looked thoughtfully at the modest decoration around them. "Some pictures in the gazettes I see still speak of that diamond necklace."

"The queen did not wish for the thing," Adrienne added, "but to not pay for the work, and such an expensive piece now sitting about, seems like such a waste. The late king should not have commissioned it in the first place." It appeared to her that there was a running trend with the monarchs and their tone deafness. The assembly hall that Gilbert's upcoming Assembly of Notables was to be hosted in was receiving quite the expensive renovation.

"All these things," Gilbert said, picking at the lace of his cravat, "I will bring to light. The Comte de Calonne will be set to speak on France's finances at the assembly."

"An irony in itself," Adrienne whispered.

"Indeed," Gilbert nodded, "he is quite the exuberant spender."

Jefferson slid another piece of fruit under the table. It did not go unnoticed by Adrienne that her youngest child was missing from her seat. The small hands reached up by the American minister's lap for more.

"Monsieur Jefferson, how is your daughter? She is still at the Abbey de Penthemont, yes? Does she enjoy it?" she asked, snapping her hand under the table for Virginie to stop bothering the man.

"Martha is quite fine, Madame, thank you for inquiring. Yes, I believe she speaks fondly of her schooling and the other young girls there."

Anastasie leaned against the table. "Monsieur, will Martha be free to join me for my dancing lessons?"

"Has she written to you about it, Mademoiselle?" Jefferson asked.

"A week or so ago!"

"Then she shall fulfill her promise. A Jefferson never lies."

Adams snorted into his glass, earning himself a heated womanly glare from his wife.

"And your children?" Adrienne asked Madame Adams. "Your son was such delightful company. He is enjoying college, I hope? And your daughter, a happy marriage?"

"Everyone is doing wonderfully. I await to embrace all of them as soon as we are called back to Massachusetts. Our family writes as often as they can to tell me of their days. Nothing in their letters ever bores me."

Virginie appeared beneath the table between Adrienne and Madame Adams, blinking with all the innocence that a four-year-old could muster.

"Yes, Maman?" she said.

"Your Papa is trying to talk with Monsieur Jefferson about work. Do you think it's wise to distract the minister?"

Virginie twisted her fingers. "No," she said. "But Papa doesn't give me treats, so my options were limited."

Gilbert perked up from his seat at the head of the table. It took a moment, but he scooted back and ducked his head under. "Virginie!" he scolded, but he was never an angry father. "Come and discuss what Papa should tell France. He will be very busy in Versailles for the next few months and he will miss your inventive mind."

"I do not care if she takes my pears," Jefferson said, handing her the whole plate. "I am saving room for your famous dessert course."

☆

More money was spent in the next *four* months, not by the French government, but by Gilbert himself on regular trips to the Versailles apothecary. Every Sunday when he returned to Paris, he'd fall face-first into bed, coughing his lungs out, saving the medicine for the days when he went back to the Assembly to speak. So heavy was his cold, he slept through mass every week and consequently through family prayers – Adrienne had taken to simply saying them in the bedroom. The children rubbed their father's back while he snored away during the Lord's prayer. He was too busy to pay much mind to Madame de Simiane's unexpected visit in March after her husband had suddenly died.

An accident, most said. *Suicide*, said she.

Though it was the Comte de Calonne that had Gilbert frothing at the mouth at night.

"He is essentially turning everyone against the clergy – against *our* class," he whispered to Adrienne. His coughs were muffled by the pillows. "I don't understand why we are all there if no one listens. There's no way to enforce whatever reforms we decide, whatever taxes they want to impose upon – of course – people who cannot afford more hardship. Ah, *mon coeur*, I think it would be better for an Estates General to be called. There is not much we can do in this hall – the king essentially falls asleep. I am trying to remain optimistic, I am sure we can achieve change, there simply needs to be equal efforts in *every* Estate."

"You've always been an amazing writer," Adrienne replied. She tucked herself under his chin. "And the people like you – let them know you are fighting for them."

"I am. I *am* fighting for them."

"And I'll fight for you."

"I know," he sighed. "My whole little family is so good to me. Otchikeita is a bright, young man; perhaps he would do me the honor of holding Calonne while I slap him about."

"Gilbert."

"I think our Oneida boy would strike fear into the hearts of the assembly."

"Oh, stop it, Otchikeita is the sweetest child, don't put him on the spot like that."

They had already splurged quite a considerable amount of money on dressing their fostered native on top of the medicine and carriages and balls through April and May. Adrienne restrained her opinion on their finances; they were digging themselves a little deeper into debt, but it wasn't something to panic over yet.

"I saved you the pictures in the gazette," she said, "about the assembly. Lots of birds."

Gilbert coughed through his laughter. "Jefferson did say we produced more puns than anything. What bird was I? A goose, I imagine."

"I was thinking more the turkey – it is an American bird, after all."

His chest was warm as she ran her hands under his shirt and up his back. She didn't need him to get feverish from this chest cold, he wouldn't stop to rest even if he did.

"This summer I think it would be best if I went down to Chavaniac to oversee the town's development. I've been in contact discussing their harvest for this year to be sure that everything is going well. We can't afford to lose the season," she said. "Would you be willing to join the family in Auvergne?"

"I'd like that," he replied. After a long minute, he added in a whisper, "Once I am able to escape Versailles, it would do well to meet with the region's officers. One goal in the assembly is to create provincial assemblies, like America and her states. Another is to adjust taxes, but I am too hopeful. This month I am to actually speak, and I will make my thoughts known. I refuse to have this assembly closed without good progress."

"You wouldn't be my Gilbert if you didn't."

Chavaniac, August 1787

Gilbert brought back birds and ham sent from Washington as well as his frustrations with government when he arrived one sunny afternoon to their mountainside château. He had made his opinions known to the public, and known to Adrienne, rapidly raising his praise from the people, but conducting a new wave of noble enemies. Court was not happy with him, but Adrienne could not be more proud to stand for the liberal ideals that they had fought for since they struck the nation. Fair distribution of taxes, religious freedom, more say for the people in government affairs – a vote… Gilbert had asked very little of the country. These were Enlightenment ideals that had been around for ages.

Adrienne was covered in dust from her rounds through the village. She had replaced her Parisienne silks with linen and tied a new apron on that experienced a baptism by fire; the bottom hem was stained with soil and dirt, as if she had been planting herself. It got under her nails and squeezed into her shoes of all places. No one could say a thing if she walked about the castle in just her stockings, arms full of paperwork ladened with numbers and finances.

Her favorite place to work was in her salon. When it was empty and the curtains were tied open, the room glowed a heavenly hue, and no musician was needed when the birds chirped away along the windowsill. The ground at times was her desk, laid out to organize and overlook. It must have been similar to what their lawyers had to do, overseeing all the debt and spending, trading and loans – only just for their family and not for a village.

"I have not been chosen to lead the Assembly of Auvergne," Gilbert said from her floor, laying on his back with the letter held aloft.

"Oh," Adrienne replied, reading over the latest from their experimental plantation. "Did you truly want that role?"

"Not really," he said, folding the paper. "I'm happy for it to go to someone else; a private member has more freedom. I'm hardly down here to speak for these people."

"If only the king realized the same," Adrienne said. She shook her head, peeking above the pages to watch Gilbert slap his arms to the side, his eyes fixed on the ceiling.

"Some members of his administration give me hope," he mulled, "but Ségur's father has resigned, that is a loss. But as a whole I hear the rest of the nominations include honest men. I would have liked to see some *military* men in the running, but I'll take anyone who can work well with his Majesty to create true reform."

"You think there will be a war?" The papers sat disarrayed on her lap.

Gilbert worked his jaw. A rectangle of light lit up his left eye, shrinking his pupil as he glanced at her. "If I am called into France's service in the next few months, I can only see it progress that way."

France couldn't afford another war.

"Would you think Auvergne would send *those* taxes to Versailles?"

Gilbert snorted. "It would make me the happiest of men to have another opportunity to make the people pleased and the government *very* displeased. Until France grows in her adoration for liberty and grants her people respect, I shall be the most stubborn of her lovers."

"A stubborn lover," Adrienne repeated. She capped the inkpot and wiped the quill's nib with a small cloth before she crawled out of her seat and onto the floor next to him. The sun had warmed his cheek, her kiss had left a pale mark on where he was definitely burning through the window. "Not stubborn to everyone, I hope."

His intense concentration on the plainness of the ceiling broke as a curious brow raised. "Why, Madame," he murmured, "on your polished floors?"

"I've had to respond to all my sisters' letters about their exploits while you've been serving your country in hall after hall. I am allowed some wanting, am I not?" She fiddled at his sleeve. "Am I?"

"You are the majesty of this house, *mon coeur*, I am at your service."

Adrienne huffed. "I am a diplomatic ruler. What is your vote, my dearest Marquis?"

Gilbert rolled onto his side, sliding the letters away with a finger. "Let's debate our options to better the state of the people: we could continue reading through correspondence until I must abscond for tomorrow's gathering, thus lengthening our time apart from each other, *or* we make extraordinary love on your freshly polished wood floors and possibly on that chaise over there. Oh dear, what a difficult vote." He tsked and tapped his chin. "I believe I speak for the country when I say that having sex will always be the best option. Good for one's health and we, as good hosts, must confirm the comfortability of that sofa for our guests, *of course.*"

His hands curved around her waist, pulling her atop of him.

"Of course," Adrienne replied. "Ah, how nice the voting system is."

"That is what I say."

Paris, January 1788

"Read it again, Monsieur, I wish to hear it again," Louis said, perching himself at the edge of his chair. His voice fought against the chimes of the cathedrals as they rang in the new year.

Adrienne sat with Louise, hugging Georges to her left and Virginie to her bosom as Gilbert paced the room with the parchment in hand. His cheeks were so flush with excitement. Possibly Washington's most generous gift, a copy of the United States' constitution, arrived and had not been put down since. Anastasie sat with her sketchbook in her lap, eyeing her father with tempered annoyance as she tried to capture his form.

"Please, Papa, stand still if you read it again," she demanded, flipping to a new page.

"Papa cannot hold still," Georges replied, "if he does, he may explode. That's what Auntie said, right?"

Louise smoothed his hair, the wild thing, and pursed her lips. "When he is excited, he is like all of you. Unstoppable, like the wind. It's been like this since he was a lanky young boy."

"Yes, yes, yes," Louis said, waving his hand to silence them all, "there are portraits, they've seen them. Shush now. Speak Gilbert; with the preamble."

"*We the people...*" Gilbert began again in English.

"Beautiful. Perfection." Louis covered his mouth, leaning back as if Christ himself had risen. "Poetry in three words, my God. Pray, continue."

It truly was an expertly written opening statement; a social contract, Adrienne thought, listening to Gilbert list off the Americans' reasoning for why their government existed. Something made for the people, written by *they* themselves. If only France was forward-thinking enough to try a thing like that.

Her thoughts drifted over to Louis. Her dear brother-in-law was love-stricken with the idea of a republic. He had resisted powdering his hair daily for years; she had never seen it cut short up front, the Noailles' dark brunette hair curled around his face like a Roman senator, his usual lengthy queue was but a little nub. Visually, Louis looked more the libertarian than Gilbert – whose red hair was still well-maintained, braided back with the perfect bow, curling only a little where the strands slipped from the ribbon in his bustling about. He managed to knock over several candles while pacing the room.

"There are a few things I have thoughts on," Gilbert said, finally pausing. His banyan rested at his ankles.

"Nay, the document is absolute," Louis argued.

Louise hummed. "It is well-crafted for such conventional men." Adrienne had to whisper the French translation the best she could to her sister where her knowledge of English failed. "Has Maman read this yet, or shall I ask for a copy to bring home tonight?"

"I'll look into making you a translation, but goodness, Louise, not tonight. I will forward it to you tomorrow, perhaps," Adrienne replied. "Or Thursday on my ride."

"You still keep to Thursdays?"

"I do when I can."

Virginie picked up her face from Adrienne's chest, her arms still wrapped around as much of her mother as she could manage. "Maman is very busy because she's very smart."

Louise puckered her lips, glancing at Adrienne before she looked at the young girl. "Yes, naturally she is."

The sofa shifted as Georges was scooped up with one long arm, the eight-year-old squawking like a gull as Gilbert took his place and dropped the boy on his lap. The constitution still remained high in his hand.

"There is no declaration of rights listed," Gilbert stated. "I find that without one, within time, a government could simply decide what their citizens can or can not do. And there is no number of years that their president must serve – is it a lifetime role? No doubt General Washington will be the first, I cannot picture a more perfect man who garners such respect and adoration of the people of America and abroad. Knowing him well, he will be opposed to accepting the role, but I will write to persuade him otherwise. He must lead."

"Here, here," Louis raised his wine glass.

Adrienne leaned against Gilbert, resting her chin on his shoulder. "A declaration of rights," she repeated. "Is that not what this country needs as well? The king and his ministers would be looked upon more kindly by the people if our fellow Frenchmen knew they had a say. Your constitutional monarchy could begin with such a declaration."

Gilbert's thumb tapped against the parchment before he rubbed at his nose. Georges held the paper for his father with both hands, trying his best to keep it steady.

"A declaration on the rights of the French man," he thought aloud, a smile on his face. "Yes, I… I think that would be exactly what the people need. If the American states can adopt this constitution, there is hope our people can adopt one as well if the rights listed are perfectly syllabic. I will talk with Jefferson of it. We have much to discuss."

"Like Ségur's letters?" Louis said. He took up lounging on his chair, a slippered foot draped over one wooden arm. "Russia fighting the Turks, the German states teetering on involvement – will England or France join the fray? Yet to be seen, but I would not be adverse to taking a few swings and stabs from a horse. Are we taking bets if his Spanish highness will join us? Nothing like a fistful of bankrupt imperial states bringing out the cannons in hopes of gaining whatever they can from other peoples. Ségur sent me a whole page consisting of just insanities – completed with one of his horrible sketches of a crying horse that I assumed must be him."

"Let the war remain in the east," Louise said, reaching over to take the wine from Louis' hand. "I am satisfied with keeping you boys here where I can see you."

"I agree," Adrienne said, biting Gilbert's shoulder softly. He tethered a pinkie around hers, finally breaking his gaze upon the mighty document.

"I'm afraid that it is likely, at least for us men, to form our army as soon as the snow ceases. To protect our home and our families, to protect freedom," he said, smothering Georges with tight embraces, "I will take up the sword again."

Paris, May 1788

He did serve in the spring, two months worth – under none other than the Duc d'Ayen himself. Gilbert was the highest officer under his command as they were stationed near Auvergne. Ten thousand soldiers marched with them in case of any foreign invader. But, already aggravating the nation's desolate bank, there was no doubt that the common soldier would either be underpaid or that taxes would be raised even higher to pay them fairly. Very likely, Adrienne mulled, both would happen.

The Hôtel de la Fayette became somewhat of an American consulate for many Frenchmen who wished to travel to the United States. Asking the Marquis for a letter of introduction to any American excellency was practically required before going abroad. Common folk presented their desires from their front door, hoping for a voice in Gilbert. He took on *everything* given to him.

Jefferson joined them often in talks of politics and government and the roadblock that the state of the King was. What role does a monarch truly play in a constitutional monarchy? How much inspiration from the United States should they take? How much from Britain's own constitutional monarchy? Britain shifting from an absolute monarchy to their current fixation did not come without bloodshed; and bloodshed was something Gilbert and Adrienne wished to avoid.

Worrying about how the French government was treating its people was making Gilbert physically sick. Too many nights, Adrienne would be rubbing at his back as he wretched into a chamberpot. Every day from Versailles produced one step forward, two steps back; they include a protestant and hate a representative, money goes one place and leaves another completely void and null, yet the Parlements demanded and demanded, and King Louis was grasping for a middle ground that did not yet exist because *indecisiveness* was his nature.

Adrienne wrote between her duties managing three estates while Gilbert kept to his military role and politics. They took up desks on Virginie's bed when she was the last of the children to be inoculated; Virginie was happy to shake up the ink or to pour the pounce on their pages, a little assistant secretary for whatever they needed.

The family's bold stance did not go without its punishments from Versailles, as less as they were compared to his contemporaries. While others who stood for the same ideals he did were thrown into the Bastille, Gilbert was merely stripped of a future army command. It was another slap on the wrist, for the ministers still wrote plainly to him.

Too radical, too conservative, the papers had a soirée arguing about what exactly the Marquis stood for. Gilbert was straightforward, and Adrienne could not see how anyone could mistake his meaning – America was a blank slate to create a sound republic, France was rooted in her aristocracy for hundreds of years: altering that so suddenly was prone to bring about catastrophe. There was a way to meld the two ideals together, it would just take careful planning and cooperation.

The latter being the apparent impossible task.

☆

Middle of the dead winter, arriving from the United States was Gouverneur Morris – the author of the preamble to the constitution that Louis and Gilbert revered. Even *he* believed that France's character was not suited to be a republican one, an opinion expressed after several weeks, and frowned upon by Gilbert, who found working with Jefferson on drafting France's declaration of rights more enthusiastic.

But Adrienne enjoyed Morris' company well enough. He had a strong stance against slavery, an amusing persona, and although unfortunate marital morals, never made any disrespectful comment towards her. Gilbert tolerated him decently, as he did bring with him letters from

Washington and all of his American friends; and it was at least one more American opinion to consider, sometimes to ignore, on what Gilbert could do next.

The waiting game now was imminent: the king had called for the Estates General Gilbert was hoping for, albeit, his Majesty left the organization in ruins. Adrienne read the drafts of her husband's and Jefferson's declaration of rights and shared them at their Aunt Tessé's salon in front of dozens of their like-minded patriots. He was busy readying to shift a country, and Adrienne was busy trying to keep their people in Auvergne from *starving* as another wheat harvest failure all throughout France darkened the horizon. Gilbert may have not been enlisted in a war like he had been before, but Adrienne saw very little of him in the days to end the year. Paris was freezing, bonfires had to be lit in the corners of the city, where the common people gathered like rats to a candle.

Famine rises faster than the devil. I have no hesitations in admitting I can see only violence in the growing hearts of the people and fear the king has little chance in quelling such a storm, Adrienne wrote her mother, who on the other side of the Seine very likely saw the same.

Chapter Twenty-Three

Versailles, June 1789

Gilbert's hand came down hard upon the door. His palm burned red as he slapped at the locked entryway again and again. He knew his vote to side with the Third Estate was a risk to his own reputation amongst the Second, but to think the nobles would lock out a whole two-thirds of the meeting procession was outright boorish. So desperate were loyalists to have their say unchallenged by a vote of populace representatives that they chose to alienate themselves from France. It wasn't good; thousands of thoughts coursed through Gilbert's mind: from the powerful rise of the Duc d'Orléans, the men he promised a say back in his countrylands, the hundreds of men who stood behind him at this moment that grew more impatient as they too realized that the Estates General had done *nothing* but exacerbate the problem. And the king? The king was now becoming a threat.

Gilbert, unsurprisingly, was in the middle of it all.

He must have looked silly to the nobles who glanced from the halls' windows: an aristocrat in his lace and feathers surrounded by clergy in their layered black garb and the merchants and commoners in their Sunday coats for the occasion. He gritted his teeth until his jaw panged, and turned to his brother.

"We will find a different location. The National Assembly must meet," he said.

Louis removed his hat, pushing the sweat on his forehead back into his hair. "I know of a hall where we can commune. And look, a few already know exactly where I think of," he replied, pointing towards the bustling of the Third Estate while the few members from the First Estate who sided with a head-count vote stalled in the courtyard. It took no delay for Louis to run off and join them, but Gilbert was chained to the ground.

Excluding the church wasn't going to bode well, Gilbert thought; not for the people nor the nobles, nor his wife who considered them an important part of the country's stability. They had opened the doors of churches to allow the Third Estate to congregate, Gilbert believed it was only fair to open doors to them.

His sword he wore was the one emblazoned with the American Congress' attestation. Carrying it brought forth the images of men in continental blue uniforms, running together, united under a common cause. It was possible in France; he refused to accept otherwise. The presentation he waited to give had to be addressed to *all* of the Estates, not just the Third. He still had his draft folded neatly in his case, gripped firmly in his right hand. Maybe he'd bring it back to Jefferson – it needed to be perfected now to appease three very different expectations.

Madame de Simiane shared the royalist view. Besides her husband's rather pitiful death, their political differences had kept Gilbert from paying her consistent visits. She was a lovely correspondent though, and he valued her insight for *what on Earth* the royalists were doing when moments for cooperation were right in front of them. She was off at her estate, so visiting her in Versailles was impossible as well as irresponsible. He didn't need more patriots to think he leaned too far to the monarchy. But if he went with the Third Estate, the king would consider him one of the radical libertines.

A stone at his feet flipped from its sun bleached side to the coarse and rugged surface as he kicked it along the road back to his carriage. Down the way he watched the stragglers enter the palace's tennis court. It had been unused since the death of the dauphin, the Court of Versailles in mourning. The dauphin was almost eight when he died – slightly younger than Georges, older than Virginie. The king shared his affinity for children, and Gilbert felt the loss like little Henriette, an aching in his chest. Yet to the people, the passing of a royal child meant nothing when the poor children starved and wasted away every day; Gilbert understood that too. The king could not waste precious time and attention in addressing his nation.

Too many armed soldiers were encircling Paris, some not even French. Bile rose in his throat. As if this were the siege of Boston. Gilbert feared a civil war – it was not at all what he imagined when he wished to bring liberty to France, to free the people from their oppressors.

The stone flew off course, stumbling off into the grass.

French people should not have to fear death at the hands of his majesty's men and mercenaries, he thought, bringing his case to his chest. He would call on Jefferson, take up his pen, and meet the nobles in the middle. There was already bloodshed in France for liberty, there was no going back.

☆

"While the Marquis de la Fayette is honorable and very appropriate in speaking for liberty as he had defended it," exclaimed Comte de Lally-Tolendal to the assembly after Gilbert presented the *Declaration of the Rights of Man* to the fully gathered three-estate assembly two weeks later, "attempting to frame an ancient government in the same process as a newborn nation is dangerous! Our subjects have never experienced a France without her king and ministers; it is imbued in our lifeblood. Such a declaration of primitive equality without the context of the rest of a constitution, publicizing these natural rights, will no doubt cause countless chaos in addition to the pandemonium already plaguing the streets!"

Gilbert sat back in his chair, Louis to his left, the Comte de Mirabeau to his right. All this pompous retort all because he left out the mention of the king from his address. No one wanted to be too specific if it favored one estate over the other, but they also did not want too *vague* where it could be interpreted out of their favor; he rolled his eyes towards the ceiling, his nails digging into the embroidery of his sleeve cuffs. It was a draft! He never stated that what he wrote should be taken word-for-word, that wasn't what an assembly, a *Congress,* was for.

"Many oversights and edits must be made," someone else had said, and Gilbert lolled his head from one shoulder to his other, staring down the row of nobles.

"As the assembly sees fit," he replied. Whatever needed to be done to suit the people – at least they did not rip up the pages outright.

Louis nudged his shoulder up against his. "His Majesty looks like he is deep in contemplation," he whispered, nodding towards the king, who sat in his throne, eyes to his folded hands. "Or sleeping again. For his sake, I hope the former. Look at the aides, they fly from this theatre with your speech in hand. No doubt Paris will hear of it before the sun falls from the sky; and America by next month. Adri must grab a copy."

"She's heard my practices a thousand times," Gilbert replied, watching the young men race out the door.

"I want a copy for myself before they are sold out and my wife is hardly as expedient."

"Should you not want to wait for us to debate the bill? For the final copy to be made up?"

"Nay, I want your unedited vigor, brother. I don't need mention of the monarchy."

Gilbert held back his smile; he was trying to look serious. "You and I still pray for different political outcomes," he said carefully, for he did not wish to wound his relationship with his friend and family.

"I know," Louis replied, "but you've always stood for what is right in the end. If somehow we manage to convince the royal family to relinquish some power to the people, I'll buy you a drink. Several even – with my dwindling fortune, if that miracle happens."

It could happen, he almost said, but he held his tongue. The ministers were still very upset with him, so much so that Gilbert had jokingly told Jefferson to claim him as an American should disappoint rise to anger. *How many people wished him dead?* He wondered.

The Comte de Mirabeau, once a noble, now a member of the Third Estate, leaned over to their conversation. "How is your family, Marquis? They are in Paris now, are they not?"

"They are," Gilbert replied.

"Despite the riots?"

"My wife refuses to leave. She is Parisian at heart."

Mirabeau smiled, his eyes crinkling as he sat back straight. "Or a patriotic noblewoman; very brave indeed."

Gilbert simply nodded. His nerves pained him hearing of the discourse so close to home; there were times when he wrote to her to go stay with her mother and father where she and the children could be more protected, but she would write back that she was not content with showing fear towards people who did not approach the Hôtel de la Fayette. The rioters were angry with their oppressors, she wrote, not with him and his family; she would remain.

Hours would droll by in which one man countered another. The Third Estate was distinctive and well-versed, Gilbert agreed quietly with every one of their points under the watchful eye of his peers. The Second Estate had a list of complaints with their requests, which Gilbert understood where they were coming from; the king: silent. But what sort of silence, Gilbert asked himself – was the man realizing what responsibility he had? King Louis wanted to be loved by the people, but he also wanted to be respected by his Court.

Gilbert rested his elbows on his knees. The declaration needed to pass soon.

☆

Paris was ablaze as his Majesty's military might closed in. Cavalry faced thrown rocks, the people faced their guns, the *Gardes Francaises* took up their bayonets against the *Royal Allemand* down the road from the Hôtel de Noailles. Gilbert held his letters from Adrienne with a forceful grip as the National Assembly roared like cannonfire.

"Your Majesty, you *must* rescind your troops!"

"Paris has grown into mob rule!"

"The people are asking for protection! We have to act."

"Give them their militia – this will cease if they are allowed their *militia*, your Majesty!"

The king stood abruptly, and like a row of dominoes, the men fell silent. Gilbert carefully rose with the rest of them as the king quietly, forcibly, uttered nothings. And he left like that, with his jaw set and his hands twitching.

Immediately, horses foaming, men were sent out to Paris to quell the potential early morning violence before it began. The National Assembly decided for itself to give the defenders of Paris what they needed: an olive branch.

Forming a militia – how very American, Gilbert mused, but his humor was deflated, the room continued in their arguing. How did hours pass so slowly yet in a blink of an eye? Air in the room was stale and dry; Gilbert only wanted to return to Paris.

In the midst of the rabble he heard his name. Someone grabbed his arm, shouting to the assembly as they pulled him forward. It was not only his name he heard, it was his rank.

"They call for General Lafayette!"

Gilbert looked towards the doorway as his hope stirred.

"For me?" he asked, hardly loud enough to be understood. The man holding a fistful of letters was sweating so profusely, his brown waistcoat was black.

"To command the militia, sir," the man rasped. "They will only trust you for the role."

A friend of Washington, one member of the Third Estate agreed; the Second Estate conceded: the Marquis de la Fayette was already speaking for the people, let him lead them towards the peace he preached, for the liberty he already defended for the New World. Gilbert's hand found his sword, and his eyes found his brother. Louis had thrown on his hat, taking the riding crop from another as he silhouetted the doorway.

"Let us go save Paris, General," he said. "Colonel Noailles is at your service!"

How bizarre it was to hear their old friend Broglie's name – who inspired them to the American Revolution – with the face of the kind man's brother, bearing a harsh countenance and orders from the king to do what was necessary to keep the disorder at bay. Was this to be an enemy? Gilbert entered the Hôtel de Ville after a hard ride, meeting with the electors and de facto leaders of the panicked militia. He wanted to change – still wearing his Second Estate ensemble, he kept his Congressional sword visible at his side. If he could help it, there would be no violence between the people and the military that day. If the Assembly could help it, they would persuade His Majesty to recall the troops and save them all the trouble.

His heart was across the river, he could see his home if he looked from the balconies. But he could also see the revolution rising in the streets, the people watching their oppressors leer down the avenues with their swords pointed at the very thing they should have been protecting and fighting for instead.

Yet, how exciting it was. The people of France were ready for change and they wanted *him* to help lead them through it. Truthfully, the thought alone made Gilbert quite giddy, the adrenaline put a little pep in his step as he converged with militia leaders to discuss strategy. There was nostalgia in it, speaking to them like brigadier generals or aides under his charge; these were the citizens who knew the streets by heart, surrounded by hired foreign troops. How could anyone *not* see the resemblance?

The sky had taken on the ruddy brown hue of the dirt and grime that swept up from Paris' streets. Disease and bellows grappled at the noses and ears of any who dared stepped outside of their dwelling. Gilbert was thankful for Louis at his side, remaining even into the late hours of the long-panned out day.

"They think His Majesty will turn on them; slaughter them like cattle," Gilbert said, picking up hurriedly written letters from the men around the city. "Why hasn't he withdrawn?"

"Because he does not want to be the coward," Louis replied. He retrieved another batch of envelopes from a militiaman. "The king who *actually* listens to his people. Pray tell when would the monarchy ever do that? D'Ayen said it himself, don't give me that look."

"I know," Gilbert said, looking out the windows to the fires that lit up around the city. "We discussed it when I was under his command last year. There are many opposing ideas within our friends and family, but I have hope for the future." All the letters in front of him complained of food, of gunpowder, lack of this, none of that. "I have to have hope."

Louis crossed the room, a hand on his hip, his eyes drifting up over the shelves of the office space inside the Hôtel de Ville. Too many people were worried of the military storming the building – militiamen posted like sentries by the windows of every door, watching the dark inkling streets like they looked out for Death.

"Give your back a good crack and have a drink with me," Louis said, reaching up to nab a dusty bottle of liquor that was very likely more vintage than he expected, for when he opened to smell it, he huffed like a horse. "If we're to be up all night, I need the energy."

"I shall pass, thank you. As should you. Soldiers should not be intoxicated while performing their duty."

"A sip or two for your intolerance would not result in being a drunkard," Louis said with a roll of his eyes. He proceeded to gag at the first sip. Gilbert sat on his desk, moving his sword to his lap. He did not need to argue that Louis already was an alcoholic and made no effort to stop his brother.

He scribbled a little line to Adrienne. No doubt on the other side of the river, she would be awake to calm the children. If he could, he would pick them all up and carry them to Auvergne himself, or better yet, across the ocean to be with his general at Mount Vernon. He missed Anastasie's twelfth birthday upon his trips to Versailles. It was not his fault it fell upon a Wednesday, but when he returned home, she was sorely disappointed in him and had held her tongue throughout every dinner hence. She looked so much like Adrienne at that age when she was pouting, it stabbed twice as hard at his heart. He prayed that Georges was not ready to join any militia; he may have had a uniform to match his father, but Gilbert wanted to delay the boy as long as he could from entering even a momentous revolution. The future Marquis would have his chance when he was of age and wiser than his current rambunctious nine-year-old self. And Virginie, little Virginie, her maman's secretary. Such a bright young lady, going to turn seven in just a few weeks. Gilbert wouldn't miss that one, he would ensure he would be home. His little family was his star, and their smiling faces made him more brave every day. Perhaps he could see them tomorrow, to give them news on what was happening within the Parisian militia and the surrounding forces, to reassure them that he was there to protect the people.

His plan, until the next day actually came.

He sent Louis in haste back to Versailles to warn the Assembly that the *Bastille* was currently under siege.

A dastardly place, that prison. Gilbert felt no remorse as the people stormed inside to release the few prisoners that remained in the tyrannical fortress. There were guardsmen only retained for refusing immoral orders to fire upon innocent crowds, and seven civilian prisoners; but regardless now, they went free, joining the revolution as it unfolded through Paris. Such a large building took a grand portion of money to upkeep its uselessness; it was to be torn down anyway for the people, at least it served some purpose to be torn away *by* the people.

Gilbert sat on his horse, the militia behind him in cockades of blue and red. They were here to restore peace — not to dissuade the revolutionaries from their righteous goal, but to quell the fires and break away the disorder — armed with weapons taken from the Hôtel des Invalides hours prior. There was no gunpowder at des Invalides; the gunpowder was moved and stored in the Bastille.

Here was the people's army, he thought, bringing about the men. There was already a growing pile of bodies as the Bastille's garrison fired upon the crowd; their leader, the Marquis de Launay, must have known they were outnumbered and on the losing side of history. Gilbert knew a leader among the armed civilians was waiting to take Launay prisoner. A proper trial, he believed, was what every wrongdoer needed for France to establish republican justice.

Republic justice, republican values... Gilbert kept his chin tall as the day of revolution continued. The sky was red as the sun penetrated the ashen clouds upon its descent; and the courtyard of the Hôtel de Ville was red with *blood* as he witnessed de Launay and the Parisian mayor lose their heads to a butcher's saw. Their faces melted like candle wax as they were thrust up onto pikes by a feverish crowd. Gilbert's knuckles whitened as he gripped the handle of his sword. Louis, sunburned and soaked in the sweat and dirt from constant riding, ran up the steps to stand beside him, unable to take his eyes off of the bloody display of freedom.

"It's begun," Louis said. "There's no going back now."

The National Assembly met in Paris the next day, squished together in the Hôtel de Ville alongside the Electors. The king had come to his senses, and with little argument, ordered the withdrawal of troops from the city. Gilbert's mouth was dry after speaking for hours, humbled only by applause and cheers for his name. It brought him immeasurable joy despite the exhaustion seeping into his bones. Another whole day had passed inside the hall; Gilbert claimed a carriage as soon as night began to fall, and made the trek to the other side of the Seine.

The Hôtel de la Fayette was untouched. The ivy along the outer walls was lush and vibrant, and members of the city's militia had set up sentinel by his property's borders: his own humble palace in the city. Decisions weighed down his feet as he pulled himself up the steps. His foyer was cool and clean and shaded; he set his blue and red cockaded hat down, and released his sword belt from his hip.

"Papa?"

Gilbert looked up to his Anastasie. The girl had blossomed into a young woman right under his nose. She was already at the height of her mother.

"Hello, sweetling," he said, and the strain in his voice startled him. She wrapped her arms around his shoulders and kissed his cheek. He kissed hers in return. "I am sorry for being gone so long, it has been an arduous several days, or one impossibly continuous single one – I cannot say for certain."

"It has been long here as well," Anastasie replied. "Papi and Mémé were by today. They left after the commotion quelled. If you had time, Papi asked that you go speak with him, but he didn't say about what."

"Allow me to greet the rest of our little family and then I shall talk with Papi, alright? You are too big for me to carry you like I used to."

"Oh, Papa!" Another too big for his own good child slid around the corner, his stockings taking Georges farther than he intended, crashing into Gilbert and his older sister with all the force momentum allowed.

Gilbert could still manage to lift his son, grunting as he squeezed a tired hug into the non-stop chattering child.

"Maman's been in the office for hours and it was so odd to see everyone here all sad and then they told Maman something and now she is sad, but beforehand we were listening to all the news that came about you; and Papa, were you leading the Assembly? Are you the king now? Does that mean we need to move to Versailles because I just started liking the boys in this quarter and it would be sad if I couldn't go out and play with them..."

"I am not the king; we are staying in Paris," Gilbert said. "Maman's sad? Why is Maman sad?" He stood up straight, regarding the hall where their office lay. Very carefully, he removed Anastasie's hands and put Georges back on the floor. He began walking even before Anastasie whispered behind him.

"Someone *died*."

He found Adrienne sitting at her desk, a hand pushed deep into her hair while the other scratched firmly against the parchment Virginie held still for her. Gilbert held his tongue, putting his hand out to stop his children from barging into the room, thankful to Anastasie for clapping a hand over her little brother's mouth.

Virginie noticed him first, her little smile made her cheeks all the more round. Yet it didn't reach her eyes; she glanced towards Adrienne and tapped the letter she wrote, like a fae breaking the spell that kept her mother's eyes towards her work.

"Mon coeur?" Gilbert called. He took the three steps to gently lay a hand on her shoulder, wincing as she jumped from under him. Her eyes were glassy — the haze after a bombardment of cannonfire. She blinked quickly as if she were the wind trying to pretend there was no smoke in the air, as if her nose was not red and her cheeks were not burned with tears.

Adrienne smiled at him, her cold hand finding his as he leaned down to kiss her lips. "You're back," she said, and she sounded almost as bad as he did. "The supper is still warm if you're hungry, I didn't have the staff clean up yet. You were at de Ville, yes? We thought at times we could hear you over the river. If we did, you sounded so grand, very eloquent."

"Thank you," he replied, although he still frowned, dragging his thumb over her cheekbone.

"You look stressed."

"I look stressed?" he laughed, and knelt by her lap. Virginie snuck around to peck his temple before she scurried away with her siblings. The doors to the office closed, and only then did he hear Adrienne's tiniest of sobs. "So many things torment my mind, but please, tell me what torments my dear heart? Who has passed? Family?"

Adrienne shook her head while he grappled to take her hands as she waved them in surrender. "I do not wish to engross your time even more with mourning on top of everything you must do for France."

"I shall find out eventually, tell me now when I am prepared for it and not when I am in the throes of quelling a mob."

"Is that what you have been doing, General la Fayette?"

"The people cease when I speak but one word, but ah," he tsked, "don't try to throw me into one of my rants, I know your ways."

She swallowed. The amber light from the candles made her cheeks all the more flushed. "Maman told me that a letter arrived from Thézan this morning. *A-anne*, she… Oh, Gilbert, her poor children, I –" He could do nothing to stop the fresh flow of tears that rolled heavily downward. "She was only twenty-six, I don't understand."

Gilbert's throat constricted. He didn't think it would be a sister they would lose. Taking Adrienne's face, he kissed her again, and up to her lashes, taking care to bump his nose as gently as he could with hers. "I am so sorry you had to be here without me to learn of this. Please forgive me, I am a terrible husband at the price of a revolution." Resting his cheek on her lap, he used her like the pew of a church. "I reign in Paris," he said, "and it is here I will be for as long as this takes. I pray it means I will have more time with you, but I can be called away at any notice."

"I will be fine," Adrienne breathed. "Do not worry about me. The children are good company; they are so clever and sweet, it is like seeing you every morning, just the way you were when I first met you."

"I am still grasping that our eldest is your age when *I* first met *you*." He pressed his face into her skirts. "Though thankful I am that she is not betrothed. I would be like Madame d'Ayen, refusing every possible suggestion."

"Yes, she did make that remark this afternoon," Adrienne said, using her fichu as a handkerchief.

"I will wear a black stock with my uniform to mourn with you, *mon coeur*."

"You do not have to. Please, I don't wish for you to get in trouble."

"Who will tell their Commander General off over his choice in neckwear? I will tell you, *amour*, certainly no one in my Guard. Certainly none of Paris."

Adrienne leaned over in her chair to press her lips to his hair, terribly oily as it was. She was quiet for a moment, needlessly carding her fingers through his curls. He could see the thoughts pass over her face before she sighed and wiped another stray tear. "I suppose we should have your peruke freshly powdered tonight before you are undoubtedly loaned out for the day tomorrow."

"You think so?"

"I have a feeling."

Adrienne's feelings were somehow always right. Gilbert received a visit from his aides-de-camp the following morning, rushing with news that the king was en route to Paris to humble himself to the people;

they had to meet him at the city limits else the people could act without order. Somber, Gilbert took up his white horse, leaving Adrienne and his children to sleep – hopeful to return to them before dark – and left for his National Guard.

Hard jibes towards the king would turn to cheers for the nation as long as Gilbert was leading the royal procession. It was quick work to line the street with the militia. He acknowledged them all as he rode by, holding his reins low and his head high. It was a little bit of a surprise to have His Majesty come at his own behest to the city, especially when the people and Assembly were still agitated at the slow speed of the foreign soldiers' withdrawal. Gilbert only needed to glance once at the man to see how resigned he was.

When the royal guard was formally left behind, it was just Gilbert and his men who led the way. He could take the king where he pleased, order his arrest if he thought it best; but of course, he brought him to the Hôtel de Ville. The weather was perfect, the organization was almost flawless. Gilbert did not miss the small flinch of the king's shoulders as the honor guard touched their swords in a ceremonial arch befitting his arrival. Louis XVI seemed prepared to be killed as he gave the large crowd around the building a slow and polite look.

Monsieur Bailly, the new elected mayor of Paris when Gilbert was elected its General, presented the king with the cockade of the Parisian colors. It was the one all the people wore, the one Gilbert wore.

"Would you join us, your Majesty?" Bailly said after a bow. "Paris and her Commune are glad to receive their monarch."

Gilbert was silent as he watched from the king's other side. Louis XVI carefully removed his hat without a word, tucked the red and blue ribbons into the stitching with the steady hand of a locksmith, and placed it back on his head.

"Long live the king!"

The timing of the crowd met Gilbert's approval. The king had endorsed their revolution, and the people welcomed their monarch with pride. It was fair progress. Now he needed to approve of the Declaration of Rights.

If he did that, Gilbert decided, he would defend the man with everything he had.

Paris, October 1789

Adrienne sat at the far end of the dining table with a gazette balanced on one leg and an angrily written letter from Louise on the other. Louise was just slightly *more* than peeved about the actions of Louis during the Assembly's early August meeting. He could not be blamed alone, however, although he did start the bout of mania that overtook the men before the session was urgently called to an end. Out went men's land and villages they owned, the feudal system in its entirety. As a vicomte and vicomtesse, Louis and Louise did not own much land at all, most money came from the Noailles' *family fund* – as Louis called it – but other men in the hysterical act certainly did benefit from feudalism, so their sudden swell of republicanism was surprising to say the least.

She placed the gazette over the letter. It was becoming more and more recent to see her husband's image depicted in the news. Any progress towards liberty that happened in Paris was attributed to him; his name was synonymous with the term. Adrienne ran her finger over the drawing of Gilbert, tall and lean, with his sword held aloft. He held the hand of *Athena*, draped in the colors of a revolutionary France, her foot stomping on the horrible monster of despotism.

In the several weeks that passed since his rise to power, he also rose to great fame. Seeing him in all his glory made her teary-eyed, and the rare mornings she had him at home, she had to sit before she made a fool of herself by swooning. Not much had changed in that aspect, she thought. He always was her knight in shining armor.

Monsieur Morris paid them a visit a few days ago. His warning to Gilbert had set the house in an peculiar mood – that he was too soft on his National Guard, a militia that still was underfunded despite Gilbert's best efforts. Morris put into Adrienne's head that someone was going to turn on the Marquis. With the pitiful efforts of the Duc d'Orléans, there were already sides to be taken between the prince and Gilbert. But

Gilbert was a beloved figure in Paris, she noted, *la Fayette was the name of Liberty.*

The rain outside was pouring sideways. Cascades of waterfalls ran down the long windows, swamping the mulch around the gardens. It had been a dark and dismal day and now it was a dark and dismal evening, where Virginie and Georges spent most of their time with their governess and tutor and Anastasie finished picking at her dinner and had moved on to staring out one window towards northern Paris.

Adrienne's dish remained untouched; the sick feeling in her gut was just going to bring up vomit if she ate anything. Gilbert had been rushed out the door early in the morning and no word from him came back since. There was rumor of yet another riot; women mostly, Adrienne heard. Paris was starving, Versailles was throwing feasts.

Seven hours, Gilbert had been gone.

Adrienne hated every one of those newsless sixty minutes.

Gilbert's face on the gazette's art was soft and gentle and held the goddess' hand with care. Adrienne set the papers on the table. She rose from her seat, eyeing the house stables from the pane glass, and turned to the maid waiting to take the plates away.

"Have my horse prepped to ride," she said, already working to unpin the house gown she had on. Anastasie's head rotated with urgency.

"Maman?"

"I won't be gone for too long, sweetling, I need to get some air."

"Maman, it's pouring out there, you'll get sick. And you couldn't possibly think about going alone? We're still in mourning."

Adrienne retrieved her dark plum redingote from her room, freshly pressed from the last ride she went out. A cloak with a hood would be adequate for heavy rain. She must have had a wool one somewhere in her trunk…

"You're ignoring me because you know I'm right," Anastasie continued to speak, catching her again in the hall. "What would Papa say? He'd say the same thing I am saying: don't go out."

"Anastasie," Adrienne said, and goodness her daughter was as brazen as any twelve-year old Noailles girl, "I am checking on your father. Go finish your reading for the evening and when I get back I expect you to be in bed with your sister –"

"Maman!"

" – *Sleeping* or needlework! Anastasie Louise, do *not* make me repeat myself." Adrienne nodded at the maid who found the cloak. It was certainly thick enough for the weather. She kept the reeling back to a minimum, she sounded like her mother but not in the way she idolized. Turning thirty was weeks away, looming about like a great beast in the shadows. Mirrors had been expertly avoided on both fronts: not to be vain, and not to acknowledge that she could just be getting uglier; it was best not to know. Louise aged gracefully like their mother, but heaven knows Adrienne never met the standard Louise kept.

She took her gloves, and when the stablehand ran up with her horse in tow, pulled up her hood and mounted the saddle. Chouchou was no longer, this chocolate gelding was named by Virginie: Gabriel. A far more mature name for a horse, although Chouchou was the best girl that Adrienne could have asked for, Gabriel was sturdy and reliable, perfect for being named after the archangel.

It was amazing to see so many women on the streets of Paris in such a rainstorm. Their petticoats were slicked with mud up to their thighs. If they had shoes on, no doubt they would have to be buckled so tightly as to not be lost within the thick sludge that Gabriel clomped heavily through. Adrienne searched for the red and blue cockade in the saddlebag, placing it on the outer folds of the cloak to easily be spotted by revolutionaries passing by with their torches held aloft. A clamour overtook alleyways, slipping between apartment buildings and larger homes. The Hôtel de Noailles, she imagined, would have their eyes on every window for Parisians who may have the gall to jump their garden walls. If the French people had anything, it was gall.

Crossing the bridge towards the Tuileries proved to be the most difficult part of the journey. The wind lifted her off her seat twice, blowing back her hood on several occasions. Gabriel kept his head low, a motion that

Adrienne was soon to copy, trying to keep a fast but safe pace to the other side. She needed to find a member of the National Guard; they would recognize her, and, perhaps, be able to point out where her husband may be. If all was well, there was a chance he could be inside the Hôtel de Ville working on simple paperwork or meetings to alleviate the growing situation. Yet Gilbert was not that type of leader – he would be in the midst of it all. And *all* was only growing.

Adrienne could not count the people in the streets, their voices rang out like thunder over the roar of water. Women, young and old, joined by their husbands and children, too much in a rage to be fearful. The torchfire lit their faces in reds and oranges, like they were the flames themselves. Through them all there was a depleting likelihood that Adrienne could find a soldier to help her.

To Versailles! Some shouted, *bring us to Versailles!*

A march on Versailles in this weather would take several hours on foot, nearly half a day. Certainly Gilbert would not condone such a thing? If the people meant to bring violence – Adrienne thought, pulling her horse back as a crowd of women ran by with spears and pikes – Gilbert would do everything in his power to stop it, even putting himself at risk.

Every week an unsightly odor was growing more potent. The poor were getting poorer, if that was possible, and the royalists were becoming less and less generous; a mixture that was irreconcilable, and one side was taking on a putrefied taint.

"Do you need a sword?" Adrienne heard from her side. A woman younger than her with a pinched face held a saber to her arm. "It isn't safe to be a woman out here without one. Should have grabbed your kitchen knives, at least."

Adrienne took the blade, one clearly taken from the storage houses in the city. How fast the world turned upside down within a few months. She found her voice, looked back at the woman and called, "Is there a goal to achieve tonight?"

"To make the king and queen hear us, of course! It isn't right they feast on diamonds and beef when all we ask for is our bread. Why should we have to die and not them? You look like you belong with a well-to-do man, Madame, it is nice to see the middling sort stand with us."

"I do stand with you," Adrienne replied. Maybe she should have brought some money with her. The thought gnawed at her conscience. "If there is anything I can do… if there is anything the la Fayettes may do –"

A rattling of a military drum was heard in the distance as if another rush of heavy rain.

"Ah, at last," the woman cried out, "we go!" She gestured to the growing image of soldiers in the streets. "Let us demand an end to this famine."

"Y-yes," Adrienne said as the crowds of rioters ran to join the march of the National Guard. She held her reins in her left hand, the gifted sword down by her right side as if she were a general watching her troops march by. At the head of the screaming lines of men and women walked the white horse anyone could have recognized miles away, and its rider, his chin low, eyes cast down towards the street while his soldiers held their bayonets high, was Gilbert.

Her chest tightened. The rain was hot acid on her cheeks. Gilbert did not look anywhere but the ground in front of him. If the rain were any harder, it may have wiped him away like wet paint on canvas.

A General for the people, she thought with a growing frown, watching the crowd continue on. *Thousands*, the number was starkly in the thousands, more than any number Adrienne had seen in court. Some women seemed pleased to see Adrienne, another female, upon a horse, as if she was the cavalry sent to protect them. She crossed herself. Gilbert and these people, at this hour, would not reach Versailles until midnight if they were lucky. Her bed would be cold without him.

God, it would take a miracle not to catch a cold, nor slip on the mud, or be overcome with the fury of the crowd and soldiers alike.

"Please," she prayed, "please protect him." Whatever was to happen, if France was to have no monarchy tomorrow, she cared little about. But if one man or woman, revolutionary or royalist, laid a hand on Gilbert, there would be a price to pay.

Gabriel huffed a hot cloud, his hooves bringing up mud to coat his legs with darker socks. The cheers and shouts were *war* in the streets. This is what her lanky country boy had to deal with in America, now in France? She wanted to wrap Gilbert up in a blanket, keep him at home with a strong cup of hot chocolate, but he always yearned for the rush of war. This couldn't possibly be what he meant. Adrienne knew he had been so caught up with maintaining peace, a tolerable middle-ground, that there were few letters sent out to his General Washington. Gilbert always thrived better when he wrote and received a line from him. Would Washington approve of this? Was this what America had done? No, Americans were not the French, she could not picture such numbers.

Song struck up as the movement left the city. Adrienne stood like a statue as she listened. Rain tasted like salt, lukewarm, yet her nose stung painfully.

She could not march to Versailles with her husband.

As desperately as she wanted to.

If she wrote to Adélaïde, perhaps she could put to light what on Earth the royalists were thinking. Gilbert had an unsent letter to her on his desk, she was always an intelligent woman to confer with on the politics Adrienne tried her best not to get involved with. Her best was simply never enough.

Leaning back in the saddle, and giving the reins a sturdy pull, she led Gabriel to back up onto the road to the bridge. Gilbert didn't need to know she came out to find him. Having the small glimpse of him was a small assurance at least. She could have his office cleaned in the meantime, or perhaps have the cook make his favorite meal if he were to come home tomorrow night. A trip to Chavaniac would do them all some good, but not when Paris needed him so urgently here. The Duc and Duchesse d'Ayen did not need to know she ventured out alone either. She could already hear the chastising her mother would give her, and the stern, worried frowning hum from her father as he would likely station his aides as secret bodyguards.

"Damn you, Adrienne," she breathed, the wind slapping her hood far over her face.

The night beyond the black clouds swallowed the city like the large fish did Jonah, a suffering silence followed the further her heart beated away from home. As Gabriel walked them to the front of the Hôtel de la Fayette and the servants rushed to assist her to the door, Adrienne let her cloak fall to the wood, leaving growing puddles in her wake. Someone handed her a towel, but she didn't look up. Her feet simply brought her to Gilbert's portrait, the copy he had done of the family. He looked directly at her, the viewer, while his hand was gesturing mere inches from her painted palm. Adrienne mirrored the movement, so close to take his hand. She should have taken it; some proof they touched. Her fingers were ice.

Forgoing her bed after she changed into her bedgown, she went instead towards the children's rooms. Virginie was curled up happily against Anastasie, a book held open on their laps by a heavy hand. Georges had his back pushed up against his older sister's other side, snoring away as his leg dangled from the blankets. Adrienne carefully pushed it back under, opening the sheets to slide in herself on the smaller bed.

"Maman, you're cold," Georges whined. Eyes still closed, he held his arm up for Adrienne to snuggle into, the way Gilbert always did on winter nights.

"Oh, thank you," she whispered, booping her nose against his. She took the book from the top of her girls before it had the chance to fall. "Go back to sleep, dear."

"We were waiting for you to get back," he said, snuggling instead into her hold. "I wasn't asleep, I just closed my eyes."

She pulled the blankets higher over Virginie and found all six of their cold-toed feet at the bottom of the bed. "You're such a gentleman."

"Is Papa well?"

Adrienne squeezed her eyes shut. "He's staying the night in Versailles, we will see him tomorrow, I'm sure. But shush now, you have your classes in the morning and we don't want to wake your sisters."

"Are *you* well?" Georges' chin dug into her sternum. She combed her nails through the red mop of his hair.

Chapter Twenty-Three

"Yes, yes, I'm alright," she lied. "Hush now."

That night, Gilbert kissed the hands of Marie-Antoinette on her balcony in front of the crowd, bringing the angry shouts to silence and then to cheers. The people of Paris promptly followed him back to the city, this time with the royal family in tow. Gilbert was gone all that day, and through the next morning for the king's first Parisian levée, and well into the night...

Chapter Twenty-Four

Paris, July 14th 1790

Glasses of champagne to a dozen tables, platters of hors d'ouvres to the others; the doors opened to the back gardens where the walkways were taken up with more tables to prepare. It wasn't hard labor; not like the digging and building that thousands of people turned out for at the *Champ de Mars*, but readying a dinner for a hundred federates today and more tomorrow and the next and on and on and on, was certainly keeping Adrienne busy.

It had rained all morning, a miserable time to prepare, but she thought of the immense crowd that showed up for the Festival of the Federation, standing out in the wind and rain for the speeches and mass. If she lifted her ear, she could hear the music and shouting voices of triumph from the park several blocks away. The sun had poked through in the late afternoon as she heard the applause for the famed General la Fayette. It brought a smile to her face, imagining him walking up to the altar. Certainly, there was a regret to missing the event, but artists from all over were encouraged to capture anything and everything from the proceedings, and so she would have to simply wait a day to see the firsts of it.

The year had started out quite well for the family. She was there when Gilbert ordered the destruction of the Bastille, and when he neatly packed the thick prison key into his parcel to General Washington. It was the beginning of a new era now that the monarchs had taken up living within the confines of Paris. Even Louis XVI labored with the people in building the grounds for this anniversary day's celebration.

Adrienne tasted every dish prepared in the kitchens. Americana dining had easily become the family's staple, and so whenever they hired a new kitchen hand, she was sure to test out their concoctions to approve the simple richness that Gilbert described from his trips. It was as extravagant as their economics could allow, yet modesty was a good patriot's goal. She could manage both, naturally, every good Catholic could.

"Leave some salt aside to add once that comes out of the oven," she said, wiping her hands as she scurried from the kitchen up to the parlor. Anastasie carried the leftover cushions from the salon into the bedchambers, dragging the large ones up the stairs until a footman came to her aid. Virginie dusted with the maids, focusing on every book just in case a federate wished to peruse their collection of American and Enlightenment writers.

"Be sure to change your apron before our guests arrive," Adrienne said, already removing her house one to leave her blue and red gown on display. Regardless of the heat, she would match her husband in his uniform, a cockade pinned neatly on her hat. Virginie saluted before she also bounded the stairs, her petticoats bunched in her fists.

It was difficult to ascertain what time the Festival would be over, the first of its kind and all that. Judging when to cook the hot food where it wouldn't burn nor go too cold was a mystical sort of math. She had sent the paperboy off down the street to report on the speech giving, promising him a few livres if he returned with how long it would be until the general took up his horse. Said boy had not returned yet, so there was time to spare.

Ducking out of the public space into Gilbert's office, she placed a pocketed letter on his desk, freshly arrived from New York where General Washington was now formally referred to as *President* Washington. If Gilbert wasn't so busy now with building republicanism in France, it would have been a perfect time to travel to the United States; the children were all decently grown and of good health, she was ready to get out of the city for a while, and dreams of the New World seeped into her exhausted slumbers.

The letter was still addressed to *The Marquis*, and Adrienne imagined it will always be so, for if Gilbert referred to Washington as his General, then to the great man, Gilbert will always be his dear Marquis. It would be the only exception allowed in France, for the Assembly put out a proclamation stemming from Louis' actions of the last year, removing titles from all nobility. Adrienne still had trouble remembering to exclude the space between the names when Gilbert formally shifted la Fayette to Lafayette – something he never thought much of, as he signed it regularly in the American army and to his American friends. In France, *Motier* was becoming a prominent name to refer to Gilbert as. "General Motier," some in the assembly called him. Although not incorrect, Adrienne read it more as a slight than as a sign of respect.

To most people, she was still Madame Lafayette, space or no space.

"Maman!"

Little Georges burst through the door, dressed in a smaller version of the National Guard uniform, complete with the ceremonial sword at his side. His hair, so red it was almost blonde, was cut shorter up front now with the latest trends, his round cheeks and wide eyes completely visible. She couldn't quite continue to call him little, the boy was already up to his father's chest.

As his smile grew, the paperboy scrambled up behind him, face pink.

"The General is on his way, Madame!" he exclaimed, huffing as he placed his hand out for the coin Adrienne had waiting for him.

"Maman, you missed it, Papa was amazing!" Georges said, his hands flying everywhere. "He couldn't even make it up to the saddle without people coming left and right to kiss him! Oh and Maman, Maman, I don't think people paid any attention to the king. God Himself opened the sky for Pa – honest."

"How did you get here so fast?" Adrienne took his shoulders and led him back out to the parlor.

"Well, goodness, Maman, like I said, Papa is trying to ride through an ocean of people. I left with Papi and we went around the main road. I think all of France is here in Paris. How many men are coming here to dine? Can me and Stas and Nini stay? They looked all dressed up so we could stay right? Papa and you *always* let us stay for supper."

"Of course, yes Georges, you three are family," Adrienne replied, signaling to the house staff to prepare for the arrival of their host and guests. She rummaged through her memory of the guest list. Years into hosting, and she finally understood how incredible her mother was for having to see faces and recall names, and where they were to be seated. A hundred names; easy when she categorized them – political, military, laypeople, clergy… Many tables, but at least she knew when it was time to eat, she'd have the chance to sit by Gilbert.

Several men were welcomed as the flood of people roamed through the streets with flags and ribbons. Adrienne received twice the amount of hand kisses as there were people in her home, her cheeks finely flushed before the man of the hour even ran inside to avoid being grabbed by his adoring Parisians at his end.

"*Mon coeur*, I am starving," he said, holding her elbows as he claimed her lips for himself. "It smells delicious. Oh look at that." Gilbert took a glass of wine as it passed them. They greeted the next arrivals together.

"Georges gave an account of the Divine intervening for you," Adrienne said, glancing up.

"Very convenient timing for the sun, yes," he replied, pausing to shake the hand of a Commune member. "If it was God, then I hope it is a good sign for the short oration I gave. I blacked out through half of it, but, ah, the reception was quite humbling, so I can assume I said some pretty words."

"You worked on that speech for weeks. And you have always been a great orator. Look at where you are, what you've already accomplished."

"In the past, I would say you were going to make me a vain man."

"You are a very generous man," she said, and gestured to the roaming food for their next guests. Forty-nine already. "I've only heard of one other banquet being hosted today and tomorrow perhaps. Here we have, six? Six planned?"

"Everyone deserves some United States splendor." His eyes followed the tray of American ham that left the kitchen. "Can people hurry up though, I need several of those slices on my plate."

Adrienne smiled. "Oh, speaking of, on your desk next to Adélaïde's letter, is one from President Washington. Just arrived while you were out."

"A marvelous day."

"*Aah*, General."

Adrienne didn't need to remember who this one was.

"Monsieur Mayor," Gilbert replied, saluting Bailly as the man politely nodded. "I apologize for the rain during your speech. You held your character to the highest standard, Monsieur, I can hear the cheers for the future reelection."

Bailly gave a small guffaw. "One can hope the Commune retains its reason on both sides and I can see your vision come to light in the month upcoming. That's all I expect, however. There's no peace, even amongst the left," he said. "Madame Lafayette, please excuse this old man's complaining. Thank you for opening your house to us, your kindness knows no bounds."

"You flatter me, Monsieur," Adrienne replied as Bailly touched his rather large nose to her knuckles. "Please, enjoy the soup while it's warm. The rain this morning was more chilly than summer should ever allow and we don't want the mayor to catch a cold."

"Madame, you are most generous; perchance, should your husband ever share you –"

"Never," Gilbert replied, hooking his arm around Adrienne's. "I am greedy and desire her only for myself. But do share some wine, tell our friends to partake in as much as they please, but not so much for them to be unfit for duty in the morning."

"And not *too* much as to run us dry," Adrienne added under her breath. "We only have twenty-seven bottles in the cellar."

"Only twenty-seven?" Gilbert whispered back while guests ninety-nine and one hundred slipped into the garden.

"Well, we have fifty already pulled up here. Supplies aren't the easiest thing to order nowadays. We can serve coffee after dinner – it's very democratic, they'll like it."

His stomach growled angrily as he made short conversation with some older guardsmen. With everyone in good spirits, the Hôtel de Lafayette quickly became as lively as any palace party, full of song and talk of the revolution. Georges put on a display with his fencing, challenging a man five times his age to a fight on the veranda, the tapping of steel conjoined with the merriment of the evening. As the sky shifted to pink, Adrienne had the footmen go around to light torches outside to keep the entertainment going. A far more tame assembly than any actual political body could conjure, the dinner was full of content liberal voices ready for France's revival as a constitutional monarchy.

It certainly felt like she was feeding the poor man's army. The speed at which the men devoured the courses served within the three-hour meal was phenomenal. Desserts and coffee broke groups into smaller side conversations, enjoying the warmth that the drink and the summer night was finally bringing. Music was simple, a few violinists claimed one side of the veranda as they strummed a little tune before taking up their bows to the instrument. Anastasie was discreet in sliding up to her mother to report that the Madame d'Ayen of all people was waiting in the front foyer.

"Maman?" Adrienne had said, quietly rushing to share a *faire la bise.* "Is everything well at the Tuileries? What are you doing here?" It was only recently when Adrienne began to note the tiny aging lines on her mother's face.

"Men drink in copious amounts, so I thought you could use some champagne. I've brought several crates anticipating that your husband may be provoked into a speech with all his compatriots. Trust me, it is bound to happen; likely within the hour." Madame d'Ayen smoothed the tiny pleats in her linen gown.

"Let me get my men to help yours, then," Adrienne replied, glancing towards the bells that would summon the servants.

"Oh no need, darling, they are busy with your guests. I've already brought plenty of help as I have men meandering about the Hôtel at this hour."

"Louis?"

"Goodness, no, he has drunken himself asleep on your sister's lap. She's due any week now so it is a blessing he's been home at all."

"You'll send for me when she goes into labor, won't you? I want to help. Anastasie is very capable as well, so please send for both of us."

The door cracked open, pushed by the butt of a man, arms full of a champagne crate. Warm air rushed down the hall, rustling the candle flames.

"Boys, boys, be careful, use both hands. Auntie d'Ayen will scold you if your mother doesn't first." Ségur shuffled sideways as his two young sons held another crate. Adrienne caught her gasp in her throat.

"Ségur!" she said, opening her arms. "You've returned from Russia? When did this happen?" Squeezing his face, she hopped up on her toes to kiss his cheek. "Are these wrinkles, sir?" His dark brown hair had taken on some gray roots.

"Don't remind me," Ségur said, gently placing the wine on the side table. "But, Madame, you, you look divine as always. Motherhood suited you well and now you are as lovely as ever."

"Louis said it just makes us Noailles' fat," Adrienne laughed.

"Louis never was a bright man," Ségur said, kissing her cheek. "From what I've heard on my voyage back, I am no longer a comte and he is partially to blame."

"It is a move towards equality between men," Adrienne explained. "Whatever helps France. We all knew it wouldn't be as simple as the Americans have done it."

"I doubt the Americans have chastised their church too," Madame d'Ayen said, sending Octave and Paul back out to retrieve another crate. "Disgusting what some men are trying to propose."

"Oh, Maman, let the festivities close before we start about what the Commune will do this fall."

"It won't be good for us, I can tell you that," she said. Holding her elbows, she let her eyes wander the parlor. Laughter rolled up from the garden. "We shouldn't keep you from your guests. Go let Gilbert know that you are now all set for the evening and for your next one, alright, chérie?"

"Yes, Maman, thank you. Give Papa and Louise my love, Rosalie too if she isn't with Auntie Tessé," Adrienne said, hearing Gilbert's crowd calming *ah-ahs* from afar. "And to Madame Ségur and your daughter. I hope her pregnancy continues well and you may call yourself a father again soon, Monsieur."

"Thank you, she will be overjoyed to hear that *the* Madame Lafayette has blessed her new baby. Hopefully it is born in France, as I have the habit of being continuously sent out on missions. I didn't need a Russian baby, and I pray it won't be German."

"It will be French," Adrienne conceded. "Bless you, Ségur. And be safe, Maman, the people outside are rowdy with excitement. Don't let them shake the carriage too much."

She saw them safely brought out to their coach, pleasantly content with the surprise of Ségur and his rapidly-growing sons and generous gifts from her mother. Her fingers tapped on the corks one by one: a dozen, two, three... It would certainly do. No man was getting completely inebriated at their house tonight, she wasn't a hostess to a den of troublemakers. Celebratory, but in moderation, that was what the homily last mass had said.

Religion wasn't very popular in Paris as of late, yet Adrienne and the rest of the Noailles sisters never claimed to want popularity – she attended every service at the church down the street with her children. If people wanted liberty, then they should stand for those who still wished to attend mass, she thought. One could not claim freedom without it extending to all. Gilbert was already in the early stages of arguing for expanding the liberties of the French man to her colonies, to the Black men who lived abroad. Monsieur Bailly was speaking for the French Jew. It was all noble stances, Adrienne knew, but there were a handful of incorrigible assembly members who would rather have lawless chaos than reasonable liberty.

Virginie, her dutiful secretary of a daughter, scurried quietly like a mouse through the halls, closing the office door behind her. She held a small folded paper in hand, hiding it amongst her ribbon belt.

"Papa wanted his notes," she said when Adrienne caught up with her. "Some of the men kept cheering for him to say something even though his glass of wine hit before the food did. And you know when Papa does that, he gets all wobbly and a little stupid."

"He doesn't get stupid," Adrienne replied with a critical tsk, "he just gets silly."

There was a temperate moisture in the air as a humid cloud barrelled off of the river and up the grass. Gilbert was standing up in the middle of the crowd of men, cheeks pink as he spoke with a slight bop in his voice. His eyes couldn't stop creasing, he was smiling so widely. Virginie looked up at the pile of men, the top of her head hardly reaching their stomachs. Adrienne knew her struggle well.

"Let me take that to your father," she said. She was hardly shoulder-height to many, but she didn't mind shoving her way through. A hostess' job was a tough one. Keeping the notes discreetly folded between her fingers, she strutted into the crowd, the first wave parted instantly as soon as her hand touched their arms, grabbing at other men to move out of her way. Adrienne maintained her pace towards Gilbert, who, now she noted, was standing on a small stool likely procured from the stables. He met her eyes at her approach, floating back to the ground to receive her as everyone else gathered around.

"When this is done, I think the bed calls for us," he whispered. "I think I am already in it, actually, my body has not caught up."

"Your tongue needs to remain for a moment longer," Adrienne replied, handing him his oration notes. "I am actively watching Georges bring you another glass of wine, but I recommend you don't sip from it until you finish speaking, *cher*."

Georges appeared behind him, a glass of champagne filled more than it needed to be, some staining the edges of his cuffs. Gilbert took it carefully, thanking him with a genteel bow of his head. Georges merely grinned and bowed back, his hand still on the sword at his side, a miniature general fit for battle.

"Settle down gentlemen," Gilbert said, loud enough for the guests to hear. "You all shall get several sentences from me and then you must go *home*, for my family and I must prepare to see you again *next* week, where perhaps I shall give you some more sentences." He held his glass aloft and his notes low. Adrienne stepped to the side, finding her daughters and pulling them to her as they listened.

"France," he said, "is seeing the most admirable progress in eons. What the enlightenment writers have written, we have read, and what we have fought for, we are finally seeing. It goes without saying the struggles and difficulties that arose these past months – you all know my ideals – I am as I was in America: a proponent for achieving liberty through the laws that we make for our nation. Without law, there is no foundation for liberty to stand upon, it rattles like a rusty nail holding our homes up. We here, of the government to make these new laws, soldiers to protect it, working men to live it: we are France. We have our king with us: he has taken the same oath we have! I can see our constitutional monarchy thriving just from the labor we have all put into the construction of the *Champs de Mars*."

A camaraderie cheer arose. Everyone's hands bore the blisters of hard work.

"So I will propose a toast," and with this another cheer accompanied by laughter filled the lawn. "To the people, a France for and by the people... And to my beautiful wife, who fed all you madmen today, huzzah." Gilbert lifted his champagne high and dumped the wine into his mouth before hopping off his platform.

"Huzzah!" Glasses clinked around, a very joyous American noise. Gilbert's hand found purchase on Adrienne's waist, squeezing her gently to him. The flush to his cheeks immediately spread to the rest of his face as the consequences of ignoring her advice and downing another drink came to pass. Georges ran by with a glass before Anastasie pulled it from his hands, holding it high above him as she clung to her father's other side.

Half-asleep finishing the festival day-one celebration, the Lafayettes spent a good hour calling coaches and wagons ensuring that every man regardless of money was escorted back towards their home safely. Coats and shoes were discarded on the wooden floors as Gilbert waved off the last of his friends, his heavy hand on the door as he pushed it shut and proceeded to slide to the ground; his children crawling over with overtired grins. Adrienne fell upon the sofa, looking over at the four as they piled onto Gilbert like he were a boat and the floor a river.

"Well, what a day this has been," Gilbert said, grunting as Virginie wrapped her arms around his neck. "You all are too big to be doing this to me."

"If we stop then you'll miss it," Anastasie reasoned, resting her head on his shoulder. "And you've been gone all week, it is only fair we compensate."

"I see your mother has been teaching you how to argue in my absence."

Adrienne smiled into the cushion as he tried to shuffle them closer to the salon. Her legs hurt from standing, but she still willed them to work one more time, as any mother must, and pulled one sleeping Georges from Gilbert's leg.

"Come now, get ready for bed and I will join you for prayers in a few minutes. You'll see your father in the morning. He needs his rest too — you know how busy he has been and how awful he handles champagne — go on. Kiss Papa goodnight and get upstairs."

She handed Georges to Anastasie, the boy wriggled in annoyance at his older sister's nagging as Gilbert prepared to receive plenty of kisses. Adrienne waited to count the number of footsteps towards the bedchambers to make sure none of them snuck off to the library. At the sight of their governess at the top of the stairs, Adrienne sighed and balanced her hands on her hips. Fashion had moved all the skirt padding to the back instead of the sides, and made her shadow look less formidable as she loomed over Gilbert. His wig from the formal affair had been discarded, leaving his hair only in its short queue. His shirt was wet from the day's rain and heat and sweat, he looked as if he dunked himself in the river.

"A bath, maybe?" he said, pulling at his cravat.

"Mn, maybe," Adrienne replied, holding out her hand. "Shall I wash your hair?"

He took it, though not quite using it to get to his feet as his knees and back cracked simultaneously. His smile lines creased when he winced. Adrienne bit her lip. Her stays were the only thing keeping her own back from cracking. Like they were an ancient elderly couple assisting each other up the stairs, they joked that perhaps they should move their master suite onto the ground floor to save themselves the trouble of tripping and groaning. He limped lazily towards the room, and Adrienne detoured towards the children'. Georges had his own room, yet it was hardly ever used. The decor was plain enough that they often used it as a guest room since Georges wanted to sleep in his sisters' chambers in a small bed to the side most of the time. His things took up a corner of the sewing supplies and books and art: a corner of his father's manuals and fencing gear, and an English book that Adrienne terribly needed to borrow to brush up on. She didn't want to completely lose the language; it had been weeks since they hosted Americans who preferred to speak English. She'd have to demand it at the next soirée.

Anastasie pulled the last pin out of Virginie's ginger hair, smoothing it with her fingers. "There we are. Georges, are you done? Maman's here for prayers, don't keep her waiting!"

"I'm done, stop bossing me around," Georges replied, appearing from behind the four paneled privacy screen in his shirt and stockings, shuffling along like all grumpy nine-year-olds did. He promptly fell to his knees next to Adrienne as she knelt by Anastasie's bed. Virginie rolled off to join her on her other side, leaving Anastasie to face her mother on the other side of the mattress.

"There we are," Adrienne said. "Virginie, I believe it's your turn to lead us?"

Virginie was soft-spoken, gentle like her papa. She said the sign of the cross and folded her hands to her lips as they recited the Lord's prayer and the Hail Mary. "Now I lay me down to sleep, I pray the Lord my soul to keep. Watch and guard me through the night, and wake me with the morning light. Dear Jesus, please keep Papa and Maman happy and safe and may my brother and sister have sweet dreams tonight so we can continue our fun game tomorrow. Amen."

"And Lord, please keep a watchful eye on our family as we try to follow in your footsteps. Keep France and your children in your divine light as we trek through unknown times," Adrienne said.

"Especially Papa," Anastasie added.

"Especially Papa," Adrienne nodded. "*Amen.*"

"Amen."

"Very good, very good, kisses goodnight, my doves," Adrienne whispered. "I'll see you all in the morning. Don't stay up reading, I will know and won't be pleased. Neither will your tutors."

"We won't, I promise."

"Goodnight, Maman."

"Tell Papa I said I love him!"

Adrienne ghosted down the hallway, already unbuttoning her bodice and working loose the first petticoat before she stepped foot into their room. The sturdy fabric fell to the floor with a thump followed by the clank of her waistcoat's several buttons.

"I love that sound," she heard Gilbert say from his place inside the tub. Sloshing, he moved to cross his arms over the edge. "That's the getting naked sound."

Adrienne shimmied out of the second petticoat, kicking it away as she made it to the bumpad underneath it. So many layers, but it was a joke now, hearing Gilbert quietly whoop and cheer for every piece of clothing lost. Her lungs expanded as soon as she worked at the ribbon keeping her stays completely closed. Gilbert's fingers wiggled from the tub and she wandered over, letting him pull the ribbon eyelet by eyelet. His hands wet her chemise underneath as he pushed the stays off her shoulders, bringing her close while he palmed her ass.

"This is nice."

Adrienne laughed. "Yours must be sore after being saddled all day."

"It could use a good hold too, I won't lie, *mon coeur*. I am surprised I've been able to stand for the rest of the evening."

"You should sleep in tomorrow. There isn't anything for you to rush to so soon. The king can have his levée without you standing there, Bailly can handle the assembly, your guard will be fine if your aides are there, and the people will be too tired after today's celebrations to cause much trouble." Adrienne combed her nails through his curls while Gilbert patted her behind in thought. "Gilbert, I cannot remember a time when you rested. You'll make yourself sick."

"I'm sorry, I've been so busy. Everything just needs to be perfect. Paris is so fragile. I feel like any wrong move and this whole revolution can capsize."

"You need to retire. Let us escape for a bit and enjoy the country."

"If only. Not yet. I need to be sure Bailly gets reelected and make some presentations to the Commune. I try to keep General Washington updated on France's affairs and I've been meaning to meet with Jefferson and Morris again." His eyes had closed while Adrienne sudsed up his hair. "Why is it that Americans can cohesively form a democratic republic even with their Tory inhabitants, yet I am faced with opposition when trying to take the middle ground? We have our king, and we will have our constitution – it is the best of both worlds and yet in government, no one is pleased. Someone is always conniving behind someone else's back, anarchy is afoot." He shook his head. "I am still facing problems inside my guard and throughout Paris' armies. They think freedom and liberty mean they are no longer accountable for anything, that law has no meaning. Oh, Adrienne, what am I to do?"

She lowered herself to the floor, his hands slid up her spine to cup the back of her head. When he opened his eyes to meet hers on equal footing, the shadows underneath them had darkened, and the joyous countenance that had held him throughout the day and over the dinner had slackened to the utter exhaustion of a man who held all of Paris on his shoulders. She kissed him slowly, through the soap bubbles and the leftover taste of champagne.

"You have always been what this country needs," she said, holding his hands to her face. "A kind, good-spirited man who, despite his aristocratic upbringing, stands for the poor and the abused. Gilbert, you have been breaking expectations since I first met you; you have loved liberty since you first heard her name. What other Frenchman can claim to have fought for it as hard as you have? Who has made more sacrifices than you? You are France's *star*. As Saint Michael followed you through one revolution, he will follow you again for this one. And God will tell you when it is time to wash your hands of the sins of man; even court martials and prison sentences cannot cure corrupted souls. You owe these anarchists *nothing*. God will see to them. Keep fighting for the downtrodden, Gilbert, and I will keep fighting for you."

Adrienne kissed him again, and this time his tongue tickled at her lips, and a tiredly desperate sigh escaped his nose. It had been weeks since they had touched each other more than a simple caress at night, or the few times she awoke to his hand on her breast as he snored. As he pleased, he pulled her into the tub, bringing her chemise and stockings with her.

"My pious wife," he murmured, wiping soap from her chin with his thumb. "My beautiful and intelligent girl." He kissed her and kissed her. They were young lovers yet.

"My steadfast and good husband," she replied. His lashes were threatening to make her giggle as he nipped down her neck, pulling her deeper into the warm water. "Gilbert! Naughty!"

"If I am breaking France's expectations, it is alright if we break this tub," he said, biting at her chemise like a dog would its own leg, expecting it to disappear with a few tugs from his teeth. "Truly, *mon coeur*, I will be so much better to work in the morning if you sit yourself right here," he gestured to his lap, "and I nuzzled a breast or two." He smiled at his coy charm, but the boyish energy didn't quite reach his eyes. Nevertheless, Adrienne made herself comfortable on his lap, walking her fingers up his navel to the rise of his collarbone, settling an open palm to his chest. His heart raced under her touch. Hers drummed a warlike tune as his hands snaked up her soaked-through shift.

"Whatever you need," she said, "I will do it."

Gilbert hummed his recognition, his acknowledgment, content in a loving distraction from what awaited Paris in the morning. What he didn't understand was just how much Adrienne meant by her words.

Paris, November 1790

"Papa, what are you doing?"

Adrienne heard Virginie follow her father and the valet around the hôtel for what felt like an hour. With every few minutes, a gust of late autumn wind penetrated the house, blowing out the candles that lit the otherwise dull and cloudy afternoon. Anastasie was with her governess, Georges with his tutor, but Virginie had woken with a frightful cough that morning and Adrienne determined the little one was to rest that day. Engulfed in a blanket, the wrapped girl waddled a few feet behind Gilbert since she had the strength to get out of bed.

Gilbert, his banyan tight over his clothing, had a deepening crevice between his brows as he pointed at each door and window to the house. His valet had unscrewed the locks and hinges, collecting them in one pile, and showed him newer and thicker ones bought from out of town.

"Papa, are you listening?"

"Papa's replacing the locks, *ma petite souris*," Gilbert said, kindly turning her about and nudging her butt back towards Adrienne who watched from her reading chair.

"Why?"

"They are getting old."

"They can't be that old. We've only lived here for eight years."

Gilbert's jaw shifted, an anxious eye lingered at Adrienne as he continued to instruct the servant where to reattach the new locks. Adrienne settled a mark in her book and set it to the side.

"Virginie, come here," she said, opening her arms. "Away from the windows, darling, I don't want your cold to worsen. Let your father work."

It was a little frightening how fast their children were growing. One would never know that Virginie was born prematurely at the height she was already at.

Her hands were freezing. Adrienne pressed the thin fingers to her lips as Virginie climbed up on the chair; a little too tall and a little too big to be sitting on her lap in such a small seat, but like any good Lafayette, they made it work. Adrienne coiled her arms around her baby girl.

"I've been reading some of Auntie Pauline's works," Virginie said, her nose stuck in Adrienne's neck. "I like them."

"Oh, do you? That's wonderful, she'll be so happy to hear that. You should write her a letter with your thoughts, I think you two would get along well. She gets rather lonely down south, you know. She doesn't have any children to keep her company like you do me."

"Being alone isn't fun."

Adrienne shook her head, watching Gilbert tighten the lock himself. "No it isn't," she said.

It didn't escape her notice how quickly Paris had grown darker, how agitated its people were, festering like an open wound. The Duc d'Orléans continued to buzz about France, the Jacobins, the Feuillants…. If there were any more groups stirring up trouble, they all began to blend together. A pile of gazettes overtook the table between chairs, advertisements that Gilbert had bought and brought home despite not knowing why he did so. They bore his face on them, which would have been reason enough, but none of the caricatures were in good humor. Adrienne narrowed her eyes at the one on top: Gilbert knelt in front of the queen, one hand upon his heart, the other over the exposed display of her genitalia. The rumor that he was sleeping with Marie-Antoinette was outrageous, and one Adrienne incredulously scoffed at. Not that Gilbert was incapable of having another affair, but the queen had grown to despise his company; it was only his belief in maintaining the crown's role in the government that he spent so much time in their presence.

"There's another one from today," Gilbert said, finally walking away from overseeing the servant's work. He pulled aside his robe and fished through his waistcoat pocket, unfolding another picture. "I am riding a phallus in this one. Quite unique, I would say."

"Gilbert!" Adrienne said, covering Virginie's eyes as if the child had not already seen it all. The artwork presented Gilbert in his National Guard uniform, with, as expected, Marie-Antoinette petting the thing like it were an animal... or a strange ostrich-penis hybrid.

He turned the pamphlet back around, staring at it for a long moment. "Truthfully I prefer this over me as a centaur. Poor Jean le Blanc doesn't deserve to be molded into some creature with me as his head. Alas, *Le Sans Tort*. It's clever."

"I hate it," Adrienne replied.

"Yes, me too." He dropped it to the growing pile. "Yet they cannot say I do not support the press, at least. I think I will avoid sending any copies to His Excellency, however. I don't believe the General will find that quite as amusing."

"I'll hold my tongue on that," she added. "I still have letters to write to the diocese. Did you know they're to replace Archbishop Juigne with this Monsieur Gobel? A good man, forced to leave France even though he, too, took the oath. He dined with us several weeks ago, but there are threats to his life! What of religious liberty, Gilbert? What is the Commune doing?"

He shook his head, eyes still scanning the pornographic art that defamed his name. His mellow humor had fallen back into a distasteful gloom. Absently, he rubbed Virginie's back. At the sides of his ginger hair, some gray was beginning to grow in. His furious speeches at the assembly had rendered his voice hoarse and his headaches far more frequent. Home was supposed to be a place for rest, and Adrienne knew he was doing his best. She tried to follow his lead, but some politics were growing ridiculous and Gilbert was still not the kind of man to shut her down for having an opinion on them.

Adrienne's frown deepened. The next cool breeze pulled her attention back to those locks. They hardly had used their locks in the first place.

"Are we in danger?" she asked.

"No." Gilbert brought his hand up to her face. "No, I wouldn't let anything happen to you."

As if he had a choice in the matter, Adrienne thought. But she nodded and kissed his palm. Plenty of houses belonging to political figures were being raided and broken into. She'd have to relocate their safe.

"This is," he struggled to find the right word to frame his delicate lie, "just precautionary."

How many people wanted her husband dead right after they profoundly sang his praises?

"You're going to hate me."

Adrienne looked up, brows raised. "Why?"

"Some of the constitutional clergy will be dining with us this season."

The priests that agreed to swear their allegiance to France over their allegiance to the Vatican. Adrienne slowly blinked, grateful his palm was there to hide the scowl that was twitching at her lips.

"But I know you are the most kind and intellectual hostess and will make them feel welcome," Gilbert said, then added with a slight sigh, "even when you politely slander their actions. I don't know how you do that: critique without bruising honor."

"Part of my education," she replied.

"I should have gone to your lessons instead of mine."

"You were more than welcome."

"Mademoiselle Maron would not have let a deranged boy like me into your lessons, please. I was stupid back then anyway, too focused on duels and – *tsk* – other things." He watched the valet test the next lock. "I'll write to Pa and tell him to check his doors. Citizens near the Tuileries can get excited when news comes out of de Ville. No need to risk break-ins. The Maréchal de Noailles took up residence not far from here, I may stop by on my route to work tomorrow."

"Gilbert, why don't we go away to Chavaniac?" Adrienne adjusted her hold on Virginie, who had quickly fallen asleep in the warm embrace.

"I cannot, *mon coeur*, I cannot. There is so much to be done. There is opposition that I am responsible for quelling. Who else could do it? It must be me." There was a thread on his banyan he continued to pull and twist while he paced a few steps around her chair. "It must be me," he repeated.

Thirty new locks added to their financial debt, Adrienne later wrote. Why no one bothered to pay Gilbert his due as General was beyond her, every livre he received came from the selling of church property to private buyers – holy land claimed by the government, and Gilbert only shoved that pay back into the National Guard as they still were somehow severely underfunded. It was charitable, and for that Adrienne felt like she should appreciate her husband's selflessness, but instead her distaste for the Commune was only growing larger as their disrespect reared its head week after week.

Every early morning, she found herself by her desk, adding more ink to her quill, adding more strikingly polite criticism to her letters. She owed no one her kindness, but for the sake of Gilbert's name, she flourished every comment she had about disrespecting the church with both prose and facts so that no one could want nor feasibly find any way to argue against them. *Why not?* Her mother was in these words, she found, giving her address a once-over. A Lafayette certainly stuck to their ideals and she was no different. Putting the wax spoon over its flame, she cleaned her pen and sealed the letter.

"Forward this to the diocese," she asked Gilbert's secretary, "as soon as you are able."

Chapter Twenty-Five

Paris, March 1791

Adrienne didn't dine out much, but when she did, she tried to dine with her family as much as possible. Gathering her mother, Louise, and Rosalie was simple: Maman and Louise hardly left Paris and Rosalie was still preparing her trip to her husband's château in Villersexel. She matched her husband, Theo, with plenty of kindness and patience; Louise commented they may not have even consummated with how shy the two of them were together. Their father had stolen Monsieur de Grammont, past marquis, and discarded upon the ladies the infallible Louis, who walked with them like a commander leading the fray of Noailles. His squared off coat cut him a fine figure and he knew it, and Louise and Adrienne knew it as they exchanged eyerolls at every other opportunity.

"Are you certain Gilbert can't join us?" Rosalie asked, her arm looped through their Maman's.

"He is dining with Monsieur Gobel," Adrienne replied.

The Madame d'Ayen scoffed. "Scoundrel, the man. The pope will never approve it, whatever the bishops claim."

"So this was a meticulously planned outing?" Louise said, pulling a strand of dark-blonde hair out of her mouth as the breeze off the river pushed it back. "You've left our poor Gil to dine with the devil?"

"I would not receive him," Adrienne replied. "Better to take myself out of the equation before something mean comes off my tongue. It's better this way. Gilbert can continue to keep his name well-received, and at least they may talk of *some* religion. Honestly, I pray Gilbert will be the one to teach Gobel a lesson on what it means to be a real Christian in this revolutionary era."

"Gilbert hasn't gone to church in years."

"That's right."

Louise huffed a laugh. Latching her finger around the wide collar of Louis in front of them, she yanked him to a stop in front of the Bouillon, the smell of food already floating down the street.

"I knew it was here," Louis coughed, adjusting his cravat, "no need to choke me."

The Bouillons of Paris had small menus and their origins catered towards the poor, but in this era, all peoples were to be equal, and the Noailles' did not mind spending some of their fortune on public meals. It was half a show of solidarity, and half a mind that the food truly wasn't so bad. They sat on only slightly tarnished chairs, the five of them sharing a long table with another few couples.

There were whispers that Adrienne duly ignored. Whether or not common people would recognize her on the street was anyone's guess; she didn't throw herself out into the public's eye as frequently as Gilbert did, but it was fair game to any federate to look over and point out the General's wife amongst her family. No doubt, it was Louis who would be regarded first – a man ever revolving around the government and the riling crowds. If it wasn't for his taste in expensive cloth, he otherwise fashioned himself like a working Frenchman. His hair was chopped so short, there was nothing for any ribbon to wrap around, and thus it fluffed up and out behind his ears. Louise looked as if she was trying very hard not to stick her hand in the short strands near his neck.

Rosalie spoke about the Château de Villersexel, of its size and estate pulled right out of a fairytale. It was half a week's journey southeast of Paris, nearing the German states, and so she had been trying to pick up some of the German language just in case. This, in turn, led Louis on a twenty minute rant about General von Steuben, which captured the attention of the men sitting nearby, who also wanted to talk of the Americans' fight for independence.

Madame d'Ayen carefully sipped on the wine, looking at Adrienne as Louise tried to pull Louis back into their own family.

"Are you getting enough sleep, Adrienne?" she asked. "You are looking fatigued."

"Everyone is fatigued, Maman," she replied. The soup course was brought to the table smelling of stewed beef and onion.

"I know, *ma petite chou*, but you know how wary I am with the Marquis' – with Monsieur Lafayette's – notoriety. With his cousin being placed at the head of the army in Nancy, I worry about consequences falling back on him, and if it is on him, then it is on you. I love both of you with all my heart; I couldn't bear seeing you or he get hurt from radical fiascoes. You know how hate trickles down families; remember when Madame de Noailles was removed from Her Majesty's service and how it affected your sister. It took months to heal that bruised honor. But that was Court, all *this* is… it feels worse. It brings an ache to my soul."

Adrienne fiddled with her spoon. "I know, Maman," she replied. "But if American women handled war at their doorsteps for several years, we must be vigilant at ours, no?"

Louis hummed. "American women, there is another story."

"Speak it and you will find yourself without a tongue," said Louise, smoothing out her dress. "Adri, that last name of yours is going to bring about all sorts of trouble, but Maman, you know her, she'd plant herself into the ground before she leaves Gilbert."

"Would you leave me, *mon loulou*?" Louis asked, downing his drink.

"If you did something so stupid," Louise replied, patting his hand, "I'd sooner take the children and go with Maman."

He shrugged. "Tis fair. I am a little offended, but fair."

Rosalie sat quietly by their mother, hands in her lap. Adrienne shared a small smile as a fiddler took up his instrument on the street corner, the music notes wafting through the windows. It must have been nerve-wracking for Rosalie, traveling far from home for the first time, leaving the rest of the family in the middle of a restless city. Pauline had already written and expressed her worry – she herself was safe in her home in southern France. Every day Adrienne thought of Chavaniac: its cool castle floors and large fields of hills to get lost in. The children could focus more on their education there and not worry about rising violence. Gilbert could leave politics.

It was a thought that replayed in her head every single night.

So maybe she wasn't getting the best sleep, but things could have been worse.

She had left Gilbert that afternoon with everything to attend to in terms of what he wished to serve Monsieur Gobel for dinner; she left the children to their governess to keep distraction out of the way while *the leech* sucked away at Gilbert's hospitality. He wasn't pleased with the scheduling either, but he had been hosting other clergy, and to not host the false archbishop of Paris would only bring him more enemies. She wondered of the *ifs* should she had remained to host. It wouldn't have been good; Adrienne did not have the longing to be liked by everyone. Likability was less important than respectability.

The Bouillon went on for another hour, the Noailles' simply eaves-dropping between their own conversations. It was pleasant to catch up. Her father had been divulging himself into science while waiting for a military command with the incredibly rising tensions between France and her monarch-led neighbors. Monsieur d'Ayen's hair had gone completely salty in the past few months, a note that the Madame was eager to compliment as "very handsome indeed," much to the delight of her daughters, and the follow up question of Louis to Louise if he too would be handsome if he went gray early on.

"Stay brown as long as you can, I am already combating my own age," Louise uttered, pulling her cap further up over her head. If she was growing white strands, it wasn't noticeable within her fair hair anyway. They were only in their early thirties, they shouldn't have been graying.

She took Louis' drink from his hand – heaven knows how many he had while Adrienne wasn't paying attention – and set it on the other far end of the table. There was a nostalgia to seeing them make the minuscule motions with each other, as if no time had passed at all. To this day, there was always a color on their clothing that matched each other completely, whether it be green or blue.

Adrienne touched the violet of her jacket. Gilbert was in a yarrow waistcoat when she kissed him goodbye. She recalled the tiny embroidered flowers on it. Anything that wasn't his uniform, she admired with such ferocity that she had been caught staring at him several times. If he was in a good mood, he'd make a little show out of it, but today his furrowed brow was present, and so there was no twirling or rolling himself against the wall like a damsel.

Perhaps she should have waited another quarter-hour before her family escorted her back across the river to Saint-Germain-des-Pres. She could have gone her whole life without coming face-to-face with Monsieur Gobel and his large crucifix hanging from his thin neck. When she heard Gilbert's voice from outside the door, in its stern and vitriolic tone, she should have retreated back into the carriage, but it was already pulling away, and she heard the door locks shift and click.

" – and she is as noble as you can imagine, Monsieur," Gilbert was saying. "But I recommend you keep my wife's name from your *fruitless* gossip, else you will find yourself, sword in that bible-holding hand, several paces from me in the field. I pray your studies of God may have included pleads for His mercy."

Adrienne threw herself around the corner of the entrance's pillar, like a lady, of course.

"General," Gobel replied. His voice was weaning, like a scolded boy. "I meant no disrespect."

"I expect not," Gilbert exclaimed, and the shadow of Gobel came upon the front stairs. "You are a man of the cloth and I of the sword. Surely, your Excellency, you have just forgotten yourself when you libel the honor of the most benevolent and pious lady in your parish."

There was a silence that followed that swallowed the air between them. Adrienne heard the click of rings to waistcoat buttons as the men bowed.

"Thank you, Monsieur, for the meal and your sound advice. I will take note of it and reflect," Gobel said, taking another step down until he had to tilt his head high to meet Gilbert's sullen expression. "Please give Madame Lafayette my regards."

"You may write your apologies to her yourself. She is at all liberty to accept or reject them, I do not rule her."

Adrienne had to press her cold fingers against her cheeks to cool herself down. If only the men glanced to the side where the bushes were into their spring blooms, they would see the very woman they spoke of as red as the roses. Divine intervention kept her hidden as the archbishop hobbled away from the house, his knuckles white with the grip of his cane as his secretary and aides who dined with him quickly followed. She counted to a hundred, not hearing the front door close nor Gilbert's feet retreating.

"How much did you hear?"

She looked up at his capricious stare as he leaned over the railing.

"Enough for me to find your ire very attractive," she replied bluntly. He sighed a laugh. "I'm sorry, did my recent letters make your dinner difficult?"

He reached his hand down, easily pulling her up onto the landing. "No," he said, "it is my privilege to defend you and your lexicon from your enemies. For anyone who comes against your principles is a rascal indeed. He made for poor conversation anyway." From his tone, it sounded like a very long-winded conversation. "How was your meal? I missed your company."

"Quite fine, actually. You mostly missed reminiscent speeches from your brother, and Rosalie's send off. She told me to give you her kisses as she takes leave in the morning."

Gilbert groaned, "dammit, I was meaning to send her along with a gift, I completely forgot."

Adrienne pulled him inside. "We can send it through post. You know how *they* love you."

"Ah, yes, of course. I might see to it before dawn tomorrow. I have to go to work early; we're still in a muck since the weapon seizure, and, ah, you know how everyone blames me. I was supposed to be in *two* places at the *same* time, you see – that is what I was told. If I was '*so high and mighty as I pretended to be, I could be in Vincennes as well as the Tuileries.*'" His hands went up and through his hair as they walked into the parlor. "Can people calm themselves and listen to reason for once in their lives? Must I worry about the nobles as much as I do the workmen? I understand revolution is an uncertain and exciting time, that great change is sometimes hard to accept, but Jesus, they do not understand I am but *one* man."

His anger wilted into prostration, collapsing onto the nearest sofa, his long legs splayed out like a stretching cat. Adrienne left her hat by the table, following him.

"I cannot stop. February was cruel, March was less than abating… I can only pray things will ease up over summer. Perhaps with the coming of our next Festival of Federation, the people will see how working together is what Paris needs, how it thrives. Every man is equal," he said, turning until his head dangled off the cushion and into Adrienne's arms. "I have a speech I must write, I've told you of the one, for citizenship for all Black Frenchmen. There is a schedule to discuss it before it goes up for vote."

"I can help you with that."

"I would be relieved for your aid," he replied. "Your persuasion may be just what we need. Not that they listen to me much anymore. Am I a puppet? Am I a dictator? Once again, I am caught between the threshold of opposites. This is all a frustrating dream where there is no coherent conclusion."

Adrienne rested her lips atop his forehead. He smelt like the lavender satchels they leave by their pillows. They fell into a silence only disturbed by the quiet clinking of silverware as the dining table was cleared in the adjoining room. From the windows outside, the river busied itself with fishermen breaking through the rest of the winter ice. A fair thought, she could order for ice cream to be made; it was a small treat that made the children happy and in turn made Gilbert very happy. Putting it on top of hot chocolate, *oh there was an idea.*

"Would you walk in the garden with me?" Gilbert asked after several minutes of Adrienne tracing lines onto his face. "I've a letter from my Hamilton and his are so rare, I feel like we must cherish it in the sanctity of the flowers. Afterwards, I'm afraid I must meet a colleague at his house briefly. I will be home before it gets too dark."

It felt as though so few of his American friends wrote to him as much as he did them. Adrienne nodded, then yelped as Gilbert rolled off the sofa instead of rising from it: a completely juvenile move.

Any excuse to spend more time with him was a good one. He paced quickly through the gardens, walking in circles around the peony bush – home to a nest of robins waiting for their eggs to hatch – as he read his dear friend's letter aloud. Adrienne had to skip every few steps to keep up with him. Being out of breath was worth it to share in his time, so much of that was spent on his horse or in the seats of the assembly. How he managed to upkeep his smile and his kindness was a miracle; and how anyone could come to hate a man who did nothing but follow his conscience was inconceivable.

Paris, July 17th 1791

Ever since the king and queen tried to escape Paris, and consequently were forgiven by the National Assembly, the sky had never shifted from its sickly green hue. Every candle did very little to add some warmth to the house, no torch provided comfort along the streets. If the monarchs did not want anything to do with Paris, then why should Paris want anything to do with their king?

Wind was replaced with the rolling thunder of anger once more. Its smell was pungent, rusty and corroding. Were there not any clocks in the Hôtel de Lafayette, it would be impossible to discern the time of day. But there were clocks, and Adrienne stared at them at every hour until the afternoon slipped into evening and the noise of dissent rattled on from down the streets. Gilbert had been called off with the National Guard for the entire day. There was no news coming back from the Champ de Mars where many of the Parisian workers were still gathering, some after their long days of labor. She only knew that Monsieur Bailly enacted martial law; and she knew that by the late morning, two people were dead.

Her heart was beating so heavily in her throat, it hurt to swallow.

She was still in her Sunday attire, appropriately well-dressed for mass with her children. Returning from the church as the workers in the city flocked down the roads to the public green, she had hastily taken their hands en route home, many other patrons opting for carriages to hurry out of the area.

There was no other wish except to hear that Gilbert was still alive. Any violent crowd was the bane of her existence until she knew he was out of harm's way.

Adrienne held her elbows, standing in the hall with her eyes toward the windows. So engrossed in waiting for news, she had not eaten. Anastasie appeared with a platter of fruit and cheese, but she was no longer hungry. Yet her daughter stood nearby, her calming presence providing a small mercy; the two of them were very used to being alone together while waiting for Gilbert's return. Anastasie was born into it.

Often through the days of riots, by evening, the crowds would move closer to de Ville or the Tuileries to extend their frustrations towards the government and king. Adrienne tilted her ear. That wasn't what she was hearing. The noise was growing louder by the second like approaching rain, slowly at first and then all at once.

The guards stationed outside the house, placed there specifically by Gilbert, were overwhelmed in an instant.

A flood of rioters ripped them off their feet, the pikes and swords held high over the mansion wall. Adrienne gasped like lightning had struck their yard. Her hand reached back to take Anastasie's, the cries rushing through the open windows.

"Death to Lafayette!"

"Maman," Anastasie said, and the glow of torchfire lit up her face.

Adrienne's mind hit a single track. She turned to Anastasie and rushed her down the hall; the servants poured into the salon, summoned by the furious blows to the gate as strangers attempted to climb into the little courtyard.

"Bar the doors, lock the windows!" she commanded, pulling her daughter up the stairs. Georges was already coming down, a sword in hand. His eyes were blown wide. "Georges turn around and get your sister. Hush, get her now. Anastasie, help me with the attic."

There was a small door that the servants used when guests overtook all the bedchambers, it melded seamlessly into the wall between large paintings and potted plants, and on the inside, the same new locks that Gilbert had installed last fall. It was a heavy door, as thick as the wall itself, opened by a thinly chained cord that matched the color of its background. Adrienne wrapped it around her wrist and pulled until the door cracked ajar, and Anastasie thrusted it open.

"Maman, what's happening?" Georges asked, running back with Virginie clinging to his sleeve.

"Get up in the attic and hide yourselves," Adrienne said, quickly kissing each of their foreheads. "Do not make a sound until I come to get you, understand?"

"Did they kill Papa?" Virginie whispered, gripping Georges as he followed Anastasie up the steps. Adrienne clenched her jaw.

"No, he's alright. They wouldn't be here if they did. Papa is coming, do you hear? Virginie, get with your siblings and say your rosary. I'll be back before you know it."

Her heart had traveled up to her head, the drumming knocking at her temples as she pushed the door closed again, locking her children away. Her palms wanted to stay holding the door shut like a shield. But there was motion in the back gardens – people had scaled over their wall, swarming the lawn.

The Hôtel was not a fortified castle like their home in Auvergne; the grounds were easily accessible from the house and the house from the garden. Adrienne pulled up her skirts and hurried back down the stairs, blowing out every candle in her path. Maids and footmen had done what she told them, pushing furniture and heavy wood against the doors and covering the dozens of windows that usually were so good at letting the soft light in, yet now they presented a growing nightmare of rabid men and women.

There was no question in her mind as to what Gilbert might have done to elicit such rage from the people. "People" was becoming a gross word for what they were, she thought, hazarding to peek out the window to the array of strange faces piling like ants against her walls.

A torch was thrown through a window, searing the edges of the drapes before a maid rushed to stomp it out, her terrified cries among the only noise within the house. Adrienne was silent. It was becoming apparent to the crowd that General Lafayette had not returned home after whatever commotion happened prior, but instead of leaving, they shifted their focus upon her.

"We'll take *your head!*" She heard, and she stepped backward into the parlor, letting the shade fall back to cover the hatred and enmity that stomped on her flowers, cracked her glass.

Pikes and lances clacked against the windows, leaving a horrid crunch that sounded off like the ticking of the clock. Tick – *crunch* – tock – *crack* – tick...

"For your husband to greet when he gets here!"

Her throat had gone dry. At least Gilbert was alive and their babies were hidden away. She didn't hear the servants whisper to her, panicked, calling for her to get to a room without the windows; but she heard the guard double back on the people outside, the swearing and crying, screaming and cursing. The commotion fluttered the drapes, casting long streaks of haunting red light across the floor and up the walls. It lit up her arm as she remained in the shadow. If she were to lean slightly to the right, she would see the violence happening where she had hosted many of these people this time last year.

Gilbert would only enforce the law. He wouldn't do the horrible things that the crowd was saying – he was no murderer, he was a soldier. Adrienne flitted through the inventory of Gilbert's valuables that remained in the house; she should hide them too, she thought, or at least have his office barred. Turning to the closest footman, she sent him down the hall to do just that. There were dueling pistols kept in the house if she wanted to grab them.

Could she shoot someone?

If they were intending on hurting her family, without a doubt, she'd damn herself to hell for them.

She wanted Gilbert home, but not now, not like this.

There was a louder crash and crumbling thud by the morning room, and a gangly man rushed out of the shadows, bare-handed, and simply barrelled into her, whatever profanities came from his mouth spat onto her face. They tumbled, briefly, her panic falling out as hastened tears as she kicked the man back with the heel of her shoe. Guards charged into the parlor to rip him away, their heavy boots cracking the broken glass strewn across the floor. A downpour of storming hooves surrounded the house, metal and snorts pushed through the jeers. Whether a cavalry came to trample her garden or the people in it, she cared not; her head throbbed, her ankle was pulsing. Two maids appeared at her side and pulled her back towards the stairs as if it were the house's redoubt.

Massacre. That was the word that continued to be thrown about.

Where was Gilbert?

If he were killed and discarded somewhere, if he faced mutiny or was held hostage, if he had fled Paris without sending word…

She melded to the staircase, looping her hands through the pillars. She didn't want to live without him even if they didn't cut her head off today.

Her eyes squeezed shut until all she felt was the pain inhabiting her blood, coursing through every limb. A prayer to God, a plea to the saints – get these people out of her home, get her husband back where he should be. She had to check on the children, they must've been so scared.

Who was to say what time it was when the clock was again audible, its ticking echoing across the tarnished floors. The green haze had invited itself in with the guard as men in their dirty boots and bloodied swords searched the property for any remaining belligerents. Adrienne half-heartedly hobbled up to the attic, wiping the dirt and tiny glass particles off her gown before she embraced Georges and Virginie, Anastasie holding them all, the only one whose eyes were dry. She was attentive to removing whatever dirt was on Adrienne's cheek and pointing out the small cut above her brow.

"Are we staying here tonight?" Georges asked, refusing to let go of her skirts.

Adrienne breathed slowly, hand on her stays. "Yes, we're safe now. Maman's going to talk to some of the men and we will make sure no one will scare us like that again," she said, keeping her voice straight.

"Can we sleep with you tonight, Maman?" Virginie wiped her eyes on Adrienne's sleeve. "Please, can we?"

"Of course. Go wait in my room. I'll have the cook make something for supper."

"I'm not hungry."

"Fine, just… just go wait, please."

Adrienne was several miles away. The children still whispered, as if their speaking voices would bring back the mob. She prayed they didn't hear their threats to her. She was already holding onto the fact no one threatened the lives of any of the three innocent Lafayettes.

Leaving her family up by the bedchambers, Adrienne returned to the salon, glass crunching underfoot. Brooms that ran in lines across the floor scratched at the wood like nails to slate. Her beautiful cushions were stained with the muggy green tint – rot and death had permeated the walls. The singed curtain was removed, taking with it the smell of ash. Down the hall, she found the shattered window, an open hole for the river's fog to broil into. She could step into the garden with ease, where the grass was kicked up and her flowers uprooted and trampled upon. Guards lined themselves around the walls, their metal ornaments glittered under the torchlight, distant flames that provided no warmth or a sense of safety. No one spoke to her. People around the city whose jeers and cries still echoed were the closest things she had to passing thoughts.

A nest lay overturned several feet from its bush. Adrienne knelt down by it, hoping that by now all the baby birds had grown enough to fly far, far away from here; that their parents never came back to the shrubbery. Bubbling sobs rushed to her throat, alone in her garden. Her fingers brought moistened dirt to her face as she tried to cover the pitiful hiccups, unable to stop her body from shaking.

"Where is my wife?"

There was one bird here, covered by its own wings. The least Adrienne could do was to put it back in its home. She used her fichu to wrap it up, tucking it into the nest as a mother would a baby in bed. If one pretended hard enough, it was just sleeping, exhausted after such a frightening evening.

"Where is she?!"

What did they have leftover in their kitchen, she wondered. Georges and Virginie had to eat something. They could split a pot of hot chocolate, that would probably make them feel a little better; the staff of the Lafayettes always knew how to make the best of the drink.

"Adrienne!"

Spurs jingled like windchimes, rushing up upon her. Sword and knees fell to the ground at her side, Gilbert's arms drawing her in with such speed and strength, Adrienne had no air in her lungs to attempt a gasp.

"I'm so sorry," Gilbert said. He kissed her cheeks and nuzzled her hair, pulling her over him until he was made the ground she sat on. "I am so sorry, *mon coeur*, I'm so sorry, forgive me, forgive me."

He was as dirty as she, his uniform askew and covered with gunpowder and nicks of blades. His skin smelt of sweat and salt, his knuckles were purple and bruised. There was a scatter of speckled burn marks upon his face, like black stars curving up his cheekbone, and rapid rivers falling down over them as he brought her attention to his eyes.

"Adrienne, talk to me, please, are you hurt? Are the children alright? I did not think they would come here – they should have just fought me. I am sorry, *mon coeur*, I've done this to you, oh God, oh God, forgive me," he murmured, finding the small cut upon her brow. He kissed it too, the red upon his lip now bringing Adrienne back to the present.

"Gilbert," she said. He really was here. "I knew you would be alive, I knew it." She wanted to bury herself in him, but didn't want to stop looking at his eyes. "What's happened? Why do they want you dead?"

His mouth quivered while he searched for words. "I'm sorry, it... it was a petition signing turned nightmare. No one would obey the martial law. Some were just there in the afternoon to provoke violence, throwing stones, harassing the troops," he shook his head. "I ordered them to disperse, but... Oh, *mon coeur*, it is like our own Boston Massacre, but I have been painted as the British regulars."

She hovered her fingertips over the burn on his cheek. "What is this?"

He took her hand away. "I looked down the barrel of a man's pistol as he stood by my horse and pulled the trigger," he replied, squeezing her hand between his. "It misfired."

In an instant, he could have been dead. There would have been a hole between his eyes. Adrienne's shoulders trembled. His embrace was so desperate.

"When I heard that part of the mob broke off and came here, I... I could not breathe. This should not have happened. H-how is our family?"

"Upstairs. They're upstairs. No one made it through the parlor." Adrienne forced herself to take a breath. "Are you done? You're not going to leave again, are you? Please tell me you're not going back out." She couldn't take it again. Her ankle curled up uncomfortably as she tried to sit up straight.

"I am here," he replied, pulling her up his chest to tuck an arm under her legs before he picked her up. It was so easy for him. "I'm done, I'm done."

He brought her back through the unbarred doors, the only crunching sound was his spurs and his sword clicking against the buttons of his coat as they climbed the stairs again. His heartbeat was strong under Adrienne's ear, picking up as he nudged their bedchamber open to the three pairs of large eyes waiting on their bed. Gilbert's strength was admirable, but even he could not remain standing under the weight of his tall children, Georges being the last to heave his father down to the mattress.

When the house was quiet, and the room softly aglow from a tiny flame kept in their fireplace; when the hot chocolate was served and Adrienne had Anastasie, Georges, and Virginie tucked under the covers, Gilbert sat on the floor by Adrienne's feet, wrapping her ankle with a thin piece of linen. His nightshirt did little to hide the bruises that dotted his shoulders and thighs, where stones and fists had connected. Any powder in his hair that he kept for the sake of formality and his link to their noble past was foremost washed away from the day. Under his curls were a few more lavender bruises. Adrienne silently bent down, holding his head as he held her calf. She was careful in not hurting him as he was the most gentle to her. Just breathing him in was a prayer. He said very little after repeating the story of the day to the children, being very concise and delicate, and leaving out the part about him almost falling victim to an assassination. He doted on them instead, praising their bravery, kissing their cheeks.

"I think," he whispered, resting his chin upon her knee, "we will prepare to return to Chavaniac."

She didn't immediately say she was relieved, although the selfish feeling raved inside her. "'We?'"

"Yes, 'we.' I do not believe I will be welcomed in Paris any longer if these factions gain too much popularity, and I do not want my little family in any more danger than I have already put you all through. I'm sorry."

"I forgive you, Gilbert, I'd always forgive you."

"Sometimes I think you should not."

"Sometimes you are just a man," she said. "And that is nothing to be ashamed of." She felt warm tears as he leaned into her leg, the minute shake of his own shoulders as he sniveled on the floor. The hero of two worlds had fallen from his pedestal and Adrienne happily caught him. A tactical retreat to Auvergne was no defeat.

Chapter Twenty-Six

Vaire, October 1791

They weren't supposed to detour on their way to Chavaniac, but it couldn't be helped. Despite Gilbert's many enemies and ill-wishers, even inside the very large extended families that the Noailles had intermingled with, he also had devoted followers and admirers nearer to home, and so they pulled into an inn to water the horses and rest for the night in the neighboring village of Vaire. Adrienne was humming to herself, trading her cloak for a shawl as she tried not to look too crazy while she paced around the common room. It had been years since she had seen her little sister, and as any Noailles girl would do, she was sneaking out from under her father-in-law's nose.

Pauline traveled lightly with so few servants, they appeared to be friends, scurrying up to the inn's doors. What a delight it was to embrace, crushing each other until their backs under their stays cracked. Gilbert was there to greet her as soon as he finished his welcome by the people who *did* support his old fame. He grew warm as Pauline reached up to kiss his forehead. She appeared to be pregnant again, but not looking so hopeful.

"Is it over?" Pauline asked, sitting down for the inn's evening meal. "The news said all the radicals fled or were arrested, but Joachim and his father insist something ugly is afoot. I believe they are planning on spending some time abroad – I am inclined to join them."

"I surely hope it is done," Adrienne said. "I am content in living out my days as a country woman and wife, seeing my brood grow into handsome young men and women from the sanctuary of Chavaniac."

Gilbert dipped his bread into Virginie's stew, stealing a few potatoes in the act. "Retirement sounds like bliss," he agreed. "I maintain my military commission, but no other beck and call could possibly pull me away from my own little heaven."

"You two are so sweet, it is nauseating," Pauline said, looking at Anastasie. "Are they like this all the time?"

Anastasie covered her smirk in her cup. "They love each other, Auntie, of course they are."

Georges nodded. "It's gross sometimes when they kiss."

Pauline gasped. "Adrienne, you two kiss? Like our Maman and Papa?" She made a face, bringing Virginie to a giggle. "My dear correspondent, you left that out of your letters."

Fighting to get some vegetables back from her father, Virginie shook her head. "Auntie, you know how much they kiss. Papa lived with you when you were our age!"

"Was I ever your age? Twenty odd years ago feels like such a long time, I'm afraid I don't remember. You will have to fill me in on how your dear father has been acting at home lately."

Adrienne basked in the unchanging silly humor that was once too often echoed by Anne in their youth; the melancholy lingered in this reunion. Pauline took every minute of their evening storytelling and doting on her nieces and nephew, speaking as though no time had passed at all. She looked like their Papa all grown up, eyes sparkling when she spoke of her work. Adrienne should have wished the man a heartier farewell, she mulled, absentmindedly taking Pauline's hand to simply hold.

They talked of the Montagu family, of Pauline's unfortunate luck with her children though she and Joachim tried often; scoring through every possible genre of polite conversation into the impolite topics once the young trio were brought to a modest sized room, leaving Adrienne, Gilbert, Pauline and her small entourage behind to sip on coffee and catch up on politics. Pauline had read Adrienne's letters regarding the treatment of the church in Paris and divulged into the story of Gilbert's treatment of the new archbishop, leaning across the table in utter disbelief.

"I know that, in rural areas, the people think that the revolution is just in Paris, and here Paris is bringing about stark change," Gilbert said. "But no one here should be put under the pretense that supporting the revolution will send you to hell. There is religious liberty; it does not mean we are sidelining Catholicism. Look at what we have opened up for Jews and Protestants alike."

"Yes, but that doesn't mean the assembly should have gone off and sold Church property; it doesn't belong to them, it belongs to the Vatican," Adrienne argued.

"Those sales funded your army, Monsieur?" Pauline asked, spinning her mug slowly in circles between her palms. "Or, *ah,* your National Guard, I mean."

Gilbert poured more cream into his drink, his lips pinched. "Not as much as I would have liked," he replied. Then sparing a glance at Adrienne, added, "there should have been other ways to fund the guard without insulting the devout. Some legislature with His Holiness, or the like. Politicians are a touchy people. I have been treading water."

"Thankfully we are done with all that," said Adrienne. She had hardly touched her drink.

"Yes, thankfully."

Pauline sat back, her attention drifting between the two. Adrienne recognized when her little sister was being particularly analytical, and if she wasn't still overjoyed at seeing her, she'd be annoyed at the insinuation that Pauline suspected any sort of disagreement between Adrienne and Gilbert. Gilbert said he was done with politics, and so Adrienne was inclined to believe him. That was that.

"Will you write me when I am an emigrant?" she quietly pleaded, shifting the subject so far off that Adrienne was thankful that she was not partaking in her drink else she would have choked.

"Pauline," she said, "of course we will, why would you think otherwise?"

Chapter Twenty-Six

A shrug. Their family wordsmith merely shrugged.

Even Gilbert seemed bewildered. "This is not the little girl I picked worms with in the garden," he decreed, moving forward to take her hand, and brought her knuckles to his lips. "A Lafayette promise, you'll hear so much from us you will wish us dead."

"I doubt that is as possible as you say," Pauline laughed. "I know you're a great correspondent, Gilbert. I pray neither of your letters miscarry; that is what I fear. Finding reliable couriers is difficult in a time like this, especially over unfriendly borders."

"Our family is everywhere, we will find a way. Aunt Tessé, even. She'd be happy to mediate and no one ever stops that woman," Adrienne said, and it was true – people went out of their way to please Madame de Tessé, even Monsieur Jefferson was an avid lover of the lady.

"Of course, of course. I'm going to miss you all until France is safe enough to return. Maybe by then you'll have a nephew or niece to meet. I'll apologize in advance if they are anything like me, but I am sure you of all people could handle that." She rested her elbow on the table. "Tell me about Louise now, the poor woman."

☆

Chavaniac came into view as they rode up the mountainside, her weathervanes pointing west and her flag billowing. It was the anniversary of Gilbert's victory at Yorktown and the moment of triumph did not blow by either of them as they watched the village folk wave happily at seeing the familiar family pass the square. Georges took it upon himself to prepare his future reputation, waving back from his seat with all the ferocity a bold preteen could muster. Anastasie's attempts to pull him back into the carriage went unabated and she ducked out of the public eye, her cheeks red. As for Virginie, accustomed to arriving at the château in the laps of her parents, she lay sprawled across them, snoring quietly into Gilbert's knee while Adrienne held onto her legs. Miraculous every time, regardless of the rocking and bumping over stones, she never stirred.

They could hear the ducks from the pool as they stepped out of the carriage in the courtyard. Poor Madame Chavaniac was on the way to losing her faculties, but she still greeted them with open arms, commenting on how tall everyone had grown, with a quiet remark to Adrienne that she was the sole exception. *Expected*, she replied, Gilbert's abnormal height genes were very powerful.

Everything was where she left it in her salon. The room had been dusted and cleaned by the tiny staff that the Madame was able to maintain since the income that accompanied titleage ceased. It was such a stark contrast to Paris. Adrienne stood in the center of the room, studying each wall that she had decorated with more flowers and vases since she last visited. It appeared that Madame Chavaniac had guessed as to what autumn blooms Adrienne would like, as the flowers were bursting with the oranges and reds that the château gardens supplied. She felt like she was in an orchard, all she needed was a basket to pick some apples. A few pumpkins were growing in the yard outside the windows – their seeds were part of a gift sent from America when the young nation heard of their favorite Frenchman's successes. Gilbert was staunch in advancing and growing the farms of Chavaniac; he was scribbling off letters to farmers he knew to visit well before they left the capital; and his architect, Monsieur Vaudoyer, was sent to liven up the hallways.

Virginie took up the duty of organizing Adrienne's desk, meticulously separating personal letters from the letters from the plantation and other estates she managed, putting her finances by a desk with an abacus next to it, trial testing all of her quills… She genuinely enjoyed the work. If she wasn't born into the lap of luxury that Adrienne and Gilbert supplied, then she would have made a very fine maid for any well-to-do household. For the first time in days, Adrienne was able to just sit back in her chair with a book, listening to her daughter scratch away on the fourth pen.

Outside sounded like Eden. Chirping and rustling of loose leaves had replaced carriage wheels and distasteful rabble, the morning sky was visible for miles as it stretched over mountains as far as the eye could see. To sleep without worrying who stalked outside their walls shattered a tower of anxiety that weighed on Adrienne. Her children were able to run reasonably amok through the grass and gardens here without hearing someone cursing their father's name.

A tickle to her hair and a kiss to her lips woke her from a slumber she didn't realize she fell into. Gilbert hovered over her from behind, eyes squinting with mirth before he gently kissed her forehead.

"Sorry to wake you, I couldn't resist walking out without stealing some," he said. He had changed into what Adrienne labeled as his country-work attire: a simple, checkered cravat tucked neatly into a deep red waistcoat that cut off at his trim waist, a straw cocked hat sat under his arm; if she could bend backward and sneak a peek at his stockings, they would likely be striped.

"You're welcome to steal anything from me – I am yours," Adrienne replied, stretching out her feet. There were two letters pinched between his fingers. "What is it you were going to give me? Work?"

"Ah, I wouldn't have you doing labor if I had any say in the matter. No, these are from your mother and father."

"What?" Adrienne sat up, the tight curls in her hair bouncing back. "Already? We've only just got here, they would have had to send them as soon as we left Paris."

"So it would seem," he said, sitting along the arm of the chair. "How about it, I open your father's and you get Maman's. We shall tackle their issue together." Gilbert handed her the single folded edge of an uncharacteristically short letter from Madame d'Ayen. Although there was no black seal, Adrienne broke it open, already fearing the worst.

"She and Louise are en route to Auvergne," she read. "Paris is not safe for nobles right now, thinks some time away would help calm some nerves. Oh, Gilbert, we have extra rooms made up, don't we?"

He was focused on his father-in-law's letter from the Royal Army's front, frown deepening. "They can have whatever room they like, naturally." Resting the letter on his leg he stared at the windows. "Louis is still in the city?"

"For now," Adrienne said, glancing back at the words. "He's had Louise send their children away. God, I could never."

"For their safety, you would."

"If Maman and Louise left not long after us, we don't have long to prepare. I'll talk with your aunt and we can sort out a menu for this week, *um...* goodness after all the trouble of saying goodbye earlier this month…" Getting up, she bustled to her desk where Virginie, too, had fallen asleep at the table. Swapping letter for child, she carried Virginie over to Gilbert, who took her in an arm with ease. "Take this duplicate girl of yours," she commanded, "drop her off in her room. I'll meet you in the kitchen in ten minutes to discuss the manor's inventory."

"As you say, Madame," Gilbert nodded, following her with his eyes until she relieved him with a quick kiss. "It shall be done."

☆

If they didn't stop to greet Pauline, they would have had more time to prepare for the arrival, as the Madame d'Ayen and Madame de Noailles arrived the following afternoon for their first visit to Chavaniac. Adrienne threw aside decorum, rushing down the steps into the courtyard to throw herself at Louise instead. Her blonde hair was growing fairer and fairer by the day; contrasting with the dark navy gown she wore, she floated like a ghost. Maman hardly aged a year despite the stress, still holding herself as high and proud as she always did.

"Welcome to Chavaniac," Adrienne said, holding out her hand for when Gilbert finally caught up to her.

"Oh, Adri, it is beautiful," Louise replied, rocking her in a tight hug. "I can see why you wandered off to the country so often. Gilbert, forgive me for mocking the south, I retract all my loving insults."

"I took no offense," he replied, bowing politely to d'Ayen before he kissed her cheek. "The grounds are open for your leisure, although I will be having some farmers come around to survey what areas are best for planting. As I am unlorded, the manor must become a farm, so please forgive any disruption."

"We will not mind, *cher*," Madame said, holding onto his arm. "Thank you for taking us in on such short notice, we promise we will not disturb your work and will depart as soon as Louis sends word."

"Please disturb me all you like, Maman. I am in absolute repose here and it is only amassing with the gathering of all the women I hold dear. Like a spoiled lover I am," he exclaimed, bringing her along to the home. "Let me introduce you to Madame Chavaniac, it's been so long since you two have been acquainted in letters. She's prepared some tea to receive you and we have a long list of Auvergne comfort foods to tickle your fancy. We expect an honest review of our cultural faire."

Adrienne nudged her head against Louise's. "Is Louis not leaving? I think it would be safer if *all* of you stayed here for the remainder of the year."

"He doesn't want to leave politics just yet," Louise said, "and thinks he can get some words of reason into the more radical of the assembly members due to his, *ah*, reputation." There was a long, exaggerated sigh before she shrugged and added, "You know how he thinks he's untouchable. I hope someone reminds him he's not before he gets himself hurt. Where is Ségur when you need him?"

"Not having a good time in Germany, I am told," Adrienne replied. "Well, regardless, if you write to your husband, tell him he is welcome here. It is as close to America as he can get."

"Unless he swims the Atlantic," Louise mumbled. She lifted her head to look up at the winding staircase inside the manor, an abrupt but pleasant smile formed as she ran her hand over the stone walls. "I can picture your face back when Gilbert first brought you here. You love this stuff."

"It is a place that is easy to love."

Bizarre yet lovely to have her mother and sister basking in her country home, Adrienne spent much of her time watching Gilbert wander around their fields as he and the English farmer he sent for pointed at grass or gestured to rocks. It had not reached chilly temperatures until the sun went down in the early days of November, and so Gilbert was working outside in the mornings as often as he could, always a diligent student.

Adrienne's salon had met her mother's approval – a great boost to her ego that had to be met with humility. She had not hosted many people since the fall of lordships, but every now and then, the priest from the local parish would take tea with them, or a small group of the village schoolmasters came and spoke with her and the children with their tutors present. She was responsible for reassuring the people that their faith and the motions of the revolution were *not* in opposition to each other, echoing Gilbert's sentiments on it even as a non-practicing man.

Louise went out to the village often, a wanton for shopping. Though little options were available, she returned with small knick-knacks, sometimes made by apprentices or women in their little downtime. Auvergne was no holiday in Italy, but it was quaint and she found some charm in the people's calm and pious attitude. Their mother doted on her grandchildren in the garden, combing through Virginie's hair while Anastasie recited poetry and sang a song for her in English and Italian, rousing a chorus of applause.

For once, using the large dining room, fit for the kings of the medieval days, was appropriate to accommodate a growing party of family and friends. The walls were grand, taken up by long windows and portraits that ate up the spaces where numerous old flags hung from the ceiling. Should the table have been round, it would have been a great beckon to tales of knights, but this was France, and so the table stretched down the room – a deep, rich wood, perfect for warming the coolness of its surroundings. They dined on the pumpkins they grew and the beef they raised, passing around wine to toast the people. Gilbert was immersed in laughter between Georges and his aunt, taken so much he could not find a breath in-between his wheezing. Adrienne had never felt so relieved in years.

Chavaniac, December 1791

Georges waited by the door of the salon with his slate-board in hand while Virginie approached her mother, who sat on her sofa, flipping the pages of her bible with a sharp snap.

"It has been requested," Virginie read from her own board, "that you understand he must follow the call to action since he is the most qualified for the position."

Adrienne bit her cheek. Damned wars, damned armies. The one thing she agreed with most of the assembly was the displeasure that Gilbert's appointment to the center army occurred so soon.

Virginie stood quietly for her response.

"Tell him: I understand, but it does not mean I will be pleased about it. He knows why."

The little girl wrote her words down, returning to Georges who erased what he had written on his and traded boards. His footsteps faded down the hall towards wherever Gilbert waited as he was barred from the salon.

With her mother and sister returning to Paris a few days into November when Louis declared that the assembly had ceased most legislative meetings and were focusing on war, and all of Paris went into their winter preparations, Adrienne was just *trying* to enjoy the days with her whole little family. When the letter giving Gilbert a command arrived, she fell back into the deep pit that was dug several years ago. It was too much war. He was supposed to be done.

Georges returned, and Virginie walked up with the new message.

"Papa says he wants to go for a ride with you before it gets too dark."

"It will be dark by the time we have the horses tacked up."

Gone and then back again. Virginie sighed, "Papa says he already has them ready. He sent Stasie out to get them fifteen minutes ago."

Adrienne closed the bible, drumming her nails against the cover. Georges, diplomat for Gilbert, leaned into the room, waving his handkerchief like a flag of truce.

"Maman, he's really sad, you should talk to him," he said. "Some of the things he says are so long, I can't fit them onto my board, but I promise he says things prettier than I can write them."

"Excuse you, I'm her liaison," Virginie replied. "He says Pa–"

Adrienne rubbed her face. "Fine. Tell your father I will meet him outside."

Georges presented a cloak handed to him from beyond the door. The pink of his cheeks grew rosy as Adrienne walked up and took it, not needing to angle herself to see Gilbert leaning a few feet away against the wall, fiddling with his fingers. She strode by to the stairs that circled down to the courtyard. He followed, swinging his coat around him as he went. Her stubbornness had set in. Upon reaching the horses that were waiting for their riders, she stepped on the mounting block and helped herself up before he could raise his hand to assist.

"Take the gloves, at least," Gilbert said, holding them aloft as his horse was brought around. Adrienne took them. The air nipped at her nose; it would be a cold winter.

Inching closer to Christmas, the grass fell frozen by evening, crunching like sand under their horses' hooves. Several acres of the property had transitioned from rolling hills of grass and wildflowers to plowed fields planted with root crops for the season under the care of their English overseer, Monsieur Desson. The town was hopeful that spring would bring a decent harvest for the cabbage and radishes.

Stars arrived early to the heavenly field, bright against the wake of the setting sun. It had not snowed yet in the week, but frost liked to settle along planted lanterns, sparkling like sapphires off of Gilbert's metal buttons.

"I cannot say why they picked me to lead," he said after they trekked a mile from the manor. "Knowing how I left Paris, I am surprised they said my name at all alongside Rochambeau and Luckner's."

If he was waiting for a reply, he did not get one. Adrienne stared plainly at her horse's ears. She heard Gilbert's long huff through his nose, and his pace caught up to remain at her side as he continued his attempted explanation.

"I've loved these quiet weeks with you. You saw how I denied every public office offered to me here. I was content in retirement. I would have refused this, believe me, *mon coeur*, I wouldn't have taken the command if our constitution was not in peril from d'Orléans. That man is a fool for threatening liberty. I will kick him back into the swamp I left him in."

"How long until the king's man arrives to take you away?" she asked, unwilling to look at him directly.

He slumped in his saddle. "I expect within the fortnight. After

Christmas, perhaps. We, *ah*, we should do something fun for Georges' birthday. Maybe see if carolers are singing a little early this year? I don't think I will be able to join the twelfth night activities."

Georges would like the attention of a country dance.

Adrienne nodded reluctantly.

"It is your arms I will long for until this war is done," he said. "And it is not so far – I will be along France's borders, never to step outside of where you can't reach me with ease. I know you have missed my letters; think of all the poetry I will write for you. You do not hate me for this, do you? Say you don't; say that you will love me still for my stubborn ideals and my stupidity for marching into the lion's den."

"Slay the lion and just come back to me. Don't make me come looking for you, else you know how cruel I can get towards your enemies." She puffed a stray hair out of her mouth. "No one wants to hear the crazed rabble of a general's wife."

His gloved hand wriggled over to take hers. "I could listen to you all day and pity the men who would have to face your pen. But it shouldn't come to that. I will be as safe as I often am: somehow, miraculously, and with sheer dumb luck."

"It isn't dumb luck. It is God; it's your star."

They came down the same sloped, waving path they always did, where the upward stream wind carried the chill with it, rustling under Adrienne's cloak and fighting to steal Gilbert's wool hat that remained fixed to his head. It was quiet here with no chirping bugs or bubble-making fish.

"Stay down south, Adrienne," Gilbert said, intense enough to be a command. Severity replaced the kindness in his features. Lines on his face were deepened by ink-blotting shadows. "I do not want to hear of you or the children coming to Paris nor anywhere near Metz, do you understand me? You wait until I return."

She wanted to retort, tell him that the family would stay together through thick and thin. But her voice remained obsolete. Gilbert's eyes reflected the lantern lights like stars upon water, wavering and desperate. She squeezed his hand and nodded once; she could certainly try to wait.

It would not be the first time, and she should have known it would not be the last.

Chapter Twenty-Seven

❧❦❧

Chavaniac, May 1792

…They await a mistake of my men on my part, but the National Guard of Paris acquitted itself perfectly in the châteauvieux affair which, in the end, became nothing more than a disgusting farce which only shows how desperate and corrupt the Jacobins have become. I return with my army back towards Austria with intention to speak to them of the partisan hazards that have befallen Paris. General Necker and I are displeased with the amount of dissent we are privy to in the factions; Rochambeau remains pessimistic and has sent his son to America. Louis, I hear, will be arriving in Boston or Philadelphia by the time this letter reaches you. How I envy him for America and loathe him for leaving our dear sister and his children behind. You do not loathe me, I hope. I am still here and count the days of returning to you and my beloved children. Perhaps a retirement in the United States will be ours sooner than later? As to my health, I am well, though my temperament flares something awful when the Jacobins spit venom into the hearts of the French people…

Adrienne could read on and on with Gilbert's letters and the pages that bore his unedited thoughts with lengthy paragraphs of worries and hopes. They fared better than the gazettes that arrived with etchings of the mechanism the Assembly had voted for as the means of judicial executions: the tall, narrow frame with a blade larger than any ax, named the guillotine. It had already tasted its first victim, some highwayman who very well deserved the decree. Reading about how the apparatus worked was nauseating, and Adrienne tossed it aside to focus on the quiet talking between Georges and his tutor, Monsieur Frestel, as they reviewed yesterday's history lesson.

Frestel – a young and unimposing man – fit in perfectly within the Lafayette household. Carrying with him a gentle demeanor and lax attitude, he would politely correct Georges' mistakes and offer different ways of remembering facts or solving problems in mathematics. He was one of the only men Adrienne would allow to be alone with her daughters as well if she were to be busy with business.

The switching of the fields went over well, and most crops were healthy and the soil, according to Monsieur Desson, was ready for summer planting. A few cows bore their calves, the small distant mooing was a cheerful noise to hear with their neighbors' chickens and goats. It was a false sense of normalcy, living the country life while wolves encircled them by the thousands. Her little garden was coming along, planting things the same way her mother taught her, although it would never be as beautiful. Adrienne came back into the house five out of the seven days of the week covered in soil and dampened from the watering can, but at least the little flowers were budding and bright. On her days inside, she still went about her normal dressing routine, her brown hair was becoming sun-bleached where her cap didn't cover. It was odd seeing the straw-colored strands and she aimlessly mentioned it in her letters back to Gilbert. He called them golden threads, but he didn't see them – they were most definitely straw.

Their fortune was growing thinner by the day. Adrienne sold off some land in France with the hopes of acquiring some funds for the year, but it was a short-term remedy that only would create a long-term problem.

Keeping in touch with their correspondents in Cayenne was a priority; Adrienne read through mountains of books to assure that she was handling affairs in the most just and humane way, cross-examining reports of the overseers and looking over the people of the plantation's education progress. Six dozen people to care for of all ages. What were the French Guineas really like? One could only live it through words unless they traveled there themselves, or if a kind and true artist sketched a landscape of the people's home. Maybe if they did retire to America… it would be right to visit.

Daydreaming caught her in its net several times a day.

She would attend mass regularly at the local church, shaking hands with her fellow villagers and accompanying many of the women to their homes to take tea. Filling her days and weeks and months with familiarity and family. She sent several letters to Louise – who no doubt suffered far worse than herself. *Louis* had grown nervous in Paris after being hounded by several men on his way back from the Assembly chambers, bringing with him a black eye and a sense of urgency to leave for the United States as soon as possible once winter had ended. It was supposed to be temporary, any emigration was, until the radicalism in France cooled. But the United States had a certain effect on any veteran who fought there, and in Louise's few returning letters, she expressed she did not foresee Louis coming back. The best Adrienne could do was insist then that Louise must take the children when they were old enough and simply meet him in America. It was a fleeting imaginary idea, having her sister and her family join Adrienne and hers one day in the land of liberty where their husbands fought. Gilbert longed for the countryland of Virginia nearest his adoptive father; but Louis, she thought, would enjoy the bustle of Philadelphia or New York City best. She couldn't say for certain – she had never been.

Monsieur Frestel gently cleared his throat, bringing Adrienne back to the present. She blinked away her dry eyes and sat up straight. The tutor folded his hands in front of him and covered his intrusion with a bow of his head.

"Georges wished to present to you the lineage of his paternal line. He recently studied it back to its founding," Frestel said. His eyes glimmered as he looked to the boy, who rocked back on his heels, waiting for Adrienne's approval.

"Oh, wonderful," Adrienne replied. Gilbert had already told her a hundred times about his family. "Please, Georges, do tell me everything."

She could listen to it a thousand more times if it meant she saw how proud Georges was of himself, listing each and every past Marquis and Marquise of a line that this present revolution was apt to erase. He glanced at Frestel when he brought up wars that lined up with the la Fayette urge to join every battle, all the way to Michel – his late grandfather who was killed a lifetime ago – and then to Gilbert, the hero of two worlds, defender of liberty, who married Marie Adrienne Françoise de Noailles, the second daughter of a very renowned, noble Parisian family.

"And then you had me!" Georges finished. "Anastasie said I was a celebratory baby when Papa surprised you in the middle of the war. Which I think is rather nice. We haven't fully learned about baby stuff yet," he said, glancing at Frestel.

Frestel rubbed his thumb to his chin, the apples of his cheeks blushing a light pink. "Perhaps, Monsieur, in a few years time. You are still quite young."

"I don't know. I turn twelve this Christmas and the older boys in the village said that's when they started learning about girls."

Adrienne couldn't imagine how she managed so long with a son without having her mother give her advice. Madame Chavaniac was her closest ally in dealing with young boys. Gilbert was brought up quickly at a young age, but he and Adrienne already agreed that they would let their children be children for as long as possible.

"But you are a gentleman, Georges," Adrienne said lightly, "so you will learn about young ladies when it is appropriate to do so. Listen to Monsieur Frestel, not the boys in the village. Back to that wonderful presentation, that was absolutely divine! Great job from both of you; you must tell your Papa when he returns, it will make him so happy to hear."

"You think so?"

"I know so."

"Did Papa say when he was coming back?"

Adrienne didn't need to glance at the letter to know it was far too soon to tell. "No," she replied, "but you know how he surprises your mother so often. We may see him soon, but for now we will keep on learning and growing and caring for Chavaniac in his absence."

Frestel collected their papers that hogged up the large part of the table. Georges came to Adrienne's side. He was growing slower than his sisters were, with Virginie already trailblazing an inch or two behind him. Adrienne was sure all her babies would overcome her in height, it was just about timing. Georges was still a ways away from hitting puberty and Adrienne was fine with that. Pinchable rosy cheeks and light, bubbling laughter were medicine for the soul. Despite Frestel still in the room and with lots of etiquette education, Georges still insisted on getting as close to Adrienne's lap as possible. She admitted she spoiled her son with *slightly* over the right amount of affection, happily hugging him and combing her fingers through the tops of his straight, queued back hair.

"I hope he comes back soon," Georges whispered into her shoulder, tightening his arms around her waist.

"Me too," she said, scratching his scalp.

The skies outside were still bright, with only a few wispy clouds on the horizon, like paint strokes on a rough canvas. Somewhere out there, Gilbert was fighting with swords in his sight and pikes in his back. What stupidity possessed these men to think Gilbert would *ever* betray the interests of a constitutional France? On her desk sat a letter from her father expressing that he did her a favor in *burning* the letter she sent him to give to some assembly members after Louis left.

"Would you care to join me for a walk? We can take your sisters after their lessons are over."

"Can I practice my geography with you? Monsieur Frestel is supposed to test me at the end of the week."

Adrienne glanced over to the young tutor. Frestel pulled his bag over his shoulder and swallowed a small laugh. "I find verbal practice to be helpful in remembering names. If Madame is in the mood," he said with a nod, "T'would be great studying."

"You know I love to hear how smart you are," Adrienne told Georges. The way his eyes creased with his smile was just like his father's.

On their promenades through the manor's sloped hills, she let the three young Lafayettes have all the shares of conversation. To see Anastasie at the age Adrienne was when she was married – incredulous – how could she ever have been ready enough to marry and be a wife? Her mother was right in wanting to keep Gilbert away from her after their vows for as long as possible. The memories of Gilbert crawling through open windows, or shoved underneath her bed while her mother bid her goodnight, hearing him giggle when she left; the powder in his hair had left a stain on the rug beneath her mattress from the amount of times he laid under there. They were naughty teenagers and Gilbert bore the scrapes from falling off her windowsill to prove it. And Adrienne, *well*, Adrienne covered the little pink bruises on her thighs for days afterwards.

The breeze was warm and ruffled the loose curls off her shoulders. There was no need to be like Romeo and Juliet anymore, they were Ferdinand and Miranda. Perhaps there was something comforting about having fictional characters to compare oneself to – and of *The Tempest*, Adrienne enjoyed hearing Gilbert read it to the family, the odd English phrases on his lips. Once, Virginie compared her Auntie Louise and Uncle Louis to Beatrice and Benedict, a comedy that Gilbert should not have read to them so young, but he did, and so he paid the price of having that comparison haunt him during a visit to the bickering Noailles couple.

Time was smoother with Gilbert around. Adrienne could waste the days away in a routine of work and mothering, cycling through the seasons like clockwork, like a songbird in its cage, but he was always the key to turn the gears, to unlock the bars.

☆

May turned into June, and June grew gray.

Cold air seeped through the windows of the salon that moistened the drapes and curled mold along the edges that the few domestics left scraped at daily. The village settled into a bizarre silence where not even the cattle stirred the fog.

June turned into July, and July charred the grass.

Promenades were impossible without keeping to the shade as the ground melted travelers' shoes. They kept to the house with games and chores. Adrienne continued to sell land to pay for the family's expenses.

July turned into August, and August came with worse news from Paris.

King Louis and Marie-Antoinette were taken from their city palace and placed in prison after a thousand bodies littered the steps of their previous abode. The gazettes removed all implications of their titles, referring to the king as Louis Capet, like he were a common man.

Gilbert was relieved of his command. The title of a gazette raised his name as an enemy of the state, *a traitor to liberty.*

Adrienne's mouth was dry. She marched with her daughters' governess and Monsieur Frestel to the girls' room and then her son's. She ordered luggage to be packed, a command that left her without a second thought on what the implications would be to her own happiness. Her daughters protested.

"Langeac is not far, Anastasie, but you cannot stay," Adrienne said, helping the servants carry their things to a wagon. "Take care of your sister and I will write to you when it is safe to come back, do you hear me?"

"Maman, please, you can't just do this without telling us what is happening," Anastasie pleaded. "Is it Papa? I saw the gazette on your desk – is he gone? Why aren't you coming with us?"

"Get in the wagon!" Adrienne exclaimed, pointing towards the borrowed thing. She couldn't afford to waste any time.

"Maman, what about me?" Georges said, grasping her skirts while Frestel quickly spoke to the carriage driver. "Why can't I go with my sisters?"

Because you are his son, she thought, and the Commune would love nothing more than to wipe France clean of any carrier of the Lafayette name.

She kissed his forehead. "You will continue studying with Monsieur Frestel, alright? He will take you to Conangles and you will improve your Latin and English there. Be as courteous and kind as I know you always are. It won't be for long, I swear." To lie uncertainty to family was like speaking fire to young flowers. There was no way of knowing what would happen next.

What she needed to do once the children were far from reach was to ride to Brioude, where the tribunal of Auvergne was held. Chavaniac must be protected. If Gilbert was considered a fugitive by escaping the country, then greedy thieves may take advantage of the law to invade and loot the manor and its grounds and Adrienne would *not* have that.

Waiting in the courtyard to say goodbye burned her insides, but she remained until they took off, three sets of frightened eyes staring back at her until they disappeared down the hill and out of sight.

She wrapped her petticoat around her hand and pulled it up, posting herself like a guard upon the castle. It took her two whole days sorting through Gilbert's office, organizing his letters and dealings. Into a locked chest and under some cabinets they went for safe keeping. A day trip into the tribunal's small town earned her a seal for safeguarding her home. Madame Chavaniac would not have to deal with ruffians storming the château she spent her life caring for.

With the arrival of letters came the arrival of officials – quills and arm desks in hand to take inventory of all that the emigrant Lafayette left behind. Madame Chavaniac followed them like a nervous dog, crying for certain items that were hers, not her dear nephews, that they couldn't take *all* the things in the manor. The men went through every hall, noting the art of the American Revolution and of George Washington, of the statues and the sculptures from the Bastille, of little things Gilbert had touched or breathed upon – all became under the ownership of the state. Some still remained in the manor, they could not carry every item away. But Adrienne watched them take her jewels, her pink topaz necklace that once graced her neck at the tender age of fourteen, her crystal, her silverware. In her hand, she gripped the last letter Gilbert wrote before he absconded: dirty along the edges and hastily folded, the seal had missed half of the wax to keep it together.

She walked silently down the ground corridor, where the ceilings were stained gold and the murals took up the stone walls, and leaned into a great divot where even God could not see her. His handwriting grew smaller and slanted when he wrote through anxiety, Adrienne remembered as she settled her attention on his words on where he was going and what had transpired to come to this point.

I am making no apology at all, either to my children or to you, for having ruined my family, he wrote, and Adrienne's heart started to chip at its hardened varnish. *Not a single one of you would have wanted to benefit from my having acted against my conscience.*

He knew his stubborn and loquacious family well, although it appeared in his following words that the confidence he had in them had diminished, as she read through his expectations of where she and the children could escape to out of France. He intended to escape to England, and then from there, implored her to meet him in the United States.

We will find the liberty that no longer lives in France, and my tenderness will seek to compensate you for the joys that you have lost because of me. Forgive your wayward husband as he laments to leave what he cherishes most behind in the hope that he will reunite with them in the sanctity of freedom soon.

"Damn it, Gilbert," Adrienne cursed through gritted teeth, crushing the letter against her forehead. She loved him with all of her being, but he was, at times, a buffoon. At some point, she ended up on the floor, her skirts falling between her legs like a broken doll. The inventory officials had come and gone, and she admired their discretion in leaving without stirring the ladies for a proper farewell. She didn't want to talk to them or thank them for at least leaving enough furniture behind to sit on. To be a phantom haunting the halls as they departed was fine, she granted them that.

Brioude, September 1792

The odds Monsieur Aulagnier was to order her incarceration grew likely, and frankly, happened far later than Adrienne expected after Gilbert's own call for arrest. Aulagnier was the commissioner of Le Puy, a straggly man whose limbs could have been supported with bent wire. When the order came, she went back to Brioude without a struggle, keeping her hands folded neatly in her lap as the carriage bustled and cracked over stones. It was only a few hours' ride, but Adrienne, alone in her thoughts, stretched the journey several more. She knew she would have a trial of some sorts, whatever it was that was granted to women of her standing. Humble as she was, she was a daughter of the Noailles family and a wife of Lafayette and she would be treated with the respect that was honored her.

Brioude was made up of mosaic basilicas and galleries, a medieval town amidst Auvergne's mountains. Its people were modest and pious in their cut-off life, the news from Paris flying like jumping fish down the river traded for wine and wood. Aulagnier's men escorted her up several stairs and down hallways laden with paintings of Christ's stations of the cross. Adrienne kept her eyes forward, her shoulders pinned far back as they made the route towards the tribunal's room. There was a stuffiness to the air that made her nostrils flare as several faces turned towards her when she entered. She had already spoken to four of the six men once before less than a month ago when they promised the house safety. They looked at her with varied contemplation, their jaws affixed, their perukes bringing out the redness of their cheeks. She never asked about her own safety; she had not considered it.

"State your name for the record," one judge said, gesturing towards a young man who had his quill and two pots of ink at the ready.

"Marie Adrienne Françoise de Noailles de la Fayette, the wife of General Lafayette," she stated, keeping her hands in front of her. A glance towards the secretary and he hesitantly wrote down the controversial name.

"Madame Noailles –"

"*Lafayette*, if you'd please."

The judge stared at her as if she held her own execution sword, his fingers numbly pinching the papers he held between them. "Madame Lafayette," he said, and the click of his teeth sounded hollow. "Your husband, upon hearing word of his impending arrest from Paris, left his station and fled from France, therefore making himself a fugitive of the law. All of his property was declared to the possession of the state, and any notion of aid in helping him to escape and/or continue to abet him will be declared as treason under penalty of death."

Adrienne listened carefully for where Gilbert may be, if he had been taken by the enemy, be it Prussia or Austria, if he were in the Netherlands or elsewhere… The judge talked for some time, reading through the long list of potential actions that would land her at the guillotine if she dared to try to help Gilbert. A thought slipped into her mind like wind hitting a sail.

"We have property in the colonies. A modest plantation for allowing its inhabitants to live a free life," she said, the sweat building up in her palms. "If you say all of his property, what will become of the people? There are families who deserve their freedom. You cannot rob them of that right as France's people, it would be abhorrent to the rights of man."

The first judge licked his lips, not expecting the specific property to be brought up so urgently. Adrienne knew that their holdings in France were not worth the fight for, as painful as it was to lose the income, but Cayenne was not income – it was far more important.

"Well, Madame," he replied, "that is something that is beyond our control at the moment. We may look into it for you, but as for the proceedings we are gathered here for, that is out of reach."

Another judge stared at her as if she were a child, leaning across the high desk to look down his nose. "The council is… *concerned* about your liability. I understand that not having your husband around is a frightening ordeal for a woman, and that you would want to seek safety, perhaps reprieve, within the members of your family – some of which we have noted here have *also* left France. We cannot say for certain that it was connected to Monsieur Lafayette's treason as they had emigrated several months before his actions, but it would be foolish of us not to take into account that he or even you, Madame, would use foreign assistance to avoid justice."

"Until Monsieur Lafayette is extradited or returns here freely, it is of the law to keep you under watch," said the first. He set his papers neatly in front of him. "Maybe then the topic of his plantation may be reasoned with."

"Your Excellencies," Adrienne said, opening her arms. "There is no need to incarcerate me within Brioude for I am not a risk for leaving Chavaniac. My aging aunt is losing her faculties and it would be negligent of me to leave her without family to comfort her; and she is too frail to leave Chavaniac – it is her grounding, her home, and she would be dead before she left it. I am not an unholy woman, your Excellencies, it is my *duty* to tend to my family."

"Should she pass away in the upcoming months, it would be unfortunate if you used the time to escape into the mountains."

"I would not."

"Understand it is difficult to take empty promises without some sort of proof. A wealthy woman alone with a dozen directions to abscond to – that is not what Commissioner Aulagnier expects us to allow, now is it?"

"No, Monsieur," Adrienne replied, ready. "I would be alone, yes, but I have no money to go anywhere. The revolution of the United States as well as here in France has taken much of our holdings. You can take a look at the overview I have constructed here," the documents worked out between her and the family lawyer listed all their expenditures and the shockingly dwindled numbers left, "and see that there is little left to pay for passage anywhere."

It took a few minutes for the tribunal to study the pages. Adrienne pulled her redingote bodice straight. She could have mentioned staying because her children were around in the south and there wasn't a thing on Earth that would make her leave without them, but the tribunal did not need to know that. As a wife, she was loaned into her husband's name, but their children bore it forever.

"Have you thought about filing for a civil divorce, Madame?" a third judge interjected. "Distancing yourself from a traitor may ease some stress from your life and you would be welcome to go with dignity as a regular citizen of France."

Her chest tightened. "No, your Excellency, I have not," she said. "I am devoted to my husband and our bond is sanctioned under *God*, not under common law. Monsieur Lafayette is not a traitor; he holds the ideals of the constitution above all else in his heart, otherwise he would not put so much of his life into serving it."

A thought.

"However," she added, "if I may propose a *compromise*, Messieurs, that could assuage yourselves as well as Commissioner Aulagnier? I am willing to disclose that through the attachment my husband and I have for each other that I am a valuable incentive for him to return to France. By imprisoning me in a cell, you will lose all hope that he will come back. But if I were to parole in the confines of my own little village, to care for my aunt and keep to my house, he will see there is some safety in returning home. I will sign under threat of perjury that I will not leave Chavaniac."

Or threat of that damned guillotine.

She did not desire to spend any nights in a prison cell alone where no letters could travel in or out of iron bars. If the judges had any reverence towards a pious, abandoned woman who only wished to care for an aging relative in her old, empty cage, they would agree to her proposition.

Adrienne waited for several minutes in the hallway after the judges pulled their lips into straight, cracking lines, wanting to deliberate to settle what best suited them. As a lady, she was always quite compliant when it suited her, and she didn't mind people-watching in the meantime; people who she didn't see as often whenever she visited Auvergne with her attention so focused on her humble adoptive village. There was a rolling cart that wobbled by with a wheel whose croaks echoed down the open-aired hallway. The smell that wafted off of the goods it carried reeked, wrapped like large sacks of wheat. She should have brought a handkerchief. Not that she wanted to visually dab at the anxiety brewing behind her eyes, but to cover her nose before the smell stirred the nausea up her throat.

The single soldier next to her hardly twitched from it, keeping his eyes ahead and his hand firm on his scabbard.

She continued to meet the secretary's eye when she was called back into the chamber. His face was so easy to read and its relaxed demeanor sent a wave of calm over her as she looked back up towards the six older men.

"After much debate," the second one said, already receiving nods from a few of the others, "we have decided to grant you house arrest in the village of Chavaniac. Any holdings you have there currently may remain for the time being."

The sixth, whom she had not met before, balled his fist tightly on the table. "However there will be strict rules and sanctions you must abide by and we reserve the right to curtail any external correspondence should their content be deemed impartial to the state. We will have the formal documentation written for your signature before you depart today."

"And Cayenne?"

"It is yet to be determined."

Adrienne shifted her knees to the side and bent them slightly, bowing her head. "Thank you, your Excellencies, I consent to the ruling."

There. She had her home to return to. Her heart finally leveled off to a normal rhythm. Yet she was still a pain to some of the men, taking her time to read through the contract of her genteel imprisonment and what they expected of her – check-ins at nondescript times, where the limits of the village were, who she was allowed to contact… Happily several names were not on the list. Dipping the pen into ink, she signed *N. de Lafayette*.

She should have been angry when she arrived home to find her daughters had already returned and that Georges was on his way back without her giving warning. How fast word must have traveled when she was at the mercy of the tribunal that even her son, who was two days away, received the news. She should have been angry, but the relief that came with embracing them overshadowed all of it. Nothing, yet *everything* had changed. She needed to get the family out of harm's way when all of France posed a threat, and to do that, she needed money.

Adrienne was already scribbling a line to Monsieur Morris.

And someone with more power than she had needed to do something for Gilbert. He was an honorary citizen of several states; diplomatically, he could be claimed as an American, it was possible. Her words flowed quickly from the quill nib as she addressed the next letter to her adoptive father-in-law, to President Washington. If he could not do anything, then no man could.

Chavaniac, January 1793

The king was dead.

Or rather, *Citoyen* Louis Capet was no more. His head was displayed high for all of Paris to see. A momentous death, joined in with the hundreds of nobles who were killed in the years past. His wife, Citoyenne Antoinette Capet, was separated from her children in her prison cell awaiting her own trial with no way of communicating to the outside world.

Adrienne silently rested her forehead at the edge of her desk.

Gilbert was now in Prussia's hands, brought east away from the French revolutionaries' fighting. Perhaps it was for the best that he was far off. She would rather picture him pacing a cell than finding his headless body at the bottom of a ditch. And it was better that her children were confined to a country castle than mildewed stone and rusted iron.

The breath she took in burned her nose as she fought to keep a frustrated sigh from escaping while Anastasie and Virginie read several feet away on the sofas. Despite the queen's grown hatred towards Gilbert, despite the horrible etchings of a faux affair, Adrienne wouldn't wish any of the torture upon her, especially to be separated from her own children. The little dauphin was hardly eight years old; he should not be without his mother now that he inherited a throne that the Assembly had poured his father's blood over. The poor daughter, just a year younger than Anastasie – who dined with her in their youth – was no doubt going to witness the tearing apart of her family.

There were no helpful words back from America. The country had done nothing to aid its dearest lover. What a betrayal it was to reach a hand out to the people who now basked in the republic so many young

Frenchmen had helped free, only for the hand to grasp incessantly at air, cold and alone. There was nothing Adrienne could do. The loan from Monsieur Morris helped as far as money could go, but it was not diplomatic intervention, it was not a country's aggression. It seemed America was too frightened of France to risk their arrogant neutrality.

Anastasie watched her when she raised her eyes, her brows pulled ever so delicately together, too young to draw lines against her face, but old enough that her wisdom was evident. She knew exactly what Adrienne was thinking.

"Come read with us, Maman?" she asked, setting her book aside. "It's from Papa's collection. We may recount it for him when we see him again."

Adrienne couldn't help the breathy laugh or the way her lungs compressed against her ribcage. Settling between her daughters, she listened to Virginie pick up from where she left off in Gilbert's books about ancient Rome. Beautiful speakers, and she did listen for some time, but her thoughts drifted back to the horrors in Paris, to where she would hide her children should the tides change. It was only a matter of time.

Her eyes wandered to the piles of correspondence on her desk while her mind went towards the hidden piles in Gilbert's office. There were indictments in the Parisian tribunals on almost anything; any small thing – plans to travel, nasty words in private letters, a written opinion from several years ago denouncing republicanism – that could find an aristocrat guilty of treason would bring about an execution sentence. And Gilbert... Gilbert was France's most willful correspondent.

A late night in the midst of a cold summer, Adrienne collected all the papers she could find in the past several years, stacking them in her salon, and burned them.

The flames in her fireplace angrily roared at the fuel. It lit the room in a sharp, white light. Shadows stretched their arms across the floor and climbed the opposing wall. Slanted, poetic inked words melted into ash. The smoke billowed from the chimney, invisibly black unless one were to gaze up to the stars that disappeared behind it. Adrienne watched every letter crumble until the fire doused itself and the wood floor was stained with soot.

No one would find anything to indict Gilbert. He would be an innocent man just as she knew he was. She would be sure of it.

Chapter Twenty-Eight

❧

Le Puy, September 1793

Adrienne had done everything right.

She felt it coming since the establishment of the *Committee of Public Safety* – a whole rerouted government run by Robespierre, Saint-Just, and all of their Jacobin allies. Like the earth shaking under the racing hooves of a dozen horses, the veil of their safety cracked and shattered.

Monsieur Frestel took Georges away once more, further, where even she did not know exactly where they would hide in the mountains of France. She sent Virginie with Anastasie and their governess out of Chavaniac wherein the villagers averted their gaze to not be complicit with knowledge of where their former lord's offspring were escaping to.

It was a mild day.

A maid left the windows of her salon open to allow the breeze to flow through the corridors, and Adrienne sat at her desk, always at her desk, tapping a dry quill against a freshly laid sheet of paper. The deep blues of her inkpot matched the indigo of her jacket, the white glaze to her shell-buttons that ran up her cuffs. It was the one thing she could focus on, flitting the feather over the small and delicate piece on the table, so often overlooked.

From outside, the rumble of horses burst through the château's gates.

She heard the startled screaming of the servants a floor below.

Gently placing the cork into the inkpot, she thought of how the ink would go bad by the time she would be able to return to it. When would be the next time she would be able to sit in her salon, her domain, surrounded by the family's art? When would the piano be played again with the sweet accompaniment of her daughters? Her fingers ran over the wood and paper, listening to the heavy stomping of boots as doors down the hall slammed against walls. The next time she returned home, it must be with Gilbert. It had been long enough, but she was quite done with waiting.

When soldiers barged into her salon, they had crossed outside of France's domain and into hers, and she remained by her desk for a moment longer, moving the inkpot exactly where it should be for her to get back to it.

Her gaze flicked upward towards the man who stamped mud onto her polished floors. He had a child's face, contorted with the discolored shades of hatred and callousness. Adrienne stood up slowly before he had the chance to open his mouth. She rose silently, elegantly, with every ounce of poise that had been drilled into her since she learned to walk.

A second time, strange men poured into her belongings, ripping apart organized shelves and bookcases. Papers flurried through the open door from the hallway as Gilbert's office was dug into with far more aggression than before. They had guns strapped to their chests, swords gripped in their hands.

Adrienne moved her attention to one soldier who bore the epaulettes, at an age closer to her father. Tilting her chin up, she asked, "what are your orders, Monsieur? So that I may expedite your mission and spare the house of chaos."

"I am to bring you to the Directory in Puy to face trial," he stated, his hand out to receive rope from another.

Adrienne folded her hands in front of her. "I will follow," she replied. Whatever got them out of the manor.

"Maman!"

The voice brought back the wringing of her gut. Anastasie pushed by two soldiers who stumbled out of the bold girl's way, her arms outstretched. She leaned down and kissed Adrienne's cheek, the mere seconds they had to exchange a conversation through one look alone.

"I am of age to be arrested with my mother," Anastasie exclaimed, turning toward the commander. She sounded so much like her father through the commanding ire in her voice. Adrienne breathed in deeply.

"You are right, sweetling," she said, squeezing her hand. "Your father would be so proud of you." As the soldiers assented to the arrest, Adrienne pulled Anastasie in close, an embrace to the outside eye, and whispered in her ear. "Where is your sister?"

"In my fireplace," Anastasie quickly answered, watching the men kick around the documents, knowing they would find nothing of interest among them. "We couldn't leave you alone in this, Maman."

They were escorted outside, joined by a persistent Madame Chavaniac, who although was aging rapidly, was determined not to allow all these men anywhere near her young grand-niece, and balked whenever any soldier moved to push Anastasie along into a wagon.

Adrienne had done everything right, but she was not expecting her daughters to have turned around on their escape to come back to her. She was angry. She was swelling with pride. Either way, her hand gripped her eldest with such vigor, Anastasie rubbed gently at her knuckles for the entire day's travel to Le Puy.

☆

The Directory was a sham, at least, to everyone's eyes but their own. The corrupt vice and lackluster organization left much to be desired as they followed the vague ideals about justice and liberty of the Jacobin Committee.

Truthfully, all the new names of government factions were growing quite old, quite fast.

"Don't you say a word to them," Madame Chavaniac said, shaking her head. They walked between armed guards into the building, arms looped around each other like a woven wall. "They want you to fumble, to convict yourself. Whatever nonsense they have cooked up to label all aristocrats as traitors. Some of us have never even stepped foot in Versailles..."

"Silence is guilt, Madame," Adrienne replied, pinching her skirt as they rose up high steps. If the Directory were to try her as the Athenians did, they needed evidence. The letter she was writing before they arrived was meant for Gilbert – it was a love letter, an innocent wife missing her beloved. Which was true. What devoted woman wouldn't plead with flowery words, the love she had for a captured man? If they were to find her guilty of anything, it was perhaps that she loved him a little too much.

Anastasie held herself like an experienced young woman. Through her was Gilbert's fury, aimed carefully in every hard click of her heels. The halls they were led through were bare and plain, no iota of God in a house of judgment, no show of wealth nor culture in decoration. For men to be equal it seemed men ought to have nothing at all.

Faces that looked familiar, like passing ghosts in the halls of Versailles, met hers where the soldiers told the three women to wait. A round up, like herded cattle. Beyond a wall, the heavy hits of a gavel broke through a constant hum of chatter. Every half-hour, the doors opened and a man or woman was brought out of the room, their eyes blank and soulless. Adrienne peeked at the rows of men that made up the Directory – mostly young, men her age or younger still. The sun shifted to the center of the sky above, casting no shadows, but bringing no bright light into the building; just a dull, limp hue to the already dusty room.

Adrienne thought she would be brought in alone to plead her case, but Madame Chavaniac and Anastasie followed behind. A powerful but stoic entourage.

Unlike the tribunal in Brioude, Le Puy was bustling. A dozen men already looked worn and ready to retire for the day by the time Adrienne was pulled before them on a small stage at the bottom of an amphitheater-like structure. It was difficult to discern who she was supposed to talk to as all sat silently looking over their papers, so she decided to simply talk to them all.

"Messieurs –"

"*Citoyenne* Lafayette," one with a punchable face interrupted, and her mouth snapped closed. Reviewing what brought her here was redundant. Everything related back to Gilbert. It was growing ridiculous: the animosity pouring off the man's tongue. A man who looked like he had served time in the military, mayhaps in the American campaign alongside him, speaking hypocrisy. Adrienne's own tongue was swelling in her mouth, her teeth acting as a dam.

"Messieurs," she said again when the lecture and the supposed crime list had ended. She maintained a soft tone, as soft as her willpower and patience allowed her, and like a repeating parrot, echoed back her sentiments of her husband. "Citoyen Lafayette has always been a name synonymous with the republic. Since he was a young boy, in the first months of our marriage, liberty was all he spoke of and it is no secret of his attachment to serving it in America that he disobeyed the monarchy in order to do so."

A quiet round of nods encircled her by those old enough to remember the news that spread rapidly through France at the Marquis' rogue nature to get to the United States.

"He always kept equality at the forefront of his heart and mind. That is why he came back to France – to bring what we hold dear now to fruition, to construct a constitution that raises the rights of the common man to where God intended man to be," she continued, her mind spinning to weave whatever words she could. "Citoyen Lafayette continued to fight for France even when her people were shifting away from his opinions; he cannot help but do it, for he loves his country so. You understand as his wife, I would have loved for him to remain in retirement in the comforts of home. But, Messieurs, I know his opinions have always been sound, and I trust in his choices completely."

"Even his choice to avoid trial, Madame?" one man asked, his hand tilted at the wrist to flop about as he spoke. "If he were an honorable Frenchman, if he had nothing to fear for his conduct, would he not show himself as he has done unannounced many times before?"

Adrienne's fingers itched to fiddle or to backhand the man. "Would you go back, Monsieur? If you were told it was a death sentence no matter what you said?"

"He betrayed the state when he decided to abandon the army and run into foreign land!"

"He was *relieved* of his *duty*, Monsieur," Adrienne said, shifting her eyes towards the outburst, "and was under threat of death. He is a man who is preserving his life for his family and for his country. I know if he were not in a German prison, because they thought his republican values were too dangerous, mind you, that he would be doing *everything* he could for the cause of liberty. When he becomes a traitor from *those ideals* for which he has held all his life that France now holds, I consent to be beheaded."

"Maman," Anastasie whispered, the horror in her voice. The Directory gawked at her, glances turning heads to neighbors as murmuring hummed through the amphitheater. The secretaries on either side of her were scribbling furiously, their quill nibs on the verge of cracking.

A part of her wondered if she had overstepped and confirmed the suspicion that both husband and wife Lafayette were as bold as they were a threat. But she was just a lady who hardly reached over five feet and two inches tall, with a family who, *although* were once powerful, were scattered over the country and Western Europe while she remained in a tiny hamlet with two main roads. Realistically, how much of a threat could she possibly be? Unless she were capable of raising up an entire army of Auvergne farmers... which was quite the American way of thinking if she admitted to herself.

No one could deny that General Lafayette committed his life towards Lady Liberty. Arguments against his support towards the late monarchy balanced the counterpoints that if he had not, then he would be a traitor to France *then* as he was declared currently. A certain messy soup the Directory had worked themselves into, as Adrienne stood quiet in prayer and contemplation, apt at keeping her address short and to the point. Behind her she heard Madame Chavaniac's constant hum of disapproval while the men continued to quarrel and throw their questions Adrienne's way. She replied politely in Gilbert's favor every time; it was almost embarrassing that they thought she would be swayed against him.

She looked up at the ceiling where the angels must have been watching in awe at the absurdity of it all.

Shadows began to cast themselves in short blobs by the standing attendees' feet as the afternoon sun found its way to a window, setting behind the Directory's heads. The golden light made the translucent whites of Adrienne's petticoats glow.

"We have decided," the leader of the Directory said while his throat bobbed, "that while there is no evidence to sentence Citoyenne Lafayette with treason, we find we do not have the proper authorization to drop the charges. Therefore the accused shall be contained within Le Puy until further instruction is sent."

Their cell at least had some fine views, with the draft of a chilled waiting room. Its one window looked towards the chapel that sat high on its distant mountain, and let in the noise from the streets of workers ending their days' labor and children playing ignorantly in the alleyways. A single bed sat along the opposite wall, the mattress stuffed with hay. It wasn't big enough for three people, hardly enough for two. Madame Chavaniac was given precedence over it, and as Adrienne made herself at home by a tiny table by the window, Anastasie knelt by her feet, resting her cheek upon Adrienne's knee.

"That was bold, Maman."

"The fact that they brought myself and other noblewomen here instead of directly to Paris speaks of their knowledge and hope of some semblance of justice," Adrienne replied. She watched the clouds roll by slowly and steady.

"What do you mean?"

"I mean," she said, then paused. After last year's massacres of the aristocracy – where dozens of lives Adrienne had personally known ended in a horrible slaughter – sending more people to the capital was a death sentence. She cleared her throat, and looked down to tuck some stray hairs under Anastasie's cap. "You know how difficult it is to get word from Paris lately. How Mémé and Auntie Louise's letters hardly ever make it to us. I would hate to have any distance from you and your siblings."

Anastasie's brow furrowed. Adrienne could see the wheels turning behind glassy eyes.

"I would come with you to Paris too," Anastasie said. "Stay in prison with you there if I must. Our family is strongest together and I will do everything in my power to be the rope that binds us all. If they take you, Maman, that's – that's not fair. To separate families, it's not right."

"I know."

There was no argument for it. She didn't even know if her family in the Hôtel de Noailles were arrested already. All the men absconded like rats; her father of all people leaving her mother behind without sending someone to retrieve her...

Would the proud Madame d'Ayen leave France? Her own Noailles stubbornness must have come from somewhere, so it would not be a surprise if the opportunity arose that the regal d'Ayen would also stay in Paris. And Louise was always destined to be a Parisian, even if her husband was off and her children were sent elsewhere.

The cell held a chill in the night, prompting all three women to cuddle desperately on the single bed. Hay was nothing like feathers, and the thin blanket brought bumps to their arms. Being a woman was perhaps best if only for their petticoats, which provided more warmth for their legs than the flimsy coarse wool sheet did. Adrienne laid with her back towards Madame Chavaniac, holding Anastasie like she did when the young woman was a baby, fresh in her arms, with a wayward father not too long ago.

Days turned into a week, then two. Adrienne only kept count through writing the dates upon the dozens of letters she turned out from the holding cell. Her letters to and from her American compatriots in France were remarkably some of the only ones able to get around as long as they did not speak to any means of an escape. An easy task. She simply wanted to raise funds to send to Gilbert and if possible, to save their assets. With no money to spare, they accepted their one meal a day and asked for nothing save for a mass each Sunday.

It was hardly into *October* when they were given leave to return to Chavaniac. Something that was meant to be joyous was overcome with the sense of dread that continued to cling to Adrienne like a dark veil. Monsieur Frestel greeted them alongside the staff, with Virginie and Georges unscathed and in perfect health, only bearing the grief of missing their mother, sister, and aunt.

Several nights she could not sleep, so she would pace the halls. Word arrived that her grandpère, the Maréchal de Noailles, had passed away, and yet she could not go to his funeral.

Thoughtlessly, she climbed the steps to the tiny door which led to the narrowly sloped roof of the château. The layered tile wobbled as she stepped across it in her ascent to the flattened top where Gilbert held her the first time she was given reign of the manor. Goosebumps stormed her skin as she sat. The stars flowed in their river overhead, moved since the summer months.

"I'm sorry," she whispered to them. "I'm sorry I can't bring him home."

The stars twinkled as wind rustled tree tops.

"I have been sent in circles and get no word of him from anyone. All this work – *all this work* and I have no assurances he is even alive, oh *God*." Adrienne covered her mouth like she could cover the idea that Gilbert was dead from her mind. It felt sacrilegious to even fathom it. The thousands of stars would not tell her if their favorite was still breathing. Adrienne's heart had not given out so it was only right she believed that his was still beating, wasn't it? She would ensure their children would survive them, but she could not promise herself. If he were dead, then she already was too – her body just hadn't realized it yet.

"I'm sorry," she said again, hoping that she would receive all the kisses that Gilbert promised with every apology she gave.

☆

Being thirty-four was far worse than being thirty-three. She felt hollow as the year passed without Gilbert. Roots along the base of her neck were coming in gray, a shocking color next to her dark strands. Sure, they could be hidden by her cap and with thoughtful styling, but what was the point?

From the Commissioner another order of arrest arrived. The queen was now *dead*. *The Law of Suspects* was merciless in its roundup. And this time, Adrienne went alone, back to the small confines of Brioude. The cell there was full of other women of nobility, whose gowns were already taking on the dust and dirt of the cramped rooms, as well as women who simply did not support the revolution one way or another. Only three of them in her cell welcomed her kindly, holding out their cold hands to grasp hers. Before the first night was up, she had already relinquished her shawl to a woman who could not stop shivering through the frightening ordeal. It was dull and a little maddening, but at least she was not alone.

The diverse characters of the ladies with her provided some comfort in between the days where Monsieur Frestel brought the children to see her. It must have been Auvergnean kindness that allowed her to greet them every other week, for she wouldn't have praised herself for her ability to seek sympathy from most people now.

"Tell me whatever you need, Madame, and I will have it done," Frestel said one afternoon through the bars. He delivered short correspondences for some of the women contained with her as well as news from Paris. His reports on the rising number of executions started to dwindle as soon as Adrienne's forehead vein throbbed hearing names of men and women she had hosted in her salon. None of her family, however; they were detained within the Hôtel de Noailles.

"Just be sure no one comes for them," Adrienne replied, holding Virginie and Georges through the bars. "Do what you must, take what you must. They are my everything, Monsieur. I need you to be a father to them."

Frestel was too sweet a man to refuse her. She didn't mean to abuse his kindness; he was young and did not deserve such responsibility. But he adjusted his cravat and nodded his head, the short hairs that slipped from his queue did nothing to hide the watering of his eyes or the redness coming over his nose.

"Georges, you take care of your sisters now, alright? I expect only the best from such an intelligent and compassionate son." He was turning the age Gilbert was when Adrienne first met him. Not as tall, but still bearing the face of his father.

Georges stiffened his lip and nodded vigorously. "Yes, Maman. You need not worry about us at all, you keep taking care of yourself. That's all we want, Maman: for you to be well enough to come right home when the Committee realizes your innocence in all this," Georges exclaimed. The sleeve of his coat came up to run under his nose. "And they will. You are the best woman in all of France."

Virginie shimmied in front of her, pulling a pearlescent rosary from her pocket. "I took my first communion, Maman. I know you would have wanted me to, so I studied and studied and Father gave it to me at Saint-Roch last week. I want you to have my prayer beads. I put a lot of extra ones in there for you just in case you need them."

"Oh," Adrienne whispered, feeling a hot tear gather at the corner of her lashes as she folded her fingers around the cross. "You're such a sweet girl, Nini, thank you. I am so proud of you, *chère*, your father would be too."

"We'll see him soon, I know it," Virginie said. And as tiny as she was, she had the biggest dreams. "Don't give up hope, Maman."

"I'm... I *am* hopeful."

Virginie's perception was almost divine. How were her children individually so perfectly wise? They were supposed to be innocent and carefree like she and Gilbert had decided, not to bear witness to a bloody massacre disguised as democracy, not to see their parents imprisoned.

But Brioude was not the worst. Its closeness to Chavaniac brought peace of mind and familiar noises from the vast mountain landscape that could hardly be seen from the windows high above their heads.

There was nowhere to hide her new gift, so one woman, a past comtesse, held Adrienne's hair flat to her head so she could slip the rosary beads around her neck and under her fichu. They spoke of their children, of the châteaus they left behind, of where their husbands had run off to... Adrienne watched their posture week by week slowly slump in their seats or succumb to lean against the icy walls. Shoe buckles would be traded for a second meal, locks of hair for hot water to hold. Adrienne twisted the cross by her bosom, unwilling to yield.

Brioude, May 1794

"No, you cannot take her – that is not fair!"

"Can't you wait for her family to see her off, then? How inhuman are you?"

"Call this justice? She has already taken ill. Send a doctor, not another cage!"

The transfer order came later than she expected. Word had already rushed down the rivers that executions in Paris were a daily occurrence. The late-king's sister met her fate at the beginning of the month. Adrienne did not speak to her much on a personal level; she knew the young woman as a holy one, and she knew that the people of Paris did not wish to see her die. But die she did. As did many others. One consolation was the lack of Noailles' mentioned in the lists. Adrienne didn't look for more beyond that. Knowing friends could have been thrown into unmarked graves was painful enough.

Amid the complaints of her cellmates, whose soft hands held her as the guards opened the door to take her away, Adrienne's head was silent.

A transfer to Paris meant a trial in front of the Committee. To most aristocracy it meant death. To the wife of the infamous Lafayette, it meant the most complicated of feelings were soon to be unfolded. Legally, she and all of her family were a danger to France. But, she prayed, there were some sympathizers among the judging politicians to remember the sacrifices Gilbert made for the cause of liberty; that there was, somewhere above, that lucky star that still shined.

Maybe her head wasn't silent.

Maybe there was so much noise that the mass of it was indescribable.

She didn't fight the guards when they pulled her from her few peers, in fact she was sure a small "thank you" escaped her lips when they held the door open for her. Her stare remained centered, ignoring the gazette pages nailed to the walls that they passed, as if advertising the damnation that awaited her in the capital. Adrienne needed to keep a brave face, if not for the other prisoners to keep their dignity, than for her to keep her own.

There was no common prison cart to take her away when she stepped outside. Instead was a post chaise carriage, Monsieur Frestel, and her children, and for a moment Adrienne felt free – that this was it: she would be going home to Chavaniac for good this time. But a soldier sat in the driver's seat, and armed men lined the walkway down to her family, who waited with their heads bowed and faces skewed.

"The household couldn't let you be taken away like a common criminal," Anastasie said into her cheek as she kissed it. "You are the *Marquise de la Fayette* and people should know you."

"My sweetling," Adrienne breathed, cupping her cheek. There were heavy tears rolling over her thumbs.

"Let me follow you," she whispered. "Let me appeal to the Directory at Puy to go to Paris. I can speak with the American minister; we have citizenship in several states we could use. Monsieur Frestel has already agreed, Maman, if you would allow me."

"There is no stopping you, my girl," Adrienne said, willful of the time they had. "Yes, of course, why not? Let them hear you."

"I will fight them all," Georges said when Adrienne kissed his forehead. He started to powder his hair again like an old aristocrat. It brought out the redness in his cheeks. "They should know we come from a long line of knights; we've fought with martyrs!"

"Hush, Georges, I know," she nodded. "Knights are to protect, Monsieur, which our family does with all of our hearts, is that right?"

"With all of our hearts," he repeated. "But I will still go to Paris and fight them one by one if I must."

Virginie was silent upon embracing Adrienne. Her fists tightened around her neck as they squeezed each other. A kiss to the temple and one last, long gaze, Virginie maintained her composure better than any old kingsguard. Monsieur Frestel looked as composed as a wrecked man would be.

"Madame," he said, taking up her hand in between his.

"Félix," she replied. Her throat was constricting. "God be with you."

He opened his mouth, but whatever he was to say, he decided against it, and nodded firmly. His hands rested on Virginie and Georges' shoulders, one in comfort while holding back the other from rushing towards Adrienne when she was led up to the carriage.

She ingrained their faces to her memory, watching them from the window with her chin held high. Thankful to the distance that they did not see it tremble while she held back a sob. No one had to tell her children that she was being transferred, no one had to allow them all to see each other one last time.

It was a small mercy; a tender, melancholic departure.

Adrienne was a lady. She should have felt grateful.

All she was fed on the week's long journey was a small ration of bread and the ever-growing anxiety that pooled up in her stomach. Watching passersby did nothing to soothe her aching – the poor were still poor, the middling were still middling. It was like nothing had changed in the countryside save for the replacement of a few hats with red caps from those who lived closer to village centers. She could try and sleep for the journey, but the constant stopping for watering the horses or to stay the night at inns kept her restless. Drinking water was starting to become a chore, she thought, staring at the canteen one soldier handed her. It tasted off – it may have been poison – and was warm and unrefreshing.

Into June they went, and Adrienne relived the days she used to ride far out on her Thursday gallivants, if she ever made it into the surrounding city, where the shops and apartment buildings were becoming somewhat recognizable. They rocked over the Seine into the right bank. Adrienne saw the rise of Notre Dame in the distance, her buttresses and gargoyles towered over everything, but the bells did not ring – it was gored from the inside.

Adrienne fanned her face with her hand wondering if the heat was from the outside or from her anger alone.

People watched the soldiers who led carriages or wagons like it were a traveling circus, trying to peek inside at the arrival of some past-noble who they may or may not recognize. The eyes grew more numerous the closer they got to their destination, the building that the driver called *La Petite Force* – the prison used for women to separate them from the men's building. It used to house Paris' prostitutes. Now it did not matter the woman's background; if she were deemed an enemy of the state, in she went. There were more active prisons in Paris than there were churches.

Adrienne was helped out of the carriage and into the prison's courtyard, walking with her hands tied in front of her after informing the guard that she was in heels and could not run far in them anyway, so tying her hands behind her back was immodest and unneeded at best. She thanked him for his gentleness.

There were still hints that La Petite Force and her brother prison were once Hôtels. Iron bars stretched over long, numerous windows overhead, and the doors that Adrienne was led through were large enough for carriage drivers to duck under. Lanterns hung every few feet down hallways, everything made of stone here, some jutted out of the walls at odd angles. She felt like she was experiencing Persephone's descent into Hades. So much noble blood filled the gaps between the uneven floors, where two years ago, massacres took place without trial. Adrienne's heel slid along the corridor, slick with humidity from the air that rushed through the barred windows. Passing by the rooms, they each seemed spacious at least, and there was no awful smell that stuck around with the windows as grand as they were.

Upon being brought to the second floor, there was a gentleman by a desk of papers, sorting through them with a constant complaint on his tongue towards a young woman who waited with one hand tied to the guard next to her.

Adrienne froze.

"Louise?"

Her sister looked over her shoulder with a small jump, her face perfectly strung in disbelief. She wore a simple white gown with a hem that looked like she had released some of the fabric to cover more of her long legs; her hair was messy for her usual tastes, with her cap coming down under her chin to keep it at bay.

"Adri –!" Louise cried, taking a step forward only to be stopped by the stoic guard who kept her by the desk. Adrienne closed the distance, throwing her tied hands up and over Louise's head, childishly knocking their foreheads together. "You are staying here? Good Lord, Adri, please say you aren't here. This is a death sentence."

"Me?" Adrienne rasped. "What of you? What are you doing here? Is Maman with you?"

"No, no. We're in the Luxembourg. Ironic, isn't it – where our dear Marquis lived before he came to us." She tilted her head towards the man stuffing paperwork into a bag. "Aunt Anne and Uncle Philippe were separated here for a few months, but they petitioned to move into a prison that let them remain in the same cell. Grandmère, Maman, and I joined them there. Some dope left Auntie's information here and she was convinced someone would try and alter it or sabotage her, so they let me come to retrieve it. This is Gronle –" Louise raised her arm to jingle the chain that was attached to the soldier. "He is quite grumpy all of the time, but he is alright."

She was so calm and charming despite the predicament. But the Luxembourg… that was hopeful. And for them to be all together too. Adrienne forced a smile. The guards behind her exchanged impatient grunts.

"Is Maman well, at least?"

"She prays for you. Constantly." Louise bumped her nose. "And as I am so happy to see you, I am scorned to inform her of where you are. Could Madame Lafayette transfer elsewhere? Can she join us?"

"Citoyenne Lafayette's business is of no concern of the Noailles," the warden replied. "Here is the file. Now go before the inspector gets here; I don't want any more trouble today."

Louise gripped the bag tightly against her side. Her eyes were the color of the sky they wouldn't see for some time: crystalline blue, and full of light. Adrienne imagined her mother with the same color, and the hug Louise was able to give with one strong arm as from their Maman too.

"You look skinny. Take my earrings, get some second meals for yourself this week."

"Louise, that's ridiculous, I am not taking your things. Save them for if the family needs it. I'm fine. I wouldn't be able to eat knowing you all could be going hungry or if Grandmère needs any doctor."

"You do overthink things, Adri," Louise said with a long sigh. Their respected guards were beginning to tug them apart, but with Adrienne's arms looped around Louise's neck, they would have to physically pick Adrienne up to remove her from her sister. From the feeling of large hands on her waist, it was a high probability. "We'll be fine, I promise. And you – you'll be alright. You have always been the one to overcome the impossible. We have a priest that visits us regularly. He's a very kind man, Abbé Carrichon. He checks on my children who are with their tutor and lets me know of their well-being. He also gives mass whenever he can. I will ask him to check on you, give some reassurance that God is ever present with us."

"Please," Adrienne replied. Her feet were hoisted from the ground and she gasped with a start. She tried to grasp her sister tighter. "Please, I will await news from you, from Maman. Tell her how I love her, say it with your prettiest words, Louise." She *was* losing weight – the guard took her with too much ease.

Louise smiled, using her shoulder to wipe away her own tears. "We will see each other soon. If not on Earth, then in Heaven!"

The guard dragged her down the stairs, where her eyes never left Adrienne's until she was pulled out of view, and Adrienne was brought to her cell where she would remain for the next fortnight. Small, but modestly dressed. It seemed appropriate to house someone who was at the foot of the scaffold at any waking moment. The women in the neighboring cells were quietly chatting and Adrienne could eavesdrop if she so wished. But she had work to do.

Fiddling through her pocket, she produced a coin to exchange for paper and a pen with the jailor. There were some names and new introductions to be made, she thought, as she addressed the embassy of the United States.

Paris, July 1794

She was transferred to *de Plessis* not long into her stay. Five-hundred meters from the Luxembourg prison, she was put in the upper floors of the old academy young Gilbert attended, alongside other women who were cramped by the small windows at floor-level. Her hands were still shaking, holding up her elbows as she quietly paced. Abbé Carrichon presented himself to her after much effort and convincing, only to give her the news of her aunt and uncle's death. He had not returned for several days.

Wherever Louis was, he was now an orphan like his favorite brother-in-law.

Robespierre's terror was in full swing. Adrienne had watched dozens of women taken from neighboring cells and from her own each day to be carted off to a trial, and very rarely did any come back. The others found watching the carts take off from the window was their only source of the outside world; Adrienne couldn't bring herself to do it.

Theoretically if she opened the windows and shouted loud enough, her sister could hear her from her prison a few blocks away. But the windows did not open, at least, not anymore.

Too many prisoners forced themselves through narrow cracks to escape the guillotine, meeting death's kiss at the ground. Adrienne didn't try to understand why they did it. They must have had their reasons.

She replayed the words of the abbé of what her mother, sister, and grandmère had passed on to her – full of piety and devotion, of calmness and love. Knowing she did not hear of any passing cart from the Luxembourg brought a sense of relief, but it was like the warmth from sheer linen – not to last.

No one in the cell bothered her, not even during her pacing episodes. Any day could be their last – they surely had more to worry about than the one mad woman who couldn't sit still longer than it took to write another letter or two. Did any letter get to the new American minister? Did they get through to Austria? Truly, it was like sending a dove and hoping it would act like a carrier pigeon.

Several fingers twisted around Virginie's rosary. So many prayers were repeated for the Comte and Comtesse de Noailles. In a Godless state, would they have been allowed absolution? Were they frightened? Resigned? And how would *she* be – approaching the guillotine? The regrets of her children, of the unknown fate of Gilbert... If he outlived her, she would be better for it, she thought. He seemed to fare better without her than she was without him.

Stop it, her heart said. *Think of something else.*

There wasn't much else to think about. Every day rolled into the next like the passing storms that summer brought. The floor, their beds here, shook as lightning struck and thunder rocked the prison. She thought of Doctor Franklin and his lightning rod. She didn't see one placed on this structure. The attic where most women were kept would be the first to go if anything caught fire.

Not that.

Rats burrowed through holes in the wall, desperate to find leftover meals from any lady who could not finish her ration. They could not bother Adrienne now, feeling one slip over her ankle as it scurried across the floor. She felt obligated to write to Louis, to his brother and sister, to tell them of their parents' fate. But once again, she fell to square one: would it even make it?

She wrote anyway; she'd be damned if she didn't try.

News straight from the gazettes about the Committee of Public Safety were sometimes read aloud if the stationed guard was literate. The disorder between factions, the everlasting debate of who is an enemy and who is simply speculated to be one amidst the madness of *the terror...* Adrienne listened carefully, one of hundreds down the shallow hall, to who was turning against who within the government walls; the name of the infamous Robespierre and his allies brought up jarring, hissing, and boos from the ladies.

By the end of July, she had piled up quite the amount of letters to her children, ready to be sent once she had the means of transportation. Her pacing stepped over some sleeping girls, for that was all that was becoming of the rest of her cellmates – just younger girls and a few older ones who preferred to lean against the walls to support their backs; the eldest among them had access to the single bed. Sometimes when the women were silent, they could hear the men far beneath them. They were kept in the basement. Screams full of resentment resounded up the walls through the rotting paths rats made, but sometimes there were songs, the deep melodic tune of gentle men who felt all the loneliness the women did. So many were the tunes of sailors, meant to be sung in a working crowd. Depending on the warden touring the attics late at night, the women sang lullabies down the holes, like heavenly angels from above, imagining their sons and husbands who could be mourning below.

But as the new month approached, there was a different bustle downstairs. *Cheers.* Thunderous applause and the banging of cell doors. Women rushed to the windows – there were no armies outside, no mobs or rioters, but there was a rush of men basking in the setting sun with open arms, free of their chains and confinement.

"He's dead!" a voice rang up the stairwells and dozens of faces showed up at their cell doors to see who was speaking. "The terror meister has fallen to his own contraption!"

A jolly guard followed behind the wardeness, clearly exalting in the news. But the short woman rushed through her papers, eyeing each cell as she passed through.

"I will call names and those names will wait by their doors with their identification," she said, firing off family names in alphabetical order. The number had dwindled exponentially, some letters only with one or two names. *J... K... L... M...*

Adrienne listened through the N names and heard nothing. She watched her cellmates rise and wait by the door on their toes, a strange nerve-wracking bounce on what it meant that Robespierre was now dead. If they were being held on one of his benign charges, Adrienne thought, then they must be getting released for there was no need to send them to trial.

There was no evidence of treason against Adrienne – she knew this. For why her name wasn't called, she could only pin the blame towards the leftover men in charge of the Committee: that they hated the name and the man connected to it. So maybe Gilbert was still too conservative for France, but perhaps her mother could have some sway in her release. No doubt what was going on in Plessis was happening across all of Paris' prisons. If there was anyone who could pull the strings of men, it was Madame d'Ayen.

Which was why when all the called women left the prison, leaving only Adrienne and a few select others behind, she didn't immediately mind the sudden silence that overtook Plessis. When she watched them embrace their family in the courtyard or run off into the city, she could handle another day or two. There *was* a plus side, she could have the bed for the first time in weeks. The hay filled mattress was as flat as the floorboards, but being elevated away from the vermin was a nice change.

She laid awake at night like a child waiting for her mother to walk through the door. Chavaniac could house them all; she would let her mother take over the garden and bring it back to life the way flowers always did when the lady handled them. She would take Louise south towards Marseille, let her shop along the shoreline to her heart's content. Grandmère would adore the ancient cathedrals that still held mass every day. They could let their hair down and don a pair of breeches and hike up the mountainside.

There was a mountain not too far from the château that Gilbert had mentioned one dreary night when they were full of wine and tangled up in each other; a mountain where the sun lit the trees' leaves gold and all the birds sang in tune. They were supposed to climb it together to take a picnic at the summit. Gilbert even sketched out an outfit for her that he said he would commission – something that would compliment her behind, he had said, while being modest up front to pass her own inspection. They were too drunk to put the sketch towards reality, and far too busy to make that hike. But when this was over, when she had her family all together again, arm in arm with everyone, they could do it.

Louise and Maman would be great help in planning a wedding for Anastasie. She had to meet some gentlemen first, that is. Adrienne already imagined the lack of arguments that she would have. She wanted her daughter to marry for love, and her mother would agree full-heartedly as she always wanted the same for her own daughters. And how lucky Adrienne had been, to marry a boy she had grown to love so dearly.

So desperately.

There was a creak up the stairs that knocked Adrienne out of her fantasy. A few times there would still be a call for a remaining woman to go face trial, many times she came back, but for one this week, she did not return. Freedom, death, it all still happened. The door opened slowly, hesitantly, as a man dressed in black entered the attic space. His knuckles were white as they held his hat, turning it inch by inch in his hand, and Adrienne got up from her bed to approach the cell door.

"Abbé Carrichon," she said. She smiled at him, pleasant to know the visitor who was so close to her family. "It's been so long since your last visit. Were you unwell or has the warden been uncivil to a man of the cloth? Hopefully just the latter, I pray you are in high spirits now that the terror has calmed."

He stopped in front of her, holding his hat up by his chest and over his cross. "Forgive me, Madame," he said. "My resolve had failed me for days and it is only now that God has given me the courage to see your face."

Adrienne curled her fingers around the bars. The poor man looked frightened. "I am well enough, Monsieur, do not fear for seeing me. You may tell Maman that I still eat my meal and pray the rosary every day as I always have. That should set her in a good spirit until we may be reunited again."

His eyes squinted involuntarily, like he had stepped on a nail and held curses behind the firmness of his teeth. "M-madame," he muttered. "I c-cannot."

"Cannot tell her? If they have still not been freed on my account, I pray for their patience and forgiveness. Do they not allow *you* to visit them anymore? That is completely barbaric, you are a man of God, how dare they—"

His hand shot out to fold over hers on the bars. Hot and a little sweaty as they squeezed her knuckles. "Madame Lafayette," he said, sternly this time, like he practiced it.

Adrienne's brow twitched. She looked at his eyes and the shadows that ran under them, the paleness to his cheeks, the thin line of water that started to reflect the scarce light of the lantern next to him.

"Monsieur Carrichon," she said, "why is it you cannot?"

Her grip on the bars tightened.

He lowered his head.

"Forgive me for not coming to you sooner to express my sincerest and utmost condolences, Madame," he said.

Adrienne's body stilled like a corpse frozen in time, but her mouth hung ajar. "When?" she asked, as if it would change something.

"The fourth of Thermador, Madame, that is, *um*, the twenty-second of July."

Not even a week before Robespierre's reign was over. So close. So damned close and they – they…

"I met them along the way," the Abbé continued, his hand was the one thing keeping her aloft. "They were composed like saints. God parted the storm for them, the light was warm and welcoming. I granted them absolution before we arrived. They are in Heaven, angels themselves."

She felt her gut cave inward, her heart pressing painfully against her chest. She didn't want to hear more. She asked for more.

"The Maréchale de Noailles was the first of the three, then the Madame d'Ayen. She never faltered, never raised her voice. Devout resignation to the sacrifice she was making to God, approaching as one does to receive holy communion. And Madame Noailles – an angel in white. She looked up towards heaven with the kindest smile I have not seen on any human being. A *martyr*, Madame." His other hand dropped his hat, and he clasped them both in hers as he prayed, "May God Almighty in his mercy bestow his blessings upon you and your family…"

He went on with more kind and holy words. If it were any other occasion, Adrienne may have listened, may have heard them. Her eyes wobbled away into oblivion, drowning beneath an ocean, hot and charring her skin. There was nothing in her stomach and yet she felt the bile rise in her throat while her gut continued to thrust inward underneath her gown.

A cold breeze took her hands as the company left her, and the torches on the walls dimmed, scattering away like ash.

They were dead.

Her mother's decapitated head rolled along the floor. Louise's in her palms, pouring crimson, her eyes opened – clear and full of hope. But Adrienne could not keep hers open any longer. She squeezed them shut. Her legs ran her blindly away, deep into her cell like a headless chicken waiting to succumb.

If the tribunal would have waited a week, they would have survived.

Her knees hit the floor with a crack.

Why was she still here – what was keeping them from executing her? Why wouldn't they just *do* it already – it was her who was the wife of their most hated emigrant, not Louise, not her mother, they *didn't* do anything wrong, they didn't do anything *wrong*, why was she still *here*, why was she doomed to be *alone*?

A sob broke through her teeth. She dug her bloodied hands into her hair and pulled until the strands gave way. Her father could have done something. Where was the new Duc de Noailles now that his mother, his wife, his oldest daughter's bodies lay somewhere in a pile of blue blood? Hate rose in her throat. Hate towards him, towards every man in the tribunal, to the citizens of Paris who sat back and watched, towards herself.

She'd always end up alone.

She wished to just lay limp until someone dragged her to her trial and execution. There was no strength in her legs, no point for her heart to beat blood anywhere anymore. It was all too much; no one was coming to console her, to pick her up and kiss her, to tell her it would be alright; she decided she would like to not open her eyes for a very long time.

Her next breath came out strangled and high-pitched, and she wept.

She wept alone.

Chapter Twenty-Eight

"Excuse me?"

Dim light from the early autumn sun was another thing that avoided Adrienne's cell every day. She watched the arch quickly rotate around the room and disappear from her spot on the floor. Her stomach growled incessantly towards a brain that could not care the least for food. The jailor at some point decided to leave the broth behind after she let the rats take the bread. She was supposedly on the schedule to be executed; but not even the judge knew the date. Why would she want to eat?

"Hello? Excuse me, Madame?"

It was accented French from a young woman, and not of any accent she had heard before.

"Madame, I beg your pardon," it slipped into English, "are you the Marquise de Lafayette?"

Adrienne's ear tuned in harder. Footsteps stopped outside of her cell. She rolled her head, eyeing the woman with a tired but curious stare. It had been ages since someone spoke English to her.

"Yes," she replied. Her voice sounded so alien.

The young woman beamed, her gloved hand took the prison bar and she turned her head down the hall and called, "James, I found her! I found her here!"

Sitting up was a task. Adrienne suddenly became aware of how much of a mess she looked as the two Americans knelt by her prison chamber. Her hair had matted against her face.

"Oh, I beg your pardon, Marquise. You see, we're quite new to the Ambassadorship and haven't had the opportunity to formally make your acquaintance. My name is Elizabeth Monroe, my husband here served with the Marquis in the War for Independence." She was delightful and petite, with black curls and a Greek nose.

Monroe appeared next to her, with hair just as dark, fashioned in the dated queue, and a deep dimple in his chin. He was far older than his wife, yet couldn't be much older than Adrienne. "At your service, Madame," he said with a bow of his head. His hand fished through his jacket pockets for a folded piece of paper. "I wished Gouverneur Morris supplied the information on what prison held you; it took some time to negotiate our visitations."

"Monsieur Morris sent you...?" Adrienne said, carefully inching towards the couple.

"Of sorts," Monroe said.

"Give us some credit," Elizabeth added, "we knew we could not leave you."

Being handed the paper, Adrienne carefully unfolded it to read the very words Monsieur Morris wrote to someone else who must have had some influence in the committee.

The family of Lafayette is beloved in America... My fellow citizens confine themselves to the grateful remembrance of his services he has rendered us, and that, therefore, the death of his wife might lessen the attachment of some among them to the French Republic... Her eyes scanned the vague threatening tone in his blunt words. *I cannot think of her existence of little consequence to this government; and that I am sure its enemies will rejoice at the destruction of anything which bears the name Lafayette...*

"What does this mean?" Adrienne asked, though her voice had not quite found itself.

Elizabeth seemed to make herself comfortable on the uneven and dirty floor. "It means we will be visiting quite often if it pleases you, Marquise. Every day perhaps. I'd love to get to know you a little better. Frankly, I have very few friends so far. James makes it difficult when he's playing politics and many of the women brought over for dinner do not make great conversationalists. I envy the knowledge that you and your husband have hosted Mister Jefferson, Mister Morris, and any other American who arrived on your shores. This is not the salon anyone was expecting, but I would *happily* take coffee here with you." She closed her statement with a wink.

Ambassadors to the United States visiting her in prison daily.

Quite tough to squeeze in an execution with that schedule.

"I would *happily* accept your company, Madame Monroe, Monsieur Ambassador. But," she paused, her heart heavy. "Can you tell me if there is any news about my husband – of Lafayette?"

Monroe took a minute, siphoning through more of his pockets. "You know," he said, taking a seat next to his wife, "I did receive some word upon my arrival. The communication lines between Americans in Europe are very tight knit. I believe General Lafayette was transferred to Olmütz, Austria this year."

He was alive.

More tears slipped down her cheeks when she thought she had dried up.

"Thank God," she breathed, wiping at her eyes. Monroe handed her his handkerchief. She could live then, knowing that. "T-thank you, thank you, I am so sorry my English is too riddled with faults to express my appreciation."

"We understand," Elizabeth said. Her hand reached in to rub Adrienne's forearm. "Trust us, Americans have been following your husband's whereabouts for *years* now. Prussia we have been able to bully lightly, but I am afraid Austria is out of our diplomatic reach, isn't it, James?"

Monroe set his thumb to tap at his dimple. "With France being at war with them, the United States is hesitant to involve themselves anywhere. Secretaries Jefferson and Hamilton have been arguing about it since before I was given the ambassadorship. It is a complicated time. But, Marquise, we will not bore you with talks of American politics. What can we do to help you?"

She was willful enough to give them all the letters she had written for her family. And as they promised, both, or on occasion just Lady Monroe, arrived at the prison to spend time with her. And every evening, Elizabeth would over-exaggerate her goodbyes and well-wishes to see her tomorrow. The jailer adjusted himself in his seat as the small American woman stared him down day after day.

Every day.

Chavaniac, February 1795

Her children smelt of home, of love, of the reminder of why she persevered. She had not even made it halfway down the country before they met her, leaving poor Monsieur Frestel behind in the dust. They held her up through her exhaustion, their cries mixed in with her cooing laughter. Madame Chavaniac was devastated. They had lost everything. The château raided and looted of all its furniture, salvaged only by what Adrienne would call a miracle.

Dearest Rosalie – young, kind Rosalie, traveling by foot with her husband and a single horse, baskets full of her infant children – arrived like an angel disguised as a shepherdess on a sunny morning. Her diamonds paid for the château, her company paid for Adrienne's utter relief. Her baby sister poured love and anguish into their embrace. Theo and Monsieur Frestel took care of setting up makeshift bedrooms in the manor while Adrienne clung to Rosalie for dear life. Anastasie settled to prepare food with Virginie while in the company of the babies Grammont.

Travel was becoming more difficult. Being spotted as nobility was still dangerous, but remaining in one spot was too risky. Adrienne's head pushed through the cobwebs as she spilled out any and all ideas she had to Rosalie. Georges needed to leave France before the government sought out the grown-enough son, step one. Meaning he was in need of a passport. She needed to get to Gilbert – *she* needed a passport. There were only a few people who could acquire such forged documents and fewer who would turn a blind eye to it all.

"Adrienne, you just were released, you should not go on such a journey," Rosalie argued. Her hands clasped her sister's wrists. "Pauline would agree with me, you would hear the same from her and Aunt Tessé. Think of your *health*. Recover; let these terrorists blow themselves up first before you risk travel."

"I cannot keep on without him," Adrienne said. "I cannot do it. Rosalie, my constitution will fail me if I don't reach him. And he needs family too. Gilbert doesn't do well in confinement."

Truthfully, Rosalie couldn't argue against that fact, knowing very well how Gilbert grew stir-crazy within the grand walls of the Hôtel de Noailles, but there were dozens of obstacles that *would* let Adrienne see the jailed General that her sister didn't seem to realize.

Staring at Adrienne as the woman's eyes looked out to the stars above, Rosalie waved her hand in front of her face. "What would you *do* when you arrive in Austria? Harass the emperor? Come now, Adri, that's delusional. It would take the hand of God to make that man even meet with you, not to say *listen*."

Chapter Twenty-Nine

Olmütz, Austria, October 1795

He could recite the book he had in hand by heart now, the only one he had with him for several months. Farming techniques would come naturally if he ever had the chance to step into a field again. There were more terms than he originally cared to know, but now he knew them too well.

Reading at the little table was better than reading on his bed. If he took to doing everything from the bed, he didn't think he would have the energy to leave it. Lugging his chains along the few feet to the chair was as much exercise as he could get within the room. In the past, he would have his companions as cellmates in tiny boxes, but he could still leave to walk with a guard, he could still receive his letters. This was different. He had not opened a letter in years, sitting on the news that death was plaguing France and her people. Gilbert couldn't sleep. He dripped with sweat and shivered from anxious fevers that gripped him on and off for weeks.

There *was* an escape attempt, one speedily planned, that ruined all his chances of a polite detainment. His dear Americans tried their best and, truthfully, if not for Gilbert's panicked ignorance, it could have possibly paid off. But he was recaptured, and any ounce of freedom he was given at first was rescinded and replaced with more guards.

Gilbert coughed into his fist and turned the worn page. *Ah yes, types of dirt. Invigorating.*

He tried to not think of the victims of Madame Guillotine. He wouldn't want to believe that his family would be brought upon her evil hand. But he made so many enemies and if they wanted to hurt him from France then his little family was the first thing they would lay their eyes on. It made him nauseous. His mind didn't win this fight very often. There was no place to tactfully retreat to.

His days were full of the same routine. Rolling out of bed, he tried a few push-ups or squats if his body allowed him, though many times it wouldn't. A few hours ticked by until his meal arrived: some bread and an uncut portion of meat not too dissimilar to war rations, or sometimes some soup, but he was forced to eat with his hands as they confiscated any sharp object from him.

Sometimes he debated if it was to stop him from being murdered in his cell or to prevent him from slicing his own wrists.

At the end of every week, the smell from the small window made him wretch. Sewage was his neighbor; the stench soaked into his meal, into the water, ruining appetites for endless days. If it weren't for the conditions he bore through the war in America, he'd no doubt fall sick more often.

He missed when his prison mates would speak with him. Some were still in this very prison. Even the mundane topics did better than days of silence. Gilbert felt crazy whenever he croaked a trepid *"ahh"* noise to be sure he still had the ability to talk. Every few weeks he would just cry at his table. He couldn't help it.

There were so many types of dirt.

Some math was involved in his stay. He counted how many paces it was to encompass this cell, leading him to decide that this one was eight feet wide and fourteen feet across. Bigger than Prussia's prison, that was certain. But the walls were always wet and the sunlight was only useful three hours out of the day, so he huddled by the single lantern hanging over his table for comfort.

Why they didn't remove *that* so he didn't *hang* himself with it was only because he was too *tall* to get off the floor before he hit the ceiling.

He checked.

Trousers felt odd on his legs. The long, tawny cloth did less to keep him warm than his stockings and breeches. But such was the poor revolutionary style now. He didn't have much clothing with him to change very often, and the days he was given a wet cloth to wash up were not numerous enough for him to feel clean. A loose robe he wore didn't compare to the silk banyans of his youth.

He could get over smelling rancid, he could accept the strange breezes that swept up his legs; he had been at war in all its challenges for months on end.

But he had friends in war. He had his brothers-in-arms to pass the days with, he had his letters he held so close to his heart.

Oh his heart.

Did it still beat?

Gilbert sat back in his seat. Then he leaned forward to rest his elbows on the table. He reread the words he already read dozens of times over. Sentences shook, not stopping even as he pressed the binding against the wood.

He heard the guard stomp by. Being on the ground floor brought terrible noise as traffic passed his door. In his mild moods, he didn't mind the sounds of life to break up the mundane. In his dour, he wished they would stop so he could wallow in peace.

The clicks and rattles of his prison cell door were startling on such a day. It wasn't a time for any of his little luxuries, there wouldn't be a washcloth nor a meal so early in the morning, and his six o'clock fire was already lit. Gilbert let his book close on his thumb, shifting slightly in his seat to not disturb the fine angle his chains remained at. The men who entered kept their blades unsheathed as the door remained open, a spared stern glance towards him brought him to his feet.

This was no merciful release, surely.

More footsteps echoed down the hall. Unfamiliar, they were not the echoes of leather boot heels or spurs, they were a rattling of tiny clicks, fast and plenty.

Gilbert couldn't remember what he thought the moment angels poured into the room, their dark hair wrapped in halos, their bright eyes searching the liminal space until they met his, and all at once they descended upon him like a rapture.

"Papa!"

These young girls were so tall, so sublime he almost did not recognize them as they peppered his cheeks with kisses, embracing his arms, squeezing his bones. Gilbert sputtered their names, his Anastasie, his Virginie.

"Nini, move for Maman, come now, move for Maman –"

Gilbert couldn't take his hands off of his wife's face as soon as she raised it from his chest. She aged in exhaustion, as did he, and her cheeks gleamed with the tears that washed the dirt from his fingers.

"Mon coeur," he said, *"mon coeur,* my wife, my Adrienne." He kissed her desperately, and again after that. His body shook to keep up with his racing heart. "My girls," he said, feeling his own outpour of tears as they fell to their knees. "What is this – what are you doing here?"

Adrienne carded her hands over his hair, pushing the overgrowth back, and studied his face. He leaned into it, lulled immediately to follow her every move and whim.

"Your whiskers," she whispered, pushing back the beard that had grown over much of his jaw. He laughed. He cried. He did all those things to kiss her again and again.

Anastasie had been holding the party together as she replied to his question. "We are here to be with you, Papa. You would not believe what it took to get here."

"To be with me?" He shook his head. "Oh, my girls, this is not the place for you." And yet he basked in their embraces and sweetness. "My brave girls, I feared the worst. I feared to never see your faces nor hear your voices again. Oh, look at how much you've grown."

He wished he had more than two arms to hold them all, to wrap them up and shield them from what they had just entered. What an awful a father he was, to have made them worry so much that they risked their lives to come to him. It should have been the opposite, he should have found his way to them.

The jingle of the guard's keys pulled his joy back to the present. Whatever Adrienne and their daughters brought with them, the soldiers were sifting through now. How feisty his little Virginie became in trying to stop them from taking their forks, their supplies, anything that would be deemed even the mildest threat.

"You better watch it – your Emperor told my maman that he would give her whatever she needed!" Virginie exclaimed.

The emperor? Gilbert blinked, becoming very aware of Adrienne's tightened grip on his robe, her nose smothered into his chest when he must've smelled awful.

"The daughters will stay in a separate cell," one guard said – Gilbert had named him *Loden* during his stay in his boredom. Loden raised his hand before anyone had the chance to protest. "There will be strict visiting times. You recall you agreed with the emperor that you shall accept whatever treatment is given to Monsieur Lafayette."

Adrienne stared at Loden for a long moment, then nodded to their girls. "I conform to that treatment with pleasure," she said. "And we are happier here in sharing in its severity *with* Monsieur Lafayette than we are anywhere else in this world without him."

In an instant, Gilbert watched their countenance harden, and they raised their chins high, as if soldiers were forming up. Anastasie must have been eighteen by now and Virginie twelve. Braver than a dozen experienced generals. He watched in astonished horror as they were led away from his room, taken from him again, yet walking with so much dignity. He gripped the small of Adrienne's back, his thoughts unscrambled to think of something to say. A tingle in his feet told him there was no use trying to stand.

"*Mon coeur,*" he mumbled, shaking his head as their door swung closed with a metallic bang. "W-what are you doing to me? Why aren't you in England? In America? I told you to go. Oh, if I could be angry with you, I would, so help me God. I am. I *am* angry with you." He tucked his nose into her hair, holding her with everything he had now. "I am so angry."

"I love you," she said into his neck. "I'm sorry, I love you."

"The emperor, Adrienne? What on… And Georges? *Mon coeur*, where is our son?" He couldn't possibly have been a victim of the terror, Gilbert refused to accept that, he was just a boy, he hadn't done anything wrong.

Adrienne politely dabbed at her own tears. "He is with his godfather by now, I pray."

"G-godfather… my general? He is –?"

"In America. With Frestel. I secured him a passport. All of us. I couldn't risk him here with your name, but for now," she said, and her hand found his beard again, "we are Motiers. I am the American wife of *Mister* Motier."

"You sent him away. *You?*"

"To keep him safe. I did."

It was almost too much, a dream perhaps. One of the best dreams he could have had within the years of transferring from prison to prison.

"Missus Motier," he said in English. Her tiny giggle was enough to spark a fire in his heart. "What can I say to you to make up for all this time? I promised you poetry, I promised you my safety and I have lied. I have sat in agony at the thought of you waiting years in Chavaniac for me while I wallowed with no way of telling you of my existence."

"I did not wait in Chavaniac," she replied, quietly, like a confession.

Gilbert frowned. "What do you mean?"

They adjusted their sitting, until Adrienne was in his open lap, kept there by the chains at his ankles. She ran her fingers over his knees, as bony and protruding as they were. He could tell she was keeping more tears back – she would wiggle her nose and blink several times in succession.

"Adrienne?"

"It's, um, it is inexplicable… the things they did, Gilbert."

"You don't have to say it all now, but," he fiddled with the silver strand that fell over her veil, "what is mine is yours and yours is mine. Let me share in your grief? If only to help ease the burden. I wish I could take all your sorrows and cast them out."

He wasn't expecting the news. It was good he was already sitting; it was merciful his Adrienne delivered horror so sweetly and agony to know she had to handle it without him by her side. Why was he an awful husband? No lovely lady should have to live through such pain if her husband could not be there to suffer it with her. Emotion rushed upon him like a bubbling stream. He clapped his hand over his mouth.

Dear God he really did grow a beard, didn't he?

The woman he knew as a second mother, his dearest sister... Adrienne was imprisoned for months because of the name she bore. He gave that to her; he endangered all of his children with it. Was it hubris that cast him so close to the sun?

"I think I am only alive," Adrienne said, folding her arms around his chest, "because God knows your name. And the young boy that ran off to America, that made that name so famous, to love or to hate throughout France – that name I took? It saved my head from the scaffold when the name I was born with gave me *nothing*."

"I am meant to console you," he sobbed. "I'm so sorry."

She shivered as she kissed him. He tasted the salt and the soap from her face while he let himself fall back to the floor with her over him. Listening to her story of the trip it took to get Chavaniac back, of meeting with her other sisters, of whom she had to write to secure passports and discreet rides to avoid highwaymen and foreign enemies; of Georges' last words for him before he was taken away from France – teenager's words of courage and sadness for his papa; Gilbert hummed as he simply touched Adrienne. The waistline of her dress went up so high, it reminded him of the days when she would be pregnant.

This was not one of those days, else he would be finding some man to wring his hands around.

Adrienne, in all of her humility, glossed over discussions with the emperor of Austria who she merely mentioned she eventually spoke to in person. He couldn't even press for more information before she changed the subject back to him – how he was faring, what his days were like, if he needed anything, anything at all.

All he could suddenly think of was how thin *she* had become. His hands circled her waist and he searched her eyes for the unfamiliar dark circles that no makeup or powder could possibly cover. "And you came for me," he breathed.

Her expression told him that his thoughts were stupid. "You've always been my knight," she replied with the smallest of breaths.

The morning light from the high-reaching window finally stretched through the bars, casting Adrienne in a holy glow – and Gilbert was not a religious man.

"You are my star," he said. "You immaculate woman."

Gilbert was certain that no other wife in France, in all of Europe, would ever have the audacity to throw themselves into the arms of a prisoner. No sane woman would do such a thing for a man, especially not a dumb man like him. So distracted by her beauty, only the sound of her sniffling laughter snapped him out of his stupor. She pulled at the hair around his mouth.

"Your whiskers are so ridiculous," she fretted, smiling as her shoulders still rocked uncontrollably.

"They would not allow me a razor to shave," he said.

"Preposterous," she said, and rose to her feet, walking a few feet to bang on the door. Her stature was too short to look through the barred window.

Gilbert sat up, moving his chains around to help, but Loden already looked through to her.

"I cannot do that," he said, the man's French needed work.

"You truly believe I would slit my husband's throat after finally reaching him and consenting to his treatment? Monsieur, I recognize you may think my intelligence lacks as a woman, but I would imagine you must consider yourself an educated enough man to understand there is no rhyme or reason in coming all this way to murder the only thing I have left in this world."

Gilbert slapped his palm to the chair to stop himself from falling over hearing the words come out of her mouth. Who was this soldier in a dress? Had Jeanne d'Arc reemerged in front of him?

"Well," Adrienne said after a small razor and a soap bowl was surrendered to her. "I don't think we will have this privilege again, so let's get you shaved. Sit down."

"Yes, Madame," he replied, falling into the chair he was in mere minutes ago, stupefied. "Do you know how to shave?" He had never grown a beard before. Truthfully he thought he wasn't capable of it because he always removed any stubble that poked out in rough patches of red fuzz. If he were still in America, he likely wouldn't be recognized with how much of a whaler he looked instead of the rosy-cheeked nobleman they knew him as.

Adrienne tutted, her brows furrowed in concentration as she smothered the bottom of his face with soapy foam and went to work. He couldn't stop watching her. His hands wanted to keep touching to make up for the years apart. She was gentle to him. Auburn hairs floated to the floor to be brushed into the fire. There were no mirrors in the cell, but he could see the way Adrienne mapped out his jaw, and felt her fingers trail up the prominent concave of his cheekbones. Her tears had dried in glossy lines; she delicately drew the blade up his neck, following each graze with the pads of her fingers.

"I am not angry with you," he said when she set the razor down. His face felt oddly cold but Adrienne was quick to hold it between her hands.

"I'm glad," she replied. Her rogue curl nipped his cheek. He took it between his fingers, watching her upside-down from the chair.

His lip quivered but he kept it down. *I'm just scared*, he wanted to admit, but he wouldn't dare. She probably already knew – this woman so divine, so close to God she was probably omnipotent.

☆

Every evening, the fire would be lit at four, and Anastasie and Virginie were allowed to join them for a few hours until curfew was called. They shared a single bed in a room half the size of Gilbert's, but they raised no complaint, and provided their father with so much extra love, he would want for nothing for at least the rest of the night.

Although most of their belongings were taken from them, Anastasie still maintained her sewing kit, and after taking one long look at Gilbert's shoes, re-soled them as they talked of everything he had missed, everything Adrienne had missed, during their time in prison. Virginie was a curious girl, Gilbert discovered, already feeling guilty over missing the rest of her young childhood. She investigated every inch of the cell from top to bottom, back and forth, as if she were the General Von Steuben overseeing the ranks. There was a mischievous glint in her eye, one Gilbert hoped wouldn't be getting her into any trouble here. He couldn't do much from his cell, and his companions who occupied other cells within the prison *certainly* couldn't do much to prevent his baby girl from putting forth whatever plot was forming in her head.

There was a worse matter he had forgotten to mention.

Worse, knowing Adrienne's piety, that is.

He did not take mass, no one in Olmütz prison did. Yet a bell tolled from a nearby church a block away. Seeing Adrienne place herself by the sewage window to try and catch the music that escaped from the church made Gilbert's stomach churn. He sat through his girls' prayers, even bowing his head, which is as much as he had done for Christ in several years it seemed.

When the girls left for the night and the evening fire dimmed to pitiful red coals, Gilbert shuffled his way over to the bed out of habit. It wasn't comfortable, but it was warmer than nothing. He tossed the blanket down halfway, plopping his ass on the hay before he noticed Adrienne pacing around their little table, cracking her knuckles as she went.

"Come on," he said. "There's no use trying to stay up. I find a routine makes the days go by a little faster, and, well, a touch easier, I suppose."

He held his palm out to her, happy only when she took it.

"I made the right decision," she said.

Gilbert quietly worked at the gown she wore, finding the ties were not where he thought they would be. Fashion was moving too fast these days. Did she make the right decision? When he looked at her smile, *yes*, he thought, seeing her and his daughters immediately brightened his mood ten-fold. Yet when she swallowed down a gag at the smells and the rut or kept her tears from him when she thought he wasn't looking, *no*, no she shouldn't have been here; she should have been in a big, comfortable home with Aunt Tessé and her sister's family. Within the German states would have been close enough. He cursed to himself, but when he untied her dress and she stepped into his arms in her stays and rump, he lost his own argument. He clasped her tighter and shook his head.

"What is it?" she asked.

"I still haven't fully processed you being here," he replied.

Her stays fell back off her shoulders. The bumroll would make for a decent pillow. Her belly was hot under her chemise, but the cold quickly bit her feet and she hopped onto the bed. The shift of weight of an additional person made the hay crunch differently, and for some reason that Gilbert couldn't explain, the noise buried itself between his legs. His brow twitched. A hand did the brain a favor and tugged at Adrienne's sleeve.

"May I touch you?" Gilbert whined, sounding like a silly teenage boy who had never learned how to talk to a girl.

She looked to the sealed off door several paces away with a firm blush coming to her face. Of course a lady wouldn't want to be overheard by strange men, but Gilbert cared little for any of them out there – hell, let them hear him make love to his wife as they stood for hours away from their own women. He wouldn't force that upon Adrienne, though, if she chose to abstain while they suffered here.

"Quietly," she whispered, pulling him from his shoulders over her.

His chains rattled at his ankles, but he went to work on loving her with everything he had. Not wanting to hurt her, he just touched and rubbed, and kissed and kneaded, swallowing all of her soft mewling between his teeth. Gilbert only managed to last a few minutes before his strength abruptly fell away and suddenly he was the one being doted on by the softest pillow with the most comforting heartbeat he had heard in eons. She combed through his greasy hair and he traced his thumb in circles over the bony rise of her pelvis.

It was the best sleep he had in his life.

Olmütz, March 1796

"Where did you get this?" Gilbert said, keeping his voice as low as a concerned father was able while confronting Virginie over a letter from his dear friend, de Faÿ – detained elsewhere in the prison.

Virginie picked at the patch her sister had sewn onto her mended jacket, rocking back on her heels while looking her father dead in the eye. "A friend," she said.

"A friend. What friend?"

"Oh, I don't know his name," Virginie replied, continuing to rock. "He passes below our cell window every few days. An official of some sorts."

Gilbert hadn't even opened the letter yet. Shaking his head, he said, "He gave you correspondence from Monsieur de Faÿ?"

"Not out of nowhere, Papa. We exchanged some pleasantries over a week or two and I convinced him to trade some food for news."

"Anastasie, did you know of this?" Gilbert asked, glancing over to where Anastasie sat with Adrienne while she dozed.

He was hushed, naturally. He never could control his tone. Adrienne had been sleeping more each day, a fatigue that struck her like lightning just as winter was ending. Her work was piled on the table: letters Gilbert wished to write but legally could not, as well as an open book covered with tiny writing that Adrienne concentrated on for hours each day until migraines forced her to stop. Her toothpick sat by a capped pot of ink.

"I've been busy," Anastasie said, holding up a pair of slippers she was making for him after replacing the soles in his shoes one too many times. "No one can stop Nini. Even the guard who drops off our food is afraid of her biting his fingers."

"There are only so many things to do," Virginie said, crossing her arms. "I've read my novels a hundred times and playing games with her gets boring after a while. Punish me if you're not pleased with the news, Papa, but I think I did something right."

It was true: he was genuinely impressed with Virginie, but coming from his loins, if he encouraged it, her hubris would surely blossom and Adrienne would not need *two* of him causing trouble. His poor lady was moving from illness to illness, scaring him one morning with her heaving into a chamberpot until she couldn't breath.

The *news* was not what he expected.

Of France, well, who could expect anything coming from that coin-flipping, anarchic excuse for a regime? No, it was that his old companion had *already* heard what Madame Lafayette had done months ago to get where she was today. And the news had not spread from the prison like he expected, but from another ally in England. People in England were hearing what his wife had done — what she said to Emperor Francis II.

On that aspect, here in their tiny cell, she did not crack. The only thing she had admitted about the ordeal was that the Holy Roman Emperor told her to inform him of anything she may need, but from the agreement of sharing in Gilbert's confinement with her own money, she was not allowed to do such a thing. She insisted what she had said was nothing out of her character, encouraging other conversation with a tender smile, and so Gilbert was left to debate with himself which of Adrienne's characters was the one to get herself permission to even bring their daughters along.

Anastasie let some information slide. "The Austrian ministers seemed embarrassed to allow it," she had said one evening while Adrienne slept on Gilbert's lap. "You know Maman's imagination soars when she is determined, the way Mémé would disapprove, but I think for this... I think she would be proud of Maman."

The late duchesse would have indeed been proud of Adrienne, Gilbert knew that without question. And he knew her mother was always in her thoughts as well as her words, as the book margins for where she wrote were covered with the great woman's life.

Gilbert put down the letter, opening his arms for Virginie to sit upon his knee. He would talk to Adrienne about anything when she was ready. "Well, my lovelies," he said, soft enough to not disturb their mother, "I'll let my scolding wait for when it is deserved, but for now how about I recount the story of General Phillips and the oddities we Lafayettes have with artillery fire?"

He was thankful for the plethora of stories he had on hand. Some from his own luck and misfortunes and others from his friends' silly or brave antics from the war. There was never a moment he could sit in silence when a good story was needed. What was being a father for, anyways?

When the girls were sent away to their rooms, he spent a long minute watching Adrienne breathe. Her legs curled up against her chest, the blanket between them to cover one leg as she quietly complained of being too hot, yet too cold to have it either way.

Damn the chains that clicked too loudly as he walked. He stirred her from her sleep, dark eyes blinking wearily up at him while he leaned down to kiss her forehead.

"I missed the girls."

"They'll be back tomorrow," Gilbert said. He pressed his hand flat against the wall behind the bed. The moisture that collected on it smelt of mold. He wiped it on the wooden post. "How are you feeling?"

Adrienne sat up and took a deep breath. "It comes and goes in waves," she answered, holding her belly the way she did when she went through morning sickness, yet it was impossible her pain was a prerequisite for a happy occasion. "I'm sorry."

"Ah-ah. It isn't your fault. You know how I am when I become ill. I make the stupid decisions and let it grow. You resting is the most intelligent thing to do."

"But I wished to spend all the time together. I've become a nuisance."

Gilbert frowned. "Adrienne, only I am allowed to be a nuisance, understand?" She looked at him like he grew three heads. "You must have my blessing to join me in absurdity and I am afraid I shan't give it."

A tired, surprised giggle. Success.

"You are something, Monsieur Lafayette."

"It is *Mister Motier*," he said, taking her hand and, continuing in English, dared to ask, "would you dance with me, *Missus* Motier?"

"Dance?" Adrienne's mouth gaped. "Gilbert, you haven't danced in years – there's little room here, and your poor legs wouldn't allow a proper minuet. Let alone the only music we have is the wind."

He carefully pulled her up to her feet, which must have bothered her as her expression twisted slightly before settling into its well-masked calm. But Gilbert was full of ideas, and so he tucked his feet under hers until she stood upon him, happily enclosed like the moon eclipsing the sun.

"There was actually some country dancing I've seen," he exclaimed. "It is very popular in the German states with people of all classes. The waltz, they call it. They held each other like this…" He placed his hand firmly at Adrienne's back and brought hers over his shoulder before balancing her fingertips with his other hand. "It was very twirly and skirts were flying everywhere, but the music was fast. We can go slow, like this."

He swayed her back and forth, taking tiny steps in a tinier circle. Her grip tightened on his shoulder, but he held her firm to his body. The people he had studied from afar appeared to step in a turning box; he didn't know the exact footwork, but neither did his beloved, and as her cheek came to rest upon his chest, he considered himself an expert.

The night breeze whistled through the tight bars of their quaint window. Not quite the music that suited the dance. He cleared his throat. *"Little angel, I am dying each time your lips touch mine,"* he sang in a low breath. *"Your mouth to mine applying delight beyond divine. One touch and bliss I knew, to be in love with loving you."*

"You remembered," she sighed. "What a memory. Almost twenty years."

His shirt was growing wet. He happily bumped his forehead against the top of her hair, humming the tune of the poetic lullaby. They stepped in their small boxy circle, something even a man as clumsy a dancer as Gilbert could do, with no one to laugh nor whisper about him behind their fans.

Adrienne's hand slipped back down his arm. He quickly compensated for it, knowing she grew tired often from reaching to such a height. He didn't mind if they turned in early. But it was more than tiredness. Adrienne continued to slip, her knees buckled beneath her and Gilbert's heart seized the moment her head lolled back as they dropped to the floor together.

"*Mon coeur?*" he said, holding her up. Color had washed from her cheeks yet she burned like an open flame. "Adrienne, *cher*, please." What was he to do – what was he supposed to do in a cage? Hoisting her up, his muscles ached, but he laid her upon the bed and moved the hair from her burning face. "Hold on, hold on," he repeated, tripping over his chain as he slammed his shoulder into the door. "Get us the doctor!"

A man who was not Loden peered at him through the door's window, not saying a word as trepidation grew in the pit of his stomach. Being ignored only made Gilbert slam on the door harder.

"Get my wife the doctor, *now!*" he dared to scream, blasting off a stream of French curses into the Austrian's ear. He didn't ever plead for himself when the prison doctor was called to his cell to inspect his own illness. Doctor Kreutschke was mellow and kind-hearted but his supply was scarce and he spoke not a lick of French. "I instruct you to tell your wretched little nobodies in Vienna to treat captives with civility, else they can go straight to –"

"Gilbert –"

"Where they are going I cannot say in front of my wife, but I expect you know our French compliments in such a phrase –"

"*Beloved.*"

His brain rattled at the speed he turned to her.

"Don't hurt yourself when they cannot understand you anyway," Adrienne mumbled. "It's just a little fever, I'll be fine."

"I'll write the emperor myself," Gilbert said, "to get you a physician."

She hummed with a slight shake of her head. He wandered back over to her, tucking his hand around her swollen fingers.

"You know your letters never make it out there," she replied, her eyes closed, and he hated that she was right. Only because her signature was needed to pay weekly bills was any of their written work allowed to leave their humble, moldy room.

Gilbert was too tired to be angry at his uselessness. He sat at her feet and rubbed listlessly at her leg while glaring down the door and the Austrian who leered back at him.

"All will be well," she said.

He had the guards bring in Kreutschke the following morning.

All the doctor could do was give a cream to relieve the agitation of where the skin along her upper chest was flaking and some tonics to help fight the ache in her muscles. And a few days later, all that the emperor could do was to offer her aid outside of the prison.

At the cost of her not returning.

"Adrienne, you must go," Gilbert exclaimed.

"I will not."

"They can not help you here; you need their doctors. Tell him you accept his proposal."

Adrienne crossed her arms and shifted to the wall. "I will not go."

"Do not risk dying just to suffer here with me," he pleaded. Anger and panic kneaded at his heart. He sank to his knees by the bed. Their daughters were due to arrive at their cell any minute and he hoped to tell them their mother was going to Vienna for help. "Anastasie could be looked at as well, *mon coeur*, think of the fevers she slips into."

He hit a heartstring; he saw it ricochet across her face as her nose grew red.

But she still shook her head. "I won't risk exposing myself to the horrors of being separated from you. Not again. I can't do it again… Now give me a pen and paper," she said, her hand shaking and stiff.

Gilbert reluctantly gave her all she asked for. She was studious as she wrote, holding the quill delicately between rigid fingers while he held the wooden board used as a lap desk steady. He was a dog, moping at the side of his mistress. Even her hand gently laid upon his head as she finished writing their captor's king a rejection letter.

What a tender-hearted, foolish, lovely woman – to rather suffer than be cured, and in doing so, still bring him comfort. She would be the death of him.

Doctor Kreutschke visited daily to do all he could to alleviate the family of some discomfort. Virginie was told to stand straight against the wall to fight back against the stoop that was forming from sitting over tables all day; Anastasie's fingertips were carefully wrapped as they blistered and tingled when she tried to hold her needles. Gilbert took up Adrienne's usual pacing, crossing the cell in half the strides.

What the doctor could not do for them medically, he discreetly offered to do for them personally. Carrying with his kit, he handed out letters and gazettes as often as he could from Vienna; and so Adrienne's recurring bouts of illness brought the little family their own messenger to take their letters out of Olmütz for them. She didn't give herself credit for producing some luck out of her pain, no one would swap her health for communication; quite the opposite, in fact. But Gilbert took what he could get and read all he had to Adrienne as they laid together each night.

England took notice of her plight, he read, where the Parliamentary politicians were singing of his wife's virtuous sacrifice after suffering so much at the hands of Robespierre. What a dishonor it was for France and Austria to keep an *innocent* family detained in a cruel place. He read of a French general Bonaparte, who was harassing Austria's ally, Sardinia; and as his reading turned to military action, Adrienne had fallen asleep on his chest.

Olmütz, September 1797

"Happy birthday, Papa!"

Virginie held up the wrapped packet full of letters spanning his friends and allies of the prison. Her little scheme had encompassed a little too much as of late, catching the attention of a young guard who scolded her in broken French but did not confiscate the collection she had hoarded.

"You worry me sometimes," Gilbert said, taking the handkerchief that Anastasie embroidered to hold it all. "Both of you. Nay, all three of my girls are too headstrong for their own good. Thank you."

"Now everyone can get to planning a surprise for *my* birthday," Virginie said, sitting on the floor next to his feet. A pattern formed to nimbly pick at his ankle cuff, the skin around it having grown used to the constant bruising and pinching.

"We aren't to be greedy," Adrienne said. She sat at the table by her expanding biography, her nails stained black from the china ink. Every few minutes, she would shift in the seat, restless and sore.

"Well, no, I don't mean to be greedy, Maman. But Anastasie got shaved ice from a guard on her birthday."

"Nini!" Anastasie hissed. "I denied it – don't treat it like he was trying to make advances on me."

"You're probably the only young lady here, why wouldn't the soldiers be –"

Gilbert closed his eyes.

"Girls," Adrienne said. "Enough. See how you stress your father?"

The quick kisses at his cheeks came with quicker apologies. Only after was he able to enjoy the letters and sketches delivered from his friends. Bells rang distantly down the road, carried by a brisk autumn breeze, the first after a boiling summer. De Faÿ sent news from their French emigrated friends in England, sharing even more from the United States, of Washington's step down from power, the presidency shifting over to Adams, of the Lafayette family's popularity with those who were tired of the violence. It was of some relief, but to not have any direct line to his American friends, nor to hear of his son...

He glanced up at Adrienne and the dark circles that shadowed her eyes. She looked forlorn, frowning but without the need to communicate her sadness. Covering a bout of coughs with her elbow, she turned away.

The Austrian emperor was growing tired of them. As a family, Gilbert admitted, they were all stubborn and duty-bound. He pulled the same move his wife did to him – refusing a deal struck that would give immediate benefit but curse them in the long-term. As Adrienne's fevers persisted, he felt the guilt gnaw at his soul.

He came upon a little ink sketch, messy only from its medium. The detail of the faces revealed his own under the grown-back beard sitting shoulder-to-shoulder with a pretty woman who could only have been Adrienne. Gilbert looked over to Anastasie, who purposefully paid him no mind, only shifting a little pink as she sipped at her drink.

How spoiled his heart allowed him to be, with such gifts that remained with him.

Several loud clicks from the door startled all four of them. It wasn't time for the girls to go, they still had three more hours of company. Gilbert shoved the letters under hay. And as if by habit, they clutched each other like a hardened chain as Loden and two more men entered the room. Loden looked at him, his nose scrunched but his eyes soft, as he fiddled with a rolled up document in his hands. It shuffled from one palm to the other.

"Sergeant?" Gilbert said.

"A fortnight," Loden replied with a nod. He raised the unsealed paper and placed it on the table between Gilbert and Adrienne. "No oaths, no ultimatums. The Madame here agrees to fund your hospitality for the next two weeks, signs, and you and your little family will be escorted out of Austria."

Adrienne slowly pulled the document towards her, unfurled it, and read it silently to herself. Gilbert said nothing, acknowledged nothing, until she finished. He clocked the slight part of her lips, the rise in her shoulders.

"All of us – together?" she asked.

Loden relaxed onto one leg, his arm draped over the hilt of his sword. "Yes, Madame. A single carriage with an officer who will be charged with making sure all four of you take your leave of the country. The emperor has far more important business to attend to than having this prison to worry about."

Gilbert held out a hand for a pen. "Then we will sign."

Adrienne nodded.

Her signature had grown messier in the last week.

☆

"You know, I really didn't expect an honest gift this year," Virginie said as they hurriedly threw their few things into a single chest. "But to see the *actual* sky again? I'm so excited. Anastasie, are you almost done?"

"Don't rush me, Nini," her sister replied. Anastasie cleared her throat for the twentieth time that morning, helping Adrienne pin her hair up properly to place her cap on.

Gilbert clicked the trunk closed, his heart thrumming heavily. Every few seconds he glanced at his wife and how thin she became and how exhausting even speaking was. Anastasie herself was in dire need of a banquet. He glanced at his baby girl, having turned fifteen, she was looking more and more like him. But her ginger hair was longing for a true bath and her skin was wanton for sun.

To be a good father and a worthy husband, Gilbert handled as much as he was able, holding back winces as the restraints around his ankles were finally released and he had to adjust to walking without the extra weight. His family would not mock him for prancing like a dog with stockings on, but he wouldn't have blamed them if they did.

A guard took their chest and Gilbert took his wife's arm over his right while Anastasie supported her from the other side, and Virginie held onto his waist from the left.

The air felt different simply stepping out of their cell and grew lighter the closer they hobbled to the exit. Like a warming up orchestra, he and his family coughed all at once at the sudden change. There couldn't have been less air, clearly there was *more* of it, but it felt like climbing a mountain or breaking to the surface of an icy cold ocean. Bright and blinding, Gilbert felt tears run down his face as he fought to focus on the sky, overblown in white until its blue hue flooded over. He wanted to run, take his family and roll over in the grass; he wanted to sleep in a bed with feathers and eat a real meal.

The carriage was more of a wagon, lightly covered, although Virginie kept her line of sight in the strips of sunlight above them. Adrienne white-knuckled a rosary, biting back gasps every time the road became too bumpy and shifted them around like cattle in the back. Gilbert pulled her atop him, so that maybe he would be a sturdier surface for her to try and rest.

"You will be well," he whispered.

Chapter Twenty-Nine

"With you," she mumbled. "I'm better with you."

"I will write to Washington. And we will hear from our son again. And with him will come all your strength and good health once more, I promise."

Part Four

Pity the man who loves the woman with broken wings.

Chapter Thirty

Wittmoldt, Germany, November 1797

Pauline's arms were warm and welcoming and came with a thick blanket as she tumbled from the boat and up the grassy dock toward Adrienne. Her face was redder than the last autumn leaves and never stopped being so as the gentlemen worked on rowing the ex-prisoners over to the quaint farmhouse of their Aunt Tessé. Adrienne held Pauline close, her little sister cried between her words of news known and unknown; she was out of France before the reign of terror – her goodbyes weren't expected to be forever.

The water, once calm when the Lafayettes arrived at the edge of the lake, was rocking with the steady traffic. Monsieur Tessé and Monsieur Montagu were sweating buckets by the time they finished ferrying everyone across, including friends of Gilbert's that were picked up along the way on the several-day-long journey north. Coats were discarded on the lawn in favor of embracing in-laws and nieces. Madame Tessé was a madwoman on the receiving dock, jumping with delight, eyes glittering before Adrienne took one step out of the boat.

She was unlike Adrienne's parents: so cheerful and eccentric in her kindness. Tessé kissed Gilbert's cheeks a dozen times before he happily lifted her from the grass, then turned to give Pauline a similar loving treatment. He returned to Adrienne's side as soon as bags and chests were grabbed, hoisted, and ready to be brought inside.

For a house holding the two Tessés, Pauline and her little family, comprising of Joachim and a small baby boy who was introduced as Adrien (much to Adrienne's already exhausted heart), and with yet another baby *clearly* on the way, squeezing in the Lafayettes was going to be difficult. Their three companions humbly offered to find lodgings nearby. The youngest brother of de Faÿ and Anastasie got along swimmingly on their journey. Their wayward glances and the batting eyes of young de Faÿ as he listened to Anastasie's stories did not escape Adrienne's notice. Yet it was Gilbert who had loudly cleared his throat or propped his shoe up between them when the carriage ride quickly became a little too cozy.

Gilbert wanted to go to America. It was one of the first things that came out of his mouth when they left Austria. They would be welcomed there, and they would be free of the turmoil of Europe. Adrienne quietly listened to his monologue while he had flipped through newspapers; he certainly said all those things, but he had lurched his dream to a halt for her sake and she knew it. Once again, she would bring disappointment to his gloom. Yet she was too tired to even cry for herself.

A peppered stone walkway led to the farmhouse's front door. The architecture was widely Danish with steep slanted roofing and a foundation more long than it was tall. Everything was done to make it appear open and airy on the inside, with windows facing the fields adjacent – home to some cows and apple trees and a small field of freshly planted wheat. There was plenty of forest to go shooting and the lake offered fresh fish. Aunt Tessé had assured them that, together, they would make ends meet. Meals were warm and clean and fresh each day; and Adrienne would find herself regularly wrapped up in a blanket upon a chair facing the fields, watching the men work.

Gilbert was back in the dirt, calling to and fro with Joachim as they brought around the cows to the growing grass. He had his hair cut a few days into their freedom and the beard was quickly shaven off. His red hair was taking on an auburn hue, but its curls were returning to the top of his head and he suddenly looked younger than he ever had before.

"You look like Maman," Pauline said from her side. Her needlework was resting on her lap as she sat on a nearby stool. Adrienne must have glanced at her oddly, for Pauline's face softened. "Elegant and mature, I mean. I can picture her here with us because of you."

"I'm sorry," Adrienne replied. "I couldn't do anything to stop them from breaking our family apart. You and Rosalie have done so much for us. There is nothing that could ever repay your kindness."

The cool wind helped excuse the tears.

"The fact that you are alive is all I will ever need to be happy again." Pauline rested her cheek against Adrienne's shoulder. "But I should tell you about Papa's letter."

"Papa?"

"He remarried. A Russian baroness."

"Oh."

Jean de Noailles was in Switzerland. The closest of anyone to where Adrienne and Gilbert were imprisoned and yet she had heard nothing from him. She wrote to him earlier in the month in the hopes of rekindling some ounce of a relationship.

"It doesn't matter," Pauline added, quickly wiping her eyes. "Maman will always be the Duchesse d'Ayen."

"De Noailles," Adrienne corrected. The clouds were moving ever so slowly. "Mémé went before her. Maman was the Duchesse de Noailles when she entered Heaven." She kept her gaze steady on the horizon, leveling the memories with the stretch of pastures and trees.

Her little sister nodded briefly, looking down at her project as she jabbed the needle through the fabric. "Good," she said.

Their rooms were small, but not in any way that brought discomfort. Each bed was by a window that overlooked greenery or the water so there truly was no bad angle. Quaint fireplaces were constantly fed throughout the winter months, filling the room with the smell of sprightly pine. Rugs were softly woven and cleaned while the walls slowly filled with more decoration and art. Everything was being done to make the house cozy and comforting. For once they did not need to wake up earlier for obligations, nor did they need to wake up to simply get out of the bed. Adrienne kicked down the covers as her skin burned hot; the frost that crept up the window threatened to push it open and she wouldn't have minded an ice bath.

"*Chère*," Gilbert muttered into his pillow. He reached down and pulled the blanket back over the two of them, leaving his arm thrown over her belly. "You are an icicle, stop doing that."

It wasn't her that was cold, it must've been Gilbert. And if he was cold and wanted to cuddle, Adrienne supposed that sweating through the morning was worth it.

But now she was awake.

An hour of reading the bible kept at her bedside did the trick of passing time. Some words wobbled and she had to reread several passages. Nothing new; she could persevere.

It was well into the afternoon by the time their door opened and Virginie poked her nose through. *Just checking in*, she would say, and always said whenever Adrienne and Gilbert slept in too long. But whenever they decided to venture into the farmhouse's morning room, there was always tea brewing and some bread and jam on the table.

If Gilbert was not assisting in outdoor work, he hunched over a desk, forming an impressive stack of letters or reclined on the sofa reading the newspapers. Adrienne, if she had the energy, rewrote her mother's biography out of the margins of the book she kept safe in Olmütz. Luckily, she had Virginie to assist when her hands were too swollen to write, or to organize the pages to be properly printed. Anastasie helped her great-aunt host their guests – always the same guests, their main friends who came with them. Including that of Charles de Faÿ.

He was three years older than Anastasie and served as a colonel in the cavalry during the recent wars; with a slightly round face, gray eyes, and a small stutter to boot, he humbled himself whenever Anastasie spoke. She did well to sit next to him at an appropriate distance while letting Madame Tessé take control of the conversations in the salon with her boisterous energy and quirky facts she had studied over the years. De Faÿ continued to glance towards the eldest Lafayette girl, and she glanced back.

Pauline held her tongue whenever talks turned political. Adrienne knew she and her husband did not approve of Gilbert's actions during the revolution, but was thankful they said nothing of it as Gilbert stood by his beliefs – still continuing on his quest for liberty and the rights of man for France. They traded knowing stares from across the room. When Pauline didn't sit for political banter, she happily brought her nieces into her study where she showed them the patterns for dressmaking.

It was true, now that Gilbert's property was confiscated by the state, the daughters would have nothing to their name.

Adrienne thumbed through the holy book while they worked. Having her girls labor all their lives was not what she wanted for them; there must've been something she could do.

She wrote often when her hand was steady enough. And taking the received correspondence from Switzerland, her teeth clenched as she stared at the blank page she must fill to send back to her distant father.

You must've foreseen, dearest Papa, how torn my heart would be at receiving your letter. I too well know the sensibility of yours to pass judgment on it. There is no reason, Papa, for you to be fearful of reawakening memories as they are present at every moment of my life, and will be present until this life ends, she wrote, still eyeing the handwriting that followed his of his new wife. *It is by making myself one with the memories of Maman that I maintain a source of strength when all else fails me. And there is no circumstance that would bring me closer to her than in my sending you wishes of all future happiness...*

Unhappy as she was, Adrienne closed off the letter in a modest tone. She wouldn't have to show Pauline or her aunt the treatment.

☆

One day simultaneously invigorated and bolstered Adrienne's mood a thousandfold and distracted all that was painful in mind and body.

It was a temperate afternoon and the windows were opened to let a breeze circle the floor. A rattle of knuckles on the door produced startled *"oh!"s* as the little family and their guests sat in their scarcely decorated parlor in quiet studies. Frankly, it shouldn't have been so surprising to have unannounced visitors, and a slight chuckle went around the room as they waited and listened for Joachim to go and answer. Adrienne sat with her sored leg elevated over Gilbert's lap – and he read through letters, bringing them a few inches *closer* to his eyes than he used to. Every time Monsieur Tessé offered his spectacles, Gilbert gawked at him. *He wasn't yet forty-two*, he argued, *he could still see* – and proceeded to hold the letters as far as his long arm could hold them… and squinted.

Joachim returned to the doorway with no color to his cheeks; his brow produced twice as many lines. So often he'd be used to introducing who it was he greeted, but his shock caught him speechless and he merely gestured to the young man who followed behind.

Tall, lean, and delightfully baby-faced, the man's hair was a light copper, straight in its pulled back queue with a dozen curled strands along his hairline. His dress, although tailored perfectly, was of American cloth, and his hat was propped neatly under his arm. Gilbert dropped the letter he was reading.

"Forgive my delayed arrival," the young man said and Adrienne gripped the arm of the sofa. "My wandering family kept moving whenever I received word of where they settled."

"Georges," Adrienne said, rushing painfully to rise from her seat. She wished she could fly to him, stumbling into arms belonging to a much stronger boy. Georges was in front of her. He was the mirror-image of his father as an experienced eighteen-year-old. The depth and timber to his voice was almost unrecognizable and made his tearful laughter all the more bittersweet.

"I've missed you, Maman." Georges let her smother his face in kisses, her hands squeezed his cheeks until his small mouth puckered into an embarrassed smile. Glassy eyes wandered up to where Gilbert rose unsteadily to his feet. The room was crossed in two steps before Adrienne felt the crushing sandwich of her husband coming to embrace him. "Papa –" Georges broke as Gilbert kissed his cheeks as well, his hand firmly on his son's shoulder.

"How you've grown," Gilbert whispered, shocked that he could look upon Georges without lowering his head.

"It's the food in Virginia, Pa," Georges replied and suddenly broke into wonderful English, "Mister Washington said there's something in the dirt that advances the speed of growth."

Gilbert laughed. "Oh, did he?"

"There's so much to tell you. I have exuberant amounts of letters and news, of the places I've stayed, of your dear friends who welcomed me. But where are my sisters? Please, I've missed them."

Virginie crashed through the pile without delay, her determination bringing her right into the crook of his free underarm. Anastasie politely waited until her Papa moved away for her to take her turn in hugging her little brother. *Goodness, they were all so tall,* Adrienne thought, feeling like the child among them. It took little prompting to get him to begin the tale of his adventure – from he and Frestel remaining in the north for some time, lodging with Colonel Hamilton and his very large family while he attended school; of the joking manner in which Hamilton delayed sending Georges down to Virginia until it was proper to do so; of how Washington was in such vivid detail. His story as well as the letters he produced enraptured his audience.

Mister Frestal has been a true Mentor to Georges. No Parent could have been more attentive to a favorite Son; and he richly merits all that can be said of his virtues – of his good sense – and of his prudence. Both your son and him carry with them the vows, and regrets of this family, and of all who know them... Washington wrote to Gilbert, and Adrienne fondly looked up at the tutor who tiredly stood with a cup of coffee behind the reunion. Félix had sacrificed more than Adrienne could ask of him. And she opened her arm to take his hand, bringing it kindly to her temple.

☆

Days rolled on like passing spring showers, and after every good meal and warm bath, Adrienne felt fine enough to walk through the house unaided, and Gilbert was gaining back some muscle he had lost over the stalemated years. The orchard bloomed flowers faster than the sun warmed the earth and one early afternoon in March, the mixed families found themselves basking amongst the buds in the fields, nursing water and potato bread, dealing with a filial argument between Pauline and Joachim about names for their baby that was due in two months time. It never grew aggressive, and Madame Tessé continued to lead the way towards topics she knew everyone would like, whether or not she realized she was doing it.

Charles de Faÿ carefully stood up from the grass, his glass of water vibrating between his fingers. Several pairs of eyes followed his movement from the rocking back and forth to the slow approach to his words as he looked at Gilbert and Adrienne. "I b-beg your pardon for interrupting our repose, but I have an important question to ask of you that I c-cannot hold in any longer."

"To ask us?" Adrienne said, slowly tilting her head towards Anastasie – who sat up straighter against Georges' side to listen.

"Monsieur, you know my brother very well, and I pray he spoke kindly of me before we made our formal acquaintance. You know I d-do not have much to offer in terms of money, my income is nary over thirty-thousand francs, but I have certainty that I love your daughter with all my soul, Monsieur, Madame. She is my b-better half in all things and I pray ask you to allow her to take me as her husband," exclaimed de Faÿ, dipping his head low so that they could not see the blush upon his cheeks as Anastasie climbed to her feet. Georges and Virginie exchanged wide-eyed glances.

Gilbert was silent.

"Oh dearest," Aunt Tessé said, throwing her knuckles to her forehead. "Only the insane get married without any money to support them!" With her fan she reached back and smacked Gilbert's shoulder thrice.

"Then I am a madman," de Faÿ replied. He sheepishly took Anastasie's hand.

Adrienne went white-lipped with how hard she suppressed a smile. Gilbert's nose flared as she turned to him. He looked angry, but his bottom lip quivered despite himself. She leaned over and pressed her lips to his other shoulder. "Gilbert," she whispered.

"That's my sweetling, you know," he said, his tone rising.

"Yes, Monsieur," de Faÿ replied.

"Papa," Anastasie pleaded. Her second hand clasped de Faÿ's arm. She was level-headed to his height and yet leaned against him.

Gilbert got to his feet, sucking in all the air he could manage to get as he crossed the grass to shake the young man's hand. "You have my blessing should Anastasie *confirm* to me this is what she wants."

Anastasie's laughter bubbled up. "Y-yes, Papa, yes, this is all I'll ever ask for. Charlie is a good boy, I promise. And Maman, he is a Christian."

Adrienne smirked. "Of course, *chère*," she said with a nod.

Virginie shrieked, leaping from the flowers with all the enthusiasm of a cricket. It was completely unladylike, but no one could care as sisters embraced and bounced and kissed their newest family addition right on the mouth. Georges applauded, a mix of French and English compliments from his tongue.

"Oh no, oh dear," Aunt Tessé said with a slow shake of her head, collecting wildflowers into a small bouquet. "Not a new baby *and* a joyous wedding to look forward to. What are we poor folk to do?"

Adrienne received Anastasie with open arms, pushing her dark curls from her face to properly kiss her cheeks. Gilbert stood where he had stepped back to witness the whole affair, his hands firmly on his hips. He was not crying, it was that rain simply had fallen right where he was and dampened his eyes.

"Damn," he said, watching Anastasie loop her arm around de Faÿ publicly for the first time. He cocked his head at Adrienne, his nose sufficiently red. "I feel like suddenly I have aged a decade in the last five minutes."

"You don't look a day over twenty-three to me," Adrienne smiled. She held her hands up for him to take. The sunshine hid any aging and wrinkles from his face – he truly did look like his young, knightly self.

"My princess, you are too kind to me. We promised not to lie to each other."

"As if I would ever think of breaking that promise."

"God," he said, planting his feet in the field while the family ran to grab wine from the small cellar to celebrate. He tucked his nose down into the crook of Adrienne's neck. "I do not think I ever contemplated that our children growing up meant that they were actually growing up. I thought we would have more time with them." Quiet for a moment, they oscillated between holding each other aloft. "I don't have regrets for what I have fought for," Gilbert said. "We've just had a bout of bad luck, that's all, but the sky is clearing for us."

"I know."

"I would do it again if I had to – if liberty was at stake, save for the pains of separation or putting you through our Austrian Bastille or sending Georges far from us again. Are you well, *mon coeur?* You're shaking."

Adrienne held his head to her neck, his voice tickled her skin. "Tired, but happy. Happy we did what we set out to do. And this may not be Chavaniac or Paris, but look – look at the young women we've raised. Our girl gets to marry for love, no contracts or deals required. That's what we wanted for them, isn't it?"

"The marital pool is full of bad choices anyway," Gilbert mumbled, nuzzling impossibly closer. "Look at what you got stuck with."

"Ah, yes, a wayward, courageous man who adores his family and his country. Clearly our guardians scraped the bottom of the pool for you."

"I should probably interview de Faÿ further. Make sure he's prepared for what kind of family he's entering into. Yes, I know he's been with us for some months now, but he has no idea the bizarre nature that tends to follow us year after year. Whenever I read letters from friends saying they have very little going on in their lives, I truly wonder if they are lying to me or if that is really possible to achieve."

Adrienne kissed his temple. "Don't scare him off, General. He's a fine boy and I will defend him with all my might. I also want to write to your aunt about all the lovely news that awaits her."

Gilbert straightened to his six foot stature and looked around at the miles of meadows and farms. "Me? Scare him off? *Mon coeur,* he has nowhere else to go."

Vianen, Batavian Republic, August 1798

De Faÿ – or Charles, rather – exchanged his bachelorhood for the hand of Anastasie that May in the Wittmoldt farmhouse's parlor. It was modest and tenderhearted and left the entire family weeping as Charles officially joined the family and Anastasie added de Faÿ de La Tour-Maubourg to her already lengthy signature.

He was now bound to them as Gilbert finally made arrangements to get a house in Holland. The extended family came with them on the journey for good luck and good company. Gilbert wasn't allowed in France: his name was still registered as an emigrant and the government, even under the rising fame of Bonaparte, was not keen on allowing people of the old regime back into the country just yet. The ride from northern Germany to Holland was agonizing to Adrienne's joints; she couldn't sit inside the carriage for longer than a few hours at a time.

The house had a lovely dining room, but otherwise lacked everything the family was used to. Adrienne was surprised they managed to lease it. She was shown the ground floor bedroom, which she made her own; having Gilbert constantly needing to help her was making her anxious.

"Knock, knock," a voice known to all entered not long after they had settled. The arrival of Rosalie united the rest of all that remained of the Noailles sisters. Somehow with even more people to receive into a smaller space than before, they managed. It was almost comical.

"Auntie Di" arrived as well – the Madame de Simiane had been exchanging letters with Gilbert since his release. It was remarkable she was still alive and Adrienne embraced her without any hint of awkward air. She was still a friend to Gilbert and a kind woman to her. Adélaïde's questions about Adrienne's health poured out as evidence of Gilbert's correspondence topics. Whatever Adrienne needed, if her husband or daughters were rarely not at her side, Adélaïde would find it amongst the many chests that the combined family still had to unpack.

That was one thing that Adrienne was not in a rush to do: become comfortable in Holland. Not that there was anything wrong with the current republic, but she knew Gilbert preferred America despite letters from his American brother Hamilton that moving now was not a sound idea, and she knew that while his lands and homes were taken from them, *hers* still had a chance.

Many things in the late duchesse's will would have been passed onto Louise in the event of her passing. The Noailles women were not emigrants and could not be considered traitors despite their unlawful executions. What was supposed to be Louise's would instead be Adrienne's as the next in line. And Adrienne left France under legal means: she had her passport and a visa.

The sores in her legs were what originally stopped her. Weeks when she could not walk were agonizing and embarrassing when her children carried her, but through it all she held her tongue. With her sisters by her side, the world was set a little more right and the pain was tolerable as long as they spoke and prayed together. In their quiet hours, Pauline continued to write and Rosalie sewed small clothes for her baby and it all painted itself as a beautifully nostalgic picture as Adrienne silently watched them from her chaise. Their infant children played with Virginie, acting as a suitable young governess despite being unable to teach them how to do much of anything but crawl or shake their rattles for proper attention.

Gilbert, in a way, carried on his socializing business, inviting guests over as if they were not scrambling for supplies. Adrienne gritted pained teeth as they welcomed more and more people to their humble home, distracted by the polite laughter at the incredulous state so many past aristocrats were enduring, sliding a joke or two in on her account as if she did not want to throw herself in an ice bath with how much her body was hurting.

He spoke of America so fondly, so full of anticipation – the idea that he could possibly go before the rest of the family to prepare the way made her nauseous. Adrienne was beginning to understand, with how often her symptoms returned to her, that she would *not* make the voyage. Gilbert was still holding on to hope; she couldn't ruin that for him. Georges fueled the fire with his stories and although Adrienne loved him perfectly, she found herself staring at an acknowledging Charles, who did his best to overcome his shyness and change the subject.

Of their guests, Gouverneur Morris took a last stop before his official return to the golden United States. Pleased to stand despite his invalidity, he told Gilbert of his desire to resign himself from the XYZ affair that was causing so much trouble between America and France. It was because of this that Gilbert was constantly being written not to attempt to cross over the Atlantic. Adrienne, once again, didn't mean to eavesdrop; she was simply in the other room and the neighboring windows were open.

"I would take a hot air balloon over if I could," he said to Morris, and there was a lapse of time that could only have been taken up by Gilbert's pacing. "Washington, Hamilton, Jefferson, they all advised me to stay, but if I arrived on American shores, I could attain what was owed to me for my services – I was offered land, offered repayment for some of my personal expenditures during the war. I didn't accept it at the time, but of course I wasn't in need of it. Mister Morris, you know I *must* provide for my family."

"It is a difficult experience for any man to go through," Morris replied. He sounded stationary, as if he was just watching Gilbert walk in circles around him.

"Naturally my wife's health lends her to remain here until she is fully recovered. And knowing my daughters – neither would wish to leave her until that time. I don't want to separate us again, but Georges and I could start the way, make it all comfortable for the ladies' arrival. I could find doctors in Virginia, I'm sure. Washington would have suggestions. American medicine isn't nearly as progressive though, but, ah, *maybe* I could bring a doctor along with his supplies. When my Adrienne is well… if… if she recovers enough. Dear God, Mister Morris, what is your opinion? Pray tell what you think I should do."

"Well," Morris said, and Adrienne imagined his tilt of the head and spin of his cane upon the floor. "It sounds to me, Lafayette, that you already know what you should do."

For once, Gilbert was silent. Adrienne held her ear towards the window, the letter in her lap. She didn't regret going to him in Austria nor any of the hardships endured in the prison; thinking if she went to America when he told her to, he could have very easily died in that cell. Then what would have been the point? No, things happened for a reason, she thought, she couldn't blame her own maladies on keeping Gilbert tied to Europe.

She did, of course, blame herself.

But the letter she had in her lap was from an old servant in Paris, one who professed great love to the Madame de Lafayette, one who offered their house in the city close-by to the *Directoire* for her to stake her claim to her family's property.

☆

Gilbert glowered at her luggage. His weight rocked from one foot to the other while Virginie packed the final pieces. Adrienne kept herself up on her own, politely defying his worry that he spent the last thirty minutes expressing. Arms crossed and tongue dry, all he managed was a continuous shake of his head until Anastasie handed him a glass of water.

"I don't like this idea," he repeated. Charles drove the small carriage up to the house, waving at Adrienne through the window. "While it is reassuring that you'll have company, I don't agree with you risking your frail constitution for such a trip."

"It is necessary, Gilbert. I have to try," she said yet again.

"Ten days is a long time in your condition; and that's if the roads to Paris are intact."

"I've been well enough this week and ten days is shorter than what we are used to."

He followed her down the hall, his hand hovering beneath her elbow. "What if I forbid it?"

Adrienne stepped aside for Charles and the girls to heave the trunks outside. Georges swayed in-between, his frown just as upsetting.

"You won't," she said, tucking Gilbert's cravat back down into his waistcoat. "The sooner I do this, the sooner you and Georges will be able to return to France. I only wish I could have gone earlier, but the fair weather will help, I'm sure of it."

"I don't like being alone," he argued.

"Do not insult your son," Adrienne replied, tugging on a button. "And you have Adélaïde to keep you company at least."

He flushed immediately, but quieted himself.

Georges held the door for her. "Let me escort you to the border at least, Maman?"

"The less the display, the better. Just take care of your father, now, would you? He needs regular walks and plenty of conversation. Also he's been breaking candle wicks, so if you could charge yourself with lighting the house, you would be quite the gentleman."

Gilbert huffed behind them, but Georges merely bit back a chuckle and nodded his agreement. "And my brother will take good care of you, isn't that right, Charlie?"

Charles blinked. "Yes! B-by God, I wouldn't let anything happen to our women."

"Good," Gilbert said. He lifted Adrienne up into the carriage, his frown ever deepening. Less of anger, and more of dejection. His attention wandered to the tied in luggage and their daughters inside. "You have everything?"

"Short of you, yes."

"And you will write me every day? I'd like a full account of how you are and what you have done, what thoughts crossed your mind – leave nothing out."

She bent down and kissed his nose. "I will."

"And have Monsieur Beauchet or his wife write me as well when you get there."

"Yes, yes."

"And be convincing when you deal with those intransigent rascals –"

"Gilbert. I can do this, but you have to let go of my waist first."

"I know," he said. "I know you can."

As hard as it was to convince the two Lafayette boys to sit back, the carriage went underway. Stretching some miles, getting out of Holland was a two day trip. A drizzle of summer rain cooled the road and lulled the passengers into short naps when convenient.

But the simple trip could never just be simple. Anastasie woke up the second morning vomiting more than the previous day, much to her embarrassment. It was easy to forgive her for the inconvenience of being in the early stages of pregnancy. She would be sent back – as would Charles. The de Faÿ name was still on the list of emigrants as well and despite Charles' promise, which he indeed kept for the time he was with them, there was no arguing against Adrienne. And she set off to Paris with only Virginie by her side.

Paris, October 1798

Gardens with hundreds of autumn flowers blossomed and lit up the gray city in magnificent color and grandeur. They were new to the streets, growing in several popular locations where the citizens of Paris roamed in their high-waisted gowns and short-cut coats. It was evident they were taken care of by a doting gardener and were a potentially lovely promenade route…

If the grounds they budded from were not the sites of the guillotine, where blood made up more of the groundwater than rain did.

Adrienne didn't touch a single stem as she marched through the circuit where her mother, Louise, and her grandmother were executed. It was like she could still smell it – the thick iron and bile that lined each crack in the stone ground. Where the rows of friends and family walked up to the scaffold was now covered in traffic of creaking wagons and wobbling carts. She could see Louise there, looking back at her with the slight tilt of her face, the pity of her smile. The Directoire did a fine job in trying to cover their past with a new name and a new look. No one would think on their visit to the grand capital that it was the city who longed to bring tens of thousands of innocents to slaughter.

Clearly Adrienne was *not* thinking that as her hold on Virginie's arm tightened. They were just two ladies on their walk towards the government building for the third time that week. The bronze of her robe took on the mood of the dying leaves above them. Talking to those who made up the Directoire felt like talking to a mass of unlicked cubs. Presenting her case overall brought them to attention, but now it was time to get down to the details.

Outside of removing her family's names from the list of exiled: she wanted her mother's estates, priority one. There were several scattered around France, but her eyes were set on the one closest to Paris. She wanted compensation for Cayenne's plantation and perhaps news on what was being done with it – praying that the people there were not separated or treated unkindly. Any mention of money that the Directoire needed to write out brought the politicians' faces into a foul grimace, but Adrienne continued, nevertheless. The properties in Brittany, she would need those too, as some income was dastardly desired to cover their debts and future expenses.

She – politely – despised every regime leader she spoke to. They were a slimy lot of men and their arrogance reflected in the strange façade of the city. Yet here she was, patient as ever, nodding along to their excuses before she laid down her argument again and again. If they wanted to use the excuse of needing paperwork to bide time, she had it on hand: receipts, lineage documents, ownership deeds and more.

Oh, and Chavaniac? She would like that back too.

If she wasn't playing lawyer against the Directoire, her dear hosts invited her to reminiscent private salons of the old elegance she was so used to and terribly fond of. Virginie took dance lessons, looking like her unfortunate father in his youth and returned back red in the face and wishing to change the clothes she was wearing. But the girls her age were walking around with gowns so sheer, their genitals were on full display, and no self-respecting Lafayette would be seen in such a state if Adrienne could help it.

Days confined to bed still brought her to write. Gilbert was testing her patience with his constant demands; his stir-craze was bleeding into his words and Adrienne for once did not have the restraint to sugar-coat her response.

Your orders to me are unnecessary as I am doing all I can to procure the nullification of your expulsion. Politicians are not generals, they do not work at the rapidity to which you desire... Despite my countenance, I am at their offices almost daily to expedite the process. Forgive me if my letters of update are agitating your suffering.

He'd reply in an instant.

I regret, mon coeur, for having quite unwillingly caused you pain; you've judged wrong in thinking your correspondence to me has caused anything but immense satisfaction. It would be very unjust if you were to think I was not counting upon the exact plan you had unfolded with me before your trip, but it was so vague then and I worry for illusionary prospects both you and myself may have divulged in. It is my greatest pleasure to admit that I was wrong and that you – as always – have been in the right. Imagine my distress to think of the anxiety and pain I have caused you.

She got Chavaniac. She lost all of Cayenne. Things were going so slow to the extremity that the officials of the Directoire were addressing, quite literally, one thing at a time, but she *did* make a grown man cry by showing up every day for two weeks in a row during November while she planned a trip to Chavaniac to see Aunt Charlotte. It was the little things.

Mass was held privately in the home. Apparently the only god allowed in Paris was the government, and so the churches were dormant of worship and prayer.

In keeping with her busy schedule, her fevers had no time to settle. Virginie summed it up quite well, albeit being scolded about it, that Adrienne must have expelled her pain onto the fainting, invalid fools who held their speaking sticks like a prostitute would a phallus.

Behind closed doors, she chuckled at the impropriety, but in the public eye, she and her young daughter kept up all the grandeur and poise a filial woman could summon.

They spent the beginning of winter in Chavaniac where they found

Aunt Charlotte had not changed in the past few years, like a portrait of her time; she was graceful as ever, and eloquent despite her pinpricked memory. The château had very few items that were saved, salvaged, or sought for. It was friends or dear servants that managed to hide pieces away from authority eyes at their own risk. Somehow she found herself looking back up at the figure of General Washington. Framed in her hand was the delicate letter he wrote to Anastasie a lifetime ago.

Now that little correspondent was due for a baby in the upcoming months.

Pinching her lips into a small circle, she blew out a long breath.

It was different to be the one away from the family – not in a prison, but actively in her own war. Planning and executing attacks, negotiating and making deals with the enemy, all she was missing was a uniform. She could don her own pink sash about her waist, use her walking stick as a sword, stare at every man in the eye and make her demands. Fighting for the liberty of her husband and of her family wasn't so different from the cause that Gilbert fought for.

There were, at times during her deliberations with the Directoire, where she gathered the best sympathy. Its president was of the kinder, dumb sort, merely a man contained in the country's current predicament of pushing for the *equal mediocrity* of its citizens while facing royalists on one side and Jacobins on the other. To save sorting out the affairs of her mother's estates until after she returned from assisting in her daughter's birthbed, the president agreed that she could have free access to the country in her travels, and that, while the Directoire was unable to allow Gilbert and his emigrée allies in, he could be tolerated in Holland.

☆

The surviving twin baby, Célestine Louise Henriette de Faÿ, was born that early spring, a dark-haired, dark-eyed and healthy infant who rather softly laughed than cried upon arriving. The crying was reserved for everyone else.

Adrienne doted upon Célestine while she went through correspondence with her French creditors, the fatigue returning by late afternoon every day.

"Did you know they consider you dead, Pauline?" she asked herself, unfolding another letter with one hand. "Your husband and dear cousin Louis are making this very difficult. No, actually, *all* our boys are making some sort of trouble."

Gilbert and Georges were on a *new* old path of desiring to fight for France against more enemies as news of her wars in Egypt brought Turkish and Russian foes into the fold. Specifically to defend France, not the government – that detail was left out of Gilbert's extensive arguments for why he supported countrymen who did not particularly like him back.

"Me too, *chère* Maman?"

She glanced up at Charles, who poured her drink, and smiled.

"Of course not, Charlie, you do well in your domesticity," she said, handing him his daughter as she cooed at his voice. Charles cradled her, well-practiced, and did not stutter once as he provided the babe with heavenly compliments. "If you would help me persuade Georges to take a smaller role in, perhaps, the Dutch military, you would be ever closer to my heart."

"I will try my best. He blames his American sabbatical for making him itch for action."

"Action with the family is certainly well enough. Tell him to retrieve some eggs from the henhouse for Madame Grammont to prepare. That should expend some action-wanton energy."

Charles masked a snort and pecked her cheek before he left the room. Adrienne hummed to herself, her desk overtaken with paperwork. A loan for Adélaïde was approved; that wasn't something Gilbert needed to know Adrienne was doing for his mistress. She had too much work to do in planning her next Parisian trip in securing the diamond amongst her ambitions.

Paris, May 1799

When Georges came with her to Paris to deal with matters of his passport, he was in for quite the surprise as it was deemed obvious that every person in the city was ready for another revolution. He hovered by Adrienne's arm like a bodyguard, but Adrienne was not concerned with the people succumbing to enough madness to hurt any woman and child on the street. She carried on with Virginie and Rosalie, leaving Monsieur Grammont to flank their other side.

Swallowing her coughs, Adrienne readily pushed through the directors as they sweated with worry about the encroaching angry people. *Take it*, they told her, presenting her with the approval of the late Henriette d'Aguesseau de Noailles' property to be divided amongst the remaining sisters as Adrienne saw fit. The pink that rose to her face was indiscernible if from joy or the choking feeling that was gathering in her throat.

She didn't even have time to share the news with Gilbert before a letter from him arrived – which for timing's sake must have been sent out a few days after she left.

My dearest Adrienne, I am back in this sad and lonely state. While I cannot say it is worse than our separation of last year, there is more than enough of it to cause me immense suffering. Often I can hold my impatience to see you until our reunion draws closer, but it has attacked me sooner than usual...

He spoke of casual news given to him of the peasants' betterment of France that, at least, came out of such a violent revolution; and of the weasel that ate the poor mother bird and her eggs that he had preoccupied his boredom in watching. One brought joy, the other melancholia.

My heart is with you, longs for you, preaches to you, and loves you very tenderly.

Adrienne's ego swelled. She pictured his face as she knew it well while she wrote of her recent achievement. The Grange-Bléneau was theirs.

Next was to push for Georges' passport before she could safely send him back to his father. Though safe was used lightly. The growing anxiety of Holland being invaded by France's new enemies swiftly returned the migraine that she tried so hard to get rid of. Gilbert needed to return to France, if not for his own safety, then for her peace of mind. Enemies of France were the ones who held him in captivity, many of whom would kill him if given the chance. And even as the dozenth government of

France crumbled beneath the weight of its own consequences, Adrienne would march herself on those tumbling stones to speak with those who could bring him home.

It is two years, mon coeur, since we left the prison to which you came, bringing to me consolation and life itself. If only, after my two years of exile and five in captivity, I could offer you much needed assurance of our being together forever in some peaceful place of retirement.

Gilbert's hand gently curled in her name, as if tenderly caressed. She kissed his letters. She could do it. She could bring him to their forever.

Chapter Thirty-One

Paris, November 1799

"Please, allow me to serve you another cup. I insist," Adélaïde said, rising from her sofa to pour more hot water into Adrienne's tea. "Virginie, would you like more as well?"

"Oh, thank you, Auntie," Virginie nodded, holding hers in the air.

The two Lafayette women were at an impasse for the winter. La Grange was far from being residential, even after Adrienne squandered the château of its rubbish and debris and spent weeks in her properties in Brittany painfully asking for rent money from the inhabitants. It went against every fiber of her being, taking from peasant folk, nauseating really. But she also did not want to take up another winter in the warm bed of her Parisian hosts while they slept in the cold garret. Everything was a lose-lose situation. Adrienne managed to rent a small room outside of the city, close enough she could still manage to walk in on foot, but far enough that her leg was sufficiently purple by the time she returned home.

Madame de Simiane's current residence was a reprieve for the little time they spent there at the end of day. She had left Gilbert in Holland with the news that he was as mopey as ever. Somehow she still looked young, with fawn colored hair that glowed in candlelight and a dewy complexion that even Virginie envied.

But Virginie was growing pretty in her own way – her posture had improved through her vigorously practiced dancing lessons. Although in the sense that she was still Gilbert's daughter, everything she did was dramatic and theatrical; her manners and looks were masculine in the daintiest of meanings. Despite the lovely gowns she wore, Adrienne was sure if Virginie were born a male, she would be all the same.

Adrienne's young daughter was also growing incredibly moody with every passing day. An apology would follow suit, and so Adrienne overlooked the self-aware, agitated grumbling of a tired teenage girl. Virginie had already done so much for her, the poor seventeen-year-old worked harder than any woman Adrienne knew.

"Madame?"

Adrienne looked back up at Adélaïde. "Pardon?"

Adélaïde smiled. "I wished to thank you," she said. "For the money. I said nothing of it to Gilbert as you asked, of course, but he should know of your kindness. But then again, he already knows of that."

"It is only proper to tend to those we hold dear," Adrienne replied. "I hope it is enough to put down a payment on your home?"

"Worry not, Madame, I will strive to persevere." She stopped, and looking towards the fireplace, her lips pursed most curiously. "Would you tell me, in greater detail, of your meeting with General Bonaparte from last month? I don't think I know a Catholic woman who would simply go straight to the highest authority instead of asking others to, well, *intercede* for her."

Virginie sat back in her seat. "He is about as tall as I, with the face of a scholar, not a military man. I found him a little unusual; I remember having to squeeze through the door to his office, right Maman?"

It was true. Entering into the building felt like walking into a puzzle. Soldiers and aides-de-camp closed each door behind them, suspicious towards the short woman allowed to speak directly to their leader. Adrienne had only Gilbert's opinions of the man to create an expectation on what the Major-General was like, but she knew that *"Napoleon"* –

as the people called him – was quickly rising in power. How odd, she thought, that the existence of a lucky star was brought up when speaking to Bonaparte's subordinates.

A man of average height and pallid color, he stood looking down at his desk full of maps and chess pieces. The king piece twiddled between his fingers, and upon seeing Adrienne arrive, it was placed centrally in Paris.

"Ah, Madame Lafayette," he had said. His voice was soft, spoken through a quaint smile, but was plain and held no emotion.

"General Bonaparte," Adrienne replied. She let the silence waver before she added, "thank you for agreeing to my interview today."

"Yes, it isn't every day I have the pleasure to meet with a lady of your caliber."

"Nor I, a man of your influence. I must say that my family and all the people who were imprisoned at Olmütz are forever grateful to you for assuring our freedom from Austria," she exclaimed.

"Yes, of course," Bonaparte said. "There was an opportunity to harass France's enemies and so it was only *logical* to take it. I am happy to see that you have recovered enough to travel; I had word that you and your family were quite ill upon the release."

"Recovered enough is well-said," Adrienne replied. "But in truth, while we are free from Austria and from prison, much of my family have not regained the liberty that was promised to all Frenchmen with the Rights of Man that my husband worked very diligently to compose." She held up the early rough drafts of the legislation that founded the basis of a republican France, saved by the American consulate from Monsieur Jefferson's desk.

General Bonaparte slightly cocked his head, eyeing the papers. "Yes," he said, "your husband's life is bound to the preservation of France's republic."

"He was given permission for his stay in Holland, but the Directoire has not sanctioned his return to France. His name as well as other members of my family are on a boorish list penned by an old political party that no longer suits the ideals of the France of today and surely not of your ideals for the France of tomorrow."

His smile tightened as the glow from the room's fireplace glittered in the dark of his eyes.

Adrienne blinked out of the memory of playing coy with the man. He very much did not give the impression that he expected anything bold out of a woman. She told Gilbert to write to the man, something short, something formal, something that wouldn't state his purpose in France, but to thank Bonaparte for his release. He did so, begrudgingly.

Balancing the desire to never again touch public affairs, but the want to be asked to help maintain the liberty of France took up the rest of Gilbert's letter to her.

I am completely satisfied with what you do, with what you say, and evermore still with what you are. I can read your heart, my love, my darling Adrienne, and mine only echoes your good and affectionate movements. How impatient I am beyond words to see you again...

Adélaïde crossed her ankles, her chin balanced between two fingers. "It is so arduous to convince people how much of a sweetheart our dear country boy is."

"We did manage to secure passage for Charles and his brother, so at least Anastasie can come back. And Georges should be clear to return as well, but refuses to come until Papa is able to," Virginie said. "Which is for the best, maybe. Papa wouldn't do well alone."

Adrienne twisted the tea in her lap. Skin around her nails was peeling, a mere fraction of how her arms were in the past month. Her mind skimmed through the interview day, of the people she saw and the notes she passed on. Everyone appeared on edge, suspicious of each other and extraordinarily wary of anyone who approached their young Citizen-General.

Something was in the works. And so, before she had left the city that day, she made a stop at the office of one who shared a painting with her husband: dear pragmatic Talleyrand.

Chapter Thirty-One

She was still in Paris when the *coup d'état* took off.

How curious it was to witness the mass of energy that overtook the city as Bonaparte's people overcame the Directoire; how busy, how chaotic everyone became as the old proclamations read a decade earlier were repeated by Napoleon: words that they heard General Lafayette say himself. *How similar these two men of liberty were,* said people in the streets.

Adrienne slipped into another office, a passport in hand. It bore a name, some benign information, and a signature of an official. What name? Something unassuming. Which official? It didn't matter – the government was amuck, any signature would do, even that of a copy. And that copy was given to an old aide of Gilbert, and that aide rode fast from the city, north into Holland, and delivered it alongside news of the rise of the *First Consulate.*

Gilbert was en route to France within hours of receiving word.

Discreet, hiding in the city, he met with allies and wrote another letter to Bonaparte. For Adrienne, her leg aching, all she wanted was to go to her husband and fall in his arms. France was brighter with him inside the borders, a founder of its liberty restored to his home.

General Bonaparte, in receiving the letter and hearing word from his intimate friends, was characteristically unhappy. The king stood on the board two spaces away from the knight who could not risk a move; and so in the next turn, Adrienne shimmied her piece right between them.

"General," she said again, standing in his new office in Paris' extravagant buildings. Her palm dryly clung to the cane centered in front of her.

Bonaparte looked the part of a man who just conquered France in under a week. His hat moved from his hand to the table, not yet reorganized with the induction of a new regime.

"Madame," he replied with a nod of his head. "Perhaps when Monsieur Talleyrand made his comment about your husband, I should have realized he meant it sincerely. You see, it is always a guessing game with that one. How unfortunate it was to learn that General Lafayette had been smuggled into France without permission, without thinking of ramifications. Madame, it puts me into an odd predicament in trying to reestablish this Republic's founding principles."

"Principles that my husband shares with you, it seems."

Bonaparte chided softly. "I do not expect you to understand, Madame, but your husband certainly would. He is no longer at the center of things happening in France; the time away has distanced himself from the people and their hearts and minds. He will admit that I am in the better position to cast correct judgment here," he said, gesturing to the zenith of government around them.

"So he will," Adrienne replied. She cocked her head. He seemed anxious. "Am I too bold to assume that you will not send *his own* National Guard to take him in, General?"

"It would cause unneeded commotion for his face or simply his name to spread about Paris overnight. No," he said, shaking his head an inch. His eyes darkened as he raised his chin to her. "No, it is not a bold assumption. He may remain in France, but I beg him, upon my kindness, that he avoid anything of public nature. I rely upon his patriotism and love for this country that he obliges me."

She kept her pride down in her gut. "Thank you, General. I assure you that a private life is all he desires." Her gaze shifted towards the decoration of the room, of the colors chosen by Lafayette and the formed Guard, drapes dancing in blues and reds. Busts of men she knew very well still remained on fireplace mantles. "Would you agree, Monsieur, that if the honest republican people of Paris heard of Lafayette's return with your favor, that you would be held in a higher esteem?"

"I am charmed at seeing you again, Madame Lafayette. You are a very intelligent woman, but forgive me when I say you know nothing of politics."

Adrienne replied coolly, "I merely saw an opportunity to bring him home to the country he loves, General. It was only *logical* for me to take it."

Bonaparte was silent, wavering. His hand shifted to rest between buttons of his coat. "To bring him to a nation that would love him today," he murmured. "Tell me how I would be assured that, should a power shift occur, the name of Lafayette would not rival my own? Like presenting the late queen of Scots to the Elizabethan English court."

"Mary Stuart was actively trying to restore her right to the throne," Adrienne replied. "My husband acquiesces to a quiet life. And as his wife, it is all I want for him as well. We have been separated far too long and it has taken a toll on my constitution. My daughters simply desire to be reunited and prosper together as a family where Monsieur Lafayette does not leave us for work on the daily."

It wasn't a mystery that Bonaparte looked upon most women like they were childish and needy, though he laced his words with a husbandly kindness. "Outside of Paris. He must live outside of Paris. I will see to the termination of his exile."

She smiled, suppressing it under a stiff lip as she curtsied politely. "Agreed, Monsieur," she said. "May I have your word?"

La Grange-Bléneau, March 1800

To her sister's new home in Fontenay, to Paris, and back and forth until her leg truly could not carry her anymore, Adrienne stumbled from her carriage into the awaiting arms of Gilbert. Behind him was their mostly completed home – the château was tall and ancient from the times of the Crusades, with five round towers and four floors on the manor. Flourishing trees draped their leaves over the bridge to the courtyard, ivy cascaded down the towers; the sounds of the lax stream bubbled with the chirps of spring birds. Adrienne had no chance to admire any of it with how much she had been working. She was pressed into more meetings, financially, diplomatically, personally… Despite having her family in the country, it was still only her and her dutiful Virginie who frequented the capital.

Her cry came out as a small whine into Gilbert's chest and Gilbert openly wept in holding her. She was not around to comfort him when the arrival of news carried from America shared the announcement of George Washington's sudden death. Paris held a grand ceremony – neither she nor Gilbert were invited.

"I'm sorry," she said.

"It is no fault of yours," he replied.

"And I need to give penance but I haven't sorted out who our closest Abbé is."

"W-why do you need to? What have you to confess, *mon coeur?*"

Adrienne peeled her wet eyes from his coat. "I admit in my latest interviews, I have thought of bashing in the heads of many a man for being so rude and uncouth."

Gilbert's hands slid down her arms, his mouth pursing to form words. He coughed a laugh, and shook his head. "Pray tell me who these men were and I will go be your divine deliverer of justice."

"Stop it, Gilbert, this is serious!"

He squinted at her with his nose wrinkled, still red from crying. Goodness, what a pair of idiots they were. He needed no prompting to step to the side to scoop her legs up in his arms. It was a walk towards the courtyard, but Gilbert didn't seem to mind. La Grange had the largest property of the estates divided amongst the Noailles sisters. It was perfect for the family to start a farm and Gilbert was beginning to put his studies to use after surveying and plotting. An apron lay over the stonework as they crossed the threshold of the château – its linen was covered in the soil that matched the marks wearing away at Gilbert's knees.

Adrienne combed idly through his hair as they ducked inside the manor's entrance. They desperately needed to decorate; rooms were still under construction, but bedchambers and a living space existed for now and it was comfortable enough with a fixed roof. She had whispered ideas to their architect unbeknownst to her husband while he was still exiled, and without hinting towards it over the months, Gilbert had not even the notion to be curious.

A mattress was under her soon enough, and Gilbert's kisses nuzzled their way under her chin. He'd been modestly patient the last few weeks in waiting for her to arrive after their brief reunion in Fontenay. Her illnesses returned like an unwanted lover and kept him from performing his *filial duty* that he so often brought up whenever they'd gone a long while without touching. But how he could still want to touch her was beyond Adrienne's intellect.

In the past two years alone she had become completely gray; only her eyebrows showed signs of a life before when her hair was dark and lush. Her reflection was startling — the eyebags and shallow cheeks were just a shown fraction of how exhausted she felt. Sometimes there was no point in applying powder and rouge to help disguise the fatigue.

Yet Gilbert still tucked his roughened palms under her dress, massaging gentle circles into her sore leg, and burrowed his nose into the soft of her tummy. She muffled her groaning with a pillow, unable to wiggle free from his grasp. All Adrienne could manage was to reach down and pull back at his mop of hair that had grown more brunet, especially in the shadows. It was in his scruff, when it grew, where the silver hairs lived, and he easily shaved them away.

"I figured," he said, rising from the pleasurable torture, "I will work out our debts and needed payments. On your next trip, you must insist on Cayenne. I don't see us taking it back from the state, but if we liquidated some of the assets..."

Adrienne was half asleep to listen as sincerely as she wished. Even with her family all back in France, somehow it was still her fate to accept separation in order to keep everything they were working for safe and secure for years to come. It often came to her to scold ministers to fulfill their promise of removing Gilbert, Charles, and the officers that were with them, off of the list of émigrés. It was ridiculous and brought her to tears in her solitude. The intransigent nature of old-harbored hatred was a thick wall to break through.

And of course, there was another problem.

"Oh!" she exclaimed, and Gilbert froze in place.

"What is it? Did I hurt you, beloved?"

"Georges' commission. I have another interview for him to attend."

"Ah," Gilbert sat to the side, his legs dangled from the bed. "For a moment I thought you'd have news about – I don't know – if Bonaparte mentioned me."

"He enjoys ignoring you, I think," Adrienne replied. Her hand turned up and he took it, tucking his fingers between hers. "Ignores me too at times. I tend to bother the other Consuls if I cannot get to him."

"You must try your best," Gilbert said. "Our friends are counting on you."

She hummed. It hurt.

Hazel eyes leaned into her limited vision. "I have every trust in you, *mon coeur*. No woman, nay, no other person in this country can accomplish as much as you do – as much as you have. I'm sorry my letters to you are heavy with my worries and how I loathe when you leave. Just know that… are you awake, Adrienne?"

☆

With every trip back to La Grange, she grew more ill, and the land grew more into what Adrienne imagined Washington's Mount Vernon looked like. Gilbert sent to import pigs from America and China, already building structures for their cows and sheep. Whenever Adrienne looked at their expenditures with an ever-intensifying frown, he assured her they would make it up with their future income. Twelve-thousand a year was not the two-hundred thousand they were used to, and she knew they had to be careful.

Gilbert's apartments in the château took up the south towers. The great pains he went into perfecting their design showcased most beautifully in his library – which occupied the highest floor of a tower, with wide windows that overlooked the land. He had scoured for his book collection, with French, English, and American friends sending some his way. Simple, yet elegant, if Adrienne did not find Gilbert outside working, then he was inside up in his tower with a book in hand, staring worldly out the window.

"Could you join me downstairs in your other tower?" she had asked, suppressing the panting that came with climbing the stairs. "There's something I wanted to show you."

And he'd help her down, slow and careful.

She'd been busy on the side of her usual business with attaining once stolen property.

In Gilbert's rounded parlor, hanged paintings of his life from boyhood to general, small artifacts sent from America, others recovered from Chavaniac and Paris. It was a very modest museum. Gilbert rounded the room to study each and every piece, opening letters saved between Washington and their daughter with a melancholic smile, and held the good gazette art of the eighties – Adrienne had no desire to save the phallus depictions of her husband.

"These will make breakfast my favorite meal again, just to sit in here every morning," he said. He leaned upon a chair to stare up at each painting.

"I hope we may find more," Adrienne replied, joining him in the center. Her hand floated up to the pink topaz brooch that she crafted into a pendant. It shimmered in the late afternoon light, dancing rose-colored hues on the central table.

Gilbert looked at her, his gaze shifting down to the piece. "Is that…?"

"I had to sell the rest of it to fund the rebuilding. I couldn't keep it all. I so wanted to, Gilbert; and in truth I should have given this piece with it for the higher deal but I was selfish, I'm sorry."

"Useless apologies," he shook his head. "I think you do it now so often that I must give you a thousand more kisses. Oh my, what a task you've given me."

She closed her eyes as he kissed her lids and the tip of her nose.

"The day you are selfish is the day I become humble. Trust me, *mon coeur*, it is an impossible insinuation." He took a minute and held the old, sparkly cross, tilting it from side to side. "You know when I purchased this for you, I had almost forgone the brooch. But as soon as I left the jeweler, something called me back to accept it."

"That would probably have been God."

"Maybe," he said. "Or the image of your mother scolding me for turning down a chance to compliment your piety. Well… that would scare any young boy into turning around."

Adrienne huffed a laugh, moseying her arms around his waist. They rocked back and forth to the sound of the birds chirping outside. Just a middle-aged couple finding music wherever they could. La Grange was odd like they were: a visage as country-like as Chavaniac, but bordering the outskirts of Paris, it felt like an extension of the Hôtel de Noailles. They never had an in-between before.

Pretending they weren't in debt for a moment, there was some good news: émigrés were no more, and the Lafayettes were duly expected to be hosting friends and family within the season. Baby Célestine was already walking when Anastasie and Charles moved into the château. She tumbled and crawled after the chickens through the yard, pleasantly providing all the entertainment the adults could need.

When Georges came back from Paris in an army hussar uniform, he brought with him his papers of his rank of lieutenant for the upcoming military campaign.

"Repeat what I said so I know you heard everything."

"Papa," Georges groaned. His helmet dangled in his hand.

Gilbert paced the parlor, his arms couldn't decide if they were to be crossed or rest on his hips, so they fluctuated in a strange motion between. *"Georges."*

"I'm older than you were when you left for war, Papa, and you were going into lands unknown. This is Italy. And I am cavalry – it is more likely the enemy will be running away from me than towards me."

"Cavalrymen are still just men and bullets and cannonfire do not show you mercy because you are on a horse. They'd more likely hope to take your regiment out as fast as they can before you draw close," Gilbert replied. "Now repeat what I've told you. Remind your old man the ways of war."

Georges sighed. His hair was finger-combed over his forehead and fluffed up at the lack of enthusiasm shown. "Always be aware of the flank; never underestimate the classic pincer movement," he said, pleading to Adrienne with his eyes. She sat on the sofa, listening intently. "It is not dishonorable to retreat to salvage an otherwise lost cause; always listen to the intelligence from trusted spies… Honestly, Papa, General Bonaparte himself will be in this war, I think we will be just fine. You said it yourself, you find an active leader involved in fighting for his country a good sign."

"Hm, yes I suppose I did say that," Gilbert mumbled. He cupped his chin in his palm. "Adrienne, my love, is there anything I am missing before our son goes and fraternizes with the Italians?"

Adrienne hugged a pillow close to her chest, her leg propped up as comfortably as she could make it. The week was not one for walking – she couldn't even if she wanted to. But wherever she made her resting fortress, her family followed to include her, and Georges especially wanted to spend all he could at her side. Her boys were gluttons for fighting, it was unsurprising. A hussar was a very active member of charges and no doubt her son would be put in imminent danger – she knew Gilbert's sadness upon hearing of Monsieur Pulaski's downfall in battle. But Georges was a smart boy and had some background of modesty in his approach to things. Being, well, half of her, he inherited some restraint.

She held out her hand and Georges knelt down in front of her to take it.

"Maman, please don't worry yourself over me," he said.

"I know this is what you've wanted," she replied, "and I am always praying to God to preserve you and I know He will. When you are far from home and look up to Heaven, know that I am too, looking up."

"Every day, Maman, I promise."

"And you will write as often as you can," Gilbert added, bringing him up into a strong hug after Georges kissed Adrienne's cheek. "No Lafayette forgets to be a good correspondent."

"Yes, General," Georges saluted. "It's time I bid my sisters adieu – they will take forever and a half to get away from, so it is best I start now."

The sunlight tickled at Gilbert's cheek as they watched their adult son wander over to his sisters who predictably trapped him in their embraces, bringing the new soldier right to the floor. Every heavy breath that came out of Gilbert's nose was followed by a clearing of the throat. Adrienne stared up at what a crybaby her husband could be; so handsome too. Her pinkie found purchase in the chains of his pocket fob.

With a tiny tug, he surrendered to her pull, and fell on the wide armrest like a ragdoll, haphazardly thumping his head against the wall.

"Ouch," Adrienne winced, and Gilbert slid sideways to take up what little space was left between her body and the back of the sofa. She patted his hip. "Don't you worry so much," she said. "It is best to raise spirits and give hope to loved ones. Your worrying will make him worried and the last thing we want is for Georges to be distracted on the field."

Gilbert's mumbled reply went straight into her gown. His rear was by her chest and so she gave it a firm and sturdy slap. He gained weight in the past year and she noticed the filling out of his breeches right away. It made watching him work in the fields all the more entertaining when she was stuck in a chair under some shade.

"Tell your son how proud you are of him before he goes off," Adrienne added. "He worked hard for his position and you know how impossible it will be for him to rise in his ranks with the name he carries."

"He knows how proud I am," Gilbert replied, his cheek resting on her knee. "And I know how proud our children are of the name they carry! Pray for me, *mon coeur,* it is my fear of losing any of you that makes me so crass."

"I pray for you, always."

His eyes were taking on more brown than green lately, as if he were becoming an autumn spirit instead of the spring that he always had been. They were still wide and gentle, and his smile was still mischievous and tender.

Gilbert raked his nails over the linen draped over her thigh, mindful of the open sores that lay wrapped beneath them. "'Raise spirits and give hope,'" he repeated. "Can't believe you would want me to lie to Georges about the abstract horror of war."

"Oh please."

"I thought we didn't lie in this family."

"We promised not to lie to *each other.* Everyone else wasn't involved in that pact if I remember our wedding day well."

"I remember," Gilbert said. "Oh, I remember you were so nervous, your hand was freezing, but, *ah,* so was I. The horror stories the lads in the academy would tell me of their engagements, of their parents' relationships, it painted an ill-boding, distant picture. I know I left for America not long afterwards, but I always intended to come back –"

Adrienne closed her eyes. His calf had joined the pillows in objects she held close, albeit it the only sturdy and shapely object in the pile. She bit it. Gilbert bit her knee in return. Two fools biting each other, she thought, and she wouldn't change a thing.

Brittany, August 1800

The month could have been going better.

"Stay back or I'll shoot!"

In fact, the entire task was completely un-Christian anyway.

"My father and brother are soldiers – I know how to use this!" Virginie stood up straight on their carriage, the pistol cocked back. It was in these instances, with her hair tied, her outfit smart, that she mirrored the image of her father. "Would you prefer your hand, Monsieur, or shall I put it right between your eyes?"

Of course threatening the handful of highwaymen that approached their driver added to the vision.

It was bound to happen. Virginie and Adrienne hired whoever owned a wagon large enough to transport them from one village to another. Adrienne felt it coming; collecting money from renters who had never met them before was a strain on her conscience. These were hard-working people trying to get by. Already, she had accepted taking as little as she could possibly manage, but her family and La Grange also needed to be cared for.

The ocean air was doing something for her health. Her lungs felt clean and the headaches cleared up, but her leg pained her daily, like a constant stirring fire that ached no matter what position she rested in; and her appetite was slimming and put her in a crotchety mood that she worked hard to overcome.

Which was probably why she bore no expression at the approach of brigands. Gilbert had already written of his worry over them: *while they have eyes only for the wealthy and declared travelers are not to be touched – I should prefer that the two travelers in whom I just so happen to be interested in should take precautions to avoid such encounters. I think on that we can agree...* But alas, Virginie had a spark that would place her among the most fearful women in Europe if someone ever compiled a list. Adrienne was nonplussed at said encounters.

"Honestly, Maman," Virginie said, flopping down in the seat next to her. She wiped at the sweat beading under her hat. "We should probably get more bullets, I've been empty since three days ago. While I'm flattered to be able to yell at men, one of these days, they're going to realize my bluff."

"If they look you in the eye and think you would not shoot, then they would justly earn our little collection," Adrienne replied. She tucked Virginie's ginger curls back into her cap. "Now would you keep reading what your father wrote?"

Even from his trip south to Chavaniac, he continued in his writing of their interior decorating arguments. Whitewashing was his newest goal, something they did not have the budget for, but now with womanly company arriving in October, he was dead-set on making the downstairs living arrangements as unnecessarily spruced up as possible. *Anything for Adélaïde,* Adrienne mused, rolling her eyes.

"Madame Chavaniac is suffering from a fever," Virginie read. "Oh, Ma, we'll have to send some prayers for her."

"That woman has Saint Raphael on her shoulder always," Adrienne said, resting her chin on her daughter's shoulder. "We'll light a candle for her as well in the next village."

Sometimes when they passed a stream, especially on particularly warm days, the traveling duo would stop and give time to their driver to rest and water the horses. The sun-bleached golden grass along the water's edge rose above her, caught in a happy little dance by a late summer's breeze. Adrienne rubbed her feet under the surface, the soft sand cushioning her heels.

Several thousand livres was what she had now. She would have something to send to the creditors at least. Not once in her life did she expect to have to be her family's breadwinner; if she hadn't already handled Gilbert's estates and expenditures, she would have walked right out of prison and into lost desperation. At least sensible desperation felt more ladylike.

Gilbert kept wanting to spend. Adrienne plopped her forehead to her knees: a small ball by the river. He pleaded innocent to spending an extraordinary amount at Chavaniac, recognizing it was now Adrienne's money that he was living under. But in his own Gilbert-fashion, he flirted and begged and whined to her through his poetic verse to get his way. And how could she let him feel anything but happy?

Just get the debts paid and live in humility. *Debts paid, humble living* – Adrienne's new mantra.

There were several other places she still needed to travel to outside of Brittany. It would be winter before she'd know it. But before she returned to La Grange, there was a dire need to proceed to Paris to check in on her project at Picpus.

It was where hundreds of bodies lay headless in the ground since the Terror. It was where her mother lay, where Louise lay.

Picpus, through the patronage of the families who survived, was to be a memorial for the murdered, under the guard of a new convent. Adrienne couldn't rest until she knew each and every name of the people who made up the ground and transcribed them in bronze.

Everyone was struggling; the project would take some time. All she could do was be certain it was still in the works.

Adrienne worked some of the water through her hair, scratching at her scalp and pulling out the knots. Taking baths was difficult when the sores on her leg opened. The soaking would cause festering, like salt to a snail.

Ah, there was a fair comparison: she was a snail.

"Excuse me?"

Jumping in her skin, Adrienne kicked back from the stream. Piles of wet sand flopped back in. To her right knelt a woman, a peasant no doubt, the bottoms of her petticoats were pulled up and old. Nostalgic, almost, for the fashions of thirty years prior. Her face was poised and, although dusty, clean and fresh; opposite her bare feet and the dirt collected under her nails.

"I'm terribly sorry," Adrienne replied, clutching her chest. "I didn't notice you. If you launder your clothes here or are looking for the perfect relaxing spot, this one is it. Let me move for you."

As she tucked her foot under her gown, the young woman waved her hand, sitting down where she was a few feet away.

"Please, don't mind me, Marquise, I was just looking for some food. If you had a spare piece of bread or a morsel of meat, perhaps?" She dipped her hands into the running water and brought it to her lips.

Adrienne nodded. "Of course," she said. Her attention flew to her bag. They were low on supplies, and would continue to be until they stopped for the night. Even with more affordable boulangeries, it was an awful shame that the poor were still suffering. Letters, check notes, money, her rosary and a prayer book – she kept her bread wrapped in linen.

"It should still be moist enough," she exclaimed, taking some chocolate from her secret stash. Everyone deserved a little luxury once in a while.

Her ears started buzzing. Virginie and the driver were waiting by the wagon already and the retired *title* that the woman called her had finally struck a chord.

"How did you–?" Turning around with the food in hand, the grassy divot was empty. Adrienne blinked hard. "Madame?" she called, looking back towards the trees and down the stream, but the young woman was gone.

A hard thud expanded in her chest, echoing like a distant bell in her ears. The golden blades of grass around her were no doubt disturbed, the woman likely just had something urgent to check on. Maybe a child or a sick relative.

Adrienne left the wrapped bread and chocolate on a nearby rock and returned to her daughter.

Chapter Thirty-Two

⁂

La Grange-Bléneau, January 1801

No tent was better than Gilbert's shirt. It kept out the cold that even the thickest blankets could not do and was all the better when Gilbert came with it.

Their first full winter in La Grange was full of guests and sprightly entertainment. Talks of politics, Napoleon, and agriculture, war, denied ambassadorship, and winter crops filtered through much of the conversations. When Adrienne couldn't bring herself to walk, she discreetly fanned out orders to Charles, Félix, and a few house servants to keep the warm drinks and light snacking continuously circling and the fire at a constant burn.

While both she and Gilbert returned from a long journey, he sprung to life at the open arms of Adélaïde and Auntie Tessé.

She? She slept for three nights straight.

Rest was required according to her nurse, and she would oblige the order. Gilbert and their family did as well, although men never changed, and so every few evenings, he would come into her bedchamber and crawl under her covers.

His chest radiated warmth against her cheek with the few curly hairs on his sternum tickling her nose. Slowly, he traced shapes into her back, counted the divots in her spine, and tucked his chin under the collar of his shirt to reach the top of her head.

"When I visited Brioude," he whispered, and she heard his heart rate shudder, "I tried to picture you amongst the women there and, well, *bah* to them. You clearly left out of your account how awful they are. Pray tell me you merely forgot their arrogance and selfishness."

"I must have," she replied, breathing through a rising cramp. "I am stubborn like that."

He hummed. "Quite."

"Thank you for staying true to your word. A gentle retirement that is well deserved must be enjoyed."

"I'm sure my words will be twisted, but," and his hand splayed out over her back, "it is important I stay away from Bonaparte's influence, I think. For a little while, at least."

Adrienne grunted. "A little while."

"I cannot speak for the me of next year. France could need me then; she could need me in a decade. All the same, I promised you truth."

If she nodded off for a few minutes, Gilbert didn't acknowledge it. His whispering made his chest rumble like a distant ocean, his heartbeat like a lullaby, she couldn't help it. She was wrapped up so tight under the blankets and his arms, sweating even, but he said nothing of it, only continuing on his story of traveling around the prison she was kept at, hating every bit.

When she woke up again, the room was dark. The fireplace's glow cast the adjacent wall in a soft red hue. Her head had been transferred above the blankets to a pillow, facing a small table that balanced her medicine and a small tray of a dinner, mostly eaten, belonging to the snoring man still situated by her side. A long leg stuck out from the blanket, kicking and tugging along a discarded banyan. He looked a mess. Adrienne let her laughter escape through her nose and into the pillow.

Sleeping through the time spent with the one person she loved most brought a fresh supply of guilt – something that she was already in full stock of. She wanted to hold as lively a conversation as Adélaïde did with him, or...

Her gaze flitted down to the thin fabric that covered his manhood.

She still remembered how to do that at least, she thought, her nail scratching into the mattress inches from him.

Who knows how long she watched her hand. Seconds felt like hours, minutes like eternity. Adrienne curled her fingers around his arm instead, pulling herself closer. He smelt like the bookish air of his library.

If his books were better company, he would have stayed in his apartments, she repeated to herself, crushing her face into his shoulder.

Nausea rose and fell like ocean waves and she was stuck on a ship, floating far away. The sooner her ailment passed, the better. She just wanted to be everything for him.

Many mornings started the same: breakfast with Gilbert before he went off into the fields to check on the vegetable crop and to grab more firewood with Charles and Félix; Adrienne would be helped to a chair overlooking the gardens to watch while she read, and if she had enough energy, a writing desk would be brought to her and she would reply to the business letters that stacked up a whole two inches.

Today she squeezed out three letters before her fingers couldn't hold her pen any longer. Even switching to a book was difficult in turning the pages with such swollen, fat hands. Her nurse brought in snow for her to place them in, as if that would help. Sleeping in did assist in conquering the fevers. *Huzzah.*

Anastasie gently massaged her mother's hands, watching Célestine rub hers over Virginie's canvas, smearing the blue sky with pink and forcing her aunt into making it a sunset piece. It shouldn't have been on the floor, Anastasie would argue, but then again, she was hogging the only easel they owned. The sunset looked pleasing to the eye, Adrienne commented, and so Célestine only received the best of praises for her artistic sense, but a small scold for messiness.

Although La Grange's decor was quite simple, they were still lacking in many aspects of the wealth they were so accustomed to. Some walls lay bare. The whitewashing was the only addition and Adrienne sighed for it *really* did help brighten the rooms. It was an expense, but it made Gilbert very pleased with the minimalism they were channeling. Just shy of Americana. They almost had it, just another harvest season or two.

"Oh, Maman," Anastasie said, looking out the far window from their seat. "Were we expecting visitors today?"

Adrienne turned her head, watching a wagon duck behind the trees and out of view towards the courtyard. There were no offers sent out nor queries for this particular week but it wasn't unusual to have wandering American guests or friends coming for a surprise. And a wagon of all modes of hired transportation was the most humble.

"Not that I had knowledge of," she replied. Gilbert would have told her if he invited someone.

Anastasie got up and crossed the room, her sister followed curiously. The gentlemen were still out back and the château's halls were silent until her daughters' slippers clicked hurriedly against the floor towards the courtyard. Their laughter echoed around the stone to where Adrienne sat waiting, merely watching Célestine fall asleep where she sat.

Her heart seized when the laughter turned to screaming.

"Anastasie?" she shouted back, her hand at the edge of the chair. "Virginie?"

No reply.

She tried again.

Quiet.

Not again, not her family – her leg crumbled beneath her after bursting forward three small steps. Her swollen hands slapped the floor, one familiarizing itself with the bold colors of Virginie's sunset, the other with the canvas sheet protecting the wood floor. Adrienne became used to falling, but her adrenaline shot up to her throat in an instant, choking on her own calls to her daughters.

The château slipped back into silence. An image of her children attacked in their own home seared itself on her mind.

Where was Gilbert? She needed Gilbert.

Crawling forward, her panicked breaths woke Célestine with a start.

The toddler looked around only to see her grandmère on the verge of tears. Adrienne cursed, her leg throbbed a dozen places every few inches she dragged herself. The babe began to sniffle, as if another crying girl was what the room needed.

A rhythmic thud was coming up the stairs and down the hall, something wood against wood. A heavy cane? An axe? Adrienne's elbows wobbled in place as she eyed the open door with anticipation.

"Maman?"

The tears welling up along her lashes overflowed as Georges' wide eyes and red cheeks turned the corner. Supporting himself under his arm was a *crutch*, a bootless foot wrapped in thick bandages precariously touched the floor.

There was no hesitation for him to discard his aid as he threw himself to the floor at his mother, pulling her up into a tight hug.

"Oh, Ma, are you alright?" he asked, glancing at the mess that followed her.

Adrienne smothered her embarrassment into his uniformed shoulder, holding her red-stained hand in the air. "Am I alright?" she laughed. "Georges, you give me a fright every time you come home. My heart cannot take it."

Georges knocked his cheek against her head. "I'm sorry," he said lightly. "My letter must've been lost, but I wrote, I swear. Stas and Nini ran to find Pa. Can I help you back to a chair, Maman? Let's not keep you on the floor."

He released her and reached for the crutch to help pull himself back up with a little hop. A spitting image of his father, and strong enough too, to lift Adrienne to her feet. He swung her arm over his shoulder and together they hobbled like invalides back to her seat.

Georges' face was healthy and full. He removed his papers from his coat pocket and set them on the table, then limped over to Célestine to pick up and bring back to a sofa. "I'll wait for Papa before I go through the whole story of what happened, but my superiors said I acted *dignified*, which was good to hear because I just remember how much it hurt," he said with a grin. "No risk of losing it, it wasn't a through-and-through bullet, a nick by the doctor's terms. But gah, Maman, the burning was astonishing. I'm just glad it missed my horse. If she'd fallen on me, I imagine I wouldn't have the strength to be allowed to leave." He bounced his niece on his good leg.

A sound like a cavalry in its own right echoed up the hall as Gilbert's form slid right passed the door before he caught the edge and pulled himself inside. His face was beat red, shoulders heaving. Georges placed Célestine on the cushion and stood, saluting his father before the man crossed the room in four strides to take him in his arms.

"I listened to everything you told me, Pa," Georges said. "It was ill-fortune that struck my ankle."

"No, no, we are simply the same," Gilbert replied, bringing him back to arm's length to look at Georges' foot. "Wounded in our first battle, but surviving, nevertheless. I'm pleased to have you back."

"I'm happy to *be* back."

The whole company soon arrived back at the parlor. Virginie's eyes grazed her painting the moment everyone began to stare at the blood-like hands on the floor that matched Adrienne's palm.

"Good Lord, Maman," Virginie said. "Forgive me, I should have moved that before running off. Are you well?"

Gilbert looked over his shoulder at what truly looked like a horrid murder scene upon the ground. Adrienne avoided his stare and brushed the dust off of her robe with her clean hand.

"I could use a washcloth," she replied. Her brow twitched. "And some more ice, perhaps." Her heart was still slowly climbing down step-by-step to a normal rate. Words came out in short bursts of air. "I'd also like… to hear Georges'… story."

"Please," Gilbert nodded. "Leave nothing to our imaginations." He squeezed Georges' arm as he backed up to take the chair closest to Adrienne's, his other arm coming back to squeeze her wrist gently without looking.

It was a little distracting, eyeing the family as they cleaned up the mess that Adrienne had caused, while Georges recounted the battle at Pozzolo and the waves of artillery fire from both sides, blackening the sky with cannon and smoke. Gilbert's thumb swung back and forth over Adrienne's skin like a clock pendulum as he continued to interview Georges on battle formations and who led what where.

A mirror took up the wall behind Georges, hanging over a console table that held candles and a vase. It helped to make the room look larger, but Adrienne scarcely looked into it. Yet when she glanced, she saw Gilbert's eyes switch over to hers and hold them. She smiled at being caught. His frown deepened.

"Are you truly well?" Gilbert asked when all others left to prepare dinner. He paced the floor around her chair. "None of those 'it is nothing' responses – you should *not* have fallen if you had someone with you. I'll be speaking with the girls about it."

"Hush, Gilbert, I didn't fall because I was alone."

"If Virginie stayed then she could have helped you."

"I wouldn't have gotten up if they weren't screaming at the sight of their brother," Adrienne argued. "I thought the worst, but how couldn't I when we've gone through so much? Don't berate the girls for being excited, I know I would have done something similar." She gestured to him. "Like fainting when you appear to me after years away."

Gilbert paused, his weight rocking up onto his toes. "Catching you has always been my joy."

"Well, letting me fall onto my face in front of a crowd would very much embarrass us both, I imagine."

"Don't make me laugh, I am angry."

Adrienne lifted her hands from the ice. They were red and numb, but not as large as before. Gilbert pulled the cloth from the chair arm and knelt in front of her, folding it over her hands and between his.

"Until you are honestly recovered, I would wish for someone to be by your side when I am working. Your nurse, Félix, our children, I don't care who it is. If you long for your sisters then I will personally call them here."

"Gilbert," she said.

"Not to give you the opportunity to argue with me, as we both are well aware of how talented you are with that, let's talk about Georges for a moment," Gilbert said, tapping his nails against the cloth as he looked around the room. "He's well into the age of marriage, I think. And of course, I don't want to tell him who he should marry – although I could think of several decent ladies that would suit him – but I was thinking of inviting some friends and well-known acquaintances over who happen to have daughters in a similar age bracket. Spring, naturally, is perfect for garden strolls. We can plant ourselves in a boat and watch some prospective coupling happen before our very eyes."

Adrienne's brows rose. "Gilbert," she said again, only this time it was laced in a laugh.

"It isn't like we are choosing a girl for him, *mon coeur*, we are merely presenting a platter of approved ladies for him to sample –"

"That is horrible phrasing!"

"As he is in La Grange to recover, he isn't going to find any lady out *here!* We must bring them *in!* And if he doesn't like one, we thank them for their company and I invite a new friend over to reconnect and encourage him to bring his family."

"Gilbert."

"Adrienne."

She leaned forward, drawing his eyes up to her as she rested her cheek on their joined hands. He queried a brow up and raised his chin.

"If you are about to double back and tell me you are well, I call bull and remind you not only of our vow, but that I have known you for twenty-nine years and you cannot coax me into yielding even with your charming intellect and big doe eyes."

Sighing, Adrienne puffed her cheeks. "Georges has to approve of this plan first," she finally said. "He will not be tricked into choosing a bride. His wound could bring him shame if the girl finds it unsightly."

"Ah, but you see my dearest Adrienne, from experience I know that a good lady loves a wounded soldier. Especially one that keeps all his faculties in check and is destined to heal perfectly fine."

If her hands were not bound, she would pinch him right then.

"And it would save you from journeying back into Paris for another damned chore," Gilbert said, sitting back on his feet. "I am still angry at your father asking you to play the commissioner when he has other daughters and their husbands, and a wife to do his work. By all means, he has *me* should I wish to trot around the city and let you be a philosopher here at home. My happiness is entirely dependent on you, I'm afraid. Am I selfish for wanting you to stay by my side?"

"Let's remain on the topic of Georges," she replied. The affairs of her father was an entire separate strain of stress that she did not wish to think back on. Any miracles she achieved in Paris for her family was enough to excuse the setbacks of other goals that would be addressed come springtime anyway. "And what people you may know."

La Grange-Bléneau, June 1801

She couldn't believe they were truly floating on a little boat watching Georges meander next to a young woman. Her leg was feeling far better after resting it for the weeks her husband and the doctors prescribed her. A pleasant breeze was medicinal for the lungs and Gilbert returning from his own audacious meeting with Bonaparte fared just as well for her peace of mind. They watched the young people idle together, catching whenever Georges glanced over to them and removed his hat to slick back his hair.

"It isn't going well," Adrienne reported.

"They've done one lap, calm yourself," Gilbert replied, dodging the swipe of Adrienne's parasol as he rowed them along. "I have at least one more person in mind, but it will have to wait until Georges and I return from Chavaniac. Which, thanks to you, all should go smoothly and we will return as quick as rain."

"Tread carefully with inheritance, Gilbert. I pray we have anything at the end of our lives to give out to our children."

"We will," he replied. "If I have an inkling of hope for the future, we will prevail. And Georges will be happily set with a wife without needing to worry of having an uncomfortable living situation. Then we can do it all again for Virginie."

"God help us," Adrienne said, hiding her face in her palm.

"You'd be proud of me if you were at my meeting with General Bonaparte," Gilbert added, watching Georges bring his walking mate to the shade of a tree, where Anastasie and Charles met them as their supervisors. "He wants to reinstate Catholicism as the national religion, but only because he wishes the Pope would crown him. I've offered my opinion that France would be happier with the American system. Your faith isn't a political statement."

His eyes glowed amber in the light that descended through the gaps of their low-hanging trees. She had never counted more freckles on him.

"Thank you," she replied. "That was very noble of you to say."

"He told me I would do the same if I were in his shoes. I replied his were far too small for me –"

"Gilbert!"

"Nay, I jest, although the thought did cross my mind," he snickered. "He's an odd man with a temper. Washington had a temper, yes, but I recall it was warranted and was followed by an apology. Not that my general ever was displeased with me for more than a minute or two."

"Bonaparte is staking his claim over that of the Bourbons," Adrienne said. "What a waste of a revolution."

"Only if he discards the ideals we've fought for. If the people are for him, then there is nothing for us to do even if his character makes him a pain in the ass at times."

"The Bourbons are not completely your friends either."

"Mm, I did humiliated at least half of them." He pulled their little boat under the willow tree and let the oars rest on his knees. "You're taking Virginie back to Brittany? Would you please take a private carriage this time? I nearly fainted when she told me of the troubles you encountered. I do not hang Georges from ours and make him wave his sword around with me like we are two musketeers in an opera. You shouldn't be having our young daughter pointing a gun at any person."

"I'll be sure to point the gun this time," Adrienne replied. "I'll wave it like a madwoman in an opera with the vocals to boot."

Gilbert smiled but shook his head. "*Mon coeur*, you simply refuse to not leave my mind. How am I supposed to do some of the work south if I am so worried over you in the west? Your health is my health."

"I'm –"

"Fine, yes, yes, I know," he groaned. "You are always fine, beloved, though I wish you were perfect. I want to hear from the doctor's lips that you are in *immaculate* health, that I did not *doom* you to suffer eternally from staying with me in that cell. No, I know you will say it was for the best and I will not argue with you on that, but I am allowed to sulk over things I feel anguish for, regardless if I can help it or not."

The river took them slowly through the branches, slapping over Gilbert's shoulders like lazy whips before they returned to the sun above.

"And you are taking Georges with you to Chavaniac, but he is to return to his regiment, is he not?" Adrienne asked, seeing their son lay on his back in the field. Gilbert followed her line of sight and nodded. "So the last friend you speak of you'll be meeting without Georges in company."

"Yes, but I'll be diligent in my interview and describe her character as I see it."

"To me as well, I hope."

"Oh, Adrienne, you will be the first to hear it. The girl will need your approval before I relay anything to Georges."

Brittany, December 1801

The girl's name was Émilie de Tracy – her father sat by Gilbert in the Estates-General and now worked under Bonaparte, but otherwise, politically agreed with the Lafayettes. Monsieur de Tracy was a slight man, and so his daughter was also.

She is charming in all the delicate womanly ways and in the best ones of a man. She inherited the sloping nose of her mother and the dark complexion of the comte. I find she only laughs with sincerity when the conversationalist is amusing, which would work well for Georges as he hates a sycophant. Her embroidery falls short of yours, mon coeur, and could use your expertise. I have bragged about you. Forgive me. Mademoiselle de Tracy was patient enough to listen to my whole prattle. I think she would do well as a Lafayette. I've forwarded you a picture dear Anastasie sketched for me that I believe suits Mme de Tracy's features. Tell me if you approve.

On another note, I've dined with Bonaparte's brother and my old colleague Lord Cornwallis after seeing family. Several pages shall be needed to describe our supper and later conversation. Trust that although I voluntarily laid my head on the executioner's block and waited, none of their criticisms were sharp enough to do damage. Imagine my surprise when they did not believe the lengths I go to defend liberty...

Gilbert's letters grew dreary the longer she remained in Brittany for business. While before she would have moped with him in his pessimism, finally, it seemed, that their funds and land distribution were working out. Adrienne grinned reading his confession of her previous right attitude and all the praises he sent to her achievements, but to tell him now of how her hard bartering and polite arguing paid off should make it all the better.

Adrienne handed Virginie a letter to Aunt Tessé to copy and forward to the Noailles sisters as well as the Duc de Noailles – who had all become loud bees swarming Gilbert's ears while she was away. She also needed to write to Gilbert about Cayenne, as the two of them were not going to give up on the plantation. That would require more trips to the capital, but now Gilbert was more or less free to travel where he wished, if she was not around to secure a deal, he could go in her stead.

The months apart from each other were grueling, and quite unfair when they were supposed to be retiring in modest bliss. Sure, her family could have picked up in places where she left off to help themselves earn back the Noailles' estates, but they were certain only Adrienne had the fundamental character to accomplish the task, and she was too humbled to argue against that. *Was this enough?* She wondered often.

Snow was falling over the ocean, covering the endless sky with light gray clouds in the late evening. It piled upon the windowsill, growing higher and higher as the hours passed and the candles shrunk.

After Paris would have to be Chavaniac, Adrienne scheduled. Only after all affairs were settled would she be free to return to La Grange.

She gently rubbed the back of Virginie, bent over the table scribbling tirelessly into the night. Her aide-de-camp was Heaven sent. Adrienne prayed her eventual wedding would not be an extra stress on her in the future.

Chavaniac, April 1802

Adrienne was a thread away from snapping as she followed her aunt-in-law around the château with a strained smile on her face. Madame Chavaniac was not yielding to agree on splitting her land or altering the interest she gave to her nephew on it all. In truth, Adrienne felt for her – Gilbert was her favorite in all matters and of course she would want her lands to go to him in its entirety if she could not split it *evenly* among her beloved grandchildren. But Georges, Gilbert's rightful heir, needed assurance of money and of property to convince his prospective fiancée's family that the wedding was worth it; he needed a *larger* share. Gilbert's letters from the de Tracy home were becoming numerous and urgent.

Adrienne forcefully slapped her hand to the wall, the noise reverberating down the walkway, bringing Aunt Charlotte to a halt.

"Madame?" she exclaimed.

"If you would please," Adrienne said, gesturing to the chairs that neighbored each other nearby. "I am growing tired of walking."

Chasing, more like it.

"I think asking me to remove Gilbert, ultimately you as well my dear Marquise, from a life-interest is a foolish move on all parts. If this young lady's family is so stuck on monetary value that Georges' ten-thousand from me is not enough in addition to your offer, then clearly they are out of their minds. Excuse my insults," Charlotte said.

Difficult as it was to argue against something she agreed with, Adrienne tried. "We cared not for money with Anastasie's match with Charles – but it was a trepid time in foreign land. France has become, somewhat, itself again, and those of us who grew up with the standards for nobility still recognize that finances are important. Georges only has a soldier's income. I am still working with Gilbert to bring back some fraction of what we've had before. The de Tracy family is involved with Napoleon's government, a Senator, and it would provide a stable support system for Georges and Émilie once all this money squabble is over with."

"You ask me to hurt the prospects of my nephew or his daughters." Her hands clapped at her knees as she shook her head.

"Gilbert is prepared to give up such an interest," Adrienne replied. The room they sat in bore the decoration that said man purchased and had arranged to his liking. Busts and shiny furniture, spent on Madame Chavaniac's wallet no doubt if he were avoiding Adrienne's wrath. "I have a proposition for you, then, that may please all parties."

Charlotte folded her hands, her aged eyes leading her head to face her niece. "Pray tell what is your offer?"

"Chavaniac's remodeling; her decor and refurbishment has cost you significantly and you allowed Gilbert to do such things because of your love for him, but as our family's executive provider, I believe we owe you a debt."

"I see."

"If we agree to, say, twenty-thousand francs," Adrienne said, citing the gift Charlotte was giving to the girls, "that we may pay off upon receiving the inheritance at your passing…"

"You would be ensuring that your daughters get the money I promised them while allowing Georges a larger share *now*," Madame Chavaniac finished. Her jaw had set, it was a waiting game now. There was no sighing or shaking her head; Charlotte just looked back up and said, "I will consent to that compromise. The dear lengths we go for our children."

Adrienne sucked in a long breath and awed. "Yes, Madame," she agreed, "yes we do."

She gave herself some time to admire the work that Gilbert and his aunt had put into the château and its grounds. Apple trees and new top soil, the flowers were blooming in full where bees and butterflies roamed in paradise. Stones that were becoming reclaimed by the grass were cleared up for walking.

Quietly, she wandered the path down to the pools and secret grotto, where memories flourished. Virginie followed several feet behind, not making a sound, as Adrienne recounted the last time she saw her mother.

It was here in Auvergne, where the duchesse enjoyed the gardens and country reprieve. Seeing her mother bask in the golden sunshine, where the only chatter was that of the otters and minks, and the army of birds in the trees, was a scene she should have had painted.

Adrienne swiped a sleeve across her cheeks. "Maman, no one holds a candle to you," she murmured to the babbling fall. "Papa has gone back to Switzerland with a woman who does not deserve my animosity, but I can't help but bite my cheek when he says her name. Everything would be so much easier if you were still here – the family would be cohesive and not arguing over inheritance. I would give it all up; you could stay at La Grange and we could watch your great-grandchildren grow." She pushed her hands into the divots of her waist before reaching into her pocket to pull out an ocean-worn letter. "And Louise, I've heard from Louis, that wayward man. He hasn't remarried, or at least makes no mention of it. Philadelphia has been his home for years, but he has taken a naval command under Rochambeau the younger. Personally I have never imagined him as a seafaring man, but you likely know his mind more than I. You'll find him in the West Indies, should you decide to guide him through rough waters or rock his ship more."

A dragonfly settled on a floating bud, its petals stretching like a star. Adrienne knelt by the water's edge and pulled aside some dirt to fit the note in its own small grave.

"Do what you wish with his letter. I have no way of reaching back out to him. I will talk to you both again in Paris, where your resting place has become holy ground," she said. "I did my best."

Two gentle hands curled around her arm. Virginie stepped by her side, bumping her temple to the top of Adrienne's head. "Maman," she said, "it looks as if it will rain soon. How about we take tea in your salon and write back to Papa? We can leave the windows open to listen, if you'd like. The next post leaves tomorrow."

"Yes, of course," Adrienne replied. She looked at Virginie and smiled. What a pretty girl she was. "We have a wedding to plan."

La Grange-Bléneau, June 1802

She may have angered some relatives by orchestrating such a private wedding, but between grand and minute politics, it was for the best. Foreign war was over and so returned Georges to meet his fiancée at last. Instead of hat lifts or genteel bowing, he blushed rather madly at the young lady who found herself quite pleased with her match. Adrienne reconnected with dear Abbé Carrichon, the man who spent the fleeting moments of the doomed Noailles ladies granting them absolution, as he agreed to lead the wedding.

Georges looked dashing in a deep blue coat, the dark linen that accentuated his wardrobe contrasted the soft, white cotton gown of delicate Émilie's. She was a head shorter than him, a detail that must have been a staple of Lafayette marriages. The ceremony was short and sweet, but not lacking applause from the immediate two families as Georges shyly kissed his new wife.

Émilie was everything Gilbert had said and more. She found the château pleasant in its modesty, and in their honeymoon, followed Georges out to the gardens with a picnic the two had prepared themselves. Gilbert and Adrienne were minding their own business as every parent should, of course, watching from his library window. He had a horn installed up in the tower, meant for talking to the fieldworkers to relay instructions. Adrienne held him down to stop him from sending comments from above.

"You are *not* going to embarrass them," she commanded over his snickering. They rolled over the rug as he weakly fought to reach the horn, knocking over a pile of unshelved books in their wake.

"Georges would think it funny," Gilbert wheezed as Adrienne's elbow shoved into his gut.

"Perhaps when he was twelve. He's a grown man, Gilbert!"

"I could offer him words of *wisdom*."

"He probably already knows all the wisdom you think you have of *that*."

He took her wrists and pulled them apart. She fell flat on his chest. "You don't think I'm good in bed?" he asked.

Adrienne rolled her eyes. "I am saying he doesn't need his father to give him lessons on consummation. You'd horrify him. And goodness, poor Émilie. Let them find it naturally."

"Bah bah bah," Gilbert replied. His head plonked against the floor and he released her hands. "Very well. If they have not already heard this struggle then perhaps it is for the best. It's not every day our children get married. We have one left now. In which we run into the same problem as before."

"Yes, about that." Adrienne slipped a letter from her sister out from her bosom. Gilbert raised his brow. "According to Pauline, she has this covered. And she is very confident in that matter."

"Oh?" Gilbert said, eyeing the paper as she waved it across his eyes. "Report, my love."

"Well-educated: *plus*," she replied. "Grew up in Malta: *questionable*, but she writes he was taken to France by his uncle. He is of good stock and, I quote: 'a very good man, both in character and to the eye.'"

"Do I know the name?"

"Lasteyrie?"

Gilbert squinted and hummed. "I will have to do some poking around for that name. If it is Pauline who suggests him, then he certainly must have made a very fine impression. Your sister is wary of all marriageable men."

Adrienne laughed. Truly, Virginie deserved a bright and handsome gentleman who could match her wit.

She sat back up on Gilbert's lap, picking at the buttons of his breeches as she watched Georges hold up a parasol for his bride. They were too far away to see faces, but Adrienne felt the smiles and the warmth already growing between them. A wave of nostalgia washed over her; to be twenty again.

Light fingers padded their way over the covered scabs on her thigh. Her legs were awful to look at, it was a mercy that, of all the changes in fashion, the hemlines remained long. But one man didn't seem to mind; they had been so busy in preparation that they had not had time to be in each other's company for months. She sighed, finding his hands. His back cracked upon his leaning up to her, and a sore laugh met her lips. Supposedly, the library floor seemed as good a place as any.

"Where is the couple I have yet to see? I've had gifts that were overlooked!" Madame de Tessé's voice echoed up the tower stairwell. Gilbert pulled back from the kiss and groaned, bonking his head back against the rug. Adrienne covered her eyes. There was a reason why she didn't invite everyone.

"One moment, Auntie," she called back. Praying to God for patience. "We'll meet you in the parlor!"

"This is cruel and unusual punishment," Gilbert said as Adrienne got to her feet and smoothed out her gown and tidied the mess they made.

"For us or for Georges?"

"Yes."

Chapter Thirty-Three

Aulnay, February 1803

Well, Adrienne thought that Louis de Lasteyrie was a delightful boy who brought with him a gentleness to meet with Virginie and a steady arm to help her across the ice of the city while Gilbert and Adrienne finally traveled as a pair to meet with their dear friends of Britain. He had clear eyes and a charming laugh and was ever so patient as to wait for Virginie to be finished with her tasks as her mother's right-hand before picking up with more conversation. Virginie, in turn, was finding the young man quite intriguing.

The love match was falling into place just as great as Gilbert was at *falling down stairs to the ground.*

Adrienne was horrified, following the doctors through the halls of Aunt Tessé's home as the muffled screams of her husband rocked the chandeliers. Of all the clumsiness he had gotten himself into – of breaking carriages and glass and friendships and more – breaking his femur was the worst of it all.

He had sweated through his shirt and waistcoat, cursing as the doctors cut through his woolen trousers to get to the massive bruise taking up his hip and leg. It was the color of deep red wine, like a spill that continued to grow. A wood board was preemptively placed between his teeth to keep him from biting his tongue off just from having to move his body another inch. Adrienne pulled a cloth from the water basin, dabbing at his face while two doctors assessed the contusion.

"The connection between your leg and your hip has been severed, General," one said, preparing a laudanum concoction. "We can think of two possible treatment methods, but they are drastically different and one is merely experimental."

Gilbert blinked quickly, his gaze shifting from the doctors to Adrienne.

"What are they?" she urged.

"The quicker option would be a simple reduction. We will try to align the fracture and you would be bed bound until it heals, but it would very likely still leave you in a crippled state."

Gilbert's forehead vein was throbbing.

"And the other?" Adrienne asked.

"A device I have been perfecting. It would be invasive, and cause far more pain for a considerable time, but should procure a better result in the end."

Spitting out the board, Gilbert's jaw was shaking. "I'll take the pain," he said.

"Gilbert." Adrienne pressed his hair back, holding his face like an infant.

"Go on, then, Doctor," he huffed. "I'm no stranger to surgery."

He took the laudanum generously while the doctors' assistant ran to retrieve the cast-like apparatus from their office, brushing past Virginie and Monsieur Lasteyrie in the hall.

"Papa," Virginie called, but Gilbert's attention was slowly waning from the drugs.

Adrienne held her arm out. "Lasteyrie, would you please escort my daughter –"

"Right away, Madame," he replied, gently holding his hand over Virginie's. "Let's get some air, Mademoiselle. There's nothing to be done here."

Gilbert's tolerance of alcohol was not good when he was younger and it hardly improved as he aged. The laudanum hit him all at once, harder than the fall. His eyes wandered around the decorated posts of the bed, squinting every few seconds as his body throbbed at the swelling injury. He was half-asleep when the assistant returned with the device in hand and a pile of additional cloth.

Adrienne refused to leave for the surgery despite being told they would be cutting into Gilbert's flesh to secure the cast to bone. She politely reinserted the block between his teeth and the look of confusion he gave her was one of a child's. All she could do was hold onto him, keeping one arm down as the assistant held the other while the doctors went to work; pressing her ear to his sweat-soaked chest and praying and praying and praying as he groaned and cried from under her.

There was so much blood to be cleared up from the room. Madame Tessé would not dare ask for the payment required to have the stains removed from her guest room sheets; it would be cheaper to buy new ones. But the apparatus was attached to Gilbert's leg, and Gilbert laid quietly breathing, asleep from the exertion and pain. His hand unconsciously squeezed Adrienne's, but she didn't mind. She picked at the curls sticking to his forehead and adjusted the blankets when he shivered.

It was unlike his wound at Brandywine. His letters of the procedure's aftermath were of annoyance but praise for the bullet's trajectory. This was a slip on ice. Far less dignified for a hero of two worlds.

"Have I died?"

Adrienne sat back. Gilbert blinked at her slowly.

"No," she whispered. "You are very much alive."

"Oh," he said. "I thought an angel was waiting by my bedside, but you must be my pretty nurse."

She smiled. He was so delirious. "And you are my very handsome patient."

He tutted. "I am married, Madame," he replied, shaking his head rather dramatically. "Only I may flirt, for I know when to stop."

"Oh, do you now?" Adrienne asked.

"Yes," he exclaimed. His half-lidded eyes wandered over to his other side. "Mn," he grumbled, "my leg hurts."

"I know, my love."

He looked up. "Does my wife know I'm alright? I was with her, I thought… I thought… I thought she was – we don't travel together very often after… Does my wife know?" Gilbert swallowed nervously, and he started to shift to try and rise.

Adrienne stood at once and pushed his shoulders back, cooing, "she knows, *cher* General. She is praying for your quick recovery. To help her, you must rest, alright? We don't want to agitate your wound."

"My wife is a good Christian," he replied, letting the pillow take him back. "Tell her I rave for her bosom, pretty nurse. She is too good to me."

She stroked his cheek as his head lolled and he continued to murmur some lovely nonsense. Tears threatened to overtake her grin, but it was better than the complaints he was apt to do when bedridden.

"Pretty nurse?" he asked, too tired to even open his eyes.

"Yes, Monsieur?"

"Could you ask my daughter if she has read any news? The news… they like to insist I've died." A true fact – *where* the rumors start from that leads a barrage of letters to arrive for Adrienne asking about his welfare, she'd never know. "I worry for my aunt. If anything were to become of me, it would no doubt kill her."

"We will keep an eye out. You may write to her as well when you wake well rested."

Of letters, word had gotten around Paris already, several asked to visit the ailing General when he had recovered enough to accept guests. Adrienne already knew he was not going to like the idea of anyone seeing him in such a state.

The room he was likely to be stuck in for some time was at least interesting to look at. The window opened to a modest garden and a street with passing carriages to watch. A shelf of Voltaire's work sat in the opposite corner, very likely to be perused by his caretakers. Upon her arrival, Anastasie brought Célestine to entertain when Gilbert was in the mood. It would be his girls that would dote on him while the men of the family tried to keep things running in their stead.

Gilbert slept for most of the first few days and was grumpy when awake. Moving to simply urinate caused a litany of swears to follow that Adrienne duly ignored. Like a moody cat, he exercised his arms with a frown on his face and a small dosage of laudanum to follow. The device made it almost impossible for him to shift himself into a sitting position, and Gilbert refused to be carried elsewhere like an *invalid*.

Adrienne didn't let the insult bother her, knowing how embarrassing the ordeal was to begin with. She was just thankful that there was no sign of infection to the incisions in his thigh.

What did bother her was his hopeless attempts to stand with the thing. It must have weighed as much as he did. Like an anchor, he lurched forward and fell again, crying more than Célestine did at her birth.

His friends from the American war, upon their visits, were attentive to Adrienne's pleas that they encourage Gilbert to remain bedside until the contraption was removed. In his state of undress, seeing them was less of a stain to his pride than the arrivals of Bonaparte's government. Virginie placed herself at the door to answer simple welfare calls, content on sending them away after reassuring them that General Lafayette lived on despite his attempts to escape her eventual engagement.

Charles got on well with Lasteyrie, as did Georges when he stopped by outside his training. The young man was facing a trial by fire – dealing with Gilbert in all his temperament – and did not utter a single complaint. Pauline spoke true: he was a good boy. When winter slipped into spring, he was sure to spend time with Virginie in the garden where her parents could supervise from Gilbert's bed, and entertained her (and them) with silly card tricks he learned from his time in the army; and she returned the favor with her dance lessons from years past. This time, Adrienne allowed Gilbert to make comments from the window, asking for them to try different moves or for Charles and Anastasie to join them for a song or two. They all willingly complied – anything for their father.

Émilie sat inside by the window with a flute, happy to add some melody while resting herself – her belly already rounded from a fairly progressed pregnancy.

Gilbert was given Adrienne's bosom to lay on, which brought up his mood significantly even through Aunt Tessé's insisting that the wedding be held in her house as she was promptly *wronged* last year. No one argued against it.

When after six weeks, the doctors returned to remove the cast, Adrienne had to look away. Surely the bones had healed by his hip, but his flesh was practically mutilated, and the strain it had put on his foot had broken more bones in its wake. Gilbert, through his tears, didn't regret choosing it. As long as he would be able to walk, he would accept the cost. Bandages now replaced the device, and Gilbert was at least capable of using crutches to swing his way around the house with minimum grunting.

New crying came from the arrival of baby Natalie du Motier. Small and strong-fisted, her bald head was perfect for decorating with embroidered caps when the ladies weren't embroidering a gown for Virginie, and her cousin Célestine did well with her first job as a naptime overseer.

Adrienne settled in a bench that overlooked her aunt's back fields where cows and low clouds roamed. Her headaches snapped back tenfold with the spotty vision to boot, and crying – from a baby or her husband – was beginning to feel like she was inside the bells of Notre Dame as they rang. She was doing so well before, why was it all coming back? Could she not go one season without feeling like vomit lived in the back of her throat?

She scratched her arm without thinking about it. Spots on her leg pricked up blood as if she was stabbed by a dozen needles. Guilt gnawed at her as she added a drop of laudanum to her drink, hoping the pain would vanish so she could focus on the happier things blossoming in the family.

"*Mon coeur?*"

Adrienne hugged her arms around her waist and leaned forward, catching Gilbert's eye from the door.

"I did not scare you away with my temper, I hope."

"No," she said. "No, I am too used to your flames to feel any burn."

"Have I been that fiery?"

"No more than the stars." Adrienne scooted to the right as Gilbert crutched himself to the bench, huffing as he carefully sat himself next to her. His left leg straightened out far in front of them accompanied by a teeth-gritted grunt. She felt his gaze turn towards her, lingering. Flakes of her skin dusted her green skirt. The sight of it made her upper lip curl back and she tried to sweep it away without causing more to peel off.

Gilbert laid his arm across her shoulders, rocking her closer to him. His breeches were stained at his left hip with the blood that soaked through the stitches and bandages. Their attention both hovered over the stains of her petticoat on her right side. At least between them were a pair of working legs.

"Louis asked if calling me Père was alright," Gilbert whispered. She felt him smile against her hair while they watched the cows graze. "I've been so used to hearing *Papa* that *Père* makes me feel old. And yet, I am also a *papi* to two cherub-cheeked girls."

Adrienne hummed. She considered herself old long ago.

"Aunt Tessé has told me to my face that I have aged like a fruit, but I think she is wrong for you have always said otherwise. Pray tell me you don't think I've become an age where all my bones are this brittle. I assure you the fall was a complete accident and could have happened to any young and sprightly man."

"Shh," she said. "You talk too much when you're anxious."

"Do I?"

"Mm." The breeze pushed back the sweat on their brow.

"You're quiet when you're unwell. Should I call the doctors back?"

She shook her head. "I don't want to take away from the celebrations."

"*Mon coeur,* I am missing a part of my handsome thigh, it would not be you who ruins the mood when the gash festers like a frying egg. They will hear my groaning like a grumpy old man. Oh dear, that's what I'll be: a crotchety geezer."

"Laughing hurts my head, Gilbert, don't say that," Adrienne said, breathless. "As long as I'm around, I will always find you a gentleman."

His good foot wiggled back and forth until Adrienne let her good leg stretch out to join it on the grass. Her toes hardly reached his calf. Perhaps she shrank; or maybe Gilbert laying on his back for months allowed him to grow without the restraints of gravity to push him down.

"Would it be medically improper if I asked you to sleep in my room tonight?" he said, watching himself nudge the slipper from Adrienne's foot. "If I lay on the left and you on the right, we could pretend nothing is the matter."

"I wouldn't be opposed to that," she replied. Flicking a piece of skin from her elbow off, some oil would be enough to stop the itching for the evening.

Gilbert's recovery was the longest time they had together under the same roof. Being on the outskirts of Paris had made Adrienne's trips short and sweet, but they hadn't laid together in months.

Émilie took her candle and met Adrienne's eye through the sliver of her door. "Is there anything else I can do for you before you retire?" she asked, her voice like a windchime.

"No, darling, thank you," Adrienne replied. "Go kiss Natalie for me. The thunder may be loud tonight and she'll need your voice for protection."

Émilie nodded, shielding the candlelight with her hand and left down the hall as the rolling storm lit the windows up with a pale blue glow. Adrienne shut her door and leaned against it until she heard the click. She couldn't take in a full breath since supper, spending the whole evening chatting about exciting nuptials and a return to La Grange. Why didn't she simply stay quiet? Sacrificing her opinions meant she focused on fighting back the pain then instead of letting it intensify for later.

Gilbert shifted on the bed, his pillow sideways to cuddle in the absence of a person. The splay of his legs created the image of a runner. Adrienne stepped around their two canes that propped up against the bottom frame of the bed, and climbed up onto the mattress. She wasn't used to him being the tired one.

Did he watch her sleep like she did him? Yearning to touch where she hadn't in ages, wanting to feel something other than the pain her body was putting her through.

She balanced her palm an inch over the rise of his pelvis, down the slight slope of his hip where the blanket was kicked down amidst his rolling. It was still healing, she didn't want to risk hurting him.

If she touched her own breast, would it feel like his hand?

Adrienne slid her hand under her chemise, curving her hand over her skin. She felt cold to the touch, empty. Closing her eyes, she tried to imagine the writing calluses of her fingers were his overworked ones. The same hands that massaged her when she was aching, combed through her hair when she was sad. She pressed her thumb against her nipple but it was all the same vexing discomfort. *Broken.* The word stung. Her hand fell limp to her lap. Adrienne had to have been capable of some pleasure still.

Thunder rumbled miles away in the hills of the country. Adrienne slipped the blanket further down Gilbert's hip.

There it was again. Just laying there.

Adrienne pushed the sleeves of her chemise up to her elbows and felt her palms. They wouldn't be too rough now, would they? Heavens, if she felt like sandpaper to him, she thought away at her lip. Maybe she should have oiled her hand as well.

Gilbert had blinked up at her, his one eye from the pillow followed her hand – tired, yet attentive. Adrienne froze. *Silly, wasn't it, to be caught pining over her husband?*

Silence took the both of them for a long minute; the sky lit up in a flash of white lightning.

"Go on," he coaxed.

Adrienne never needed more encouragement.

His throat bobbed as he watched her reach for him. The slight intake of breath from both of them as she traced her thumb and forefinger up the length of it, to Gilbert's muffled sigh, brought a spark of interest to Adrienne's gut. She remembered how to please him, finding the motions that elicited soft whines and bit back moans that curled his good leg up to support himself.

Gilbert tugged at her nightgown, pulling the drawstring until it loosened and fell down her shoulder and there was his hand on her breast, hot and weathered. He cupped and held it with a firm tenderness, and when his thumb glided over the tip, a shudder of bliss lit up goosebumps across her body.

He rose to meet her, cupping her head with his other hand. She leaned on him, finding his lips to claim, pulling his little gasps into her breath. Her head throbbed angrily, but her sex throbbed with delight at the sudden intimacy. His hand that held her breast had greedily wormed its way down and soon Gilbert too was eating up her whimpers.

Adrienne steadied her shaking body. Their noses continued to bump and her working hand was inching precariously closer to his. It was a bad idea. It was a great idea. In their state, they could seriously hurt each other. She felt so good; she loved hearing all the small noises he made. He kissed her neck while she let her breath go in one shallow moan, covered under the closing in storm. Rain splattered against the windows and roof in sharp bursts as the clouds moved in, progressing to a steady pour that resonated through the floors.

Her body felt hot simply in his grasp. Gilbert tugged her down atop of him, humming his contentment when her breasts squished against his chest and he held on firm to her ass. She traced her thumbs over his cheekbones and lines, unable to process anything he was saying to her. His blinking was slow, as was hers. When he mouthed words with a grin, she grinned back. His happiness was hers – she felt it in her heart, the joyful beating against his own.

And she thought, if they still held each other like this for the next fifty years, she'd happily grow old with him to become kind, old grandparents together.

La Grange-Bléneau, March 1804

Marching back and forth between chambers to pack for another trip was Adrienne's recent exercise. Rosalie was due for another baby after a strenuous pregnancy and asked for her to be there. Who was Adrienne to deny her youngest sister?

Virginie flipped through papers at the desk, brooding as her new husband was already sent off to the army for the season. "Did you know Anastasie is pregnant again?" she said over her shoulder. Adrienne carried a different gown over from the chest.

"She hasn't told me yet," Adrienne replied, "and so I will pretend not to hear you. I asked for current news."

"Émilie might be too. I heard she and Georges were trying again before he left."

"Virginie, they will tell me when they are ready. Could you help me find my hat? Your father tends to throw them on high shelves when he's in a mood."

"It's on the one above the mantle," Virginie sighed, her elbow on the table. "Maman, how long does it take to get pregnant?"

Adrienne scrunched her face, reaching for the lace that dangled from the bonnet. "It entirely depends on the woman – where she is on her courses, if she's been eating well. Of course if the man, ah, *finishes* during intercourse." She popped the bonnet between some petticoats and tilted the chest lid closed. At least that was out of the way. "News, Virginie?"

Her daughter lazily glanced at the gazettes and correspondence laid out. "President Jefferson insists Papa moves to the Louisiana territory on account that he may be in danger if Bonaparte goes to war with England."

"We've already made our decision to remain in France," Adrienne said, leaning on her bedpost to take weight off her leg. Gilbert would reply to his friend with the same answer as before. And that man still needed to pack as well. "What else?"

"Do you think there's something wrong with me, then?" Virginie asked. Her hands moved to her flat stomach. "Louis and I tried so much before he left for training."

Ah, that worry.

Adrienne looked over her daughter wearily. Their time at Olmütz very well could have caused detrimental damage to Virginie's maturing if her being premature from her own birth did not bring its own issues. But

Virginie had never displayed any signs of infertility nor suffered from as much sickness as her sister had.

"You cannot rush things," she said. "God will let you know when you are ready. Until then, all you can do is try again when Louis returns."

Women were having their children later and later it seemed anyway. Virginie was still young. If Adrienne wasn't worried yet, then she had no reason to be either.

A calling card twirled between her fingers. "Oh," Virginie said, "and Uncle Ségur is downstairs."

Adrienne slapped her hand to the bedpost. "Virginie! How long has he been waiting?"

"Probably twenty minutes. Papa was still down by the cornfield."

Ségur was not expected whatsoever. Very hesitant to return to France, she had not heard from him nor her aunt in some time, but he had joined the parade of interested men in the rising new regime. Adrienne gripped her walking stick and left her room thinking of apologies for keeping the man waiting for so long.

His once dark hair had taken to a salted finish, still styled long and bagged in the back. He watched some of the château's fieldworkers through the windows of the reception room while they tilled and replanted for the season, tapping his foot along to the clang of hoes and rakes. From the silk of his black coat to the cut of his trousers, it appeared he was doing quite well. Ségur chuckled at the window as Gilbert appeared at the top of the fields with his cane and constantly moving tongue and jumped when he realized Adrienne was in the doorway.

"Dear me, Madame," he said, holding his chest. "What a vision that has surprised me."

"A nightmare, I imagine," she replied, walking up to kiss his cheeks. "Forgive me, my daughter decided to tell me now you were here. Did you not look for my husband first on your way in?"

"I've been enjoying watching him waddle around. The limp reforms all his gooselike qualities that I have so missed from his youth," Ségur said with a smile that didn't quite reach his eyes. "As for my waiting, that is quite alright. I don't visit nearly as much as I should. Please accept my apologies; I'll be a steadier correspondent and a good uncle. Elisabeth is doing well and sends her love. She is planning our daughter's wedding after a long debacle, but I shall spare the details for now."

"You sound resigned," Adrienne noted. Her hands were growing clammy. "What is it?"

He gestured to the chair nearby and Adrienne hesitantly took it, a worrying pulse finding itself at her temple. "Let us wait for Lafayette to join us," he said. "I fear I do not have the courage to say it twice."

Gilbert took another quarter hour before he walked by the reception room covered in pollen and soil. His cane dug into the wood floor at the sight of Ségur, expressions ranging from joyful surprise to an agitated confusion. He removed his cravat to wipe the grime from his forehead, appearing like a poor farmer welcoming a state official.

"You look like a walking black seal," Gilbert said, his features settling into a blank frown.

Ségur reached into his pocket and pulled out a uniformly folded letter, bearing such a seal. "Yes, I'm afraid I do," he replied. "Would you like to sit, Monsieur?"

"No," Gilbert replied. "I am fine as I am."

Adrienne rested her hand on his back, watching Ségur's every move.

"Tis from Rochambeau younger," Ségur said. "Of our naval war in the Caribbean."

Her fingers pinched into her husband's shirt.

"It would seem our Noailles was mortally wounded in the midst of a French victory this past winter. I'm afraid it does not go into much detail, just that he passed with dignity and all the zeal of the Noailles family."

Tears immediately overflowed from Adrienne's eyes while Gilbert took the letter to read himself. She heard Gilbert's shaken inhale, joined by the crinkle of Ségur's sleeve as he placed his arm over his friend and nephew's shoulders, pollen stains be damned.

"W-we must invite his children here," Adrienne exclaimed, wiping her cheeks. They were all adults at this point, but no matter the age, becoming an orphan after an estranged father's death had to have been difficult. Angry as she was with Louis' decision to leave Louise, she did not want him to die, he didn't deserve to die.

"I've already written to Alexis at his place in Paris, Madame," Ségur said. "As heir, he was the first to know and should, hopefully, break the news to his siblings with some grace. On my way, I will be glad to forward your invitation."

"What a bastard," Gilbert said, holding up the letter. Adrienne reeled back, but he continued, "Upstaging us even in death."

Ségur wept through a laugh. "Yes," he agreed. "I imagine he'd think passing in retirement is the coward's way out. He never did anything without flair."

Delaying her trip to the Grammont home and Gilbert's to Adélaïde's would be necessary, but not detrimental. The last thing anyone wanted was to plan a funeral for a family member whose body was likely on foreign shores or at the bottom of the ocean, but it would be horrible not to. She prayed that if Louis remained a Christian, that he would see Louise long enough for her to give him a good thrashing.

Fleeting scenes from the last time she saw Louise crossed Adrienne's mind, the bubbling sobs compressed by a stiffening of her jaw. Her nails sunk into Gilbert's shirt further, but if he noticed, he said nothing.

La Grange-Bléneau, September 1804

No politician wanted to leave the family alone when it came to chiding Gilbert on what side he would take after Bonaparte crowned himself emperor. Retirement was what was originally asked of him and he was content to live it. It wasn't his fault that Bonaparte saw his mere existence as a threat. Not even the children were safe from questioning and demands when they traveled to and from the capital, and Georges and Virginie's Louis bore the brunt of Emperor Bonaparte's disapproval: stuck in their stations with no hope for promotions. But if there was anything the family at La Grange held dear, it was their beliefs and dignity. No complaint arose from *either* of Adrienne's boys.

A summer's rest brought some strength back to Adrienne, happily partaking in the growing families' affairs that made up for all the grief of early spring. Gilbert, fantastic at ignoring correspondence from Paris, was almost always out in the fields with the animals. An acting tour guide, a shepherd, a farmer, he was everything he needed to be at La Grange. He threw himself across the grass with his stiff leg at speeds their guests needed to brisken their walk to keep up with. Every evening he would return with sun kissed cheeks and more freckles on his nose, and they would entertain their household staff at the end of their work week. Fiddles made for excellent waltzing, inside or out. Gilbert swung Adrienne around inelegantly with the servants until they were light-headed and laughing, others joining in on the poor footwork, falling back into the grass as the lanterns hanging in the trees replaced the sun and the stars reflecting on the river acted as their own fireflies.

Everything felt all right in La Grange. Somehow its forest and pallid roads kept them safe from the outside world and from the ailments that persisted whenever they traveled. Adrienne would have been in Heaven if Georges and Louis returned home for good. All the gazettes and rumors circulating around the emperor's rise in power did not bode well in foreign nations, and Adrienne could smell the stench of wartime brewing yet again.

A letter sat in her pocket. She hadn't opened it in fear of ruining another joyous day with friends and family. The seal was regular, ink was not poisoned, and the paper was not crumpled in a panic.

But the sender's name was her father's, and so the letter weighed heavily in that pocket.

Chapter Thirty-Four

Rolle, Switzerland, July 1805

She had talked herself into it. Knowing her family was en route to Chavaniac, she set off alone towards the border of Switzerland. The road was, in layman's terms, terrible. Erasing almost all the year's progress on resting her leg, she tried to lay it flat where a companion would have sat, but the bumpy path was testing her limits.

Lake Geneva was a mirror-image of the sky and mountains that surrounded it. A calm sea that bustled with merchant ships and leisure boats alike. It was morning, but she imagined the night reflection was just as magnificent, fantastic for astronomers to practice their science.

Adrienne didn't want to admit it, but it looked like the perfect place for a man such as her father.

His address led to a quaint home, unlike anything he would stay at in Paris, it was clear only a couple lived here with room for a guest or two. The garden consisted of a few flowers and trees that led to a rocky drop off, descending down the hill to the city below. It hardly compared in grandeur to the gardens her mother would tend to.

Her mind was empty, walking across the stones to the house. There was no speech prepared, no berating or scolding, nor letters from her sisters to give. Quite rudely, she did not even send advance word that she was close.

An older man opened the door to her, his spectacles high on his nose. While he was surely acting the role of a butler, his suit was French and all brown, and instead of averting his gaze, he greeted her with a familiar smile.

"My Madame, what a shock it is to see you again," he said with a bow of his head.

Adrienne pursed her lips, looking at his short hair as gray as hers, and her recognition returned with a sharp snap. "Oh, *Monsieur Dameron!*" she cried, her arms wide like a child as she took the old friend into a happy embrace. The secretary, polite as ever, let her handle all of the intimacy. "I didn't know Papa hired you back. How are you?"

"I am well. Still piling papers at times, but my son is a great help."

"And you've a son," Adrienne said, glowing. "How wonderful!"

"Yes," he exclaimed, "he works at the docks as an apprentice. I live with my wife and him at the bottom of this very hill. But please, enough about me. You must be tired from your trip and your father has been waiting to hear of your arrival."

She stepped up into the home, the foyer of a light wood, decorated with glass and landscapes. "Is he here?"

"Yes, I had left him to retrieve some coffee. He's been paying close attention to that Napoleon. Worried for the family in Paris. Would you prefer to stop in the powder room or should you like to see him now?"

Her head buzzed. "Now, please, if you don't mind."

Letting him prepare himself to see her wasn't fair when she wasn't prepared at all to see him. How did he look? Did he still address himself as a duc here? One of the most influential and well-known aristocrats in all of France could not possibly just be sitting in a rocking chair in self-imposed exile. She was readying herself to feel anger, to feel bitterness, if that woman was with him.

His office was far different from the one at the Hôtel de Noailles. Where it was cramped and dark before, the room was bright and airy. Hanging plants replaced chandeliers, the rows of shelves were taken up with science books rather than correspondence and official documents, and windows that stretched a whole wall were open instead of closed up and covered. The light smell of mint wafted in the air.

"Monsieur de Noailles," Dameron said, "your daughter, Madame de Lafayette."

Her father looked up from his desk – a modest size that served more as a side-table to rest his arm upon as he read – and removed his reading spectacles right away. He looked well for a man approaching his seventies. Wrapped in a house robe of unspectacular fabric, he held his bosom and rose from the chair.

They stared at each other, words on their tongues but no courage to say them. Dameron nodded to himself and stepped from the room with a short excusal.

The breeze meant to roll down the hill to the water busied itself over the pages of her father's books.

"I, um, have been studying Kant in lieu of his passing last year," he said, gesturing to the collection. "Have you read Kant?"

Adrienne swallowed the lump in her throat. "I have listened to his critiques," she said with a tilt of her chin.

Her father smiled quickly, nervously. "Yes, of course. You were all very intelligent girls – Henriette made sure of that… she always did things ineffably well. Ah," he gestured around the room and settled on the chair, "would you like to sit or should you like a tour?"

She looked at the armed chair facing him by the window and set her cane by the arm before sitting down. Folding her hands in her lap, she watched the man swallow stiffly and return to his seat.

"Are you thirsty, Adrienne? It's a little warm for chocolate, but we may have some swiss made. I haven't tried it yet–"

"I'm alright, Papa," she replied. Her heart twanged watching him mouth the endearment.

"Pray tell, is Gilbert well? Your children?"

"Gilbert is accosted from all sides as he always has been," she said a little too harshly. She reined it back. "His leg pains him, but he's in otherwise excellent health. The girls as well."

Chapter Thirty-Four

"Wonderful. That's wonderful, darling."

The awkward strain was becoming too much for even Adrienne. Pressure built up behind her eyes and stuffed her nose; she turned to face the windows, hoping that the air would give a reasonable excuse to why she was beginning to cry.

Jean held out a handkerchief and asked no more questions.

"You haven't come to see my home once, Papa," she said, dabbing under her eyes. "It feels like you are avoiding it because it was Maman's, but you should have seen how much work I've put into it, how much she would have loved it. The grounds are flourishing, the stone is polished and it is full of family all year round. You left France before I had the chance to see you years ago and all I was given was *hearsay* of your love and affection."

Why was it so difficult to lay the grounds of truth out to her father when she was capable of doing it a hundred times over to men of much higher consequence?

"And furthermore," she said, shaking her head, "to remarry so soon after Maman's murder? We languished for years without your comfort. And the first news I had of you is that you've discarded her so quickly, as if she were a *nobody*, for a baroness?"

Her father's eyes were glassy. He pressed his lips tightly together and dipped his head. A hand, having gained more lines since the last she saw him, gestured to the window. "Would you like to meet her?" he asked, his voice still.

"I – Pardon?"

"Wilhelmine takes walks every morning while I have my coffee," he replied. "She will be back in a moment. No one from my family has greeted her as of yet, but she has always been attentive of my rambling. Her husband passed away not long after the terror. I do not think her son blames her for remarrying."

"That's different," Adrienne declared. "A woman needs security in this day and age."

"And a widower must wallow for eternity?" he asked. "If I had the courage to come back to France, I would have tried harder. I am a coward, but I did not fathom they would touch my wife, my darling daughter… Would you have preferred I prolong my sorrow and mourn for ten years? Twenty?"

The sincerity in his tone made the questioning all the worse. Adrienne hated it. She hated that she couldn't just hate him and she hated that she would never wish him to be lonely; her mother wouldn't have wanted that either.

"I wished you all the happiness in the world, Papa, and I meant it."

"Come and meet her."

"I don't know if I want to."

Jean rose from his seat, offering his arm. "It will be a difficult stay if you are to avoid your hostess while you're here. Not impossible, but dinners will be hard to coordinate without our guest present."

With his support, Adrienne did not need her walking aid, and for a brief passing moment, she felt the brush of her wedding gown slipping across the floor as he led her out to the hall. She clasped her hand over his elbow. No good daughter would say all the horrible rumors and expectations she had garnered about his wife. Pauline declared her Russian, but her title included French lands; was it insulting if she looked like Maman, or more insulting if she were entirely different? She married into the Noailles family when they had almost nothing, but to a widow baroness, a duc's nothing was still much.

Dameron was a steady constant to focus on as he brought a coffee tray outside to wait on a rock slab, straightened to act as a table and sheltered by the few trees that grew on the property. From between bushes, a pebbled path descended gently, rounding the hill and out of sight. Between the mountains and the lake, Rolle was pleasantly temperate. Adrienne imagined if walking sloping paths were not painful, she may have enjoyed them as well.

"Adrienne," her father said, guiding her to a woven chair. "Your work has been nothing short of miraculous." He held his finger up to stop her interjection. "Picpus is a *marvel*, my darling. I walked through it myself when I finished my business in Paris. Your mother would be so proud of you."

That wasn't fair, she thought, to be melting into an emotional mess before she was supposed to meet a woman formally known as her stepmother. She pushed her father's arm and sobbed furiously, and all the more for crying in front of company her face grew red. Dameron produced a fan and a wet cloth as if on cue, as a rising straw hat appeared behind the bushes.

"Good morning, Jean. Have you watered the edelweiss yet?" the woman, Wilhelmine, asked. She pushed her hat up and out of her eyes – eyes the color of the lake – and paused at the sight of Adrienne. "Forgive me, I wouldn't have gone out if I knew we would have company. Please excuse my attire, Madame."

"Wilhelmine, this is my second daughter, Adrienne," Jean replied. "So fear not for formalities; I am just an old man in his robe. And yes, those ugly things have been taken care of."

"Papa," Adrienne whispered, "mind your tone."

Wilhelmine did not address his sass, only focusing on her as she walked up to the shaded seating, hands lifted to her navel, touching the ring upon her left. "You are the Madame de Lafayette?" she said. Her accent was strange, a slavic sound to her vowels in an otherwise perfect French flow. "I am so very pleased to make your acquaintance. Jean has told me many stories of you and your husband when you two were but children together and how brave you were during the trials of Robespierre. What an honor it is to finally meet you."

"It's," Adrienne uttered, sizing the woman up. She had no extraordinary detail about her face except her eyes. Striking as they were, they were not cold like the mountain waters, but welcoming and sincere. "It is a pleasure to meet you as well, Madame."

"Now, I do not wish to take up your time with your father this morning," she said. "Let me prepare your room. You are a Roman Catholic, is that right? If you would like, there is a church just over a mile from here for Catholics. They hold their mass at eight in the morning on Sundays."

Adrienne blinked. "Thank you. That's kind of you to tell me."

Wilhelmine lifted her shoulders in a happy shrug before she absconded back to the house, squeezing Jean's hand as she passed. He took up his coffee, a drink Adrienne hardly ever saw him enjoy before, and sipped at it gingerly.

"Not so horrid, I hope," he said, sitting down in the chair next to his daughter. "First impression, my darling?"

"She is charming enough," Adrienne admitted, deflating.

"It doesn't have to be said in defeat. I still love your mother; she was an incredible woman and no one could replace the tender hold she has on my heart and the utter respect I had for her." He twisted the two rings on his finger. "Men need security as well, believe it or not. Perhaps not of an economic kind, but for his very being. It is *lovely* to be loved again."

"And she grows flowers?"

"She certainly tries," he mused.

"And you are happy, Papa?"

Jean lowered his cup. The brown of his eyes had taken on a milky hue that she only noticed as he looked up at the sky around them. "The evidence presented would conclude that this is a reliable theory."

Adrienne shook her head, fanning away her melancholy to the best of her ability. He had only grown into more of a science philosopher than ever. "Then I will be amicable in getting to know Madame a little better while I am here."

Her room was small and cozy. Without a companion, the bed felt cold, but she filled the time with writing to Gilbert of her father and of her new stepmother; including all the bits about her health that he always wanted to hear of. There were some companions in Switzerland that she would like to see again, and whose life Gilbert would also be itching to hear. The post would take less than a week to travel from Rolle to Chavaniac, so they would not have to wait long to hear from each other. Adrienne kissed every letter she sent.

Through the week, her father showed her all his new gadgets and theory notes from a small group of self-proclaimed scientists in the province. Everything he did, he focused all of his attention on, satisfied with discovering even a wrong hypothesis. Wilhelmine devoted much of her conversation about her own son who was sent off towards China and of whom she had not heard much from. Bringing up her late husband did not bother Jean in the slightest, the two of them content with existing in each other's company. Adrienne found it warmed her heart to see her father retired in good spirits. Anger towards him shifted to insistence that he and Wilhelmine must visit La Grange at their earliest convenience.

Arguably, Chavaniac would be an easier visit, but Gilbert was firing off every hearth in the château to test its new insulation, and no doubt the rooms and his person would be covered in soot. *Summer*, she wrote back to his reports, *is perhaps not the greatest time to be perfecting heat.*

If we sweat sufficiently in these weeks, it is destiny that we may sweat tears of joy as the snow falls later. I find standing bare in your salon does well for my health, he replied.

News of the French army's shifting was noticed right away in the Noailles' Swiss home where merchants crossing the lake spread swift gossip of Bonaparte's indecisiveness. Britain or Europe? Where would he go? Where would Adrienne's son and son-in-law be taken to next? Preferably home, but she knew that was wishful thinking. It was through friends of the family that she relied on Georges' safety as an aide-de-camp, hopping from staff to staff.

"Is there any supplies we can get you before you return?" her father asked, handing her a wrapped block of ice while Wilhelmine packed Adrienne's belongings.

Adrienne placed it on her leg. "No, I'll be alright. Rosalie's is hardly two days north and she always welcomes me there when Gilbert isn't around. And La Grange isn't much farther after that."

"Does that boy always have you traveling alone?"

"This is a rarity, actually. Your granddaughter is usually my secretary, but Madame Chavaniac wanted to see her and Anastasie to discuss the matter of her will."

Jean eyed her leg with apprehension. "That is something I've been editing every year, but pray you do not need to discuss it with me any time soon. I think the mountain air adds some longevity to an old man like myself."

Adrienne closed her journal that filled in as a miniature ledger and travel itinerary. The pages were becoming worn from heavy use. "I've taken a look at mine as well," she professed. "You know the one from my marriage contract. After Olmütz I thought it was for the best that I had my things in order. I wasn't fairing very well."

"But you are now." A disguised question.

"I'm *managing*, Papa. Rest and good company helps. If you would come to La Grange next spring, you can see Anastasie's babes: Célestine is growing so fast and Louise was delivered last autumn," she said, and his eyes softened at the namesake. "Natalie is chubby like Georges' was at her age. Émilie gave birth to Matilde in the advent season. We have a lovely full house for you to see all your great-grandchildren."

"All my great-granddaughters, you mean," Jean said, leaning against the doorframe. He laughed and crossed his arms. "How I imagine Gilbert is, having inherited an all female household. God bless and preserve him."

"It wasn't so bad for you, Papa."

"No, I've managed fairly well with my brood of smart and scathing girls once I accepted my fate. But I relied heavily on your mother; as Gilbert relies heavily on you."

She didn't want to admit everyone was relying on her, that was placing herself in too much of an important role, but she was more active than she wished to be. Going back home and sleeping for a good week sounded like the best plan. It wasn't likely to happen.

Her father didn't need to know that.

La Grange-Bléneau, November 1805

She held the mug of hot chocolate close while Gilbert led her around the farm on horseback. They had just the one for now, inundated with more livestock and their shelters to be able to afford a stable for more than two at a time. Every source of income was swept away in a litany of expenses and debts to be paid; staring at the ledger was a source of great anxiety. Staring at the row of cabbages that Gilbert had planted was the opposite. He waved his arm over the perfect patch, his smile contagious.

"Not much for a birthday gift, but just you wait until we have the best stews this winter," he declared, bringing her around to see all the late blooms along the moat.

"You are too much sometimes." The chocolate itself was a marvelous gift to be given. "Would you have some?" She held out the mug.

He stopped and leaned on his cane, staring up at her with a debating pout. "Me thinks I would be satisfied with a taste from thy maiden's lips," he said, scooting the scarf tied around his neck down and raising himself on the toes of his good foot. Adrienne tutted, ignoring the cramp that came with leaning over to reach him, kissing his cocky grin straight on. *"Delicious!"*

Gladly, he picked some of the chrysanthemums, handing them in a small bouquet up to her. It was always busy on the day of her birth – All Soul's Day. If she were well enough, they would take the trip to Picpus. But La Grange was lit to be a memorial in itself for the dearly departed. Warm against a cool gray sky. Adrienne tucked some chrysanthemum petals into the curls around Gilbert's head, an orange halo crown to bring out what was left of his ginger color.

She watched him as they continued to walk, boots and hooves crunching the fallen leaves as they went. So handsome. He truly was. More admirable than a carved statue, she could look at him every morning and every night and still find new things to love. His hand rested firmly on the top of her shoe, clicking his tongue to lead the horse along.

"I love you," she said matter-of-factly. And there rose his wide eyes and shocked goofy face as if he did not hear those words uttered a thousand times before.

"Mon coeur," he replied. "You make me woozy when I hear that phrase. What if my leg gave out? I have been trying to hold myself together just witnessing you sitting astride. Jealous of my own saddle."

"Fear not, beloved, you make a far more comfortable seat."

Gilbert stumbled, gripping onto the stirrups. "Adrienne, the children can see! Don't make their Papi embarrass himself." He nodded his head up to the windows of the château where three young girls stood with their faces and palms against the glass. They looked exactly how she remembered Anne, Pauline, and Rosalie did when they were their age.

Adrienne's smile waned.

Chapter Thirty-Five

Villersexel, February 1806

I t was never easy, bringing medicine and comfort to a grieving mother, especially when the mother was a sister. Rosalie, never fairing well with her pregnancies, had lost the one she carried over winter, and the depression seldom brought talk and movement. Monsieur Grammont wrote to Adrienne himself, worried for his wife who spent the days in bed staring blankly out the window. Adrienne could hardly bore herself in the high ceiling château with its illustrious rose-colored wood and libraries to die for.

But she was here for her baby sister. The things she brought with her were expensive, but Grammont was sure to pay her back over time. Money was tight, yet Adrienne wasn't going to fret over caring for Rosalie, especially after all she did for her.

Found in her bedchamber, Rosalie lay on her side, hugging a small pillow to her chest. The windows were cracked open, letting the cold winter air remove the smell of blood and fluid from the room.

Adrienne knew Rosalie had given birth to a son last year. Little Ferdinand must have only been around for a few weeks before she was pregnant again. It wasn't unsurprising that the womb would still be volatile.

"Before I get settled, may I grab you some wine? Water, even?" Adrienne asked, setting the basket of herbs and vials on the armoire.

Rosalie shook her head.

"Very well. Maybe some tea in an hour, then." She walked over to the side Rosalie faced, blocking the window with her body. "What would you like first: a prayer or a hug?"

"I just want to disappear," Rosalie breathed.

"I'm afraid that isn't one of the options I offered," Adrienne replied. She tucked her gown under herself as she sat on the bed and removed her bonnet. "I am sorry for your loss, Rose. May I hold you?"

Her sister's head would never be heavy to her. She stroked through dirty blonde waves, muttering all the prayers that were made for such moments. In some instances, she knew the words alone meant very little to thick walls of grief, but faith was all that they had, that God would be there behind the wall ready to break it down and replace all sadness with love and memories.

"He was such a little thing," Rosalie said, holding her palm open to Adrienne. "No bigger than the tiniest sunflower, covered in yellow fuzz."

"Your tournesol," Adrienne replied. "Henriette will take great care of all your little flowers. She was always so attentive." Taking the open hand, she brought it to her lips and tucked it under her chin. "Philippine and Rosie look well. Their governess is doing a wonderful job with their manners, I thought I walked into a palace, for certain."

Rosalie hummed, some of her tears pooling in the crook of Adrienne's neck. "I just don't understand why I am so horrible at bearing children."

"Sometimes there are no answers. We can't know God's plans."

"You and Gilbert are still intimate," Rosalie said, "but nothing comes from it. Is that God's will too?"

Adrienne found the wavering branch by the window that Rosalie was so enraptured by.

"I'm sorry, that was mean of me."

She shook her head. "It's alright," she said. "I haven't had regular courses since Virginie. And after Austria, they have ceased altogether. It is as it is; I have no room to complain with how lovely my children have become and the healthy grandchildren they have given me."

"All three of mine have been," a breath, "in perfect health. For now, at least. But I worry if they fall ill or hurt themselves or –"

Adrienne shushed her. "There's nothing we can do about that now. We have today for the time being, and tomorrow to wait for."

She was terrified for her own children *constantly*. Virginie had come down most of the way with her, but her destination was the German states where Louis' uncle was stationed within the Black Forest. It was as close as she could get to her husband without appearing on the front lines. The idea gave Gilbert agita, but he couldn't talk her out of it; and Adrienne had to admit if she were in Virginie's place, she would have also wanted to be as close to Gilbert in war as she could manage. There were no rewards when risks were not taken.

Rosalie eventually agreed to the tea. Adrienne brewed it herself in the large kitchen downstairs to make sure it was perfectly how their mother made it. The short, steep steps of the servants stairwell were terrible on her leg, making rising to the ground floor take twice as long as coming down.

While managing her own ledger, helping Rosalie get back to her usual business took up the rest of her time. Coming out of depression wasn't an immediate thing, Adrienne knew that well, and she stood in her place in greeting the children each day, organizing dinners, and attending to the charities that Rosalie was focused on over the last three years.

Be mindful, Gilbert wrote from La Grange, *of your own health. Keep up with your medicine and get as much rest as you can. We have teethers in our midst. Louise found the edge of your embroidered pillows I keep in my library very soothing...*

By the time she would have to reply to him, it was two in the morning.

Fontenay, May 1806

Seeing more nieces and nephews was a delight despite fatigue coming on fast after a two week journey to the other side of France. When the letter came from Monsieur Montagu, she packed her belongings, bid adieu to Rosalie, and came straight to her other sister.

A doctor was already in house, willing to tell Adrienne all he knew about what ailment was causing Pauline's fevers. She slept most of the day with Adrienne doting by her side with cool cloth and cups of fresh water. Diligently, she prayed more prayers than a Sunday mass until Pauline woke up long enough to have conversation with her.

"Would you let Gilbert know I do not hate him for his poor taste in politics now that we share a loathing for our current leader?" Pauline said, indecisive if she wanted the bedsheets at her chin or by her lap.

Adrienne rubbed her face and grinned. "He will joyfully love to hear it from you personally once you've recovered. I try to keep my mouth closed on such matters, so ill-talk will strictly be reserved between you two."

"Oh, excellent. I will look forward to it."

"And bring your family, we will make room for everyone. Gilbert needs all the attention he can get while I am away."

Pauline's tired cheerfulness suddenly stopped. "While you're away?"

Forehead throbbing, Adrienne cocked her head. "If I'm at Aunt Tessé's or checking up on the lands in Brittany, I mean," she said. "Nothing else by it. You're half-asleep, Pauline, get some rest."

There was always plenty to be done, having her run around France was nothing new; Pauline knew that. She sent Adrienne on many errands before and would do so again. And Adrienne was ready to do for Pauline what she already did for Rosalie – but it was a little helpful having more grown children in Fontenay to assist.

Dinners.

Charities.

Helped Joachim with running the house.

Paid the servants.

Treated niece Stéphanie's bee sting.

Wrote the poems that Pauline rambled from her bed.

Washed her sister; washed herself.

Alone in the rather homey rectangle of her guest room, Adrienne grabbed the chamberpot from under her bed and collapsed on her knees, retching until her stomach had nothing else in it. No matter how much she blinked, her eyes were still full of tears. For days, the constant dull pain would light up like fireworks inside. It squeezed her skull, it made food impossible to keep down. Sweat dripped down her neck even as goosebumps lined her arms.

Please come home, Adrienne. I do not like when our doctor cannot see to you right away when your symptoms start up again. Come back to La Grange where I can tend to you. You've done enough. It hurts me to not have you here.

Surely, she could ask Rosalie to come and tend to Pauline in her stead. But she was already here and settled with a routine; breaking it would bother too many people. Adrienne wiped her mouth and pulled a pillow from the bed to comfort herself on the floor. She would be fine after a night's rest, she reassured herself. Pauline was in much worse shape than she. Perhaps if she traveled to the abbey in town, some holy water could add some benefit to the herbal medications Pauline was taking. It was worth a try. Adrienne enjoyed looking at the church's architecture.

Breathing in through the nose, out through the mouth, *repeat*. She only threw up one more time before her stomach settled into an immobile pinch. Sleeping just once on the floor would be alright.

Aulnay, October 1806

"You remember our anniversary last year, don't you, Adrienne?" Aunt Tessé asked, bustling around her parlor with new decor to set up. She spoke of her golden wedding anniversary with her husband who hardly spoke a word to her nowadays. It was an odd event, Adrienne thought, most couples their age lived apart and cared little for the occasion. "I had ferns all along the foyer. Well, I was thinking something similar, but maybe little pumpkins. I bought a few from your quaint farm and they are the cutest, obscene things. Definitely would make quite the conversation piece for my dinner party. Very small party, naturally. I've heard it all from you before about what little we have to go around, but parties are necessary to lift one's spirits!"

Adrienne nodded, watching the cows wander by in the field. There were baby ones now, following their mothers as they munched on dying grass.

Her headaches had stirred up into such a fury, it was difficult to focus on anything for too long. She hardly remembered why her aunt called her here on her way back home. Was it just that she was in the area? Did she need information on her nieces' health? Adrienne hid her face in her hands and popped her head back up whenever her aunt walked by her, smiling and agreeing without purpose. Tessé was bound to mention it eventually if she hadn't already.

"That chapel built by your Picpus cemetery," Tessé moved on. "I went by it last Tuesday and I think they should add some color to the walls. Everything in Paris just feels so plain as of late. Some *color* will really perk it up, I believe. If I were a ghost, I would want something pretty to look at by my resting grounds. Perhaps a garden nearby? The nuns could take care of that, don't you think? Now those would brighten a chapel up right away."

"It used to be a garden before they needed to dig more to fit all the *bodies*, Auntie," Adrienne replied. "Bring it up to Pauline. She's the president of the committee that tends to it now, I'm sure some flowers could be arranged in your name."

"In my... Ah, *yes*, of course. In my name, I'd be happy to donate."

Was she being too harsh on her aunt? It couldn't be helped that her tone was so aggrieved by the lackluster state of her own head.

Tessé switched to a different topic. Something about Bonaparte's dramatic government and gossip given to her by Ségur of all people. It may have been rude, but Adrienne could not care a little bit about the Emperor and his court of foolhearted, enslaved Frenchmen. The animosity to which he treated her family was enough to cast the man into Adrienne's pit of apathy. She took up the pillow sitting next to her and smothered herself with it, hoping the dark and silence would give her the chance to at least nap for an hour or two.

Her dreams were of her mother, in the ruby red draped room of the

Hôtel de Noailles where they worked on their stitches and talked of their lessons after the days had come to a close. She remembered how soft and crunchy her mother's gown was, grasped in her hand in hopes she could sit next to the woman. The duchesse's laugh sounded like church bells, her scolding was full of love. No words shared with her mother were boring; the silence between them was insightful and relaxing.

Knock.

Adrienne should have had her remain in Chavaniac where the mountains would have shielded them longer, or sent her away with Anastasie and Virginie. She *shouldn't* have agreed that Paris was safe enough just because one crazed party was replaced by another. Why didn't she think of the future when the months were so fleeting? Why *didn't* she hold onto her gown tighter?

Knock.

How much could she have done in Paris when she saw Louise leaving that prison? She could have fought back, held onto her longer. Kissed her cheek one more time. If she wrote to the *right* people, argued with the *right* words, maybe, if not sparing their lives, she could have *stalled* execution until the terror ended – the terror that ceased days after their beheading, she could have pleaded for a few days, if she just did something *different.* Why didn't they come for her next? What name was so important that her neck was spared of all people? She *should* have died, she *would* have died –

"*Mon coeur*, I'm here."

The pillow lifted from her eyes, she blinked awake as an arm was tucked under her head and another by her knees. Everything in the room seemed to blur, like a washed away watercolor painting except her savior's face. She had not seen it in months.

"She had agreed to help me host my party, I would not have kept her if she told me."

"Auntie, she's burning up, tell me how you could not see?"

He shouldn't have been picking her up, she realized. He needed his cane.

"Gilbert," she said, throwing her arm out to fight back. "Your leg! You'll hurt yourself. Don't do this, I can walk. I can walk."

"I'm bringing you home," he replied, his jaw set.

"You're angry." The ceiling was replaced with a dusty sky as he carried her outside.

He was still handsome when he was angry. How lucky she was.

"Yes, I am angry," Gilbert said.

"With me?"

His brow twitched, lifting the both of them into the carriage. Was that Charlie in the driver's seat? She couldn't tell.

"No. Yes. A little. I'm a little angry with you," he grumbled, slamming the door shut twice with his foot. Her luggage hadn't yet been unpacked; he must have heard she stopped here right away to have traveled from La Grange. "You should be angry too at the *stupid* choice you made to not come home when I begged you to."

Adrienne looped her arms around his neck, the carriage too small for her to lay down flat. "But Aunt Tessé –"

"Damn Aunt Tessé!" Gilbert exclaimed, slapping the roof. His temper flared. "She is very capable of hosting her own dinners. What use would you be like this anyway? If you fainted in front of everyone or… or fainted alone with no one to check on you? Twas stupid, Adrienne, *stupid!*"

The rocking of the carriage shot pains up her spine. That was why she started crying; it must have been.

"*Mon coeur*, I can't… I can't," he stuttered, his head thumping against the wall. "You are going to make me cry, stop it."

"I'm sorry." She tried to wipe her cheeks, but the tears kept coming.

"No," he said, closing his eyes. "No, *I'm* sorry. I should have come to get you at Fontenay. You are a good woman. I know you always put your family first, but damn it all, if you put me first, please remember that you are my everything, Adrienne. Please stop if you cannot go; and do not go if I can't reach you."

"I'm sorry."

"Stop." He kissed her forehead. "We're going to get you into bed. The doctor has already been called. These are all things we've dealt with before and you are going to pull through just as you always do." They both winced as the dirt road turned to pebbles. "And Virginie's letters. Beloved, you will love to read them."

"O-of course."

"Ask me why."

"W-why will I love them?"

Smiling into her hair, he said, "because she is with child." Her scalp felt damp, but whether or not he was crying or she was simply sweating was undetermined.

That's where all Virginie's letters went. Her daughter thought she would be at home so late in the year. Adrienne giggled, tasting her own salty lips. "That is wonderful," she whispered. Over two years into their marriage, Virginie and Louis finally were given a blessing. All they needed now was an end to the war so they could return to La Grange safely.

Gilbert's arms encircled her as she leaned against him like a chaise. He gently rubbed her stomach and blew air on her neck until she began to nod off again. Flashes of her mother in church, the replaying image of Louise before she was dragged down the steps of prison.

"We will see each other again soon!"

Chapter Thirty-Six

La Grange-Bléneau, April 1807

Adrienne liked when the blossoms bloomed right on time every spring when the eleventh of April rolled around. She wrapped herself in pink to sit among the tulips and roses, watching the apple blossoms twirl from their branches to the stream below. They had music playing up in the château, but the songbirds were plentiful enough for her. All the attention was too much. As always, her wedding anniversary was a joyous memory, but her fevers were a dime a dozen, sometimes lasting a day, maybe two, with the headache to follow. If she wandered off for some quiet, the family would understand. The doctor had said she was out of any danger after she insisted that rest was great enough medicine. It worked before and should work again.

Virginie was glowing so late into her pregnancy, as if the weight of the world was lifted from her shoulders. Letters from the warfront were hopeful of their boys' eventual return. Men could only withstand being stuck in one position for so long. Throw the army away, Adrienne had said, they can make do at La Grange.

A passing shower from yesterday made the grass by the river slick with dew. It slid from one long blade to another, some dotted three to a leaf. From where the sun hit it, they glistened like diamonds.

It would have been smart to bring a book with her out here in the fresh air. But the tranquility never bothered her, knowing that up the hill, Lafayettes, Faÿs, and Lasteyries danced and sang together: an obnoxious and lovely sound to hear. Her leg allowed her a twirl or two, but she wasn't supposed to be greedy.

She had, at last, a small miniature of Gilbert to keep her company, a made pair in their current age.

"A loud bunch, aren't they?"

She didn't recognize the voice, looking up from the stream and around the trees. A man stood by the low hanging branch, no older than Gilbert; he was not one of the field workers nor a hired contractor that she knew was interviewed. He looked well-off, if not slightly out of fashion for the year.

"I beg your pardon, can I help you?" she asked. He pivoted on his heel, facing Adrienne with a rather young face. If anything, he was the one that looked surprised to see *her*.

"I am terribly sorry," he said. "I believe I got lost somewhere on my path and ended up here. It wasn't my intention to sneak up on you." Removing his hat, a mass of curly auburn hair tied into a queue slipped over his shoulder as he bowed. "If I may, Madame, may I ask where 'here' is?"

Adrienne's head could not cock any further. He must've been a little mad, but did not seem to her a dangerous man. "This is La Grange. You're just outside of Paris, Monsieur."

"'Grange?' Grange… certainly not my Grange," he muttered, walking in a small circle. "Paris, you say?"

"Yes. Have you not been?"

"I've never been to France, Madame. *'Grange.'* This isn't the Grange of the Marquis, is it?"

A spark lit up in her mind. "You are an American," she said, her mouth twitching up into a smile. No wonder he was lost. "Yes, we receive a lot of my husband's old colleagues here."

"Your husband?" he asked. Slowly he approached her, keeping a reasonable distance. His eyes were a cornflower blue, squinted from the height of his cheekbones. A keen smile split his lips. "My dear Marquise, what an honor it is to make your acquaintance. I've heard so much about you from Lafayette during the war."

"You know him well, I presume?"

"We have shared plenty of tents," the man said. "I've held his hair back when he was absolutely sloshed at officer parties, although he tried not to drink as much afterwards. May I sit, Madame Marquise?"

"If you'd like. My husband is in the château if you would like to see him. I'm sure he would be happy to receive a friend. It is funny, not many Americans speak French. Your accent is very good."

He settled down into the grass without disturbing the glossy dew. "My mother was Huguenot; taught me at a young age."

Adrienne pulled her shawl tighter around her arms. The spring air held a chill between trees. "How did you and General Lafayette meet? On a battlefield, perhaps?" It was rare for her to hear new stories before Gilbert had the chance to edit them.

"If Philadelphia counts as a battlefield," he laughed. "I was sent to retrieve a recently arrived French boy who was given the rank of major-general and escort him to a tavern. Not many people on the staff were as fluent as I, and it was very easy to boss me around while complimenting my lexicon; I was only twenty at the time."

"I hope he made a good first impression," she said, of which he must have, otherwise it would be silly for this American to venture so far to see him.

"I have never met a more awkward man in my life," he replied. "But he grows on you quickly – like a weed. I remember him always asking, *'Alexandre, could you check my English,'* or *'how do you tell another general to lick my boot?'"*

Alexandre.

Adrienne pursed her lips. That did sound like Gilbert. "You must mean General Lee," she said, calling back to his war stories.

Alexandre pushed loose hair from his forehead. "One mustn't speak ill of the dead," he replied while simultaneously nodding along. He looked around at the pastel canopy over them to the clear water a few feet in front of them. "You have a lovely home. The biggest I've seen, actually."

"Thank you," she said, blushing at the smallest compliment. "It is very cozy for fitting my rather *loud* family."

It was his turn to flush, spinning a finger around a blade of grass. "I could argue my Grange is cozier with my brood."

A contest? Adrienne rested her cheek on raised knees. "How many children do you have, Monsieur?"

He clicked his tongue. "Eight," he said, paused, then nodded. "My poor wife."

"We may be tied on how many we squeeze into our walls, but I suppose I am blessed for the size of mine. I've heard American homes are quite economic." Adrienne picked at a pebble by her feet, rolling it down the slope to the water's edge. "I do insist you speak to Gilbert. We are celebrating and have plenty of food for an honored guest."

He seemed to be preoccupied with his waistcoat, his perky demeanor shifted down. Adrienne lowered her gaze to his side, where the color of the linen was starting to run.

"Are you injured?" she asked, her heart rising to her throat.

"Oh, no, tis alright," he replied, getting to his feet. "I really wasn't supposed to be here anyway, you see. Lost, remember?"

Adrienne moved to her knees, the grass too slick to stand up as fast as she wanted. "Please, by God, come into the house. Let my husband and I help." She struggled to get up, and the man's brows fell in pity. He stepped over to her and reached out his hand.

"Come now, a gentlewoman should not worry."

"How could I not worry?" she asked, taking the hand and pulling herself up to the flat of the hill.

Gilbert sighed, twisting her hand around to take it in a gentle embrace. "That is not what I said," he exclaimed with a small smile. "I said *don't disappear in such a hurry.* I would have joined you if you asked me to. Thirty-four years, and still the same."

The hair on Adrienne's neck sprung up in an instant. She looked behind him, around the trees and back towards the river. "I don't understand," she said, pulling Gilbert along to the low hanging branch. "Where did your friend go?"

Gilbert shook his head. "My friend?"

"Your American friend. A-a-an *Alexandre*, he mentioned. Said he knew you."

His forehead bonked against hers. "You are warm again, *mon coeur*," he said with a tsk. "We must break this habit of yours, I do not like it."

Feverish or not, Adrienne gripped his waistcoat. "He was bleeding, Gilbert! We have to find him."

"Adrienne!" he shouted, taking her wrists. "Beloved, you were alone. I approached you alone. This… this *Alexandre* is not here; he cannot possibly *be* here, my love."

She stammered a complaint. She wasn't losing it, she couldn't have been growing mad. The fear in Gilbert's eyes was real and what a horror it was for her to have put it there.

A small laugh escaped her lips. "Of course," she chuckled. "I'm overtired, that's all."

"Yes, I think so," Gilbert smiled back. "Let me walk you back now. I can have some blossoms brought into your room so you don't have to come out here alone anymore."

Gripping onto his arm, Adrienne let her gaze linger across the garden. He felt too detailed to have been made up by her ailing mind. Gilbert also felt too attentive of her on their way to her room. She reassured him it was just her fever, it couldn't have been anything else. All the excitement of the day must have manifested itself. He agreed with her. It must've been the fever.

☆

Pauline de Lasteyrie, to no surprise, was a little girl. Gilbert looked thoroughly pleased, surrounded by his girls in white wreaths of flowers, holding her in place of her father through her baptism within the château's small chapel. Her namesake and godmother was a flurry of tears and kisses, gifting Virginie with pen after journal, desk after cradle.

"I have become an expert on holding daughters," Gilbert declared, refusing to give up his youngest to his other youngest. "Do not deprive me of my right as the favorite Papi."

"Gilbert, let her hold her baby," Adrienne said, interceding to scoop the bundle of lace and cotton from his arms. Virginie was all smiles and it melted into all the crevices of La Grange.

When Georges and Louis returned, they sealed the deal, all little families were right where they belonged, sitting together in the morning room, enjoying the rush of a summer rain by the open windows. Louis was far tanner on his face and hands, holding baby Pauline like she were made of glass, very proud of himself and Virginie for having accomplished making a child in the middle of a war. It couldn't have been comfortable, but maybe that was what they needed. Georges made do with Natalie draped across his back, humming along to all the stories he shared while he held onto Matilde's wiggling toes as Émilie fed her.

Charles returned with beverages balanced in one hand and dragging Célestine by the leg with the other, the young girl giggling for her mother to take notice; Anastasie rocked Louise in her arms.

Adrienne sat between them all, her hand placed lightly on Gilbert's thigh. Wholly content with listening to them talk of everythings and nothings, stories retold from the letters sent to everyday chores they put themselves through at camp. The medicine she took with her drink left her tired early on in the day, but she'd push herself through time for family; it was all she looked forward to outside of business.

Gilbert's hand slipped over hers. Warm as always, she missed his little touches whenever Adélaïde and his other guests were visiting. She studied him as he spoke. There were his gray hairs, curled around his ears in such scarcity one wouldn't even notice! Summer freckles had returned in greater numbers, at least two dozen on each high cheekbone. He started brushing his hair over his forehead like Georges, except his curls had to be flattened or styled with pomade to remain there, and it hid much of his high hairline. Adrienne missed it, but he looked dashing regardless.

"Would it be alright," he asked in the night as he walked her to her room, their canes clicking with every few steps, "if Georges and I travel to Chavaniac this autumn? There are some things I wish to show him there and it is always healthy to check in on Aunt Charlotte as much as possible in her old age. Her last letter makes me worried, although she does tend to dramatize."

"Goodness, Gilbert, by all means. Give Madame all my love."

"You would be well? I know you know how much I worry about you. From what I've seen, though you're ill often, you have always been strong enough to overcome it. But still," he said, holding the candle by her door while she unlatched it. "I've not taught my heart how to function without yours. And if you feel like anything is out of the ordinary, speak the word and I will delay my trip."

Adrienne knew at once that she was far from ordinary. There was a shadow that lingered behind her that never felt like her own as the weeks ticked on by. But holding him back was cruel, if he wanted to take a trip with Georges to see his ailing aunt then he had every right to do so. Why would she place herself above Madame Chavaniac now?

"I'm perfect," she lied. "Let me write something for your aunt before you go. We can prepare a basket."

Gilbert's smile broke through with a relieved sigh. "That would be delightful. I'm sure she will love it even if it were –"

"Cabbages?"

"Cabbages, yes." He knocked his nose against hers. She could smell the wine on his breath as he leaned back again, finding intrigue in the loose strands of her hair that glowed white against the candlelight. "Goodnight, my snow-kissed delight."

Her cheeks warmed. "Goodnight."

The bliss that tickled her skin as he departed for his own apartment around the corner quickly cracked and shifted to horror at the *lie* that had crawled from the pit of her soul. She felt revolted if not more sick than ever as nausea climbed up her gut, inch by inch.

La Grange-Bléneau, September 1807

Nothing remained down. Through her own shame, she had woken

her daughters in the middle of the night with her crying. With a third chamberpot in front of her, half-full of anything else she had left inside her, the rest of it was pooling from her own sweat and tears. It would have been better to throw up on the floor, not on the bed where the blankets had already cost so much.

"Hang on, Maman," Virginie said, running into the room with towels and a large bowl from the kitchen. "Anastasie is writing Doctor Lobinhes right now. Louis will ride it to Paris."

"It hurts," she moaned, grasping onto the bowl until her nails cracked.

"I'm sorry, Maman. Hold on." There was the sound of water and Virginie returned to the bed, climbing right onto the mattress with a damp cloth for the back of her neck and across her mouth. With her other hand, she rubbed Adrienne's back in circles, slow and steady. "Does that feel any better? Do you want to lay down on your side?"

She shook her head no when she meant yes. Nothing made any sense to her when every muscle ached so profoundly. Virginie's rosary laid on the table in front of her. Adrienne focused on that, counting and praying through every heaving convulsion that dragged out until she was coughing and dry.

Anastasie came into the room with a basket full of chipped ice from the icebox. "Nini, help cool her fever until the doctor arrives. Tuck this under her shift."

The ice was melting faster than it was cooling her skin. Adrienne wanted to cry out for Gilbert. He had only left a few days ago, it wasn't fair to pull him back so soon only to pity her for a few days. She couldn't do this every time he left her. She told him to go. This was hers to bear.

"We're going to alter your diet," the doctor said, removing his contraption from her belly. "It's important you consume hearty foods that would be easy to digest. I suggest a very brothy stew, slow cook all the veal and chicken until it is easy to pull apart into small pieces. You may find quinquina as your drink of choice, as we've tested that before and you responded well to it."

Virginie sat by Adrienne's bed, vigorously writing all instructions.

"I've been told you have been traveling frequently. One of your sisters' illnesses may have led you to a relapse from your sickness in Austria. But you are still young and a *relapsed* illness is far more likely to be conquered with the right technique and treatment than something entirely new." Lobinhes left a container of the quinquina with Anastasie. "I'll return in the next day or two to see how you are taking to the diet. In the meantime, rest does wonders for the body and mind."

Adrienne stared at the ceiling.

This didn't feel the same, but if the doctor thought it was as it had been before, then she would try.

She waited as her daughters and Émilie took to the kitchens like harpies, following all of what was said Adrienne needed. Her sons-in-law acted as the dual patriarchs of La Grange, making sure all the farm work and pay was taken care of. Every night, one would be chosen to sit by her bed, reading or praying like clockwork. Disappointed when she threw up her meal or enthused when she kept it down, everything was going as it always did.

Two days in.

One week in.

Two weeks in.

From her own bed, she must have ran a mile from how fast she was breathing. The room was so hot; *was there a fire?* She didn't smell smoke, *but what if there was?* Maybe she was moved to a desert country, somewhere like Egypt. It was impossible to sleep with how wet the sheets were from the sweat that dripped off her skin. Apologies poured out when she saw the scrunched faces of her family when they entered her room; she must have been revolting.

Someone was packing things into a chest. Their form was a ghostly blur around the room. Where were they going? Was she to go with them? *Where was Gilbert?* Oh, right, he was in Chavaniac.

What a good man he was to check on his aunt.

Chapter Thirty-Six

Aulnay, October 1807

Taking the lead by tongue despite its bitter taste was better than having it spread over the open sores in her leg. They stung and bubbled and took all her energy not to curse at the process that was supposed to purify her blood. A month of a fever and that was the doctor's prognosis. In a time of awareness, Adrienne's daughters did tell her that she was being moved to Aunt Tessé's, as her home was closer to the doctor for him to keep a steadier eye on the treatment.

When she could, she *still* loved to read to Célestine about the line of David in the Bible or of the saints to whom her Papi was named after. But her energy only lasted a few minutes every morning and evening, when she slept all through the night and afternoons.

She enjoyed, at least, the sight of roaming cows outside and the bird's nest that nestled itself between the stone surrounding the window and the bushes of the garden. It was the same room Gilbert was stuck in for months; how fitting it was for her now.

Some nights she hardly dreamed. Others, it was unsure when exactly she awoke. When Aunt Tessé arrived with breakfast, she was dressed so *oddly* for the climate of Egypt. If she walked outside, she would burn in an instant.

"Where's your veil, Auntie?" she asked, pointing to the window. "See how sunny it is? You'll want to cover your skin."

It wasn't an obscene suggestion. The look of alarm Tessé gave worried her, and she took the bowl that was originally meant for her from frozen hands.

"Forgive me, I didn't mean to sound rude."

"Dear," Tessé said, "you weren't rude at all. I am just confused, love. It's overcast today, don't you see?" She moved to the window and shifted the blinds that covered the miles of sand and rippling horizon. Adrienne squinted. Her aunt must have been the one that was mistaken, but she wouldn't dare let her know her age was catching up to her, so Adrienne nodded and smiled.

Vomiting the following night placed her back in the outskirts of Paris, hunched over the bed in the guest room. Adrienne wiped her face, feeling the sweat that came from her own fever, not a desert. Her chamberpot had all of the broth wasted. And splattered over the surface were the tiniest dots of blood.

~~Syria, 840 BC~~ Paris, November 1807

They were now in a smaller apartment of her aunt's, that much she understood, and being visited by Bonaparte's *personal* doctor gave Adrienne the greatest sense of embarrassment. It was deemed best for her to keep her mouth shut while the doctor assessed her, lest she say something completely deranged.

Adélaïde was the first to greet her in the morning, a sincere smile that she was glad to see. They both understood why the family was hesitant to speak with Adrienne, it must have been scary to see her at her thinnest and most tired, like an old hag.

"It is just one of my fevers," Adrienne assured Adélaïde. "You see how well I am being taken care of, I will get over it soon."

"Gilbert is due to arrive soon," Adélaïde replied, and seeing how nervous Adrienne became, rested her hand atop of hers. "His cheekiness always does wonders, doesn't it?"

"It does… isn't it a dangerous road from the palace? He… he should be careful of raids," Adrienne said, shaking her head. "There is so much infighting."

The tension between those that worshiped God and those of the false prophets amounted to countless deaths; Gilbert should be careful where he traveled through if he were coming for her.

☆

Her leg grew numb from more medicine that was rubbed into her wounds. Like rocking on a ship or trying to find north in a sandstorm, Adrienne was incapable of keeping even water down over the next who knows how many days.

It was just a bad fever, she would get better.

Everyone was being so attentive to her, how troublesome she was being.

All she could do was thank each person who walked by her, whether or not they aided her in some way. She worried that if they did and she didn't notice, she'd insult them. Virginie stared at her with a benign look when she talked about her day over supper.

When her star arrived, Adrienne couldn't keep herself from blushing, pulling herself under her covers, hiding her face in her pillow.

"Oh," she said, as Gilbert carefully took the walls of her fortress down piece by piece. "Oh." He sat by her side and tilted his head. Reaching out a hand, she felt the firmness of his arm all the way up to his shoulder, to the fuzz at his chin. "Thank God," she breathed.

He was real.

"Has your body betrayed you so much, my dear Adrienne," he said with a shake of his head, "that they've trapped you in Paris? When I heard, I rushed home as fast as I could expecting the worst, but here you are, my better half."

"I am sorry for making you worry. This is nothing, I only wanted you to enjoy your trip with our son. Oh, Gilbert."

"Anastasie mentioned you haven't been keeping down food," Gilbert said, removing his coat. "Can we try that again? Do you think you could beat your stomach into submission?"

Adrienne nodded. If he was here, she could certainly do anything.

He held the bowl for her even when she fiddled with the spoon. He taste tested every other bite, assuring her that it was just normal broth when she asked.

There wasn't much to talk about from bed, but Gilbert took the reins and spoke about his trip and about their southern home and Aunt Charlotte. He laid his head next to hers at night and continued speaking so softly and tenderly, she heard him in her dreams.

But where was peace when someone was out there trying to kill her?

Dozens of scorpions, scratching their way across her legs and under her chemise, *biting* her and *stabbing* her with their pronged tails – she shrieked, kicking a few off, trying to swipe the rest off of her bed but they avoided her fingers, tearing at her skin.

"*Mon coeur.*"

"Stop! Stop, make them stop!" She covered her face. What if the Baalites got to her children? Where were her grandchildren?

"Adrienne, it's not real. None of it is real," Gilbert said firmly. He held her cheeks between his hands, thumbing her jaw until she opened her eyes. "It's all in your head. Nothing is going to hurt you."

"Th-the babies," she whispered.

"They are all fine, *mon coeur*. They're asleep. Do you want to see?"

She nodded. She had to be sure.

Helping her out of bed, a clear bed with no scorpions, he walked her to the guest bedrooms where Anastasie and Virginie lay sleeping with their husbands, where the children cuddled each other in their cribs. She counted them all and listened to their breath. *Of course they were all alright,* she thought.

"I'm sorry," she said, turning around into Gilbert's hold. Her shoulders rocked as she whimpered into his shirt. "I did not mean to wake you. You must be so tired." Sniffling through his rubbing her back, she wiped her nose and looked up at the shadows under his eyes. "Would you like hot chocolate? I'll make you a pot."

"Let's have some tomorrow," he offered. "I think some rest is in order, don't you?"

"You do not have to wait on me."

"I insist on staying. Would you come to bed, beloved?"

She fiddled with her hands. "Well, if you wait next to me, I'll fall asleep quietly."

What patience he had for her. Adrienne couldn't think of a sweeter man who smiled at her with all the endearment of a new lover. He was the only one to point out the falsehoods she saw, and did so in a way that made the room lighter, agreeing with some of the tall tales and quotes of wisdom; and she merely laughed at herself for all the silly things she said. Eventually she caught some errors the moment she commented about them, and could at least know that if she woke up in the desert once more that no scorpions nor raids would befall her or the family.

Thank you were her primary words. There was never a day of her sicknesses where she was not cared for, but someone was with her now through every moment. Through the fits of burning when her leg was wishing to fall away, to days where she slept for twenty hours at a time, when she woke there was a dear keeping vigil.

The evening she watched Gilbert stand by the door with a priest was the moment she understood that she was dying.

She didn't know if everyone else was coming to that realization, but that feeling of perpetual ache that settled everywhere but her heart and soul was coming into focus. Her thank yous, as numerous as they were, were accompanied by her asking if there was anything she could do in return. Almost always she was denied, they only wished for her to rest and get better. But around her bouts of delirium, Gilbert *finally* agreed to that pot of hot chocolate.

He carried her to the kitchen late one night, where the fire was already awaiting something to heat. She shook her head, catching him on his attempt to help her, but thanked him all the same. Sitting by the embers, she twirled the kettle around to get an even melt from the inside lest there would be chunks in their drink. Some sugar and cream and a few more strokes of a ladle and it should be done. Gilbert lifted the pot while she prepared their mugs.

"Where did you go?" he asked, standing by the table.

"On the floor, of course," she said, peeking through the doorway. The floor of a city kitchen was certainly not the polished wood of a bedchamber hall, but times changed.

Gilbert limped over, wincing with a growing grin at the elaborate display set before him. "You really have been waiting for me to agree," he noted.

"Yes, well, I had some time to ask Virginie if anyone in the House of Judah knew how to make macarons, but then I realized we have very talented daughters and she did me the honor of making some for us..." Peeking up at him, Gilbert regarded her with a gentle softness she quickly came to know. "I said something silly, didn't I?"

"No," he replied, pouring the hot chocolate into her mug. "I was just admiring your tender compassion for everyone."

Adrienne didn't want to sip hers until he had his, watching for his approval, waiting for his smile. Only when she finally got it did she try. It didn't need as much sugar as she put in there, but it was fine enough, melting on her tongue. She giggled. All Gilbert needed was to show off his shapely calf and she would be thirteen again.

"Gilbert," she said, and he was at her beck and call.

"Yes, my dear?"

"Why was it you decided to call me *mon coeur?*"

Every man in some capacity called their wife by an endearment; at times for love, others because it was easier to say than a name. Maman was always *chérie* to Papa, it was simple and to the point. Louis called Louise *mon loulou,* a childish nickname that also meant sweetheart. Gilbert did not invent the endearment, but she could not recall any other men referring to their women as such.

"You just are," he said. "We've been together almost every day through everything, I cannot think of you beyond myself. And while *mon amour* is also true when I speak of you, I have used it with other women in the past, I will admit. But *mon coeur… Mon coeur* has always been reserved only for you."

She caught her fingers between each other, twisting them shyly. "To be the heart of the great Lafayette," she said. "What an honor, Monsieur."

Gilbert laughed, his gleaming eyes full of mirth, and he drummed his fist to his chest and uttered, "The honor is undoubtedly *mine.*"

He rubbed her back in countless circles as she vomited the next morning until she couldn't keep her eyes open any longer.

Chapter Thirty-Seven

With Him, December 24th, 1807

Advent was always a beautiful time in church with the hundreds of candles lit and the altar draped in purple, rose, and gold. It was such a shame she couldn't attend, but how kind her family was to bring a priest in for her. She didn't need it. Her daughters pleaded with sore voices for her absolution, to be sure her soul was safe, but it wasn't necessary.

Adrienne did not fear death. She knew where she was going and of the lovely faces that would greet her at Heaven's divine gates. Hell was not within an inch of her mind for the life that she had lived. For all the people in her room, she only saw their sincerity and goodness and love and knew that they were all safe for eternity.

Talking must have been her solace, for after some time, her head ached from the energy she exerted at the sight of her lovely children, so grown and charming. No worries would come from their future endeavors.

If there was one regret she had, it was how *long* she would have to wait to see *him* again, because fifty for a healthy man was still a very young age to be departing from the world.

She asked for him to stay in the tiny room, even when its walls blurred and the fire sounded like a distant, faraway dream. Whether or not others remained or left or traded spots, she took no notice. She only desired that he was there the whole time, from her confession to her final prayers. And he stood by now like he did for her every day. If he needed to be elsewhere, though, she did not want to keep him; no one desired a burdensome wife, and he was a very busy man.

How peculiar, he wore a *rose* waistcoat on a purple week, she thought.

His cheeks were flushed with the outpouring of affection she was to give him as she held out her hand towards the chair by her bed. He took the seat and moved it all the more closer, the way she did for the times he was bedridden.

"How grateful I am for God to have given me a duty so conforming with my passion," she told him. "There has not been a day past where I have not been so happy and blessed to be your wife."

While she fumbled to hold his hand, he took it up with ease, holding it close to his lips. "I could not have asked for a most excellent and beautiful soulmate. There is not enough paper on Earth, nor words in any language I know to tell you how much I love you."

What joy, she beamed, that a man as handsome and kind thought so much of her. "Is that true? You love me? Will you say it again? I will say it too, that I love you with all my being and more if God had left me my strength to show you."

Gilbert didn't let his gaze linger on the condition of her body, where she was bruised and bloodied like a madman had attempted to remove her flesh by grating it with nails.

"Forgive the state I am in," she said. "I do look atrocious."

He dusted the hair from her forehead and pressed his lips together before he shook his head. "You are always beautiful."

Adrienne raised her brow – how silly he was to say so. The kindness it took to lie so softly. The stories she may have drolled on in her accepted madness, he was ever so truthful.

She was attentive to his mood at every hour and how quickly it changed when she asked of a friend or of himself; if he did not answer with a truth, he answered with his silence. Today he was tired, melancholic, like he wished for nothing more than a long rest.

"Are you a Christian?" she asked, and his face contorted and scrunched in the way it did when he wanted to reply no. "Oh, wait, I know," clicking her tongue, "you are a *Fayettist!*"

Gilbert sputtered, the first lopsided grin she managed that evening. "That would make me quite egotistical, would it not?" he said, scratching his nose. "Are you a Fayettist?"

"Absolutely," she replied without hesitation, for all her energy was focused on him. "I would happily give my life to that creed. But… but you do admire Christ, don't you?"

He twisted their entwined hands from one side to the other. "Yes, I do. I don't know when I lost my time for Him, I'm afraid." Breathing warm air onto her fingers, he sighed. "Maybe the wars, perhaps it was politics."

"Then you will find Him again, I am sure of it!"

"You have always had enough faith for both of us."

Adrienne was not used to all Gilbert's affectionate compliments to her character. He merely said everything that he was *more* of: good, compassionate, gentle, but he held his argument that *she* was above him in all these things, and she didn't have the gallantry to tell him how much he was exaggerating. His recounts of the days when their lives together were starting made her smile all the more wide and her cheeks redden to the same color as his waistcoat.

Snow was falling outside in a thin blanket over the lines of buildings and towers that made up the Parisian skyline. Adrienne watched them float angelically beyond the window. "If you go to see our children now," she said after a long moment, "bless me – would you give me your blessing?"

"I am not leaving you, *mon coeur*. But you have it all the same."

"I'll be seeing my mother soon," she exclaimed, watching two snowflakes bump into each other, holding on for the rest of their voyage.

Though the window became dark in a few blinks of her eyes, she felt like no time had ticked by at all. Gilbert was suddenly replaced with Pauline. She had already spoken with her dear sister in days past, she was sure of it, readying of all she was to do as the incoming oldest Noailles sister. It was a difficult task, but Pauline was always capable of running operations smoothly once she put her mind to it. And she would *have* to put her mind to it as Adrienne was going to be very unavailable.

She was growing tired, whatever her sister wanted to say could be answered through divine intervention. Where was her husband? *Bring that man back*, she thought, tapping her sister's leg until she rose from the chair and a chain of whispers echoed out like ghosts.

Sounds of church bells rang, and *oh!* It was her son's birthday! Gilbert must have been so proud to have a son.

Yes, he was, Adrienne remembered, his pride and joy. How blessed her children were; they must have known how dearly she loved them.

When the chair creaked, her eyes refocused on him. He carried dark circles under his eyes that did not fit his character at all. She tutted, retook his hand, and brought it to her lips as she prayed. If she were to see him again in Heaven, all the pains of a short and challenging life would have been worth it.

His breathing was loud and broken, and in some semblance of clarity, Adrienne looked him in the eye and asked, "would you come near, and rest your head upon my bosom?"

Like a hurting child, he obeyed her request and clamored to the edge of her bed. Bending his head to her chest, he rested his cheek over her heart. If she breathed, she did it for him, as she did all things for him with all the strength of her being. Gilbert inhaled when she did, exhaled with her. He was listening to it after all, his heart.

Adrienne looked over to her nurse, who waited alongside blurred faces at the foot of the bed, those of whom could have been there the entire time. "Worry not," she said, "I am in no pain."

The crackle of the fire was soothing, the last thing to cast a glow over her one love. He watched her with tears that finally fell over his lashes, and cascaded down to her skin. So sweet of such a good man to love a childish sap as her. She carded her stiff fingers through the curls of his hair. His shoulders rocked, his teeth were not sturdy enough to contain the bubbling mewls that escaped his lips.

"You are all my happiness in this world," he replied only to her.

God was gracious as He sent this man as a boy to wed her. Everything Gilbert had was hers and she prayed she took care of it well. A large, beautiful family, a humble estate, all safe, all secure, she made sure of it.

Ah, the rose waistcoat. They wore pink when they first met. How delightful he remembered such little things.

She wasn't afraid, for she was always in good hands, she thought, kissing his fingers for the thousandth time and holding them to her cheek.

"I am all yours," she breathed.

Epilogue

⇨⇦

Paris, May 1834

Where the news gathered their sources must have been from some downtrodden *idiot* who needed a penny to get by for the day, for the Marquis de Lafayette had died for the *third* time that spring. Gazettes were crumpled into balls to fuel the fire, and he had plenty of them, mumbling his annoyance to the flames as he tossed in the next one. It landed three feet from the coals, joining a growing pile of misses.

It had not stopped raining during the week, and every day of the year felt more bland and gray than the last for an old man who left politics behind him for the thousandth time. He was multi-faceted: a flirtatious oaf, a starch defender of liberty, a man who hated every king who followed the fall of Bonaparte, but supported the country anyway… His character had not blurred with the years, although his limp worsened and he had to become adept at holding several of his great-grandchildren at a time.

A cough trembled its way through his lungs, wet and haggard. He didn't want Georges to come rushing again to his aid, nor any secretary, or to-be-hero flying in with new medicine or a contraption that cured the body of whatever *nonsense* they came up with next. Balking as he did at his bout of pneumonia earlier in the year, he sure asked for it while out on horseback in the midst of thunderstorm season. What was the sky to

He who was determined to ride every Thursday?

There was nothing for him to worry about. All matters of La Grange, of Chavaniac, of his will and debts were all taken care of by his son, just as the boy did before almost thirty years ago when the Marquis could not. In a way, he did not fear dying – he was tired and moody, and ready to lie down for a while. Any man in his late seventies was entitled to do so.

Tearing off his coat was a new exercise, bringing an ache to his shoulders that never belonged there in the first place. His cravat never tied the same way. His slow fingers fumbled over the knots. *Fashion changed too quickly,* he thought. He couldn't keep up with the widening shoulders and nipped-in waist of tasteful men. Anastasie and Virginie arrived in the most colorful of garb to see him, their hair tied like odd sculptures, adorning decorations that would make the Catholic Church envious.

A snap and a rattle came from his shirt, and out tumbled a polished gold pendant down his leg to the floor.

The old Marquis gasped as if he were shot — and he might as well have been. He scurried after it, snatching the round charm from the ground before it could become tainted with dirt. His thumb smoothed over the words *bless me* on the back as he stumbled to his bed that creaked and moaned under his weight. His heart raced while he spoke a jumbled mess in-between his tired coughs.

"Forgive me," he lamented. "I should have been more careful."

"Monsieur," the dreaded stalking voice of his valet called from beyond the door. "I heard some clamour – are you well? You did not fall, Monsieur?"

The Marquis' thinning patience set in the firmness of his jaw. *"Leave me be, for the love of God!"* he shouted back. It was rude to be interrupted in general, but to try and interfere with his evening routine was just about sacrilegious.

He ignored the quiver of his voice – it had been a long day.

Turning the pendant over between his palms once, twice, three times before he opened it, he gently pressed his lips to its inhabitant.

"Was this you telling me to watch my stupidity? *Mon coeur,* my reputation is based on my foolishness in this decade, don't you know?"

Tracing the frame of the miniature, he mouthed the engraving by her chest, *I am all yours*, to himself again and again.

"This morning I finished the last book you asked me to read, which I had put off for so long because I am a fool, as you know, and clearly for good reason – it was terrible," he told the portrait. "I would have preferred it more if you read it to me instead. I may have fallen asleep, but you wouldn't have said anything about that."

He did this daily, morning and night, for twenty-six years: speak to her. But although it was evening and he was inclined to put himself to bed early with the cold that was rapidly brewing, it was understandable for a senile old man to speak to his departed wife before he closed his eyes. Maybe this night would be the one. And if not tonight, then tomorrow.

For Gilbert thought his one Christian thought: if God and the angels were always listening, would it not be reasonable for her to hear him when he called her name? And if she heard him like she always had, she would no doubt come for him again.

About the Author

Kiley Knott is an 18th century reenactor, researcher, and author. Native to Rhode Island, she studied Intelligence Analysis and National Security at American University in Washington, DC. but started writing sci-fi and fantasy stories since her 7th grade English class had a lot of creative writing time, and expanded to historical fiction the next year. When she isn't writing, Kiley can easily be found playing Dungeons & Dragons, working on cosplay, or hanging out with friends at the Nathanael Greene Homestead and other reenactment events.

You can connect with me on:

🌐 https://linktr.ee/ladiesofthegreene